Anthologies

FROM THE HEART
A LITTLE MAGIC
A LITTLE FATE

MOON SHADOWS
(with Jill Gregory, Ruth Ryan Langan, and Marianne Willman)

The Once Upon Series
(with Jill Gregory, Ruth Ryan Langan, and Marianne Willman)

ONCE UPON A CASTLE
ONCE UPON A STAR
ONCE UPON A KISS

ONCE UPON A ROSE
ONCE UPON A DREAM
ONCE UPON A MIDNIGHT

* * *

SILENT NIGHT
(with Susan Plunkett, Dee Holmes, and Claire Cross)

OUT OF THIS WORLD
(with Laurell K. Hamilton, Susan Krinard, and Maggie Shayne)

BUMP IN THE NIGHT
(with Mary Blayney, Ruth Ryan Langan, and Mary Kay McComas)

DEAD OF NIGHT
(with Mary Blayney, Ruth Ryan Langan, and Mary Kay McComas)

THREE IN DEATH

SUITE 606
(with Mary Blayney, Ruth Ryan Langan, and Mary Kay McComas)

IN DEATH

THE LOST
(with Patricia Gaffney, Mary Blayney, and Ruth Ryan Langan)

THE OTHER SIDE
(with Mary Blayney, Patricia Gaffney, Ruth Ryan Langan, and Mary Kay McComas)

THE UNQUIET
(with Mary Blayney, Patricia Gaffney, Ruth Ryan Langan, and Mary Kay McComas)

Also available . . .

THE OFFICIAL NORA ROBERTS COMPANION
(edited by Denise Little and Laura Hayden)

CHASING FIRE

NORA ROBERTS

J

JOVE BOOKS, NEW YORK

THE BERKLEY PUBLISHING GROUP
Published by the Penguin Group
Penguin Group (USA) Inc.
375 Hudson Street, New York, New York 10014, USA

Penguin Group (Canada), 90 Eglinton Avenue East, Suite 700, Toronto, Ontario M4P 2Y3, Canada (a division of Pearson Penguin Canada Inc.) • Penguin Books Ltd., 80 Strand, London WC2R 0RL, England • Penguin Group Ireland, 25 St. Stephen's Green, Dublin 2, Ireland (a division of Penguin Books Ltd.) • Penguin Group (Australia), 250 Camberwell Road, Camberwell, Victoria 3124, Australia (a division of Pearson Australia Group Pty. Ltd.) • Penguin Books India Pvt. Ltd., 11 Community Centre, Panchsheel Park, New Delhi—110 017, India • Penguin Group (NZ), 67 Apollo Drive, Rosedale, Auckland 0632, New Zealand (a division of Pearson New Zealand Ltd.) • Penguin Books (South Africa) (Pty.) Ltd., 24 Sturdee Avenue, Rosebank, Johannesburg 2196, South Africa

Penguin Books Ltd., Registered Offices: 80 Strand, London WC2R 0RL, England

This is a work of fiction. Names, characters, places, and incidents either are the product of the author's imagination or are used fictitiously, and any resemblance to actual persons, living or dead, business establishments, events, or locales is entirely coincidental. The publisher does not have control over and does not have any responsibility for author or third-party websites or their content.

CHASING FIRE

A Jove Book / published by arrangement with the author

PUBLISHING HISTORY
G. P. Putnam's Sons hardcover edition / April 2011
Jove mass-market edition / April 2012

Copyright © 2011 by Nora Roberts.
Excerpt from *Vision in White* copyright © 2009 by Nora Roberts.
NR® is a registered trademark of Penguin Group (USA) Inc.
Cover design by Richard Hasselberger.
Stepback photograph: Riger Archibald / Aurora Photos.

ISBN: 978-0-515-15063-6

JOVE®
Jove Books are published by The Berkley Publishing Group, a division of Penguin Group (USA) Inc., 375 Hudson Street, New York, New York 10014. JOVE® is a registered trademark of Penguin Group (USA) Inc. The "J" design is a trademark of Penguin Group (USA) Inc.

PRINTED IN THE UNITED STATES OF AMERICA

10 9 8 7 6 5 4 3 2 1

ALWAYS LEARNING   PEARSON

To Bruce

For understanding me, and loving me anyway

INITIAL
ATTACK

Soon kindled and soon burnt.
WILLIAM SHAKESPEARE

1

Caught in the crosshairs of wind above the Bitterroots, the jump ship fought to find its stream. Fire boiling over the land jabbed its fists up through towers of smoke as if trying for a knockout punch.

From her seat Rowan Tripp angled to watch a seriously pissed-off Mother Nature's big show. In minutes she'd be inside it, enclosed in the mad world of searing heat, leaping flames, choking smoke. She'd wage war with shovel and saw, grit and guile. A war she didn't intend to lose.

Her stomach bounced along with the plane, a sensation she'd taught herself to ignore. She'd flown all of her life, and had fought wildfires every season since her eighteenth birthday. For the last half of those eight years she'd jumped fire.

She'd studied, trained, bled and burned—outwilled pain and exhaustion to become a Zulie. A Missoula smoke jumper.

She stretched out her long legs as best she could for a moment, rolled her shoulders under her pack to keep them loose.

Beside her, her jump partner watched as she did. His fingers did a fast tap dance on his thighs. "She looks mean."

"We're meaner."

He shot her a fast, toothy grin. "Bet your ass."

Nerves. She could all but feel them riding along his skin.

Near the end of his first season, Rowan thought, and Jim Brayner needed to pump himself up before a jump. Some always would, she decided, while others caught short catnaps to bank sleep against the heavy withdrawals to come.

She was first jump on this load, and Jim would be right behind her. If he needed a little juice, she'd supply it.

"Kick her ass, more like. It's the first real bitch we've jumped in a week." She gave him an easy elbow jab. "Weren't you the one who kept saying the season was done?"

He tapped those busy fingers on his thighs to some inner rhythm. "Nah, that was Matt," he insisted, grin still wide as he deflected the claim onto his brother.

"That's what you get with a couple Nebraska farm boys. Don't you have a hot date tomorrow night?"

"My dates are always hot."

She couldn't argue, as she'd seen Jim snag women like rainbow trout anytime the unit had pulled a night off to kick it up in town. He'd hit on her, she remembered, about two short seconds after he'd arrived on base. Still, he'd been good-natured about her shutdown. She'd implemented a firm policy against dating within the unit.

Otherwise, she might've been tempted. He had that open, innocent face offset by the quick grin, and the gleam in the eye. For fun, she thought, for a careless pop of the cork out of the lust bottle. For serious—even if she'd been looking for serious—he'd never do the trick. Though they were the same age, he was just too young, too fresh off the farm—and maybe just a little too sweet under the thin layer of green that hadn't burned off quite yet.

"Which girl's going to bed sad and lonely if you're still dancing with the dragon?" she asked him.

"Lucille."

"That's the little one—with the giggle."

His fingers tapped, tapped, tapped on his knee. "She does more than giggle."

"You're a dog, Romeo."

He tipped back his head, let out a series of sharp barks that made her laugh.

"Make sure Dolly doesn't find out you're out howling," she commented. She knew—everyone knew—he'd been banging one of the base cooks like a drum all season.

"I can handle Dolly." The tapping picked up pace. "Gonna handle Dolly."

Okay, Rowan thought, something bent out of shape there, which was why smart people didn't bang or get banged by people they worked with.

She gave him a little nudge because those busy fingers concerned her. "Everything okay with you, farm boy?"

His pale blue eyes met hers for an instant, then shifted away while his knees did a bounce under those drumming fingers. "No problems here. It's going to be smooth sailing like always. I just need to get down there."

She put a hand over his to still it. "You need to keep your head in the game, Jim."

"It's there. Right there. Look at her, swishing her tail," he said. "Once us Zulies get down there, she won't be so sassy. We'll put her down, and I'll be making time with Lucille tomorrow night."

Unlikely, Rowan thought to herself. Her aerial view of the fire put her gauge at a solid two days of hard, sweaty work.

And that was if things went their way.

Rowan reached for her helmet, nodded toward their spotter. "Getting ready. Stay chilly, farm boy."

"I'm ice."

Cards—so dubbed as he carried a pack everywhere—wound his way through the load of ten jumpers and equipment to the rear of the plane, attached the tail of his harness to the restraining line.

Even as Cards shouted out the warning to guard their reserves, Rowan hooked her arm over hers. Cards, a tough-bodied vet, pulled the door open to a rush of wind tainted with smoke and fuel. As he reached for the first set of streamers, Rowan set her helmet over her short crown of blond hair, strapped it, adjusted her face mask.

She watched the streamers doing their colorful dance against the smoke-stained sky. Their long strips kicked in the turbulence, spiraled toward the southwest, seemed to roll, to rise, then caught another bounce before whisking into the trees.

Cards called, "Right!" into his headset, and the pilot turned the plane.

The second set of streamers snapped out, spun like a kid's wind-up toy. The strips wrapped together, pulled apart, then dropped onto the tree-flanked patch of the jump site.

"The wind line's running across that creek, down to the trees and across the site," Rowan said to Jim.

Over her, the spotter and pilot made more adjustments, and another set of streamers snapped out into the slipstream.

"It's got a bite to it."

"Yeah. I saw." Jim swiped the back of his hand over his mouth before strapping on his helmet and mask.

"Take her to three thousand," Cards shouted.

Jump altitude. As first man, first stick, Rowan rose to take position. "About three hundred yards of drift," she shouted to Jim, repeating what she'd heard Cards telling the pilot. "But there's that bite. Don't get caught downwind."

"Not my first party."

She saw his grin behind the bars of his face mask—confident, even eager. But something in his eyes, she thought. Just for a flash. She started to speak again, but Cards, already in position to the right of the door, called out, "Are you ready?"

"We're ready," she called back.

"Hook up."

Rowan snapped the static line in place.

"Get in the door!"

She dropped to sitting, legs out in the wicked slipstream, body leaning back. Everything roared. Below her extended legs, fire ran in vibrant red and gold.

There was nothing but the moment, nothing but the wind and fire and the twist of exhilaration and fear that always, always surprised her.

"Did you see the streamers?"

"Yeah."

"You see the spot?"

She nodded, bringing both into her head, following those colorful strips to the target.

Cards repeated what she'd told Jim, almost word for word. She only nodded again, eyes on the horizon, letting her breath come easy, visualizing herself flying, falling, navigating the sky down to the heart of the jump spot.

She went through her four-point check as the plane completed its circle and leveled out.

Cards pulled his head back in. "Get ready."

Ready-steady, her father said in her head. She grabbed both sides of the door, sucked in a breath.

And when the spotter's hand slapped her shoulder, she launched herself into the sky.

Nothing she knew topped that one instant of insanity, hurling herself into the void. She counted off in her mind, a task as automatic as breathing, and rolled in that charged sky to watch the plane fly past. She caught sight of Jim, hurtling after her.

Again, she turned her body, fighting the drag of wind until her feet were down. With a yank and jerk, her canopy burst open. She scouted out Jim again, felt a tiny pop of relief when she saw his chute spread against the empty sky. In that pocket of eerie silence, beyond the roar of the plane, above the voice of the fire, she gripped her steering toggles.

The wind wanted to drag her north, and was pretty insistent about it. Rowan was just as insistent on staying on the course she'd mapped out in her head. She watched the ground as she steered against the frisky crosscurrent that pinched its fingers on her canopy, doing its best to circle her into the tailwind.

The turbulence that had caught the streamers struck her in gusty slaps while the heat pumped up from the burning ground. If the wind had its way, she'd overshoot the jump spot, fly into the verge of trees, risk a hang-up. Or worse, it could shove her west, and into the flames.

She dragged hard on her toggle, glanced over in time to see Jim catch the downwind and go into a spin.

"Pull right! Pull right!"

"I got it! I got it."

But to her horror, he pulled left.

"Right, goddamn it!"

She had to turn for her final, and the pleasure of a near seamless slide into the glide path drowned in sheer panic. Jim soared west, helplessly towed by a horizontal canopy.

Rowan hit the jump site, rolled. She gained her feet, slapped her release. And heard it as she stood in the center of the blaze.

She heard her jump partner's scream.

THE SCREAM followed her as she shot up in bed, echoed in her head as she sat huddled in the dark.

Stop, stop, stop! she ordered herself. And dropped her head on her updrawn knees until she got her breath back.

No point in it, she thought. No point in reliving it, in going over all the details, all the moments, or asking herself, again, if she could've done just one thing differently.

Asking herself why Jim hadn't followed her drop into the jump spot. Why he'd pulled the wrong toggle. Because, *goddamn it,* he'd pulled the wrong toggle.

And had flown straight into the towers and lethal branches of those burning trees.

Months ago now, she reminded herself. She'd had the long winter to get past it. And thought she had.

Being back on base triggered it, she admitted, and rubbed her hands over her face, back over the hair she'd had cut into a short, maintenance-free cap only days before.

Fire season was nearly on them. Refresher training started in a couple short hours. Memories, regrets, grief—they were bound to pay a return visit. But she needed sleep, another hour before she got up, geared up for the punishing three-mile run.

She was damn good at willing herself to sleep, anyplace, anytime. Coyote-ing in a safe zone during a fire, on a shuddering jump plane. She knew how to eat and sleep when the need and opportunity opened.

But when she closed her eyes again, she saw herself back on the plane, turning toward Jim's grin.

Knowing she had to shake it off, she shoved out of bed. She'd grab a shower, some caffeine, stuff in some carbs, then do a light workout to warm up for the physical training test.

It continued to baffle her fellow jumpers that she never drank coffee unless it was her only choice. She liked the cold and sweet. After she'd dressed, Rowan hit her stash of Cokes, grabbed an energy bar. She took both outside where the sky was still shy of first light and the air stayed chill in the early spring of western Montana.

In the vast sky stars blinked out, little candles snuffed. She pulled the dark and quiet around her, found some comfort in it. In an hour, give or take, the base would wake, and testosterone would flood the air.

Since she generally preferred the company of men, for conversation, for companionship, she didn't mind being outnumbered by them. But she prized her quiet time, those little pieces of alone that became rare and precious during the season. Next best thing to sleep before a day filled with pressure and stress, she thought.

She could tell herself not to worry about the run, remind herself she'd been vigilant about her PT all winter, was in the best shape of her life—and it didn't mean a damn.

Anything could happen. A turned ankle, a mental lapse, a sudden, debilitating cramp. Or she could just have a bad run. Others had. Sometimes they came back from it, sometimes they didn't.

And a negative attitude wasn't going to help. She chowed down on the energy bar, gulped caffeine into her system and watched the day eke its first shimmer over the rugged, snow-tipped western peaks.

When she ducked into the gym minutes later, she noted her alone time was over.

"Hey, Trigger." She nodded to the man doing crunches on a mat. "What do you know?"

"I know we're all crazy. What the hell am I doing here, Ro? I'm forty-fucking-three years old."

She unrolled a mat, started her stretches. "If you weren't crazy, weren't here, you'd still be forty-fucking-three."

At six-five, barely making the height restrictions, Trigger Gulch was a lean, mean machine with a west Texas twang and an affection for cowboy boots.

He huffed through a quick series of pulsing crunches. "I could be lying on a beach in Waikiki."

"You could be selling real estate in Amarillo."

"I could do that." He mopped his face, pointed at her. "Nine-to-five the next fifteen years, then retire to that beach in Waikiki."

"Waikiki's full of people, I hear."

"Yeah, that's the damn trouble." He sat up, a good-looking man with gray liberally salted through his brown hair, and a scar snaked on his left knee from a meniscus repair. He smiled at her as she lay on her back, pulled her right leg up and toward her nose. "Looking good, Ro. How was your fat season?"

"Busy." She repeated the stretch on her left leg. "I've been looking forward to coming back, getting me some rest."

He laughed at that. "How's your dad?"

"Good as gold." Rowan sat up, then folded her long, curvy body in two. "Gets a little wistful this time of year." She closed ice-blue eyes and pulled her flexed feet back toward the crown of her head. "He misses the start-up, everybody coming back, but the business doesn't give him time to brood."

"Even people who aren't us like to jump out of planes."

"Pay good money for it, too. Had a good one last week." She spread her legs in a wide vee, grabbed her toes and again bent forward. "Couple celebrated their fiftieth anniversary with a jump. Gave me a bottle of French champagne as a tip."

Trigger sat where he was, watching as she pushed to her feet to begin the first sun salutation. "Are you still teaching that hippie class?"

Rowan flowed from Up Dog to Down Dog, turned her head to shoot Trigger a pitying look. "It's yoga, old man, and yeah, I'm still doing some personal trainer work off-season. Helps keep the lard out of my ass. How about you?"

"I pile the lard on. It gives me more to burn off when the real work starts."

"If this season's as slow as last, we'll all be sitting on fat asses. Have you seen Cards? He doesn't appear to have turned down any second helpings this winter."

"Got a new woman."

"No shit." Looser, she picked up the pace, added lunges.

"He met her in the frozen food section of the grocery store in October, and moved in with her for New Year's. She's got a couple kids. Schoolteacher."

"Schoolteacher, kids? Cards?" Rowan shook her head. "Must be love."

"Must be something. He said the woman and the kids are

coming out maybe late July, maybe spend the rest of the summer."

"That sounds serious." She shifted to a twist, eyeing Trigger as she held the position. "She must be something. Still, he'd better see how she handles a season. It's one thing to hook up with a smoke jumper in the winter, and another to stick through the summer. Families crack like eggs," she added, then wished she hadn't as Matt Brayner stepped in.

She hadn't seen him since Jim's funeral, and though she'd spoken with his mother a few times, hadn't been sure he'd come back.

He looked older, she thought, more worn around the eyes and mouth. And heartbreakingly like his brother with the floppy mop of bleached wheat hair, the pale blue eyes. His gaze tracked from Trigger, met hers. She wondered what the smile cost him.

"How's it going?"

"Pretty good." She straightened, wiped her palms on the thighs of her workout pants. "Just sweating off some nerves before the PT test."

"I thought I'd do the same. Or just screw it and go into town and order a double stack of pancakes."

"We'll get 'em after the run." Trigger walked over, held out a hand. "Good to see you, Hayseed."

"You too."

"I'm going for coffee. They'll be loading us up before too long."

As Trigger went out, Matt walked over, picked up a twenty-pound weight. Put it down again. "I guess it's going to be weird, for a while anyway. Seeing me makes everybody . . . think."

"Nobody's going to forget. I'm glad you're back."

"I don't know if I am, but I couldn't seem to do anything else. Anyway. I wanted to say thanks for keeping in touch with my ma the way you have. It means a lot to her."

"I wish . . . Well, if wishes were horses I'd have a rodeo. I'm glad you're back. See you at the van."

SHE UNDERSTOOD Matt's sentiment, couldn't seem to do anything else. It would sum up the core feelings of the men, and four women including herself, who piled into vans for the ride out to the start of the run for their jobs. She settled in, letting the ragging and bragging flow over her.

A lot of insults about winter weight, and the ever-popular lard-ass remarks. She closed her eyes, tried to let herself drift as the nerves riding under the good-natured bullshit winging around the van wanted to reach inside and shake hands with her own.

Janis Petrie, one of the four females in the unit, dropped down beside her. Her small, compact build had earned her the nickname Elf, and she looked like a perky head cheerleader.

This morning, her nails sported bright pink polish and her shiny brown hair bounced in a tail tied with a circle of butterflies.

She was pretty as a gumdrop, tended to giggle, and could—and did—work a saw line for fourteen hours straight.

"Ready to rock, Swede?"

"And roll. Why would you put on makeup before this bitch of a test?"

Janis fluttered her long, lush lashes. "So these poor guys'll have something pretty to look at when they stumble over the finish line. Seeing as I'll be there first."

"You are pretty damn fast."

"Small but mighty. Did you check out the rookies?"

"Not yet."

"Six of our kind in there. Maybe we'll add enough women for a nice little sewing circle. Or a book club."

Rowan laughed. "And after, we'll have a bake sale."

"Cupcakes. Cupcakes are my weakness. It's such pretty country." Janis leaned forward a little to get a clearer view out the window. "I always miss it when I'm gone, always wonder what I'm doing living in the city doing physical therapy on country club types with tennis elbow."

She blew out a breath. "Then by July I'll be wondering what I'm doing out here, strung out on no sleep, hurting everywhere, when I could be taking my lunch break at the pool."

"It's a long way from Missoula to San Diego."

"Damn right. You don't have that pull-tug. You live here. For most of us, this is coming home. Until we finish the season and go home, then that feels like home. It can cross up the circuits."

She rolled her warm brown eyes toward Rowan as the van stopped. "Here we go again."

Rowan climbed out of the van, drew in the air. It smelled good, fresh and new. Spring, the kind with green and wildflowers and balmy breezes, wouldn't be far off now. She scouted the flags marking the course as the base manager, Michael Little Bear, laid out requirements.

His long black braid streamed down his bright red jacket. Rowan knew there'd be a roll of Life Savers in the pocket, a substitute for the Marlboros he'd quit over the winter.

L.B. and his family lived a stone's throw from the base, and his wife worked for Rowan's father.

Everyone knew the rules. Run the course, and get it done in under 22:30, or walk away. Try it again in a week. Fail that? Find a new summer job.

Rowan stretched out—hamstrings, quads, calves.

"I hate this shit."

"You'll make it." She gave him an elbow in the belly. "Think of a meat-lover's pizza waiting for you on the other side of the line."

"Kiss my ass."

"The size it is now? That'd take me a while."

He snorted out a laugh as they lined up.

She calmed herself. Got in her head, got in her body, as L.B. walked back to the van. When the van took off, so did the line. Rowan hit the timer button on her watch, merged with the pack. She knew every one of them—had worked with them, sweated with them, risked her life with them. And she wished them—every one—good luck and a good run.

But for the next twenty-two and thirty, it was every man—and woman—for himself.

She dug in, kicked up her pace and ran for, what was in a very large sense, her life. She made her way through the pack and, as others did, called out encouragement or jibes, whatever worked best to kick asses into gear. She knew there would be knees aching, chests hammering, stomachs churning. Spring training would have toned some, added insult to injuries on others.

She couldn't think about it. She focused on mile one, and when she passed the marker, noted her time at 4:12.

Mile two, she ordered herself, and kept her stride smooth, her pace steady—even when Janis passed her with a grim smile. The burn rose up from her toes to her ankles, flowed up her calves. Sweat ran hot down her back, down her chest, over her galloping heart.

She could slow her pace—her time was good—but the stress of imagined stumbles, turned ankles, a lightning strike from beyond, pushed her.

Don't let up.

When she passed mile two she'd moved beyond the burn, the sweat, into the mindless. One more mile. She passed some, was passed by others, while her pulse pounded in her ears. As before a jump, she kept her eyes on the horizon—land and sky. Her love of both whipped her through the final mile.

She blew past the last marker, heard L.B. call out her name and time. *Tripp, fifteen-twenty.* And ran another twenty yards before she could convince her legs it was okay to stop.

Bending from the waist, she caught her breath, squeezed her eyes tightly shut. As always after the PT test she wanted to weep. Not from the effort. She—all of them—faced worse, harder, tougher. But the stress clawing at her mind finally retracted.

She could continue to be what she wanted to be.

She walked off the run, tuning in now as other names and times were called out. She high-fived with Trigger as he crossed three miles.

Everyone who passed stayed on the line. A unit again, all but willing the rest to make it, make that time. She checked her watch, saw the deadline coming up, and four had yet to cross.

Cards, Matt, Yangtree, who'd celebrated—or mourned— his fifty-fourth birthday the month before, and Gibbons, whose bad knee had him nearly hobbling those last yards.

Cards wheezed in with three seconds to spare, with Yangtree right behind him. Gibbons's face was a sweat-drenched study in pain and grit, but Matt? It seemed to Rowan he barely pushed.

His eyes met hers. She pumped her fist, imagined herself dragging him and Gibbons over the last few feet while the seconds counted down. She swore she could see the light come on, could see Matt reaching in, digging down.

He hit at 22:28, with Gibbons stumbling over a half second behind.

The cheer rose then, the triumph of one more season.

"Guess you two wanted to add a little suspense." L.B. lowered his clipboard. "Welcome back. Take a minute to bask, then let's get loaded."

"Hey, Ro!" She glanced over at Cards's shout, in time to see him turn, bend over and drop his pants. "Pucker up!"

And we're back, she thought.

2

Gulliver Curry rolled out of his sleeping bag and took stock. Everything hurt, he decided. But that made a workable balance.

He smelled snow, and a look out of his tent showed him, yes, indeed, a couple fresh inches had fallen overnight. His breath streamed out in clouds as he pulled on pants. The blisters on his blisters made dressing for the day an . . . experience.

Then again, he valued experience.

The day before, he, along with twenty-five other recruits, had dug fire line for fourteen hours, then topped off that little task with a three-mile hike, carrying an eighty-five-pound pack.

They'd felled trees with crosscut saws, hiked, dug, sharpened tools, dug, hiked, scaled the towering pines, then dug some more.

Summer camp for the masochist, he thought. Otherwise known as rookie training for smoke jumpers. Four recruits had already washed out—two of them hadn't gotten past the initial PT test. His seven years' fire experience, the last four on a hotshot crew, gave Gull some advantage.

But that didn't mean he felt fresh as a rosebud.

He rubbed a hand over his face, scratching his palm over bristles from nearly a week without a razor. God, he wanted a hot shower, a shave and an ice-cold beer. Tonight, after a fun-filled hike through the Bitterroots, this time hauling a hundred-and-ten-pound pack, he'd get all three.

And tomorrow, he'd start the next phase. Tomorrow he'd start learning how to fly.

Hotshots trained like maniacs, worked like dogs, primarily on high-priority wilderness fires. But they didn't jump out of planes. That, he thought, added a whole new experience. He shoved a hand through his thick mass of dark hair, then crawled out of the tent into the crystal snowscape of predawn.

His eyes, feline green, tracked up to check the sky, and he stood for a moment in the still, tall and tough in his rough brown pants and bright yellow shirt. He had what he wanted here—or pieces of it—the knowledge that he could do what he'd come to do.

He measured the height of the ponderosa pine to his left. Ninety feet, give or take. He'd walked up that bastard the day before, biting his gaffs into bark. And from that height, hooked with spikes and harness, he'd gazed out over the forest.

An experience.

Through the scent of snow and pine, he headed toward the cook tent as the camp began to stir. And despite the aches, the blisters—maybe because of them—he looked forward to what the day would bring.

Shortly after noon, Gull watched the lodgepole pine topple. He shoved his hard hat back enough to wipe sweat off his forehead and nodded to his partner on the crosscut saw.

"Another one bites the dust."

Dobie Karstain barely made the height requirement at five six. His beard and stream of dung brown hair gave him the look of a pint-sized mountain man, while the safety goggles seemed to emphasize the wild, wide eyes.

Dobie hefted a chain saw. "Let's cut her into bite-sized pieces."

They worked rhythmically. Gull had figured Dobie for a washout, but the native Kentuckian was stronger, and sturdier, than he looked. He liked Dobie well enough—despite the man's distinctly red neck—and was working on reaching a level of trust.

If Dobie made it through, odds were they'd be sawing and digging together again. Not on a bright, clear spring afternoon, but in the center of fire where trust and teamwork were as essential as a sharp Pulaski, the two-headed tool with ax and grub hoe.

"Wouldn't mind tapping that before she folds."

Gull glanced over at one of the female recruits. "What makes you think she'll fold?"

"Women ain't built for this work, son."

Gull drew the blade of the saw through the pine. "Just for baby-making, are they?"

Dobie grinned through his beard. "I didn't design the model. I just like riding 'em."

"You're an asshole, Dobie."

"Some say," Dobie agreed in the same good-natured tone.

Gull studied the woman again. Perky blond, maybe an inch or two shy of Dobie's height. And from his point of view, she'd held up as well as any of them. Ski instructor out of Colorado, he recalled. Libby. He'd seen her retaping her blisters that morning.

"I got twenty says she makes it all the way."

Dobie chuckled as another log rolled. "I'll take your twenty, son."

When they finished their assignment, Gull retaped some of his own blisters. Then, as the instructors were busy, taped Dobie's fresh ones.

They moved through the camp to their waiting packs. Three miles to go, Gull thought, then he'd end this fine day with that shave, shower and cold beer.

He sat, strapped on the pack, then pulled out a pack of gum. He offered a stick to Dobie.

"Don't mind if I do."

Together they rolled over to their hands and knees, then pushed to standing.

"Just imagine you're carrying a pretty little woman," Dobie advised, with a wiggle of eyebrows in Libby's direction.

"A buck-ten's pretty scrawny for my taste."

"She'll feel like more by the time we're done."

No question about it, Gull mused, and the instructor didn't set what you'd call a meandering pace along the rocky, quad-burning trail.

They pushed one another, that's how it was done. Ragged one another, encouraged one another, insulted one another, to get the group another step, another yard. The spurring fact was, in a few weeks it would be real. And on the fire line everyone's life depended on the other.

"What do you do back in Kentucky?" Gull asked Dobie while a hawk screamed overhead and the smell of group sweat competed with pine.

"Some of this, some of that. Last three seasons I doused fires in the national forest. One night after we beat one down, I got a little drunk, took a bet how I'd be a smoke jumper. So I got an application, and here I am."

"You're doing this on a bet?" The idea just appealed to his sense of the ridiculous.

"Hundred dollars on the line, son. And my pride that's worth more. You ever jump out of a plane?"

"Yeah."

"Takes the crazy."

"Some might say." Gull passed Dobie's earlier words back to him.

"What's it feel like? When you're falling?"

"Like hot, screaming sex with a beautiful woman."

"I was hoping." Dobie shifted his pack, winced. "Because this fucking training better be worth it."

"Libby's holding up."

"Who?"

Gull lifted his chin. "Your most recent bet."

Dobie gritted his teeth as they started up yet another incline. "Day's not over."

By the time it was, Gull got his shower, his shave, and managed to grab a brew before falling facedown on his bunk.

MICHAEL LITTLE BEAR snagged Rowan on her way into the gym. "I need you to take rookie training this morning. Cards was on it, but he's puking up his guts in the john."

"Hangover?"

"No. Stomach flu or something. I need you to run them on the playground. Okay?"

"Sure. I'm already on with Yangtree, on the slam-ulator. I can make a day eating rooks. How many do we have?"

"Twenty-five left, and they look pretty damn good. One beat the base record on the mile-and-a-half course. Nailed it in six-thirty-nine."

"Fast feet. We'll see how the rest of him does today."

She knocked thirty minutes off her planned ninety in the gym. Taking the recruits over the obstacle course would make up for it, and meant she'd just skated out of a stint sewing personal gear bags in the manufacturing room.

Damn good deal, Rowan thought as she put on her boots.

She grabbed the paperwork, a clipboard, a water bottle and, fixing a blue ball cap on her head, headed outside.

Clouds had rolled in overnight and tucked the warm in nicely. Activity swarmed the base—runners on the track or the road, trucks off-loaded supplies, men and women crossed from building to building. A plane taxied out taking a group up for a preseason practice jump.

Long before the fire siren screamed, work demanded attention. Sewing, stuffing, disassembling equipment, training, packing chutes.

She started toward the training field, pausing when she crossed paths with Matt.

"What're you on?" he asked her.

"Rook detail. Cards is down with some stomach deal. You?"

"I'm up this afternoon." He glanced skyward as the jump plane rose into the air. "I'm in the loadmaster's room this morning." He smiled. "Want to trade?"

"Hmm, stuck inside loading supplies or out here torturing rookies? No deal."

"Figured."

She continued on, noting the trainees were starting to gather on the field. They'd come in from a week of camping and line work, and if they had any brains would've focused on getting a good night's sleep.

Those who had would probably feel pretty fresh this morning.

She'd soon take care of that.

A few of them wandered the obstacle course, trying to get a gauge. Smart, she judged. Know your enemy. Voices and laughter carried on the air. Pumping themselves up—and that was smart, too.

The obstacle course was a bitch of the first order, and it was only the start of a long, brutal day. She checked her watch as she moved through the wooden platforms, took her place on the field.

She took a swig from her water bottle, then set it aside. And let out a long, shrill whistle. "Line up," she called out. "I'm Rowan Tripp, your instructor on this morning's cakewalk. Each of you will be required to complete this course before moving on to the next exercise. The campfire songs and roasted marshmallows of the last week are over. It's time to get serious."

She got a few moans, a few chuckles, some nervous glances as she sized up the group. Twenty-one men, four women, different sizes, shapes, colors, ages. Her job was to give them one purpose.

Work through the pain.

She consulted her clipboard, did roll call, checked off the names of those who'd made it this far. "I hear one of you rooks beat the base record on the mile-and-a-half. Who's the flash?"

"Go, Gull!" somebody shouted, and she watched the little guy elbow-bump the man next to him.

About six-two, she judged, dark hair clean and shaggy, cocky smile, easy stance. "Gull Curry," he said. "I like to run."

"Good for you. Speed won't get you through the playground. Stretch out, recruits. I don't want anybody crying about pulled muscles."

They'd already formed a unit, she determined, and the smaller connections within it. Friendships, rivalries—both could be useful.

"Fifty push-ups," she ordered, noting them down as they were completed.

"I'm going to lead you over this course, starting here." She gestured at the low platform of horizontal squares, moved on to the steep steel walls they'd need to hurdle, the ropes they'd climb, hand over hand, the trampoline flips, the ramps.

"Every one of these obstacles simulates something you will face during a fire. Get one done, hit the next. Drop out? You're done. Finish it, you might just be good enough to jump fire."

"Not exactly Saint Crispin's Day."

"Who?" Dobie asked at Gull's mutter.

He only shrugged, and figured by the sidelong glance the bombshell blonde sent him, she'd heard the remark.

"You, Fast Feet, take the lead. The rest of you, fall in behind him. Single file. If you fall, get your ass out of the way, pick up the rear for a second shot."

She pulled a stopwatch out of her pocket. "Are you ready?"

The group shouted back, and Rowan hit the timer. "Go!"

Okay, Rowan thought, fast feet and nimble feet.

"Pick up those knees!" she shouted. "Let's see some energy. For Christ's sake, you look like a bunch of girls strolling in the park."

"I am a girl!" a steely-eyed blonde shouted back, and made Rowan grin.

"Then pick up those knees. Pretend you're giving one of these assholes a shot in the balls."

She kept pace with Gull, jogging back as he raced for, charged up, then hurdled the first ramp.

Then the little guy surprised her by all but launching over it like a cannon.

They climbed, hurdled, crawled, clawed. L.B. was right, she decided. They were a damn good group.

She watched Gull execute the required flips and rolls on the tramp, heard the little guy—she needed to check his name—let out a wild yee-haw as he did the same.

Fast feet, she thought again, still in the lead, and damned if he didn't go up the rope like a monkey on a vine.

The blonde had made up ground, but when she hit the rope, she not only stalled, but started to slip.

"Don't you slide!" Rowan shouted it out, put a whiplash

into it. "Don't you slide, Barbie, goddamn it, and embarrass me. Do you want to start this mother over?"

"No. God, no."

"Do you want to jump fire or go back home and shop for shoes?"

"Both!"

"Climb it." Rowan saw the blood on the rope. A slide ripped the skin right off the palms, and the pain was huge. "Climb!"

She climbed, forty torturous feet.

"Get down, move on. Go! Go!"

She climbed down, and when she hurdled the next wall, left a bloodstain on the ramp.

But she did it. They all did, Rowan thought, and gave them a moment to wheeze, to moan, to rub out sore muscles.

"Not bad. Next time you have to climb a rope or scale a wall it might be because the wind shifted and fire just washed over your safe zone. You'll want to do better than not bad. What's your name—I'm a Girl Barbie?"

"Libby." The blonde rested her bloody hands on her knees, palms up. "Libby Rydor."

"Anybody who can climb up a rope when her hands are bleeding did better than not bad." Rowan opened the first-aid kit. "Let's fix them up. If anybody else got any boo-boos, tend to them, then head in, get your gear. Full gear," she added, "for practice landings. You got thirty."

Gull watched her apply salve to Libby's palms, competently bandage them. She said something that made Libby—and those hands had to hurt—laugh.

She'd pushed the group through the course, hitting the right combination of callous insult and nagging. And she'd zeroed in on a few as they'd had trouble, found the right thing to say at the right time.

That was an impressive skill, one he admired.

He could add it to his admiration of the rest of her.

That blonde was built, all maybe five feet ten inches of her. His uncle would have dubbed her statuesque, Gull mused. Himself? He just had to say that body was a killer. Add big, heavy-lidded blue eyes and a face that made a man want to look twice, then maybe linger a little longer for a third time, and you had a hell of a package.

A package with attitude. And God, he had a hard time resisting attitude. So he stalled until she crossed the field, then fell into step beside her.

"How are Libby's hands?"

"She'll be okay. Everybody loses a little skin on the playground."

"Did you?"

"If you don't bleed, how do they know you've been there?" She angled her head, studied him with eyes that made him think of stunning arctic ice. "Where are you out of, Shakespeare? I've read *Henry the Fifth*."

"Monterey, mostly."

"They've got a fine smoke-jumper unit in Northern California."

"They do. I know most of them. I worked Redding IHC, five years."

"I figured you for a hotshot. So, you're wanted in California so you headed to Missoula?"

"The charges were dropped," he said, and made her smile. "I'm in Missoula because of Iron Man Tripp." He stopped when she did. "I'm figuring he must be your father."

"That's right. Do you know him?"

"Of course. Lucas 'Iron Man' Tripp's a legend. You had a bad one out here in 2000."

"Yeah."

"I was in college. It was all over the news, and I caught this interview with Iron Man, right here on base, after he and his unit got back from four days in the mouth of it."

Gull thought back, brought it into the now in his head. "His face is covered with soot, his hair's layered with ash, his eyes are red. He looks like he's been to war, which is accurate enough. The reporter's asking the usual idiot questions. 'How did it feel in there? Were you afraid?' And he's being patient. You can tell he's exhausted, but he's answering. And finally he says to the guy, 'Boy, the simplest way to put it is the bitch tried to eat us, and we kicked her ass.' And he walks away."

She remembered it as clearly as he did—and remembered a lot more. "And that's why you're in Missoula looking to jump fire?"

"Consider it a springboard. I could give you the rest of it over a beer."

"You're going to be too busy for beer and life stories. Better get your gear on. You've got a long way to go yet."

"Offer of beer's always open. Life story optional."

She gave him that look again, the slight angle of the head, the little smirk on the mouth that he found sexily bottom-heavy. "You don't want to hit on me, hotshot. I don't hook up with rookies, snookies or other smoke jumpers. When I've got the time and inclination for . . . entertainment, I look for a civilian. One I can play with when I'm in the mood over the long winter nights and forget about during the season."

Oh, yeah, he did like attitude. "You might be due for a change of pace."

"You're wasting your time, rook."

When she strolled off with her clipboard, he let himself grin. He figured it was his time to waste. And she struck him as a truly unique experience.

GULL SURVIVED being dragged up in the air by a cable, then dropped down to earth again. The not-altogether-fondly-dubbed slam-ulator did a damn good job of simulating the body-jarring, ankle-and-knee-shocking slam of a parachute landing.

He slapped, tucked, dropped and rolled, and he took his lumps, bumps and bruises. He learned how to protect his head, how to use his body to preserve his body. And how to *think* when the ground was hurtling up toward him at a fast clip.

He faced the tower, climbing its fifty feet of murderous red with his jump partner for the drill.

"How ya doing?" he asked Libby.

"I feel like I fell off a mountain, so not too bad. You?"

"I'm not sure if I fell off the mountain or on it." When he reached the platform, he grinned at Rowan. "Is this as much fun as it looks?"

"Oh, more." Sarcasm dripped as she hooked him to the pully. "There's your jump spot." She gestured to a hill of sawdust across the training field. "There's going to be some speed on the swing over, so you're going to feel it when you hit. Tuck, protect your head, roll."

He studied the view of the hill. It looked damn small from where he was standing, through the bars of his face mask.

"Got it."

"Are you ready?" she asked them both.

Libby took a deep breath. "We're ready."

"Get in the door."

Yeah, it had some speed, Gull thought as he flew across the training field. He barely had time to go through his landing list when the sawdust hill filled his vision. He slammed into it, thought *fuck!*, then tucked and rolled with his hands on either side of his helmet.

Willing his breath back into his lungs, he looked over at Libby. "Okay?"

"Definitely on the mountain that time. But you know what? That was *fun*. I've got to do it again."

"Day's young." He shoved to his feet, held out a hand to pull her to hers.

After the tower came the classroom. His years on a hotshot crew meant most of the books, charts, lectures were refreshers on what he already knew. But there was always more to learn.

After the classroom there was time, at last, to nurse the bumps and bruises, to find a hot meal, to hang out a bit with the other recruits. Down to twenty-two, Gull noted. They'd lost three between the simulator and the tower.

More than half of those still in training turned in for the night, and Gull thought of doing so himself. The poker game currently under way tempted him so he made a bargain with himself. He'd get some air, then if the urge still tickled, he'd sit in on a few hands.

"Pull up a chair, son," Dobie invited as Gull walked by the table. "I'm looking to add to my retirement account."

"Land on your head a few more times, you'll be retiring early."

Gull kept walking. Outside, the rain that had threatened all day fell cool and steady. Shoving his hands into his pockets, he walked into the wet. He turned toward the distant hangar. Maybe he'd wander over, take a look at the plane he'd soon be jumping out of.

He'd jumped three times before he'd applied for the program, just to make sure he had the stomach for it. Now he was anxious, eager to revisit that sensation, to defy his own instincts and shove himself into the high open air.

He'd studied the planes—the Twin Otter, the DC-9—the most commonly used for smoke jumping. He toyed with the idea of taking flying lessons in the off-season, maybe going for his pilot's license. It never hurt to know you could take control if control needed to be taken.

Then he saw her striding toward him through the rain. Dark and gloom didn't blur that body. He slowed his pace. Maybe he didn't need to play poker for this to be his lucky night.

"Nice night," he said.

"For otters." Rain dripped off the bill of Rowan's cap as she studied him. "Making a run for it?"

"Just taking a walk. But I've got a car if there's somewhere you want to go."

"I've got my own ride, thanks, but I'm not going anywhere. You did okay today."

"Thanks."

"It's too bad about Doggett. Bad landing, and a hairline fracture takes him out of the program. I'm figuring he'll come back next year."

"He wants it," Gull agreed.

"It takes more than want, but you've got to want it to get it."

"I was just thinking the same thing."

On a half laugh, Rowan shook her head. "Do women ever say no to you?"

"Sadly, yes. Then again, a man who just gives up never wins the prize."

"Believe me, I'm no prize."

"You've got hair like a Roman centurion, the body of a goddess and the face of a Nordic queen. That's a hell of a package."

"The package isn't the prize."

"No, it's not. But it sure makes me want to open it up and see what's in there."

"A mean temper, a low bullshit threshold and a passion for catching fire. Do yourself a favor, hotshot, and pull somebody else's shiny ribbon."

"I've got this thing, this . . . focus. Once I focus on something, I just can't seem to quit until I figure it all the way out."

She gave a careless shrug, but she watched him, he noted, with care. "Nothing to figure."

"Oh, I don't know," he said when she started into the dorm. "I got you to take a walk in the rain with me."

With one hand on the door, she turned, gave him a pitying smile. "Don't tell me there's a romantic in there."

"Might be."

"Better be careful then. I might use you just because you're handy, then crush that romantic heart."

"My place or yours?"

She laughed—a steamy brothel laugh that shot straight to his loins—then shut the door, metaphorically at least, in his face.

Damned if he hadn't given her a little itch, she admitted. She liked confident men—men who had the balls, the brains and the skills to back it up. That, and the cat-at-the-mousehole way he looked at her—desire and bottomless patience—brought on a low sexual hum.

And picking up that tune would be a mistake, she reminded herself, then tapped lightly on Cards's door. She took his grunt as permission to poke her head in.

He looked, to her eye, a little pale, a lot bored and fairly grungy. "How're you feeling?"

"Shit, I'm okay. Got some bug in my gut this morning. Puked it, and a few internal organs, up." He sat on his bed, cards spread in front of him. "Managed some time in manufacturing, kept dinner down okay. Just taking it easy till tomorrow. Appreciate you covering for me."

"No problem. We're down to twenty-two. One of them's out with an injury. I think we'll see him back. See you in the morning then."

"Hey, want to see a card trick? It's a good one," he said before she could retreat.

Tired of his own company, she decided, and gave in to friendship and sat across from him on the bed.

Besides, watching a few lame card tricks was a better segue into sleep than thinking about walking in the rain with Gulliver Curry.

3

Gull lined up in front of the ready room with the other recruits. Across the asphalt the plane that would take them up for their first jump roared, while along the line nerves jangled.

Instructors worked their way down, doing buddy checks. Gull figured his luck was in when Rowan stepped to him. "Have you been checked?"

"No."

She knelt down so he studied the way her sunflower hair sculpted her head. She checked his boots, his stirrups, worked her way up—leg pockets, leg straps—checked his reserve chute's expiration date, its retainer pins.

"You smell like peaches." Her eyes flicked to his. "It's nice."

"Lower left reserve strap attached," she said, continuing her buddy check without comment. "Lower right reserve strap attached. Head in the game, Fast Feet," she added, then moved on up the list. "If either of us misses a detail, you could be a smear on the ground. Helmet, gloves. You got your letdown rope?"

"Check."

"You're good to go."

"How about you?"

"I've been checked, thanks. You're clear to board." She moved down to the next recruit.

Gull climbed onto the plane, took a seat on the floor beside Dobie.

"You looking to tap that blonde?" Dobie asked. "The one they call Swede?"

"A man has to have his dreams. You're getting closer to owing me twenty," Gull added when Libby ducked through the door.

"Shit. She ain't jumped yet. I got ten right now says she balks."

"I can use ten."

"Welcome aboard," Rowan announced. "Please bring your seats to their full upright position. Our flying time today will depend on how many of you cry like babies once you're in the door. Gibbons will be your spotter. Pay attention. Stay in your heads. Are you ready to jump?"

The answer was a resounding cheer.

"Let's do it."

The plane taxied, gained speed, lifted its nose. Gull felt the little dip in the gut as they left the ground. He watched Rowan, flat-out sexy to his mind in her jumpsuit, raise her voice over the engines and—once again—go over every step of the upcoming jump.

Gibbons passed her a note from the cockpit.

"There's your jump site," she told them, and every recruit angled for a window.

Gull studied the roll of the meadow—pretty as a picture— the rise of Douglas firs, lodgepole pines, the glint of a stream. The job—once he took the sky—would be to hit the meadow, avoid the trees, the water. He'd be the dart, he thought, and he wanted a bull's-eye.

When Gibbons pigged in, Rowan shouted for everyone to guard their reserves. Gibbons grabbed the door handles, yanked, and air, cool and sweet with spring, rushed in.

"Holy shit." Dobie whistled between his teeth. "We're doing it. Real deal. Accept no substitutes."

Gibbons stuck his head out into that rush of air, consulted

with the cockpit through his headset. The plane banked right, bumped, steadied.

"Watch the streamers," Rowan called out. "They're you."

They snapped and spun, circled out into miles of tender blue sky. And sucked into the dense tree line.

Gull adjusted his own jump in his head, mentally pulling on his toggles, considering the drift. Adjusted again as he studied the fall of a second set of streamers.

"Take her up!" Gibbons called out.

Dobie stuffed a stick of gum in his mouth before he put on his helmet, offered one to Gull. Behind his face mask, Dobie's eyes were big as planets. "Feel a little sick."

"Wait till you get down to puke," Gull advised.

"Libby, you're second jump." Rowan put on her helmet. "You just follow me down. Got it?"

"I got it."

At Gibbons's signal, Rowan sat in the door, braced. The plane erupted into shouts of Libby's name, gloved hands slammed together in encouragement as she took her position behind Rowan.

Then Gibbons's hand slapped down on Rowan's shoulder, and she was gone.

Gull watched her flight; couldn't take his eyes off her. The blue-and-white canopy shot up, spilled open. A thing of beauty in that soft blue sky, over the greens and browns and glint of water.

The cheer brought him back. He'd missed Libby's jump, but he saw her chute deploy, shifted to try to keep both chutes in his eye line as the plane flew beyond.

"Looks like you owe me ten."

A smile winked into Dobie's eyes. "Add a six-pack on it that I do better than her. Better than you."

After the plane circled, Gibbons looked in Gull's eyes, held them for a beat. "Are you ready?"

"We're ready."

"Hook up."

Gull moved forward, attached his line.

"Get in the door."

Gull leveled his breathing, and got in the door.

He listened to the spotter's instructions, the drift, the wind, while the air battered his legs. He did his check while the plane circled to its final lineup, and kept his eyes on the horizon.

"Get ready," Gibbons told him.

Oh, he was ready. Every bump, bruise, blister of the past weeks had led to this moment. When the slap came down on his right shoulder, he jumped into that moment.

Wind and sky, and the hard, breathless thrill of daring both. The speed like a drug blowing through the blood. All he could think was, Yes, Christ yes, he'd been born for this, even as he counted off, as he rolled his body until he could look through his feet at the ground below.

The chute billowed open, snapped him up. He looked right, then left and found Dobie, heard his jump partner's wild, reckless laughter.

"Now *that's* what I'm talking about!"

Gull grinned, scanned the view. How many saw this, he wondered, this stunning spread of forest and mountain, this endless, open sky? He swept his gaze over the lacings of snow in the higher elevations, the green just beginning to haze the valley. He thought, though he knew it unlikely, he could smell both, the winter and the spring, as he floated down between them.

He worked his toggles, using instinct, training, the caprice of the wind. He could see Rowan now, the way the sun shone on her bright cap of hair, even the way she stood—legs spread and planted, hands on her hips. Watching him as he watched her.

He put himself beside her, judging the lineup, and felt the instant he caught it. The smoke jumpers called it on the wire, so he glided in on it, kept his breathing steady as he prepared for impact.

He glanced toward Dobie again, noted his partner would overshoot the spot. Then he hit, tucked, rolled. He dropped his gear, started gathering his chute.

He heard Rowan shouting, saw her running for the trees. Everything froze, then melted again when he heard Dobie's shouted stream of curses.

Above, the plane tipped its wings and started its circle to

deploy the next jumpers. He hauled up his gear, grinning as he walked over to where Dobie dragged his own out of the trees.

"I had it, then the wind bitched me into the trees. Hell of a ride, though." The thrill, the triumph lit up his face. "Hell of a goddamn ride. 'Cept I swallowed my gum."

"You're on the ground," Rowan told them. "Nothing's broken. So, not bad." She opened her personal gear bag, took out candy bars. "Congratulations."

"There's nothing like it." Libby's face glowed as she looked skyward. "Nothing else comes close."

"You haven't jumped fire yet." Rowan sat, then stretched out in the meadow grass. "That's a whole new world." She watched the sky, waiting for the plane to come back, then glanced at Gull as he dropped down beside her. "You had a smooth one."

"I targeted on you. The sun in your hair," he added when she frowned at him.

"Jesus, Gull, you *are* a romantic. God help you."

He'd flustered her, he realized, and gave himself a point on his personal scoreboard. Since he hadn't swallowed his gum, he tucked the chocolate away for later. "What do you do when you're not doing this?"

"For work? I put in some time in my dad's business, jumping with tourists who want a thrill, teaching people who think they want, or decide they want, to jump as a hobby. Do some personal training." She flexed her biceps.

"Bet you're good at it."

"Logging in time as a PT means I get paid to keep fit for this over the winter. What about you?"

"I get to play for a living. Fun World. It's like a big arcade— video games, bowling, bumper cars, Skee-Ball."

"You work at an arcade?"

He folded his arms behind his head. "It's not work if it's fun."

"You don't strike me as the kind of guy to deal with kids and machines all day."

"I like kids. They're largely fearless and open to possibilities. Adults tend to forget how to be either." He shrugged. "You spend yours trying to get couch potatoes to break a sweat."

"Not all of my clients are couch potatoes. None are when I'm done with them." She shoved up to sit. "Here comes the next group."

With the first practice jump complete, they packed out, carrying their gear back to base. After another stint of physical training, classwork, they were up again for the second jump of the day.

They practiced letdown in full gear, outlined fire suppression strategies, studied maps, executed countless sit-ups, pull-ups, push-ups, ran miles and threw themselves out of planes. At the end of a brutal four weeks, the numbers had whittled down to sixteen. Those still standing ranged outside Operations answering their final roll call as recruits.

When Libby answered her name, Dobie slapped a twenty into Gull's hand. "Smoke jumper Barbie. You gotta give it to her. Skinny woman like that toughs it through, and a big hoss like McGinty washes."

"We didn't," Gull reminded him.

"Fucking tooting we didn't."

Even as they slapped hands a flood of ice water drenched them.

"Just washing off some of the rookie stink," somebody called out. And with hoots and shouts, the men and woman on the roof tossed another wave of water from buckets.

"You're now one of us." From his position out of water range, L.B. shouted over the laughter and curses. "The best there is. Get cleaned up, then pack it in the vans. We're heading into town, boys and girls. You've got one night to celebrate and drink yourself stupid. Tomorrow, you start your day as smoke jumpers—as Zulies."

When Gull made a show out of wringing out his wet twenty, Dobie laughed so hard, he had to sit on the ground. "I'll buy the first round. You're in there, Libby."

"Thanks."

He smiled, stuffed the wet bill in his wet pocket. "I owe it all to you."

Inside, Gull stripped off his dripping clothes. He took stock of his bruises—not too bad—and for the first time in a week took time to shave. Once he'd hunted up a clean shirt and pants, he spent a few minutes sending a quick e-mail home to let his family know he'd made it.

He expected that news to generate mixed reactions, though they'd all pretend to be as happy as he was. He slid a celebratory cigar into his breast pocket, then wandered outside.

The e-mail had cost him some time, so he loaded into the last of the vans and found a seat among the scatter of rookies and vets.

"Ready to party, rook?" Trigger asked him.

"I've been ready."

"Just remember, nobody gets babysat. The vans leave and you're not in one, you find your own way back to base. If you end up with a woman tonight, the smart thing is to end up with one who has a car."

"I'll keep that in mind."

"You dance?"

"You asking?"

Trigger hooted out a laugh. "You're almost pretty enough for me. The place we're going has a dance floor. You do it right, dancing with a woman's the same as foreplay."

"Is that the case, in your experience?"

"It is, young Jedi. It surely is."

"Interesting. So . . . does Rowan like to dance?"

Trigger raised his eyebrows. "That's what we call barking up the wrong tree."

"It's the only tree that's caught my interest and attention."

"Then you're going to have a long, dry summer." He gave Gull a pat on the shoulder. "And let me tell you something else from my vast experience. When you've got calluses on your calluses and blisters on top of that, jerking off isn't as pleasant as it's meant to be."

"Five years as a hotshot," Gull reminded him. "If the summer proves long and dry, my hands'll hold up."

"Maybe so. But a woman's better."

"Indeed they are, Master Jedi. Indeed they are."

"Have you got one back home?"

"No. Do you?"

"Had one. Twice. Married one of them. Just didn't take. Matt's got one. You got a woman back home in Nebraska, don't you, Matt?"

Matt shifted, angled around to look back over his shoulder. "Annie's back in Nebraska."

"High-school sweethearts," Trigger filled in. "Then she went off to college, but they got back together when she came home. Two minds, one heart. So Matt doesn't dance, if you get my drift."

"Got it. It's nice," Gull continued, "having somebody."

"No point in the whole screwed-up world if you don't." Matt shrugged. "No point doing what we do if nobody's waiting for us once we've done it."

"Sweetens the pot," Trigger agreed. "But some of us have to settle for a dance now and again." He rubbed his hands together as the van pulled up in a lot packed with trucks and cars. "And my toes are already tapping."

Gull scanned the long, low log building as he stepped out of the van, contemplated a moment on the flickering neon sign.

"'Get a Rope,'" he read. "Seriously?"

"Cowboy up, partner." Trigger slapped him on the shoulder, then strutted inside on his snakeskin boots.

An experience, Gull reminded himself. You could never have too many of them.

He stepped into the overamplified screech and twang of truly, deeply bad country music performed by a quartet of grungy-looking guys behind the dubious protection of a chicken-wire fence. At the moment the only things being hurled at them were shouted insults, but the night was young.

Still, people crowded the dance floor, kicking up boot heels, wiggling butts. Others ranged along the long bar or squeezed onto rickety chairs at tiny tables where they could scarf up dripping nachos or gnaw on buffalo wings coated with a suspicious substance that turned them cheese-puff orange. Most opted to wash that combo down with beer served in filmy plastic pitchers.

The lights were mercifully dim, and despite the smoking ban dingy blue clouds fogged the air that smelled like a sweat-soaked, deep-fried, overflowing ashtray.

The only reasonable thing to do, as Gull saw it, was to start drinking.

He moved to the bar, elbowed in and ordered a Bitter Root

beer—in a bottle. Dobie squeezed beside him, punched him in the arm. "Why do you wanna drink that foreign shit?"

"Brewed in Montana." He passed the bottle to Dobie, ordered another.

"Pretty good beer," Dobie decided after a pull. "But it ain't no Budweiser."

"You're not wrong." Amused, Gull tapped his bottle to Dobie's, drank. "Beer. The answer to so many questions."

"I'm going to get this one in me, then cut one of these women out of the herd, drive 'em on the dance floor."

Gull sipped again, studied the fat-fingered lead guitar player. "How do you dance to crap like this?"

Dobie's eyes slitted, and his finger drilled into Gull's chest. "You got a problem with country music?"

"You must've busted an eardrum on your last jump if you call this music. I like bluegrass," he added, "when it's done right."

"Don't bullshit me, city boy. You don't know bluegrass from bindweed."

Gull took another swig of beer. "I am a man of constant sorrow," he sang in a strong, smooth tenor. "I've seen trouble all my days."

Now Dobie punched him in the chest, but affectionately. "You're a continual surprise to me, Gulliver. Got a voice in there, too. You oughta get up there and show those shit-kickers how it's done."

"I think I'll just drink my beer."

"Well." Dobie tipped up the bottle, drained it. Let out a casual belch. "I'm going for a female."

"Good luck with that."

"Ain't about luck. It's about style."

Gull watched Dobie bop over to a table of four women, and decided the man had a style all of his own.

Enjoying the moment, Gull leaned an elbow back on the bar, crossed his ankles. Trigger, true to his word, already had a partner on the dance floor, and Matt—true to his Annie—sat with Little Bear, a rookie named Stovic and one of the pilots they called Stetson for his battered and beloved black hat.

Then there was Rowan, chowing down on the orange-coated nachos at a table with Janis Petrie, Gibbons and Yangtree. She'd pulled on a blue T-shirt—snug, scoop-necked—that molded her breasts and torso. For the first time since he'd met her she wore earrings, something that glittered and swung from her ears when she shook her head and laughed.

She'd done something to her eyes, her lips, he noted, made them bolder. And when she let Cards pull her to her feet for a dance, Gull saw her jeans were as snug as her shirt.

She caught his eye when Cards swung her into a spin, then stopped his heart when she shot him a wide, wicked smile. He decided if she was going to kill him, she might as well do it at closer range. He ordered another beer, carried it over to her table.

"Hey, fresh meat." Janis toasted him with a dripping nacho. "Want to dance, rookie?"

"I haven't had enough beer to dance to whatever this is."

"They're so bad, they're good." Janis patted Rowan's empty chair. "A few more drinks, they'll be nearly good enough to be bad."

"Your logic tells me you've walked this path before."

"You're not a Zulie until you've survived a night at Get a Rope." She glanced toward the door as a group of three men swaggered in. "In all its glory."

"Local boys?"

"Don't think so. They're all wearing new boots. High-dollar ones." She topped off her beer from the pitcher on the table. "I'm guessing city, dude-ranch types come to take in some local color."

They headed toward the bar, and the one in the lead shoulder-muscled his way through the line. He slapped a bill on the bar.

"Whiskey and a woman." He punched his voice up, deliberately, Gull imagined, so it carried above the noise. The hoots and laughter from his friends told Gull it wouldn't be their first drink of the night.

A few people at the bar edged over to give the group room while the bartender poured their drinks. The lead guy tossed it back, slapped down the glass, pointed at it.

"We need us some *females*."

More group hilarity ensued. Looking for trouble, Gull concluded, and since he wasn't, he went back to watching Rowan on the dance floor.

Janis leaned toward him as the band launched into a painful cover of "When the Sun Goes Down." "Ro says you work in an arcade."

"She talked to you about me?"

"Sure. We pass notes in study hall every day. I like arcades. You got pinball? I kill at pinball."

"Yeah, new and vintage."

"Vintage?" She aimed a narrow look with big brown eyes. "You don't have High Speed, do you?"

"It's a classic for a reason."

"I love that one!" Her hand slapped the table. "They had this old, beat-up machine in this arcade when I was a kid. I got so good at it, I'd play all day on my first token. I traded this guy five free games on it for my first French kiss." She sighed, sat back. "Good times."

Following her gaze as it shifted to the bar, Gull glanced back in time to see the whiskey-drinker give a waitress passing by with a full tray a frisky slap on the ass. When the woman looked around, he held up both hands, smirked.

"Asshole. You can't go anywhere," Janis said, "without running into assholes."

"Their numbers are legion." He shifted a little more when Rowan stepped off the dance floor.

"That's my seat."

"I'm holding it for you." He patted his knee.

She surprised him by dropping down on his lap, picking up his beer and drinking deep. "Big spender, buying local brew by the bottle. Don't you dance, moneybags?"

"I might, if they ever play something that doesn't make my ears bleed."

"You can still hear them? I can fix that. Time for shots."

"Count me out," Gibbons said immediately. "The last time you talked me into that I couldn't feel my fingers for a week."

"Don't do it, Gull," Yangtree warned him. "The Swede has an iron gut. Got it from her old man."

Rowan turned her face close to Gull's and smirked. "Aw, do you have a tender tummy, hotshot?"

He imagined biting her heavy bottom lip, just one fast, hard nip. "What kind of shots?"

"There's only one shot worth shooting. Te-qui-la," she sang it, slapping her palm on the table with each syllable. "If you've got the balls for it."

"You're sitting on my balls, so you ought to know."

She threw back her head on that sexy saloon girl laugh. "Hold them for a minute. I'll get us set up."

She hopped up, swung around a couple times when Dobie grabbed her hand and gave her a twirl. Titania to Puck, Gull thought.

Then she hooked her thumbs in her front pockets and joined him in some sort of boot-stomping clog thing that had some of the other dancers whistling and clapping.

She shot a finger at Gull—and damn, there went his heart again—then danced over to the bar.

"Hey, Big Nate." Rowan leaned in, hailed the head bartender. "I need a dozen tequila shots, a couple saltshakers and some lime wedges to suck on."

She glanced over, gave the man currently grabbing his crotch a bored look, shifted away again. "I can take them over if Molly's busy."

The crotch-grabber slapped a hundred-dollar bill on the bar in front of her. "I'll buy your shots and ten minutes outside."

Rowan gave the bartender a slight shake of the head before he could speak.

She turned, looked the drunk, insulting bastard in the eye. "I guess since you lack any charm, and the only way you can get a woman is to pay her, you think we're all whores."

"You've been wiggling that ass and those tits out there since I came in. I'm just offering to pay for what you've been advertising. I'll buy you a drink first."

At the table, Gull thought, *shit*, and started to rise. Gibbons put a hand on his arm. "You don't want to get in her way. Trust me on this."

"I don't like drunks hassling women."

He shoved up, noted the noise level had diminished, so he

clearly heard Rowan say in a tone sweet as cotton candy, "Oh, if you'll buy me a drink first. Is that your pitcher?"

She picked it up and, with her height, had no trouble upending it over the man's head. "Suck on that, fuckwit."

The man moved pretty quick for a sputtering drunk. He shoved Rowan back against the bar, grabbed her breasts and squeezed.

And she moved faster. Before Gull was halfway across the room she slammed her boot on the man's instep, her knee into the crotch he'd been so proud of, then knocked him on his ass with an uppercut as fine as Gull had ever seen when the drunk doubled over.

She back-fisted one of his buddies who'd been foolish enough to try to yank her around. She grabbed his arm, dragged him forward, past her. The boot she planted on his ass sent him careening into his friend as the man started to struggle to his feet.

She whipped around to man number three. "You want to try for me?"

"No." This one held up his hands in a don't-shoot-me gesture. "No, ma'am, I don't."

"Maybe you've got half a brain. Use it and get your idiot friends out of here before I get mad. Because when I get mad, I just get *crazy*."

"I guess she didn't need any help," Dobie observed.

"That does it." Gull laid a hand over his heart, beat it there. "I'm in love."

"I don't think I'd want to fall in love with a woman who could wipe the floor with me."

"No risk, no point."

He hung back as a half dozen Zulies moved in to help the three men to the door. And out of it.

Rowan gave her T-shirt a fussy tug. "How about those shots, Big Nate?"

"Coming right out. On the house."

Gull took his seat again, waiting for Rowan to carry the tray over.

"Are you ready?" she asked him.

"Line them up, sweetheart. You want some ice for your knuckles?"

She wiggled her fingers. "They're okay. It was like punching the Pillsbury Doughboy."

"I hear he's a mean drunk, too." ·

She laughed, then dropped down into the chair Gibbons pulled over for her. "Let's see what kind of drunk you are."

4

Gull watched her eyes as he and Rowan knocked back the first shot, as the tequila hit his tongue, his throat, and took that quick, hot slide to the belly.

That, he realized, was her first appeal for him. Those clear, cool blue eyes held so much *life*. They sparkled now with challenge, with humor, and there was something in the way they leveled on his that made the moment intimate—as much of a hot slide through the system as the tequila.

Matching his pace to hers, he picked up the next shot glass.

Then there was her mouth, just shy of wide, heavy on the bottom—and the way it so naturally, so habitually formed a smirk.

Small wonder he lusted for a good, strong taste of it.

"How ya doing, hotshot?"

"I'm good. How about you, Swede?"

In answer she tapped her third shot glass to his before they tossed back the contents together. She brought the lime wedge to her mouth. "Do you know what I love about tequila?"

"What do you love about tequila?"

"Everything." After a wicked laugh, she drank the fourth

with the same careless gusto as the first three. Together they slapped down the empties.

"What else do you love?" he asked her.

"Hmm." She considered as she downed number five. "Smoke jumping and those who share the insanity." She toasted them to a round of applause and rude comments, then sat back a moment with her full glass. "Fire and the catching of it, my dad, ear-busting rock and roll on a hot summer night and tiny little puppies. How about you?"

Like her, he sat back with his last shot. "I could go along with most of that, except I don't know your dad."

"Haven't jumped fire yet either."

"True, but I'm predisposed to love it. I have a fondness for loud rock and tiny little puppies, but would substitute heart-busting sex on a hot summer night and big, sloppy dogs."

"Interesting." They tossed back that last shot, in unison, to more applause. "I'd've pegged you for a cat man."

"I've got nothing against cats, but a big, sloppy dog will always need his human."

Her earrings swung as she cocked her head. "Like to be needed, do you?"

"I guess I do."

She pointed at him in an *aha* gesture. "There's that romantic streak again."

"Wide and long. Want to go have heart-busting sex in anticipation of a hot summer night?"

She threw back her head and laughed. "That's a generous offer—and no." She slapped a hand on the table. "But I'll go you another six."

God help him. "You're on." He patted his pocket. "I believe I'll take a short cigar break while we get the next setup."

"Ten-minute recess," Rowan announced. "Hey, Big Nate, how about some salsa and chips to soak up some of this tequila? And not the wimpy stuff."

The woman of his dreams, Gull decided as he opted to go out the back for his smoke. A salsa-eating, tequila-downing, smoke-jumping stunner with brains and a wicked uppercut.

Now all he had to do was talk her into bed.

He lit up in the chilly dark, blew smoke up at a sky sizzling with stars. The night struck him as pretty damn perfect. Crappy music in a western dive, cheap tequila, the companionship of like-minded others and a compelling woman who engaged his mind and excited his body.

He thought of home and the winters that engaged and absorbed most of his time. He didn't mind it, in fact enjoyed it. But if the past few years had taught him anything, it was he needed the heat and rush of the summers, the work and, yes, the risk of chasing fires.

Maybe it was just that, the combination of pride and pleasure in what he'd accomplished back home, the thrill and satisfaction of what he knew he could accomplish here that allowed him to stand in a chilly spring night in the middle of almost-nowhere and recognize perfection.

He wandered around the building, enjoying his cigar, thinking of facing Rowan over another six tequila shots. Next time—if there was a next time—he'd make damn sure they had a bottle of Patrón Silver. Then at least he'd feel more secure about the state of his stomach lining.

Amused, he came around the side of the building. He heard the grunts first, then the ugly sound of fist against flesh. He moved forward, toward the sounds, scanning the dark pockets of the parking lot.

Two of the men Rowan had dealt with in the bar held Dobie while the third—the big one—whaled on him.

"Shit," Gull muttered, and, tossing down his cigar, rushed forward.

Over the buzz of rage in his ears, Gull heard one of the men shout. The big man swung around, face full of mean. Gull cocked back his fist, let it fly.

He didn't think; didn't have to. Instinct took over as the other two men dropped Dobie in a heap and came at him. He embraced the madness, the moment, punch, kick, elbow strike, as he scented blood, tasted his own.

He felt something crunch under his fist, heard the whoosh of expelled air as his foot slammed into belly fat. Someone dropped to his knees and gagged after his elbow jabbed an exposed throat. Out of the corner of his eye, Gull saw Dobie had managed to gain his feet and limped over to the retching man to deliver a solid kick in the ribs.

One of the others tried to run. Gull caught him, flung him so he skidded face-first over the gravel.

He didn't clearly remember knocking the big guy down, getting on top of him, but it took three of his fellow jumpers to pull him off.

"He's had enough. He's out." Little Bear's voice penetrated that buzz of rage. "Ease off, Gull."

"Okay. I'm good." Gull held up a hand to signal he was done. As the grips on him loosened, he looked over at Dobie.

His friend sat on the ground surrounded by other jumpers, a few of the local women. His face and shirtfront were both a bloody mess, and his right eye was swollen shut.

"Did a number on you, pal," Gull commented. Then he saw the dark stain on Dobie's right pant leg, and the dripping pool. "Christ! Did they knife you?"

Before Gull reached him, Dobie two-fingered a broken bottle of Tabasco out of his pocket. "Nah. Busted this when I went down. Got a few nicks is all, and a waste of good Tabasco."

L.B. crouched to get a better look at Dobie. "You carry Tabasco in your pocket?"

"Where else would I carry it?"

Shaking his head, Gull sat back on his heels. "He dumps it on everything."

"Damn right." To prove it, Dobie shook out the little left on the ass of one of the semiconscious men. "I came out for a little air, and the three of them jumped me. Laying for me—or any of us, I reckon. You sure came along at the right time," he said to Gull. "You know kung fu or some shit?"

"Something like that. Better go get patched up."

"Oh, I'm okay."

Rowan moved through, crouched in front of Dobie. "They wouldn't have gone after you if they hadn't been pissed at me. Do me a favor, okay? Go get patched up so I don't have to feel guilty." Then she leaned over, kissed his bruised and bloody cheek. "I'll owe you."

"Well . . . if it'll make you feel better."

"Do you want me to call the law?" Big Nate asked him.

Dobie studied the three men, shrugged. "Looks to me more like they need an ambulance." He shrugged again. "I don't care if they go to jail, to fiery hell or back wherever they came from."

"All right then." Big Nate stepped over, toed the man sitting up nursing his face in his hands. "You fit to drive?" When the man managed a nod, Big Nate toed him again a little harder. "You're going to get in your truck with the fuckers you travel with. You're going to drive, and keep on driving. If I see you around my place or any other place I happen to be, you're going to wish to God almighty I had called the law. Now get off my property."

To expedite the matter, several of the men hoisted the barely conscious big guy and his moaning companions into the truck, then stood like a wall until it drove away.

Gull received a number of shoulder and back slaps, countless offers of a drink. He wisely accepted all of them to avoid an argument as he watched Libby, Cards and Gibbons help Dobie into one of the vans.

"Do you want a doc to look you over?" Little Bear asked him.

"No. I've had worse falling out of bed."

Little Bear watched the van as Gull did. "He'll be all right. It takes more than three assholes to down a smoke jumper." He gave Gull a last shoulder slap, then turned back toward the bar when the van pulled out of the lot.

Gull stayed where he was, trying to reach for his calm again. He knew it was in there, somewhere, but at the moment, elusive.

"Is this yours?"

He turned to see Rowan holding his cigar.

"Yeah. I guess I dropped it."

"Butterfingers." She took a few puffs until the tip glowed true again, then helped herself to one long, deep drag. "Prime cigar, too," she added, then offered it back. "Shame to waste it."

Gull took it, studied it. "That's it," he decided.

He flung it down again and, grabbing her, yanked her against him. "That's it," he repeated before his mouth crushed down on hers.

A man could only take so much stimulation before demanding release.

She slapped both hands on his chest, shoved. "Hey."

For a moment he figured he'd experience her excellent uppercut up close and personal. Then she mirrored his initial move and yanked him back.

Her mouth was as he'd imagined. Hot and soft and avid. It met his with equal fervor, as if a switch had been flipped in each of them from stop to go. She pressed that killer body to his without hesitation, without restraint, a gift and a challenge, until the chilly air under the sizzling stars seemed to smoke.

He tasted the sharp tang of tequila on her tongue, a fascinating contrast to the scent of ripe peaches that clung to her skin; felt the hard, steady gallop of her heart that matched the pace of his own.

Then she drew back, looked in his eyes, held there a moment before drawing away.

"You've got skills," she stated.

"Ditto."

She blew out a breath—a long one. "You're a temptation, Gull, I can't deny it. Stupid to deny it, and I'm not stupid."

"Far from it."

She rubbed her lips together as if revisiting his taste. "The thing is, once you mix sex into it, even smart people can get stupid. So . . . better not."

"No's your choice. Mine's to keep trying."

"I can't hold that against you." She smiled at him now, not her usual smirk but something warmer. "You fight like a maniac."

"I tend to get carried away, so I try to avoid it when I can."

"That's a good policy. What do you say we postpone the tequila and get some ice on that jaw of yours?"

"That's fine."

As they started back, she glanced over at him. "What was that technique you were using on those bastards?"

"An ancient form called kicking ass."

She laughed, gave him a friendly hip bump. "Impressive."

He returned the hip bump. "Sleep with me and I'll give you lessons."

She laughed again. "You can try harder than that."

"I'm just getting warmed up," he told her, then opened the door to the overheated bar and lousy music.

ROWAN ZIPPED her warm-up jacket as she stepped outside.
She'd put in some time in the gym, and checked the jump list
on the board in Operations. She was first load, fourth man.
Now she wanted a solid run on the track, maybe some chow.
She'd already checked and rechecked her gear. If the siren
sounded, she'd be ready.

Otherwise . . .

Otherwise, she thought as she shot a wave to one of the
mechanics, there was always work, always training. But the
fact was she was ready, more than ready, to jump her first fire
of the season. She cast a look up at the sky as she walked
toward the track. Clear, wide and as pretty a spring blue as
anyone could want.

Below it, the base chugged along in early-season morning
mode. Jumpers and support staff stayed busy, washing vehicles or tuning them up—or tuning themselves with calisthen-
ics on the training field. After the night's revelry, plenty were
getting a slow start, but she wanted air and effort.

And saw as she looked toward the track, she wasn't the
only one.

She recognized Gull not only by the body, but the speed.
Fast feet, she thought again. Obviously tequila shots and a bar
fight hadn't slowed him down.

She had to admire that.

As she jogged closer she noted that despite the cool air he'd
worked up a good sweat, one that ran a dark vee down the
faded gray tee he wore.

She had to admire that, too. She liked a man who pushed
himself, who tested his limits even when he was in his own world.

Though she'd already loosened up, she paused to stretch
before peeling off her jacket. And timed her entrance to the
track to veer on beside him.

"What're you up to?"

He held up two fingers, saving his breath.

"Going for three?" When he nodded, she wondered if he
could keep up that killing pace for another mile. "Me too. Go
ahead, Flash, I can't keep up with you."

She fell off his pace, found her own rhythm.

She loved to run, loved it with a pure heart, but imagined if she'd had Gull's speed, she'd have adored it. Then she forgot him, tuned into her own body, the air, the steady slap of her shoes on the track. She let her mind empty so it could fill again with scattered thoughts.

Personal supply list, juggling some time in for sewing some PG bags, Gull's mouth, Dobie. She should give her father a buzz since she was on call and couldn't get over to see him. Why did Janis paint her toenails when nobody saw them anyway? Gull's teeth scraping over her bottom lip. Assholes who ganged up on a little guy.

Gull kicking ass in a dark parking lot.

Gull's ass. Very nice.

Probably better to think of something else, she told herself as she hit the first mile. But hell, nothing else was as appealing. Besides, thinking wasn't doing.

What she needed—what they all needed—was for the siren to blast. Then she'd be too busy to fantasize about, much less consider, getting tangled up with a man she worked with.

Too bad she hadn't met him in the winter, though how she'd have run into him when he lived in California posed a problem. Still, say she'd taken a vacation, dropped into his arcade place. Would she have experienced that sizzle if she'd met him across the lane in the bowling alley, or over a hot game of Mortal Kombat?

Hard to say.

He'd have looked as good, she reminded herself. But would there have been that punch if she'd looked into those green eyes when he sold her some tokens?

Wasn't at least part of the zip because of what they both did here, the training, the sweat, the anticipation, the intense satisfaction of knowing only a select few could make the cut and be what they were?

And, hello, wasn't that the reason she didn't get sexually or romantically involved with other jumpers? How could you trust your feelings when they were pumped through the adrenaline rush? And what did you do with those feelings when and if—and most likely when—things went south? You'd still have to work with, and trust your life to, somebody you'd been sleeping with and weren't sleeping with anymore. And one or both of you had to be fairly pissed about it.

Entirely better to meet somebody, even if he sold you tokens in an arcade, have a nice, uncomplicated short-term relationship. Then go back to doing what you do.

She kicked up her pace to hit the last mile, then eased off to a cool-down jog. Her eyebrows lifted when Gull fell into pace beside her.

"You still here?"

"I did five. Felt good."

"No tequila haze this morning?"

"I don't get hangovers."

"Ever? What's your secret?" When he only smiled, she shook her head. "Yeah, yeah, if I sleep with you, you'll tell me. How's the jaw, et cetera?"

"It's okay." Banging like a drum after the five miles, but he knew that would subside.

"I heard Dobie nixed the overnight for observation. L.B.'s got him off the jump list until he's fit."

Gull nodded. He'd checked the list himself. "It won't take him long. He's a tough little bastard."

She slowed to a walk, then stopped to stretch. "What were you listening to?" she asked, gesturing to the MP3 player strapped to his arm.

"Ear-busting rock," he said with a smile. "You can borrow it the next time you run."

"I don't like music when I run. I like to think."

"The best thing about running is *not* thinking."

As he stretched, she checked out the body she'd been thinking about. "Yeah, you're probably right."

They started the walk back together.

"I didn't come out here because I saw you on the track."

"Well, hell. Now my day's ruined."

"But I did admire your ass when you were whizzing by."

"That's marginally satisfying," he considered, "but I find it doesn't fully massage my ego."

"You're a funny guy, Gull. You tend to use fancy words, and read fancy books—I hear. You're mean as a rattler in a fight, fast as a cheetah and spend your winters with foosball."

He bent to snag her jacket off the ground. "I like a good game of foosball."

As she tied the sleeves around her waist, she gave his face a long study. "You're hard to figure."

"Only if you're looking for one size fits all."

"Maybe, but—" She broke off as she spotted the truck pulling up in front of Operations. "Hey!" she shouted, waved her arms, then ran.

Gull watched the man get out of the truck, tall and solid in a battered leather jacket and scarred boots. Silver hair caught by the wind blew back from a tanned, strong-jawed face. He turned, then opened his arms so Rowan could jump into them. Gull might have experienced a twinge of jealousy, but he recognized Lucas "Iron Man" Tripp.

And it was a pretty thing, in his opinion, to see a man give his grown daughter a quick swing.

"I was just thinking about you," Rowan told her father. "I was going to give you a call later. I'm on the second stick, so I couldn't come by."

"I missed you. I thought I'd check in, grab a minute and see how it's all going." He pulled off his sunglasses, hooked them in his pocket. "So, a strong crop of rooks this year."

"Yeah. In fact . . ." Rowan glanced around, then signaled to Gull so he'd change direction and join them. "Here's the one who broke the base record on the mile-and-a-half. Hotshot out of California." She kept her arm around her father's waist while Gull walked to them.

"Gulliver Curry, Lucas Tripp."

"It's a genuine pleasure, Mr. Tripp," Gull told him as he extended a hand.

"You can drop the mister. Congratulations on the base record, and making the cut."

"Thanks."

She had her father's eyes, Gull noted as they covered the small talk. And his bone structure. But what made more of an impression was the body language of both. It said, simply and unquestionably, they were an unassailable unit.

"There's that son of a bitch." Yangtree let the door of Operations slap behind him, and came forward to exchange one-armed hugs with Lucas.

"Man, it's good to see you. So they let you skate through again this year?"

"Hell. Somebody's got to keep these screwups in line."

"When you're tired of riding herd on the kids, I can always use another instructor."

"Teaching rich boys to jump out of planes."

"And girls," Lucas added. "It's a living."

"No packing in, packing out, no twenty hours on a line. You miss it every day," Yangtree said, and pointed at him.

"And twice on Sunday." Tripp ran a hand down Rowan's back. "But my knees don't."

"I hear that."

"We'll get you a couple rocking chairs," Rowan suggested, "and maybe a nice pot of chamomile tea."

Lucas tugged her earlobe. "Make it a beer and I'm there. Then again, I heard the bunch of you had plenty of those last night, and got into a little ruckus."

"Nothing we couldn't handle," Yangtree claimed, and winked at Gull. "Or you couldn't handle, right, Kick Ass?"

"A momentary distraction."

"Did the momentary distraction give you that bruise on your jaw?" Lucas wondered.

Gull rubbed a hand over it. "I'd say you should see the other guys, but it's hard to be sure how they looked since they ran off with their tails tucked."

"From having them rammed into your fists." Lucas nodded at Gull's scraped and swollen knuckles. "How's the man they ganged up on?"

"Do you know everything?" Rowan demanded.

"Ear to the ground, darling." Lucas kissed her temple. "My ear's always to the ground."

"Dobie's a little guy, but he got some licks in." Yangtree turned his head, spat on the ground. "They beat on him pretty good until Kick Ass here came along. Of course, before all that, your girl put two of them on their asses."

"Yeah, I heard about that, too."

"I didn't start it."

"So I'm told. Starting it's stupid," Lucas stated. "Finishing it's necessary."

Rowan narrowed her eyes. "You didn't come by to check in, you came by to check *on*."

"Maybe. Want to fight about it?"

She gave her father a poke in the chest, grinned.

And the siren went off.

Rowan kissed her father's cheek. "See you later," she said, and took off running. Yangtree slapped Lucas's shoulder and did the same.

"It was good to meet you."

Tripp took the hand Gull offered, studied the knuckles. "You're off the list because of these."

"Today."

"There's tomorrow."

"I'm counting on it."

Gull headed to the ready room. He was off the jump list, but he could lend a hand to those on it. Already jumpers were suiting up, taking their gear out of the tall cabinets, pulling on Kevlar suits over the fire-retardant undergarments. By the time he spotted her, Rowan had dropped into one of the folding chairs to put on her boots.

He helped with gear and equipment until he could work his way to her.

Over the sound of engines and raised voices, he shouted at her, "Where?"

"Got one in the Bitterroots, near Bass Creek."

A short enough flight, he calculated, to warrant a buddy check prior to boarding. He started at her bootstraps, worked his way up. He'd already gotten past the state of his knuckles, and his temporary leave from the jump list.

No point in regrets.

"You're clear." Gull squeezed a hand to her shoulder, met her eyes. "Make it good."

"It's the only way I know."

He watched her go, thought even the waddle enforced by the suit and gear looked strong and sexy on her.

As he walked out to watch the rest of the load, he saw Dobie hobbling over. And in the distance Lucas "Iron Man" Tripp stood, hands in his pockets.

"Fuckers screwed our chances." Puffing a little, his face a

crescendo of bruises, his brutalized eye a vivid mix of purple and red, Dobie stopped beside Gull.

"Others to come."

"Yeah. Shit. Libby's on there. I never thought she'd catch one before me."

Together they stood as the plane taxied, as its nose lifted. Gull glanced down to where Lucas stood, saw him lift his face to the sky. And watch his daughter fly toward the flames.

5

The heart of the wildfire beat hot and hard. Cutting through it loosed a waterfall of sweat that ran down Rowan's back in constant streams. Her chain saw shrieked through bark and wood, spitting out splinters and dust that layered her clothes, gloves, hard hat. The roar and screams of saws, of cracking wood, crashing trees fought to smother that hard, hot beat.

She paused only to chug down water to wet her throat and wash out the dust and smoke or to swipe off her goggles when the sweat running down her face blurred them.

She stepped back when the ponderosa she'd killed to save others whooshed its way to the forest floor.

"Hey, Swede." Gibbons, acting as fire boss, hailed her over the din. Ash blackened his face, and the smoke he'd hiked through reddened his eyes. "I'm taking you, Matt and Yangtree off the saw line. The head's shifted on us. It's moving up the ridge to the south and building. We got spots frigging everywhere. We need to turn her while we can."

He pulled out his map to show her positions. "We got hotshots working here, and Janis, Trigger, two of the rooks, flanking it here. We've got another load coming in, and they'll take the saw line, chase down spots. We've got repellent on the way, should dump on the head in about ten, so make sure you're clear."

"Roger that."

"Take them up. Watch your ass."

She grabbed her gear, pulled in her teammates and began the half-mile climb through smoke and heat.

In her mind she plotted escape routes, the distance and direction to the safe zone. Small, frisky spot fires flashed along the steep route, so they beat them out, smothered them before continuing up.

Along their left flank an orange wall pulsed with heat and light, sucked oxygen out of the air to feed itself as it growled and gobbled through trees. She watched columns of smoke build tall and thick in the sky.

A section of the wall pushed out, skipped and jumped across the rough track in front of them, and began to burn merrily. She leaped forward kicking dirt over it, using her Pulaski to smother it while Yangtree beat at it with a pine bough.

They beat, shoveled and dug their way up the ridge.

Over the din she caught the rumble of the tanker, pulled out her radio to answer its signal. "Take cover!" she shouted to her team. "We're good, Gibbons. Tell them to drop the mud. We're clear."

Through the smoke, she watched the retardant plane swing over the ridge, heard the thunder of its gates opening to make the drop, and the roar as the thick pink rain streaked down from the sky.

Those fighting closer to the head would take cover as well, and still be splattered with gel that burned and stung exposed skin.

"We're clear," she told her team as Yangtree gnawed off a bite of an energy bar. "We're going to jag a little east, circle the head and meet up with Janis and the others. Gibbons says she's moving pretty fast. We need to do the same to keep ahead of her. Let's move! Keep it peeled for spots."

She kept the map in her head, the caprices of the fire in her guts. They continued to chase down spot fires, some no bigger than a dinner platter, others the size of a kid's swimming pool.

And all the while they moved up the ridge.

She heard the head before she saw it. It bellowed and

clapped like thunder, followed that with a sly, pulsing roar. And felt it before she saw it, that rush of heat that washed over her face, pushed into her lungs.

Then everything filled with the flame, a world of vivid orange, gold, mean red spewing choking clouds of smoke. Through the clouds and eerie glimmer she saw the silhouettes, caught glimpses of the yellow shirts and hard hats of the smoke jumpers, waging the war.

Shifting her pack, she pushed her way up the ridge toward the ferocious burn. "Check in with Gibbons," she shouted to Matt. "Let him know we made it. Yo, Elf!" Rowan hailed Janis as she hurried forward, waving her arms. "Cavalry's here."

"We need it. We got scratch lines around the hottest part of the head. The mud knocked her down some, and we've been scratching line down toward the tail. Need to widen it, and down the snags. Jesus."

She took a minute to gulp some water, swipe at the sweat dripping into her eyes. The pink goo of repellent pasted her hat and shirt. "First fire of the season, and this bitch has a punch. Gibbons just told me they're sending in another load of jumpers, and they put Idaho on alert. We gotta cut off her head, Swede."

"We can start on widening the line, downing the snags. Hit a lot of spots on the way up. She keeps trying to jump."

"Tell me. Get started. I got the rooks up there, Libby and Stovic. Keep 'em straight."

"You got it."

Rowan dug, cut, beat, hacked and sweated. Hours flashed by. She sliced down snags, the still-standing dead trees the fire would use for fuel. When she felt her energy flag, she stopped long enough to stuff her mouth with the peanut-butter crackers in her PG bag, wash it down with the prize of the single Coke—nearly hot now—she'd brought with her.

Her clothes sported the pink goo from a second drop of repellent, and under it her back, legs, shoulders burned from the heat and the hours of unrelenting effort.

But she felt it, the minute it started to turn their way.

The massive cloud of smoke thinned—just a little—and through it she saw a single hopeful wink of light from the North Star.

Day had burned into night while they'd battled.

She straightened, arched her back to relieve it, and looked back, into the black—the burned-out swatch of the forest the fire had consumed, the charred logs, stumps, ghostly spikes, dead pools of ash.

Nothing to eat there now, she thought, and they'd cut off the supply of fuel at the head.

Her energy swung back. It wasn't over, but they'd beaten it. The dragon was beginning to lie down.

She downed a dead pine, then used one of its branches to beat out a small, sneaky spot. The cry of shock and pain had her swinging around in time to see Stovic go down. His chain saw bounced out of his hands, rolled, and the blood on its teeth dripped onto the trampled ground.

Rowan let her own drop where she stood, lunged toward him. She reached him as he struggled to sit up and grab at his thigh.

"Hold on! Hold on!" She pushed his hands away, tore at his pants to widen the jagged tear.

"I don't know what happened. I'm cut!" Beneath the soot and ash, his face glowed ghastly white.

She knew. Fatigue had made him sloppy, caused him to lose his grip on the saw or use it carelessly enough, just for a second, to allow it to jerk back.

"How bad?" he demanded as she used a knife from her pack to cut the material back. "Is it bad?"

"It's a scratch. Toughen up, rook." She didn't know either way, not yet. "Get the first-aid kit," Rowan ordered when Libby dropped down beside her. "I'm going to clean this up some, Stovic, get a better look."

A little shocky, she determined as she studied his eyes, but holding.

And his bitter litany of curses—a few of them Russian delivered in his Brooklyn accent—made her optimistic as she cleaned the wound.

"Got a nice gash." She said it cheerfully, and thought, Jesus, Jesus, a little deeper, a little to the left, and bye-bye, Stovic. "The blade mostly got your pants."

She looked him in the eye again. She'd have lied if necessary, and her stomach jittered with relief she didn't need the

lie. "You're going to need a couple dozen stitch
shouldn't slow you down for long. I'm going to do a f...
ing that'll hold you until you get back to base."

He managed a wobbly smile, but she heard the click i...
throat as he swallowed. "I didn't cut off anything essent...,
right?"

"Your junk's intact, Chainsaw."

"Hurts like hell."

"I bet."

He gathered himself, took a couple slow breaths. Rowan
felt another wave of relief when a little color eked back into his
face. "First time I jump a fire, and look what I do. It won't keep
me grounded long, will it?"

"Nah." She dressed the wound quickly, competently. "And
you'll have this sexy scar to impress the women." She sat back
on her haunches, smiled at him. "Women can't resist a
wounded warrior, right, Lib?"

"Damn right. In fact, I'm holding myself back from jumping you right now, Stovic."

He gave her a twisted grin. "We beat it, didn't we, Swede?"

"Yeah, we did." She patted his knee, then got to her feet.
Leaving Libby tending him, she walked apart to contact Gibbons and arrange for Stovic to be littered out.

Eighteen hours after jumping the fire, Rowan climbed back
onto the plane for the short flight back to base.

Using her pack as a pillow, she stretched out on the floor,
shut her eyes. "Steak," she said, "medium rare. A football-size
baked potato drowning in butter, a mountain of candied carrots, followed by a slab of chocolate cake the size of Utah
smothered in half a gallon of ice cream."

"Meat loaf." Yangtree dropped down beside her while
somebody else—or a couple of somebody elses by the stereo-
phonics—snored like buzz saws. "An entire meat loaf, and I'll
take my mountain in mashed potatoes with a vat of gravy.
Apple pie, and make that a gallon of ice cream."

Rowan slid open her eyes to see Matt watching her with a
sleepy smile. "What's your pick, Matt?"

"My ma's chicken and dumplings. Best ever. Just pour it in
a five-gallon bucket so I can stick my head in and chow it
down. Cherry cobbler and homemade whipped cream."

"Everybody knows whipped cream comes in a can."

"Not at my ma's house. But I'm hungry enough to eat five-day-old pizza, and the box it came in."

"Pizza," Libby moaned, then tried to find a more comfortable curl on her seat. "I never thought I could be this empty and live."

"Eighteen hours on the line'll do it." Rowan yawned, rolled over, and let the voices, the snoring, the engines lull her toward sleep.

"Gonna hit the kitchen when we get back, Ro?" Matt asked her.

"Mmm. Gotta eat. Gotta shower off the stink first."

The next thing she knew they were down. She staggered off the plane through a fog of exhaustion. Once she'd dumped her gear she stumbled to her room, ripped the wrapper off a candy bar. She all but inhaled it while she stripped off her filthy clothes. Barely awake, she aimed for the shower, whimpered a little as the warm water slid over her. Through blurry eyes she watched it run dingy gray into the drain.

She lathered up, hair, body, face, inhaling the scent of peaches that apparently tripped Gull's trigger. Rinse and repeat, she ordered herself. Rinse and repeat. And when, at last, the water ran clear, she made a halfhearted attempt to dry off.

Then fell onto the bed wrapped in the damp towel.

THE DREAM crept up on her in the twilight layer of sleep, as her mind began to float back from the deep pit of exhaustion.

Thundering engines, the whip of wind, the heady leap into the sky. The thrill turning to panic—the pound, pound, pound of heart against ribs as she watched, helplessly, Jim plunge toward the burning ground.

"Hey. Hey. You need to wake up."

The voice cutting through the scream in her head, the rough shake on her shoulder, had her bolting up in bed.

"What? The siren? What?" She stared into Gull's face, rubbing one hand over her own.

"No. You were having a nightmare."

She breathed in, breathed out, slitting her eyes a little. It was morning—or maybe later—she could tell that much. And Gulliver Curry was in her room, without her permission.

"What the hell are you doing in here?"

"Maybe you want to hitch that towel up some? Not that I mind the view. And, in fact, could probably spend the rest of the day admiring it."

She glanced down, saw she was naked to the waist, and the towel that had slipped down wasn't covering much below either. Baring her teeth, she yanked it up and around. "Answer the question before I kick your ass."

"You missed breakfast, and you were heading toward missing lunch."

"We worked the fire for eighteen hours. I didn't get to bed till about three in the morning."

"So I hear, and good job. But somebody mentioned you didn't get to eat, and have a fondness for bacon-and-egg sandwiches, with Jack cheese. So . . ." He jerked his thumb at the bedside table. "I brought you one. I was going to leave it on the nightstand, but you were having a bad one. I woke you up, you flashed me—and just let me insert you have the most magnificent rack it's ever been my privilege to view—and that brings us up to date."

She studied the sandwich, the bottle of soda beside it. This time when she breathed in, the scent nearly made her weep with joy. "You brought me a bacon-and-egg sandwich?"

"With Jack cheese."

"I'd say you earned the flash."

"I can go get you another if that's all it takes."

She laughed, yawned, then secured the towel before grabbing the plate. The first bite had her closing her eyes in ecstasy. Wrapped in pleasure, she didn't order him off the bed when she felt it give under his weight.

"Thanks," she said with her mouth full of bite two. "Sincerely."

"Let me respond, sincerely. It was way worth it."

"I do have exceptional tits." She reached for the drink, twisted the top off. "The fire kept changing direction on us, spitting out spots. We'd get a line down, and she'd say, Oh, you want to play that way? Try this. But in the end, she couldn't beat the Zulies. Have you got any word this morning on Stovic?"

"Now known as Chainsaw. He and his twenty-seven stitches are doing fine."

"I should've kept a closer eye on him."

"He passed the audition, Rowan. Accidents happen. They're part of the job description."

"Can't argue, but he was part of my team, and I was senior member in that sector." She shrugged. "He's okay, so that's okay."

She shifted her gaze. "Your hands look better."

"Good enough." He flexed them. "I'm back on the jump list."

"Dobie?"

"He's coming along, but it'll be a couple more days anyway. Little Bear discovered Dobie can sew like Betsy Ross, so he's been keeping Dobie chained to a machine. I won fifty-six dollars and change at poker last night, and Bicardi—one of the mechanics—got half lit and sang Italian opera. That, I believe, is all the news."

"I appreciate the update, and the sandwich. Now go away so I can get dressed."

"I've already seen you naked."

"It'll take more than a breakfast sandwich for you to see me naked again."

"How about dinner?"

God, he made her laugh. "Out, hotshot. I need to hit the gym, put my time in and work out some of these kinks."

"To show what a classy guy I am, I'll refrain from making any of the obvious comments to that statement." He rose, picked up the empty plate. "You're one gorgeous female, Rowan," he said as he walked out. "It keeps me up at night."

"You're one sexy male, Gulliver," she murmured when he'd gone. "It's messing with my head."

She put in ninety in the gym, but kept it light and slow to avoid overworking her system, then hit the cookhouse.

Feeling human again, she texted the basics to her father.

Killed the fire. Am A-OK. Love you, Ro

She headed to the loft to check the chute she'd hung the night before. She began to check for holes, snags, defects.

She glanced up when Matt and Libby came in.

"Well, don't you look flat-tailed and dull-eyed."

"Remind me never to eat like a pig before crawling into bed." Libby pressed a hand to her belly. "I couldn't settle till after five, then lay there like a beached whale."

"You didn't make it to the cookhouse," Matt commented when he brought his chute over.

"By the time I scraped off the stink, I barely made it from the shower to the bed. Slept like a rock," she added, smiling at Libby. "Had room service, put in my ninety PT, ate more, and here I am ready to do it all again."

"Sweet." Libby spread out her chute. "Room service?"

"Gull brought me a breakfast sandwich."

"Is that what they call it in Missoula?"

Rowan pointed a finger. "Just the sandwich, but he did earn some points. Have either of you seen Chainsaw?"

"Yeah, I poked in before I ran into Matt. He showed me his stitches."

"Is that what they call it in California?"

"Walked right into that one."

"He's lucky," Matt said. "Only hit meat. An inch either way, different story."

"It comes down to inches, doesn't it?" Libby ran her fingers over her chute. "Or seconds. Or one tiny lapse of focus. The difference between having an interesting scar or . . ."

She trailed off, paled a little. "I'm sorry, Matt. I wasn't thinking."

"It's okay. You didn't even know him." He continued his inspection, cleared his throat. "To tell you the truth, I didn't know, not for sure, if I was going to be able to really do it again until yesterday. In the door, looking down at the fire, waiting for the spotter's hand to come down on my shoulder. I didn't know if I could jump fire again."

"But you did," Rowan murmured.

"Yeah. I told myself I did it for Jim, but until I actually did it . . . Because you're right, Libby. It is about inches and seconds. It's about fate. It's why we can't let up. Anyway." He let out a long breath. "Did you know Dolly's back?" he asked Rowan.

"No." Surprised, Rowan stopped what she was doing. "When? I haven't seen her on base."

"She came back yesterday, while we were on the fire. She came by my room this morning after breakfast." He kept his gaze fixed on his chute. "She looks okay. Wanted to apologize for how she was after Jim died."

"That's good." But Rowan felt a twist in her belly as she completed her chute inspection.

"I told her she ought to do the same to you."

"Doesn't matter."

"Yeah, it does."

"Can I ask who Dolly is?" Libby wondered. "Or should I mind my own business?"

"She was one of the cooks," Rowan told her. "She and Jim had a thing. Actually, she tended to have things with a variety, but she'd narrowed it down to Jim most of last season. She took it hard when he died. Understandable."

"She came at you with a kitchen knife," Matt reminded her. "There's nothing understandable about that."

"Well, Jesus."

"She sort of came at me," Rowan corrected as Libby gaped at her.

"Why?"

"I was Jim's jump partner that day. She needed to blame somebody. She went a little crazy, waved the knife at me. But basically she blamed all of us, said we'd all killed him."

Rowan waited a beat to see if Matt would comment, but he kept his silence.

"She took off right after. I don't think anyone expected she'd be back, or get hired back, for that matter."

Matt shifted his feet, looked at her again. "Are you okay with it?"

"I don't know." Rowan rubbed the back of her neck. "I guess if she doesn't wave sharp implements at me or try to poison me, I'm cool with it."

"She's got a baby."

It was Rowan's turn to gape. "Say what?"

"She told me she had a baby, a girl, in April." His eyes watered up a little, so he looked away. "Dolly named her Shiloh. Her ma's looking after her while Dolly's working. She said it's Jim's."

"Well, God, you didn't know before? Your family doesn't know?"

He shook his head. "That's what she apologized for. She asked if I'd tell my mother, my family, and gave me some pictures. She said I could go see it—her—the baby—if I wanted."

"Did Jim know?"

Color came and went in his face. "She said she told him that morning, before the jump. She said he was really excited, that he picked the name. Boy or girl, he told her, he wanted Shiloh. They were going to get married, she said, in the fall."

He drew a wallet-sized photo out of his pocket. "Here she is. This is Shiloh."

Libby took the picture. "She's beautiful, Matt."

His eyes cleared at that, and the smile spread. "Bald as a melon. Jim and I were, too, and my sister. I've got to call my ma," he said as Libby passed the photo to Rowan. "I can't figure out how to tell her."

Rowan studied the chubby-cheeked, sparkle-eyed infant before handing the photo back. "Go take a walk, work it out in your head. Then call your mother. She'll be happy. Maybe a little mad she didn't know sooner, but overall she'll be happy. Go on. I'll take care of your chute."

"I can't get it off my mind, so I guess you're right. I can finish the chute later."

"I'll take care of it."

"Thanks. Thanks," he repeated, and wandered out like a man in a dream.

"It's a lot to deal with," Libby commented.

"Yeah, it's a whole lot."

She let it simmer in the back of her mind while she worked. Others came in, and since word of Dolly Brakeman's return spread, it reigned as the hot topic of the day.

"Have you seen her yet?"

Rowan shook her head at Trigger. Since she'd finished clearing her own chute, she focused on Matt's.

"Word is she came in yesterday afternoon, with her mother and her preacher."

"Her *what*?"

"Yeah." Trigger rolled his eyes. "Some Reverend Latterly.

The word is it's her mother's preacher guy, and Dolly's going to church regular now. And so they closeted up with L.B. for an hour. This morning, she's in the kitchen with Lynn and Marg, frying up the bacon."

"She can cook."

"Yeah, that was never her problem."

She met Trigger's eyes, gave another quick shake of her head. "She's got a kid now." Rowan kept her voice low. "There's no point shaking all that out."

"You think the kid's Jim's, like she says?"

"They were banging like bunnies, so why not?" Because, neither of them said, she had a habit of hopping to lots of male bunnies. "Anyway, it's not our business."

"He was one of ours, so you know that makes it our business."

She couldn't deny it, but she tuned out the gossip and speculation until she had stowed the chutes. Then she hunted out Little Bear.

He straightened from his hunch over his desk, gestured for her to close the door. "I figured you'd be stopping by."

"I just want to know if I need to watch my back. I'd as soon not end up with a bread knife between my shoulder blades."

He rubbed a spot between his eyebrows. "Do you think I'd let her on base if I thought she'd give you any trouble?"

"No. But I wouldn't mind hearing that right out loud."

"She worked here three years before Jim. The only problem we ever had was the wind from how fast she'd throw up her skirts. And nobody much had a problem with that, either."

"I don't care if she gave every rookie, snookie, jumper and mechanic blow jobs in the ready room." Rowan jammed her hands in her pockets, did a little turn around the room. "She's a good cook."

"She is. And from what I heard, a lot of men missed those bj's once she hooked up with Jim. And she's got a kid now. From the timing of it, and from what she says, it's his." L.B. puffed out his cheeks. "She brought her preacher with her. Her mother got her going to church. She needs the work, wants to make amends."

He waved a hand in the air. "I'm not going to deny I felt sorry for her, but I'd've turned her off if I hadn't believed she wanted a fresh start for her and the baby. She knows if she gives you or anybody else any trouble, she's out."

"I don't want that on my head, L.B."

He gave Rowan a long look out of solemn brown eyes. "Then think of it on mine. If you're not all right with this, I'll take care of it."

"Hell."

"She's singing in the choir on Sundays."

"Give me a break." She shoved her hands in her pockets again as L.B. grinned at her. "Fine, fine." But she dropped down in a chair.

"Not fine?"

"Did she tell you she and Jim were going to get married, and he was all happy about the baby?"

"She did."

"The thing is, L.B., I know he was seeing somebody else. We caught that fire last year in St. Joe, and were there three days. Jim hooked up with one of the women on the cook line; he seemed to go for cooks. And I know they met at a motel between here and there a few times when he was off the jump list. Others, too."

"I know it. I had to talk to him about expecting me to cover for him with Dolly."

"And the day of his accident, I told you, he was jittery on the plane. Not excited but nervous, jumpy. If Dolly dropped the pregnancy on him before we got called out, that's probably why. Or part of why."

He tapped a pencil on the desk. "I can't see any reason Dolly has to know any of that. Do you?"

"No. I'm saying maybe she found God, or finds some comfort in singing for Jesus, but she's either lying or delusional about Jim. So it's fine with me if she's back, as long as we understand that."

"I asked Marg to keep an eye on her, let me know how she does."

Satisfied, Rowan stood up again. "That's good enough for me."

"They're getting some lightning strikes up north," L.B. told her as she started out.

"Yeah? Maybe we'll get lucky and jump a fire, then everybody can stop talking about the return of Dolly. Including me."

She might as well clear it up altogether, Rowan decided, and made the cookhouse her next stop.

She found dinner prep under way, as she'd anticipated.

Marg, the queen of the cookhouse, where she'd reigned a dozen years, stood at the counter quartering red-skinned potatoes. She wore her usual bib apron over a T-shirt and jeans, and her mop of brown hair secured under a bright pink do-rag.

Steam puffed from pots on the stove while Lady Gaga belted out "Speechless" from the playlist on the MP3 Marg had on the counter.

Nobody but Marg determined kitchen music.

She sang along in a strong, smoky alto while keeping the beat with her knife.

Her Native American blood—from her mother's grandmother—showed in her cheekbones, but the Irish dominated in the mild white skin dashed with freckles and the lively hazel eyes.

Those eyes caught Rowan's now, and rolled toward the woman washing greens in the sink.

Rowan lifted her shoulders, let them fall. "Smells good in here." She made sure her voice carried over the music.

At the sink, Dolly froze, then slowly switched off the water and turned.

Her face was a bit fuller, Rowan noted, and her breasts as well. She had her blond hair in a high, jaunty ponytail, and needed a root job.

But that was probably unkind, Rowan thought. A new mother had other priorities. The rose in her cheeks came from emotion rather than blush as she cast her gaze down and dried her hands on a cloth.

"We got pork roasting to go with the rosemary potatoes, butter beans and carrots. Veggies get three-cheese ravioli. Gonna put a big-ass Mediterranean salad together. Pound cake and blueberry crumble for dessert."

"Sign me up."

Rowan opened the refrigerator and took out a soda as Marg went back to her potatoes.

"How are you doing, Dolly?"

"I'm fine, and you?" She said it primly, chin in the air now.

"Good enough. Maybe you could take a quick break, catch a little air with me?"

"We're busy. Lynn—"

"Better get her skinny ass back in here right quick," Marg interrupted. "You go on out, and if you see her, send her in."

"I need to dry these greens," Dolly began, but shrunk—as all did—under Marg's steely stare. "Okay, fine." She tossed aside her cloth, headed for the door.

Rowan exchanged a look with Marg, then followed.

"I saw a picture of your baby," Rowan began. "She's beautiful."

"Jim's baby."

"She's beautiful," Rowan repeated.

"She's a gift from God." Dolly folded her arms as she walked. "I need this job to provide for her. I hope you're Christian enough not to do anything that gets me fired."

"I don't think about it being Christian or otherwise, Dolly. I think about it as being human. I never had a problem with you, and I'm not looking to have one now."

"I'll cook for you just like I cook for the rest. I hope you'll show me the respect of staying clear of me and I'll do the same. Reverend Latterly says I have to forgive you to get right with the Lord, but I don't."

"Forgive me for what?"

"You're the reason my baby's going to grow up without her daddy."

Rowan said nothing for a moment. "Maybe you need to believe that to get through, and I find I don't give a shit either way."

"I expect that from you."

"Then I'm happy not to disappoint you. You can claim to have tripped over God or to've been born again, I don't care about that, either. But you've got a baby, and you need work. You're good at the work. What you're going to have to suck up, Dolly, is to keep the work, you have to deal with me. When I feel like coming into the kitchen, I will, whether you're around or not. I'm not going to live my life around your stipulations or misplaced grudges."

She held up a hand before Dolly could speak. "One more thing. You got away with coming at me once. You won't get away with it again. New baby or not, I'll put you down. Other than that, we won't have a problem."

"You're a heartless whore, and one day you'll pay for all you've done. It should've been you instead of Jim that day. It should've been you, screaming your way to the ground."

She ran back to the kitchen.

"Well," Rowan mumbled, "that went well."

6

Rowan slept poorly, and put the blame squarely on Dolly. She'd checked the radar, the logs, the maps before turning in. Fires sparked near Denali in Alaska and in the Marble Mountains of Northern California. She'd considered—half hoped—she'd be called up and spend part of her night on a transport plane. But no siren sounded, no knock banged on her door.

Instead, she'd dreamed of Jim for the second night in a row. She woke irritated and itchy, and annoyed with her own subconscious for being so easily manipulated.

Done with it, she promised herself, and decided to start her day with a good, hard run to blow the mood away.

As her muscles warmed toward the first quarter mile, Gull fell into step beside her.

She flicked him a glance. "Is this going to be a habit?"

"I was running first yesterday," he reminded her. "I like putting in a few miles first thing. Wakes me up."

He'd gotten a look at her, too, and decided she looked a little pissed off, a little shadowed around the eyes. "Are you going for time or distance?"

"I'm just going for the run."

"We'll call it distance then. I like having an agenda."

"So I've noticed. I think three."

He snorted. "You've got more than that. Five."

"Four," she said just to keep him from getting his way. "And don't talk to me. I like being in my head when I run."

Obligingly he tapped the MP3 playing on his arm and ran to his music.

They kept the pace steady for the first mile. She was aware of him beside her, of the sound of their feet slapping the track in unison. And found she didn't mind it. She could speculate on what music he ran to, what *agenda* he'd laid out for the rest of his day. How that might tumble apart if they caught a fire.

They were both first stick on the jump list.

When they crossed the second mile she heard the sound of an engine above, and saw one of her father's planes glide across the wide blue canvas of sky. Flying lesson, she determined—business was good. She wondered if her father or one of his three pilots sat as instructor, then saw the right wing tip down twice, followed by a single dip on the left.

Her dad.

Face lifted, she shot up her arm, fingers stretched high in her signal back.

The simple contact had the dregs of annoyance that the run and Gull's companionship hadn't quite washed away breaking apart.

Then her running companion picked up the pace. She increased hers to match, knowing he pushed her, tested her. Then again, life without competition was barely living as far as she was concerned. The building burn in her quads and her hamstrings scorched away even those shattered dregs.

Her stride lengthened at mile three. Her arms pumped, her lungs labored. The bold sun the forecasters had promised would spike the temperatures toward eighty by afternoon skinned her in a thin layer of sweat.

She felt alive, challenged, happy.

Then Gull glanced her way, sent her a wink. And left her in his dust.

He had some kind of extra gear, she thought once he kicked in. That's all there was to it. And when he hit it, he was just fucking gone.

She dug for her own kick, found she had a little juice yet. Not enough to catch him—not unless she strapped herself to a rocket—but enough not to embarrass herself.

The last half-mile push left her a little light-headed, had her breath whooping as she simply rolled onto the grass beside the track.

"You'll cramp up. Come on, Ro, you know better than that."

He was winded—not gasping for air as she was, but winded, and she found a little satisfaction in that.

"Minute," she managed, but he grabbed her hands, pulled her to her feet.

"Walk it off, Ro."

She walked her heart rate down to reasonable, squeezed a stream from the water bottle she'd brought out with her into her mouth.

Watching him, she stood on one leg, stretched her quads by lifting the other behind her. He'd worked up a sweat, and it looked damn good on him. "It's like you've got an engine in those Nikes."

"You motor along pretty good yourself. And now you're not pissed off or depressed anymore. Was that your father doing the flyover?"

"Yeah. Why do you say I was pissed off and depressed?"

"It was all over your face. I've been making a study of your face, and that's how I tagged the mood."

"I'm going to hit the gym."

"Better stretch out those hamstrings first."

Irritation crawled up her back like a beetle. "What are you, the track coach?"

"No point getting pissed at me because I noticed you were pissed."

"Maybe not, but you're right here." Still, she dropped down into a hamstring stretch.

"From what I've heard, you've got cause to be."

She lifted her head, aimed that icy blue stare.

"Let me sum up." He opened the kit bag he'd tossed on the edge of the track, took out some water. "Matt's brother and the blond cook spent a good portion of last season tangling the sheets. Historically, said cook tangled many other sheets with dexterity and aplomb."

"Aplomb."

"It's a polite way of saying she banged often, well and without too much discrimination."

"That also sounded polite."

"I was raised well. In addition, Jim also tended to be generous with his attentions."

"Get you."

"However," Gull continued, "during the tangling and banging, the cook decided she was in love with Jim—that I got from Lynn, who got it from the blonde—and the blonde broke the hearts of many by focusing her dexterity exclusively on Jim, and closed her ears and eyes to the fact he didn't exactly reciprocate."

"You could write a book."

"The thought's crossed. Toward the end of this long, hot summer, the cook gets pregnant, which, rumor has it, since she avoided this eventuality previously, may have been on purpose."

"Probably." It was one of the things she'd already considered, and one of the things that depressed her.

"Sad," he said, and left it at that. "The cook claims she told Jim, who greeted the news with joy and exaltation. Though I didn't know him, that strikes me as sketchy. Plans to marry were immediately launched, which strikes sketchier yet. Then more sadly yet, Jim's killed during a jump which the ensuing investigation determines was his error—but the cook blamed his jump partner, which would be you, and tried to stab you with a kitchen knife."

"She didn't exactly try to stab me." The hell of it was, Rowan thought, she couldn't figure out why she kept defending the lunatic Dolly on that score. "Or didn't have time to because Marg yanked the knife away from her almost as soon as she'd picked it up."

"Points for Marg." He watched her face as he spoke, cat eyes steady and patient. "Grief takes a lot of forms, and a lot of those are twisted and ugly. But blaming you, or anyone on that load, for Jim's accident is just stupid. Continuing to is mean and stupid, and self-defeating."

She didn't want to talk about this. Why was she? She couldn't seem to help it, she realized, with him watching her intently, speaking so calmly.

"How do you know she still blames me?"

The sunlight picked out the gold in his brown hair as he drank down more water. "To wind it up, the cook takes off, and finds religion—or so she claims and maybe even believes. Not enough grace and faith to tell the father's grieving family about the baby, until she comes back to base looking for work. So I call bullshit on the God factor."

"Okay." Maybe she couldn't help it because he'd laid it out flat, and in exactly the way she saw it. "Wow."

"Not quite finished. You seek out the cook, engage her in private conversation. Though, of course, privacy is slim pickings around here. During the not-so-private conversation, the cook becomes very steamed, does a lot of snarling and pointing, then storms off. Which leads me to conclude finding religion didn't include finding forgiveness, charity or good sense."

"How did you get all this? And I do mean all."

"I'm a good listener. If you care, the general consensus on base is she had Jim's kid—and Matt's niece—so she should get some support. In fact, Cards is taking donations for a college fund in Jim's name."

"Yeah," Rowan replied. "He'd think of that. He's just built that way."

"The consensus continues that if she gives you grief or talks trash about you, she gets one warning. Second time, we meet with L.B., lay it out and she goes. You've got no say in it."

"I—"

"None." The single syllable remained calm, and absolutely final. "Everybody pretty much wants her to keep her job. And nobody's going to let her keep it if she causes trouble. So if you don't agree with that, you're outvoted. You might as well stop being pissed off and depressed because it's not going to do you any good."

"I guess I don't agree because it's me. If it was somebody else, I'd be right there."

"I get that."

"Leaving out a lot of stuff I'm not in the mood to talk about, my mother died when I was twelve."

"That's hard."

"They weren't together, and . . . that's the lot of stuff I'm not in the mood to talk about. My father raised me, with his parents taking a lot of the weight during the season when he was still jumping. What I'm saying is, I know it's not easy to be a single parent, even with help and support. I'm willing to cut her some slack."

"She's getting slack already, Rowan. She's working in the kitchen. It'll be up to her if she stays."

They'd walked back while they talked. Now he gestured toward the gym. "Feel like lifting?"

"Yeah. Can I use this?" She tapped his MP3 player. "I want to check out your playlist."

"Working out without the tunes is a sacrifice." He pulled it off, handed it to her. "Consider that when you're lining up the reasons to sleep with me."

"I'll put it at the top of the list."

"Nice. So . . . what did it bump down?"

She laughed and walked inside ahead of him.

Once she finished her daily PT, cleaned up, she hiked to the cookhouse to fuel up on carbs.

In the dining hall, Stovic chowed down on bacon and eggs and biscuits while Cards ragged on him for being a malingerer between forkfuls of pancakes. Gull had beaten her there and was already building a stack of his own from the breakfast buffet.

Rowan grabbed a plate. She flopped a pancake onto it, laid two slices of bacon over that, added another pancake, two more slices of bacon. She covered that with a third pancake over which she dumped a hefty spoonful of berries.

"What do you call that?" Gull asked her.

"Mine." She carried it to the table, dropped into a chair. "What's the word, Cards?"

"Plumbago."

"That's a good one. Sounds like a geriatric condition, but it's a flower, right?"

"Shrub. Half point for you."

"The flower on the shrub, or plant, is also called plumbago," Gull pointed out.

Cards considered. "I guess that's true. Full point."

"Yippee." Rowan dumped syrup over her bacon pancakes. "How's the leg, Chainsaw?"

"Stitches itch." He glanced over as Dobie wandered in, grinned. "But at least it's not my face."

"At least I didn't do it to myself," Dobie tossed back, and studied the offerings. "If I hadn't lost that bet, I'd've joined up just for the breakfasts." To prove it, he took a sample of everything.

"Your eye looks better," Rowan told him.

He could open both now, and she recognized the symphonic bruising as healing.

"How are the ribs?"

"Colorful, but they don't ache much. L.B.'s got me doing a shitload of sit-down work." He pulled out a bottle of Tabasco, pumped it over his eggs. "I asked if I could have some time today. I figured I'd walk on down, check out your daddy's operation. Watch some of those pay-to-jump types come down."

"You should. A lot of people make a picnic of it. Marg would pack you up something."

"Maybe I'll go with you."

Dobie wagged an impaled sausage at Stovic. "You've got that gimp leg."

"The walk'll take my mind off the itch."

It probably would, Rowan thought, but just in case. "I'll give you the number for the desk. If you can't make it, they'll send somebody to get you."

Marg stepped in, scanned the table as she walked over and set a tall glass of juice in front of Rowan. "Are you all going to be wandering in and out of here all morning, and lingering at my table half the day? What you need is a fire."

"Can't argue with that." Rowan picked up the glass, sampled. "Carrots, because there are always carrots, celery, I think, some oranges—and I'm pretty sure mango."

"Good for you. Now drink it all."

"Marg, you're looking more beautiful than ever this morning."

Marg cast a beady eye on Dobie. "What do you want, rookie?"

"I heard tell you might could put together a bag lunch if me and my fellow inmate here mosey on down to Rowan's daddy's place to watch the show."

"I might could. You tell Lucas, if you see him, it's past time he came in to pay a call on me."

"I'll sure do that."

AS HE HAD a short window before a tandem jump, Lucas made a point of walking out when he got word a couple of the rookies from the base were on the grounds.

A lot of tourists and locals came by to watch the planes and the jumpers, with plenty of them hooking the trip to his place with a tour of the smoke jumpers' base. He figured it was good for business.

He'd started with one plane, a part-time pilot and instructor, with his mother handling the phones. When they rang. His pop ran dispatch, helped with the books. Of course in those days, he'd only been able to give the half-assed business his attention off-season, or when he was off the jump list.

But he'd needed to build something for his daughter, something solid.

And he had. He took pride in that, in his fleet of planes, his full-time staff of twenty-five. He had the satisfaction of knowing one day, when she was ready, Rowan could stand on what he'd built and have that solidity under her.

Still there were days he watched a plane rise into the sky from the base, knew the men and women on it were flying to fire, that he missed it like a limb.

He knew, now, what it was to be on the ground and know someone he loved more than anything in the world and beyond was about to risk her life. He wondered how his parents, his daughter, even the wife he'd had so briefly had ever stood that constant mix of fear and resignation.

But today, so far, the sirens stayed silent.

He stopped a moment to watch one of the students—a sixty-three-year-old banker from town free-fall from the Otter. Applause broke out in the audience of watchers when the chute deployed.

Zeke had been Lucas's banker for close to forty years, so Lucas watched a moment longer, gave a nod of approval at the form, before he walked over to the blanket where the two men from the base stretched out with what he recognized as one of Marg's famous boxed lunches.

"How's it going?" he asked, and crouched down beside them. "Lucas Tripp, and you must be Dobie. I heard you got in a scuffle at Get a Rope the other night."

"Yeah. I'm usually prettier. It's a pleasure meeting you," Dobie added as he held out a hand. "This one's Chainsaw, as he likes to use one to shave his legs."

"Heard about that, too. If you're going to get banged up, it might as well be early in the season, before things heat up."

"It's a real nice operation you got here, Mr. Tripp," Stovic commented.

The polite deference made Lucas feel old as an alp. "You can hang the mister around my father. We're doing pretty well here. See that one." He gestured toward where Zeke touched down and rolled. "He won't see sixty again. Bank manager out of Missoula. Granddaddy of eight with two more coming. Known him longer than either of you have been alive, and up until a couple months ago, he never said a word to me about wanting to jump. *Bucket List*," Lucas told them with a grin. "Since that movie came out, we're getting a lot of clients and students with some age on them coming in.

"I've got a tandem jump coming up. Client's due in about fifteen. Fifty-seven-year-old woman. High-school principal. You never know who's got a secret yen to fly."

"Do you miss it?" Dobie asked him. "Jumping fire."

"Every day." Lucas shrugged as he watched his banker wave to a trio of his grandkids. "But old horses like me have to make room for you young stallions."

"You must have a lot of stories from back in the day."

And older yet, Lucas thought, but grinned at Stovic. "Get a couple beers in me, I'll tell them all, whether you want to hear them or not."

"Anytime," Dobie said. "Anyplace."

"I might take you up on it. I better get on, give the principal the thrill of her life." Lucas pushed to his feet. "Enjoy your day off. You won't get many more of them."

"I don't see how he could come to give it up," Dobie commented. "I don't think I could."

"You haven't jumped fire yet," Stovic pointed out.

"In my head I have." Dobie bit into a drumstick Marg had fried to a crispy turn. "And I didn't try to castrate myself with a chain saw."

Stovic gave him a good-natured punch in the arm. "It got the Swede's hands on my thigh. Worth every stitch."

"You try to move on that, Gull'll give you more than a few stitches. His eyes're homed in that direction."

"I ain't blind. But she's sure got a nice touch." Stovic dug into the potato salad as they watched the next jumper.

LUCAS CHECKED HIS LOGS, the aircraft, had a quick conversation with his mechanic and the pilot for the tandem. Even if the client arrived on time, Marcie—his service rep—would sit her down for an overall explanation, have the client fill out the necessary forms. Since she'd ordered the DVD package, he swung through to make sure his videographer was lined up for the go.

When he walked into the operations building, he spotted Marcie and the client at one of the tables dealing with the paperwork. His first thought was a cliché, but true nonetheless.

They hadn't made principals like that when he'd been in high school.

She had red hair, and a lot of it, that kind of swept around her face, and eyes like forest shadows. Deep and green. When she smiled at something Marcie said, shallow dimples popped out in her cheeks, and her lips turned up in a pretty bow.

He wasn't shy around women—unless he was attracted to one. He felt the wash of embarrassed heat run up the back of his neck as he approached the table.

"And here's your jump master," Marcie announced, "and the owner of Zulie Skydiving. Lucas, I was just telling Mrs. Frazier she's about to experience the thrill of a lifetime, and she's got the top dog to take her through it."

"Well," Lucas managed as the heat spread to the top of his skull.

"If I'm going to be thrilled, I like knowing it's with the top dog." She offered her hand—narrow, slender-fingered. Lucas took it loosely, released it quickly, worried he might crush it.

"Mrs. Frazier's son bought her the package for Christmas," Marcie added.

"Make it Ella, since we'll be jumping out of a plane together. He heard me say I wanted to try skydiving one day, and took me seriously, even though I believe I'd had several glasses of wine at the time." Those lips bowed up again; the dimples popped. "He and his family are out poking around, as are my daughter and hers. They're all excited to watch."

"That's good. That's nice."

"So . . ." Ella waited a beat. "When do we start?"

"We'll get you suited up." Though she beamed smiles, Marcie slid a puzzled look up at Lucas. "While we do, you'll watch a short instructional video. Then the boss will give you a little training, answer any questions. That'll take about thirty minutes, so you'll be familiar with the equipment, feel comfortable and learn how to land."

"Landing would be key. I don't want to traumatize my grandchildren." She said it with a sparkle in her eye.

Married. Lucas's brain caught up with the rest of him. With kids. With grandkids. Knowing she was married eased the shyness. Now he could just admire how pretty she was, seeing as she was off-limits.

"No worries about that." He was able to grin back at her. "They'll remember today as the day they watched their grandmother fly. If you're done with the paperwork, we'll get you your flight suit."

He changed into his own while Marcie got the client outfitted. He generally enjoyed doing tandems with first-timers, soothing their nerves if they had them, answering questions, giving them the best experience possible, and a memory they'd carry for the rest of their lives. He expected this run would be no exception.

The client looked fit, which helped. He glanced at his copy of the form and noted he'd been on the mark on her statistics. Five-five, 123 pounds. No physical problems.

He stepped outside to wait for her.

"I feel official." She laughed and did a little turn in her flight suit and jump boots.

"Looking good. I know Marcie went over the procedure with you, but I can go over it again, answer any questions you've got."

"Marcie was thorough, and the video was great. The harness attaches me to you, start to finish, which is very important from my point of view."

"It's a good way to make a first jump. Low stress."

She bubbled out a laugh. "Easy for you to say. I guess you're used to screamers."

"Don't worry about that. I'm betting you're going to be too happy and too dazzled by the view to scream." He led her to a small training field. "We'll go up to about fourteen thousand feet. When you're ready, I'll take you on a trip into that big sky. The free fall's a rush, exhilarating. It'll last about a minute before the chute deploys. Once it does, you'll float, and listen to the kind of quiet only jumpers know."

"You love it."

"Absolutely."

"I'm doing this for a couple of reasons. First for my son. I just couldn't disappoint him. And second, I realized on the way here, to remind myself I used to be fearless. Tell me, Mr. Tripp—"

"Lucas."

"Lucas, how many people chicken out once they're up there?"

"Oh, there's some, sure. I can usually peg them before we get off the ground." He gave her an easy smile. "You won't be one of them."

"Because?"

"You were fearless once. You don't forget what you are. Sometimes you just put it aside awhile."

The dimples fluttered in her cheeks. "You're right. I've learned that lesson the last few years."

He showed her how to land, how to use him, her own body for a soft touchdown. He strapped the harness so she could get accustomed to the feel of it, and having his body against hers.

The little jump in the belly he felt had him relieved to remind himself she was married.

"Any questions? Concerns?"

"I think I've got it. I'm supposed to relax and enjoy—and hope I don't scream the whole way down so the DVD shows me with my mouth wide open and my eyes squeezed shut."

"Hey, Mom!"

They looked over at the group hovering at the edge of the field.

"The family. Do you have time to meet them before we do this?"

"Sure."

He walked over with her, made some small talk with her son—he looked pale and nervous now that it was zero hour—her daughter, the three children, including the one watching him like an owl from his daddy's hip.

"You're sure about this? Because if—"

"Tyler." Ella rose to the toes of her jump boots, kissed her son's cheek. "I'm revved and ready. Best Christmas present ever."

"Nana's gonna do this." A boy of about five shot the toy parachutist from their gift shop into the air. It floated down on a bright red chute.

"You bet I am. Watch me."

After hugs and kisses, she walked off with Lucas toward the waiting Twin Otter. "I'm not nervous. I'm not going to be nervous. I'm not going to scream. I'm not going to throw up."

"Look at that sky. It doesn't get prettier. Until you're floating in it. Here's Chuck. He'll be videographing your entire experience."

"Chuck." She shook hands. "You'll get my best side, right?"

"Guaranteed. Nobody gives a tandem like Iron Man, ma'am. Smooth as silk."

"Okay." She blew out a breath. "Let's do it, Iron Man."

She turned, waved to her family, then got onboard.

She shook hands with the pilot, and to Lucas's eye stayed steady and attentive through the flight. He expected more questions—about the plane, the equipment, his experience—but she played it up for the camera, obviously determined to give her family a fun memento.

She mugged, pretended to faint and surprised Lucas by crawling into his lap and telling her kids she was flying off to Fiji with her jump master.

"We need to go back for a bigger plane," he told her, and made her laugh.

When they reached jump altitude he winked at her. "Ready to harness up?"

Those lips bowed up with nerves around the edges. "Let's rock and roll."

He went over the procedure again, his voice soothing, easy, as he hooked them together.

"You're going to feel a rush of air, hear more engine noise when we open the door. We're miked, so Chuck will pick up what we say for your DVD."

As he spoke he felt her breathing pick up. When the door opened, he felt her jerk, felt her tremble.

"We don't go until you say go."

"I swam naked in the Gulf of Mexico. I can do this. Let's go."

"We're go." He nodded to Chuck, who jumped first. "Watch the sky, Ella," he murmured, and leaped with her.

She didn't scream, but after a strangled gasp, he heard her clearly shout, "Holy fucking shit!" and wondered if they'd want that edited out for the grandchildren.

Then she laughed, shot her arms out like wings.

"Oh, my God, oh, my God, oh, my *God* ! I did it. Lucas!"

She vibrated against him, and in tune with her he recognized exhilaration rather than fear.

The chute deployed, a rush of wings, and the whippy dive became a graceful float.

"It was too fast, over too fast. But, oh, *oh*, you were right. This is . . . religious."

"Put your hands on the toggles. You can drive awhile."

"Okay, wow. Look at Nana, Owen! I'm a skydiver. Thank you, Tyler! Hi, Melly, hi, Addy, hi, Sam!" She tipped her head back. "I'm in the sky, and it's blue silk."

She fell silent, then sighed. "You were right about the quiet. You were right about everything. I'll never forget this. Oh, there they are! They're waving. You'd better take over so I can wave back."

"You have a beautiful family."

"I really do. Oh, gosh, oh, wow, here comes the ground."

"Trust me. Trust yourself. Stay relaxed."

He brought her down soft.

With excited screams, wild cheers, her family jumped and waved. When Lucas detached the harness, she dropped into an exaggerated curtsy, blew kisses.

Then she spun around, her face glowing, and stunned him

by throwing her arms around him and kissing him firmly on the mouth.

"I'd have done that in midair if I could have because, my God, that was orgasmic. I don't know how to thank you."

"I think you just did."

She laughed, made him laugh by doing a quick victory dance. "I jumped out of a damn plane. My ex-husband said I'd be crazy to do it, the jerk. But I *feel* crazy, because I'm going to do it again."

Still laughing, she ran over, arms wide, to her family.

"Ex-husband," Lucas managed. And the heat spread up the back of his neck again.

7

With the siren silent, Rowan spent most of her time in the loft checking, clearing or mending chutes. She'd caught up on paperwork, repacked her personal gear bag, checked and rechecked her own chute, readied her jump gear.

She remained first jumper, first stick.

"Going stir-crazy here," Cards said when he got up from the machine.

"Aren't we all. And the word of today is . . ."

"Fastidious. We've been doing dick-all but cleaning and organizing. The ready room's freaking fastidious enough to suit my mother's scary standards."

"It can't last much longer."

"I hope to Christ not. I had to kick my own ass for cheating at solitaire yesterday, and I'm starting to think about crafts. We'll be knitting next."

"I'd like a nice scarf to match my eyes."

"It could happen," he said darkly. "At least I had phone sex with Vicki last night." He pulled the deck of cards from his shirt pocket, shuffling as he paced. "It's fun while it lasts, but it doesn't really do the job."

"And gone are the days you'd hunt up a companion for actual sex?"

"Long gone. She's worth it. I told you she and the kids are coming out next month, right?"

"You mentioned it." One or two thousand times, Rowan thought.

"Gotta get in some time now, so I can take a couple days next month. I need to work, need the pay, need—"

"To resist trolling the aisle of the craft store," Rowan finished.

"I won't be trolling alone if this lull lasts much longer. Have you got anything to read? All Gibbons has are books that give me a headache. I read one of Janis's romance novels, but that doesn't help keep my mind off sex."

"Nothing deep, nothing sexy. Check." She signed and dated the tag on the repaired chute. "What're you after?"

"I want something gory, where people die miserable deaths at the hands of a psycho."

"I could fix you up. Come on. We'll peruse my library."

"Dobie's in the kitchen with Marg," Cards told her, passing a hand over Rowan's head, then flipped out an ace of spades. "He got some recipe of his mother's, and he's in there cooking up some pie or other."

Cooking, knitting—that bake sale could be next. Then struck, Rowan paused. "Is Dobie hitting on Marg?"

Cards only shook his head. "She's got twenty years on him."

"Men routinely hit on women twenty years younger."

"I'm bored, Ro, but not bored enough to get into a tangle on that with you."

"Coward." But when they stepped outside, she paused again. "Look, check out those clouds."

"We got scouts." His face brightened as he studied the clouds over the mountains. "A nice string of them."

"Could mean smoke today. With any luck, we'll have that ready room messed up again before afternoon. Do you still want that book?"

"Might as well. I'll get myself all settled in, good book, good snack. It's like guaranteeing we'll fly today."

"It's the slowest start to a season I remember. Then again,

my father once told me when it starts cool, it ends hot. Maybe we shouldn't be so eager to get going."

"If it doesn't get going, what're we here for?"

"No argument. So . . ." She tried for a casual tone as they crossed to her end of the barracks. "Have you seen Fast Feet this morning?"

"In the Map Room. Studying. At least he was about an hour ago."

"Studying. Huh." She wasn't interested in settling down with a book, but a little byplay with Gull might be just the solution to boredom she needed.

Inside, she led the way to her quarters. "Gruesome murder," she began. "Do you want just violence, or sex and violence? As opposed to romantic sexy."

"I always want sex."

"Again, it's hard to—" She broke off as she opened her door. The slaughterhouse stench punched like a fist in the throat.

A pool of blood spread over the bed. Dark rivers of it ran down hills of clothes heaped on the floor. On the wall in letters wet and gleaming dripped the statement:

BURN IN HELL!

In the center of the ugliness, Dolly whirled to face the door. Some of the blood in the canister she held splattered on her shirt.

"Son of a *bitch*!" Fists up, her mind as red and vicious as the blood, Rowan charged. A war-paint line of pig's blood splatted on her face as Dolly screamed and dropped to the ground—seconds before Cards grabbed Rowan's arms.

"Wait a minute, wait a minute."

"Fuck you." Rowan pushed off her feet, adding to the blood when the back of her head connected sharply with Cards's nose and had it spurting.

He yelped, and through sheer grit managed to hold on for another second or two.

"You're so dead!" Rowan shouted at Dolly, and, blind to anything but payback, jabbed her elbow into Cards's ribs, sprang free.

Shrieking, scrabbling back, Dolly pitched the canister. Globs of blood flew, striking wall, ceiling, furniture, when Rowan batted it away.

"You like blood? Let's see how you like painting with yours, you crazy *cunt*."

Rowan clamped her hands on Dolly's ankles when Dolly tried to crawl under the bed. Even as she hauled Dolly across the blood-smeared floor, men who'd come running at the commotion dived in to grapple Rowan back.

Rowan didn't waste her breath. She punched, kicked, jabbed and kneed, heedless of where blows landed, until she ended up facedown on the floor, pinned.

"Just stay down," Gull said in her ear.

"Get off me. Goddamn you, get off me. Do you see what she did?"

"Everybody sees it. Jesus, somebody get that screaming idiot out of here before *I* punch her."

"I'm going to kick every square inch of her skanky ass. Let me *up*! You hear that, you psycho? First chance I get it won't be pig's blood you're wearing, it'll be your own. Let me the fuck *up*!"

"You're down until you calm down."

"Fine. I'm calm."

"Not even close."

"She's got Jim's blood on her," Dolly wept as Yangtree and Matt pulled her from the room. "You all have his blood on you. I hope you all die. I hope you all burn alive. All of you."

"I think she lost her religion," Gull commented. "Listen to me. Rowan, you listen. She's gone, and if you try to go after her and take a shot at her now, we're just going to put you down again. You already bloodied Cards's nose, and I'm pretty sure Janis is going to be sporting a black eye."

"They shouldn't have gotten in my way."

"If they, and the rest of us, hadn't, you'd have punched a pathetic lunatic, and you'd be off the jump list until it got sorted out."

That, he noted, had her taking the first calming breath. He signaled for Libby and Trigger to let go of her legs and, when she didn't try to kick them, pointed to the door.

Libby shut it quietly behind them.

"I'm letting you up." He eased his grip on her arms, braced to grab them again if necessary. Then, cautiously, he shifted off her, sat on the floor.

Blood covered both of them, but he was pretty sure she had the worst of it. It smeared her face, dripped from her hair, coated her arms, her shirt. She looked as if she'd been whacked with an ax. And it made him sick.

"You know, it's a goddamn pigsty in here."

"That's not funny."

"No, it's not, but it's the best I got." He eyed her coolly as she pushed up to sit, watched her right hand bunch into a fist. "I can take a punch if you need to throw one."

"Just get out."

"No. We're just going to sit here awhile."

Rowan used her shoulder to wipe at her face, smeared it with more blood. "She got that crap all over me. All over my bed, the floor, the walls."

"She's sick and she's stupid. And she deserved to have every square inch of her skanky ass kicked. She'll get fired, and everybody on base and within fifty miles will know why. That might be worse."

"It's not as satisfying." She looked away a moment as, with the wild heat of temper fading, tears wanted to sting. She clamped her hands together; they'd started to shake.

"It smells like a slaughterhouse in here."

"You can sleep in my room tonight." He hitched a bandanna out of his pocket, used it to wipe blood from her face. "But everybody who sleeps in my room has to be naked."

She huffed out a tired breath. "I'll bunk with Janis until I get it cleaned up. She has the naked rule, too."

"Now that was just mean."

She looked at him then, just sat and looked while he ruined his bandanna on a hopeless job. It helped to see he wasn't as calm as he sounded, helped to see the temper and disgust on his face.

Oddly, seeing it calmed her just a little.

"Did I give you that bloody lip?"

"Yeah. Back fist. Not bad."

"I'll probably be sorry for it at some point, but I can't work it up right now."

"It took five of us to take you down."

"That's something. I have to go wash up."

She started to rise when L.B. knocked briskly on the door, opened it. "Give us a minute, will you, Gull?"

"Sure." Before he stood, Gull leaned over, laid a hand on Rowan's knee. "People like her? They never get people like you. It's their loss."

He pushed to his feet, and closed the door on his way out.

L.B. looked around the room, rubbed a hand over his face. "Jesus, Ro. Jesus. I'm sorry. I can't tell you how sorry."

"You didn't do it."

"I shouldn't have hired her on. I shouldn't have taken her back. This is on me."

"It's on her."

"She got the chance to come at you this way because I gave her one." He hunkered down so their faces were on level. "We've got her in my office, with a couple of the guys watching her. She'll be fired, banned from base. I'm going to call the law on this. Do you want to press charges?"

"I do because she earned it." The tears had backed off, thank God. Now she only felt sick, sick and tired. "But the baby didn't. I just want her gone."

"She's gone," he promised. "Come on, you need to get out of here. We'll have some of the cleaning crew deal with it."

"I need to get some air. Apologize to some people. I need to take a shower, wash this off me." She blew out another breath as she looked down at herself. "I probably need the full *Silkwood*."

"Take as long as you need. And nobody needs you to apologize."

"I need me to. But this shit's all over my stuff. I need to clean some of it up myself."

She got up, opened the door. Looked back. "Did she love him this much? Is this love?"

L.B. stared at the bloody words on the wall. "It's got nothing to do with love."

THE SIREN SOUNDED as she stepped out of the shower.

"Perfect," she muttered. She dragged on underwear without

bothering to dry off, pulled on a shirt, her pants, and zipped them on the run.

The nine other jumpers on the list beat her to the ready room. She listened to the rundown as she suited up. Lightning strikes on Morrell Mountain. She and Cards had judged those morning clouds correctly. The lookout spotted the smoke about eleven, around the time she'd surprised Dolly and her goddamn pig's blood.

Over the next hour or so, the fire manager officer had to consider letting it burn, do its work of clearing out some brush and fallen trees, or call in the smoke jumpers.

A few more lightning strikes and unseasonably dry conditions made the natural burn too big a risk.

"Ready for the real thing, Fast Feet?" She put her let-down rope in her pocket while Gull grabbed gear from the speed rack.

"Jumping the fire, or you and me making some?"

"You'd better keep your mind off impossible dreams. This isn't a practice jump."

"Looking good." Dobie slapped Gull on the back. "Wish I was going with you."

"You'll be off the disabled list soon. Save me some pie," Rowan called out, and shambled over to the waiting plane.

She tucked her helmet in the crook of her elbow. "Okay, boys and girls, I'll be your fire boss today. For a couple of you, this is your first fire jump. Do it by the numbers, don't screw up, and you'll do fine. Remember, if you can't avoid the trees . . ."

"Aim for the small ones," the crew responded.

Once they were airborne she sat next to Cards. "At least the nose didn't ground you."

He pinched it gently to wag it back and forth. "So I don't have to be pissed at you. Like I said, Swede, the girl's batshit."

"Yeah. And it's done." She took the note passed back to her from the cockpit. "We're going to hold off while they drop a load of mud. It was a hard winter in that area, and there's a lot of downed trees fueling this one. It's moving faster than they figured."

"Almost always does."

She pulled out her map, scanned the area. But in moments

she only had to look out the window to see what they were dealing with.

A tower of smoke spewed skyward, gliding along the mountain's ridge. Trees, standing and downed, fueled the wall of fire. She scanned for and found the stream she'd scouted out on the map, calculated the amount of hose they had on board, and judged they'd be able to use the water source.

The plane bucked and trembled in the turbulence while jumpers lined the windows to study the burning ground. And bucking, they circled to wait for the mud drop on the head that shot up flames she estimated at a good thirty feet.

She waddled over to L.B., who'd come on as spotter.

"See that clearing?" he shouted. "That's our jump spot. A little closer to the right flank than I'd like, but it's the best in this terrain."

"Saves us a hike."

"The wind's whipping her up. You want to keep clear of that slash just east of the spot."

"You bet I do."

Together they watched the tanker thunder its load onto the head. The reddened clouds of it made her think of the blood soiling her room.

No time for brooding, she reminded herself.

"That'll knock her down a little." When the tanker veered off, L.B. nodded at her. "Are you good?"

"I'm good."

He gave her arm a squeeze, a tacit acknowledgment. "Guard your reserves," he called out, and went to the door.

From his seat, Gull watched Rowan as the wind and noise rushed in. About an hour earlier she'd been spitting mad with blood on her face and blind vengeance in her fists. Now, as she consulted with their spotter over the flight of the first streamers, the cool was back in those gorgeous, icy eyes. She'd be the first out, taking that ice into fire.

He didn't see how the fire had a chance.

He looked out the window to study the enemy below. In his hotshot days, he'd have gone in, one of twenty handcrew, transported in The Box—the crew truck that became their home away from home every season.

Now he'd get there by jumping out of a plane.

Different methods, same goal. Suppress and control.

Once he was down, he knew his job and he knew how to take orders. He shifted his gaze back to Rowan. No question she knew how to give them.

But right at the moment, it was all about the getting there. He watched the next set of streamers, tried to judge for himself the draft. With the plane bucking and rocking beneath them, he understood the wind wasn't going to be a pal.

The plane bumped its way up to jump altitude at L.B.'s order, and as Rowan fixed on her helmet and face mask, as Cards—her jump partner—got into position behind her, Gull felt his breathing elevate. It climbed just as the plane climbed.

But he kept his face impassive as he worked to control it, as he visualized himself shoving out the door, into the slipstream and past it, hurtling down to do his job.

Rowan glanced over briefly so he caught that flash of blue behind her mask. Then she dropped down into position. Seconds later, she was gone. Gull shifted back to the window, watched her fly, and Cards after her. As the plane circled around, he changed angles, saw her chute open.

She slid into the smoke.

When the next jumpers took positions, he strapped on his helmet and mask, calmed and cleared his mind. He had everything he needed, equipment, training, skill. And a few thousand feet below was what he wanted. The woman and the blaze.

He made his way forward, felt the slap of the wind.

"Do you see the jump spot?"

"Yeah, I see it."

"Wind's going to kick, all the way down, and it's going to want to shove you east. Try to stay out of that slash. See that lightning?"

Gull watched it rip through the sky, strike like an electric bullet.

"Hard not to."

"Don't get in its way."

"Got it."

"Are you ready?"

"We're ready."

"Get in the door."

Gaze on the horizon, Gull dropped down, pushed his legs out into the power of the slipstream. Heat from the fire radiated against his face; the smell of smoke tanged the air he drew into his lungs.

Once again L.B. stuck his head out the door, scanning, studying the hills, the rise of trees, the roiling walls of flame.

"Get ready!"

When the slap came down on his shoulder, Gull propelled himself out. The world tipped and turned, earth, sky, fire, smoke, as he took a ninety-mile-an-hour dive. Greens, blues, red, black tumbled around him in a filmy blur while he counted in his head. The sounds—a roaring growl—amazed. The wind knocked him sideways, clawed him into a spin while he used strength, will, training to revolve until he was head up, feet down, stabilized by the drogue.

Heart knocking—adrenaline, awe, delight, fear—he found Trigger, his jump partner, in the sky.

Wait, he ordered himself. Wait.

Lightning flared, a blue-edged lance, and added a sting of ozone to the air.

Then the tip and tug. He dropped his head back, watched his chute fly up, open in the ripping air like a flower. He let out a shout of triumph, couldn't help it, and heard Trigger answer it with a laugh as Gull gripped his steering toggles.

It was a fight to turn to face the wind, but he reveled in it. Even choking on the smoke that wind blew smugly in his face, hearing the bomb-burst of thunder that followed another crack of lightning, he grinned. And with his chute rocking, his eyes tracking the ugly slash, the line of trees, the angry walls of flames—close enough now to slap heat over his face—he aimed for the jump site.

For a moment he thought the wind would beat him after all, and imagined the discomfort, embarrassment and goddamn inconvenience of hitting those jack-sawed trees. And on his first jump.

He yanked down hard on his toggle, shouted, "No fucking way."

He heard Trigger's wild laugh, and seconds before he hit, Gull pulled west. His feet slapped ground, just on the east end of the jump spot. Momentum nearly tumbled him into the slash, but he flipped himself back in a sloppy somersault into the clearing.

He took a moment—maybe half a moment—to catch his breath, to congratulate himself on getting down in one piece, then rolled up to gather his chute.

"Not bad, rook." Cards gave him a waggling thumbs-up. "Ride's over, and the fun begins. The Swede's setting up a team to dig fire line along the flank there." He pointed toward the wicked, bellowing wall. "And you're elected. Another team's going to set up toward the head, hit it with the hoses. Mud knocked her back some, but the wind's got her feeling sexy, and we're getting lightning strikes out the ass. You're with Trigger, Elf, Gibbons, Southern and me on the line. And shit, there goes one in the slash and the other in the trees. Let's haul them in and get to work."

Gull trooped over to assist Southern, but stopped when his fellow rookie got to his feet among the jagged, jack-sawed trees.

"You hurt?" Gull shouted.

"Nah. Damn it. A little banged, and my chute's ripped up."

"Could've been worse. Could've been me. We're on the fire line."

He maneuvered through the slash to help Southern gather his tattered chute. After stowing his jumpsuit, Gull headed over to where Cards was ragging on Gibbons.

"Now that Tarzan here has finished swinging in the trees, let's do what we get paid for."

With his team, Gull hiked half a mile in full pack to the line Rowan had delegated Cards to dig.

They spread out, and with the fire licking closer, the sounds of pick striking earth, saw and blade slicing tree filled the smoky air. Gull thought of the fire line as an invisible wall or, if they were lucky, a kind of force field that held the flames on the other side.

Heroic grunt work, he thought while sweat ran rivulets through the soot on his face. The term, and the job, satisfied him.

Twice the fire tried to jump the line, skipping testing spots like flat stones over a river. The air filled with sparks that swarmed like murderous fireflies. But they held the flank.

Now and then, through the flying ash and huffing smoke, Gull spotted a quick beam of sunlight.

Little beacons of hope that glowed purple, then vanished.

Word came down the line that the hose crew had to fall back, and with the flank under control, they would move in to assist.

After more than six hours of laying line, they hiked their way up the mountain and across the black where the fire had already had her way.

If the line was the invisible wall, he thought of the black as the decimated kingdom where the battle had been waged and lost. The war continued, but here the enemy laid scourge and left what had been green and golden a smoldering, skeletal ruin.

The thin beams of sun that managed to struggle through the haze only served to amplify the destruction.

Limping a little, Southern fell into step beside him.

"How're you holding up?" Gull asked him.

"I'd be doing better if I hadn't landed in that godforsaken slash," he said in the fluid Georgia drawl that gave him his nickname. "I thought I knew what it was. I've got two seasons in on wildfires, and that's before we'll-whoop-your-ass recruit training. But it's shit-your-pants hard is what it is. I nearly did just that when I saw I was going to miss the jump spot."

Gull took a heat-softened Snickers out of his pack, pulled it in two. "Snickers really satisfies," Gull said in the upbeat tone of a TV voice-over.

Southern grinned, bit in. "It sure enough does."

They hit the stream, veered northeast toward the sounds of engines and saws.

Rowan came out of a cloud of smoke, a Viking goddess through the stink of war.

"Dry lightning's kicking our ass." She paused only to chug down some water. "We'd beat the head down, nearly had her, then we had a triple strike. We got crown fire along the ridge due north, and the head's building back up west of that. We gotta cut through the middle, stop them from meeting up. Hold here until we're clear. They're sending another load of mud. We got another load from base coming in to take the rear flanks and tail, keep them down. Bulldozer made it through, and he's clearing brush and downed trees. But we need the line."

She scanned faces. "You've got about five minutes till the drop. Make the most of it—eat, drink, because you won't see another five minutes clear today."

She went into a confab with Cards. Gull waited until they stepped apart, then walked to her. Before he could speak, she shook her head.

"Wind changed direction on a dime, and she just blew over. She melted fifty feet of hose before we got clear. Then boom! Boom! Boom! Fourth of July. Trees went up like torches, and the wind carried it right over the tops."

"Anybody hurt?"

"No. Don't look for clean sheets and a pillow tonight. We'll be setting up camp, and going back at her tomorrow. She's not going to die easy." She looked skyward. "Here comes the tanker."

"I don't see it."

"Not yet. You can hear it."

He closed his eyes, angled his head. "No. You must have super hearing. Okay, now I hear it."

She pulled her radio, spoke with the tanker, then with the crew on the ridge.

"Let it rip," she mumbled.

The pink rain tumbled down, caught little stray rainbows of sunlight.

"We're clear!" Rowan shouted. "Let's move. Watch your footing, but don't dawdle."

With that, she disappeared into the smoke.

THEY HACKED, CUT, BEAT at it into the night. Bodies trained to withstand all manner of hell began to weaken. But resolve didn't. Gull caught sight of Rowan a few times, working the line, moving in and out as she coordinated with the other teams and with base.

Sometime toward one, more than twelve hours after he'd landed in the clearing, the fire began to lie down.

To rest, Gull thought, not to surrender. Just taking a little nap. And hell, he could use one himself. They worked another hour before word came down they'd camp a half mile east of the fire's right flank.

"How's the first day on the job going, rook?"

He glanced over at Cards's exhausted face as they trudged. "I'm thinking of asking for a raise."

"Hell, I'd settle for a ham on rye."

"I'd rather have pizza."

"Picky Irishman. You ever been there? Ireland?"

"A couple times, yeah."

"Is it really as green as they say, as it looks in the pictures?"

"Greener."

Cards looked off into the smoky dark. "And cool, right? Cool and damp. Lots of rain."

"That's why it's green."

"Maybe I'll go there one of these days, take Vicki and the kids. Cool and damp and green sounds good after a day like this. There we are." He lifted a chin to the lights up ahead. "Time to ring the supper bell."

Those who'd already arrived had set up tents, or were doing so. Some just sat on the ground and shoveled their Meals Ready to Eat into their mouths.

Rowan, using a rock near the campfire as a table, worked over a map with Gibbons while she ate an apple. She'd taken off her helmet. Her hair shone nearly white against her filthy face.

He thought she looked beautiful, gloriously, eerily so—and was forced to admit she'd probably been right. He was, under it all, a romantic.

He dumped his gear, felt his back and shoulders weep with relief before they cramped like angry fists.

No Box to crawl into this time, he mused as he popped his tent. Then like the others, he dropped down by the campfire and ate like the starving. The cargo drop included more MREs, water, more tools, more hose and, God bless some thoughtful soul, a carton of apples, another of chocolate bars.

He ate his MRE, two apples, a candy bar—and stuffed another in his PG bag. The vague nausea that had plagued him on the hike to camp receded as his body refueled.

He rose, walked over to tap Rowan on the shoulder. "Can I talk to you a minute?"

She stood up, obviously punchy and distracted, and followed him away from the campfire, into the shadows.

"What's the problem? I've got to hit the rack. We're going to be—"

He just yanked her in, covered her mouth with his and feasted on her as he had on the food. Exhaustion became an easier fatigue as he fueled himself with her. The twinges in his back, his arms, his legs gave way to the curls of lust low in the belly.

She took back in equal measure, gripping his hips, his hair, pressing that amazing body against him, diving straight into those deep, greedy kisses.

And that, he thought, was what made it so damn good.

When he drew back he left his hands on her shoulders, studied her face.

"Is that all you have to say?" she demanded.

"I'd say more, but the rest of the conversation requires more privacy. Anyway, that should hold you for the night."

Humor danced into her eyes. "Hold *me*?"

"The crew boss works harder than anybody, to my way of thinking. So, I wanted to give you a little something more to take to bed."

"That's very considerate of you."

"No problem." He watched her eyes shift from amused to puzzled as he tipped down, brushed a kiss on her sooty brow. "'Night, boss."

"You're a puzzle, Gulliver."

"Maybe, but not that hard to solve. See you in the morning."

He went to his tent, crawled in. He barely managed to get his boots off before he went under. But he went under with a smile on his face.

8

Rowan's mental alarm dragged her out of sleep just before five A.M. She lay where she was, eyes closed, taking inventory. A world of aches, a lot of stiffness and a gut-deep hunger, but nothing major or unexpected. She rolled out of her sleeping bag and, in the dark, stretched out her sore muscles. She let herself fantasize about a hot shower, an ice-cold Coke, a plate heaped with one of Marg's all-in omelets.

Then she crawled out of her tent to face reality.

The camp slept on—and could, she calculated, for about an hour more. To the west the fire painted the sky grimy red. A waiting light, she thought. Waiting for the day's battle.

Well, they'd be ready for it.

She rinsed the dry from her mouth with water, spat it out, then used the glow of the campfire to grab some food. She ate, washing down the rations with instant coffee she despised but needed while reviewing her maps. The quiet wouldn't last long, so she used it to strategize her tasks, directions, organizing teams and tools.

She radioed base for a status report, a weather forecast, scribbling notes, quick-drawing operational maps.

By first light, she'd organized her tools, restocked her PG

bag, bolted another sandwich and an apple. Alert, energized, ready, she gathered in her small pocket of alone time.

She watched the forest come to life around the sleeping camp. Like something out of a fairy tale, the shadows of a small herd of elk slipped through morning mists veiling the trees like wisps of smoke. The shimmer of the rising sun haloed the ridge to the east, spreading its melting gold. The shine of it trickled down the tree line, flickering its glint on the stream, brushing the green of the valley below.

Birds sang their morning song, while overhead in that wakening sky a hawk soared, already on the hunt.

This, she thought, was just one more reason she did what she did, despite the risks, the pain, the hunger. There was, to her mind, nothing more magical or more intensely real than dawn in the wilderness.

She'd fight beyond exhaustion alongside the best men and women she knew to protect it.

When Cards rolled out of his tent, she smiled. He looked like a bear who'd spent his hibernation rolling in soot. With his hair standing up in grungy spikes, his eyes glazed with fatigue, he grunted at her before stumbling off for a little privacy to relieve his bladder.

The camp began to stir. More grunts and rustles, more dazed and glassy eyes as smoke jumpers grabbed food and coffee. Gull climbed out, his face shadowed by soot and scruff. But his eyes were alert, she noted, and glinted at her briefly before he wandered off into the trees.

"Wind's already picking up." Gibbons came to stand beside her, gulped coffee.

"Yeah." She looked toward the smoke columns climbing the sky. Orange and gold flared through the red now. Like the sky, the magic, the camp, the dragon woke. "We're not going to get any help from the weather gods today. Wind's variable, fifteen to twenty, conditions remain dry with the temps spiking past eighty. She'll eat that up."

Rowan pulled out her hand-drawn maps. "We held her flank along here, but we lost ground at our water source, and when she crowned, she swept straight across this way. The hotshots hit that, kicked her back to about here, but she turned on them, about midnight, and then had to RTO," she added, speaking of reverse tool order, "and retreat back to this line."

"Was anybody hurt?"

"Minor burns, bumps and bruises. Nobody had to be evaced." She glanced over her shoulder as Gull walked up. "They're camped here." She unfolded the main map to show Gibbons. "I'm thinking if we can pump water on the head from about here, and lay line along this sector, intersect the low point of the hotshot line, then cross. We'll head up while they work over. We could box her in. It's a hell of a climb, but we'd smother her tail, block her left flank, then meet up with the pump team and cut off her head."

Gibbons nodded. "We're going to have to hold this line here." He jabbed a finger at the map. "If she gets through that, she could sweep up behind. Then it's the line team that's boxed in."

"I scouted this area yesterday. We've got a couple of safe spots. And they're sending in more jumpers this morning. We'll be up to forty. I want ten on the water team, and for you to head that up, Gib. You're damn good with a hose. Take the nine you want for it."

"All right." He glanced back at the fire. "Looks like recess is over."

"Where do you want me?" Gull asked her when Gibbons stepped off to pick his team.

"Saw line, under Yangtree. You hold that line, or you're going to need those fast feet. If she gets behind you, you make tracks, straight up the ridge and into the black. Here." She looked into his eyes as she laid a finger on the map. "You got that?"

"We'll hold it, then you can buy me a drink."

"Hold the line, cut it up and around to the water team, and maybe I will. Get your gear." She walked over toward the campfire, lifted her voice. "Okay, boys and girls, time to kick some ass."

She caught a ride partway on a bulldozer, then hopped off for a brutal hike to check the hotshots' progress firsthand.

"Winsor, right? Tripp," she shouted at the lean, grim-faced man over the roar of saws. Fire sounded its throaty threat while its heat pulsed strong enough to tickle the skin. "I've got a team working its way up to cross with you. Maybe by one this afternoon."

A scan of the handcrew told her what she'd suspected. They'd downplayed injuries. She gestured to one of the men wielding a Pulaski. His face glowed with sweat and showed raw and red where his eyebrows had been singed off. "You had a close one."

"Shit-your-pants close. Wind bitched on us, and she turned on a freaking dime, rolled right at us. She let out that belly laugh. You know what I mean."

"Yeah." It was a sound designed to turn your bowels to ice. "Yeah, I do."

"We RTO'd. Couldn't see a goddamn thing through the smoke. I swear she chased us like she wanted to play tag. I smelled my own hair burning. We barely got clear."

"You're holding her now."

"These guys'll work her till they drop, but if we don't knock that head down, I think she's going to whip around and try for another bite."

"We're pumping on her now. I'm going to check in with the team leader, see if he wants another drop." She faced the fire wall as ash swirled around her like snow. "They underestimated her, but we're going to turn this around. Look for my team to meet up with yours about one."

"Stay cool," he called after her.

She hiked back around, filling her lungs when she moved into clearer air. Moving, always moving, she checked in with her teams, with base, with the fire coordinator. After jumping a narrow creek, she angled west again. Then stopped dead when a bear crossed her path.

She checked the impulse to run; she knew better. But her feet itched to move. "Oh, come on," she said under her breath. "I'm doing this for you, too. Just move along."

Her heart thumped as he studied her, and running didn't seem like such a stupid idea after all. Then he swung his head away as if bored with her, and lumbered away.

"I love the wilderness and all it holds," she reminded herself when she worked up enough spit to swallow.

She hiked another quarter of a mile before her heart settled down again. And still, she cast occasional cautious looks over her shoulder until she heard the muffled buzz of chain saws.

She picked up her speed and met up with the fresh saw line.

After a quick update with Yangtree, she joined the line. She'd give them an hour before hiking up and around again.

"Pretty day, huh?" Gull commented as they sliced a downed tree into logs.

She glanced up, and through a few windows in the smoke, the sky was a bold blue. "She's a beauty."

"Nice one for a picnic."

Rowan stamped out a spot the size of a dinner plate that kindled at her feet. "Champagne picnic. I always wanted to have one of those."

"Too bad I didn't bring a bottle with me."

She settled for water, then mopped her face. "We're going to do it. I'm starting to feel it."

"The picnic?"

"The fire's a little more immediate. You've got a good hand with the saw. Keep it up."

She headed up to confer with Yangtree again over the maps, then, ripping open a cookie wrapper, headed back into the smoke.

While she gobbled the cookie, she considered the bear—and told herself he was well east by now. She clawed her way up the ridge, checked the time when she met the hotshot line.

Just noon. Five hours into the day, and damn good progress.

She cut up and over, her legs burning and rubbery, to check on the pumpers.

Arcs of water struck the blaze, liquid arrows aimed to kill. Rowan gave in, bent over, resting her hands on her screaming thighs. She couldn't say how many miles she'd covered so far that day, but she was damn sure she felt every inch of it.

She pushed herself up, made her way over to Gibbons. "Yangtree's line is moving up well. He should meet up with the hotshots within the hour. She tried to swish her tail, but they've got that under control. Idaho's on call if you need more on the hoses."

"We're holding her. We're going to pump her hard, go

through the neck here. If you get those lines down, cut them
across, we'll have her."

"I want to pull out the fusees, start a backfire here." She
dug out her map. "We could fold her back in on herself, and
she'd be out of fuel."

"I like it. But it's your call."

"Then I'm making it." She pulled her radio. "Yangtree,
we're going with the backfire. Split ten off, lead them up. I'm
circling back down. Keep drowning that bitch, Gib."

Rowan stuffed calories into her system by way of an energy
bar, hydrated with water as she backtracked. And considered
herself lucky when she didn't repeat her encounter with a bear.
Nothing stirred in the trees, in the brush. She cut across a trail
where the trees still towered—trees they fought to save—and
the wildflowers poked their heads toward the smoke-choked
sky. Birds had taken wing so no song, no chatter played
through the silence.

But the fire muttered and growled, shooting its flames up
like angry fists and kicking feet.

She followed its flank, thought of the wildflowers, took
their hope with her as she hiked to the man-made burn she'd
ordered.

At Yangtree's orders, Gull peeled off from the saw line to
deal with spot fires the main blaze spat across the border. Most
of his team were too weary for conversation, and as speed
added a factor, breath for chat was in limited supply.

Water consumed poured off in sweat; food gulped down
burned off and left a constant, nagging hunger.

The trick, he knew from his years as a hotshot, was not to
think about it, about anything but the fire, and the next step
toward killing it.

"Get your fusees." Gibbons relayed the information in a
voice harsh from shouting and smoke. "We're going to burn
her ass, pull her back till she eats herself."

Gull looked back toward the direction of the tail. Their line
was holding, the cross with the hotshots' cut off her flank—
so far. Spot fires flared up, but she'd lost her edge of steam
here.

He considered the timing and strategy of the backfire dead-
on. Despite his fatigue, it pleased him when Yangtree pulled

him off the line and sent him down with a team to control the backfire.

With the others he hauled up his tools, left the line.

He saw the wildflowers as Rowan had, and the holes woodpeckers had drilled into the body of a Douglas fir, the scat of a bear—a big one—that had him scanning the hazy forest. Just in case.

Heading the line, Cards limped a little as he kept in contact with Rowan, other team leaders on his radio. Gull wondered what he'd hurt and how, but they kept moving, and at an urgent pace.

He heard the mumble of a dozer. It pushed through the haze, scooping brush and small trees. Rowan hopped off while it bumped its way along a new line.

"We're going to work behind the Cat line. We got hose." She pointed to the paracargo she'd ordered dropped. "We've got a water source with that stream. I want the backfire hemmed in here, so when she rolls back she burns herself out. Watch out for spots. She's been spitting them out everywhere."

She shifted her gaze to Gull. "Can you handle a hose as well as you do a saw?"

"I've been known to."

"You, Matt, Cards. Let's get pumping. Everybody else, hit those snags."

He liked a woman with a plan, Gull thought as he got to work.

"We light it on my go." Rowan offered Cards one of the peanut-butter crackers from her PG bag. "Are you hurt?"

"It's nothing. Tripped over my own feet."

"Mine," Matt corrected. "I got in the way."

"My feet tripped over his feet. It was pretty crazy on the line for a while."

"And now it's so sane. Soak it down," she told them. "Everything in front of the Cat line, soak it good."

Manning a pumping fire hose took muscle, stability and sweat. Within ten minutes—and hours on the saw and scratch line—Gull's arms stopped aching and just went numb. He dug in, sent his arcs of water raining over the trees, soaking into the ground. Over the cacophony of pump, saw and engine, he heard Rowan shout the order for the light.

"Here she goes!"

He watched fusees ignite, burst.

Special effects, he thought, nothing like it, as flames arrowed up, ignited the forest. It roared, full-throated, and would, if God was good, call to the dragon.

"Hold it here! We don't give her another foot."

In Rowan's voice he heard what flooded him—wonder and determination, and a fresh energy that struck his blood like a drug.

Others shouted, too, infected with the same drug. Steam rose from the ground, melded with smoke as they pushed the backfire forward. Firebrands rocketed out only to sizzle and drown on the wet ground.

This was winning. Not just turning a corner, not just holding ground, but winning. An hour passed in smoke and steam and ungodly heat—then another—before she began to lie down, this time in defeat.

Rowan jogged over to the water line. "She's rolled back. Head's cut off and under control. Flanks are receding. Take her down. She's done."

The fire's retreat ran fitful and weak. By evening she could barely manage a sputter. The pulse of the pump silenced, and Gull let his weeping arms drop. He dug into his pack, found a sandwich he'd ratted in at dawn. He didn't taste it, but since it awakened the yawning hunger in his belly, he wished he'd grabbed more of whatever the hell it was.

He walked to the stream, took off his hard hat and filled it with water. He considered the sensation of having it rain cool over his head and shoulders nearly as good as sex.

"Nice work."

He glanced over at Rowan, filled his hat again. Standing, he quirked a brow. She laughed, took off her helmet, lifted her face, closed her eyes. "Oh, yeah," she sighed when he dumped the water on her. She blinked her eyes open, cool, crystal blue. "You handle yourself pretty well for an ex-hotshot rookie."

"You handle yourself pretty well for a girl."

She laughed again. "Okay, even trade." Then lifted her hand.

He quirked his brow again, the grin spreading, but she shook her head. "You're too filthy to kiss, and I'm still fire boss on this line. High five's all you get."

"I'll take it." He slapped hands with her. "We were holding her, kicking her back some, but we beat her the minute you called for the backfire."

"I'm second-guessing if I should have called it earlier." Then she shrugged. "No point in what-ifs. We took her down." She put her hard hat back on, lifted her voice. "Okay, kids, let's mop it up."

They dug roots, tramped out embers, downed smoldering snags. When the final stage of the fight was finished, they packed out, all but asleep on their feet, shouldering tools and gear. Nobody spoke on the short flight back to base; most were too busy snoring. Some thirty-eight hours after the siren sounded, Gull dragged himself into the barracks, dumped his gear. On the way to his quarters he bumped into Rowan.

"How about a nightcap?"

She snorted out a laugh. He imagined she'd braced a hand on the wall just to stay on her feet. "While a cold beer might go down good, I believe that's your clever code for sex. Even if my brain was fried enough to say sure, I don't believe you could get it up tonight—today—this morning."

"I strongly disagree, and would be willing to back that up with a demonstration."

"Sweet." She gave him a light slap on his grimy face. "Pass. 'Night."

She slipped into her room, and he continued on to his. Once he stripped off his stinking shirt, pants, and fell face-down and filthy on top of his bed, he had time to think, thank God she hadn't taken him up on it, before he zeroed out.

IN THE BUNK in his office, where he habitually stayed when Rowan caught a fire at night, Lucas heard the transport plane go out. Heard it come back. Still, he didn't fully relax until his cell phone signaled a text.

Got nasty, but we put her down. I'm A-OK. Love, Ro

He put the phone aside, settled down, and slid into the first easy sleep since the siren sounded.

LUCAS JUMPED with an early-morning group of eight, posed for pictures, signed brochures, then took the time to discuss moving up to accelerated free fall with two of the group.

When he walked them in to Marcie to sign them up, his brain went wonky on him. Ella Frazier of the red hair and forest-green eyes turned to smile at him.

With dimples.

"Hello again."

"Ah . . . again," he managed, flustered. "Um, Marcie will take you through the rest, get you scheduled," he told the couple with him.

"I watched your skydive." Ella turned her smile on them. "I just did my first tandem the other day. It's amazing, isn't it?"

He stood, struggling not to shuffle his feet while Ella chatted with his newest students.

"Have you got a minute for me?" she asked him.

"Sure. Sure. My office—"

"Could we walk outside? Marcie tells me you've got two more tandems coming in. I'd love to watch."

"Okay." He held the door open for her, then wondered what to do with his hands. In his pockets? At his sides? He wished he had a clipboard with him to keep them occupied.

"I know you're busy today, and I probably should've called."

"It's no problem."

"How's your daughter? I followed the fire on the news," she added.

"She's fine. Back on base, safe and sound. Did I tell you about Rowan?"

"Not exactly." She tucked her hair behind her ear as she angled her face toward his. "I Googled you before I signed up. I love my son, but I wasn't about to jump out of an airplane unless I knew something about who I was hooked to."

"Can't blame you." See, he told himself, sensible. Any man should be able to relax around a sensible woman. A grandmother, he reminded himself. An *educator*.

He managed to unknot his shoulders.

"Your experience and reputation turned the trick for me. So, Lucas, I was wondering if I could buy you a drink."

And his shoulders tensed like overwound springs while his brain went to sloppy mush. "Sorry?"

"To thank you for the experience, and giving me the chance to show off to my grandchildren."

"Oh, well." There went that flush of heat up the back of his neck. "You don't have to . . . I mean to say—"

"I caught you off-guard, and probably sounded like half the women who come through here, hitting on you."

"No, they . . . you—"

"I wasn't. Hitting on you," she added with a big, bright smile. "But now I have to confess to a secondary purpose. I have a project I'd love to speak to you about, and if I could buy you a drink, soften you up, I'm hoping you'll get on board. If you're in a relationship, you're welcome to bring your lady with you."

"No, I'm not. I mean, there isn't any lady. Especially."

"Would you be free tonight? I could meet you about seven, at the bar at Open Range. I could thank you, soften you up, and you can tell me more about training for the AFF."

Business, he told himself. Friendly business. He discussed friendly business over drinks all the damn time. No reason he couldn't do the same with her. "I don't have any plans."

"Then we're set? Thanks so much." She shot out a hand, shook his briskly. "I'll see you at seven."

He watched her walk away, so pretty, so breezy—and reminded himself it was just friendly business.

9

As she had done in her tent, Rowan lay with her eyes closed and took morning inventory. She decided she felt like a hundred-year-old woman who'd been on a starvation diet. But she'd come out of it—as fire boss—uninjured, her crew intact, and the fire down.

Added to it, she thought as she opened her eyes, tracked her gaze around her quarters, during her two days out the pig-blood fairies had not only mopped and scrubbed but rolled a fresh coat of paint on her walls.

She owed somebody, and if she could drag herself out of bed she'd find out who.

When she did, her calves twinged, her quads protested. The bis and tris, she noted, shed bitter tears. The hot shower she'd all but slept through had helped, a little, but the eight hours in the rack after two arduous days required more.

Fuel and movement, she ordered herself. And where was Gull with his breakfast sandwich when she needed one? She settled for a chocolate bar while she dressed, then hobbled off to the gym.

She wasn't the only one hobbling.

She grunted at Gibbons, who grunted back, watched Trigger wince through some floor stretches. She studied Dobie—wiry little guy—as he bench-pressed what she judged to be his body weight.

"I'm back on the jump list tomorrow," he told her as he pumped up with an explosion of breath. "I'm ready. Hell of a lot readier than you guys, from the looks of it."

She shot him the finger, then moaned into a forward bend. She stayed down, just stayed down and breathed for as long as she could stand it, then with her palms on the floor, arched her back and looked up.

The yellow bruising on Dobie's red-with-effort face made him look like a jaundiced burn victim. And he'd shaved off his scraggly excuse for a beard—an improvement, to her mind, since he looked less like a hillbilly leprechaun.

"Somebody cleaned up and painted my room."

"Yeah." With another explosion of breath, he pushed the weights up, then clicked them in the safety. "Stovic and me, we had time on our hands."

She brought herself back to standing. "You guys did all that?"

"Mostly. Marg and Lynn did what they could with your clothes. Salt's what gets blood out; that's what my ma uses."

"Is that so?"

"Doesn't work so well on walls, so we got them painted up. It kept us from going stir-crazy while the rest of you were having all the fun. Hell of a mess in there, and smelled like a hog butchering. Made me homesick," he added with a grin. "Anyhow, that broad must be crazy as a run-over lizard."

She walked over, bent down, kissed him on the mouth. "Thanks."

He wiggled his eyebrows. "It was a big, stinkin' *hell* of a mess."

This time she drilled her finger into his belly. After walking back to her mat, she stretched out her muscles, soothed her mind with yoga. She'd moved to floor work when Gull came in. Fresh, she thought. He looked fresh and clean, with his gait loose and easy as he crossed to her.

"I heard you'd surfaced." He crouched down. "You're looking pretty limber for the morning after."

"Just need some fine-tuning."

"And a picnic."

She lifted her nose from her knee. "I need a picnic?"

"With a big-ass hamper loaded with cuisine by Marg and a fine bottle of adult beverage enjoyed in the company of a charming companion."

"Janis is going with me on a picnic?"

"I've got the big-ass hamper."

"There's always a catch." Danger zone, she warned herself. The man was a walking temptation. "It's a nice thought, but—"

"We're not on the jump list, and L.B. cleared us for the day. Now that we've been through fire together, I think we can take a short break, have some food and conversation. Unless you're afraid a little picnic will drive you into uncontrollable lust until you force yourself on me and take advantage of my friendly offer."

Temptation and challenge—both equally hard to resist. "I'm reasonably sure I can control myself."

"Okay then. We can leave whenever you're ready."

What the hell, she decided. She lived and breathed danger zones. She could certainly handle one appealingly cocky guy on a picnic.

"Give me twenty. And you'd better pick your spot close by because I'm starving."

"I'll meet you out front."

She hunted up Stovic first, gave him the same smack on the lips as Dobie. She paid her debts. She had a report to write and turn in on the fire, but that could wait a couple hours. Check and reorganize her gear, she thought as she pulled on cropped khakis. Deal with her chute, repack her PG bag. She buttoned on a white camp shirt, slapped on some makeup and sunscreen and considered it good enough for a friendly picnic with a fellow jumper.

She shoved on her sunglasses as she walked outside, then narrowed her eyes behind them. Gull leaned on the hood of a snazzy silver convertible chatting it up with Cards.

She sauntered over. "How's the leg?" she asked Cards.

"Not bad. Knee's a little puffy yet. I'm going to ice it down again." He patted the hood beside Gull's hip. "That's some ride, Fast Feet. Some hot ride. Today's word's got to be virile, 'cause that machine's got balls. You kids have fun." He winked at Rowan and, still limping, went back in.

Hands on her hips, Rowan took a stroll around the hot ride. "This is Iron Man's car."

"Since I doubt you're claiming I stole it from your father, I conclude you're a woman who knows her superheroes and her motor vehicles."

She stopped in front of him. "Where's the suit?"

"In an undisclosed location. Villainy is everywhere."

"Too true." She angled her head, skimming a finger over the gleaming fender while she studied Gull. "Iron Man's a rich superhero. That's why he can afford the car."

"Tony Stark has many cars."

"Also true. I'm thinking, smoke jumping pays pretty well, in season. But I can't see selling tokens and tracking games at an arcade's something that pays for a car like this."

"But it's entertaining, and I get free pizza. It's my car," he said when she just kept staring at him. "Do you want to see the registration? My portfolio?"

"That means you *have* a portfolio, and I'm damned if you built one working an arcade." Considering, she pursed her lips. "Maybe if you owned a piece of it."

"You have remarkable deductive powers. You can be Pepper Potts." He stepped over, opened her door. She slid in, looked up.

"How big a piece?"

"I'll give you the life story while we eat if you want it."

She thought it over as he skirted the hood, got behind the wheel. And decided she did.

He drove fast, had a smooth, competent hand on the stick shift—both of which she appreciated.

And God, she did love a slick machine.

"Do I have to sleep with you before you let me drive this machine?"

He spared her a single, mild glance. "Of course."

"Seems fair." Enjoying herself, she tipped her face up to the wind and sky, then lifted her hands up to both. "Riding in it's a pretty decent compromise. How did you manage to get this all set up?"

"Staggering organizational skills. Plus I figured I'd grab a few hours while I had them. The food was the easy part. All I had to do was tell Marg I was taking you on a picnic, and she handled the rest of that section. She's in love with you."

"It's mutual. Still, I'd've had a hard time planning anything when I managed to crawl out of bed."

"I have staggering recuperative powers to go with the organizational skills."

She tipped down her sunglasses to eye him over them. "I know sex bragging when I hear it."

"Then I probably shouldn't add that I woke up feeling like I'd been run over by a sixteen-wheeler after I hauled a two-hundred-pound bag of bricks fifty miles. Through mud."

"Yeah. And it's barely June."

When he turned off on Bass Creek Road, she nodded. "Nice choice."

"It's not a bad hike, and it ought to be pretty."

"It is. I've lived here all my life," she added as he pulled into the parking area at the end of the road. "Hiking the trails was what I did. It kept me in shape, gave me a good sense of the areas I'd jump one day—and gave me an appreciation for why I would."

"We crossed into the black yesterday." He hit the button to bring up the roof. "It's harsh, and it's hard. But you know it's going to come back."

They got out, and he opened the hood with its marginal storage space.

"Jesus, Gull, you weren't kidding about big-ass hamper."

"Getting it in was an exercise in geometry." He hefted it out.

"There's just two of us. What does that thing weigh?"

"A lot less than my gear. I think I can make it a mile on a trail."

"We can switch off."

He looked at her as they crossed to the trailhead. "I'm all about equal pay for equal work. A firm believer in ability, determination, brains having nothing to do with gender. I'm even cautiously open to women players in the MLB. Cautiously open, I repeat. But there are lines."

"Carting a picnic hamper is a line?"

"Yeah."

She slid her hands into her pockets, hummed a little as she strolled with a smirk on her face. "It's a stupid line."

"Maybe. But that doesn't make it less of a line."

They walked through the forested canyon. She heard what she'd missed during the fire. The birdsong, the rustles—the life. Sun shimmered through the canopy, struck the bubbling, tumbling waters of the creek as they followed the curve of the water.

"Is this why you were studying maps?" she asked him. "Looking for a picnic spot?"

"That was a happy by-product. I haven't lived here all my life, and I want to know where I am." He scanned the canyon, the spills of water as they walked up the rising trail. "I like where I am."

"Was it always Northern California? Is there any reason we have to wait for the food to start the life story?"

"I guess not. No, I started out in LA. My parents were in the entertainment industry. He was a cinematographer, she was a costume designer. They met on a set, and clicked."

The creek fell below as they climbed higher on the hillside.

"So," he continued, "they got married, had me a couple years later. I was four when they were killed in a plane crash. Little twin engine they were taking to the location for a movie."

Her heart cracked a little. "Gull, I'm so sorry."

"Me too. They didn't take me, and they usually did if they were on the same project. But I had an ear infection, so they left me back with the nanny until it cleared up."

"It's hard, losing parents."

"Vicious. There's the log dam," he announced. "Just as advertised."

She let it go as the trail approached the creek once more. She could hardly blame him for not wanting to revisit a little boy's grief.

"This is worth a lot more than a mile-and-a-half hike," he said while the pond behind the dam sparkled as if strewn with jewels.

Beyond it the valley opened like a gift, and rolled to the ring of mountains.

"And the hamper's going to be a lot lighter on the mile-and-a-half back."

Near the pond, under the massive blue sky, he set it down.

"I worked a fire out there, the Selway-Bitterroot Wilderness." He stood, looking out. "Standing here, on a day like this, you'd never believe any of that could burn."

"Jumping one's different."

"It's sure a faster way in." He flipped open the lid of the hamper, took out the blanket folded on top. She helped him spread it open, then sat on it cross-legged.

"What's on the menu?"

He pulled out a bottle of champagne snugged in a cold sleeve. Surprised, touched, she laughed. "That's a hell of a start—and you just don't miss a trick."

"You said champagne picnic. For our entrée, we have the traditional fried chicken à la Marg."

"Best there is."

"I'm told you favor thighs. I'm a breast man myself."

"I've never known a man who isn't." She began to unload. "Oh, yeah, her red potato and green bean salad, and look at this cheese, the bread. We've got berries, deviled eggs. Fudge cake! Marg gave us damn near half of one of her fudge cakes." She glanced up. "Maybe she's in love with *you*."

"I can only hope." He popped the cork. "Hold out your glass."

She reached for it, then caught the label on the bottle. "Dom Pérignon. Iron Man's car and James Bond's champagne."

"I have heroic taste. Hold out the glass, Rowan." He filled it, then his own. "To wilderness picnics."

"All right." She tapped, sipped. "Jesus, this is not cheap tequila at Get a Rope. I see why 007 goes for it. How'd you get this?"

"They carry it in town."

"You've been into town today? What time did you get up?"

"About eight. I never made it to the shower last night, and smelled bad enough to wake myself up this morning."

He opened one of the containers, and after breaking off a

chunk of the baguette, spread it with soft, buttery cheese. Offered it. "I'm not especially rich, I don't think."

She studied him as flavors danced on her tongue. Caught in a pretty breeze, his hair danced around his face in an appealing tangle of brown and sun-struck gold.

"I want to know. But I don't want bad memories to screw your picnic."

"That's about it for the bad. I'm not sure I'd remember them, or more than vaguely, if it wasn't for my aunt and uncle. My mother's sister," he explained. "My parents named them as my legal guardians in their wills. They came and got me, took me up north, raised me."

He took out plates, flatware as he spoke, while she gave him room for the story.

"They talked about my parents all the time, showed me pictures. They were tight, the four of them, and my aunt and uncle wanted me to keep the good memories. I have them."

"You were lucky. After something horrible, you were lucky."

His gaze met hers. "Really lucky. They didn't just take me in. I was theirs, and I always felt that."

"The difference between being an obligation, even a well-tended one, and belonging."

"I never had to learn how wide that difference is. My cousins—one's a year older, one's a year younger—never made me feel like an outsider."

That played a part in the balance of him, she decided, in the ease and confidence.

"They sound like great people."

"They are. When I graduated from college, I had a trust fund, pretty big chunk. The money from my parents' estate, the insurance, all that. They'd never used a penny, but invested it for me."

"And you bought an arcade."

He lifted his champagne. "I like arcades. The best ones are about families. Anyway, my younger cousin mostly runs it, and Jared—the older one—he's a lawyer, and takes care of that sort of thing. My aunt supervises and helps plan events, and for the last couple years my uncle's handled the PR."

"For families by family. It's a good thing."

"It works for us."

"How do they feel about your summers?"

"They're okay with it. I guess they worry, but they don't weigh me down with that. You grew up with a smoke jumper." They added chicken and salad to plates. "How'd you handle it?"

"By thinking he was invincible. Talk about superheroes. Mmm," she added when she bit through crisp skin to tender meat. "God bless Marg. I really considered him immortal," Rowan added. "I never worried about him. I was never afraid for him, or myself. He was . . . Iron Man."

Gull poured two more glasses. "I'll definitely drink to Iron Man Tripp. He's why we're both here."

"Weird, but true." She ate, relaxed in the moment and felt easier with him, she realized, than she'd expected to be. "I don't know how much of the story you've heard. About my parents."

"Some."

"A lot of some's glossed over. My father—you've probably seen pictures—he was, still is, pretty wow."

"He passed the wow down to you."

"In a Valkyrie kind of way."

"You're not the sort who decides to die in the battle."

"You know your Norse mythology."

"I have many pockets of strange, inexplicable knowledge."

"So I've noticed. In any case, a man who looks like Iron Man, does what he does . . . women flock."

"I have the same problem. It's a burden."

She snorted, ate some potato salad. "But he wasn't one for coming off a fire, or out of the season, and looking for the handy bang."

She arched a brow as Gull merely grinned. "It's not his way. Like me, he's lived here all his life. If he'd had that kind of rep, it would've stuck. He met my mother when she came to Missoula, picked up work as a waitress. She was looking for adventure. She was beautiful, a little on the wild side. Anyway, they hooked up, and oops, she got knocked up. They got married. They met in early July, and by the middle of September they're married. Stupid, from a rational point of view, but I have to be grateful seeing as I'm sitting here telling the tale."

He'd known he'd been wanted, all of his life. How much did it change the angles when you, as she did, considered yourself an oops?

"We'll both be grateful."

"I think it must've been exciting for her." Rowan popped a fat blackberry into her mouth as she spoke. "Here's this gorgeous man who wore a flight suit like some movie star, one of the elite, one at the top of his game, and he picks her. At the same time, she's rebelling against a pretty strict, stuffy upbringing. She was nearly ten years younger than Dad, and probably enjoyed the idea of playing house with him. Over the winter, he's starting up his business, but he's around. My grandparents are, too, and she's carrying the child of their only son. She's the center. Her parents have cut her off, just severed all ties."

"How do people do that? How do they justify that, live with that?"

"They think they're right. And I think that added to the excitement for her. And in the spring, there I am, so she's got a new baby to show off. Doting grandparents—a husband who's besotted, and still around."

She chose another berry, let it lie on her tongue a moment, sweet and firm. "Then a month later, the season starts, and he's not around every day. Now it's about changing diapers, and walking a squalling baby in the middle of the night. It's not such an adventure now, or so exciting."

She reached for another piece of chicken. "He's never, not once, said a word against her to me. What I know of that time I got from reading letters he'd locked up, riffling through papers, eavesdropping—or occasionally catching my grandmother when she was pissed off and her tongue was just loose enough."

"You wanted to know," Gull said simply.

"Yeah, I wanted to know. She left when I was five months old. Just took me over to my grandparents, asked if they'd watch me while she ran some errands, and never came back."

"Cold." He couldn't quite get his mind around that kind of cold, or what that kind of cold would do to the child left behind. "And clueless," he added. "It says she decided this isn't what I want after all, so I'll just run away."

"That sums it. My dad tracked her down, a couple of times. Made phone calls, wrote letters. Her line, because I saw the letters she wrote back, was it was all his fault. He was the cold and selfish one, had wrecked her emotionally. The least he could do was send her some money while she was trying to recover. She'd promise to come back once she had, claimed she missed me and all that."

"Did she come back?"

"Once, on my tenth birthday. She walks into my party, all smiles and tears, loaded down with presents. It's not my birthday party anymore."

"No, it's her Big Return, putting her in the center again."

Rowan stared at him for a long moment. "That's exactly it. I hated her at that moment, the way a ten-year-old can. When she tried to hug me, I pushed her away. I told her to get out, to go to hell."

"Sounds to me that at ten you had a good bullshit detector. How'd she handle it?"

"Big, fat tears, shock, hurt—and bitter accusations hurled at my father."

"For turning you against her."

"And again, you score. I stormed right out the back door, and I'd have kept on going if Dad hadn't come out after me. He was pissed, all the way around. I knew better than to speak to anyone like that, and I was going back inside, apologizing to my mother. I said I wouldn't, he couldn't make me, and until he made *her* leave, I was never going back in that house. I was too mad to be scared. Respect was god in our house. You didn't lie and you didn't sass—the big two."

"How did he handle it?"

"He picked me right up off the ground, and I know he was worked up enough to cart me right back in there. I punched him, kicked him, screamed, scratched, bit. I didn't even know I was crying. I do know if he'd dragged me in, if he'd threatened me, ordered me, if he who'd never raised a hand to me had raised it, I wouldn't have said I was sorry."

"Then you'd've broken the other big one, by lying."

"The next thing I knew we were sitting on the ground in the backyard, I'm crying all over his shoulder. And he's hugging me, petting me and telling me I was right. He said, 'You're right, and I'm sorry.' He told me to sit right there, and he'd go in and make her go away."

She tipped back her glass. "And that's what he did."

"You got lucky, too."

"Yeah, I did. She didn't."

Rowan paused, looked out over the pond. "A little over two years later, she goes into a convenience store to pick up something, walks in on a robbery. And she's dead, wrong place, wrong time. Horrible. Nobody deserves to die bleeding on the floor of a quick market in Houston. God, how did I get on all this when there's fudge cake and champagne?"

"Finish it."

"Nothing much left. Dad asked me if I'd go to the funeral with him. He said he needed to go, that if I didn't need or want to, that was okay. I said I'd think about it, then later my grandmother came into my room, sat on the bed. She told me I needed to go. That as hard as it might be now, it would be harder on me later if I didn't. That if I did this one thing, I would never have to have any regrets. So I went, and she was right. I did what I needed to do, what my father needed me to do, and I've got no regrets."

"What about her family?"

"Her parents cold-shouldered us. That's who they are. I've never actually spoken to them. I know her sister, my aunt. She made a point of calling and writing over the years, even came out with her family a couple times. They're nice people.

"And that concludes our exchange of life stories."

"I imagine there's another chapter or two, for another time."

She eyed him as he refilled her glass. "You stopped drinking, and you keep filling my glass. Are you trying to get me drunk and naked?"

"Naked's always the goal." He said it lightly as he sensed she needed to change the mood. "Drunk? Not when I've witnessed you suck down tequila shots. I'm driving," he reminded her.

"Responsible." She toasted him. "And that leaves more for me. Did you know Dobie and Stovic scrubbed up and painted my room?"

"I heard Dobie got to first base with you."

She let out that big, bawdy laugh. "If he considers that first base, he's never hit a solid single." She took her fork, carved off a big mouthful of cake right out of the container. Her eyes laughed as she stuffed it in, then closed on a long, low moan. "Now, that is cake, and the equivalent of a grand slam. Enough fire and chocolate, and I can go all season without sex."

"Don't be surprised if the supply of chocolate disappears in a fifty-mile radius."

"I like your style, Gull." She forked up another hefty bite. "You're pretty to look at, you've got a brain, you can fight and you do what needs doing when we're on the line. Plus, you can definitely hit a solid single. But there are a couple of problems."

She stabbed another forkful, this time offering it to him.

"First, I know you've got deep pockets. If I slept with you now, you might think I did it because you're rich."

"Not that rich. Anyway." He considered, smiled. "I can live with that."

"Second." She held out more cake, then whipped it around, slid it into her own mouth. "You're a smoke jumper in my unit."

"You're the kind of woman who breaks rules. Codes, no. Rules, yes."

"That's an interesting distinction."

Full, she stretched out on the blanket, studied the sky. "Not a cloud," she murmured. "The long-range forecast is for hot and dry. There won't be a lot of champagne picnics this season."

"Then we should appreciate this one."

He leaned down, laid his lips on hers in a long, slow, upside-down kiss. She tasted of champagne and chocolate, smelled of peaches on a hot summer day.

She carried scars, body and heart, and still faced life with courage.

When her hands came to his face he lingered over those

flavors, those scents, the fascinating contrasts of her, sliding just a little deeper into the lush.

Then she eased his face up. "You're swinging for a double."

"It worked for Spider-Man."

"He was hanging upside down, in the rain—and that was after he'd kicked bad-guy ass. Not to mention, he didn't get to second."

"I'm in danger of being crazy about you, if only for your deep knowledge of superhero action films."

"I'm trying to save you from that fate." She patted the blanket beside her. "Why don't you stretch out in the next stage of picnic tradition while I explain?"

Gull shifted the hamper aside, lay down hip-to-hip with her.

"If we slept together," Rowan began, "there's no doubt we'd bang all the drums, ring all the bells."

"Sound all the trumpets."

"Those, too. But after, there's the inevitable tragedy. You'd fall in love with me. They all do."

He heard the humor in her voice, idly linked his fingertips with hers. "You have that power?"

"I do and, though God knows I've tried, can't control it. And you—I'm telling you this because, as I said, I like your style. You, helpless, hopeless, would be weak in love, barely able to eat or sleep. You'd spend all the profits you make off quarters pumped into Skee-Ball on elaborate gifts in a vain attempt to win my heart."

"They could be pretty elaborate," he told her. "Skee-Ball's huge."

"Still, my heart can't be bought. I'd be forced to break yours, coldly and cruelly, to spare you from further humiliation. And also because your pathetic pleas would irritate the shit out of me."

"All that," he said after a moment, "from one round in the sack?"

"I'm afraid so. I've lost count of the shoes I've had to throw away because the soles were stained with the bleeding hearts I've crushed along the way."

"That's a fair warning. I'll risk it."

He rolled over, took her mouth.

For a moment, she thought the top of her head simply shot off. Explosions, heat, eruptions burst through her body like a fireball. She lost her breath, and what she thought of as simple common sense, in the wicked whir of want.

She arched up to him, her hands shoving under his shirt—eager to feel her need pressed to him, his skin, his muscles under her hands.

There was a wildness here. She knew it lived inside her, and now she felt whatever animal he caged in leap out to run with hers.

She made him crazy. That lush, greedy mouth, those quick, seeking hands, the body that moved under his with such strength, such purpose, even as, for just a moment, it yielded.

Her breasts, full and firm, filled his hands as her moan of pleasure vibrated against his lips. She was sensation, and bombarded him with feelings he could neither stop nor identify.

He imagined pulling off her clothes, his own, taking what they both wanted there, on a borrowed blanket beside a shining pond.

Then her hands came between them, pushed. He gave himself another moment, gorging on that feast of feelings, before he eased back to look down at her.

"That," he said, "is the next step in a traditional picnic."

"Yeah, I guess it is. And it's a winner. It's a good thing I got off on that fudge cake because you definitely know how to stir a woman up. In fact . . ." She wiggled out from under him, grabbed what was left of the cake and took a bite. "Mmm, yeah, that takes care of it."

"Damn that Marg."

Her lips curved as she licked chocolate from her fingers. "This was great—every step."

"I've got a few more steps in me."

"I'm sure you do, and I have no doubt they'd be winners. Which is why we'd better go."

Her lips had curved, he thought when they began to pack

up, but the smile hadn't reached her eyes. He waited until they'd folded the blanket back into the well-depleted hamper.

"I got to second."

She laughed, as he'd hoped, then snickered with the fun of it as they started the hike back.

10

Lucas poked his head in the kitchen of the cookhouse.
"I heard a rumor about blueberry pie."

Marg glanced back as she finished basting a couple of turkeys the size of Hondas. "I might have saved a piece, and maybe could spare a cup of coffee to go with it. If somebody asked me nicely."

He walked over, kissed her cheek.

"That might work. Sit on down."

He took a seat at the work counter where Lynn prepped hills and mountains of vegetables. "How's it going, Lynn?"

"Not bad considering we keep losing cooks." She shot him a smile with a twinkle out of rich brown eyes. "If you sit here long enough, we'll put you to work."

"Will work for pie. I heard about the trouble. I was hoping to talk to Rowan, but they tell me she's on a picnic with the rookie from California."

"Fast Feet," Lynn confirmed. "He sweet-talked Marg into putting a hamper together."

"Nobody sweet-talks me unless I like the talk." Marg set a warmed piece of blueberry pie, with a scoop of ice cream gently melting over the golden crust, in front of Lucas.

"He's got a way though," Lynn commented.

"Nobody has their way with Rowan unless she likes the way." Marg put a thick mug of coffee beside the pie.

"I don't worry about her." Lucas shrugged.

"Liar."

He smiled up at Marg. "Much. What's your take on this business with Dolly?"

"First, the girl can cook but she doesn't have the brains, or the sense, of that bunch of broccoli Lynn's prepping." Marg waved a pot holder at him. "And don't think I don't know she tried getting her flirt on with you a time or two."

"Oh, golly," Lynn said as both she and Lucas blushed to the hairline.

"For God's sake, Marg, she's Rowan's age."

"That and good sense stopped you, but it didn't stop her from trying."

"Neither here nor there," Lucas mumbled, and focused on his pie.

"You can thank me for warning her off before Rowan got wind and scalped her. Anyway, I'd've butted heads with L.B. about hiring her back, but we needed the help. The cook we hired on didn't last through training."

"Too much work, she said." Lynn rolled her eyes as she filled an enormous pot with the mountain of potatoes she'd peeled and quartered.

"I was thinking about seeing if we could bump one of the girls we have who helps with prep sometimes, and with cleanup, to full-time cook. But then Dolly has the experience, and I know what she can do. And, well, she's got a baby now."

"Jim Brayner's baby." Lucas nodded as he ate pie. "Everybody needs a chance."

"Yeah, and that bromide ended up getting Ro's quarters splattered with pig blood. Nasty business, let me tell you."

"That girl's had it in for Ro since their school days, but this?" Lucas shook his head. "It's just senseless."

"Dolly's lucky Cards was there to hold Ro back long enough for some of the other guys to come on the run and wrestle her down. It would've been more than some oinker's blood otherwise."

"My girl's got a temper."

"And was in the right of it, if you ask me—or anybody else around here. And what does Dolly do after L.B. cans her?" Marg's eyes went hot as she slapped a dishcloth on the counter. "She comes crying to me, asking, can't I put in a word for her? I gave her a word, all right."

Lynn snorted. "Surrounded by others, as in: Get the *word* out of my kitchen."

"I'm sorry for her troubles, but it's best she's gone. And away from my girl," Lucas added. As far as he was concerned, that ended that. "How would you rate the rookies this season?"

Marg hauled out a couple casserole dishes. "The rook your girl's eating fried chicken with, or all of them?"

"All of them." Lucas scraped up the last bit of pie. "Maybe one in particular."

"They're a good crop, including one in particular. I'd say most are just crazy enough to stick it out."

"I guess we'll see. That was damn good pie, Marg."

"Are you after seconds?"

"Can't do it." He patted his belly. "My days of eating like a smoke jumper are over. And I've got some things I've got to get to," he added when he rose to take his plate and mug to the sink. "When you see Ro, tell her I stopped by."

"Will do. You're close enough not to be such a stranger."

"Business is good, and good keeps me pinned down. But I'll make the time. Don't work too hard, Lynn."

"Come back and say that in October, and I might be able to listen."

He headed out to walk down to where he'd left his truck. As always, nostalgia twinged, just a little. Some of the jumpers got in a run on the track. Others, he could see, stood jawing with some of the mechanics.

He spotted Yangtree, looking official in his uniform shirt and hat, leading a tour group out of Operations. Plenty of kids being herded along, he noted, getting a charge out of seeing parachutes, jumpsuits and the network of computer systems— vastly improved since his early days.

Maybe they'd get lucky and see somebody rigging a chute. Anyway, it was a nice stop for a kid on summer vacation.

That made him think of school, and school led him to the high-school principal he'd agreed to meet for a drink.

Probably should've just taken her into the office, had the sit-down there. Professional.

Friendly business started to seem more nerve-racking as the day went on.

No way around it now, he reminded himself, and dug his keys out of his pocket. As he did, he turned toward the lion's purr of engine, frowned a little as he watched his daughter zip up in the passenger seat of an Audi Spyder convertible.

She waved at him, then jumped out when the sleek beast of a car growled to a stop.

"Hey! I was going to try to get over and see you later." She threw her arms around him—was there anything more wonderful than a hard hug from your grown child? "Now I don't have to, 'cause here you are."

"I almost missed you. Gull, right?"

"That's right. It's good to see you again."

"Some car."

"I'm happy with it."

"What'll she do?"

"Theoretically, or in practice—with your daughter along?"

"That's a good answer, without answering," Lucas decided.

"Do you want to try her out?" Gull offered the key.

"Hey!" Rowan made a grab for them, missing as Gull closed his hand. "How come he rates?"

"He's Iron Man."

Rowan hooked her thumbs in her pockets. "He said I had to sleep with him before I could drive it."

Gull sent her smirk a withering look. "She declined."

"Uh-huh. Well, I wouldn't mind giving her a run. I'll take a rain check on it since I've got to get along."

"Can't you stay awhile?" Rowan asked. "We can hang out a little. You can stay and mooch dinner."

"I wish I could, but I've got a couple of things to see to, then I'm meeting a client for a drink—a meeting. An appointment."

Rowan slid off her sunglasses. "A client?"

"Yeah. Yeah. She's, ah, got some project she wants to talk to me about, and she's interested in trying for AFF. So I guess we're going to talk about it. That. Anyway . . . I'll get back over soon, mooch that dinner off you. Maybe try out that machine of yours, Gull."

"Anytime."

Lucas took Rowan's chin in his hand. "See you later."

She watched him get in the truck, watched him drive away.

"Meeting, my ass."

Gull opened the nose to maneuver the hamper out. "Sorry?"

"He's got a date. With a woman."

"Wow! That's shocking news. I think my heart skipped a beat."

"He doesn't date." Rowan continued to scowl as her father's truck shrunk in the distance. "He's all fumbling and flustered around women, if he's attracted. Didn't you see how flustered he was when he talked about his *appointment*? And who the hell is she?"

"It's hard, but you've got to let the kids leave the nest someday."

"Oh, kiss ass. His brain goes to mush when he's around a certain type of woman, and he can be manipulated."

Fascinated with her reaction, Gull leaned on his car. "It's just a wild shot, but it could be he's going to meet a woman he's attracted to, and who has no intention of manipulating him. And they'll have a drink and conversation."

"What the hell do you know?" she challenged, and stomped off toward the barracks.

Amused, Gull hauled the basket back to Marg.

He'd no more than set it down on the counter when someone tapped knuckles on the outside door.

"Excuse me. Margaret Colby?"

Gull gave the man a quick summing-up—dark suit with a tightly knotted tie in dark, vivid pink, shiny shoes, hair the color of ink brushed back from a high forehead.

Marg stood where she was. "That's right."

"I'm Reverend Latterly."

"I remember you from before, from Irene and Dolly."

Catching her tone, and the fact she didn't invite the man in, Gull decided to stick around.

"May I speak with you for a moment?"

"You can, but you're wasting your breath and my time if you're here to ask me to try to convince Michael Little Bear to let Dolly Brakeman back in this kitchen."

"Mrs. Colby." He came in without invitation, smiled, showing a lot of big white teeth.

Gull decided he didn't like the man's tie, and helped himself to a cold can of ginger ale.

"If I could just have a moment in private."

"We're working." She shot a warning glance at Lynn before the woman could ease out of the room. "This is as private as you're going to get."

"I know you're very busy, and cooking for so many is hard work. Demanding work."

"I get paid for it."

"Yes." Latterly stared at Gull, let the silence hang.

In response, Gull leaned back on the counter, drank some ginger ale. And made Marg's lips twitch.

"Well, I wanted a word with you as you're Dolly's direct supervisor and—"

"Was," Marg corrected.

"Yes. I've spoken with Mr. Little Bear, and I understand his reluctance to forgive Dolly's transgression."

"You call it a transgression. I call it snake-bite mean."

Latterly spread his hands, then linked them together for a moment like a man at prayer. "I realize it's a difficult situation, and there's no excuse for Dolly's behavior. But she was naturally upset after Miss Tripp threatened her and accused her of . . . having low morals."

"Is that Dolly's story?" Marg just shook her head, as much pity as disgust in the movement. "The girl lies half the time she opens her mouth. If you don't know that, you're not a very good judge of character. And I'd think that'd be an important skill to have in your profession."

"As Dolly's spiritual advisor—"

"Just stop there because I'm not overly interested in Dolly's spirit. She's had a mean on for Rowan as long as I've known her. She's always been jealous, always wanted what somebody else had. She's not coming back here, not getting another chance to kick at Rowan. Now, L.B. runs this base, but I run this kitchen. If he took it into his head to let Dolly back in here, he'd be looking for another head cook and he knows it."

"That's a very hard line."

"I call it common sense. The girl can cook, but she's wild, unreliable, and she's a troublemaker. I can't help her."

"She is troubled, still trying to find her way. She's also raising an infant on her own."

"She's not on her own," Marg corrected. "I've known her mother since we were girls, and I know Irene and Leo are doing all they can for Dolly. Probably more than they should, considering. Now you're going to have to excuse me."

"Would you, at least, write a reference for her? I'm sure it would help her secure another position as a cook."

"No, I won't."

Gull judged the shock that crossed the man's face as sincere. Very likely the reverend wasn't used to a flat-out no.

"As a Christian woman—"

"Who said I'm a Christian?" She jabbed a finger at him now, pointedly enough to take him back a step. "And how come that's some sort of scale on right and wrong and good and bad? I won't write her a reference because my word and my reputation mean something to me. You advise her spirit all you want, but don't come into my kitchen and try advising me on mine. Dolly made her choices, now she'll deal with the consequences of them."

She took a step forward, and those hazel eyes breathed fire. "Do you think I haven't heard what she's been saying about Rowan around town? About me, L.B., even little Lynn there? About everybody? I hear everything, Reverend Jim, and I won't give a damn thing to anyone who lies about me and mine. If it wasn't for her mother, I'd give Dolly Brakeman a good swift kick myself."

"Gossip is—"

"What plumps the grapes on the vine. If you want to do her a favor, tell Dolly to mind her mouth. Now I've got work to do, and I've given you and Dolly enough of my time."

Deliberately she turned back to the stove.

"I apologize for intruding." He spoke stiffly now, and without the big-toothed smile. "I'll pray the anger leaves your heart."

"I like my anger right where it is," Marg shot back as Latterly backed out the door. "Lynn, those vegetables aren't going to prep themselves."

"No, ma'am."

On a sigh, Marg turned around. "I'm sorry, honey. I'm not mad at you."

"I know. I wish I had the courage to talk like that to people—to say exactly what I think and mean."

"No, you don't. You're fine just the way you are. I just didn't like the sanctimonious prick." She aimed a look at Gull. "Nothing to say?"

"Just he's a sanctimonious prick with too many teeth and an ugly tie. My only critique of your response is I think you should have told him you were a Buddhist woman, or maybe a Pagan."

"I wish I'd thought of that." She smiled. "You want some pie?"

He didn't know where he'd put it after the fudge cake, but understanding the sentiment behind the offer, he couldn't say no.

LUCAS'S STOMACH JITTERED when he walked into the bar, but he assured himself it would settle once they started talking about whatever she wanted to talk about.

Then he saw her, sitting at a table reading a book, and his tongue got thick.

She'd put on a dress, something all green and summery that showed off her arms and legs while her pretty red hair waved to her shoulders.

Should he have worn a tie? he wondered. He hardly ever wore ties, but he had a few.

She looked up, saw him, smiled. So he had no choice but to cross over to the table.

"I guess I'm late. I'm sorry."

"You're not." She closed the book. "I got here a little early, as the errands I had didn't take as long as I thought." She slipped the book into her purse. "I always carry a book in case I have some time on my hands."

"I've read that one." There, he thought, he was talking. He was sitting down. "I guess I figured doing what you do, you'd be reading educational books all the time."

"I do plenty of that, but not with my purse book. I'm liking it a lot so far, but then I always enjoy Michael Connelly."

"Yeah, it's good stuff."

The waitress stepped up. "Good evening. Can I get you a drink?"

When she shifted, Ella's scent—something warm and spicy—drifted across the table and fogged Lucas's brain.

"What am I in the mood for?" she wondered. "I think a Bombay and tonic, with a twist of lime."

"And you, sir? Sir?" the waitress repeated when Lucas remained mute.

"Oh, sorry. Ah, I'll have a beer. A Rolling Rock."

"I'll get those right out to you. Anything else? An appetizer?"

"You know what I'd love? Some of those sweet potato skins. They're amazing," she told Lucas. "You have to share some with me."

"Sure. Okay. Great."

"I'll be right back with your drinks."

"I so appreciate you taking the time to come in," Ella began. "It gives me an excuse to sit in a pretty bar, have a summer drink and some sinful food."

"It's a nice place."

"I like coming here, when I have an excuse. I've come to feel at home in Missoula in a fairly short time. I love the town, the countryside, my work. It's hard to ask for more."

"You're not from here. From Montana." He knew that. Hadn't he known that?

"Born in Virginia, transplanted to Pennsylvania when I went to college, where I met my ex-husband."

"That's a ways from Montana."

"I got closer as time went by. We moved to Denver when the kids were ten and twelve, when my husband—ex—got a difficult-to-refuse job offer. We were there about a dozen years before we moved to Washington State, another job offer. My son moved here, got married, started his family, and my girl settled in California, so after the divorce I wanted fresh. Since I like the mountains, I decided to try here. I get fresh, the mountains, and my son and his family, with my daughter close enough by air I can see her several times a year."

He couldn't imagine the picking up and going, going then

picking it all up again. Though his work had taken him all over the West, he'd lived in Missoula all his life.

"That's a lot of country, a lot of moving around."

"Yes, and I'm happy to be done with it. You're a native?"

"That's right. Born and bred in Missoula. I've been east a few times. We get hired off-season to work controlled burns, or insect eradication."

"Exterminating bugs?"

He grinned. "Bugs that live up in tall trees," he explained, jerking a thumb at the ceiling. "We—smoke jumpers, I mean—are trained to climb. But most of my life's been spent west of St. Louis."

The waitress served their drinks, and Ella lifted hers. "Here's to roots—maintaining them and setting them down."

"Washington State, that's pretty country. I jumped some fires there. Colorado, too."

"A lot of country." Ella smiled at him. "You've seen the most pristine, and the most devastated. Alaska, too, right? I read you fought wildfires there."

"Sure."

She leaned forward. "Is it fantastic? I've always wanted to see it, to visit there."

For a minute, he lost the rhythm of small talk in her eyes. "Ah . . . I've only seen it in the summer, and it's fantastic. The green, the white, the water, the miles and miles of open. All that water's a hazard for jumping fire, but they don't have the trees like we do here, so it's a trade-off."

"Which is more hazardous? Water or trees?"

"Land in the water with all your gear, you're going to go down, maybe not get up again. Land in the trees, land wrong, maybe you just get hung up, maybe you break your neck. The best thing to do is not land in either."

"Have you?"

"Yeah. I hit my share of both. The worst part's knowing you're going to, and trying to correct enough so you'll walk away from it. Any jump you walk away from is a good jump."

She sat back. "I knew it. I knew you'd be perfect for what I'd like to do."

"Ah—"

"I know they give tours of the base, and groups can see the operation, ask some questions. But I had this idea, specifically for students. Something more intimate, more in-depth. Hearing firsthand, from the source, what it takes, what you do, what you've done. Personal experiences of the work, the life, the risks, the rewards."

"You want me to talk to kids?"

"Yes. I want you to talk to them. I want you to teach them. Hear me out," she added when he just stared at her. "A lot of our students come from privilege, from parents who can afford to send them to a top-rated private school like ours. Everyone knows about the Zulies. The base is right here. But I'll guarantee few, if any, unless they have a connection, understand what it really means to be what you are, do what you do."

"I'm not a jumper anymore."

"Lucas." The soft smile teased out the dimples. "You'll always be one. In any case, you gave it half of your life. You've seen the changes in the process, the equipment. You've fought wilderness fires all over the West. You've seen the beauty and the horror. You've felt it."

She laid a fisted hand on her heart. "Some of these kids, the ones I'd especially like to reach with this, have attitudes. The hard work, the dirty work, that's for somebody else—somebody who doesn't have the money or brains to go to college, launch a lucrative career. The wilderness? What's the big deal? Let somebody else worry about it."

She'd tripped something in him the minute she'd said he'd always be a jumper. The minute he saw she understood that.

"I don't know how me talking to them's going to change that."

"I think listening to you, being able to ask you questions, having you take them through, from training to fire, will open some of those young minds."

"And that's what your work is. Even though you don't teach anymore, you'll always be a teacher."

"Yes. We understand that about each other." She watched him as she sipped her drink. "I intend to talk to the operations officer at base. I'd like to, with parental permission, have a group, or groups, go through training. A shortened version obviously. Maybe over a weekend after the fire season."

"You want to put them through the wringer," he said with a glimmer of a smile.

"I want to show them, teach them, bring it home to them that the men and women who dedicate themselves to protecting our wilderness put themselves through the wringer. I have ideas about photographs and videos, and . . . I have ideas," she said with a laugh. "And we'd have all summer to put the project together."

"I think it's a good thing you're trying to do. I'm not much good at speaking. Public speaking."

"I can help you with that. Besides, I'd rather you just be who you are. Believe me, that's enough."

She picked up one of the potato skins the waitress had served while she'd laid out her plan.

She'd caught him up in it, he couldn't deny it. The idea of it, the passion behind it. "I can give it a try, I guess. At least see how it goes."

"That would be great. I really think we can do something that has impact—and some fun. And that brings me to two things." She took another drink. "Let me just get this off the table. I was married for twenty-eight years. I uprooted myself, then my kids as well to support and suit my husband. I loved him, almost all of those twenty-eight years, and for the last of them, I believed in the marriage, the life we'd built. I believed in him. Until on my fifty-second birthday, he took me out to dinner. A beautiful restaurant, candles, flowers, champagne. He even had a rather exquisite pair of diamond earrings for me to top it off."

She sat back a little, crossed her legs. "All of this to set it up, so I wouldn't cause a public scene when he told me he was having an affair with his personal assistant—a woman young enough to be his daughter, by the way. That he was in love with her and leaving me. He still thought the world of me, of course, and hoped I'd understand that these things happened. Oh, and the heart wants what the heart wants."

"I'm sorry. I'm trying to think what I should say, but nothing that's coming into my head seems appropriate."

"Oh, it can't be any less appropriate than what I said—after I picked up the champagne bucket and dumped the ice over his head. When I went to a lawyer—the very next day—she asked if I wanted to play nice or cut him off at the balls. I went for castration. I'd finished playing nice."

"Good for you."

"I wondered if I would regret it. But so far, no. I'm telling you this because I think it's only fair that you understand, right now, I can be mean, and that both my marriage and my divorce taught me to understand myself, virtue and flaw, and to not waste time in going after what I want."

"Time's always wasted if you're not aiming for what you want."

"An excellent point. Which brings me to the second thing. I lied to you earlier today when I said I wasn't hitting on you. I was. I am."

It wasn't just that his mind went blank, but that his whole system hit overload and snapped to an abrupt halt. He couldn't quite manage the simple act of swallowing as he stared into her sparkling eyes.

"I don't believe in absolute honesty in all things," she continued, "because I think a little shading now and then not only softens the edges, but makes things more interesting. But in this case, I decided on the bald truth. If it scares you off, it's better to know at this point, where there really isn't anything on the line for either of us."

She took a small sip from her glass. "So . . . Have I scared you off?"

"I . . . I'm not very good at this."

"I should have put in there that whether you're interested or not, I'm very sincere and serious about the project, and about learning how to skydive. Both of those things might be connected to me being attracted to you, but they're not contingent on it. Or you reciprocating."

She sighed. "And that sounded like a high-school principal when I'd hoped not to. I'm a little nervous."

The idea of that stopped the degeneration of his brain cells. "You are?"

"I like you, and I'm hoping you're interested enough to want to spend time with me, on a personal level. So, yes, I'm a little nervous that pushing that forward so soon might put you off. But it's part of my don't-waste-time policy, so . . . If you're interested, or inclined to consider being interested, I'd like to take you to dinner. There's a nice restaurant a couple blocks away. It's an easy walk—and I made a reservation, just in case."

He considered, shook his head. "No."

"Well. Then we'll just—"

"I'd like to take *you* to dinner." He could hardly believe the words came out of his mouth, and didn't cause a single hitch. "I heard there's a nice restaurant a couple blocks away, if you'd like to take a walk."

He loved watching the way the smile bloomed on her face. "That sounds great. I'm just going to go freshen up first."

She got up from the table, moved toward the restroom.

The minute the door closed behind her, she did a high-stepping dance in the bold purple peek-toe pumps she'd bought that afternoon.

On a foolish giggle, she walked to the sink, studied her giddy face in the mirror. "Let the adventure begin," she said, then took out her lipstick.

A few years before, she'd wondered, worried, all but assumed her life was essentially over. In a way, it had been, had needed to be to push her to start again.

So far, the new life of Ella Frazier brimmed with interesting possibilities.

And one of them was about to take her to dinner.

She nodded to her reflection, dropped the lipstick back in her purse. "Thanks, Darrin," she declared to her ex-husband. "It took that kick in the teeth to wake me up." She tossed her hair, did a stylish half turn. "And just look at me now. I am wide awake."

ROWAN RESISTED calling or texting her father's cell. It struck her as a little too obviously checking up on him. Instead, she opted for his landline at home.

She fully expected him to answer. She'd waited until nine thirty, after all, busying herself with her paperwork. Or trying to. When his machine picked up, she was momentarily at a loss. She had to grope for the excuse it had taken her nearly a half hour to come up with.

"Oh, hey. I'm just taking a quick break from writing up my reports and realized I didn't get the chance to tell you of my brilliance as fire boss. If I can't brag to you, who can I brag to? I'll be at this for another hour or so, then I'll probably take a walk to clear the administrative BS out of my head. So give me a call. Hope your meeting went well."

She rolled her eyes as she clicked off. "Meeting-schmeeting," she muttered. "A drink with a client doesn't go for two and a half hours."

She brooded awhile. It wasn't that she thought her father wasn't entitled to a social life. But she didn't even know who this *client* was. Lucas Tripp was handsome, interesting, a successful businessman. And a prime target for an opportunistic woman.

A daughter held a solemn duty to look after her single, successful, naive and overly-trusting-of-women father. She wanted him to get home and call her back, so she could do just that.

Maybe she should try him on his cell, just in case—

No, no, no, she ordered herself. That crossed the line into interfering. He was sixty, for God's sake. He didn't have a curfew.

She'd just finish the stupid report, take that walk. He was bound to call before she'd gotten it all done.

But she finished the report, sent it to L.B. She took a long, admittedly sulky walk, before going back to her quarters and taking twice as long as necessary to get ready for bed.

Annoyed with herself, she shut off the light. During a brutal mental debate about the justification of trying her father's cell after midnight, she fell asleep.

VOICES WOKE HER. Voices raised outside her window, outside her door. For a bleary moment she thought herself in the recurring dream—the aftermath of Jim's tragic jump when everyone had been shouting, rushing. Scared, angry.

But when her eyes opened in the half-light, the voices continued. Something's wrong, she thought, and instinct had her out of bed, out the door before fully awake.

"What the hell?" she demanded as Dobie pushed by her.

"Somebody hit the ready room. Gibbons said it looks like a bomb went off."

"What? That can't—"

But Dobie continued to run, obviously wanting to see for himself. In the cotton pants and tank she'd slept in, Rowan raced out in her bare feet.

The morning chill hit her skin, but what she saw in the faces of those who hurried with her, or quick-stepped it toward Operations, heated her blood.

Something's *very* wrong, she realized, and quickened her pace.

She hit the door to the ready room in step with Dobie.

A bomb wasn't far off, she thought. Parachutes, so meticulously and laboriously rigged and packed, lay or draped like tangled, deflated balloons. Tools scattered on the torn silks with gear spilling chaotically out of lockers. From the looks of it, tools, once carefully cleaned and organized, had been used to hack and slice at packs, jumpsuits, boots, damaging or destroying everything needed to jump and contain a fire.

On the wall, splattered in bloody-red spray paint, the message read clearly:

JUMP AND DIE

BURN IN HELL

Rowan thought of pig's blood.

"Dolly."

With his hands fisted at his sides, Dobie stared at the destruction. "Then she's worse than crazy."

"Maybe she is." Rowan squatted, slid a hand through the slice in silk. "Maybe she is."

EXTENDED ATTACK

A little fire is quickly trodden out;
Which, being suffered, rivers cannot quench.

WILLIAM SHAKESPEARE

11

Every able hand worked in manufacturing, in the loadmaster's room, in the loft. They spread through the buildings, making Smitty bags, ponchos, finishing chutes already in for repair, rigging, repacking. Under the hum and clatter of machines, the mutters, Rowan knew everyone's thoughts ran toward the same destination.

Let the siren stay silent.

Until they repaired and restocked, rerigged, inspected, there was no jump list.

Nothing in the ready room could be touched until the cops cleared it. So they worked with what they had in manufacturing, running against the clock and the moods of nature.

"We could maybe send eight in." Cards worked opposite Rowan, painstakingly rigging a chute. "We can put eight together right now."

"I can't think about it. And we can't rush it. It's a damn good thing she didn't get in here. Bad enough as it is."

"Do you really think Dolly did that?"

"Who else?"

"That's just fucked up. She was sort of one of us. I even . . ."

"A lot of the guys even."

"Before Vicki," Cards added. "Before Jim. Anyway, I mean, she worked right here on base, joking and flirting around in the dining hall. Like Marg and Lynn."

"Dolly's never been like Marg and Lynn."

Focusing, Rowan arranged the chute's lines into two perfect bundles. One tangled cord could be the difference between a good jump and a nightmare. "Who else is pissed off and crazy besides Dolly?"

"Painting that crap on the wall, too," Cards agreed. "Like she did in your room. I was up till damn near one, and didn't hear a goddamn thing. Wrecking the place that way, she had to make some noise."

"She snuck onto base late, after everyone was bunked down." Rowan shrugged. "It's just not that hard, especially if you know your way around. It happened, that's for damn sure."

"It doesn't make any sense." Gull stopped on his way to another table with a repaired chute. "If there's a fire when we're not squared away, they'll send in jumpers from other bases. Nobody's going to jump until our equipment's cleared. Who's she trying to hurt?"

"Crazy doesn't have to make sense."

"You've got a point. But all that mess down there accomplishes is to cost time and money—and piss everybody off. Not to mention cops knocking at your door, when you slid by that one last time."

"Vindictive doesn't have to make sense either."

Gull started to speak again, but Gibbons hailed Rowan. "Cops want to talk to you, Ro. To all of us," he added as the machines hummed into silence. "But you're up."

"I'm going to finish packing this chute. Five minutes," she estimated.

"L.B.'s office. Lieutenant Quinniock."

"Five minutes."

"Cards, when you're finished there, you can go on over to the cookhouse. The other one, Detective Rubio'll talk to you there."

Cards jerked his head in acknowledgment. "Looks like you got the short straw, Ro. At least I'll get some breakfast."

"Gull, Matt, Janis, when the cops give us the go-ahead, you'll be working with me on cleanup and inventory. You want chow, Marg's got a buffet set up. Fill your bellies because we're going to be at it awhile. Fucking mess," he said in disgust as he walked out.

Cards signed his name, the time and date on the repacked chute.

"I'll walk down with you," Gull told Cards, and brushed a hand down Rowan's back as he walked by her.

She finished the job, choking down everything but the task at hand. When she was done, she labeled the pack. Chute by Swede.

She shelved it, then gladly left the headachy din of manufacturing. But she detoured to the ready room.

She wanted to see it again. Maybe needed to.

Two police officers worked with a pair of civilians—forensics, Rowan concluded. She knew the woman currently taking photos of the painted message. Jamie Potts, Rowan thought. They'd been stuck in Mr. Brody's insanely boring world history class together their junior year in high school. She recognized one of the cops as well, as she'd dated him awhile about the same time as Mr. Brody.

She started to speak, then just backed out, realizing she didn't want conversation until she had no choice.

Besides, looking at the torn and trampled, the strewn and defaced, only heated up her already simmering temper.

She shoved her hands into the pockets of the hoodie she'd pulled on over her nightclothes.

Halfway to Operations, Gull cut across her path. He handed her a Coke. "I thought you could use it."

"Yeah, thanks. I thought you'd headed down for breakfast."

"I'll get it. It's a bump, Ro."

"What?"

"This." He gestured behind them, toward the ready room. "It's a bump, the kind that gives you a nasty jolt, but it doesn't stop you from getting where you're going. Whoever did that? They didn't accomplish a thing but make everybody on this base more determined to get where we're going."

"Glass half full?"

She honestly couldn't say why that grated on her nerves. "Right now my glass is not only mostly empty, it has a jagged, lip-tearing chip in it. I'm not ready to look at it in sunny terms. I might be once her vindictive batshit crazy ass is sitting in a cell."

"They'll have to call in the rangers or the feds, I guess. U.S. Forest Service property that got messed with, so it's probably a felony. I don't know how it works."

That stopped her. She hadn't thought it through. "L.B. called the locals. The feds aren't going to waste their time with this."

"I don't know. But I'd think if somebody wanted to push it, that's where it would go. Destruction of federal property, that could land her a stiff stint in a cell. What she needs is a big dose of mandatory therapy."

The man, she concluded, was a piece of work. Good work at the core, and right now that core of good made her want to punch something.

Possibly him.

"You're telling me this because you're not sure if I want her to do time in Leavenworth, or wherever."

"Do you?"

"Damn it. Right now I wouldn't shed a tear over that, but at the bottom of it, I just want her out of our hair, once and for all."

"Nobody can argue with that. Whoever did that to the ready room has some serious problems."

"Look, you've had a few weeks' exposure to Dolly. I've had a lifetime, and I'm finished having her problems become mine."

"Nobody can argue with that, either." He cupped a hand at the back of her neck, catching her off-guard with the kiss. "Let's see if we can squeeze in a run later. I could use one."

"Will you *stop* trying to settle me down?"

"No, because you probably don't want to talk to a cop when you're pissed off enough to bite out his throat if he happens to push the wrong button."

He took her shoulders, got a good grip. And, she noted, his eyes weren't so calm, weren't so patient. "You're smart. Be smart. The ready room wasn't a personal attack on you; it was a sucker punch at all of us. Remember that."

"She's—"

"She's nothing. Make her nothing, and focus on what's important. Give the cop what he needs, go back to work on fixing the damage. After that, take a run with me."

He kissed her again, quick and hard, then walked away.

"Take a run. I'll give you a run," she muttered. She veered off toward L.B.'s office, and realized Gull unsettled her nearly as much as Dolly's sudden bent for violence.

Lieutenant Quinniock sat at L.B.'s overburdened desk with a mug of coffee and a notebook. Black-framed cheaters perched on the end of his long, bladed nose while eyes of faded-denim blue peered over them. A small scar rode high on his right cheek, a pale fishhook against the ruddiness. And like a scar, a shock of white, like a lightning bolt blurred at the edges, shot through his salt-and-pepper hair between the left temple and the crown.

She'd seen him before, Rowan realized—in a bar or a shop—somewhere. His wasn't a face easily overlooked.

He wore a dark, subtly pin-striped suit like an executive—pressed and tailored, with a perfectly knotted tie of flashy red.

The suit didn't go with the face, she thought, and wondered if the contrast was deliberate.

He stood when she came into the room. "Ms. Tripp?"

"Yeah. Rowan Tripp."

"I appreciate you taking a few minutes. I know it's a stressful day. Would you mind closing the door?"

The voice, she decided, mild, polite, engaging, fit the suit.

"Have a seat," he told her. "I have a few questions."

"Okay."

"I've met your father. I imagine most around these parts have at some time or other. You're following in big footprints, and I'm told you're doing a good job of filling them."

"Thanks."

"So . . . you and a Miss Dolly Brakeman had an altercation a few days ago."

"You could call it that."

"What would you call it?"

She wanted to rage, to jab a finger in the middle of that flashy tie. Be smart, Gull had said—and damn it, he was right.

So she ordered herself to relax in the chair and speak

coolly. "Let's see, I call it trespassing, vandalism, defacing private property and generally being a crazy bitch. But that's just me."

"Apparently not just you, as others I've spoken with share that point of view. You discovered Miss Brakeman in your quarters here on base in the act of pouring animal blood on your bed. Is that correct?"

"It is. And that would be after she'd poured it, tossed it, splattered it over the walls, the floor, my clothes and other assorted items. After she wrote on my wall with it. 'Burn in hell,' to be precise."

"Yes, I've got the photographs of the damage Mr. Little Bear took before the area was cleaned and repainted."

"Oh." That set her back a moment. She hadn't realized L.B. had documented with photos. Should have figured he would, she thought now. That's why he was in charge.

"And what happened when you found her in your quarters?"

"What? Oh, I tried to kick her ass, but several of my colleagues stopped me. Which, given the current situation, is even more of a damn shame."

"You didn't notify the police."

"No."

"Why not?"

"Partially because I was too pissed off, and partially because she got fired and kicked off the base. That seemed enough, considering."

"Considering?"

"Considering, at that time, I figured she was just sublimely stupid, that her stupidity was aimed solely at me—and she's got a baby. Plus, within an hour we caught a fire, so she wasn't a top priority for me after that."

"You and your unit had a long, hard couple of days."

"It's what we do."

"What you do is appreciated." He sipped his coffee as he scanned his notes. "The baby you mentioned is purported to have been fathered by James Brayner, a Missoula smoke jumper who died in an accident last August."

"That's right."

"Miss Brakeman blames you."

It hurt still; she supposed it always would. "I was his jump partner. She blames the whole unit, and me in particular."

"Just for my own edification, what does 'jump partner' mean?"

"We jump in two-man teams. One after the other once we get the go from the spotter. The first one out, that would've been me in this case, checks the location and status of the second man. You might want to make adjustments in direction, trajectory, give the second man a clear stream. If one of you has any problems, the other should be able to spot it. You look out for each other, as much as you can, in the air, on landing."

"And Brayner's accident was ruled, after investigation, as his error."

Her throat burned, making it impossible to keep the emotion out of her voice. "He didn't steer away. We hit some bad air, but he just rode on it. He pulled the wrong toggle, steered toward instead of away. There was nothing I could do. His chute deployed; I gave him space, but he didn't come around. He overshot the jump site, kept riding, and went down into the fire."

"It's difficult to lose a partner."

"Yeah. Difficult."

"At that time Miss Brakeman was employed as a cook on base."

"That's right."

"Did you and she have any problems prior to the accident?"

"She cooked. I ate. That's pretty much it."

"I'm under the impression the two of you knew each other for quite some time. That you went to school together."

"We didn't run in the same circle. We knew each other. For some reason she was always jealous of me. I know a lot of people. I know Jamie and Barry, down doing their cop thing in the ready room; went to school with them, too. Neither one of them ever pulled a Carrie-at-the-prom on my quarters."

He watched her over that long, narrow nose. "Were you aware she was pregnant at the time of Brayner's death?"

"No. As far as I know nobody was aware except, from what she said when she came back, Jim. She took off right after the accident—I don't know where, and don't care. As far as I can tell she came back with the baby, got religion and came here looking for work, armed with her mother, her minister and pictures of her chubby-cheeked baby. L.B. hired her."

To give herself a moment, she took a long drink from her Coke. "I had one conversation with her, figuring we should clear the air, and during which she made it crystal she hated every linear inch of my guts, wished me to hell. She dumped blood all over my room. L.B. fired her. And that brings us up to date."

She shifted in her chair, tired of sitting, tired of answering questions she suspected he already had the answers to. Focus on what's important, she remembered. "Look, I know you've got ground to cover, but I don't see why my past history with Dolly applies. She broke into the ready room and damaged equipment. Essential equipment. It's a lot more than inconvenient and messy. If we're not ready when we're called, people can die. Wildlife and the forests they live in are destroyed."

"Understood. We'll be talking to Miss Brakeman. At this time, the only possible link between her and the vandalism in your ready room is her confirmed vandalism of your quarters."

"She said she wanted us all to die. All of us to burn. Just like she wrote on the wall. I guess she couldn't get her hands on any more pig's blood, so she used spray paint this time."

"Without equipment, you can't jump. If you can't jump, you're not in harm's way."

"Logical. But then logic isn't Dolly's strong suit."

"If it turns out she's responsible for this situation, I'd have to agree. Thanks for your time, and your frankness."

"No problem." She pushed to her feet, stopped on her way to the door. "I don't see how there's any 'if.' People around here understand what we do. We're part of the fabric. Everybody on base is a thread in the fabric, and we do what we do because we want to. We depend on each other. Dolly's the only odd man out."

"There are three men who got their asses kicked last month outside Get a Rope who might enjoy fraying those threads."

She turned fully back into the room. "Do you really think those assholes came back to Missoula, snuck on base, found the ready room and did that crap?"

Quinniock removed his cheaters, folded them neatly on the desk. "It's another 'if.' It's my job to consider all the 'ifs.'"

The interview left Rowan more annoyed than satisfied. Though her appetite barely stirred, she hit the buffet, built herself a breakfast sandwich. She ate on the way back to manufacturing.

Nobody complained. Not about the extra work or the tedium of doing it. While she'd been with Quinniock, Janis set up her MP3 with speakers so R&B, country, rock, hip-hop softened the clamor of the machines. She watched Dobie do a little boot-scoot across the floor to Shania Twain with a load of Smitty bags in his arms.

Could be worse, she thought. It could always be worse, so the smart thing to do was to make the best out of the bad. When Gull hauled in chutes for repair, she figured the cops had cleared the ready room.

She left her machine to go to the counter and help him spread the silks.

"How bad is it?" she asked him.

"Probably not as bad as it looked. Everything's tossed around, but there's not as much actual damage as we thought. Or I thought, anyway. A lot just needs to be sorted and repacked."

"Silver lining." She marked tears and cuts.

"With a rainbow. Maintenance is setting up tables outside. Rumor is Marg is putting a barbecue together, and she's got a truckload of ribs."

Rowan marked another tear. Men who hadn't bothered to shave or shower that morning were singing along with Taylor Swift. It was just a little surreal.

"When the going gets tough," she decided, "the tough eat ribs. We've got nearly all the chutes that were in for rigging and repair done, and nearly all of those packed. Coming along on PG bags, Smitties, ponchos and packs."

She paused, met his eyes. "If it keeps moving, maybe we'll fit in that run."

"Ready when you are."

"I hate being wrong."

"Anybody who doesn't probably has low self-esteem. Low self-esteem can lead to a lot of problems, many of them sexual."

She knew when she was being ribbed, so nodded solemnly. "I'm lucky I have exceptionally high self-esteem. Anyway, I hate being wrong about thinking this was a shot at me. I'd rather she'd taken a shot at me. I'd rather be pissed off about a personal vendetta than this."

"It sucks, but there's something to be said about listening to Southern and Trigger singing a duet of 'Wanted Dead or Alive.'"

"They weren't bad. No Bon Jovi, but not bad."

"If your glass is half empty and has a chip in it, you might as well belly up to the bar and order a fresh one. I've gotta get back."

Bright side, she thought. Silver lining. Maybe it took her longer to find them—or want to—but what the hell. She might as well toss away her crappy glass.

She examined every inch of the chute before turning it over to repair, then started on the next. She was so focused on what she thought of as an assembly line of life and death, she didn't hear L.B. walk up beside her.

His hand came down on her shoulder like a spotter's in the door. "Take a break."

"Some of these need rigging, but most of the ones coming up just need patching."

"I've been getting updates. Let's get some air."

"Fine." The bending, hunching, peering left her stiff and knotted up. She wanted that run, she decided, wanted to burn off the tension and hours of standing.

Then she caught a whiff of the ribs smoking on the grills, and decided she wanted those even more.

"Holy God, that smells good. Marg knows exactly the way to get the mind off problems and on the belly."

"Wait'll you see the cornbread. I just got off the phone with the police."

"Did they arrest her? No," she said before he could speak. "I can tell by your face. Goddamn it, L.B."

"She claims she was home all night. Her mother's backing her up."

"Big surprise."

"The thing is, they can't prove she wasn't. Maybe when

they go through everything, they'll find some evidence. You know, fingerprints or something."

He thumbed out a Life Savers to go with the one already in his mouth, and made her realize the stress had him jonesing for a Marlboro.

"But right now," he continued with cherry-scented breath, "she's denying it. They talked to the neighbors, too. Nobody can say for sure if she was home or wasn't. And since none of us saw her, they can't charge her with anything."

L.B. puffed out his cheeks. "Quinniock wanted us to know she's making noises about suing us for slander."

"Give me a break."

"Right there with you, Ro. She won't, but he thought we should know she got up a pretty good head of steam when I questioned her."

"The best defense is offense."

"That could be it, sure." He looked out over the grill and she imagined the dozens of things on his mind, the load of weight on his shoulders.

"Hell, all that's for cops and lawyers anyway."

"Yeah. The main thing is if we get called out, we're okay. We can send out twenty at this point."

"Twenty?"

"Some of the mechanics pitched in to help out the ready room team. They've been working like dogs. We've got gear and supplies for twenty squared away. I've already requisitioned replacements for what's damaged or ruined. This isn't going to slow us down. You're back on the jump list."

"I guess it wasn't as bad as it looked."

"Well, it looked pretty damn bad." She watched him, very deliberately, roll off some of that weight. "We're smoke jumpers, Swede. We can saw a line from here to Canada. We can sure as hell handle this."

"I want her to pay."

"I know, and by God, so do I. If they find anything to link her to that ready room, I want them to toss her in a cell. I felt sorry for her," he said in disgust. "I gave her a second chance, then a third one when I fired her instead of calling the cops. So believe me, nobody wants her to pay more than I do."

The phone in her pocket jingled.

"Go ahead and take it. I'm going to pass the word on lunch." He headed back, turned around briefly to walk backward. "Keep clear of the stampede," he warned.

Laughing, she pulled out her phone. Seeing her father's ID reminded her of the messages she'd left him.

"Well, it's about time."

"Honey, I'm sorry I didn't get back to you. I got in late, and didn't want to chance waking you up. I've been busy all morning."

"Here, too." She told him about the ready room, the police, about Dolly.

"For God's sake, Ro, what's wrong with that girl? Do you want more help? I can reschedule some things, or at least send over a couple men."

"I think we've got it, but I'll ask L.B."

"Quinniock, you said. I know him a little. I met him when I did one of those charity grip and grins last year. He came out with his kids. We gave them a tour."

"That's where I saw him. He's been through here, too. So . . . how was your meeting last night?"

"It was good. I'm going to work on this project for some of the high-school kids. And Ella—the client—she's signing up for AFF training."

"All that? That was some drink."

"Ha. Well. Ah, you'll probably meet her. She wants to connect up with the base, too. For this project. I've got a group coming in, but you tell L.B. to let me know if he wants extra hands. I can put in some time."

"I will, but I think we're good. You could come over after you close up. You can always put in some time with me."

"I've got a dinner meeting with the accountant on the slate tonight. How about we plan on it tomorrow? I'll come by after work."

"Works for me. See you tomorrow."

She clicked off, then started over to join the horde spilling out of manufacturing in a beeline for the tables.

Her mood improved. Progress, a full stomach, an upcoming date with her best guy. After which, she promised herself, she'd turn in early and bank some sleep.

It lifted her a little more to hear Matt laugh at something Libby said, to watch Cards dazzle one of the rookies with some sleight of hand, to listen to Trigger and Janis bitterly debate baseball.

As irritating as it was, Gull had been right. The Dolly crap? Just a bump.

She nudged him as they started back to their respective work areas. "Four o'clock, on the track."

"I'll be there."

Asking for trouble, she thought, and admitted she liked it. So maybe she'd bend her rule just a little—or a whole lot—for him. Maybe think about it awhile, and stretch out the heat, that sizzle of tension. Or just jump in, go full blast, burn it up, burn it out.

They were both grown-ups. They both knew the score. When the fire between them lay down, they could just step away again. No scars, no worries.

If she opted for the jump, that's just how she'd approach it. Two healthy, single adults who liked each other enjoying some good, tension-snapping sex.

"That's a big, smug smile you're wearing," Janis said as she joined Rowan at the table.

"I'm deciding if I'm going to have sex with Gull sooner or later."

"That would put a big, smug smile on my face. He's just sooo purty—" She gave a shoulder wiggle that sent her pony-tail, circled with bluebirds, dancing. "In a manly way. But what happened to the rule?"

"I'm thinking I'll temporarily rescind it. But do I wait, keep getting off, so to speak, on the sexual tension, innuendo, by-play and pursuit? Or do I dive headlong into the hot, steamy, sexy goodness?"

"Both are excellent uses of time. However, I've found, occasionally, that building anticipation can also overbuild expectation. Then nobody can fully meet the overbuild."

"That's a problem, and another factor to consider. The thing is, I don't think I'd be considering it, at least not yet, if this hadn't happened. The Dolly Crapathon. It's thrown me off, Janis."

"If you let that tiny-brained, coldhearted, self-pitying

skank throw you off, you're letting her win. If you let her win, you're going to piss me off. If you piss me off, I'm going to beat the snot out of you."

Rowan went *pfftt*. "You know you can't take me."

"That has not yet been put to the test. I got my fourth-degree black belt this winter. When I make martial arts noises, thousands flee in terror. Don't test me."

"Can you hear that? It's my knees knocking."

"They're wise to fear me. Go, have sex for fun and orgasms, and forget about the Dolly Crapathon."

"You are wise as well as short."

"I can also break bricks with my bare hands." And examined her manicure.

"That's a handy skill if you ever find yourself walled up in the basement of an abandoned house by a psychopath."

"I keep it in my pocket for just that eventuality." She glanced over as Trigger walked between tables on his hands. "A sure sign we're going stir-crazy. Plenty to do, but we're doing it grounded."

"The way we're going, especially with Super-Sewer Dobie, we're going to be in better shape on gear and equipment than before *The Nightmare on Dolly Street*."

"I hope the cops put the fear of God into her." Janis lowered her voice. "Matt gave her five thousand."

"What?"

"For the baby. I heard her crying to Matt after L.B. gave her the boot. How was she going to pay off the hospital bills now, and the pediatrician? He said he could spare five thousand to help her clear up the bills, tide her over until she got work. I guess I get it. His brother's kid and all. But she's going to keep tapping him, you know she is."

"Why work when you can sob-story your dead lover's brother into passing you cash? If he wants to help out with the baby, he should give money to Dolly's mother, or pay some of those bills directly."

"Are you going to tell him that?"

"I just might." Rowan gathered up the chute to take to repair. "I damn well might."

She considered offering unsolicited advice and opinion—which everybody hated—or just staying out of it. By the time she took a break for her run, she'd all but exhausted ideas for a third choice. Maybe the PT would help her think of one.

She changed into her running gear, grabbed a bottle of water. Gull joined her as she walked out of the barracks.

"Right on time," he commented.

"If I'd had to spend another hour indoors, I'd've hurt someone. What've you got in you today?"

"We'll have to find out. I'll tell you this, the ready room looks like Martha Stewart stocked and organized it. And I'm well past done with anything approaching domestic work, but I am looking to get some more rigger training."

"So you've been studying there, too?"

"Knowing how something works isn't the same as making it work. You're a certified Master Rigger. You could tutor me."

"Maybe." She already knew him for a quick study. "Are you looking to work toward your Senior Rigger certification, or to spend more time with me?"

"I'd call it multitasking."

They stopped on the side of the track where Rowan shed her warm-up jacket, laid her water bottle on it. "Distance or time?"

"How about a race?"

"Easy for you to say, Fast Feet."

"I'll give you a head start. Quarter mile of three."

"A quarter mile?" She did a little toe-heel to loosen her ankles. "You think you can beat me with that much of a spread?"

"If I don't, I'll have plenty of time to enjoy the view."

"Okay, sport, if you want my ass in your sights, you've got it."

She took the inside lane, cued her stopwatch, then took off.

Damn nice view, Gull thought as he strolled onto the track, plugged in his earbuds. He took a moment to loosen up, shaking out his arms, lifting his knees. When she hit the quarter mile, he ran.

And God, it felt good to move, to breathe, to have music banging in his head. Warm, dry air streamed over him, the sun splashed on the track, and he had Rowan's curvy body racing ahead of him.

It didn't get much better.

He built up his pace gradually, so by the first mile had cut her lead in half. She'd changed into shorts that clung to her thighs, and a tank that molded her torso. As he closed more distance he let himself enjoy the sexy cut of her calf muscles, the way the sun played on those strong shoulders.

He wanted his hands on both.

Totally in lust with that body, he admitted. Completely fascinated with her mind. The combo left him unable to think of anyone else, and uninterested.

At two miles he advanced to a handful of paces behind her. She glanced back over her shoulder, shook her head and dug for more speed.

Still, at two and a half, he ran with her, shoulder to shoulder. He considered easing off—a sop to her labored breathing—but his competitive spirit kicked in. He hit mile three a dozen strides ahead.

"Jesus, Jesus!" Rowan bent over to catch her wind. "I ought to be pissed off. That was humiliating."

"I thought about letting you win, but I respect you too much to patronize."

She wheezed out a laugh. "Gee, thanks."

"You bet."

"Still." She examined the stopwatch she'd clicked at the finish. "That was a personal best for me. Apparently you push me to excel."

Her face glowed with exertion and sweat; her eyes held his, cool and clear.

He hadn't run far enough, Gull realized. He hadn't nearly run off the need. He hooked his fingers in the bodice of the tank, jerked her to him.

"Hold on. I haven't got my breath back."

"Exactly."

He wanted her breathless, he thought as he took her mouth. Hot and breathless and as needy as he. She tasted like a melted lemon drop, tart and warm. The heat from the run, and from that dominating lust, pulsed off both of them while her heart galloped against his.

For the first time she trembled, just a little. He didn't know whether it came from the run or the kiss. He didn't care.

From somewhere nearby, someone let out a hoot and whistle of approval. And for the first time, like a lemon drop in the sun, she began to melt.

The siren sounded.

They tore themselves apart, their breath quick and jerky as they looked toward the barracks.

"To be continued," Gull told her.

12

In the air the next afternoon, with a golf pro harnessed to him, Lucas watched the base scramble below. He and his daughter wouldn't eat dinner together tonight after all.

The disappointment ran keen, reminding him how many times he'd had to cancel plans with her during his seasons. He wished her safe; he wished her strong.

"This is the best time of my life!" his client shouted.

You're young yet, Lucas thought. Best times come and go. If you're lucky enough, they keep coming.

Once they'd landed, once the routine of photographs, replays, thanks wound down, he read the text on his phone.

Sorry about dinner. Caught one. See you later.

"See you later," he murmured.

Lucas called base to get a summary of the fire.

The one the day before had only required a four-man crew, and they'd been in and out inside ten hours.

This one looked trickier.

Camper fire, off Lee Ridge, load of sixteen jumping it. And his girl was in that load.

Though he could bring the area into his head, he consulted his wall map. Ponderosa and lodgepole pines, he mused, Douglas fir. Might be able to use Lee Creek as a water source or, depending on the situation, one of the pretty little streams.

He studied the map, considered jump sites, and the tricky business of jumping into those thick and quiet forests.

She'd be fine, he assured himself. He'd do some paperwork, then grab some dinner. Then settle in to wait.

He stared at his computer screen for five full minutes before accepting defeat. Too much on his mind, he admitted.

He considered going over to the base, using the gym, maybe scoring a meal from Marg. But it felt too much like what it was. Hovering.

It had been nice to eat in a restaurant the other night, he remembered. Drink a little wine, have some conversation over a hot meal. He'd gotten too used to the grab-and-go when Rowan wasn't around. Not that either of them excelled at cooking, but they managed to get by.

Alone, he tended to hit the little cafe attached to his gift shop, if he remembered before business closed for the day. Or slap a sandwich together unless he wandered down to base. He could mic a packaged meal; he always stocked plenty at home. But he'd never gotten used to sitting down to one without the company of teammates.

There had been times, he knew, when he'd been jumping that he'd felt intensely lonely. Yet he'd come to know he hadn't fully understood loneliness until the nights spun out in front of him in an empty house.

He pulled out his phone. If he let himself think about it, he'd never go through with it. So he called Ella before he had a clear idea what to say, or how to say it.

"Hello?"

Her voice sounded so cheerful, so breezy. He nearly panicked.

Iron Man, my ass, he thought.

"Ah, Ella, it's Lucas."

"Hello, Lucas."

"Yeah, hello."

"How are you?" she asked after ten seconds of silence.

"Good. I'm good. I had a really good time the other night."
Jesus Christ, Lucas.

"So did I. I've had a lovely time thinking about it, and you,
since."

"You did?"

"I did. Now that you've called, I'm hoping you're going to
ask to do it again."

He felt the pleasure rise up from his toes and end in a big,
stupid grin. This wasn't so hard. "I'd like to have dinner with
you again."

"I'd like that, too. When?"

"Actually, I— Tonight? I know it's short notice, but—"

"Let's call it spontaneous. I like spontaneity."

"That's good. That's great. I could pick you up at seven."

"You could. Or we can both be spontaneous. Come to dinner, Lucas, I'm in the mood to cook. Do you like pasta?"

"Sure, but I don't want to put you out."

"Nothing fancy. It's supposed to be a pretty evening; we
could eat out on the deck. I've been working on my garden,
and you'd give me a chance to show it off."

"That sounds nice." A home-cooked meal, an evening on a
deck by a garden—two dinners within three days with a pretty
woman? It sounded flat-out amazing.

"Do you need directions?"

"I'll find you."

"Then I'll see you around seven. Bye, Lucas."

"Bye."

He had a date, he thought, just a little stunned. An official
one.

God, he hoped he didn't screw it up.

HE THOUGHT ABOUT ROWAN while he drove home to
change for dinner. She'd be in the thick of it now, in the smoke
and heat, taking action, making decisions. Every cell in her
body and mind focused on killing the fire and staying alive.

He thought of her when he walked in the house, only minutes from the base. A good-sized place, he reflected. But when
Rowan was home, she needed her space, and his parents came
home several times a year and needed theirs.

Still, during the long stretches without them, the empty seemed to grow.

He kept it neat. All the years of needing to grab whatever he needed the minute he needed it carried over to his private life. And he kept it simple.

His mother liked to fuss, enjoyed having *things* around the place, which he packed up whenever she wasn't in residence and stored away until the next time she was.

Less to dust.

He did the same with the colorful pillows she liked to toss all over the sofa, the chairs. It saved him from shoving them on the floor every time he wanted to stretch out.

In his room a plain brown spread covered his bed, a straight-backed tan chair stood in the corner. Dark wood blinds covered the windows. Even Rowan despaired at the lack of color or style, but he found it easy to keep clean.

Shirts hung tidily in his closet, sectioned off from pants by a set of open shelves he'd built himself for shoes.

Nothing fancy, Ella had said, but what did that mean? Exactly?

When panic tried to tickle his throat, he grabbed his basics. Khaki trousers and a blue shirt. After he'd dressed, he checked in for another fire report.

Nothing to do but wait, he thought, and for a few hours, this time, he wouldn't wait alone.

Because Ella had mentioned her garden, he stopped on the way and bought flowers. Flowers were never wrong, that much he knew.

He plugged her address into the GPS in his truck as backup. He knew the area, the street.

He wondered what they'd talk about. He wondered if he should've bought wine. He hadn't thought of wine. Would wine and flowers be too much?

It was too late to buy wine anyway, plus how would he know what kind?

He pulled into the drive, parked in front of the garage of a pretty, multilevel house in a bold orange stucco he thought suited her. A lot of windows to take in the mountains, flowers in the yard, with more in an explosion of color and shape spiking and tumbling in big native pots on the stones of the covered front entrance.

Now he wondered if the yellow roses he'd bought were over-kill. "Flowers are never wrong," he mumbled to himself as he stepped out of the truck on legs gone just a little bit weak.

He probably should've gotten a burger and fries from the cafe, hunkered down in his office. He didn't know how to do this. He was too *old* to be doing this. Women had never made any sense to him, so how could he make sense to a woman?

He felt stupid and clumsy and tongue-tied, but since retreat wasn't an option, rang the bell.

She answered, her hair swept back and up, her face warm and welcoming.

"You found me. Oh, these are beautiful." She took the roses, and as a woman would, buried her face in the buds. "Thank you."

"They reminded me of your voice."

"My voice?"

"They're pretty and cheerful."

"That's a lovely thing to say. Come in," she said, and, taking his hand, drew him inside.

Color filled the house, and the *things* his mother would have approved of. Bright and bold, soft and textured, a mix of patterns played throughout the living area where candles filled a river stone fireplace.

"It's a great house."

"I love it a lot." She scanned the living area with him with an expression of quiet satisfaction. "It's the first one I've ever bought, furnished and decorated on my own. It's probably too big, but the kids are here a lot, so I like having plenty of room. Let's go on back so I can put these in water."

It was big, he noted, and all open so one space sort of spilled casually into the next. He didn't know much—or any-thing, really—about decorating, but it felt like it looked. Bright, happy, relaxed.

Then the kitchen made his eyes pop. It flowed into a dining area on one side and a big gathering space—another sofa, chairs, big flat-screen—on the other. But the hub was like a magazine shot with granite counters, a central island, shiny steel appliances, dark wood cabinets, many of them glass-fronted to display glass and dishware. A few complicated small appliances, in that same shiny steel, stood on the counters.

"This is a serious kitchen."

"That and the view sold me on the place. I wanted it the minute I saw it." She chose a bottle of red from a glass rack, set it and a corkscrew on the counter. "Why don't you open this while I get a vase?"

She opened a door, scanned shelves and selected a tall, cobalt vase. He opened the wine while she trimmed the stems under running water in the central island's sink.

"I'm glad you called. This is a much nicer way to spend the evening than working on my doctorate."

"You're working on your doctorate?"

"Nearly there." She held up one hand, fingers crossed. "I put it off way too long, so I'm making up time. Red-wine glasses," she told him, "second shelf in the cupboard to the right of the sink. Mmm, I love the way these roses look against the blue. How did work go today?"

"Fine. We had a big group down from Canada, another in from Arizona, along with some students. Crowded day. Yesterday even more. I barely had time to get over to the base and check after they had the trouble."

"Trouble?" She looked up from her arranging.

"I guess you wouldn't have heard. Somebody got into the ready room over there yesterday—or sometime during the night—tore the place up."

"Who'd do such a stupid thing?"

"Well, odds are it was Dolly Brakeman. She's a local girl who had a . . . a relationship with the jumper who was killed last summer. She had his baby back in the spring."

"Oh, God, I know her mother. We're friends. Irene works at the school. She's one of our cooks."

He'd known that, Lucas realized, known Irene worked in the school's kitchen. "Look, I'm sorry. I shouldn't have said anything about Dolly."

"Irene's one thing, Dolly's another—and believe me, I know that very well." Ella stabbed a trimmed stem into the vase. "That girl's put Irene through hell. In any case, what happened to the father of Dolly's baby—that's tragic for her, but why would she want to vandalize the base?"

"You know Dolly used to be a cook there, and they hired her back on?"

"I knew she'd worked there. I haven't talked to Irene since I went by to take a baby gift. I knew she and Leo went out to . . . Bozeman, I think it was—to bring her and the baby home—so I've been hanging back a little, giving them all time to settle in. I didn't realize Dolly had gone back to work at the base."

"They gave her a chance. You know? She went off after Jim's accident. Before she did, she went after Rowan."

"Your daughter? Irene never mentioned . . . Well, there's a lot she doesn't mention about Dolly. Why?"

"Ro was Jim's partner on that jump. It doesn't make any sense, but that's how Dolly reacted. And she hadn't been back at base but a handful of days when Ro walked in on her splashing pig's blood all over Ro's room."

"For God's sake."

When she planted fisted hands on her hips, Lucas dubbed it her hard-line principal look.

He liked it.

"I haven't heard anything about this." Those deep green eyes flashed as she poured wine. "I'll have to call Irene tomorrow, see if she needs . . . anything. I know Dolly's troublesome, to put it mildly, but Irene really believed the baby, getting Dolly to go to church, taking her back in the house, would settle her down. Obviously not."

Full of sympathy now, and a touch of worry, her eyes met his. "How's your daughter dealing with it?"

"Ro? She deals. They've been working on repairs and manufacturing since, and must've gotten enough done to take some calls. A four-man jump yesterday, basically an in-and-out."

"That's good. Maybe they'll have time to catch their breath."

"Not much chance of that. The siren went off about four-thirty today."

"Rowan's out on a fire? Now? I didn't hear about that, either. I haven't had the news on all day. Lucas, you must be worried."

"No more than usual. It's part of the deal."

"Now I'm even more glad you called."

"And got you upset and worried about Irene."

"I'm glad I know what's going on with her. I can't help if I don't know." She reached out, laid a hand over his. "Why don't you take your wine and the bottle out on the deck? I'll be right out."

He went out wide glass doors to the deck that offered views of the mountains, the endless sky—and her yard that struck him—again—like something out of a magazine.

A squared-off area covered by the colorful, springy mulch he'd seen in playgrounds held a play area for her grandkids. Swings, ladders, bars, seesaws, even a little playhouse with a pint-sized umbrella table and chairs.

He found it as cheerful as the house—and it told him she'd made a home here not just for herself, but for her family to enjoy.

And still, her flowers stole the show.

He recognized roses—he knew that much—but the rest, to his eyes, created fairyland rivers and pools of color and shape all linked together with narrow stone paths. Little nooks afforded space for benches, an arbor covered with a trailing vine, a small, bubbling copper fountain.

While he watched, a Western meadowlark darted to the wide bowl of a bird feeder to help himself to dinner.

Lucas turned when she came out with a tray.

"Ella, this is amazing. I've never seen anything like it outside the movies."

Her dimples winked in cheeks pinked up with pleasure. "My pride and joy, and maybe just a little bit of an obsession. The people who owned the house before were keen gardeners, so I had a wonderful foundation. With some changes, some additions and a whole lot of work, I've made it my own."

She set the tray on a table between two bright blue deck chairs.

"I thought you said no fuss." He looked at the fancy appetizers arranged on the tray.

"I'll have to confess my secret vice. I love to fuss." She picked up her wine. "I hope you don't mind."

"My mother didn't raise a fool."

She sat, angling toward him while her wind chimes picked up the tune of the summer breeze. The meadowlark sang for his supper.

"I love sitting out here, especially this time of day, or early in the morning."

"Your grandkids must love playing out here."

They drank wine, ate her fancy appetizers, talked of her grandchildren, which boosted him to relate anecdotes from Rowan's childhood.

He wondered why he'd had those moments of panic. Being with her was so comfortable once he got off the starting blocks. And every time she smiled, something stirred inside him. After a while it—almost—didn't seem strange to find himself enjoying a pretty summer evening, drinking soft wine, admiring the view while talking easily with a beautiful woman.

It—almost—blocked out memories of how he'd spent so many other summer evenings. How his daughter was spending hers now.

"You're thinking of her. Your Ro."

"I guess it stays in the back of my mind. She's good, and she's with a solid unit. They'll get the job done."

"What would she be doing now?"

"Oh, it depends." So many things, he thought, and all of them hard, dangerous, necessary. "She might be on a saw line. They'd plot out a position, factor in how the fire's reacting, the wind and so on, and take down trees, cut out brush."

"Because those are fuel."

"Yeah. They've got a couple water sources, so she might be on the hose. I know they dropped mud on her earlier."

"Why would they drop mud on Rowan?"

His laugh broke out, long, delighted. "Sorry. I meant the fire. Mud's what we call the retardant the tanker drops. Believe me, no smoke jumper wants to be under that."

"And you call the fire *her* because men always refer to dangerous or annoying things they have to deal with as female."

"Ah . . ."

"I'm teasing you. More or less. Come inside while I start dinner. You can keep me company and tell me about mud."

"You don't want to hear about mud."

"You're wrong," she told him as they gathered up the tray, the glasses, the wine. "I'm interested."

"It's thick pink goo, and burns if it hits your skin."

"Why pink? It's kind of girlie."

He grinned as she got out a skillet. "They add ferric oxide to make it red, but it looks like pink rain when it's coming down. The color marks the drop area."

She drizzled oil into the skillet from a spouted container, diced up garlic, some plump oval-shaped tomatoes, all the while asking him questions, making comments.

She certainly *seemed* interested, he thought, but he was having a hard time concentrating. The way she moved, the way her hands looked when she chopped and diced, the way she smiled and smelled, the way his name sounded when it came from her lips.

Her lips.

He didn't mean to do it. That's what happened when he acted before he thought. But he was a little in her way when she turned away from the work island, and their bodies bumped and brushed. She tipped her face up, smiled, maybe she started to speak, but then . . .

A question in her eyes, or an invitation? He didn't know, didn't think. Just acted. His hands slid onto her shoulders, and he laid his lips over hers.

So soft. So sweet. Yielding under his even as her hands ran up his back, linked there to hold them together. She rose onto her toes, and the sensation of her body sliding up his simmered heat under the soft.

He wanted to burrow into her as he would a blanket at the end of a cold winter's night.

He gave up her lips, rested his forehead to hers.

"It's your smile," he murmured. "It makes it hard for me to think straight."

She framed his face, lifted his head until she could look in his eyes. Sweet man, she thought. Sweet, sweet man.

"I think dinner can wait." She eased away, turned the heat off under the oil, then leaned back to look at him again. "Do you want to go upstairs with me, Lucas?"

"I—"

"We're not kids. We've both got more years behind us than ahead. When we have a chance for something good, we ought to take it. So . . ." She held out a hand. "Come upstairs with me."

He took her hand, let out a shaky breath as she led him through the house. "You don't just feel sorry for me, do you?"

"Why would I?"

"Because I so obviously want . . . this."

"Lucas, if you didn't, I'd feel sorry for me." Humor sparkled over her face when she tipped it up to his. "I've wondered since you called if we'd take each other to bed tonight, then I had to do thirty minutes of yoga to stop being nervous."

"Nervous? You?"

"I'm not a kid," she reminded him as she drew him into her bedroom, where the light through the windows glowed soft. "Men your age often look at thirty-somethings, not fifty-somethings. That's twenty years of gravity against me."

"What would I want with someone young enough to be my kid?"

When she laughed at that, he grinned. "Hell. It'd just make me feel old. I'm already worried I'll mess this up. I'm out of practice, Ella."

"I'm pretty rusty myself. I guess we'll see if we tune up as we go. You could start by kissing me again. We both seemed to have that part down."

He reached for her, and this time her arms went around his neck. He felt her rise up to her toes again as their lips met, as they parted for the slow, seductive slide of tongues.

He let himself stop thinking, stop worrying *what if*. Just act. His hands stroked down her back, over her hips, up her sides, then up again to pull the pins out of her hair.

It tumbled over his hands, slid through his fingers while she tipped back her head so his lips could find the line of her throat.

Nerves floated away on an indescribable mix of comfort and excitement. She shivered when he eased back to unbutton her shirt. As he did when she did the same for him.

She slipped out of her sandals; he toed off his shoes.

"So far . . ."

"So good," he finished, and kissed her again.

And, oh, yes, she thought, he definitely had that part down.

She pushed his shirt aside, splayed her hands over his chest. Hard and fit from a lifetime of training, scarred from a lifetime of duty. She laid her lips on it as he drew her shirt off to join his on the floor. When he took her breasts in his hands, she forgot about gravity. How could she worry when he looked at her as though she were beautiful? When he kissed her with such quiet, such total intensity?

She unhooked his belt, thrilled to touch and be touched, to remember all the things a body felt when it desired, and was desired. The pants it had taken her twenty minutes to decide on after he'd called slid to the floor. Then her heart simply soared as he lifted her into his arms.

"Lucas." Overcome, she dropped her head to his shoulder. "My whole life I've wanted someone to do that. To just sweep me up. You're the first who has."

He looked into her dazzled eyes, and felt like a king as he carried her to bed.

In the half-light, they touched and tasted. They remembered, and discovered. Rounded curves, hard angles, with all the points of pleasure to be savored.

When he filled her, she breathed his name—the sweetest music. Moving inside her, each long, slow stroke struck his heart, hammer to anvil. She met him, matched him, her fingers digging into his hips to urge him on.

The king became a stallion, rearing over his mate.

When she cried out, fisting around him in climax, his blood beat in triumph. And letting himself go, he rode that triumph over the edge.

"Well, God," she said after several moments where they both lay in stunned, sated silence. "I have all these applicable clichés, like it *is* just like riding a bike, or it just gets better with age like wine and cheese. But it's probably enough to simply say: Wow."

He drew her over where she obligingly curled at his side, her head on his shoulder. "Wow covers it. Everything about you is wow to me."

"Lucas." She turned her face into the side of his throat. "I swear, you make my heart skip. Nobody's ever said those kinds of things to me."

"Then a lot of men are just stupid." He twirled her hair around his finger, delighted he could. "I'd write a poem to your hair, if I knew how to write one."

She laughed and had to blink back tears at the same time. "You are the sweetest, sweetest man." She pushed up to kiss him. "I'm going to make you the best pasta you've ever eaten."

"You don't have to go to all that trouble. We could just make sandwiches or something."

"Pasta," she said, "with fresh Roma tomatoes and basil out of my garden. You're going to need the fuel, for later."

As her eyes twinkled into his, he patted her bare butt. "In that case, we'd better get down there and start cooking."

13

As her father slept the sleep of the righteously exhausted in Ella's bed, Rowan headed into her eighth hour of the battle. They'd had the fire cornered, and nearly under control, when a chain of spot fires ignited over the line from a rocket shower of firebrands. In a heartbeat, the crew found itself caught between the main fire and the fresh, spreading spots.

Like hail from hell, embers ripped through the haze, battering helmets, searing exposed skin. With a bellowing roar, a ponderosa torched, whipping flame through clouds of eye-stinging smoke. Catapulted by the wind the fire created, burning coal flew over the disintegrating line, turning near victory into a new, desperate battle.

On the shouted orders, Rowan broke away with half the crew, hauling gear at a run toward the new active blaze.

"Escape route's back down the ridge," she called out, knowing they'd be trapped if the shifting flank fed into the head. "If we have to go, drop the gear and run like hell."

"We're going to catch her. We're going to kill her," Cards yelled back, his face fervent with dragon fever.

They knocked down spots as they went, beating, digging, sawing.

"There's a stream about fifty yards over," Gull said, jogging beside her.

"I know it." But she was surprised he did. "We'll get the pump in, get the hoses going and build a wet line. We'll drown the sister."

"Nearly had her back there."

"Gibbons and the rest will knock the head down." She looked at him, his face glowing in the reflection of the fire while hoarse shouts and wild laughter tangled with the animal growl of the fire.

Dragon fever, she knew, could spread like a virus—for good or ill. It pumped in her own blood now, because make or break was coming.

"If they don't, Fast Feet, grab what gear you can, haul it as far as you can. The way you run, you ought to be able to outrace the dragon."

"You got it."

They worked with demonic speed, dumping gear to set up the pump, run the hose, while others cut a quick saw line.

"Let her rip!" Rowan shouted, planting her feet, bracing her body as she gripped the hose. When it filled, punched out its powerful stream, she let out a crazed whoop.

Her arms, already taxed with the effort of hours of hard, physical work, vibrated. But her lips peeled back in a fierce grin. "Drink this!"

She glanced back over at Gull, laughed like a loon. "Just another lazy, hazy summer night. Look." She jerked her chin. "She's going down. The head's dying. That's a beautiful sight."

AN HOUR shy of dawn, the wildfire surrendered. Rather than pack out, the weary crew coyote'd by the stream, heads pillowed on packs to catch a couple hours' sleep before the mopup. Rowan didn't object when Gull plopped down beside her, especially when he offered her a swig of his beer.

"Where'd you get this?"

"I have my ways."

She drank deep, then lay back to watch the stars break through the thinning haze of smoke.

This, she thought, was the best—the timeless moment

between night and day—the hush of forest, mountain and sky. No one who hadn't fought the war could ever feel such intense satisfaction in winning it.

"A good night's work should always be followed by beer and starlight," she decided.

"Now who's the romantic?"

"That's just because I'm dazed by the smoke, like a honeybee."

"I dated a beekeeper once."

"Seriously?"

"Katherine Anne Westfield." He gave a little sigh of remembrance. "Long-legged brunette with eyes like melted chocolate. I had the hots enough to help her out with the hives for a while. But it didn't work out."

"You got stung."

"Ha. The thing was, she insisted on being called Katherine Anne. Not Katherine, not Kathy or Kate or Kat, not K.A. It had to be the full shot. Got to be too much trouble."

"You broke up with a woman because her name had too many syllables?"

"You could say. Plus, I have to admit, the bees started to creep me out, too."

"I like to listen to them. Sleepy sound. Cassiopeia's out," she said as the constellation cleared. Then her eyes closed, and she went out.

SHE WOKE curled up against him with her head nestled on his shoulder. She didn't snuggle, Rowan thought. She liked her space—and she sure as hell didn't snuggle while coyote camping with the crew.

It was just embarrassing.

She started to untangle herself, but his arm tucked her in, just a little closer.

"Give it a minute."

"We've got to get started."

"Yeah, yeah. Where's my coffee, woman?"

"Very funny." Actually, it did make her lips twitch. "Back off."

"You'll note I'm the one still in his assigned space, and

you're the one who scooted over and wrapped around me. But am I complaining?"

"I guess I got cold."

He turned his head to kiss the top of hers. "You feel plenty warm to me."

"You know, Gull, this isn't some romantic camping trip in the mountains. We've got a full day's mop-up ahead of us."

"Which I'm happy to put off for another couple minutes while I fantasize we're about to have wake-up sex on our romantic camping trip in the mountains. After which you'll make me coffee and fry me up some bacon and eggs, while wearing Daisy Duke shorts and one of those really skinny tank jobs. After that I have to wrestle the bear that lumbers into camp. Naturally, I dispatch him after a brutal battle. And after *that* you tenderly nurse my wounds, and after *that*, we have more sex."

She didn't snuggle, Rowan thought, and charm cut no ice with her. So why was she snuggling, and why was she charmed? "That's an active fantasy life you've got there."

"Don't leave home without it."

"What kind of bear?"

"It has to be a grizzly or what's the point?"

"And I suppose I'm wearing stilettos with my Daisy Dukes."

"Again, what would be the point otherwise?"

"Well, all that sex and cooking and tending your wounds made me hungry." She pushed away, sat up. "Twenty minutes in a hot, bubbling Jacuzzi, followed by a hot stone massage. That's my morning fantasy."

Rowan dug into her pack for an energy bar. Devoured it while she studied him. He'd scrubbed some of the dirt off his face, but there was plenty left, and his hair looked like he'd used it to mop the basement floor.

Then she looked away, to the mountains, the forest, shimmering away under the bright yellow sun. Who needed fantasies, she thought, when you could wake up here?

"Get moving, rook." She gave him a light slap on the leg. "The morning's wasting."

Gull helped break out some of the paracargo so he could

get to a breakfast MRE—and more importantly, the coffee. He dropped down next to Dobie.

"How'd it go for you?"

"Son, it was the hardest day of my young life." Dobie drenched his hash browns and bacon with Tabasco before shoveling them in as if they were about to be banned. "And maybe the best. You think you know," he added, wagging the bacon, "but you don't. You can't know till you do."

"She gave you a few kisses."

Dobie reached up to rub the burns on the back of his neck. "Yeah, she got in a couple licks. I thought when she started raining fire we might be cooked. Just for a minute. But we beat her back down. You ought to see Trigger. Piece of wood blew back off a snag he was taking down. Got him right here." Dobie tapped a finger to the side of his throat. "When he yanked it out, the hole it left looked like he'd been stabbed with a jackknife."

"I didn't hear about that."

"It happened after your team hightailed it toward the spot on the ridge. Blood all over. So he slaps some cotton on it, tapes it up and hits the next snag. It made me think, if I got cooked, I'd be cooked with the best there is."

"And now we get to sit here and eat breakfast with this view."

"Can't knock it with a hammer," Dobie said, and grabbed another MRE. "What're you going to do about that woman?"

He didn't have to ask what woman, and glanced over in Rowan's direction. "All I can."

"Better pick up the pace, son." Dobie shook his ever-present bottle of Tabasco. "Summer don't last forever."

GULL THOUGHT about that as he worked, sweating through the morning and into the afternoon. He'd approached her along the lines he might have if they'd met outside—where time was abundant, as were opportunities to go to dinner, or the movies, a long drive, a day at the beach. This world and that didn't have much crossover when you came down to it.

Maybe it was time to approach her as he did the work.

Nothing wrong with champagne picnics, but there were times a situation required a less . . . elegant approach.

By the time they packed out, Gull figured all he wanted in the world was to feel clean again, to enjoy a real mattress under him for eight straight.

Hardly a wonder, he decided as he dropped down in the plane, women, despite their wondrous appeal, hit so low on his priority list most seasons.

He shut off his mind and was asleep before the plane nosed into the sky.

With the rest of the crew, he trudged off, dealt with his gear, hung his chute. He watched Rowan texting as she headed for the barracks. He went in behind her, fully intending to walk straight to his quarters, peel off his fire shirt and pants, get his feet out of the damn boots that currently weighed like lead. Everything in him pulsed with fatigue, tension and an irritation that stemmed from both.

If he was hungry, it wasn't for a woman, or for Rowan Tripp in particular. If he was tired, it was because if he wasn't knocked-out exhausted, he spent too much time thinking about her in the middle of the night. So he'd stop. He'd just stop thinking about her.

When she turned into her room, he went in right behind her.

"What do—"

He shut the door—and her mouth—by pushing her back against it. The kiss burned with temper, smoldered with the frustration he'd managed to ignore for the past weeks. Now he let them both go. The hell with it.

He jerked back an inch, his gaze snapping to hers. "I'm tired. I'm pissed off. I don't know exactly why, but I don't give a damn."

"Then why don't you—"

"Shut up. I have something to say." He crushed his mouth to hers again, cuffing her wrists in his hands. "This has gotten stupid. I'm stupid, or maybe you're stupid. I don't care."

"What the hell do you care about?" she demanded.

"Apparently you. Maybe it's because you're goddamn beautiful, and built, and manage to be smart and fearless at the same time. Maybe it's just because I'm horny. That could be it. But something's clicked here; we both know it."

Since she hadn't told him to go to hell, or kneed him in the groin—yet—he calculated he had a short window to make his case.

"So it's time to stop playing around, Rowan. It's time to toss that asinine rule of yours out the window. Whatever we've got going here, we need to hit it head-on. If it's just a flash, fine, we'll take it down and move on. No harm, no foul. But I'm damned if I'm going to keep slapping away at the spot fires. You're in or you're out. Now how do you want to play it?"

She hadn't expected temper and force from him, which, considering she'd seen him take on three men with a ferocity she'd admired, made that her mistake. She hadn't expected anything could stir up her juices after a thirty-six-hour jump, but here he was, looking at her as if he couldn't decide if he wanted to kiss her or strangle her, and those juices were not only stirring, but pumping strong.

"How do I want to play it?"

"That's right."

"Let's drown it." She fisted her hands in his hair, yanked his mouth back to hers. Then she reversed their positions, shoved him back against the door. "In the shower, rookie." She made quick work unbuttoning his shirt.

"Funny, that was first on my list before I got pissed off." He pulled her shirt off as he backed her toward the bathroom. "Then all I could think about was getting my hands on you." He unhooked her pants.

"Boots," she managed as they groped each other. She dropped down on the toilet, fingers flying on laces. He dropped to the floor to do the same.

"This shouldn't be sexy. Maybe I am just horny."

"Just hurry up!" Laughing, she yanked off her pants, then stood to peel off the tank, the bra beneath.

"Sing hallelujah," Gull murmured.

"Get naked!" she ordered, then, wiggling out of her panties, flicked on the water in the shower.

Crazy, she thought. A crazy thing to do, but she felt crazy. Another type of dragon fever, she decided, and turned to pull him in with her under the spray.

"We're very dirty," she said, linking her arms around his neck, pressing her body to his.

"And about to get dirtier. Let's turn up the heat." Reaching behind her, he clicked the hot water up a notch, then gave himself the pleasure of those waiting, willing lips.

Good, so good, she thought, the water on her skin, his hands spreading the wet and hot over her. Why deny what she'd known the first time they'd locked eyes? They'd always been heading here, to this. She ran her hands down his back, over hard planes, tough muscle, instinctively working her fingers over the knots tied tight by hours of brutal effort.

He moaned as she worked her way to his shoulders.

He fixed his teeth at the side of her neck, pressed his own fingers in a line down her spine, then up again until he found points of pain and pleasure at the base of her neck.

"Let me take care of this." She poured shampoo in her palm, rubbed her hands together lightly as she watched him, then slid her fingers through his hair. While she rubbed, massaged, he filled his hands with her shower gel. The shower filled with the scent of ripe peaches as he glided circles, slow circles, over her breasts, her belly.

Lather foamed and dripped, frothing fragrantly between their bodies as he trailed a hand down, his fingers teasing, just teasing when he cupped her.

Her head fell back, and a low sound of pleasure hummed in her throat. Watching her absorb sensation, he gave her a little more, a little more until her hips, her breath picked up the rhythm.

Not yet, he thought, not yet, and made her groan when he turned her to face the wet wall.

"Gull, Jesus—"

"I need to wash your back. Love your back." At the small of it, a tattoo of a red dragon breathed gold flame. He ran his lathered hands over her, followed them with his lips. "Your skin's like milk."

He indulged himself with the subtle curve of the back of her neck, exposed and vulnerable to his teeth and tongue, and when her arm hooked back to press him closer, he glided his hands around, filled them with her breasts.

So firm, so full.

He spun her around, replaced his hands with his mouth.

Not what she'd expected or prepared for. Never what she

expected, she thought as her body quivered. The angry man who'd shoved her against the door should have stormed her. Instead he seduced. She didn't know if she could bear it.

With steam billowing like smoke, he trailed that mouth down her body, until every muscle trembled, until anticipation and sensation squeezed to a pulsing ache inside her.

Then he used his mouth on her until the hot flood of release swamped her.

When she was weak, in that shivering instant where body and mind surrendered, he plunged inside her.

No seduction now, no slow hands or teasing mouth. He gripped her hips and let himself take, and take, and take. Need raged through him, incited by the harsh sound of wet flesh slapping wet flesh, the pounding beat of the water, the wild thrust of her hips as she gave herself over to what they fueled in each other.

The chains of control shattered; madness broke free.

Through the haze of steam and passion he watched her eyes go blind. Still he drove her, himself, greedy for more until pleasure ripped through him and emptied him out.

She let her head drop on his shoulder until she could get her breath back. Might be a while, she realized, as she was currently panting like an old woman.

"Need a minute."

She made some sound of agreement to the statement.

"If we try to move now, we're both going to end up going down and drowning—after we fracture our skulls."

"We're lucky we didn't do that already."

"Probably. But we'd die clean and satisfied. I'm going to turn off the water. It's going cold."

She'd have to take his word for it. Her body still pumped enough heat to melt an ice floe. She managed her first full breath when he brushed his lips over her hair. She simply didn't know how to react to sweetness—after.

"Got your legs under you?" he asked her.

"Steady as a rock." Hopefully.

He let her go to reach out and grab towels. "It's a sacrifice to give you anything to cover up that body with." Before she could take it, he wrapped it around her, laid a warm, lingering kiss on her lips.

"Problem?" he asked her.

"No. Why?"

He trailed a fingertip between her eyebrows. "You're frowning."

"My face is reflecting the mood of my stomach, which is wondering why it's still empty." Which was true enough. "I'm starving." She relaxed again, smiled again. "Between the jump and the shower bonus, I'm out."

"Right there with you. Let's go eat."

She started to move past him to the bedroom, turned. "I've said it before, but it bears repeating. You've got skills."

"I also work well horizontally."

Her laugh rolled out as she pulled out a T-shirt and jeans. "I think you're going to have to prove it."

"Now or after food?"

She shook her head as she pulled on clothes. "After, definitely. I'm in the mood for . . . Aren't you getting dressed?"

"I'm not putting that stinking mess back on. I need to borrow your towel."

She thought of the state of the clothes they'd both dragged off. "Just hang on a minute. I'll get you some clothes."

"Really?"

"I know where your quarters are." She breezed out, strolled into his room.

He kept it tidy, she thought as she pulled open a drawer. Inside spaces, too. She grabbed what she figured he needed, took another quick look around. When she noticed the photograph, she stepped over for a closer study.

Gull, she noted, with what had to be his aunt and uncle, his cousins, all arm in arm in front of big, bright red doors.

Great-looking group, she thought, and the body language spoke of affection and happy. In front of the arcade, which, she realized by what she could see of it, was a lot bigger than she'd envisioned.

She took the clothes back, pushed them into his hands. "Hurry up and get dressed before I start gnawing on my own hand."

"Hurry up and get undressed, hurry up and get dressed. Orders, orders." He sent her an exaggerated smoldering look. "Dominant females make me hot."

"I'll see if I can find my whip and chain later."

"Ah, a brand-new fantasy to explore."

"Don't forget to call me 'Mistress.'"

"If you promise to be gentle. By the way, I like the tat."

"Good-luck charm," she told him. "If I wear the dragon, the dragon doesn't wear me. How about yours?" She walked around to tap the letters scrolled over his left shoulder blade. "Teine," she said.

"It's pronounced 'teen,' not 'The-ine.' Old Irish for fire. I guess if I wear the fire, it doesn't wear me."

"It just gets to try us both on from time to time. How'd you get that one?" she asked, gesturing to the scar along his left ribs.

"Bar fight in New Orleans."

"No, seriously."

"Well, it was, technically, outside the bar. I went down for Mardi Gras one year. Have you ever been?"

"No."

"Not to be missed." His hair, still damp from the shower, curled at the collar of the shirt he pulled on. "I was in college, went down with some friends. After the revelry, we hit a bar. This asshole went after this girl. Sort of like the asshole who hassled you, but this one was drunker and meaner, and she didn't have your style."

"Few do," she said with a grin.

"No argument. So, when I suggested he cease and desist, he objected. One thing led to another. Apparently he didn't like the fact I was kicking his ass in front of witnesses, so he pulled a knife."

The grin changed to openmouthed shock. "Well, sweet baby Jesus, he *stabbed* you?"

"Not exactly. The knife sort of skimmed along my ribs." Gull motioned a careless finger over the spot. "He didn't get much of me, and I had the pleasure of breaking his jaw. The girl was really grateful, so a night well spent."

He tied his sneakers. "I have a spotted and unruly past."

"You're a puzzler."

"Okay." He held out a hand. "How about I buy you dinner and a couple of cold beers?"

"I say since meals come with the job, that makes you a cheapskate, but what the hell."

LATER, AFTER GULL PROVED he did indeed work well horizontally, Rowan gave him a sleepy nudge. "Go home."

"Nope." He simply tucked her in against his side.

"Gull, neither of us is what you'd call petite, and this bed isn't exactly built for two." Besides, sleeping with a guy was different from sex.

"It worked pretty well so far. We'll manage. Besides, you saw the jump list. We're first and second man, first stick. If we get a call, all we have to do is put on the clothes currently strewn all over the floor, and hit it. It's efficient."

"So you always sleep with your jump partner for the sake of efficiency."

"I'm trying it out with you first. Who knows, if it saves enough time, it might become regulation. If we're clear, do you want to take a run in the morning?"

His hand, trailing lightly up and down her back, felt good—soothing. It was late anyway, she thought, she could make an exception on the sleeping rule this one time. Except she'd already made an exception on the sex, and now . . .

"Are we going to keep doing this?" she wondered.

"Okay, but you're going to have to give me about twenty minutes."

"Not tonight. I think we've rung the bell on that."

"Oh, you mean as a continuing series." He gave her ass a light, friendly pat. "Definitely."

"If we continue the series, there's a rule."

"Of course there is."

"If I sleep with a guy, I don't sleep with other guys, or sleep with that guy if he's banging anyone else. If either of us decide someone else looks good, that's fine. Series over. That one's firm. No exceptions."

"That's fair. One question. Why would I want anybody else when I get to take showers with you?"

"Because people tend to want what they don't have."

"I like what I've got." He gave her an easy squeeze. "Ergo, I'm happy to abide by your rule on this matter."

"Ergo." She chuckled, closed her eyes. "You're something else, Gulliver."

Right then, tucked up with Rowan in bed, an owl hooting dourly in the night and the moon shafting through the window, Gull figured he was exactly who, and where, he wanted to be.

IT TOOK LESS TIME to burn a body than a forest. An uglier business, but quicker. Still, collateral damage couldn't be avoided, and probably served as an advantage. She didn't weigh much, considering, so carrying her up the trail, through the lodgepole pines, wasn't as hard as it might have been.

The shimmer of moonlight helped light the way—like a sign—and the music of night creatures soothed.

The trail forked, steepened, but the climb wasn't altogether unpleasant in the cool, pine-scented air.

Better not to think of the unpleasant, of the horror. Better to think of moonlight and cool air and night birds.

In the distance, a coyote called out, high and bright. A wild sound, a *hungry* sound. Burning her would be humane. Better than leaving her for the animals.

They'd probably come far enough.

The task didn't take much effort or require too many tools. Just hacking away some dried brush and twigs, soaking them, her clothes. Her.

Don't think.

Soaking it all with gas from the spare can.

Try not to look at her face, try not to think of what she'd said and done. What had happened. Stick to what had to be done now.

Light the fire. Feel the heat. See the color and shape. Hear the crackle and snap. Then the whoosh of air and flame as that fire began to breathe.

A thing of beauty. Dazzling, dangerous, destructive.

So beautiful and fierce, and *personal*, when started with your own hands. Never realized, never knew.

It would purge. Erase her. Send her to hell. She belonged there. The animals wouldn't get her, tear at her as the dogs had torn at Jezebel. But she'd earned hell.

No more harm, no more threat. No more. In the fire, she would cease to be.

Watching it take her brought a horrible thrill, a bright

tingle of unexpected excitement. Power tasted. No tears, no regrets—not anymore.

That thrill, and the rising voice of the fire, followed down the trail while smoke began to climb toward the shimmering moon.

14

For the second time Rowan woke curled up to Gull with her head on his shoulder. This time she wondered how the hell he could sleep with her weight pressing on him.

Then she wondered, since she was shoehorned into the narrow bed with him, why the hell she wasn't taking advantage of it. She bit his earlobe as her hand trailed down his chest. As she'd expected, she found him already primed.

"I'd've put money on it," she murmured.

"I like your hand on it better."

"Now this . . ." She swung a leg over him, taking him in slowly. Slowly until she sheathed him in the warm and the wet. "This is what I call efficient."

Thinking there was no finer way to greet the morning, he got a firm grip on her hips. "A plus."

When she bowed back, the sun slanting light and shadow over her body, casting diamonds through her crown of hair, a snippet of Tennyson flitted through his mind.

A daughter of the gods, divinely tall, and most divinely fair.

She was that, in that moment, and in that moment took command of his romantic heart.

His grip gentled to a caress. And she began to move, undulating over him in a slow, fluid rhythm. Sensation spooled through him, unwinding a lovely, lazy delight.

Her eyes closed, her hands stroked up her own body, inciting them both.

Through the bars of light, the building beauty, he reached for her. He thought they could drift like this, leisurely awakening body, blood, heart, forever.

The siren screamed.

"Shit!" Her eyes popped open.

"Give me a fucking break." He held on to her for one frustrating moment, then they broke apart to scramble for clothes.

"You did this," she accused him. "You called it last night with that damn efficiency crack."

"Ten minutes more, it would've been worth it."

Instead, in ten minutes they suited up in the ready room.

"Spotted smoke at first light." L.B. gave the outline. "Lolo National Forest, between Grave Creek and Lolo Pass. It's fully active on the south slope above Lolo Creek. Conditions dry. Rowan, I want you in as fire boss; Gibbons, you're on the line."

The ground thundered as the tanker began to roll with the first load of mud.

The minute she boarded the jump ship, Rowan pulled out the egg sandwich and Coke she'd stuck in pockets. She ate and drank while she coordinated with the pilot, the spotter.

"There she is." She pressed her face to the window. "And, damn, she's frisky this morning."

A hundred acres, maybe a hundred and twenty, she estimated, already fully active in some of the most primitive and pristine areas of Lolo. Lewis and Clark had traveled there, and now the fire wanted it for breakfast.

Here we come, she thought, and guarded her reserves as wind rushed in through the open door.

She felt fresh and fueled and ready—and couldn't deny the ride down was beautiful. She checked on Gull, shot him a huge grin. "It's not sex, but it doesn't suck," she shouted.

She heard his laugh, understood exactly what ran through him. It ran through her, free and strong into the sky, the smoke, and down to the soft landing on a sweet little meadow.

Once the unit and the paracargo hit the ground, she strategized with Gibbons. She decided to do a recon up the right flank while the crew headed in to start the line.

She traveled at a trot, gauging the area, the wind, and keeping twenty yards off the flank as the fire burned hot. She heard the head calling in that grumbling, greedy roar as it tossed spot fires into the unburned majesty of forest.

Not going to have it, she thought, using her Pulaski and her bladder pump to smother the spots as she went. It wants to run, wants to feed. She smelled the sharp resin as trees burned, heard their crackling cries, felt the air tremble with the power already unleashed. Smoke spiraled up where spitting embers met dry ground.

She yanked out her radio. "She wants to run, and she's fast, L.B. She's fast. We need another load of mud on the head, and another down the right flank. She's throwing a lot of spots along that line."

"Copy that. Are you clear?"

"I will be." She kept moving, away from a spot that ate ground the size of a tennis court. "We need to contain these spots now, L.B. We're at critical. Gibbons is on the line, southwest, and I'm doubling back."

"Stay clear. We've got another load of jumpers on alert. Say the word and we'll send them in."

"Copy that. Let me finish this recon, check in with Gibbons."

"Tankers on the way. Don't get slimed, Swede."

"I'm clear," she repeated. "And I'm out."

She ran, charging her way down as she checked in with Gibbons, making for the trail where Lewis and Clark had once traveled. At the roar behind her, she cursed, ran through the falling embers, the missiles of burning pinecones hurled by the blasting wind of a blowup. When the ground shook under her feet, she charged through the heart of the fire.

Safer inside it, she thought while smoke gushed through the lick of orange flames.

In the black she took a moment to pull out her compass and get her bearings, to plot the next moves. Gibbons would have sent the crew up the ridge on attack, she thought, and then—

She nearly ran over it. Instinct and atavistic horror stumbled her back three paces from the charred and blackened remains of what had been human. It lay, the crisp bones of its arms and legs curled in. Contracted by the heat, she knew that, but in that terrible moment it seemed as if the dead or dying had tried to tuck into a ball the fire might overlook.

Her fingers felt numb when she pulled out her radio. "Base."

"Base here, come back, Swede."

"I've got a body."

"Say again?"

"I'm maybe ten yards from the Lobo Trail, near the southeast switchback, in the black. There's a body, L.B." She blew out a breath. "It's crisp."

"Ah, Christ. Copy that. Are you safe there?"

"Yeah. I'm in the black. I'm clear."

"Hold there. I'll contact the Forest Service, then get back to you."

"L.B." She rubbed her fingers between her eyebrows. "I can't tell for sure, but the ground under and around the remains, the pattern of the burn . . . Hell, I think maybe somebody lit him—her—up. And there's . . . I don't know, but the angle of the head. It looks like the neck's broken."

"Sweet Jesus. Don't touch anything. Do you copy, Rowan? Don't touch anything."

"Believe me, I won't. I'll radio Gibbons, give him a SITREP. Jesus, L.B., I think it's a woman or a kid. The size . . ."

"Hang in, Rowan. I'll come back."

"Copy that. Out."

She steeled herself. She'd seen burned bodies before. She'd seen Jim, she thought, when they'd finally recovered his remains. But she'd never stumbled over one, alone, in the middle of an operation.

So she took a breath, then radioed Gibbons.

It took her more than an hour and a half to get back to her crew, after holding her position, and guiding two rangers in. She welcomed the heat, the smoke, the battle after her vigil with the dead.

As she'd expected, Gibbons had the crew up the ridge, and the line held.

"Holy shit, Ro." Gibbons swiped a forearm over his blackened face. "You okay?"

The time, the vigil, the hard reality of giving a statement hadn't completely settled the raw sickness in her belly. "I'm a lot better than whoever's back there. The rangers are down there now, and a Special Agent Somebody's coming in. And an arson guy."

"Arson."

"It might be this fire was deliberately set, to cover up murder." Because it felt as if it squeezed her skull, she shifted her helmet—but it did nothing to relieve the steady throbbing.

"They don't know yet," she told him as he cursed. "Maybe it was some dumb kid messing around, but it looked to me like that could've been the point of origin. Putting the fire down's first priority. The feds'll handle the other. Where do you want me?"

"You know you can pack out, Ro. Nobody'll blame you."

"Let's finish this."

She worked the saw line, while another part of the crew reinforced the scratch lines riding up toward the head. A fresher crew of jumpers attacked the other flank, down toward the tail.

Countless times during the hours on the line, she pulled off to radio the other crew for progress, updated base, consulted with Gibbons.

A few more hours to finish her off and mop up, she thought, and the crew would sleep in beds tonight.

"What's up?" Gull stopped by her side. "There are rumors up and down the line something is, and you're the source."

She started to brush him off, but he looked her dead in the eye.

"You can tell me now or tell me later. You might as well get it done."

She'd shared her body with him, she reminded herself, and her bed. "We've got her caged. If Gibbons can spare you, you can come with me to scout out smokes."

Cleared, they moved away from the line. Rowan beat out a spot the size of a basketball, moved on.

And told him.

"You think the person was murdered, and whoever did it started the fire to try to cover it up?"

"I can't know." But her gut, roiling still, told her differently.

"Smarter to bury it." His matter-of-fact tone slowed the churning. "A fire like this brings attention. Obviously."

"I've never done it, but it seems to me killing somebody might impair logic. Or maybe the fire added to it. Plenty of people get off starting fires."

"They spotted this one at first light. From the progress it made by the time we jumped, it must've started late last night, early this morning. It was burning damn hot, had at least a hundred acres involved when we jumped at, what, about eight?"

Odd, she realized, that talking it through, picking out the practical, calmed the jitters. "Yeah."

"The campground's not that far west, but with that burned-out area between where you found the body and the campground, the fire sniffed east. Lucky for the campers."

The drumming inside her skull backed off, a little. Thinking was doing, she decided. Up until now she'd done too much reacting, not enough doing.

"Maybe they were from the camp," she speculated. "And came out on the trail, got into a fight. By accident or design, he kills her."

"Her?"

"The size of the body. I think it was a woman or a kid, and since I don't want to think it was a kid, I'm going with woman. He'd drag or carry her off the trail. Maybe he thinks about burying her, and went back to get tools. Fire's quicker and takes less effort. Dry conditions, some brush."

"If you started it around two, three in the morning," Gull calculated, "it would get a pretty good blaze up by dawn, and buy you a few hours."

Yes, she thought. Sure. Survival had to be the first priority.

"Pack it up, and you're way gone by dawn." She nodded, steadied by working it as a problem to be solved. "It'll take time to identify her, so that buys you more yet. And the fact is, if I hadn't taken that route back to the line, maybe it's hours more, even days, before she's found. I wasn't going that route, but the blowup sent me in and over."

They continued to find and kill spots as they talked. Then she stopped. "I didn't think I wanted to think about it. I found her, I called it in, now it's for the USFS to deal with. But it's been gnawing at me ever since. It . . . it shook me," she confessed.

"It would shake anybody, Rowan."

"Have you ever seen somebody after they've been—"

"Yeah. It sticks with you." And he knew talking about it, thinking about the hows and whys, helped.

"Summers are usually about this." She drowned a bucket-sized spot before it had a chance to grow. "Putting out fires, mopping them up, training and prepping to jump the next. But this summer? We've got crazy Dolly, my father going on a date, dead people."

"Your father dating ranks with vandalism and possible homicide and arson?"

"It's just different. Unusual. Like me sleeping with a rookie—which I haven't done, by the way, since I was one."

"Points for me."

She shifted direction, angled south. Points for him, maybe, but to her mind change, exceptions, the different screwed up the order of things.

After nearly two hours on spots, they rejoined the crew and shifted to mop-up mode.

She pulled out her radio to take a call from the operations desk.

"We want the first load to demob," L.B. told her. "Second load and ground crew will complete the mop-up."

"I hear that."

"The fed wants to talk to you when you get back."

"Can't it wait until tomorrow? I talked to the rangers, gave them all the details."

"Doesn't look like it. You can pack out. There'll be ground transportation for you at the trailhead."

"Copy that." What the hell, she thought, at least this way she'd get it all over with in one day.

SHE'D PLANNED on getting a shower first, but she'd no more than dumped her gear when the fed came looking for her.

"Rowan Tripp?"

"That's right."

"Special Agent Kimberly DiCicco. I have some questions."

"The rangers already have my answers, but since we both work for a bureaucracy, I know how it goes."

"Mr. Little Bear offered his office so we can speak in private."

"I'm not stinking up L.B.'s office. In case you haven't noticed, I'm pretty ripe with smoke and sweat."

She had to notice, Rowan thought. The agent's compact body was tucked into a black suit of classic lines with a pristine white shirt. Without a hair out of place, her sleek nape-of-the-neck bun left her refined-boned, coffee-with-a-splash-of-cream face unframed.

DiCicco's eyebrows arched over tawny eyes as she angled her head. "You've put in a long day. I'm aware. I'll make it as brief as possible."

"Then let's walk and talk." Rowan stripped down to her tank and trousers. "Maybe I'll air out a little."

"Heads up."

She turned, caught the cold bottle of Coke Gull sent her in a smooth underhand pass. "Thanks. Save me some lasagna."

"I'll do what I can."

"Okay, Agent DiCicco." At Rowan's gesture, they walked outside. "You ask, I'll answer."

"You could start by telling me how you came upon the body."

Already covered, Rowan thought, but went through it again. "With the way the fire was running," she continued, "I had to cut off the recon and make for a safe zone. I headed in, then hiked across the old burnout section and into the black. The area adjacent to where the fire had passed through. I was heading for Lolo Trail. I could take that most of the way back to my crew. And I found her."

"Her?"

"I don't know. The remains were on the small side for a grown man."

"You'd be correct. The victim was female."

"Oh. Well." Rowan stopped, blew out a breath. "That's better than the alternative."

"Excuse me?"

"It could've been a kid. The size again."

"You contacted your operations desk immediately on the discovery?"

"That's right."

"So, if I have this correct." DiCicco read back Rowan's movements, the times she'd radioed in her position and the situation through her recon to the report of the body. "That's a considerable area in a short amount of time."

"When you catch fire, you're not out on a stroll or a nature hike. You move, and you move fast. It's my job to assess the situation on the ground, strategize a plan and approach with Gibbons, the line boss on this one, to recon and to keep Ops apprised of the situation and any additional support we might need."

"Understood. When you contacted Operations, you stated you believed the victim had been murdered and the fire started to cover up the crime."

Should she have kept her mouth shut? Rowan wondered. Would this be done if she'd kept her speculations to herself?

Too late now, she reminded herself.

"I said what it looked like. I've been jumping fires for five years, and I worked with a hotshot crew for two before that. I'm not an arson expert, but I know when a fire looks suspicious. I'm not a doctor, but I know when a head's twisted wrong on a neck."

And now, damn it, *damn* it, that image carved in her brain again. "I acted on what I observed so the proper authorities could be contacted. Is that a problem?"

"I'm gathering facts, Ms. Tripp." DiCicco's tone made a mild counterpoint to Rowan's snap. "The medical examiner's preliminary findings indicate the victim's neck had been broken."

"She was murdered." Better or worse? Rowan wondered.

"The ME will determine if this is homicide, accidental, whether the neck injury was cause of death or postmortem."

"Have you checked with the campground? Lolo Campground isn't far from where I found her, not for a day hike."

"We're working on identifying her. You had some trouble here recently?"

"What?" Rowan pulled her mind back from speculating on just how much force it took to break a neck. "The vandalism?"

"That's plural, isn't it?" DiCicco kept unreadable eyes on Rowan's face. "According to my information, one Dolly Brakeman, employed at that time as a cook here, vandalized your room. You caught her in the act and had to be physically restrained from assaulting her."

Temper burned through fatigue like a brushfire. "You walk into your quarters, DiCicco, and find somebody pouring animal blood on your bed. See how you react. If you want to call my reaction 'attempted assault,' you go right ahead."

"Ms. Brakeman was also questioned by the police regarding the vandalism of the ready room here on base."

"That's right. That little number cost us hours of time and could have cost more if we'd gotten a call out before we'd repaired the damage."

"You and Ms. Brakeman have a history."

"Since you already know that, I'm not going over the ground again. She's a pain in the ass, a vindictive one, and an unstable one. If the locals turned over the vandalism here to your agency, good. I hope it scares the shit out of her. Now look, I'm tired, I'm hungry and I want a goddamn shower."

"Nearly done. When did you last see Dolly Brakeman?"

"Jesus, when she trashed my room."

"You haven't seen or spoken with her since?"

"No, I haven't, and I'd be thrilled if I can keep that record. What the hell does Dolly have to do with me finding a dead woman burned to a crisp in Lolo?"

"We'll need to wait for confirmation of identification, but as Dolly Brakeman failed to return home last night—a home she shares with her parents and her infant daughter—as the victim and Ms. Brakeman are the same height, and thus far the investigation has turned up no other female missing, it's a strong possibility the victim is Dolly Brakeman."

"That's . . ." Rowan felt her belly drop, the blood just drain out of her head while those unreadable eyes never shifted off her face. "A lot of women are Dolly's height."

"But none of them has been reported missing in this area."

"She's probably hooked up with some guy. Take a look at that part of her history." But she had a baby now, Rowan thought. Jim's baby. "Dolly wouldn't be on the trail, in the forest. She likes town."

"Can you tell me your whereabouts last night, from eight P.M. until you reported to the ready room this morning?"

"I'm a suspect?" Anger and shock warred—a short, bloody battle before anger won. "You actually think I snapped her neck, hauled her into the forest, then started a fire? A fire men and women I work with, live with, eat with every day would have to jump. Would have to risk their lives, their *lives*, to beat down?"

"You tried to assault her. Threatened to kill her."

"Fucking A right I did. I was pissed. Who wouldn't be pissed? I wish I'd gotten a punch in, and that's a hell of a long way from killing somebody."

"It'd be easier if you could tell me where you were last night between—"

"I'll make it real easy," Rowan interrupted. "I had dinner in the cookhouse about seven, maybe seven-thirty. About thirty of the crew were in there at the same time, and the kitchen staff. We hung out, bullshitting until close to ten. Then I went to my quarters, where I stayed until the siren went off this morning. Squeezed into bed with the hottie you saw toss me this Coke."

"And his name?" DiCicco asked without a blink of reaction.

"Gulliver Curry. He's probably in the cookhouse by now. Go ask him. I'm getting a goddamn shower."

She stormed off, outrage burning a storm in her belly, slammed into the barracks.

Trigger had the misfortune of getting in her way. "Hey, Ro, are you—"

"Shut up and move." She shoved him aside, then slammed

into her quarters. She kicked the door, then the dresser, causing the little dish she tossed loose change into to jump off and crash onto the floor.

Her boots stamped the shards.

"Stiff-necked, tight-assed *bitch*! And it wasn't Dolly!" Fuming, she tore at the laces of her jump boots, then hurled them.

Dolly was the type who just kept rolling, she thought as she yanked off her clothes, balled them up and threw them. She made people feel sorry for her, or—if they were men—sweetened the pot with sex or the promise of it. She was the type who did whatever the hell she wanted, then blamed somebody else if it didn't work out.

Her mother's type, Rowan decided, and maybe that was just one more reason she'd never liked Dolly Brakeman. Selfish, scheming, whining . . .

Her mother's type, she thought again. Her mother had died bleeding on the floor. Murdered.

Not the same, she told herself firmly. Absolutely not the same.

In the shower, she turned the water on full, braced her hands on the wall and let it run over her. Watched it run black, then sooty gray.

She'd had enough of this shit, enough of the sucker punches.

What right did that federal bitch have to accuse her? She was the reason the body was found so quickly, the reason the feds had been called in the first damn place.

By the time she'd all but scrubbed herself raw, the leading edge of temper had dulled into a sick fear.

Her hands shook as she dressed, but she told herself it was hunger. She hadn't eaten in hours and had burned thousands of calories. So she was shaky. That's all it was.

When the door opened, she whirled, felt the shaking increase as Gull closed it quietly behind him.

"Did you tell that bitch you spent the night nailing me?"

"I told her we spent the night in here, in a bed small enough if you'd managed to roll over I'd've known it."

"Good. Good. She can stick that up her federal ass." She

pushed him back when he came to her. "I don't want to be coddled. Appreciate the alibi and all that. It looks like breaking my rule just keeps paying off. Whoopee."

She pushed at him again, but this time he got his arms around her, hard and tight, and just held on while she struggled against him.

"I said I didn't want to be coddled. I've got a right to blow off some steam after being questioned as a killer, an arsonist, as somebody who'd betray everything that matters to squash some little pissant—"

She broke off, broke down. "Oh, God, oh, God, they think it's Dolly. They think Dolly's dead and I killed her."

"Listen to me." His hands firm on her shoulders, he eased her back until he could see her eyes. "They don't know who it is at this point. Maybe it is Dolly."

"Oh, Jesus, Gull. Oh, God."

"There's nothing anybody can do about that if it is. If it is, nobody thinks you had anything to do with it."

"DiCicco—"

"Was just informed you and I were together all night. There are plenty of people in the barracks who know we came in here together, and we came out together. So, if you're a suspect, I'm one, too. I don't think that's going to play for DiCicco or anyone else. She had a job to do. She did it, and now that part's over."

He ran his hands down her arms until he could link them with hers. "You're beat, you're shaky. She wouldn't have gotten to you like this if you'd been in top form."

"Maybe not, but boy, did she."

"Screw her." He kissed Rowan's forehead, then her lips. "Here's what we're going to do. We're going to go get dinner. You can listen to the rest of the unit express their pithy and colorful opinions over the fed asking you for an alibi."

"Pithy." That nearly got a smirk out of her. "I guess that would feel good."

"Nothing like solidarity. Then, we're going to come back here so I can give you an alibi for tonight."

Now the smirk formed, quick and cocky. "Maybe I'll be the one giving you an alibi."

15

After her morning PT, Rowan made a point of going to the cookhouse kitchen. If there was one person who knew something about everything, and most everything about something, it was Marg.

"Lynn's reloading the buffet now," Marg told her. "Or are you looking for a handout?"

"I wouldn't mind."

With silver hoops dancing at the sides of her do-rag—yellow smiley faces over bright blue today—Marg reached for a pitcher. "You don't want to have breakfast with your boyfriend?"

Rowan answered Marg's smirk with an eye roll. "I don't have boyfriends, I have lovers. And I take them and cast them off at my will."

"Ha." Marg poured a glass of juice. "That one won't cast off so easy. Drink this."

Obliging, Rowan pursed her lips. "Your carrot base, some cranberry, and . . ." She sipped again. "It's not really orange. Tangerine?"

"Blood orange. Gotcha."

"Sounds disgusting, and yet it's not. Any word on Dolly?"

Marg shook her head as she whisked eggs. Not a negative gesture, Rowan recognized, but a pitying one.

"They found her car, down one of the service roads in the woods off of Twelve, with a flat tire."

"Just her car?"

"What I heard is her keys were still in it, but not her purse. Like maybe she had some car trouble, pulled off."

"Why would she pull off the main highway if she had a flat?"

"I'm just saying what I heard." After pouring the eggs into an omelet pan, Marg added chunks of ham, cheese, tomatoes, some spinach. "Some of the thinking is maybe she walked on back to the highway, or somebody followed her onto the service road. And they took her."

"They still don't know if the remains in the fire . . . they can't know that for sure."

"Then there's no point in worrying about it."

Marg tried for brisk, but Rowan heard the hitch in her voice that told her Marg worried plenty.

"I wanted to hurt her, and seriously regretted not getting my fist in her face at least once. Now, knowing somebody might've hurt her, or worse? I don't want to feel guilty about Dolly. I hate feeling guilty about anything, but I *hate* feeling guilty about Dolly."

"I've never known anybody better at bringing trouble and drama onto herself than Dolly Brakeman. And if L.B. hadn't fired her, I'd have told him flat he'd have to choose between her and me. I don't feel guilty about that. I can be sorry if something's happened to her without feeling guilty I wanted to give her the back of my hand more than once."

Marg set the omelet and the wheat toast with plum preserves she'd prepared in front of Rowan. "Eat. You've shed a few pounds, and it's too early in the season for that."

"It's the first season I've needed an alibi for a murder investigation."

"I wouldn't mind having an alibi like yours."

Rowan dug into the omelet. "Do you want him when I'm done with him? Ow." Rowan laughed when Marg cuffed the side of her head. "And after I offer you such a studly guy." She smiled, shooting for winsome.

"When do you think you'll be done with him? In case I'm in the market for a stud."

"Can't say. So far he's playing my tune, but I'll let you know."

When Marg set a Coke down by her plate, Rowan leaned into her just a little. "Thanks, Marg. Really."

In acknowledgment, Marg gave her a hard one-armed hug. "Clean your plate," she ordered.

After breakfast, she tracked down L.B. in the gym where he'd worked up a sweat with bench presses.

"I'm on the bottom of the jump list," she said without preamble.

He sat up, wiped his face with his towel. His long braid trailed down his sweaty, sleeveless workout shirt. "That's right." He picked up a twenty-pound free weight and started smooth, two-count bicep curls.

"Why?"

"Because that's where I put you. I'd have taken you off completely for a day or two, but they've caught one down in Payette, and Idaho might need some Zulies in there."

"I'm fit and I'm fine. Move me up. Christ, L.B., you've got Stovic ahead of me, and he's still limping a little."

"You've been on nearly every jump we've had this month. You need a breather."

"I don't—"

"I say you do," he interrupted, and switched the weight to his other arm while he studied her face. "It's my job to decide that."

"This is about what happened yesterday, and that's not right. I need the work, I need the pay. I'm not injured, I'm not sick."

"You need a breather," he repeated. "Put some time in the loft. We're still catching up there. I'll take a look at the list tomorrow."

"I find remains, which I dutifully report, and I get grounded."

"You're still on the list," he reminded her. "And you know jumping fire's not all we do here."

She also knew that when Michael Little Bear used that mild, reasonable tone, she'd have better luck arguing with smoke. She could sulk, she could steam, but she wouldn't change his mind.

"Maybe I'll go down and see my father for a bit."

"That's a good idea. Let me know if you decide you want to go farther off base."

"I know the drill," she grumbled. She started to shove her hands in her pockets, then went stiff when Lieutenant Quinniock walked in. "Cops are here," she said quietly.

L.B. set down his weight, got to his feet.

"Mr. Little Bear, Ms. Tripp. I've got a few follow-up questions."

"I'll get out of your way," Rowan began.

"Actually, I'd like to speak with you, too. Why don't we step out. You can finish your workout," he said to L.B., "then we could talk in your office."

"I'll be there in twenty."

"That works. Miss?" Quinniock, in his polished shoes and stone-gray suit, gestured toward the gym doors.

"Don't 'Miss' me. Make it Tripp," she said as she shoved open the door ahead of him. "Or Rowan, or Ro, but don't 'Miss' me unless you're sad I've gone away."

He smiled. "Rowan. Would you mind if we sat outside? This is a busy place."

"Do you want me to go over my—what would you call it?—altercation with Dolly?"

"Do you have anything to add to what you've already told me?"

"No."

"She got the pig's blood from a ranch, if you're interested. From one of the people who goes to her church."

"Onward, Christian soldiers." She dropped down on a bench outside the barracks.

"She acquired it the day before she came here to ask for work." He nodded when Rowan turned to stare at him. "It leads me to conclude she meant to cause you trouble, even before you and she spoke the day she was hired back on."

"It wouldn't have mattered what I said or did."

"Probably not. I understand you spoke with Special Agent DiCicco."

"She's a snappy dresser. You too."

"I like a good suit. It complicated things for you, finding the remains."

"Complicated because it was during a fire, or because Dolly's missing?"

"Both. The missing person's end is MPD's case, at this time. We're cooperating with the USFS while they work to identify the body. In that spirit, I've shared information with Agent DiCicco."

"My history, as she called it, with Dolly."

"That, and the fact Dolly told several people you were to blame for what happened to James Brayner. You, and everyone here. She's been vocal about her resentment for some time, including the period of time she was away from Missoula."

It didn't surprise her, could no longer anger her. "I don't know how she could work here, be involved with jumpers, and not understand what we do, how we do it, what we deal with."

She looked at Quinniock then, the dramatic hair, the perfectly knotted tie. "And I'm not sure I understand why you're telling me this."

"It's possible she planned to continue to cause trouble—for you, for the base. It's possible she came back here for work so she had easier access. And it's possible she had help. Someone she convinced to help her. Did you see her with anyone in particular after she came back?"

"No."

"She and Matthew Brayner, the brother."

Rowan's back went up. "She blindsided Matt, the Brayner family, with the baby. I know they all took a natural interest in the baby and, being the kind of people they are, would do whatever they could for Dolly. It took guts for Matt to come back here, to work here after what happened to Jim. Any idea you may have that he'd help Dolly destroy my quarters or equipment is wrong and insulting."

"Were they friendly while his brother was alive?"

"I don't think Matt gave Dolly two thoughts, but he was, and is, friendly with everyone. And I'm not talking about another jumper behind his back."

"I'm just trying to get a feel for the dynamics. I'm also told several of the men on base had relationships with Dolly, at least until she became involved with James Brayner."

"Sex isn't a relationship, especially blow-off-some-steam sex with a woman who was willing to pop the cork with pretty much anybody. She popped plenty of corks in town, too."

"Until James Brayner."

"She zeroed in on him last season, and as far as I know that was a first for her. Look, he was a cute guy, fun, charming. Maybe she fell for him, I don't know. Dolly and I didn't share our secrets, hopes and dreams."

"You're probably aware by now that we found her car."

"Yeah, word travels." She squeezed her eyes shut a moment. "It's going to be her, when they finish the ID. I know that. You just have to triangulate the town, where you found the car, where I found the remains, and it's heavy weight on it. I didn't like her. I didn't like her a whole bunch of a lot, but she didn't deserve the way she ended up. Nobody deserves the way she ended up."

"People are always getting what they don't deserve. One way or the other. Thanks for the time."

"When will they know?" she asked when he stood up. "When will they know for sure?"

"Her dentist is local. They'll verify with her dental records, and should have confirmation later today. It's not my case, but just out of curiosity, in your opinion, how long would it take to get from the trailhead to where you found the remains, adding in carrying about a hundred and ten pounds, in the dark."

She got to her feet so they'd be eye to eye. "It depends. It could take an hour. But if you were fit, an experienced hiker, and you knew the area, you could do it in less than half that."

"Interesting. Thanks again."

She sat back down when he walked toward Operations, tried to work her mind around the conversation, the information.

And decided, as much as she hated to admit it, maybe L.B. was right. Maybe she did need a breather. So she'd walk down to see her father, touch base with the rest of his crew. The walk might clear her head, and God knew having a little time with her father never hurt.

She went back in for a bottle of water and a ball cap, then crossed paths with Gull as she came back out.

"I saw you with the cop. Do I need to post that bail?"

"Not so far. They found her car, Gull."

"Yeah, I heard."

"And . . . there's other stuff. I have to get my head around it. I'm going to walk down to the school, see my father."

"Do you want company?"

"I need some solo time."

He ran his knuckles down her cheek in a casually affectionate gesture that threw her off. "Look me up when you get back."

"Sure. You're second load," she called back as she started the walk. "Idaho might need some Zulies. If you jump, jump good."

She watched the show as she walked. Planes nosing up; skydivers drifting down. Clouds gathered in the west, hard and white over the mountains. Smaller, she noted, and puffier overhead and north, drifting east on a slow, leisurely sail.

She heard mechanics working in the hangars, the twang of music, the clink of metal, the roll of voices, but didn't stop as she might have another day. Conversation wasn't what she was after.

Solo time.

The killer had a car, or truck, she decided. Nobody would've carried Dolly from where she'd stopped to where she ended up. Did he kill her when she pulled off 12, dump her body in the trunk of the car, bed of the truck? Or did he give her a ride, maybe park at the trailhead, then do it? Or force her up the trail, then—

Jesus, any way it had happened, she'd ended up dead, and her baby daughter an orphan.

Why had she been heading south on 12, or had she been heading back from farther away? To meet a lover? To meet this theoretical person she'd enlisted to cause trouble? Plenty of motels to choose from. Hard to meet a lover—and Dolly had been famous for using sex as barter—when you lived at home with your parents and your baby.

Why couldn't she have loved the baby enough to just make a life? To treasure what she had, and put some goddamn effort into being a good mother instead of letting this obsession eat away at her?

All the time she'd spent planning her weird revenge,

harboring all that hate, could've been spent on living, on nuzzling her baby.

"Oh, mother issues much?" Annoyed with herself, she quickened her pace.

Enough solo time, she decided. Solo time was overrated. She should've taken Gull up on his offer to come with her. He'd have distracted her out of this mood, made her laugh, or at least annoyed her so she'd stop feeling sad and angry.

When she moved around the people scattered over the lawn, the picnic tables at her father's place, she looked up, as they were.

Coming on final, she thought, watching the plane. She crossed to the fence, tucked her hands in her back pockets and decided to enjoy the show. Her smile bloomed as the skydiver jumped—and taking a breather didn't seem so bad after all. When the second figure leaped out, she settled in, studying their forms on the free fall.

The first, definitely a student, but not bad. Not shabby. Arms out, taking it in. Check out that view! Feel that wind!

And the second . . . Rowan angled her head, narrowed her eyes. She couldn't be sure, not yet, but she'd have laid decent money down Iron Man Tripp rocketed down toward the student.

Then came the moment. The chutes deployed, one then two—to applause and cheers—the blue-and-white stripes of the student's, and the chute she'd designed and rigged for her father's sixtieth birthday with the boldly lettered IRON MAN in red (his favorite color) over a figure of a smoke jumper.

She loved watching him like this, and always had. Perfect form, she thought, absolute control, riding the air from sky to earth while the sun streamed through those drifting clouds.

She'd been exactly right to come here, she realized, when the world tipped crazily all around her. Here, what she loved held constant. Whatever happened, she could count on him.

She willed the stress of the morning into a corner. She couldn't dismiss it, but she could shove it back a little and focus on what made her happy.

She'd hang out here with her father for a while, have lunch with him, talk over what was going on. He'd listen, let her spew, and somehow pull her back in, steady her again.

She always thought more clearly, felt less overwhelmed, after a session with her father.

The student handled the drop well, Rowan observed, managed a very decent landing and was up on his—no her, Rowan realized—feet quickly. Then the Iron Man touched down, soft as butter, smooth as silk.

She added her applause to the rest, sent out a high whistle of approval before waving her arms in hopes of snagging her father's attention.

The student unhooked her harness, pulled off her helmet. Gorgeous red hair seemed to explode in the sunlight. As the woman raced toward her father, Rowan grinned. She understood the exuberance, the charge of excitement, had seen this same scene play out countless times between student and instructor. She continued to grin as the woman leaped into Lucas's arms, something else she'd seen again and again.

What she hadn't seen, and what had her grin shifting to a puzzled frown, was her father swinging a student in giddy circles while said student locked her arms around his neck.

And when Lucas "Iron Man" Tripp leaned down and planted a long, very enthusiastic kiss (and the crowd went wild) on the student's mouth, Rowan's jaw dropped to the toes of her Nikes.

She would've been more shocked if Lucas had pulled out a Luger and shot the redhead between the eyes, but it would've been a close call.

The woman had her hands on Lucas's cheeks, a gesture somehow more intimate than the kiss itself. It spoke of knowledge, familiarity, of privilege.

Who the hell was this bimbo, and when the hell had Iron Man started kissing students? Kissing *anyone*?

And in public.

The woman turned, her face—which didn't look bimboish—warm from the kiss, bright with laughter, and executed a deep, exaggerated curtsy for the still cheering crowd. To Rowan's continued shock, Lucas simply stood there grinning like the village idiot.

Was he on drugs?

Her brain told her to ease back, to find some quiet place to absorb the shock. Her gut told her to hurdle the fence, march right up and demand, what the fuck?!

But her fingers had curled around the fence, and she couldn't seem to uncurl them.

Then her father spotted her. His loopy grin aimed her way as he—Jesus—took the redhead's hand, gave it a little swing. He waved at Rowan with his free hand before he said something to the face-caressing redhead, who actually had the *nerve* to smile in Rowan's direction.

Still holding hands, they strolled toward the fence and Rowan.

"Hi, honey. I didn't realize you were here."

"I . . . I'm low on the jump list, so."

"I'm glad you came by." He laid his fingers over the ones she had curled on the fence, effectively linking the three of them. "Ella, this is my daughter, Rowan. Ro, Ella Frazier. She just did her first AFF."

"It's great to meet you. Lucas has told me so much about you."

"Oh, yeah? Funny, he hasn't told me a thing about you."

"You've been pretty busy." Obviously oblivious, Lucas spoke cheerfully. "We keep missing each other. Ella's principal of Orchard Homes Academy."

A high-school principal. Tony private school. Another strike against bimbo status. Damn it.

"Her son bought her a tandem jump as a gift," Lucas went on, "and she got hooked. You should've had your family here for this, Ella," he continued. "Your grandkids would've loved it."

And a *grandmother*? What kind of father-face-sucking bimbo was this?

"I wanted to make sure I handled it before they came to watch. Next time. In fact, I'm going to go in and talk to Marcie about setting it up. It was nice to meet you, Rowan. I hope we see more of each other."

Though her voice was mild and polite, the quick clash when the two women's gazes met made it clear they understood each other.

"I'll see you inside, Lucas."

Yeah, keep walking, Rowan thought. Make tracks.

"So what did you think?" Lucas asked, eagerly. "I've been hoping you'd get a break so you could meet Ella. It's cool you happened to be here for her first AFF."

"Her form's not bad. She had a good flight. Listen, Dad, why don't we grab some lunch in the cafe? There's—"

"Ella and I are having a picnic lunch out here to celebrate her dive. Why don't you join us? It'll give the two of you a chance to get to know each other."

Was he kidding? "I don't think so, but thanks. Riding third wheel doesn't suit me."

"Don't be silly. If I know Ella, she made plenty. She's a hell of a cook."

"Just—just—" She had to untangle her tongue. "How long has this been going on? *What's* going on? Kissing on the jump spot, hand-holding, picnic lunches? Jesus, Dad, are you *sleeping* with her?"

He pokered up, a look she knew meant she'd hit a nerve.

"I think that would come under the heading of my personal business, Rowan. What's your problem here?"

"My problem, other than the kissing, holding and so on in front of God, crew and visitors, is I came over here because I needed to talk to my father, but you're obviously too busy with Principal Hotpants to spare any for me."

"Watch it." His fingers tightened on hers before she could jerk away. "Don't you use that tone with me. I don't give a damn how old you are. If you need to talk to me, come inside. We'll talk."

"No, thanks," she said, coldly polite. "Go ahead and take care of your personal business. I'll take care of my own. Excuse me." She pulled her fingers free. "I have to get back to base."

She recognized the combination of anger and disappointment on his face, something rarely seen and instantly understood. She swung away from it, strode away from him, her back stiff with resentment. And her heart aching with what she told herself was betrayal.

Her temper only built on the walk back, then took a bitter spike when she heard the siren blast. She broke into a run, covering the remaining distance to the base where she could already see jumpers on the scramble and the jump plane taxiing onto the runway.

She hit the ready room, shoving aside the bitterness as she had the stress—as something to be taken out and examined later.

She grabbed gear off the speed rack for Cards. "Payette?"

"That's the one." He zipped his let-down rope into the proper pocket. "Zulies to the rescue!"

She looked in his eyes. "Have a good one."

"It's in the cards." He let out a chortle before waddling toward the waiting plane.

She went through the same procedure with Trigger while Gull helped Dobie.

In minutes she stood watching the plane take off without her.

"Secondary blaze blew up," Gull told her. "Idaho's already spread thin. One of their second load got hung up on the jump, broke his arm, and they've got two more injuries on the ground."

"Aren't you well informed?"

"I like to keep up with current events." He re-angled his ball cap to gain more shade from the bill as he followed the plane into the sky. "Such as the dry lightning doing a smack-down up in Flathead. You didn't spend much time at your dad's."

"Are you keeping track of me?"

"Just using my keen powers of observation. They also tell me you're severely pissed."

"I don't like being grounded when I'm fit to jump."

"You're on the list," he reminded her. "And?"

"And, what?"

"And what else has you severely pissed?"

"You and your keen powers of observation are about to, so aim them elsewhere." She started to stalk off, then, too riled to hold it in, stalked back. "I go up to see my father, spend some time with him, talk this crap over with him because that's what we do. When I get there he's doing an AFF with a student. A student who happens to be a woman. A redhead. One who, the minute they're on the ground, jumps him like my old dog Butch used to jump a Frisbee. Then he's swinging her around, and then he's kissing her. Kissing her, right there, a serious lip-locking, body-twining kiss no doubt involving tongues."

"The best do. So . . . I'm working my way through that report, trying to pinpoint what pissed you off."

"Did I just tell you my father kissed that redhead?"

"You did, but I'm having a tough time seeing why that flipped your switch. You're acting like you've never seen your old man kiss a woman before."

When she said nothing, only stood with her eyes like smoldering blue ice, he let out a half laugh of genuine surprise. "Seriously? You've seriously never seen him kiss a woman? The man has to have superhuman discretion."

Gull stopped again, shook his head and gave her a light slap on the shoulder. "Come on, Ro. You're not going to tell me you think he actually hasn't bumped lips with a female in—how old are you, exactly?"

"He doesn't date."

"So you said when he had the date with the lady client for drinks . . . Aha. Now my intrepid deductive skills mesh with my keen powers of observation to conclude this would be the same woman."

"She *says* she's a high-school principal. It's pretty damn clear they're sleeping together."

"I guess getting called into the principal's office has taken on a whole new meaning for your dad."

"Fuck you."

"Whoa." He caught her arm as she spun around. "You're jealous? You're actually jealous because your father's interested in a woman—who's not you?"

Heat—temper, embarrassment—slapped into her cheeks. "That's disgusting and untrue."

"You're pissed and jealous, and genuinely hurt because your father may be in a romantic relationship with a woman. That's not disgusting or untrue, Rowan, but it sure strikes me as petty and selfish."

Something very akin to the disappointment she'd just seen on her father's face moved over Gull's. "When's the last time he threw a tantrum because you were involved with someone?"

Now she felt petty, and that only fueled her temper. "My feelings and my relationship with my father are none of your business. You don't know a damn thing about it, or me. And you know what, I'm pretty goddamn sick of being dumped on, from Dolly and vindictive bullshit, to tight-assed special agents, my father's disappointment to your crappy opinion of me. So you can just—"

The shrilling siren sliced off her words.

"Looks like me and my crappy opinion have to get going." Gull turned his back on her and walked back to the ready room.

It was almost more than she could swallow, standing on the ground again while the plane flew north.

"If this keeps up, they'll have to send us up."

She glanced over at Matt. "The way my luck's going, L.B.'ll cross me off and send Marg if we get another call. How did you rate the basement?"

"He feels like I'm too twisted up about Dolly, because of my niece. Maybe I am."

"I'm sorry. I wasn't thinking."

"It's okay. I keep expecting them to come back, say it's all a mistake." He held his cap in his hands, turning it around and around in them and leaving his floppy cornsilk hair uncovered.

"It can't be right, you know, for a baby to lose her father before she's even born, then her mother so soon after." He turned to Rowan, and she thought he looked unbearably young and exposed.

"It isn't right," she said.

"But things, I guess things just aren't always right. I guess . . . it's like fate."

He leaned into her a little when she hooked an arm around his waist. "It's harder on you, maybe," he said, "than me."

"Me?"

"You found her. If it's her. Even if it's not, finding whoever it was. It's awful you were the one who found her."

"We'll both get through it, Matt."

"That's what I keep telling myself. I keep thinking of Shiloh, and telling myself that whatever happens, we'll make sure she's okay. I mean, she's just a baby."

"The Brakemans and your family will take care of her."

"Yeah. Well, I guess I'll go up to the loft, try to get my mind on something else."

"That's a good idea. I'll be up in a few minutes."

She went back to her quarters first, locked herself in. Though she knew it was self-pity, that it was useless, she sat on the floor, leaned back against the bed and had a good cry.

16

The cry emptied out the temper and the self-pity. For a trade-off she accepted the splitting headache, and downed the medication before splashing cold water on her face.

One of the problems with being a true blonde with fair skin, she mused, giving herself the hard eye in the mirror, was that after a jag she resembled someone who'd gotten a brutal sunburn, through cheesecloth.

She splashed some more, then wrung out a cold cloth. She gave herself ten minutes flat on her back on the bed, the cloth over her face, to let the meds and the cool do their job.

So she'd overreacted, she thought. Beat her with a brick.

She'd apologize to her father for sticking her nose in his business since he now had business he didn't want her to stick her nose into.

And she damn well expected the same courtesy from a certain fast-footed, hotshot rookie, so he'd better come back safe.

She checked her face again, decided she'd do. Maybe she didn't look her best, but she didn't look as if she'd spent the last twenty minutes curled up on the floor, blubbering like a big baby.

On her way toward Operations to check on the status of the crews, she caught sight of Special Agent DiCicco walking toward her.

"Ms. Tripp."

"Look, I know you've got a job to do, but we've got two loads out. I'm heading to Ops, and don't have time to go over ground I've already gone over."

"I'm sorry, but I will need to speak with you, as well as members of the crew and staff. The remains you discovered yesterday have been positively identified as Dolly Brakeman."

"Hell." Sick, Rowan pressed her forehead, and rubbed it side to side. "Oh, hell. How? How did she die?"

"Since some of those details will make the evening news, I can tell you cause of death was a broken neck, possibly incurred in a fall."

"A fall? You'd have to fall really hard and really wrong. Not an accidental fall, not when she left her car one place and ended up in another."

DiCicco's face remained impassive, her eyes level. "This is a homicide investigation, coordinated with an arson investigation. Your instincts on both counts appear to have been right on target."

"And being right makes me a suspect."

"I'm not prepared to eliminate anyone as a suspect, but you have an alibi for the time frame. The fact is, you and the victim had an adversarial relationship. It's an avenue I need to explore."

"Explore away. Be Magellan. I didn't look for trouble with her. If I could've punched her on the infamous day of the blood of the pigs, I would have. And she'd have earned it. I think she should've been charged for what she did to our equipment, and spent some quality time in jail. I don't think she should've died for either of those offenses. She was—"

Rowan broke off as a truck roared in, fishtailing as it swerved in her direction. She grabbed DiCicco's arm to yank her back even as DiCicco grabbed hers to do the same.

The truck braked with a shriek, spewed up clouds of road dust.

"Jesus Christ! What the hell are you . . ." She trailed off as she recognized the man leaping out of the truck as Leo Brakeman, Dolly's father.

"My daughter is dead." He stood there, meaty hands balled into white-knuckled fists at his sides, his former All-State left tackle's body quivering, his face—wide and hard—reddened.

"Mr. Brakeman, I'm sorry for—"

"You're responsible. There's nothing left of her but burned bones, and you're responsible."

"Mr. Brakeman." DiCicco stepped between Rowan and Brakeman, but Rowan shifted to the side, refusing the shield. "I explained to you that I and the full resources of my agency will do everything possible to identify your daughter's killer. You need to go home, be with your wife and your granddaughter."

"You'll just cover it up. You work for the same people. My daughter would be alive today if not for that one." When he pointed his finger, Rowan felt the raging grief behind it stab like a blade.

"She got Dolly fired because she couldn't stand being reminded of how she let Jim Brayner die. She got her fired so Dolly had to drive all the way down to Florence to find work. If she didn't kill my girl with her own hands, she's the reason for it."

"You think you're so important?" he raged at Rowan. "You think you can ride on your father's coattails, and because your name's Tripp you can push people around? You were jealous of my girl, jealous because Jim tossed you over for her, and you couldn't stand it. You let him die so she couldn't have him."

"Leo." L.B., with a wall of men behind him, moved forward. "I'm sorry about Dolly. Every one of us is sorry for your loss. But I'm going to ask you once to get off this property."

"Why don't you fire her? Why don't you kick her off this base like she was trash, the way you did my girl? Now my girl's dead, and she's standing there like it was *nothing.*"

"This isn't a good time for you to be here, Leo." L.B. kept his voice low, quiet. "You need to go home and be with Irene."

"Don't tell me what I need. There's a baby needs her ma. And none of you give a damn about that. You're going to pay for what happened to my Dolly. You're going to pay dear, all of you."

He spat on the ground, slammed back into his truck. Rowan saw tears spilling down his cheeks as he spun the wheel and sped away.

"Ro."

"Not now, L.B. Please." She shook her head.

"Now," he corrected, and put an arm firm around her shoulders. "You come inside with me. Agent DiCicco, if you need to talk to Rowan, it's going to be later."

DiCicco watched the wall of men close ranks like a barricade, then move into the building behind Rowan.

Inside, L.B. steered her straight to his office, shut the door on the rest of the men. "Sit," he ordered.

When she did, he shoved his hands through his hair, leaned back on his desk. "You know Leo Brakeman's a hard-ass under the best of circumstances."

"Yeah."

"And these are beyond shitty circumstances."

"I get it. It has to be somebody's fault, and Dolly blamed me for everything else, so I'm the obvious choice. I get it. If she told him—people—I was doing the deed with Jim before he tossed me over, why wouldn't his father think I had it out for his kid? And just to clarify, Jim and I were never—"

"You think I don't know you? I'll be talking to DiCicco and setting her straight on that front."

Rowan shrugged. Oddly she'd felt her spine steel up again under Brakeman's assault. "She'll either believe it or she won't. It doesn't matter. I'm okay, or close to being okay. You don't have time to babysit me, L.B., not with our crews out.

"I'm sorry for Brakeman," she said, "but that's the last time he'll use me as an emotional punching bag. Dolly was a liar, and her being dead doesn't change that."

She got to her feet. "I told you this morning I was fit and fine. That wasn't a lie but it wasn't completely true, either. Now it is. Nobody's going to treat me like Dolly and her father have and make me feel bad about it. I'm not responsible for the baggage full of shit they've hauled around. I've got plenty of my own."

"That sounds like you're fit and fine."

"I can help out in Ops if you want, or head up to the loft, see what needs doing there."

"Let's go see how our boys and girls are doing."

DiCicco MADE HER WAY to the cookhouse kitchen, found it empty, unless she counted the aromas she dubbed as both comforting and sinful. She started to move into the dining area when a movement out the window caught her eye.

She watched the head cook, Margaret Colby, weeding a patch of an impressive garden.

Marg looked up at the sound of the back door opening, pushed at the wide brim of the straw hat she wore over her kitchen bandanna.

"That's some very pretty oregano."

"It's coming along. Are you looking for me, or just out for a stroll?"

"I'd like to talk to you for a few minutes. And to the other cook, Lynn Dorchester."

"I let Lynn go on home for the afternoon since she was upset. She'll be back around four." Marg tossed weeds into the plastic bucket at her feet, then brushed off her hands. "I could use some lemonade. Do you want some?"

"If it's not too much trouble."

"If it was, I wouldn't be getting it. You can have a seat there. I spend enough time in the kitchen on pretty days, so I take advantage of being out when I can."

DiCicco sat in one of the lawn chairs, contemplated the garden, the lay of the land beyond it. The big hangars and outbuildings, the curve of the track some distance off. And the rise and sweep of the mountains dusted with clouds.

Marg came out with the lemonade, and a plate of cookies with hefty chocolate chunks.

"Oh. You hit my biggest weakness."

"Everybody's got one." Marg set the tray down, sat comfortably and toed off her rubber-soled garden shoes.

"We heard it was Dolly. I let Lynn go, as it hit her hard. They weren't best of friends, Dolly didn't have girlfriends. But they'd worked together awhile now, and got along all right for the most of it. Lynn's got a soft core, and punched right into it."

"You worked with Dolly for some time, too. Were her supervisor."

"That's right. She could cook—she had a good hand with it, and she never gave me a problem in the kitchen. Her problem was, or one of them was, she looked at sex as an accomplishment, and as something to bargain with."

Marg picked up a cookie, took a bite. "The men around here, they're strong. They're brave. They've got bodies you'd be hard-pressed not to notice. Dolly wasn't hard-pressed.

"A lot of them are young, too," she continued, "and most all of them are away from home. They're going to risk life and limb and work like dogs, sometimes for days at a time in the worst conditions going. If they get a chance to roll onto a naked woman, there's not many who'd say no thanks. Dolly gave plenty of them a chance."

"Was there resentment? When a woman gives one man a chance, then turns around and gives the same chance to another, resentment's natural."

"I don't know a single one who ever took Dolly seriously. And that includes Jim. I know she said he was going to marry her, and I know she was lying. Or just dreaming. It's kinder to say just dreaming."

Though he'd used different words, L.B. had stated the same opinion.

"Was Jim serious about Rowan Tripp?"

"Ro? Well, she helped train him as a recruit, and worked with him. . . ." Marg trailed off as the actual meaning of *serious* got through. Then she sat back in the chair and laughed until her sides ached. She waved a hand in the air, drank some lemonade to settle down.

"I don't know where you got that idea, Agent DiCicco, but if Jim had tried to *get serious* with Ro, she'd've flicked him off like a fly. He flirted with everything female, myself included. It was his way, and he was so damn good-natured about it. But there was nothing between him and Ro but what's between all of them. A kind of friendship I expect war buddies understand. Added to it, Rowan's never gotten involved with anybody in her unit—until this season. Until Gulliver Curry. I'm enjoying watching how that one comes along."

"Leo Brakeman claims that Rowan and Jim were involved before he broke it off to be with Dolly."

Marg drank more lemonade and contemplated the mountains as DiCicco had. "Leo's grieving, and my heart hurts for him and Irene, but he's wrong. It sounds to me like something Dolly might've said."

"Why would she?"

"For the drama, and to try to take some of the shine off Rowan. I told you, Dolly didn't have girlfriends. She got on with Lynn because she didn't see Lynn as a threat. Lynn's married and happy, and the men tend to think of her as a sister, or a daughter. Dolly always saw Rowan as a threat, and more, she knew Rowan considered her . . . cheap, we'll say."

"It's obvious they didn't get along."

"Up until Jim died they tolerated each other well enough. I've known both of them since they were kids. Rowan barely noticed Dolly. Dolly always noticed Ro. And if you're still thinking Rowan had anything to do with what happened, you're wasting a lot of time better spent finding out who did."

Time wasn't wasted, in DiCicco's opinion, if you found out *something*.

"Did you know anything about Dolly getting work in Florence?"

"No. I don't know why she would. Plenty of places right around here would hire her on, at least for the season."

Marg loosed a long sigh. "I wouldn't give her a reference. Her preacher came out, tried to get me to write her one. I didn't like his way, that's one thing, but I wouldn't do it anyway. She didn't earn it with the way she behaved.

"I guess I'm sorry for that if she felt she had to leave Missoula to work. But there are plenty of places she could've gotten work without a reference."

Marg sat a moment, saying nothing. Just studying the mountains.

"Was she coming back from there when it happened? From work in Florence?"

"It's something I'll check out. I hate exaggeration,

so you know I'm giving it to you straight when I say this is the best cookie I've ever eaten."

"I'll give you some to take with you."

"I wouldn't say no."

THE CREW IN IDAHO had the fire caged in by sundown. But up north, the battle raged on.

She could see it. As Rowan stepped outside to take the air, she could see the fire and smoke, and the figures in yellow shirts brandishing tools like weapons.

If they called for another load, if they needed relief or re-enforcement, L.B. would send her. And she'd be ready.

Her back stiffened at the glint of headlights, the silhouette of an approaching pickup. Then loosened again, a little, when she saw it wasn't Leo Brakeman back for another shot at her.

Lucas stepped out of the truck, walked to her.

Some anger there, she noted. Still some mad on.

He proved it when he clamped his hands on her shoulders, gave her a little shake. "Why the hell didn't you tell me what happened? Finding the remains, about Dolly, about *any* of it."

"I figured you knew."

"Well, I damn well didn't."

"You've been busy."

"Don't pull that crap with me, Rowan. Your landing text said A-OK."

"I was. I wasn't hurt."

"Rowan."

"I didn't want to tell you in a text, or on the phone. Then it was one thing and another. I came down this morning to talk to you about it, but—"

He simply yanked her against him and hugged.

"I'm a suspect."

"Stop it," he murmured, and pressed his lips to the top of her head.

"The Forest Service agent's questioned me twice. I had altercations with Dolly, then out of all the acres up there, I stumble right over what's left of her. Then, Leo Brakeman came here today."

She unburdened, stripped it out and off because he was there to cover her again.

"Leo's half mad with grief. In his place, I don't know what I'd do." Couldn't bear to think of it. "They'll find whoever did it. Maybe it'll help like they say it does, though I swear I don't know how."

"He was crying when he drove away. I think that was the moment I stopped feeling sorry for myself, because I'd been having a real good time with that."

"You were never able to stretch that out for long."

"I was going for the record. Dad, about before. I'm sorry."

"So am I." He wiped a hand through the air, a familiar gesture. "Clean slate."

"Squeaky clean."

"Where's that guy you've been hanging around with?"

"He's on the Flathead fire."

"Let's go check with Ops, see how they're doing."

"I want him back safe, want all of them back safe. Even though I'm pissed at him. Especially pissed because I think he had a point about a couple things."

"I hate when that happens. Besides, who does he think he is, having a point?"

She laughed, tipped her head to his shoulder. "Thanks."

SHE KEPT VIGIL in Operations, helped update the map tracking the crew's progress and the fire's twists and turns, and watched the lightning strikes blast on radar.

Sometime after two while a booming thunderstorm swept over the base, and up north Gull and his crewmates crawled into tents, she dropped into bed.

And almost immediately dropped into the dream.

The roar of thunder became the roar of engines, the scream of wind the air blasting through the plane's open door. She saw the nerves in Jim's eyes, heard them in his voice and, tossing in bed, ordered herself to stop him. To contact base, alert the spotter, talk to the fire boss.

Something.

"It is what it is," he said to her, with eyes now filled with sorrow. "It's, you know, my fate."

And he jumped as he always did, taking that last leap behind her. Into the mouth of the fire, screaming as its teeth tore through him.

This time she landed alone, the flames behind her snarling, throaty growls that built until the ground shook. She ran, sprinting up the incline, heat drenching her skin while she shoved through billowing clouds of smoke.

She shouted for Jim—there was a chance, always a chance—searching blindly. Fire climbed the trees in pulsing strings of light, blew over the ground in a deadly dance. Through it, someone called her name.

She changed direction and, shouting until her throat burned, stumbled into the black. Charred branches punched out of smoldering spots and beckoned like bony fingers. Snags hunched and towered, seemed to shift and sway behind the curtain of smoke. The scorched earth crackled under her feet as she continued to run toward the sound of her name.

Silence dropped, like a breath held. She stood in that void of sound, dismayed, disoriented. For a moment it was as if she'd become trapped in a black-and-white photo. Nothing moved, even as she ran on. The ground stayed silent under her feet.

She saw him, lying on the ground the fire had stripped bare, facing west, as if positioned to watch the sunset. Her voice echoed inside her head as she called his name. Dizzy with relief, she dropped down beside him.

Jim. Thank God.

She pulled out her radio, but like the air around her, it answered with silence.

I found him! Somebody answer. Somebody help me!

"They can't."

She tumbled back when Jim's voice broke the silence, when behind his mask his eyes opened, behind his mask his lips curved in a horrible smile.

"We burn here. We all burn here."

Flames ignited behind his mask. Even as she drew breath to scream, he gripped her hand. Fire fused her flesh to his.

She screamed, and kept screaming as the flames engulfed them both.

ROWAN DRAGGED HERSELF out of bed, stumbled to the window. She shoved it up, gulping in the air that streamed in. The storm had moved east, taking the rain and the boiling thunder with it. Sometime during the hideous dream the sky had broken clear of the clouds. She studied the stars to steady herself, taking comfort in their cool bright shine.

A bad day, that was all, she thought. She'd had a bad day that had brought on a bad night. Now it was done, out of her system. Put to rest.

But she left the window open, wanting that play of air as she got back in bed, and lay for a time, eyes open, looking at the stars.

As she started to drift something about the dream tapped at the back of her brain. She closed down to it, thought of the stars instead. She kept that cool, bright light in her mind's eye as she slipped into quiet, dreamless sleep.

ROWAN AND A MOP-UP TEAM jumped the Flathead mid-morning. While grateful for the work, the routine—however tedious—she couldn't deny some disappointment that Gull and his team packed out as she came in.

While she did her job, Special Agent Kimberly DiCicco did hers. She met Quinniock at a diner off Highway 12. He slid into the booth across from her, nodded. "Agent."

"Lieutenant. Thanks for meeting me."

"No problem. Just coffee," he told the waitress.

"I'll get right down to it, if that's okay," DiCicco began when the waitress had turned over the cup already in place, filled it and moved off.

"Saves time."

"You know the area better than I do, the people better than I do. You know more of the connections, the frictions, and you just recently questioned the victim over the vandalism. I could use your help."

"The department's always happy to cooperate, especially since your asking saves me from coming to you trying to wrangle a way in. Or working around you if you refused."

"Saves time," she said, echoing him, "and trouble. You have a good reputation, Lieutenant."

"As do you. And according to Rowan Tripp, we're both snappy dressers."

DiCicco smiled, very faintly. "That is a nice tie."

"Thanks. It appears we've taken the time and trouble to check each other out. My thinking, it's your jurisdiction, Agent Di-Cicco, but the victim is one of mine. We'll get what we both want quicker if we play to our strengths. Why don't you tell me who you're looking at, and I might be able to give you some insight."

"Let's take the victim first. I think I have a sense of her after reviewing the evidence, compiling interviews and observations. My leading conclusion is Dolly Brakeman was a liar, by nature and design, with some self-deception thrown in."

"I wouldn't argue with that conclusion. She was also impulsive, while at the same time being what I call a stewer. She tended to hoard bad feelings, perceived insults, and let them stew—then act impulsively with the switch flipped."

"Taking off when Jim Brayner died," DiCicco said, "even though it was a time she'd have most needed and benefited from home, family, support."

"She had a fight with her father."

DiCicco sat back. "I wondered."

"I got this from Mrs. Brakeman, when I talked to her after the vandalism at the base. Dolly came home out of her mind after learning of Jim's accident, and that's when she told her parents she was pregnant, and that she'd quit her job. Brakeman didn't take it well. They went at each other, and he said something along the lines of her getting her ass back to base, getting her job back or finding somebody else to freeload on. Dolly packed up and lit out. A little more maneuvering got me the fact that she packed up her parents' five-hundred-dollar cash emergency envelope for good measure."

"Five hundred doesn't take you far."

"Her mother sent her money now and again. And when Dolly called from Bozeman, in labor, the Brakemans drove out, patched things up."

"Babies are excellent glue."

"Dolly claimed to have been saved, and joined her mother's church when they all came home."

"Reverend Latterly's church. I got that, and I've spoken to him. He made a point of telling me Leo Brakeman didn't attend church." She thought of what Marg had said over lemonade and cookies. "I can't say I liked his way. His passive-aggressive way," she added, and Quinniock nodded agreement. "He seems to feel Little Bear, Rowan Tripp, the rest of them failed to show Christian charity to a troubled soul. As harsh as it was, I prefer Leo Brakeman's honest grief and rage."

"Whatever his way, Irene Brakeman claims he helped the three of them—herself, her husband and Dolly, come to terms once she was back. What Dolly left out when she called her parents for help, and I found after some poking around, was she'd made arrangements for a private adoption in Bozeman, which had paid her expenses."

"She planned to give the baby up?"

"She's the only one who knows what she planned, but she didn't contact the adoptive parents when she went into labor, nor the OB they'd paid for. Instead she went to the ER of a hospital across town and gave her Missoula address. By the time the other party found out what had happened, she was on her way back here. Since birth mothers have a right to change their minds, there wasn't much they could do."

DiCicco flipped open her notebook. "Do you have their names?"

"Yeah. I'll give you all of it, but I don't think we're going to find either of these people tracked Dolly down here and killed her, then set fire to the forest."

"Maybe not, but it's a strong motive."

"Are you still looking at Rowan Tripp?"

DiCicco sat back as the waitress breezed by to top off their coffee. "Let me tell you about Rowan Tripp. She's got a temper. She's got considerable power—physical strength, strength of will. She disliked Dolly intensely, on a personal level and in general terms. Her alibi is a man she's currently sleeping with. Men will lie for sex."

DiCicco paused to tip a fraction of a teaspoon of sugar into her coffee. "Dolly claimed Rowan had it in for her because Brayner tossed Rowan over for her. She was a liar," DiCicco added before Quinniock could respond. "Rowan Tripp isn't. In fact, she's almost brutally up-front. If Dolly had had her face punched in, I'd put my finger on Tripp. But the kill spot off the road, the broken neck, the arson? That doesn't jibe with my observations. Whoever killed her and put her in the forest might have expected the fire to burn her to ash, or at least for it to take more time for the remains to be discovered. It would've been monumentally stupid for Tripp to call the discovery in, and she's not stupid."

"We agree on that."

"Sticking with the victim, I've spent some time trying to verify her claim she had work in Florence. So far, I haven't been able to verify. I've started checking places like this, along the highway, but I haven't found any that hired her, or anyone who remembers her coming in looking for work. And, given her history, I'm wondering why she'd go to the trouble of looking for work down this way when she recently deposited ten thousand dollars in two hits of five—I traced it back to Matthew Brayner—in a bank in Lolo. Not her usual bank," DiCicco added, "which leads me to believe she didn't want anyone knowing about it. Which likely includes her parents."

He hadn't hit on the money—yet—and money always mattered. "She might've been thinking about running again."

"She might have. There's another pattern in her history. Men. Which is why I'm going to start checking motels along the route from Florence to Missoula. Maybe she decided to try out the other Brayner brother."

"Sex and money and guilt." Quinniock nodded. "The trifecta of motives. Want to get started?"

17

Gull sat on his bed with his laptop. He'd answered personal e-mail, attached a couple of pictures he'd taken that morning of the mountains, of the camp. He'd done a little business and now brought up his hometown paper to scan the sports section.

He knew the jump ship was back, and wondered how long it would take Rowan to knock on his door.

She would, he thought, even if just to pick up the fight where they'd left off. She wasn't the avoid-and-evade type, and, even if she were, it was damn near impossible to avoid and evade him while working on the same base.

He could wait.

Out of curiosity he did a Google search for wildfire arson investigation, and while he sifted through the results, considered heading into the lounge to see what was up, or maybe see if Dobie wanted to drive into town.

Always easier to wait when you're occupied, he thought. Then an article caught his interest. He answered the knock on the door absently.

"Yeah, it's open."

"Unlocked is different than open."

He glanced over. Rowan leaned on the jamb.

"It's open now."

She left the door ajar as she stepped in, and angled to see the laptop screen. "You're boning up on arson?"

"Specific to wildfire. It seemed relevant at the moment. How'd the mop-up go?"

"You left a hell of a mess." She shifted her gaze from the screen to his face. "I heard things got hairy up there."

"There were moments." He smiled. "Missed you."

"Because I'm so good or so good-looking?"

"All of the above." He shut down the computer. "Why don't we take a walk, catch the sunset."

"Yeah, all right."

When they went out, she pulled her sunglasses out of her pocket. "The fact that I'm surprised and not happy that my father's involved with a woman I don't know and he didn't tell me about doesn't make me jealous."

"Is that what we're calling it? Surprised and not happy. I'd've defined it as outraged and incensed."

"Due to the surprise." She clipped the words off.

"I'll give you that," Gull decided, "since you've apparently gone your entire life without witnessing a lip-lock."

"I don't think I overreacted. Very much."

"Why quibble about degrees?"

"I'm not apologizing for telling you to butt the hell out."

"Then I don't have to be gracious and accept a nonexistent apology. I'm not apologizing for expressing my opinion over your not very much of an overreaction."

"Then I guess we're even."

"Close enough. It's a hell of a sunset."

She stood with him, watching the sun sink toward the western peaks, watched it drown in the sea of red and gold and delicate lavender it spawned.

"I don't have to like her, and I sure as hell don't have to trust her."

"You're like a dog with a bone, Rowan."

"Maybe. But it's my bone."

Silence, Gull thought, could express an opinion as succinctly as words. "So. I heard about Dolly's father coming down on you."

"Over and done."

"I don't think so."

"Are you butting in again, Gull?"

"If you want to call it that. You've got to have sympathy for a man dealing with what he's dealing with, so maybe he gets a pass this time. But that's what's over and done. Nobody lays into my girl."

"Your girl? I'm not your girl."

"Are we or are we not together here and watching the sunset? And isn't it most likely you and I will end up naked in bed together tonight?"

"Regardless—"

"Regardless, my ass." He grabbed her chin, pulled her in for a kiss. "That makes you my girl."

"Holy hell, Gull, you're making my back itch."

Amused, he scratched it, then hooked an arm around her shoulders and kept walking. "So, later. Your place or mine?"

With the light softening, she pulled her sunglasses off, then swung them by the earpiece. "Some people are intimidated or put off by a certain level of confidence."

"You're not."

"No, I'm not. Fortunately for you, I like it. Let's—" She jerked back at the sharp crack in the air. "Jesus, was that—"

The breath whooshed out of her lungs when Gull knocked her to the ground and landed on top of her.

"Stay down," he ordered, and saw a bullet dig into the ground six feet away. "Hold on to me. We're going to roll." The minute her arms clamped around him, he pushed his body over, felt her do the same, so they covered the ground in a fast, ungainly roll to shield themselves behind one of the jeeps parked outside a hangar.

A third report snapped, pinging metal overhead.

"Where's it coming from? Can you tell?"

Gull shook his head, keeping his body over hers while he waited for the next shot. But silence held as seconds ticked by, then shattered with the shouts and rushing feet.

"For Christ's sake, get down, get cover," he called out. "There's a sniper."

Dobie bolted for the jeep, dived. "Are you hit? Are you— Goddamn, Gull, you're bleeding."

Rowan bucked under him. "Get off, get off. Let me see."

"Just scraped up from the asphalt. I'm not shot. Stay down."

"Rifle." Dobie shifted to a crouch. "I know a rifle shot when I hear one. From over there in the trees, I think. Damn good thing he's a shitty shot 'cause the two of you were sitting ducks. Standing ducks."

"Hey!" Trigger called from the far side of the hangar. "Is anybody hurt?"

"We're okay," Rowan answered. "Don't come out here. He may be waiting for somebody to step into the clear."

"L.B.'s got the cops coming. Just stay where you are for now."

"Copy that. Get off me, Gull."

"He tackled you good," Dobie commented when Gull pushed off. "You know he played football in high school. Quarterback."

"Isn't that interesting?" Rowan muttered it as she turned Gull's arm over to examine the bloody scrapes on his elbows and forearms. "You got grit in these."

"I liked basketball better," Gull said conversationally. "But I didn't have the height to compete. Had the speed, but I'd topped out at six feet until senior year when I had a spurt and added two more. Baseball, now, I like that better than either. Had a pretty good arm back in the day."

Maybe talking kept his mind off the scrapes, she decided, because they had to sting like hell.

"I thought you were the track star."

"My best thing, but I like sports, so I dabbled. Anyway, I liked collecting letters. I graduated a four-letter man."

Rowan studied him in the fading light. "We're sitting behind this jeep, hiding from some nutcase with a rifle, and you're actually bragging about your high-school glory days?"

"It passes the time. Plus I had very impressive glory days." He brushed dirt off her cheek. "We're okay."

"If you two are going to get sloppy, I'm not looking the other way." Dobie leaned back against the tire. "Wish I had a beer."

"Once this little interlude's over," Gull told him, "the first round's on me."

"I was thinking about going to the lounge, kicking back

with some screen and a beer. Just stepped outside for a minute, and *bam! bam!*"

"So you ran out, in the open, instead of back in?" Rowan demanded.

"I wasn't sure if either of you were hit or not, the way you both went down."

Rowan leaned over Gull, kissed Dobie on the mouth. "Thanks."

"I'm not kissing you. He's gone," Gull added. "He took off after the third shot."

"I expect so," Dobie agreed. "It's full dusk now. He can't see squat, unless he's got infrared."

"Let's go." Rowan pushed up to her haunches. "If he wants to shoot us, he could circle around in the dark and get us while we're sitting here."

"She's got a point. Don't run in a straight line. That's what they say in the movies," Gull pointed out. "Barracks?"

"Barracks," Dobie agreed.

Before either man could react, Rowan sprang up, a runner off the blocks, and revved straight into a sprint.

"Goddamn it."

Gull raced after her—could have caught her, passed her, they both knew. But he stayed at her back, zigging when she zigged, zagging when she zagged.

"We're coming in!" Rowan called out, then hit the door.

"What the hell were you thinking?" Gull grabbed her, spun her around. "Taking off like that?"

"I was thinking you weren't going to be my human shield twice in one day. I appreciate the first, I'm not stupid."

"You don't get to decide for me."

"Right back at you."

They shouted at each other while people shouted around them. Libby let out a piercing whistle. "Shut up! Shut the hell up. Everybody!" She shoved her hands through the hair dripping from the shower she'd leaped out of. "Gull, you're bleeding on the floor. Somebody get a first-aid kit and clean him up. The cops are on their way. Okay, the cops are here," she amended when the sirens sounded. "L.B. wants everybody inside until . . . until we know something."

"Come on, Gull." Janis gave him a light pat on the butt. "I'll be Nurse Betty."

"Is everybody accounted for?" Rowan asked.

"Between here, the cookhouse and Operations, we're all good." Yangtree stepped forward, drew her in for a hug that nearly cracked her ribs. "I was watching TV. I thought it was a backfire. Then Trig came running through, said somebody was shooting, and you were out there." He drew her back. "What the fuck, Ro?"

"My thought exactly. Why would somebody shoot at us?"

"People are batshit." Dobie shrugged. "Maybe one of those government's-our-enemy types. Y'all got those militia types out here."

"Three shots isn't much of a statement."

"It would've been," Trigger pointed out, "if one of them had hit you or Gull."

"Your father's going to hear about this, Ro," Yangtree commented. "You call him now before he does, tell him you're okay."

"Yeah, you're right." She glanced down toward Gull's quarters before she stepped into her own to make the call.

Steaming, Gull endured the sting as Janis cleaned out cuts and scrapes. "What the hell's wrong with her?"

"Since the blood on her appeared to be mostly yours, not much. And I know you're talking about how she thinks or acts, but you'll have to be more specific."

"How can somebody trained to be a team player, who *is* a team player in ninety percent of her life, be the damn opposite the other ten?"

"First, smoke jumpers work as a crew, but you know damn well we all have to think, act and react individually. But more to the point, with Rowan it's defense mechanism, pride, an instinctive hesitation to trust."

"Defense against what?"

"Against having her pride smacked and her trust betrayed. Personally, I think she's dealt pretty well with being abandoned by her mother as an infant. But I don't think anybody ever gets all the way over being abandoned. Okay, I'm going to need to use the tweezers to get some of this debris out. Feel free to curse me."

He said, "Fuck," then gritted his teeth. "You trust every time you get in the door. The spotter, the pilot, yourself. Hell, you have to trust fate isn't going to send a speeding bus your way every time you step out of your house. If you can't take that same leap with another human being, you end up alone."

"I think she's always figured she would. She's got her father, us, a tight pack of people. But a serious, committed one-to-one? She's not sure she believes in them in general, much less for herself."

A bit of gravel hit the bowl with a tiny ting. "I've worked with Ro a long time. She's a proactive optimist in general. In that she—or we, depending—will find a way to make this work. In her personal life, she's a proactive pessimist who has no problem living in the moment because this isn't going to last anyway."

"She's wrong."

"Nobody's proven that to her yet." She glanced up. "Can you?"

"If I don't bleed to death from this sadistic game of Operation you're playing."

"I haven't hit the buzzer yet. You're the first guy, in my opinion, who has a shot at proving her wrong. So don't screw it up. There." She dropped more grit into the bowl. "I think that's it. You lost a lot of skin here, Gull," she began as she applied antiseptic. "Banged up your elbows pretty good, but it could've been a hell of a lot worse."

"Not to knock the results, but I keep wondering why it wasn't a hell of a lot worse."

He looked over at the rap on the door frame. As she had earlier, Rowan leaned on the jamb, but now she had two beers hooked in her fingers. "I brought the patient a beer."

"He could probably use one." Janis bandaged the gouges around his right elbow. "Any word?"

"The cops have the grounds lit up like Christmas. If they've found anything, they're not sharing it yet."

"Okay. You're as done as I can do." Janis picked up the bowl filled with grit, bloodied cloths and cotton swipes. "Take two ibuprofen and call me in the morning."

"Thanks, Janis."

She gave his leg a squeeze as she rose. "None but the brave," she said, then walked out.

Rowan stepped over, offered a beer. "Do you want to fight?"

Watching her over the bottle, he took a long swallow. "Yeah."

"Seems like a waste, considering, but fine. Pick your topic."

"Let's start with the latest—we can always work back—and how you ran, alone, into the open out there."

"We'd decided to try for the barracks, so I did."

"Of the three of us, I'm the fastest—and the one best qualified to draw and evade fire, if there'd been any."

"I said I like overconfidence, but this idea you can dodge bullets might be taking it too far. I can and do take care of myself, Gull. I do it every day. I'm going to keep doing it."

He considered himself a patient, reasonable man—mostly. But she'd just about flipped his last switch.

"The fact you can and do take care of yourself is one of the most appealing things about you. You idiot. Handling yourself on a jump, in a fire or in general, no problem. This was different."

"How?"

"Have you ever been shot at before?"

"No. Have you?"

"First time for both of us, and clearly a situation where you should have trusted me to take care of you."

"I don't want anybody to take care of me."

"You know, that's just stupid. Janis just took care of me, yet somehow my pride and self-esteem remain unbattered and unbowed."

"Bandaging somebody up isn't the same as falling on them like they were a grenade you were going to smother with your own body to save the guys in the trenches. And look at you, Gull. I've barely got a scrape because you took the brunt of that roll instead of letting me take my share."

"I protect what I care about. If you've got a problem with that, you've got a problem with me."

"I protect what I care about," she tossed back at him.

"Were you protecting a fellow smoke jumper, or me?"

"You *are* a fellow smoke jumper."

He stepped closer. "Is it what I do, or who I am? And don't try the 'you are what you do' because I'm a hell of a lot more, and less, and dozens of other things. So are you. I care about you, Rowan. The you who's got a laugh like an Old West saloon girl, the you who picks out constellations in the night sky and smells like peaches. I care about that woman as much as I do the fearless, smart, tireless one who puts her life on the line every time the siren goes off."

Wariness clouded her eyes. "I don't know what to say when you talk like that."

"Is the only thing you see when you look at me another jumper you'll work with for the season?"

"No." She let out an unsteady breath. "No, that's not all, but—"

"Stop at no." He cupped a hand at the back of her neck. "Do us both a favor and stop at no. That's enough for now."

She moved into him, wrapping her arms tight around his waist when their lips met. She felt her equilibrium shift, as if she'd nearly overbalanced on a high ledge. With it came a flutter, under her heart, at the base of her throat. She gripped harder, wanting to find the heat, the buzz, an affirmation that they were both alive and whole.

Nothing more than that, she told herself. It didn't have to be more than that.

"Getting a room's not always enough," Trigger said from the doorway. "Sometimes you gotta close the door."

"Go ahead," Gull invited him, then slid back into the kiss.

"Sorry, they want you in the lounge."

"Who are 'they'?" Rowan demanded, and gave Gull's bottom lip a nip.

"The lieutenant guy and the tree cop. If you're not interested in finding out who the hell *shot* at you tonight, I can tell them, gee, you're out on a date."

Gull lifted his head. "Be right there." He looked at Rowan, ran his hands over her shoulders, down her arms. "My place," he said. "The decision that was so rudely interrupted earlier. My place tonight because it's closer to the lounge."

"Not a bad reason." She picked up the beers, handed him his. "Let's get this done so we can close the door."

DiCicco sat with Quinniock and L.B. in the lounge. Generally at that time of the evening, people sprawled on sofas and chairs watching TV, or gathered around one of the tables playing cards. Somebody might've buzzed up some microwave pizza or popcorn. And there would always be somebody willing to talk fire.

But now the TV screen remained blank and silent, the sofas empty.

L.B. got up from the table, walked quickly over to wrap an arm around Gull and Rowan in turn. "You're okay. That matters most. Next is finding the bastard."

"Did they find anything?" Rowan asked.

"If we could get your statements first." DiCicco gestured to the table. "It should help us get a clearer picture."

"The picture's clear," Rowan countered. "Somebody shot at us. He missed."

"And when you file a fire report, does it just say: 'Fire started. We put it out'?"

"If we could just take it from the beginning." Quinniock held up his hands for peace. "The witness, Dobie Karstain, says he stepped outside the barracks around nine thirty. A few minutes later, he noticed the two of you walking together between the training field and the hangar area, approximately thirty yards from the trees. Does that sound accurate?"

"That's about right." Gull took the lead, as it seemed obvious to him DiCicco put Rowan's back up. "We went for a walk, took a couple of beers, watched the sunset. You'd narrow down where we were if you find the bottles. We dropped them when the shooting started."

He took them through it, step by step.

"Dobie said it sounded like rifle fire," he continued, "and it was coming from the trees. He grew up hunting in rural Kentucky, so I'm inclined to believe he's right. We couldn't see anyone. The first shot fired right around sunset. The whole thing probably only lasted about ten minutes. It seemed longer."

"Have either of you had trouble with anyone, been threatened?" When Rowan merely arched her eyebrows, DiCicco inclined her head. "Other than Leo Brakeman."

"We're a little too busy around here to get into arguments with the locals or tourists."

"Actually, there was an incident with you, Mr. Curry, Ms. Tripp and Mr. Karstain in the spring."

"That would be when Rowan objected to one of those three yahoos' behavior toward her, and them sopping their pride by ganging up on Dobie when he came out of the bar."

"And you kicking their asses," Rowan concluded. "Good times."

"The same holds true on them as it did when we had the vandalism," Gull continued. "It's pretty hard to see them coming back here. And harder still to see any one of them staking us out from the woods and taking shots at us when we went for a walk. We're in and out all the damn time anyway. Together, separately. It's stretching it even more to figure those bozos from Illinois came all the way back, then got lucky when Ro and I walked out to give them some target practice."

"How do you know they're from Illinois?" DiCicco asked.

"Because that's what the plate on the pickup said—and I did some checking on it after the ready room business."

"You never told me that."

Gull shrugged at Rowan. "It didn't amount to anything to tell you. The big guy—and he was the alpha—owns a garage out in Rockford. He's an asshole, and he's had a few bumps for assaults—bar fights his specialty—but nothing major." He shrugged again when DiCicco studied him. "The Internet. You can find out anything if you keep looking."

"All right. You two have recently become involved," Di-Cicco said. "Is there anyone who might resent that? Any former relationship?"

"I don't date the kind of woman who'd take a shot at me." He gave Rowan the eye. "Until maybe now."

"I shoot all my former lovers, so your fate's already set."

"Only if we get to the former part." He covered her hand with his. "It was either a local with a grudge against one or both of us specially, or the base in general. Or a wacko who wanted to shoot up a federal facility."

"A terrorist?"

"I think a terrorist would've used more ammo," Gull said to DiCicco. "But any way you slice it, he was a crap shot.

Unless he's a really good shot and was just trying to scare and intimidate."

Rowan's gaze sharpened. "I didn't think of that."

"I think a lot. I can't swear to it, but I think the closest one hit about six or seven feet away from where we hit the ground. That's not a comfortable distance when bullets are involved, but it's a distance. Another sounded like it hit metal, the hangar. Way above our heads. Maybe it'll turn out to be a couple of kids on a dare. Smoke jumpers think they're so cool, let's go make them piss their pants."

"It's a theory," he claimed when Rowan rolled her eyes.

"Lieutenant." A uniformed cop stepped in.

"Hi, Barry."

"Ro. Glad you're okay. Sir, we found the weapon, or what we believe to be the weapon."

"Where?"

"About twenty yards into the trees. A Remington 700 model—bolt action. The special edition. It was covered up with leaves."

"Stupid," Rowan mumbled. "Stupid to leave it there."

"More stupid if it's got a brass name plaque on the stock," L.B. said. "I went hunting with Leo Brakeman last fall, and he carried a special edition 700. He was real proud of it."

Rowan's hand balled into a fist under Gull's. "So much for theories."

When DiCicco and Quinniock went out to examine the weapon, L.B. walked over to the coffeemaker.

"You know," Ro said, "she told those lies to her father. All those lies, and they drove him to come out here with a gun and try to kill me."

"I'd say you're half right." L.B. sat with his coffee, sighed. "The lies drove him to come out here with a gun, but, like I said, I've been hunting with Leo. I saw him take down a buck with that rifle, at thirty yards with the buck on the run. If he'd wanted to put a bullet in you, you'd have a bullet in you."

"I guess it was my lucky day then."

"Something snapped in him. I'm not excusing him, Ro. There's no excuse for this. But something's snapped in him. What the hell's Irene going to do now? Her daughter murdered, and her husband likely locked up, an infant to care for. She hasn't even buried Dolly yet, and now this."

"I'm sorry for them. For all of them."

"Yeah, it's a damn sorry situation. I'm going to go see if the cops will tell me what happens next." He went out, leaving his untouched coffee behind.

18

Too wound up to sit, Rowan pushed up, wandered the room, peeked out the window, circled back. Gull propped his feet on the chair she'd vacated and decided to drink L.B.'s abandoned coffee.

"I want to *do* something," Rowan complained. "Just sitting here doesn't feel right. How can you just sit here?"

"I'm doing something."

"Drinking coffee doesn't count as something."

"I'm sitting here, I'm drinking coffee. And I'm thinking. I'm thinking if it's Brakeman's rifle, and if Brakeman was the one shooting it, did he just go stand in the trees and assume you'd eventually wander out into range?"

"I don't know if it had to be me. He's pissed at all of us, just mostly at me."

"Okay, possible." He found the coffee bitter, wished for a little sugar to cut the edge. But just didn't feel like getting up for it. "So Brakeman stands in the woods with his rifle, staking out the base. He gets lucky and we come along. If he's as good a shot as advertised, why did he miss?"

"Because it has to be a hell of a lot different to shoot a

human being than a buck. Nerves. Or he couldn't bring himself to kill me—us—and decided to scare us to death instead."

"Also possible. Why leave the weapon? Why leave a special edition, which had to cost, which he cared enough about
to put his name on, under a pile of leaves? Why leave it behind
at all when he had to know the cops would do a search?"

"Panic. Impulse. He wasn't thinking clearly—obviously.
Hide it, get out, come back for it another time. And maybe
take a few more shots." She stopped, rubbed at the tension in
the back of her neck as she studied Gull. "And you don't think
Leo Brakeman shot at us."

"I think it might be interesting to know who had access to
his gun. Who might've liked causing him trouble, and
wouldn't feel too bad about scaring you doing it." He sipped at
the coffee. "But it could've been Brakeman following impulse,
getting lucky, being nervous and panicking."

"When you say it like that, it's a lot to swallow."

She plopped down in L.B.'s chair as Gull had opened her
mind to alternatives. And thinking *was* doing, she reminded
herself.

"I guess his wife would have access, but I have a hard time
seeing her doing this. Plus, I've never heard of her going hunting or target shooting. She's more the church-bake-sale type.
And it's easier to believe she might panic because she's more
the quiet, even a little timid, type. If you get past the first step,
her actually coming out here with a rifle, the rest goes down.

"Maybe a double bluff," she considered aloud. "He left the
rifle so he could say, hey, would anybody be that stupid? But I
don't know if he'd be that cagey. I just don't know these people
very well. We've never had much interaction, even when Dolly
worked here. Which means I don't know if anybody's got a
grudge against Brakeman, or would know enough to use him
as a fall guy. It's easier if it's Brakeman. Then it would be
done, and there wouldn't be anything to worry about."

"It's up to the cops anyway. We can let it go."

"That's passive, and that's what's driving me crazy. Who
killed Dolly? That's the first question. Jesus, Gull, what if her
father did?"

"Why?"

"I don't know." She hooked her feet around the legs of the

chair, leaned forward. "Say they had a fight. Say she's coming back from Florence—if she got work there like she claimed—gets the flat. Calls her father to come fix it. I can't picture Dolly with a lug wrench and jack. He comes out, and they get into it over something. Her dumping the baby on her mother so much, maybe having the kid in the first place, or just dragging him out that time of night. Things get out of hand. She takes a fall, lands wrong, breaks her neck. He freaks, puts her body in the truck. He's got to figure out what to do, decides to destroy the evidence—and the rest follows. He knows the area, the trails, and he's strong enough to have carried her in."

"Plausible," Gull decided. "Maybe he confesses to his wife, and you get part two. There's another hypothesis."

"Share."

"You said you didn't know Dolly that well, but you had definite opinions about her. Jim died last August. We're moving toward July. Is she the type to be without a man for a year?"

Rowan opened her mouth, shut it again, then sat back. "No. And why didn't I think of that? No, she'd never go this long without a man. There's a stronger case for that knowing that her whole I-found-Jesus deal was bogus."

"Maybe the current guy's in Florence. Maybe that's why she got work there, or said she did. Or maybe they just met up in a motel on Twelve or thereabouts."

"Lovers' quarrel, and *he* kills her. If there's a he. There had to be—it's Dolly. Or her father found out, and so on. But if she had one on the line in Florence, why come back here anyway? Why not just go there, be with him? Because he's married," Rowan said before Gull could comment. "She fooled around with married men all the time."

"If so, it's more likely he's in Missoula. She came back here, got work here at the base. She'd want to be close to whoever she was sleeping with. Say, he's married, or there's some other reason why they can't be open about a relationship. Then you have the meet-up somewhere away from where people know you, would recognize you."

"You're good at this."

"It's like playing a game. You work the levels." He took her hand again. "Except it's not characters, it's real people."

"It still feels better to play it through. And here's another thing. Dolly wasn't nearly as smart or clever as she liked to think. If she was sleeping with somebody, she'd have dropped hints. Maybe to Marg. More likely to Lynn. She was going to church, so maybe to somebody she made friends with there."

"It would be interesting to find out."

"It would." She needed to move again, do more than think. "Why don't we go outside, see what's going on?"

"Good idea."

"Quinniock likes me, I think. Maybe he'll give us a couple of nibbles."

When they went out, she spotted Barry heading toward his patrol car. "Hey, Barry. Is Lieutenant Quinniock around?"

"He and Agent DiCicco just left. Do you need something, Ro?"

She gave Gull a quick glance. "I could sure use a little reassurance. I'd sleep better tonight."

"I can tell you the weapon we found is Leo Brakeman's. The lieutenant and DiCicco are on their way to his place to talk to him."

"Talk."

"That's the first step. I had to back up Little Bear when he told them Leo's a damn good shot. I don't know if it makes you feel better or not, but I don't think he was aiming for you."

"It doesn't make me feel worse."

"He was wrong blaming you for what happened to Dolly. Some people just can't get their lives together."

"I meant to ask Lieutenant Quinniock if they found out where she'd gotten work. Maybe somebody she knew or met there killed her."

Barry hesitated, then shrugged. "It doesn't look like she was working. It's nothing for you to worry about, Ro."

"Barry." She put a hand on his arm. "Come on. I'm in the middle of this whether I want to be or not. What was she doing coming back from down that way if she didn't have a job?"

"I can't say for sure, and I shouldn't say at all." He puffed out his cheeks as she kept looking into his eyes. "All I know is the police artist is scheduled to work with somebody tomorrow. The word is it's a maid from some motel down off Twelve.

Whoever he is, if we can ID him, the lieutenant's going to want to talk to him."

"Thanks, Barry." She moved in to hug him. "Erin got lucky with you. Tell her I said so."

"I'll do that. And you don't worry. We're looking out for you."

Gull slipped his hands in his pockets as Barry got in the car. "You didn't come down on him for saying he was looking out for you."

"Cops are supposed to look out for everybody. Besides, Barry gets a pass. He was my first. Actually we were each other's firsts, a scenario I don't necessarily recommend unless both participants have a solid sense of humor. That was several years before he met Erin, his wife, and the mother of his two kids."

"My first was Becca Rhodes. She was a year older and experienced. It went quite smoothly."

"Are you still friends with Becca Rhodes?"

"I haven't seen her since high school."

"See? Humor wins out. Dolly never worked in Florence," Rowan added. "Our little what-if session hit a mark. A man, a motel—possibly a murderer." She tipped her head back, found the sky. "I feel less useless and victimized. That counts for a lot. I'm going to talk to Lynn first chance I get, just to see if Dolly dropped any crumbs."

Time to put it away for the night, Gull decided, and draped an arm over her shoulders. "Pick one out for me. A constellation. Not the Dippers. Even I can find them. Usually."

"Okay. Then you'll spot Ursa Minor there." She took his hand, used it to outline the connection of stars. "Now, the stars in this one aren't very bright, but if you follow that west, connect the dots, going south and over—it winds around the Little Dipper, see? There. You've got Draco. The dragon. It seems apt for a couple of smoke jumpers."

"Yeah, I get it. Pretty cool. Now that we've got our constellation, we just need to decide on our song."

He lightened her load, she thought. No doubt about it. "You're so full of it, Gulliver."

"Only because I have so much depth."

"Hell." She turned into him, indulged them both with a deep, dreamy kiss. "Let's go to bed."

"You read my mind."

"DID YOU FIND who killed my girl?" Leo demanded the minute he opened the door.

"Let's go inside and sit down," Quinniock suggested.

He and DiCicco had discussed their approach on the drive, and, as agreed, Quinniock took the lead. "Mrs. Brakeman, we'd like to talk with both of you."

Irene Brakeman linked her hands together at her heart. "It's about Dolly. You know who hurt Dolly."

"We're pursuing several avenues of investigation." DiCicco kept her voice clipped. It wasn't quite good cop/bad cop, but more cold cop/warm cop. "There are some matters we need to clear up with you. To start with, Mr. Brakeman—"

Quinniock touched a hand to her arm. "Why don't we all sit down? I know it's late, but we'd appreciate if you gave us some time."

"We answered questions. We let you go through Dolly's room, through her things." Leo continued to bar the door with his knuckles white on the knob. "We were going up to bed. If you don't have anything new to tell us, just leave us in peace."

"There is no peace until we know who did this to Dolly." Irene's voice pitched, broke. "Go up to bed if you want to," Irene told her husband with a tinge of disgust. "I'll talk to the police. Go on upstairs and shake your fists at God, see if that helps. Please, come in."

She moved forward, a small woman who pushed her burly husband aside so that he stepped back, his head hung down like a scolded child's.

"I'm just tired, Reenie. I'm so damn tired. And you're wearing yourself to the bone, tending the baby and worrying."

"We're not asked to lift more than we can carry. So we'll lift this. Do you want some coffee, or tea, or anything?"

"Don't you worry about that, Mrs. Brakeman." Quinniock took a seat in the living room on a chair covered with blue and red flowers. "I know this is hard."

"We can't even bury her yet. They said you need to keep

her awhile more, so we can't give our daughter a Christian burial."

"We'll release her to you as soon as we can. Mrs. Brakeman, the last time we spoke, you said Dolly got a job in Florence, as a cook."

"That's right." She twisted her fingers together in her lap, a working woman's hands wearing a plain gold band. "She felt like she didn't want to take a job in Missoula after what went on at the base. I think she was embarrassed. She was embarrassed, Leo," Irene snapped as he started to object. "Or she should have been."

"They never treated her decent there."

"You know that's not true." She spoke more quietly now, briefly touched a hand to his. "You can't take her word as gospel now that she's gone when you know Dolly didn't tell the real truth half the time or more. They gave her a chance there," she said to Quinniock when Leo lapsed into brooding silence. "And Reverend Latterly and I vouched for her. She shamed herself, and us. She got work down there in Florence," Irene continued after she'd firmed quivering lips. "She was a good cook, our girl. It was something she liked, even when she was just a little thing. She could be a good worker when she put her mind to it. The hours were hard, especially with the baby, but the pay was good, and she said she could go places."

"You didn't remember the name of the restaurant when we spoke before," DiCicco prompted.

"I guess she never mentioned it." Irene pressed her lips together again. "I was angry with her about what she did to Rowan Tripp, and embarrassed my own self. It's hard knowing Dolly and I were at odds when she died. It's hard knowing that."

"I have to tell you, both of you, that Agent DiCicco and I have contacted or gone to every restaurant, diner, coffee shop between here and Florence, and Dolly didn't work in any of them."

"I don't understand."

"She wasn't working in a restaurant," DiCicco said briskly. "She didn't get a job, didn't leave here the night she died to go to work."

"Hell she didn't," Leo protested.

"On the night she died, and on the afternoon prior, the evening prior to that, Dolly spent several hours in a room at the Big Sky Motel, off Highway Twelve."

"That's a lie."

"Leo, hush." Irene gripped her hands together tighter.

"Several witnesses identified her photograph," Quinniock continued. "I'm sorry. She didn't spend those hours alone. She met a man there, the same man each time. We have a witness who'll be working with our police artist to reconstruct his face."

With tears trickling down her face, Irene nodded. "I was afraid of it. I knew in my heart she was lying, but I was so upset with her. I didn't care. Just go on then, I thought. Go on and do what you want, and I'll have this baby to tend. Then, after . . . after it happened, I took that out of my mind. I told myself I'd been harsh and judgmental, a cold mother.

"I knew she was lying," she said, turning to her husband. "I knew all the signs. But I couldn't let myself believe it when she was dead. I just couldn't have that inside me."

"Do you have any idea who she was involved with?"

"I swear to you I don't. But I think maybe it'd been going on awhile now. I know the signs. The way she'd whisper on the phone, or how she'd say she just needed to go out for a drive and clear her head, or had to run some errands so could I watch Shiloh? And she'd come home again with that look in her eye."

She let out a shuddering breath. "She never meant to change." Dissolving, Irene turned to press her face to Leo's shoulder. "Maybe she just couldn't."

"Why do we have to know this?" Leo demanded. "Why do you have to tell us this? You don't leave us anything."

"I'm sorry, but Dolly was with this man the night she died. We need to identify him and question him."

"He killed her. This man she gave herself to, this man she lied to us about."

"We need to question him," Quinniock repeated. "If you have any idea who she was meeting, we need to know."

"She lied to us. We don't know anything. We don't have anything. Just leave us alone."

"There's something else, Mr. Brakeman, we need to discuss." DiCicco took the ball. "At approximately nine thirty tonight, Rowan Tripp and Gulliver Curry were fired on while walking on the base."

"That's nothing to do with us."

"On the contrary, a Remington 700 special edition rifle was found hidden in the woods flanking the base. It has your name engraved in a plaque on the stock."

"You're accusing me of trying to kill that woman? You come into my home, tell me my daughter was a liar and a whore and say I'm a killer?"

"It's your gun, Mr. Brakeman, and you recently threatened Ms. Tripp."

"My daughter was *murdered*, and she . . . My rifle's in the gun safe. I haven't had it out in weeks."

"If that's the case, we'd like you to show us." DiCicco got to her feet.

"I'll show you, then I want you out of my house."

He lunged up, stomped his way back to the kitchen to yank open a door that led to a basement.

Or a man cave, DiCicco thought as she followed. Dead animal heads hung on the paneled wall in a wildlife menagerie that loomed over the oversized recliner and lumpy sofa. The table that fronted the sofa showed scars from years of boot heels and faced an enormous flat-screen television.

The room boasted an ancient refrigerator she imagined held manly drinks, a worktable for loading shot into shells, a utility shelf that held boxes of clay pigeons, shooting vests, hunting caps—and, oddly, she thought, several framed family photos, including a large one of a pretty baby girl with one of those elasticized pink bows circling her bald head.

A football lamp, a computer and piles of paperwork sat on a gray metal desk shoved in a corner. Above it hung a picture of Leo and several other men beside what she thought was a 747 aircraft, reminding her he worked at the airport as a mechanic.

And against the side wall stood a big, orange-doored gun safe.

Pumping off waves of heat and resentment, Leo marched to the safe, spun the dial for the combination, wrenched it open.

DiCicco had no problems with guns; in fact she believed in them. But the small arsenal inside the safe had her eyes widening. Rifles, shotguns, handguns—bolt action, semiauto, revolvers, under and overs, scopes. All showing the gloss of the well-cleaned, well-oiled, well-tended weapon.

But her scan didn't turn up the weapon in question, and her hand edged toward her own as Leo Brakeman's breathing went short and quick.

"You have an excellent collection of firearms, Mr. Brakeman, but you seem to be missing a Remington 700."

"Somebody stole it."

Her hand closed over the butt of her weapon when he whirled around, his face red, his fists clenched.

"Somebody broke in here and stole it."

"There's no record of you reporting a break-in." Quinniock stepped up.

"Because I didn't *know*. Somebody's doing this to us. You have to find out who's doing this to us."

"Mr. Brakeman, you're going to have to come with us now." She didn't want to draw on the man, hoped she wouldn't have to, but DiCicco readied to do so.

"You're not taking me out of my home."

"Leo." Quinniock spoke calmly. "Don't make it worse now. You come quietly, and we'll go in and talk about this. Or I'm going to have to cuff you and take you in forcibly."

"Leo." Irene simply collapsed onto a step. "My God, Leo."

"I didn't do anything. Irene, as God is my witness. I've never lied to you in my life, Reenie. I didn't do anything."

"Then let's go in and talk this out." Quinniock moved a step closer, laid a hand on Leo's quivering shoulder. "Let's try to get to the bottom of it."

"Somebody's doing this to us. I never shot at anybody out at the base, or anywhere else." He jerked away from Quinniock's hand. "I'll walk out on my own."

"All right, Leo. That would be best."

Stiff-legged, he walked toward the steps. He stopped, reached for his wife's hands. "Irene, on my life, I didn't shoot at anybody. I need you to believe me."

"I believe you." But she dropped her gaze when she said it.

"You need to lock up now. You be sure to lock up the house. I'll be home as soon as we straighten this out."

ROWAN GOT THE WORD when she slipped into the cookhouse kitchen the next morning.

Lynn set down the hot bin of pancakes she carried, then wrapped Rowan in a hug. "I'm glad you're all right. I'm glad everybody's all right."

"Me too."

"I don't know what to think. I don't know what to say." Shaking her head, she picked up the bin again. "I have to get these on the buffet."

At the stove, Marg scooped bacon from the grill, set it aside to drain before shifting over to pour a glass of juice. She held it out to Rowan. "Drink what's good for you," she ordered, then turned back to pull a batch of fresh biscuits from the oven. "They picked up Leo Brakeman last night."

Rowan drank the juice. "Do you know what he's saying?"

"I don't know a lot, but I know they talked to him for a long time last night, and they're holding him. I know he's saying he didn't do it. I'm feeling like Lynn. I don't know what to think."

"I think it was stupid to leave the rifle. Then again, the cops would do their CSI thing since they found at least one of the bullets. Then again, with his skill, at that range, he could've put all three of them into me."

"Don't say that."

At the crack of Marg's voice, Rowan walked over, rubbed a hand down Marg's back. "He didn't, so I can come in here and drink a juice combo of carrots, apples, pears and parsnips."

"You missed the beets."

"So that's what that was. They're better in juice than on a plate."

Marg moved aside to take a carton of eggs out of the refrigerator. "Go on in and eat your breakfast. I've got hungry mouths to feed."

"I wanted to ask you. I wanted to ask both of you," she said when Lynn came back with another empty tub. "Was Dolly seeing someone? Did she say anything about being involved?"

"She knew better than to start that business up around me," Marg began, "when she kept saying how she was next thing to a grieving widow, and finding her comfort in God and her baby. But I doubt she stepped outside on a break to giggle on her cell phone because she'd called Dial-A-Joke."

"She didn't tell me anything, not directly," Lynn put in. "But she said, a couple of times, how lucky I was to have a daddy for my kids, and how she knew her baby needed one, too. She said she spent a lot of time praying on it, and had faith God would provide."

Lynn shifted, obviously uncomfortable. "I don't like talking about her this way, but the thing is, she was a little sly when she said it, you know? And I thought, well, she's already got her eye on a candidate. It wasn't very nice of me, but it's what I thought."

"Did you tell the cops?"

"They just asked if she had a boyfriend, and like that. I told them I didn't know of anybody. I wouldn't have felt right telling them I thought she was looking for one. Do you think I should have?"

"You told them what you knew. I think I'm going to go get in my run, work up an appetite." She saw Lynn bite her lip. "The cops have the rifle, and they have Brakeman. I can't spend my life indoors. I'll be back with an appetite."

She walked outside. The shudder that went through her as she glanced toward the trees only stiffened her spine. She couldn't live her life worried she had a target on her back. She put on the sunglasses—the ones Cards found where Gull had tackled her—and started the walk toward the track.

She could run on the road, she considered, but she was on the jump list, first load. The clouds over the mountains confirmed the forecast from the morning briefing. *Cumulus overtimus*, she thought, knowing the buildup could hurl lightning. She'd likely jump fire today, and get plenty of that overtime.

Better to stay on base in case.

"Hey." Gull caught up with her at a light jog. "We running?"

"I thought you had things to do."

"I said I wanted coffee, maybe some calories. And that was

mostly to give you time to talk to Marg and Lynn. A straight three miles?"

"I . . ." Behind him, she saw Matt, Cards and Trigger come out of the cookhouse and head in her direction. Her eyes narrowed. "Did Lynn go in and tell the dining hall I was heading to the track?"

"What do you think?"

Now Dobie, Stovic and Gibbons herded out.

"Did she call up the Marines while she was at it? I don't need a bunch of bodyguards."

"What you've got is people who care about you. Are you really going to carp about that?"

"No, but I don't see why . . ." Yangtree, Libby and Janis headed out from the direction of the gym. "For Christ's sake, in another minute the whole unit's going to be out here."

"It wouldn't surprise me."

"Half of you aren't even in running gear," she called out.

Trigger, in jeans and boots, reached her first. "We don't wear running gear on a fire."

She considered him. "Nice save."

"When you run, we all run," Cards told her. "At least everybody who's not on duty with something else. We voted on it."

"I didn't get a vote." She jabbed a finger at Gull. "Did you get a vote?"

"I got to add mine to the unanimous results this morning, so your vote is moot."

"Fine. Dandy. We run."

She took off for the track, then geared up to a sprint the minute she hit its surface. Just to see who'd keep up, besides Gull, who matched her stride for stride. She heard the scramble and pounding of feet behind her, then the hoots and catcalls as Libby zipped up to pass.

"Have a heart, Ro," she shouted. "We've got old men like Yangtree out here."

"Who're you calling old!" He kicked it up a notch, edged out of the pack on the turn.

"Gimps like Cards hobbling back there in his boots."

Amused, Ro glanced over her shoulder to see Cards shoot

up his middle finger. And Dobie begin to run backward to taunt him.

She cut her pace back a bit because he was hobbling just a little, then laughed herself nearly breathless when Gibbons jogged by with Janis riding on his shoulders pumping her arms in the air.

"Bunch of lunatics," Rowan decided.

"Yeah. The best bunch of lunatics I know." Gull's grin widened as Southern puffed by with Dobie on board. "Want a ride?"

"I'll spare you the buck and a half on your back. Show them how it's done, Fast Feet. You know you wanna."

He gave her a pat on the ass and took off like a bullet to a chorus of cheers, insults and whistles.

By the time she made her three, Gull was sprawled on the grass, braced on his elbows to watch the show. Highly entertained, she stood, hands on hips, doing the same. Until she saw her father drive up.

"It's a good thing he didn't get here sooner," she commented, "or he'd have been out on the track, too."

"I'm betting he can hold his own."

"Yeah, he can." She started toward him, trying for an easy smile. But the expression on his face told her easy wouldn't work.

He grabbed her, pulled her hard against him.

"I'm okay. I told you I was A-OK."

"I didn't come to see for myself last night because you asked me not to, because you said you had to talk to the cops, and needed to get some sleep afterward." He drew her back, took a long study of her face. "But I needed to see for myself."

"Then you can stop worrying. The cops have Brakeman. I texted you they found his gun and were going to get him. And they got him."

"I want to see him. I want to look him in the eye when I ask him if he thinks hurting my daughter will bring his back. I want to ask him that before I bloody him."

"I appreciate the sentiment. I really do. But he didn't hurt me, and he's not going to hurt me. Look at that bunch." She gestured toward the track. "I came out here for my run, and every one of them came out of their various holes."

"All for one," he murmured. "I need to talk to your boy-friend."

"He's not my . . . Dad, I'm not sixteen."

"Boyfriend's the easiest term for me. Have you had breakfast?"

"Not yet."

"Go on in, and I'll sweet-talk Marg into feeding me with you—when I'm done talking to your boyfriend."

"Just use his name. That should be easy."

Lucas merely smiled, kissed her forehead. "I'll be in in a minute."

He crossed over to Gull, slapped hands with Gibbons, gave Yangtree a pat on the back as the man bent over to catch his breath.

"I want to talk to you a minute," he said to Gull.

"Sure." Gull pushed to his feet. His eyebrows lifted when Lucas walked away from the group, but he followed.

"I heard what you did for Rowan. You took care of her."

"I'd appreciate it if you wouldn't say that to her."

"I know better, but I'm saying it to you. I'm saying I'm grateful. She's the world to me. She's the goddamn universe to me. If you ever need anything—"

"Mr. Tripp—"

"Lucas."

"Lucas, first, I figure mostly anyone would've done what I did, which wasn't that big a deal. If Rowan's instincts had kicked in first, she'd have knocked me down, and I'd've been under her. And second, I didn't do it so you'd owe me a favor."

"You scraped a lot of bark off those arms."

"They'll heal up, and they're not keeping me off the jump list. So. No big."

Lucas nodded, looked off toward the trees. "Am I supposed to ask what your intentions are regarding my daughter?"

"God, I hope not."

"Because to my way of thinking, if you were just in it for the fun, me saying I owed you wouldn't put your back up. So I'm going to give you that favor whether you want it or not. And here it is." He looked back into Gull's eyes. "If you're serious about her, don't let her push you back. You'll have to hold on until she believes you. She's a hard sell, but once she believes, she sticks.

"So." Lucas held out a hand, shook Gull's. "I'm going to go have breakfast with my girl. Are you coming?"

"Yeah. Shortly," Gull decided.

He stood alone a moment, absorbing the fact that Iron Man Tripp had just given his blessing. And thinking over just what he wanted to do with it.

He mulled it over, taking his time walking toward the cookhouse. The siren sounded just before he reached it. Cursing the missed chance of breakfast, Gull turned on his heel and ran for the ready room.

19

After forty-eight hours battling a two-hundred-acre wildfire in the Beaverhead National Forest, getting shot at a few times added up to small change. Once she'd bolted down the last of a sandwich she'd ratted away, Rowan worked with her team, lighting fusees in a bitter attempt to kick the angry fire back before it rode west toward the national battlefield.

The head changed direction three times in two days, snarling at the rain of retardant and spitting it out.

The initial attack, a miserable failure, moved into a protracted, vicious extended one.

"Gull, Matt, Libby, you're on spots. Cards, Dobie, we're going to move west, take down any snags. Dig and cut and smother. We stop her here."

Nobody spoke as they pushed, shoved, lashed the backfire east. The world was smoke and heat and noise with every inch forward a victory. About time, Rowan thought, about damn time their luck changed.

The snag she cut fell with a crack. She positioned to slice it into smaller, less appetizing logs. They'd shovel and drag limbs and coals away from the green, into the black, into a bone pile.

Starve her, Rowan thought. Just keep starving her.

She straightened a moment to stretch her back.

She saw it happen, so fast she couldn't shout out much less leap forward. A knife-point of wood blew out of the cut Cards was carving and shot straight into his face.

She dropped her saw, rushing toward him even as he yelped in shock and pain and lost his footing.

"How bad? How bad?" she shouted, grabbing him as he staggered. She saw for herself the point embedded in his cheek, half an inch below his right eye. Blood spilled down to his jaw.

"For fuck's sake," he managed. "Get it out."

"Hold on. Just hold on."

Dobie trotted up. "What're you two . . . Jesus, Cards, how the hell did you do that?"

"Hold his hands," Rowan ordered as she dug into her pack.

"What?"

"Get behind him and hold his hands down. I think it's going to hurt when I pull it out." She set a boot on either side of Cards's legs, pulled off her right glove. She clamped her fingers on the inch of jagged wood protruding from his cheek. "On three now. Get ready. One. Two—"

She yanked on two, watched the blood slop out, watched his eyes go a little glassy. Quickly, she pressed the pad of gauze she'd taken out of her pack to the wound.

"You've got a hell of a hole in your face," she told him.

"You said on three."

"Yeah, well, I lost count. Dobie, hold the pad, keep the pressure on. I have to clean that out."

"We don't have time for that," Cards objected. "Just tape it over. We'll worry about it later."

"Two minutes. Lean back against Dobie."

She tossed the bloody pad aside, poured water over the wound, hoping to flush out tiny splinters. "And try not to scream like a girl," she added, following up the water with a hefty dose of peroxide.

"Goddamn it, Ro! Goddamn, fucking shit!"

Ruthless, she waited while the peroxide bubbled out dirt and wood, then doused it with more water. She coated another pad with antibiotic cream, added another, then taped it over what she noted was a hole in his cheek the size of a marble.

"We can get you out to the west."

"Screw that. I'm not packing out. It was just a damn splinter."

"Yeah." Dobie held up the three-inch spear of wood. "If you're fifty feet tall. I saved it for you."

"Holy shit, that's a fucking missile. I got hit with a wood missile. In the face. My luck," he said in disgust, "has been for shit all season." He waved off Rowan's extended hand. "I can stand on my own."

He wobbled a moment, then steadied.

"Take some of the ibuprofen in your PG bag. If you're sure you're fit, I want you to go switch off to scout spots. You're not running a saw, Cards. You know better. Switch off, or I'll have to report the injury to Ops."

"I'm not leaving this here until she's dead."

"Then switch off. If that hole in your ugly face bleeds through those pads, have one of your team change it."

"Yeah, yeah." He touched his fingers to the pad. "You'd think I cut off a leg," he muttered, but headed down the line. When he'd gone far enough, she pulled out her radio, contacted Gull. "Cards is headed to you. He had a minor injury. I want one of you to head up to me, and he'll take your place down there."

"Copy that."

"Okay, Dobie, get that saw working. And watch out for flying wood missiles. I don't want any more drama."

The backfire held. It took another ten hours, but reports from head to tail called the fire contained.

The sunset ignited the sky as she hiked back to camp. It reminded her of watching the sun set with Gull. Of bullets and blind hate. She dropped down to eat, wishing she could find that euphoria that always rose in her once a fire surrendered.

Yangtree sat down beside her. "We're going to get some food in our bellies before we start mop-up. Ops has eight on tap for that. It's up to you since he was on your team, but I think Cards should demob, get that wound looked at proper."

"Agreed. I'm going to pack out with him. If they can send eight, let's spring eight from camp."

"My thinking, too. I tell you, Ro, I say I'm too old for this, but I'm starting to mean it. I might just ask your daddy for a job come the end of the season."

"Hell. Cards is the one with the hole in his face."

He looked toward the west, the setting sun, the black mountain. "I'm thinking I may want to see what it's like to sit on my own porch on a summer night, drink a beer, with some female company if I can get it, and not have to think about fire."

"You'll always think about fire, and sitting on a porch, you'd wish you were here."

He gave her a pat on the knee as he rose. "It might be time to find out."

She had to browbeat Cards into packing out. Smoke jumpers, she thought, treated injuries like points of pride, or challenges.

He sulked on the flight home.

"I get why he's in a mood." Gull settled down beside her. "Why are you?"

"Sixty hours on fire might have something to do with it."

"No. That's why you're whipped and more vulnerable to the mood, but not the reason for the mood."

"Here's what I don't get, hotshot: why, after a handful of months, you think you know me so damn well. And another is why you spend so much time psychoanalyzing people."

"Those are both pretty easy to get. The first is it may be a handful of months, but people who live and work together, particularly under intense conditions, tend to know and understand each other quicker than those who don't. Add sleeping together, and it increases the learning curve. Second."

He pulled out a bag of shelled peanuts, offered her some, then shrugged and dug in himself when she just glowered at him.

"Second," he repeated. "People interest me, so I like figuring them out."

He munched nuts. Whatever her mood or the reasons for it, he wasn't inclined to lower his to match it. A hot shower and hot food, followed by a bed with a warm woman in it, ranged in his immediate future.

Who could ask for better?

"You're starting to think about what's waiting back at base. All the crap we've been too busy to worry about. What's happened while we were catching fire, if the cops charged Brakeman, found Dolly's killer. If not, what next?"

He glanced over toward Cards, who snored with his head on his pack, a fresh bandage snowy white against his soot-smeared face. "And you're mixing in worrying how bad Cards messed his face up. Whatever Yangtree and you talked about before we demobbed topped it off."

She said nothing for a moment. "Know-it-alls are irritating." Leaning her head back, she closed her eyes. "I'm getting some sleep."

"Funny, I think having somebody understand you is comforting."

She opened one eye, cool, crystal blue. "I didn't say you were an understand-it-all."

"You've got me there." Gull shut his eyes as well, and dropped off.

ROWAN HEADED STRAIGHT to the barracks after unloading her gear. To settle down, Gull decided, as much as clean up. Maybe she'd label it as "taking care of her," and that was too damn bad, but he postponed his own agenda to hunt down L.B.

He waited in Operations while L.B. coordinated with the mop-up crew boss.

"Got a minute?"

"For the first time in three days, I've got a few. I'm stepping out," L.B. announced, then jerked his head toward the door. "What's on your mind?"

"You telling me the status of things around here so I can pass it on to Rowan."

"I don't know how much they're keeping me in the loop, but let's find a place to sit down."

WHEN ROWAN STEPPED OUT of the bathroom wrapped in a towel, a still filthy Gull was sitting on the floor.

"Is something wrong with your shower?"

"I don't know. I haven't been in it yet."

"I've got a lot to do before I'm done, so we'll have to reschedule the hot-sex portion of the evening."

"You've got a one-track mind, Swede. I like the track, but there are more than one."

She opened a drawer, selected yoga pants and a top.

"I'll give you the rundown," Gull began. "Trigger dragged Cards to the infirmary. The wound's clean. No infection, but it's pretty damn deep. Plastic surgeon recommended, and after some bullshit, he's going into town to see one in the morning. He wants to keep his pretty face."

"That's good." She pulled on the pants and top without bothering with underwear—something Gull appreciated whatever the circumstances. "And it'll be fun to rag him about plastic surgery," she added, stepping back into the bath to hang the towel. "We ought to get some fun out of it."

"Trigger already suggested they suck the lard out of his ass while they're at it."

"That's a start."

"They've charged Leo Brakeman."

He watched her jerk, just a little, then cross over to sit on the side of the bed. "Okay. All right."

"His rifle, prior threats and the fact he can't verify his whereabouts for the time of the shooting. He admitted he and his wife had a fight, and he went out to drive around for a couple hours. He'd only just gotten back when the cops showed up at the door."

"His wife could've lied for him."

"He never asked her to. Some of this came from the cops, some of it's via Marg. I could separate it out, but being a know-it-all, I figure Marg's intel is as solid as the cops'."

"You'd be right."

"They fought about him coming out here, going off on you. About Dolly in general. I think losing a child either sticks the parents together like cement, or rips them up."

"My father had a brother. A younger one. You probably know that, too, since you studied Iron Man."

Gull said nothing, gave her room. "He died when he was three of some weird infection. He'd never been what you'd call robust, and, well, they couldn't fix it. I guess it cemented my grandparents. Has he admitted it? Brakeman?"

"No. He's claiming he was driving around, just tooling the backroads, that somebody broke in, took his rifle. Somebody's framing him. His wife finally convinced him to get a lawyer. They held the bail hearing this morning. She put up their house to post his bond."

"Jesus."

"He's not coming back around here, Ro."

"That's not what I mean. She's dealing with more than anybody should have to deal with, and it just doesn't feel like any of it's her doing. I don't know how she's standing up to it."

"She's dealing with more yet. They identified a man Dolly met at a motel off Twelve the night she died. One she met there a number of times in the past few months. Reverend Latterly."

"Their pastor? For the love of—" She broke off, slumped back. "Dolly was putting out for her mother's *padre*, all the while claiming she'd been washed in the light of the Lord or whatever. It makes sense," she said immediately. "Now it makes sense. God will provide. That's what she said to Lynn. Her baby would need a father, and God would provide."

"I don't think God had the notion to provide Dolly with a married man who's already got three kids. He's denying it, all righteously outraged, and so far, anyway, his wife's sticking with him. The cops are working on picking that apart."

"He met her the night she was killed. She wanted a father for her baby, and Dolly always pushed when she wanted something. She pushed, maybe threatened to tell his wife, ruin him with his congregation. And he kills her."

"Logical," Gull agreed.

"It still doesn't explain why he didn't just leave her, why he took her into the forest, started the fire. But odds are it's the first time he killed anyone. It's probably hard to be rational after doing something like that.

"Gull . . . If he and Dolly were heating the sheets, all this time—and he's been preaching to Mrs. Brakeman for years—he could've gotten into their house."

She tilted her head. "And you've already thought about that."

"Speculated. I expect he's had Sunday dinner there a time or two, he and his wife probably brought a covered dish to summer cookouts and so on. Yeah, I think he knew how to get in, and he might've known or been able to access the combination to the safe."

"It would be a way to have the cops looking at Brakeman, and that worked. Maybe have them speculating. This violent man, this man with a violent temper, one who'd already pushed his daughter out of the house once, has been known to have heated arguments with her. It could be."

"It's not out of the realm. You lost your mood."

She smirked, just a little. "Know-it-all. Maybe I was feeling useless again, a comedown from three days when I know everything I did mattered, made a difference, was needed. Then I'm coming back here where I can't do a damn thing. I can't be in charge, so I guess it helps some to think it all through, and to figure out what I'd do if I could be in charge. Maybe it helps to talk it through with somebody who understands me." She smirked again. "At least understands parts of me."

"You know, I could sit here and look at you all night. All gold and cream and smelling like a summer orchard. It's a nice way to transition back after an extended attack. But, how about I clean up, and we go get ourselves a late supper?"

"That's a solid affirmative."

"Great." He pushed to his feet. "Can I use your shower?"

She laughed, waved toward the bathroom. Since she had some time she decided to call the other man who understood her.

"Hi, Dad."

ELLA TURNED when Lucas opened the door to the deck. She'd slipped out when his cell phone rang to give him some privacy for the call, and to admire the fairy lights she'd strung on the slender branches of her weeping plum.

"Everything okay?"

"Yeah. Rowan just wanted to check in, and to update me on what's going on."

"Is there anything new?"

"Not really." As he sipped a glass of the wine they'd

enjoyed with dinner, he brushed his fingertips up and down her arm.

She loved the way he touched her—often, like a reassurance she was with him.

"She sounded steady, so I feel better about that. With Ro, when bad things happen, or wrong things, she tends to take it in. What could she have done to prevent it, or what should she do to fix it?"

"I can't imagine where she gets that from. Who's been fiddling around here every chance he gets? Fixing the dripping faucet in the laundry room sink, the drawer that kept sticking in that old table I bought at the flea market?"

"I have to pay for all those dinners you cook me. And breakfasts," he added, gliding his hand down to her waist.

"It's nice to have a handy man around the house."

"It's nice to be around the house, with you." He hooked his arm around her waist so they looked out at the garden together, at the pretty lights, the soft shadows. "It's nice to be with you."

"I'm happy," she told him. "I tend to be a happy person, and I learned how to be happy on my own. It was good for me, to have that time, to find out a little bit more about myself. What I could do, what I could do without. I'm happier with you."

She hooked an arm around his waist in turn. "I was standing here before you came out thinking how lucky I am. I've got a family I love and who loves me, a career I'm proud of, this place, good friends. Now the bonus round. You."

Lights sparkling, she thought, in her garden, and in her heart. And all the while her friend lived in the terrible dark.

"I talked with Irene earlier."

"She's got a terrible load to carry now."

"I went to see her, hoping to help, but . . . I can't even begin to conceive what she's lost. The most devastating loss a mother can know. What she may lose yet. Nothing in her life is certain now, or steady or happy. She's burying her daughter, Lucas. She's facing the very real possibility her husband will go to prison. The man she trusted with her spiritual guidance, her faith, betrayed her in a horrible way. The only thing she has to hold on to now is her grandchild, and caring for that sweet little girl must bring Irene incredible pain and joy.

"I'm lucky. And I guess I'm enough like you and Rowan to wish there were some way I could fix things. I wish I knew what I could do or say or be to help Irene."

"You're helping her plan the service, and you'll be there for her. That'll matter. Do you want me to go with you?"

"Selfishly yes. But I think it would embarrass her if you did."

He nodded, having thought the same. "If you think it's right, you could tell her I'm sorry for her loss, sorry for what she's going through."

"I've made us both sad, and here I was thinking about being happy."

"People who are together get to share both. I want to . . . share both with you."

Almost, she thought as butterflies on the wing filled her belly. They were both almost ready to say it. Had she said she felt lucky? She'd been blessed.

"Let's take a walk in the moonlight," she decided. "In the garden. We can finish drinking this wine, and make out."

"You always have the best ideas."

USING A DEAD WOMAN'S phone to lure a man to his death felt . . . just. A man of God should understand that, should approve of the sentiment of an eye for an eye. Though Latterly was no man of God, but a fraud, a liar, an adulterer, a fornicator.

In a very real sense Latterly had killed Dolly. He'd tempted her, led her onto the path—or if the temptation and leading had been hers, he had certainly followed.

He should have counseled her, advised her, helped her be the decent person, the honorable woman, the good mother. Instead he'd betrayed his wife, his family, his God, his church, for sex with the daughter of one of his faithful.

His death would be justice, and retribution and holy vengeance.

The text had done its job, so simple really.

it wasnt me u have 2 come bring money dont tell not yet
talk first need to know what 2 do meet me 1 am Lolo Pass
Vistor Center fs rd 373 2 gate URGENT Can help u Dolly

Of course, the soon-to-be-dead man called the dead woman. The return text when the call went unanswered had been full of shock, panic, demands. Easy enough to deflect.

must c u face 2 face explain then will do what u say when you know what i know cant txt more they might find out

He'd come. If he didn't, there would be another way.

Planning murder wasn't the same as an accident. How would it feel?

The car rolled in ten minutes early, going slow. A creep along the service road.

Easy after all. So easy. Should there be talk first? Should the dead man know why he was dead? Why he would burn in fiery hell?

He called for Dolly, his voice a harsh whisper in the utter peace of the night. At the gate, he sat in his car, silhouetted in the moonlight.

Death waited patiently.

He got out, his head turning right, left, as he continued to call Dolly's name. As he continued up the road.

Yes, it was easy after all.

"An eye for an eye."

Latterly looked over, his face struck with terror as shadow moved to moonlight.

The first bullet struck him in the center of the forehead, a small black hole that turned terror to blank shock. The second pierced his heart, releasing a slow trickle of blood that gleamed black in the shimmer of light.

Easy. A steady hand, a just heart.

No shock, no grief, no trembling, not this time.

A long way to drag a body, but it had to be done right, didn't it? Anything worth doing was worth doing well. And the forest at night held such beauty, such mystery. Peace. Yes, for a little while, peace.

All the effort came to nothing in that moment when the body rested at the burn site, on the pyre, already prepared.

Reverend Latterly didn't look so good, didn't look so *pious* now with his clothes and flesh torn and dirty from the trail.

A click of the lighter, that's all it took to send him to hell.

Flames kindled with a whoosh as they gulped fuel and oxygen. Burning the body as the soul would burn. Peace settled while the fire climbed and spread.

How did it feel to murder and burn?

It felt right.

20

The fire chewed its way east, consuming forest and meadow, its head a rage of hunger and greedy glee leading the body across two states.

Gull dug his spikes into a lodgepole pine, climbing up, up into a sky of sooty red. Sweat dripped down his face to soak the bandanna he'd tied on like a latter-day outlaw as he ground the teeth of his saw through bark and wood. Logs tumbled, crashed below as he worked his way down.

The blaze they sought to cage danced, leaped nimbly up trees to string their branches with light as it roared its song.

He hit the ground, unhooked his harness, then moved down the saw line.

He knew Rowan worked the head. Word traveled down the crew, and the jumpers from Idaho had twice had to retreat due to unstable winds.

He heard the roll of thunder, watched the tanker pitch through the smoke. So far the dragon seemed to swallow the retardant like candy.

He'd lost track of the hours spent in the belly of the beast since the siren had sounded that morning. Only that morning, looking into Rowan's eyes as she moved under him, feeling her body rise and fall beneath him. Only that morning he'd had the taste of her skin, warm from sleep, on his tongue.

Now he tasted smoke. Now he felt the ground move as another sacrificial tree fell to earth. He looked into the eyes of the enemy, and knew her lust.

What he didn't know, as he set down his saw to gulp down water, was if it was day or night. And what did it matter? The only world that mattered lived in this perpetual red twilight.

"We're moving east." Dobie jogged out of the smoke, his eyes red-rimmed over his bandanna. "Gibbons is taking us east, digging line as we go. The hoses are holding her back on the right flank at Pack Creek, and the mud knocked her back some."

"Okay." Gull grabbed his gear.

"I volunteered you and me to go on south through the burn-out and scout spots and snags along the rim, circle on up toward the head."

"That was real considerate of you to include me in your mission."

"Somebody's got to do it, son." Those red-rimmed eyes laughed. "It's a longer trip, but I bet we beat the rest of the crew to the head, get back into the real action sooner."

"Maybe. The head's where I want to be."

"Fighting ass-to-ass with your woman. Let's get humping."

Spots bloomed like flowers, burst like grenades, simmered like shallow pools. The wind colluded, thickened the smoke, giving loft to sailing firebrands.

Gull smothered, dug, doused, beat, then laughed his way through the nasty work as Dobie started naming the spots.

"Fucking Assistant Principal Brewster!" Dobie stomped out the licking flames. "Suspended me for smoking in the bathroom."

"High school sucks."

"Middle school. I got an early start."

"Priming your lungs for your life's work," Gull decided as he moved on to another.

"That's fucking Gigi Japper. Let me at her. She dumped me for a ball player."

"Middle school?"

"Last year. Bastard plays slow-pitch softball. Can you beat that? Slow-pitch softball. How does that count for anything?"

"You're better off without her."

"Damn straight. Well, Captain, I believe we've secured this line, and recommend we cut across from here and start scouting north. I'm still looking for crazy old Mr. Cotter, used to shoot at my dog just because the pup liked to shit in his petunias."

"We'll beat the hell out of old Mr. Cotter together."

"That's a true friend."

They ate lunch, dinner, breakfast—who the hell knew?— on the quickstep hike, chowing down on Hooah! bars, peanut-butter crackers, and the single apple from Gull's pack they passed back and forth.

"I love this job," Dobie told him. "I didn't know as I would. I knew I could do it, knew I would. Figured I'd like it okay. But I didn't know it's what I was after. Didn't know I was after anything."

"If it gets its hooks in you, you know it's what you were after." That, Gull thought, covered smoke jumping and women.

Murdered trees stood, black skeletons in the thinning smoke. Wind trickled through, sending them to moan, scooping up ash that swirled like dirty fairy dust.

"It's like one of those end-of-the-world movies," Dobie decided. "Where some meteor destroys most every goddamn thing, and what's left are mutant scavengers and a handful of brave warriors trying to protect the innocent. We can be the warriors."

"I was counting on being a mutant, but all right. Look at that." Gull pointed east where the sky glowed red above towers of flame. "Half the time I can't understand how I can hate it and still think it's beautiful."

"I felt that way about fucking Gigi Japper."

Laughing, somehow completely happy to be hot and filthy alongside his strangely endearing friend, Gull studied the fire as they hiked—the breadth of it, the colors and tones, the shapes.

On impulse, he pulled his camera out of his PG bag. A

photo couldn't translate its terrifying magnificence, but it would remind him, over the winter. It would remind him.

Dobie stepped into the frame, set his Pulaski on his shoulder, spread his legs, fixed a fierce expression on his face. "Now, take a picture. 'Dragon-slayer.'"

Actually, Gull thought when he framed it in, the title seemed both apt and accurate. He took two. "Eat your heart out, Gigi."

"Fucking A! Come on, son, time's a'wasting."

He took off with a swagger as Gull secured his camera.

"Gull."

"Yeah." He glanced up from zipping his PG bag to see Dobie in nearly the same pose, reversed with his back to him. "Camera's secured, handsome."

"You better come on over here. Take a look at this."

Alerted by the tone, Gull moved fast, stared when Dobie pointed. "Is that what I think it is?"

"Aw, shit."

The remains lay, a grim signpost on the charred trail.

"Jesus, Gull, looks like the mutants have been through here." Dobie staggered a few feet away, braced his hands on his knees, and puked up his energy bars.

"Like Dolly," Gull murmured. "Except . . ."

"Christ, I feel like a pussy. Losing my lunch." Bone-white beneath the layer of soot, Dobie took a pull of water, spat it out. "He started the fire, the cocksucker, right here. Like with Dolly." He rinsed again, spat again, then drank. "He did all this."

"Yeah, except I don't think he did this to try to hide the body, or destroy it. Maybe it's so we'd find it, or for attention, or because the son of a bitch likes fire. And it's not like Dolly because this one's got what's got to be a bullet hole dead in the forehead."

Bracing himself, Dobie stepped over again, looked. "Christ, I think you're right about that."

"I guess I should've taken that bet." Gull pulled out his radio. "Because I don't think we're going to get back to action before the rest of the crew."

While they waited, Dobie took two mini bottles of Kentucky bourbon from his bag, took a swig. "Who do you think it is?" he asked, and passed the second bottle to Gull.

"Maybe we've just got some homicidal firebug picking people at random. More likely it's somebody connected to Dolly."

"Jesus please us, I hope it's not her ma. I really hope it's not her ma. Somebody's got to take care of that baby."

"I saw her mother that day she and the preacher came to thank L.B. for hiring Dolly again. She's short, little like Dolly was. I think what's there's too tall. Pretty tall, I think."

"Her daddy, maybe."

"Maybe."

"If I hadn't volunteered us, somebody else would've found it. It's right on the damn trail. Ro said Dolly was off it. Right on the trail. The rangers would've found it if we hadn't. It really makes you think about what the fire'll do to you, it gets the chance."

Gull looked out at the red, the black, the stubborn lashing gold. And downed the bourbon.

The rangers let them go to rejoin the war. The fury built up in Gull all the way up to that snarling, snapping head. He channeled that fury into the attack so every strike of his ax fed his anger. This war wasn't fought against God or nature or fate, but against the human being who'd given birth to the fire for his own pleasure or purpose or weakness.

For those hours the battle burned, he didn't care about the reasons why. He only cared about stopping it.

"Take a breath," Rowan told him. "We've got her now. You can feel it. Take a breath, Gull. This isn't a one-man show."

"I'll take a breath when she's down."

"Look, I know how you feel. I know exactly how—"

"I'm not in the mood to be reasonable." He pushed her hand off his arm, eyes hot and vivid. "I'm in the mood to kill this bitch. We can discuss our mutual traumas later. Now let me do my job."

"Okay, fine. We need men up on that ridge digging line before she rides this wind and shifts this way for fresh eats and builds again."

"All right."

"Take Dobie, Matt, Libby and Stovic."

—————

NIGHT, HE THOUGHT—or morning, probably—when he dragged himself to the creek. The fire trembled in its death throes, coughing and sputtering. Overhead, stars winked hopefully through thinning smoke.

He pulled off his boots, his socks, and stuck his abused feet in the gorgeously cool water. The postfire chatter ran behind him in voices raw with smoke and adrenaline. Jokes, insults, rewinds of the long fight. And the expected what-the-fuck? question about what he and Dobie had found.

More work waited, but would keep until daybreak. The fire hadn't lain down to rest. She'd lain down to die.

Rowan sat down beside him, dropped an MRE in his lap, pushed a drink into his hand. "They dropped a nice load down for camp, so I made you dinner."

"A woman's work is never done."

"More in the mood to be reasonable, I see."

"I needed to burn it off."

"I know." She touched a hand to his briefly, then picked up the fork to shovel in beef stew. "I put some of Dobie's famous Tabasco in this. Nice kick."

"I was taking his picture. Him standing there in the black, and behind him the fire, and the sky. Surreal. I'd just taken his picture when we found it. It didn't get to me, really, until we started up to meet you, and it just got bigger and bigger in me. Christ, I wasn't even thinking about some guy burned to bone after taking a shot in the head."

"Shot?"

Gull nodded. "Yeah, but I wasn't thinking about him. All I could think about was this, and us. All the loss and waste, the risks, the sweat and blood. And for what, Ro? Since I couldn't beat the hell out of whoever caused it, I had to beat the hell out of the fire."

"Matt got hung up on the jump. He let down okay, but it could've gone bad. A widowmaker as thick as my arm nearly hit Elf when we had to retreat, and Yangtree's got a Pulaski gash on his calf to go with his swollen knee. One of the Idaho crew took a bad fall, broke his leg. You were right to be mad."

For a while, they ate in silence. "They want you back in the morning, you and Dobie, so DiCicco and Quinniock can talk to you. I can pack out with you."

He glanced over, grateful—grateful enough not to mention she was taking care of him. "That'd be good."

"I figured you're pretty tired, so I can save you the time popping your tent. You can share mine."

"That'd be even better. I love this job," he said after a moment, thinking of Dobie. "I don't know why exactly but what this bastard's done makes me love it even more. The cops have to find him, catch him, stop him. But we're the ones cleaning up his goddamn mess. We're the ones doing whatever it takes to keep it from being worse. The wild doesn't mean anything to him, what lives in it, lives off it. It means something to us."

He looked at her then, slowly leaned in to take her lips in a kiss of surprising gentleness. "I found you in the wild, Rowan. That's a hell of a thing."

She smiled, a little uncertainly. "I wasn't lost."

"Neither was I. But I'm found, too, just the same."

When they walked the short distance to the tents, they crossed paths with Libby.

"How you doing, Gull?"

"Okay. Better since I hear I get to skate out of mop-up. Have you seen Dobie?"

"Yeah, he just turned in. He was feeling . . . I guess you know. Matt and I sat up with him awhile after the rest bunked down. He's doing okay."

"You did good work today, Barbie," Rowan told her.

"Never plan to do any other kind. Good night."

Rowan yawned her way into the tent and, with her mind and body already shutting down, worked off her boots. "Don't wake me unless there's a bear attack. In fact, even then."

She stripped down to her tank and panties. As she rolled toward the sleeping bag, Gull considered.

"You know, thirty seconds ago I figure I was too tired to scratch my own ass. And now, strangely, I'm filled with this renewed energy."

She opened one eye, shut it again. "Do what you gotta do. Just don't wake me up doing it."

He climbed in beside her, smiling, drew her already-limp-

with-sleep body to his. When he closed his eyes he thought of
her, of nothing but her, and slid quietly into the dark.

IT WAS HER KNEE pressing firmly into his crotch that woke
him. His eyes crossed before they opened. Easing back
relieved the worst of the pressure on his now throbbing balls.

Had she aimed, he wondered, or had it just been blind luck?
Either way, perfect shot.

She didn't budge when he rolled out to pull on his pants,
fresh socks, boots. He left the pants and boots unfastened and
crawled out into soft morning light.

Nothing and no one stirred. Then again, as far as he knew
the other tents held occupants of one—with no one to jab a
knee into their balls. Should they have them.

He stood, adjusted himself—carefully—then chose a direction out of camp to empty his bladder. Coffee, and filling his
belly, would be next on the list, he decided. Being the first
awake meant he had first dibs on the breakfast MREs. He'd sit
outside, maybe down by the creek, give Rowan the tent for
more sleep and enjoy a quiet, solitary if crappy meal until . . .

He stopped and looked. Looked over a meadow brilliant
with wild lupines, regally purple. The faintest ground mist
shimmered through them, giving them the illusion of floating
on a thin, white river while dozens of deep blue butterflies
danced over those bold lances.

Untouched, he thought. The fire hadn't touched this. They'd
stopped it, and now the wildflowers bloomed, the butterflies
danced in the misty morning light.

It was, he thought, as beautiful, as vivid as the finest work
of art. Maybe more. And he'd had a part in saving it, and the
trees beyond it, and whatever lay beyond the beyond.

He'd fought in the smoke and the blistering red air, walked
through the black that stank with death. And to here, where
life lived, where it thrived in quiet and simple grace.

To here, which held all the answers to why.

HE BROUGHT HER THERE, dragging her away from camp
before they packed out.

"We've got to get going," she protested. "If we haul our asses down to the visitors' center, they can van us back to base. Clean bodies, clean clothes. And, *God*, I want a Coke."

"This is better than a Coke."

"Nothing's better than a Coke first thing in the morning. You coffee hounds have it all wrong."

"Just look." He gestured. "That's better than anything."

She'd seen meadows before, seen the wild lupine and the butterflies it seduced. She started to say so, grumpy with caffeine withdrawal, but he looked so . . . struck.

And she got it. Of course she got it. Who better?

Still, she had to give him a dig, one with the elbow in the side, the other verbal. "There's that mushy romantic streak again."

"Stand right there. I'm going to get a picture."

"Hell you are. Jesus, Gull, look at me."

"One of my favorite occupations."

"If you want a shot of a woman in front of a meadow of flowers, get one with clean, shiny hair and a flowy white dress."

"Don't be stupid, you look exactly right. Because you're part of why it's here. This is like a bookend to the one I took of Dobie in the black. It shows how and why and who go into everything between those two points."

"Romantic slob," she repeated. But it moved her, the truth of it, the knowing they shared.

So she hooked her thumbs in her front pockets, cocked her hip and sent him and his camera a big, bold grin.

He took the shot, lowered the camera slowly and just stared at her as he had at the meadow. Struck.

"Here, switch off. I'll take one of you."

"No. It's you. It's Dobie in the black, the fire raging behind him, telling me how much he loves this job, what he's found in it. And it's you, Rowan, in the sunlight with preserved beauty at your back. You're the end of the goddamn rainbow."

"Come on." Mildly embarrassed, she shrugged it off, started toward him. "You must be punchy."

"You're the answer before I even asked the question."

"Gull, it weirds me out when you start talking like that."

"I think you're going to have to get used to it. I've fallen pretty deep in . . . care with you. We'll go with that for now, because I think it's more, and that's a lot to figure out."

A touch of panic speared through embarrassment. "Gull, getting wound up in . . . care for people like us—for people like me—it's a sucker bet."

"I don't think so. I like the odds."

"Because you're crazy."

"You have to be crazy to do this job."

She couldn't argue with that. "We've got to get going."

"Just one more thing."

He took her shoulders, drawing her in. His fingers glided up to her face as he guided them into a kiss made for meadows and summer shine, the flutter of butterflies and music of birdsong.

Unable to find a foothold, she tumbled into it, lost herself in the sweetness, the promise she told herself she didn't want. Her heart trembled in her chest, ached there.

And, for the first time in her life, yearned there.

Unsteady, she stepped away. "That's just heat."

"Keep telling yourself that." He hooked an arm around her shoulders in a lightning switch to friendly. The man, she thought, could make her dizzy.

DiCicco and Quinniock stepped out of Operations even as the vans pulled up to base.

"It'd be nice if they let us clean up first," Gull commented, then he got off the van, nodded to the cop and the fed. "Where do you want to do this?"

"L.B.'s office is available for us," Quinniock told him.

"Look, there are tables outside the cookhouse. I wouldn't mind airing out some and getting some food while we're at it. I expect Dobie feels the same."

"You got that right, son. Did you figure out who's dead?"

"We'll talk about it," DiCicco told him.

"We'll take care of your gear." Rowan gestured to Matt, Janis. "Don't worry about it."

"Appreciate it." Gull gave her a quick look.

"Are we suspects?" Dobie wanted to know as they walked toward the cookhouse.

"We haven't made any determinations, Mr. Karstain."

"Loosen up, Kim," Quinniock suggested. "We have no reason to suspect you in this matter. You can tell us where you were the night before you jumped the fire, between eleven P.M. and three A.M., if you'd like."

"Me? I was playing cards with Libby and Yangtree and Trigger till about midnight. Trig and me had a last beer after. I guess we bunked down about one."

"I was with Rowan," Gull said, and left it at that.

"We'd like to go over the statements you gave the rangers on scene." DiCicco sat at the picnic table, pulled out her notebook, her mini recorder. "I'd like to record this."

"Dobie, why don't you go ahead? I'll go see what Marg can put together for us. Do you two want anything?" Gull asked.

"I wouldn't mind a cold drink," Quinniock told him, and, remembering the lemonade, DiCicco nodded.

"That'd be good. Now, Mr. Karstain—"

"Can you leave off calling me mister? Just Dobie."

"Dobie."

He went over what happened. What he'd seen, done, what he'd already told the rangers.

"You know, the black looks like a horror show anyhow, then you add that. Gull said it must be connected to Dolly."

"Did he?" DiCicco said.

"Makes sense, doesn't it?" Dobie looked from one to the other. "Is it?"

"Dobie, how was it only you and Mr. Curry were in that area?"

Dobie shrugged at DiCicco just as Gull came out, two steps in front of Lynn. Both carried trays.

"We needed most everybody up at the head, digging line toward it, but somebody still needed to scout spots along the flank. So I volunteered me and Gull."

"You suggested that you and Mr. Curry take that route?"

"She's big on the misters," he said to Gull. "Yeah. It's a longer hike, but I like killing spots. Me and Gull, we work good together. Thanks." He gave Lynn a smile when she set a loaded plate in front of him. "It sure looks good."

"Marg said to save room for cherry pie. You just let me know if you need anything else."

"Let's save some time." Gull took his seat. "We took that route because we were scouting spots. You see a spot, you put it out, and you move on. We had that duty while making our way east to join the rest of the crew. The fire'd been moving east, but the winds kept changing, so the flanks shifted. We found the remains because we cut across the burnout, heading to the far flank in case any spots broke out and took hold. If they did, and we didn't, it could've put the visitor center in the line. Nobody wanted that. Clear?"

"That's the way it is." Dobie took his bottle of Tabasco out of his pocket, lifted the top of his Kaiser roll and dumped some on the horseradish Marg had piled on his roast beef.

Gull shook his head when Dobie offered the bottle. "Mine's fine as it is. And, yeah, I speculated this body was related to Dolly. It could be we've got a serial killer–arsonist picking victims at random, but I like the odds on connection a lot better."

"Shot this one," Dobie said with his mouth full. "Couldn't miss the bullet hole."

"Jumpers got hurt on that fire. I heard on the way in a couple of hotshots I know were injured. I watched acres of wilderness go up. I want the person responsible to pay for it, and I want to know why killing wasn't enough. Because I can speculate again that the fire was just as important as the kill. Otherwise, there wasn't a reason for it. The fire itself had to matter."

"That's an interesting speculation," DiCicco commented.

"Since we've already told you what we know, speculation's all that's left. And since neither of you look particularly stupid, I have to assume you've already entertained those same speculations."

"He's feeling a little pissed off 'cause he's out here talking to cops instead of taking a shower with the Swede."

"Jesus, Dobie." Then Gull laughed. "Yeah, I am. So, since you cost me, maybe you could tell us if you've identified the remains."

"That information . . ." DiCicco caught Quinniock's look, huffed out a breath. "While we're waiting for verification, we found Reverend Latterly's car parked on the service road alongside the visitors' center. His wife can't tell us his whereabouts, only that he wasn't home or at his church when she got up this morning."

"Somebody shot a preacher?" Dobie demanded. "That's hell for sure."

"The Brakemans' preacher," Gull added. "And the one rumor has it Dolly was screwing around with. I heard Leo Brakeman made bail."

"Sumbitch better not come back around here."

DiCicco gave Dobie a glance, but kept her focus primarily on Gull. "We'll be speaking to Mr. Brakeman after his daughter's funeral this afternoon."

"I've got a couple of men on him," Quinniock added. "We've got a list of his registered weapons, and we'll take another look at his gun safe."

"It'd be pretty stupid to use one of his own guns, at least a registered weapon, to kill the man who was screwing his daughter and preaching to his wife."

"Regardless, we'll pursue every avenue of the investigation. We can speculate, too, Mr. Curry," DiCicco added. "But we have to work with facts, with data, with evidence. Two people are dead, and that's priority. But those wildfires matter. I work for the Forest Service, too. Believe me, it all matters."

She got to her feet. "Thanks for your time." She offered Gull the ghost of a smile. "Sorry about the shower."

"Why, Agent DiCicco," Quinniock said as they walked away, "I believe you just made an amusing, smart-ass comment. I feel warm inside."

"Well, hold on to it. Funerals tend to cool things off."

BLOWUP

To burn always with this hard, gem-like flame,
to maintain this ecstasy, is success in life.

WALTER PATER

21

Rowan dawdled. She lingered in the shower, took her time selecting shorts and a top as if it mattered. She even put in a few minutes with makeup, pleased when the dawdling transformed her into a girl.

Time enough, she decided, and went to hunt for Gull.

When she stepped out of her quarters, Matt stepped out of his.

"Wow." She gave him and his dark suit and tie a lusty eyebrow wiggle. "And I thought I looked good."

"You do."

"What, do you have a hot date? Going to a wedding, a funer—" She broke off, mentally slapped herself. "Oh, God, Matt, I forgot. I wasn't thinking. You're going to Dolly's funeral."

"I thought I should, since we're off the fire."

"You're not going by yourself? I'd go with you, but I've got to be the last person the Brakemans want to see today."

"It's okay. I'm just . . . I feel like I have to, to represent Jim, you know? I don't want to, but . . . the baby." He shoved at his floppy, sun-bleached hair with his fingers. "I almost wish we were still out on the fire, so I couldn't go."

"Get somebody to go with you. Janis packed out with us, or Cards would go if he's up to it. Or—"

"L.B.'s going." Matt stuck his hands in his pockets, pulled them out again to tap his fingers on his thigh. It reminded her painfully of Jim. "And Marg and Lynn."

"Okay then." She walked over, fussed with his tie though it didn't need it. "You're doing the right thing by your family by going. If you want to talk later, or just hang out, I'll be around."

"Thanks." He put a hand over hers until she met his eyes. "Thanks, Rowan. I know she caused you a lot of trouble."

"It doesn't matter. Matt, it really doesn't. It's a hard day for a lot of people. That's what matters."

He gave her hand one hard squeeze. "I'd better get going."

She changed direction when he left, headed to the lounge. Cards sprawled on the sofa watching one of the soaps on TV.

"This girl's telling this guy she's knocked up, even though she's not, because he's in love with her sister but banged her— the one who's not knocked up—when she put something in his drink when she went over to his place to tell him the sister was cheating on him, which she wasn't."

He slugged down some Gatorade. "Women suck."

"Hey."

"Fact is fact," he said grimly. "So I'm riveted. I could get hooked on this stuff taking my afternoon, medically ordered lie-down. I get to malinger for another day while I get pretty again."

She sat, studied the bandage over his cheek. "I don't know. The hole in your face added interest, and it would've distracted from the fact your eyes are too close together."

"I have the eyes of an angel. And a hawk. An angel hawk."

"Matt's leaving to go to Dolly's funeral."

"Yeah, I know. He's wearing Yangtree's tie."

"We should get a couple more of the guys to go with him. Libby's still on mop-up, but Janis packed out."

"Let it be, Ro. You can't fix every damn thing."

He hissed through his teeth when she said nothing. "Look, L.B.'s going to stand for the base, and Marg and Lynn, because they worked with her. Matt, well, he's like kin now with Jim's baby and all. But L.B. and I talked about it. The way things ended up here with Dolly, it's probably best to keep it to a minimum. Probably be easier on Dolly's mom."

"Probably," she agreed, but frowned as she studied him. She knew that face, with or without the hole, and those big camel eyes. "What's up?"

"Nothing except your interrupting my soap opera. Orchid's going to get hers when Payton finds out she's been playing him for a sap."

She knew a brood when she was sitting next to one. "You're sulking."

"I've got a frigging hole in my face and I'm watching soap operas, then you come along and start carping about dead Dolly and funerals." He shot her a single hot look. "Go find somebody else to rag on."

"Fine."

She shoved up.

"Women suck," he repeated with a baffled bitterness that had her easing down again. "We're better off without them."

She opted not to remind him she happened to be a woman. "Altogether, or one in particular?"

"You know the one I hooked up with last winter."

Since he'd mentioned her about a hundred times, shown off her picture, Rowan had a pretty good idea. "Vicki, sure."

"She was coming out in a couple weeks, with the kids. I was getting a few days off to show her around. The kids were all juiced up to see the base."

Were, Rowan thought. "What happened?"

"That's just it. I don't know. She changed her mind, that's all. She doesn't think it's a good idea—I've got my life, she's got hers. She dumped me; that's it. She won't even tell me why, exactly, just how she has to think of the kids, how she needs a stable, honest relationship and all that shit."

He turned, aiming those angry, baffled eyes at Rowan. "I never lied to her, that's the thing. I told her how it was, and she said she was okay with it. Even that she was proud of what I did. Now she's done, just like that. Pissed off, too. And . . . she cried. What the hell did I do?"

"I guess . . . the theory of being attached to somebody who does what we do is different from the reality. It's hard."

"So I'm supposed to give it up? Do something else? Be something else? That's not right."

"No, it's not right."

"I was going to ask her to marry me when she came out."

"Hell. I'm sorry."

"She won't even talk to me now. I keep leaving messages, and she won't answer. She won't let me talk to the kids. I'm crazy about those kids."

"Write her a letter."

"Do what?"

"Nobody writes letters anymore. Write her a letter. Tell her how you feel. Lay it all out."

"Shit, I'm not good at that."

"And that'll make it even better. If you're hung up enough to want to marry her, you can write a damn letter."

"I don't know. Maybe. Hell."

"Women suck."

"Tell me about it. Write a letter," he repeated, brooded into his Gatorade. "Maybe. Talk about something else. If I keep talking about her, I'm going to try to call her again. It's humiliating."

"How about those Cubs?"

He snorted. "I need more than baseball to get my mind off heartbreak, especially since the Cubbies suck more than women this year. We've got murder, and fire starters. I heard there was another one, another body. And whoever did it started the fire. The cops better catch this bastard before he burns half of western Montana. We can all use the fat wallet, but nobody wants to earn it that way."

"He got a good chunk of Idaho, too. It's scary," she said because they were alone. "We know fire wants to kill us when we're going there. We know nature couldn't give a damn either way. But going in, knowing there's somebody out there killing people and lighting it up who maybe wants to see some of us burn. Maybe doesn't give a shit either way. That's scary. It's scary not knowing if he's done, or if the next time the siren sounds, it's because of him."

She looked over as Gull came in. "What did the cops say?" she demanded.

"It's not official, but it's a pretty good bet what we found out there is what's left of Reverend Latterly."

Cards bolted up. "The priest?"

"Loosely." Gull dropped down in a chair. "They found his car out there, and nobody can find him. So, either we did, or he's taken off. They're going to be talking to Brakeman after the funeral."

"They think he killed him and burned him up?" Cards said. "But . . . wouldn't that mean . . . or do they think he killed Dolly and— Her own father? Come on."

"I don't know what they think."

"What do you think?" Rowan asked him.

"I'm still working on it. So far I think we've got somebody who's seriously pissed off, and likes fire. I've got to clean up."

Rowan followed him into his quarters. "Why do you say 'likes fire'? Using it's not the same as liking it."

"I guess since you're dressed—and you look good, by the way—you're not going to wash my back."

"No. Why do you say 'likes fire'?"

Gull pulled off his shirt. "I increased my passing acquaintance with arson after Dolly."

"Yeah, you study. It's a thing with you."

"I like to learn. Anyway," he continued, dragging off his boots. "Arsonists usually fall into camps. There's your for-profit—somebody burning property to collect insurance, say, or the torch who lights them up for a fee. That's not this."

"You've got the torching to cover up another crime. I have a passing acquaintance, too," she reminded him as he took off his pants. "Murder's sure as hell another crime."

"Maybe that's what it was with Dolly." Naked, he walked into the bathroom, turned on the shower. "The accident or on purpose, the panic, the cover-up. But this, coming on top of it, when the first didn't really work?"

He stepped under the spray, let out a long, relieved groan. "All hail the god of water."

"Maybe it was a copycat. Somebody wanted to kill Latterly. Brakeman had motive, so did Latterly's wife if she found out about him and Dolly. One of his congregation who felt outraged and betrayed. And they mirrored Dolly because of the connection. It's the same motive."

"Could be."

She whipped back the shower curtain. "It makes the most sense."

"In or out, Blondie." He skimmed those feline eyes down her body. "I'd rather in."

She whipped the curtain back closed. "The third type doesn't play out, Gull. The firebug who gets off starting fires, watching them burn. It doesn't play because of the murders."

"Maybe he's getting a twofer."

"It's bad enough if it's to cover the murders. That's plenty bad enough. What you're thinking's worse."

"I know it. If the vibe I got from the cops is right, it's something they're thinking about, too."

She leaned her hands on the sink, stared at her own reflection. "I don't want it to be somebody I know."

"You don't know everybody, Ro."

No, she didn't know everybody, and was suddenly, desperately grateful she knew only a few people who were connected to Dolly and Latterly.

But . . . what if it was one of those few?

"Dolly's funeral. Where can they have it?" she wondered. "They couldn't have planned on Mrs. Brakeman's church, even before this happened."

"Marg said they're having the service in the funeral parlor. They don't expect much of a crowd."

"God." She shut her eyes. "I hated her like a hemorrhoid, but that's just depressing."

He shut off the water, pulled back the curtain. "You know what you need?" He reached for a towel.

"What do I need? Gee, let me guess."

"Gutter brain. You need a drive with the top down and an ice-cream cone."

"I do?"

"Yeah, you do. We're third load on the jump list, so we can cruise into town, find ourselves an ice-cream parlor."

"I happen to know where one is."

"Perfect. And you look nice. I should take my girl out for ice cream."

"Cut that out, Gull."

"Uh-uh." He wrapped the towel around his waist and, still dripping, grabbed her in for a kiss.

"You're getting me wet!"

"Sex, sex, sex. Fine, if that's what you want."

He managed to chase the blues away, make her laugh as she shoved him back. "I want ice cream." Since he'd already dampened her shirt, she grabbed his face, kissed him again. "First. Get dressed, big spender. I'll go check with Ops, make sure we're clear for a few hours."

PHOTOGRAPHS OF DOLLY BRAKEMAN, from birth to death, were grouped together in a smiling display. Pink roses softened with sprigs of baby's breath flanked them. The coffin, closed, bore a blanket of girlish pink and white mums over polished gloss.

As she'd helped Irene by ordering her choice of flowers, Ella sent pink and white lilies. She noted a couple other floral offerings, and even such a sparse tribute overpowered the tiny room with scent.

Irene, pale and stark-eyed in unrelieved black, sat on the somber burgundy sofa with her sister, a woman Ella knew a little who'd come in from Billings with her husband. The man sat, stiff and grim, on a twin sofa across the narrow room with Leo.

Sacred music played softly through the speakers. No one spoke.

In her life, Ella thought, she'd never seen such a sad testament to a short life, violently ended.

Ella crossed the room, took her friend's limp hands. "Irene."

"The flowers look nice."

"They do."

"I appreciate you taking care of that for me, Ella."

"It was no trouble at all."

Irene's sister nodded at Ella, then rose to sit with her husband. "The photographs are lovely. You made good choices."

"Dolly always liked having her picture taken. Even as a baby," she said as Ella sat down beside her, "she'd look right at the camera. I don't know how to do this. I don't know how to bury my girl."

Saying nothing—what was there to say?—Ella put her arms around Irene.

"I've got pictures. All I've got's a lot of pictures. That one there, of Dolly and the baby, is the last one I have. My sister Carrie's bringing the baby soon. She's been a help to me, coming up from Billings. She's bringing Shiloh. I know Shiloh won't understand or remember, but I thought she should be here."

"Of course. You know you can call me, anytime, for anything."

"I don't know what to do, with her things, with her clothes."

"I'll help you with that when you're ready. There's Reverend Meece now."

Irene's hand clutched at Ella's. "I don't know him. It's good you asked him to come do the service, but—"

"He's kind, Irene. He'll be kind to Dolly."

"Leo didn't want any preacher. Not after what . . ." Her eyes welled again. "I can't think about that now. I'll go crazy if I think about that now."

"Don't. Remember the pretty girl in the photographs. Let me bring Reverend Meece over. I think he'll be a comfort to you. I promise."

Though she wasn't much of a churchgoer, Ella liked Meece, his gentle ways. Irene needed gentle now.

"Thank you so much for doing this, Robert."

"No need for thanks. It's a hard day," he said, looking at the coffin. "The kind of day that shakes a mother's faith. I hope I can help her."

As she led him to Irene, she saw a trio of staff from the school come in. Thank God, she thought. Someone came. Leaving Irene with Meece, she went over to take on greeter duties, as Irene's older sister seemed unwilling or unable to shoulder the task.

She excused herself when Irene's younger sister arrived with the baby, her husband and her two children. "Carrie, would you like me to take the baby? I think Irene could use you."

As people formed their groups, quiet conversations began, Ella cuddled the chubby, bright-eyed orphan.

And Leo surged to his feet. "You've got no business here. You've got no right to be here."

The outraged tone had Shiloh's lip quivering with a whimper. Ella murmured reassurance as she turned, saw the small contingent from the base.

"After what you did? The way you treated my girl? You get out. You get the hell *out*!"

"Leo." Across the room, Irene sank back into the sofa. "Stop. Stop." Covering her face with her hands, she burst into harsh sobs.

Ignoring Leo, Marg marched straight to Irene, sat to embrace the woman, to let Irene cry on her shoulder.

"Mr. Brakeman." Irene watched a ruddy-faced, towheaded young man step forward—his jaw as clenched as Leo's fists. "That baby there is my blood as much as yours, and Dolly was her ma. Wasn't a year ago I buried my brother. We both lost something, and Shiloh's what we've got left. We've come to pay Shiloh's ma our respects."

The livid color in Leo's cheeks only deepened. For one horrible moment, Ella imagined the worst. Fists, blood, chaos. Then Lieutenant Quinniock and a woman stepped in, and fear flickered briefly in Leo's eyes.

"Stay away from me," he told the young man. Matt, Ella realized. Matt Brayner.

"That's your uncle," Ella whispered. "That's Uncle Matt. It's okay now."

Leo turned his back, moved as far away as the narrow confines of the room allowed, folded his arms over his chest.

Ella stepped to Matt. "Would you hold her? I'd like to take Irene out for a minute or two, get her some fresh air."

"I'd be pleased." Matt's eyes watered up when the baby reached a chubby hand to his face.

"She favors Jim a little." Lynn spoke quietly. "Don't you think, Matt? She favors Jim?"

Matt's throat worked as he nodded, as he bent his head to press his cheek to Shiloh's.

"Come on with us, Irene." With Marg's help, Ella got Irene to her feet. "Come on with us for a bit."

As they led the sobbing woman out, Ella heard Meece's gentle voice coat over the ugly tension in the room.

ROWAN LICKED her strawberry swirl, enjoying the buzz of pedestrian and street traffic as she strolled with Gull.

"That's not really ice cream," she told him.

"Maple walnut is not only really ice cream, it's macho ice cream."

"Maple's for syrup. It's like a condiment. It's like mustard. Would you eat mustard ice cream?"

"I'm open to all flavors, even your girlie strawberry parfait."

"This is refreshing." As the drive had been, she thought. A long, aimless drive on winding roads, and now a slow, purposeless stroll along the green shade of boulevard trees toward one of the city's parks.

With two of the four-hour breaks ahead of them, she could let go, relax. Unless the phones in their pockets signaled a call back to base.

For now she'd just appreciate the respite, the ice cream, the company and the blissful rarity of a free summer afternoon.

"I'll ignore your syrup ice cream because you had a really good idea. Twenty-four hours ago, we're in the belly of the beast, and here we are poking along like a couple of tourists."

"One makes the other all the more worthwhile."

"You know what, if we're not catching fire, we should complete our tequila shot competition tonight. We can pick up a bottle of the good stuff before we head back."

"You just want to get me drunk and take advantage of me."

"I don't have to get you drunk for that."

"Suddenly I feel cheap and easy. I like it."

"Maybe we can get Cards into it. He could use the distraction."

She'd told Gull the situation on the drive in. "The letter's a good idea. He should follow through."

"Maybe you could help him."

"Me?"

"You've got good words."

"I don't think Cards wants me playing Cyrano for his Roxanne."

"See?" She drilled a finger into his arm, and put on a bumpkin accent. "You got all that there book-larning."

"Rowan?"

She glanced over at the sound of her name. Feeling awkward, mildly annoyed and uncertain what came next, Rowan lowered her ice cream. "Ah, yeah. Hi."

Ella stayed seated on the bench. "It's nice to see you. I heard you got back this morning." Ella mustered up a smile for Gull. "I'm Ella Frazier, a friend of Rowan's father."

"Gulliver Curry." He stepped over, offered his free hand. "How're you doing?"

"Honestly? Not very well. I've just come from Dolly's funeral, which was as bad as you can imagine. I wanted to walk it off, then I thought I could sit it off. It's so pretty here. But it's not working."

"Why were you . . . Mrs. Brakeman works at your school," Rowan remembered.

"Yes. We've gotten to be friends the last year or so."

"How is she . . . It's stupid to ask how she's doing, if she's okay. She couldn't be okay."

"She's not, and I think it may be worse yet. The police were there, too, and took Leo in for questioning after the service. Irene's in the middle of a nightmare. It's hard to watch a friend going through all this, knowing there's little to nothing you can do to help. And I'm sorry." She caught herself, shook her head. "Here you are on what I'm sure is very rare and precious free time, and I'm full of gloom."

"You need ice cream," Gull decided. "What flavor?"

"Oh, no, I—"

"Ice cream," he repeated, "is guaranteed to cut the gloom. What would you like?"

"You might as well pick something," Rowan told her. "He'll just keep at you otherwise."

"Mint chocolate chip. Thank you."

"I'll be back in a minute."

Only more awkward now, Rowan thought as Gull jogged back in the direction of the ice-cream parlor. "I guess you saw the group from the base."

"Yes. Leo started to cause a scene, which might have escalated. But between Matt, then the police coming in, it died off into awful tension, resentment, grief, smothered rage. And, enough." She closed her eyes. "Just enough of all that. Will you sit? You know your delightful man took off not only to get me ice cream but to give us a few minutes on our own."

"Probably. He likes to put things in motion."

"He's gorgeous, and strikes me as tough and sweet. That's an appealing blend in a man." Ella angled on the bench, putting them face-to-face. "You're uncomfortable with me, with my relationship with your father."

"I don't know you."

"No, you don't. I feel like I know you, at least a little, because Lucas talks about you all the time. He loves you so much, is so proud of you. You have to know there's nothing he wouldn't do for you."

"It's mutual."

"I know it. Just as I know if you made it a choice between you and me, I wouldn't stand a chance."

"I'm not going to—"

"Just let me finish, because you don't know me and, at this point, don't particularly like me. Why should you? But since we have this opportunity I'm going to tell you your father is the most wonderful, the most endearing, the most exciting man I've ever known. I made the first move, he was so shy. Oh, God." She pressed a hand to her heart, her face lighting up in the dappled sunlight. "I'd hoped we'd get to know each other, date, enjoy each other's company. And we did. What I never expected was I'd fall in love with him."

Battling a dozen conflicting emotions, Rowan stared at her melting ice cream.

"You're so young. And I know you don't think you are. But you're so young, and it has to be impossible to understand how someone my age can fall just as hard, as deep and terrifyingly as someone yours. But I have, and I know where the power is, Rowan. I hope you'll give me a chance."

"He's never . . . He hasn't been involved with anyone since my mother."

"I know. That makes me very, very lucky. Here comes Gull. From where I'm sitting, we're both very lucky."

Gull skimmed his gaze over Rowan's face before shifting to Ella. "Here you go."

"That was quick."

"We call him Fast Feet." Not sure what to think, Rowan attacked the drips running down her cone.

"Thank you." After the first taste, Ella smiled, tasted again. "You were right, this cuts the gloom. Take my seat," she said as she got up. "I think I can walk this off now. It was nice to talk to you, Rowan."

"Yeah. You too." Sort of, Rowan thought, as Ella walked away.

Gull sat, looked after her. "She's hot."

"Jesus Christ. She's old enough to be your mother."

"My aunt's also hot. A guy doesn't have to want to sleep with a woman to acknowledge the hotness."

"She said she's in love with my father. What am I supposed to say to that? Do about that? Feel about that?"

"Maybe that she has good taste in men." He patted her thigh. "You've got to let these crazy kids work these things out on their own. Anyway, my first—if brief—impression. I liked her."

"Because she's hot."

"Hot is a separate issue. She was sitting here grieving for a friend's loss, worried for that friend and what she might still have to face. Empathy and compassion. She's pissed off at Leo Brakeman, which shows good sense and a lack of hypocrisy. She told you how she felt about your father, when it's pretty clear you're not too crazy about the whole matchup. That took guts, and honesty."

"Maybe you could be her campaign manager." Rowan sat back. "She dropped it in my court, and that was smart. I have the power. So you can add smart to her list of virtues."

"Would you rather see your dad with somebody dumb, selfish, cold-hearted and hypocritical?"

"You're no dummy, either. Hell, let's buy two bottles of tequila. I could use a good drunk tonight."

"Who says I'm a good drunk?"

ROWAN CHECKED in on Matt when they got back to base, and found him sitting on the side of his bed tying his running shoes.

"I heard it was pretty bad."

"It was, but it could've been worse. Why he wants to blame me and L.B. and, jeez, Marg and Lynn for Dolly getting fired? She brought that on herself."

Good, she thought, he was pissed off, not broody. "Because people suck and generally want anything crappy to be somebody else's fault."

"At the damn funeral? He starts yelling and threatening us at his daughter's funeral?"

"At my mother's funeral, her parents wouldn't even speak to me. They wouldn't speak to me really loud."

"You're right. People suck."

"We're going to have a tequila shooter contest in the lounge later. You're on third load, too. I'll float your entry fee."

That got a smile. "You know I can't compete with you there. I'm going for a run. It's cooled off a little." He fixed on his cap. "I got to see the baby anyway, and even held her a few minutes. I'm thinking my parents ought to talk to a lawyer, about custody or rights and all that."

"That's a tough call, Matt."

He gave the bill of his cap a quick jerk into place as he frowned at Rowan. "She's their blood, too. I don't want to screw with Mrs. Brakeman. I think she's a good person. But if that dickhead she's married to goes to jail, how is she supposed to take care of Shiloh all alone? How's she supposed to pay for all the stuff Shiloh needs on her salary cooking in the school cafeteria?"

"It's a hard situation, and, well, I know you already gave Dolly money for the baby."

Those faded blue eyes flattened out. "It's my money, and my blood."

"I know that. It was good of you to want to help with Shiloh's expenses, to stand in for Jim that way."

He relaxed a little. "It was the right thing to do."

"And it's not always easy to do the right thing in a hard situation. I guess I'd worry bringing lawyers in might murk it up even more. At least right now."

"It doesn't hurt to talk. Everybody should do whatever's best for the baby, right?"

"They should. I . . . I'm probably the wrong person to ask about something like this. Maybe, I don't know, Matt, if your mother came out . . . if she and Mrs. Brakeman talked about everything, they could work out what's best, what's right."

"Maybe. She looks like a Brayner, you know? The baby? Even Lynn said so. I've got to think about it."

She supposed they did, Rowan decided when he headed out for his run. Matt, his family, the Brakemans, they'd all have to think about it. But she knew what it was to be the child everybody was thinking about.

It wasn't an easy place to be.

22

Rowan watched Dobie painfully swallow shot number ten. His eyes had gone glassy on eight, and now his cheeks took on a faint, sickly green hue.

"That's twenty."

"Count's ten, Dobie," Cards, official scorekeeper, told him.

"I'm seeing double, so it's twenty." Laughing like a loon, he nearly tipped out of his chair.

Janis, official pourer, filled shot number eleven for Yangtree. "Experience," he said, and knocked it back smooth. "That's the key."

Rowan smirked, licked salt off the back of her hand, then drank hers down. "I'd like to thank the soon-to-be loser for springing for the prime."

"You're welcome." Gull polished off eleven.

"I got another in me." Stovic lifted his glass, proved he did—before he slid bonelessly to the floor.

"And he's out." Cards crossed Stovic off the board.

"I am not out." From the floor, Stovic waved a hand. "I'm fully conscious."

"You leave your chair without calling for a piss break, you're out."

"Who left the chair?"

"Come on, Chainsaw." Gibbons got his hands under Stovic's arms and dragged him out from under the table.

Dobie made it to thirteen before surrendering. "It's this foreign liquor, that's what it is. Oughta be homegrown bourbon." He got down, crawled on his hands and knees and lay down next to a snoring Stovic.

"Rookies." Yangtree got number fourteen down, then laid his head on the table and moaned, "Mommy."

"Did you mean uncle?" Cards demanded, and Yangtree managed to shoot up his middle finger.

Rowan and Gull went head-to-head until Janis split the last shot between them. "That's all there is, there ain't no more."

"Shoulda bought three bottles." Rowan closed one eye to focus and click her glass to Gull's. "On three?"

Those still conscious in the room counted off, then cheered when the last drops went down.

"And that's a draw," Cards announced.

"I'm proud to know you." Janis dropped a hand on each shoulder. "And wish you the best of luck with tomorrow's hangover."

"Gull doesn't get 'em."

He smiled, a little stupidly, into Rowan's eyes. "This might be the exception. Let's go have lotsa drunk sex before it hits."

"'Kay. Drunk sex for everybody!" She waved her hands and smacked a barely awake Yangtree in the face. "Oops."

"No, I needed that. Everybody still alive?"

"Can't make that much noise dead." Rowan gestured to snoring-in-stereo Stovic and Dobie as she swayed to her feet. "Follow me, stud."

"I'm with the blonde." Gull staggered after her.

"We can do this." She fumbled at his shirt when he booted the door shut on the third try. "Soon as the room stops spinning around."

"Pretend we're doing it on a merry-go-round."

"Naked at the carnival." On a wild laugh she defeated his shirt, but started to teeter. When he grabbed for her, she took them both onto the floor, hard.

"I think that hurt, but it's better down here, 'cause of the gravity."

"Okay." He shifted off her to struggle with her clothes. "We should do naked tequila shots. Then we wouldn't have to take them off after."

"Now you think of it. Alley-oop!" She held up her arms to help him strip off her shirt. "Gimme, gimme." She locked her legs around his waist, her arms around his neck, then latched her mouth onto his.

The heat burned through the tequila haze, fired in the senses. The world rolled and turned, yet she remained constant, chained around him. Caged, he met the desperate demand of her mouth, rocking center to center until he thought he'd go mad.

The chains broke. She rolled on top of him, biting, grasping, lapping, then rolled off again.

"Get naked," she ordered. "Beat ya."

They tugged at shoes, clothes in a panting race. With clothes still landing in heaps, they dived at each other. Wrestling now, skin damp and slick, they rolled over the floor. Knees and elbows banged, and still her laughter rang out. The moonlight turned her dewed skin to silver, glowing and precious, irresistible.

Breathless with pleasure, crazed with a whirling, spinning need, she threw her head back when he plunged into her.

"Take me like you mean it."

And he did, God, he did, filling her up, wringing her out while she pushed for more. Catching fire, she thought, leaping into the heart of the blaze. She rode the heat until it simply consumed her.

"Merry-go-round," she murmured. "Still turning. Stay right here." This time she drew him close before they slept.

ANOTHER FIRE WOKE HER, the fire that killed, that hunted and destroyed. It growled behind her, pawing at the ground as she ran. She flew through the black, yet still it came, stalking her to the graveyard where the dead lay unburied on the ground. Waiting for her.

Jim's eyes rolled up in the sockets of the charred skull. "Killed me dead."

"I'm sorry. I'm so sorry."

"Plenty of that going around. Plenty of dragon fever. It's not finished. More to come. Fire can't burn it away. But it can sure try."

From behind her, it breathed, and its breath ignited her like kindling.

"HEY, HEY." Gull pulled her to sitting, shaking her by the shoulders on the way. "Snap out of it."

She shoved at him, gulping for air, but he tightened his grip. He couldn't see her clearly, but he could feel her, hear her. The shakes and tremors, the cold sweat, the whistle of air as she fought for breath.

"You had a nightmare." He spoke more calmly now. "A bad one. It's done."

"Can't breathe."

"You can. You are, just too fast. You're going to hyperventilate if you keep it up. Slow it down, Rowan."

Even as she shook her head, he started rubbing her shoulders, moving up her neck where the muscles strained stiff as wire. "It's a panic attack. You know that in your head. Let the rest of you catch up. Slow it down."

He saw her eyes now as his own vision adjusted, wide as planets. She pressed a hand to her chest where he imagined the pressure crushed like an anvil. "Breathe out, long breath out. Long out, slow in. That's the way. Let go of it. Do it again, smooth it out. You're okay. Keep it up, in and out. I'm going to get you some water."

He let her go to roll to her cooler, grab a bottle.

"Don't guzzle," he warned her. "We're in slow mode." When she gulped the first swallow, he tipped the bottle down. "Easy."

"Okay." She took another, slower sip. She stopped, went back to breathing, with more control, less trembling. "Wow."

He touched her face, leaned in to rest his brow on hers. The shudder he'd held back rocked through him.

"You scared the shit out of me."

"That makes two of us. I didn't scream, did I?" She glanced toward the door as she asked.

Trust her, Gull thought, to worry about embarrassing herself with the rest of the crew. "No. It was like you were trying to and couldn't get it out."

"I was on fire. I swear I could feel my skin burning, smell my hair going up. Pretty damn awful."

"How often do you have them?" Now that the crisis had passed, he could coddle her a little—a comfort to himself, too. So he touched his lips to her forehead as he shifted to rub her back and shoulders.

"I never used to have them. Or just the usual monster-in-the-closet deal once in a while when I was a kid. But I started having them after Jim. Replaying the jump, then how we found him. They eased off over the winter, but started coming back at the start of the season. And they're getting worse."

"You found another fire victim, someone else you knew. That would kick it up some."

"He's started to talk to me in them—cryptic warnings. I know it's my head putting words in his mouth, but I can't figure it out."

"What did he say tonight?"

"That it wasn't finished. There'd be more coming. I guess I'm worried there will be, and that's probably all there is to it."

"Why are you worried?"

"Well, Jesus, Gull, who isn't?"

"No, be specific."

"Be specific at half past whatever in the morning after twisting myself up into a panic attack?"

The irritation in her tone settled him down. "Yeah."

"I don't know. If I knew, I'd . . . Dolly and Latterly, obviously that's connected. The odds of them both running afoul of some homicidal arsonist are just short of nil. If we were dealing with random, that would be cause for some serious worry. But this isn't, and they're probably going to bust Brakeman for the whole shot. But . . ."

"But you're having a hard time buying he'd set fire to his own daughter's body. So am I."

"Yeah, but that's what makes the most sense. He finds out Dolly's not only lying but screwing the preacher. They fight about it, he kills her—in a rage, by accident, however. Then panics, does the rest. It broke something in him."

Tears running down his face, she remembered.

"He shoots at us, kills Latterly. Case closed."

"Except you don't quite believe it. Hence—"

"Hence," she repeated, and snickered.

"That's right. Hence you have nightmares where Jim—who's connected to you and to Dolly—verbalizes what you're already thinking, at least on a subconscious level."

"Thanks, Dr. Freud."

"And your fifty minutes are up. You should catch the couple hours' sleep we've got left."

"We're still on the floor. The floor was most excellent, but for sleep, the bed's better."

"The bed it is." He rose, grabbed her hand to pull her up. Then, to make her laugh, swept her up in his arms.

Laugh she did. "I may have shed a few this season, but I'm still no lightweight."

"You're right." He dropped her onto the bed. "Next time, you carry me." He stretched out beside her. "One thing, it looks like your nightmare blew any potential tequila hangover out of me."

"Always the bright side."

He snuggled her in, gently stroking her back until he felt her drop off.

AFTER THE MORNING BRIEFING, she got in her run, some weight training and power yoga with Gull for company. She had to admit, having someone who could keep up with her, and more, made the daily routine more fun.

They hit the dining hall together where Dobie slumped over a plate of toast and what Rowan recognized as a glass of Marg's famed hangover cure.

"Mmm, look at these big, fat sausages." Rowan clattered the top back on the warmer. "Nothing like pig grease in the morning."

"I'll hurt you when I can move without my head blowing up."

"Hangover?" she asked sweetly. "Gosh, I feel *great*." There might have been a dull, gnawing ache at the base of her skull, but all things considered, small price to pay.

"Hurt you, and all your kin. Your pets, too."

She only grinned as she sat down with a full plate. "Not much appetite this morning?"

"I woke up on the floor with Stovic. I may never eat again."

"How's Stovic?" Gull asked.

"Last I saw him, his eyes were full of blood, and he was crawling toward his quarters. If I ever pick up a glass of tequila again, shoot me. It'd be a mercy."

"Drink that," Rowan advised. "It won't make you jump up and belt out 'Oh, What a Beautiful Morning,' but it'll take the edge off."

"It's brown. And I think something's moving in there."

"Trust me."

When he picked up the Tabasco Lynn kept on the table for him, Rowan started to tell him he wouldn't need it—then smiled to herself as she cut into a sausage.

Dobie doused the concoction liberally, gave a brisk, bracing nod. "Down the hatch," he announced. Closing his eyes, he drank it down fast.

And his eyes popped open as his face went from hangover gray to lobster red. "Holy shitfire!"

"Burns like a helitorch." Struggling with laughter, Rowan ate more sausage. "It may scorch some brain cells while it's at it, but it fires through the bloodstream. You've been purified, my child."

"He's not going to speak in tongues, is he?" Gull asked.

"Holy shitfire. *That's* a drink. All it needs is a shot of bourbon. Man, makes me sweat."

Fascinated, Gull watched sweat pop out on Dobie's red face. "Flushing out the toxins, I guess. What the hell's in there?"

"She won't tell. She makes you start with the M-and-M Breakfast—Motrin and Move-Free—with a full glass of water, then drink that, eat toast, drink more water."

"Said I had to do my run, too."

"Yeah." Rowan nodded at Dobie. "And by lunchtime, you'll feel mostly human and be able to eat. Somebody ought to drag Stovic down here—and Yangtree. Hey, Cards," she said when he walked in. "How about hauling Stovic's and Yangtree's pitiful asses down here so we can pour some of Marg's hangover antidote into them?"

He said nothing until he'd taken the chair beside hers, angled it toward her. "L.B. just got word from the cops. The rangers found a gun, half buried a few yards from where they found the preacher's car. They ran it. It's one of Brakeman's."

"Well." Deliberately she spread huckleberry jelly on a breakfast biscuit. "I guess that answers that."

"They went to pick him up this morning. He's gone, his truck's gone."

Jelly dripped off her knife as she stared at him. "You don't mean as in gone to work."

"No. It looks like he took camping gear, a shotgun, a rifle, two handguns and a whole hell of a lot of ammo. His wife said she didn't know where he'd gone, or that he'd packed up in the first place. I don't know if they believe her or not, but from what L.B. says, nobody seems to have the first goddamn clue where he is."

"I thought— I heard they were going to take him in after the funeral yesterday."

"For questioning, yeah. But he has a lawyer and all that, and until they had the gun, Ro, they didn't have anything on him for this shit."

"For Christ's sake," Gull exploded. "Didn't they have him under surveillance?"

"I don't know. I don't know dick-all about it, Gull. But L.B. says he wants you to stay on base, Ro, unless we catch a fire. He wants you to stay inside as much as possible until we know what the fuck. And he doesn't want to hear any carping about it."

"I'll work in the loft."

"They'll get him, Ro. It won't take them long."

"Sure."

He gave her arm an awkward pat. "I'll roust Yangtree and Stovic. It'll be fun watching the smoke come out of their ears when they drink the hangover cure."

In the silence that followed Cards's exit, Dobie got up, poured himself coffee. "I'm going to say this 'cause I have a lot of respect for you. And because Gull's got more than that for you. If I took off into the hills back home, if I had the gear—hell, even without it, but if I had the gear, a good gun, a good knife, I could live up there for months. Nobody'd find me I didn't want finding me."

Rowan made herself continue eating. "They'll find his truck, maybe, but they won't find him. He'll lose himself in the Bitter-roots, or the Rockies. His wife'll lose her home. She put it up for his bond, and he just fucking broke that. I didn't believe he'd done it—or not Dolly. He's running, and left his wife and grand-daughter twisting in the wind. He abandoned them.

"I hope he screws up." She shoved to her feet. "I hope he screws up and they catch him, and they toss him in a hole for the rest of his life. I'll be in the loft, sewing goddamn Smitty bags."

As she stomped out, Dobie dumped three heaping spoons of sugar into his coffee. "How do you want to play this, son?"

"Intellectually, I don't think Brakeman's coming back around here, or worrying about Rowan right now."

"Mmm-hmm. How do you want to play it?"

He looked over. Sometimes the most unlikely person became the most trusted friend. "When we're on base, some-body's with her, round the clock. We make sure she has plenty to do inside. But she needs to get out. If we hole her in, she'll blow. I guess we mix up the routine. We usually run in the mornings, early. We'll start running in the evening."

"If everybody wore caps, sunglasses, it'd be a little harder to tell who's who at a distance. The trouble is, that woman's built like a brick shithouse. You just can't hide that talent. I don't guess she'd transfer to West Yellowstone, or maybe over to Idaho for a stretch."

"No. She'd see that as running. Abandonment."

"Maybe. But maybe not, if you went, too."

"She's not there yet, Dobie."

Dobie pursed his lips, watching Gull as he drank coffee. "But you are?"

Gull stared down at his half-eaten breakfast. "Fucking lupines."

"What the hell's lupines?"

Gull just shook his head. "Yeah, I'm there," he said as he got to his feet. "Goddamn it."

Southern, Gibbons and Janis came in, still sweaty from PT, as Gull stormed out.

"What's that about?" Gibbons demanded.

"Sit down, boys and girls, and I'll tell you."

———————

TEMPER BUBBLING, Gull tracked down L.B. outside a hangar in conversation with one of the pilots.

"How the fuck did this happen?"

"Do you think I didn't ask the same damn thing?" L.B. tossed back. "Do you think I'm not pissed off?"

"I don't care if you're pissed off. I want some answers."

L.B. jerked a thumb, headed away from the hangar and toward one of the service roads. "If you want to jump somebody's ass, find a cop. They're the ones who screwed this up."

"I want to know how."

"You want to know how? I'll tell you how." L.B. picked up a palm-sized rock, heaved it. "They had two cops outside the Brakeman house. Shit, probably looking at skin mags and eating donuts."

He found another rock, heaved that. "My fucking brother's a cop, over in Helena, and I know he doesn't do that shit. But goddamn it."

Gull leaned over, picked up a rock, offered it. "Go ahead."

"Thanks." After hurling it, L.B. rolled his shoulder. "They were out in the front, watching the house. Brakeman's truck is around the side, under a carport. So he loads it up sometime in the middle of the night, then he pushes it right across the backyard, cuts a truck-sized hole in the frigging fence, then pushes it right across the neighbor's yard to the road. Then God knows where he went."

"And the cops don't see the truck's gone until this morning."

"No, they fucking don't."

"Okay."

"Okay? That's it?"

"It's an answer. I do better with answers. She's third load. Can you put her on Ops if we get a call for one or two?"

"Yeah." L.B. picked up another rock, just stared at it a moment, then dropped it again. "I'd figured on it. I just wanted to wait until she'd cooled off."

"I'll tell her."

"She's been known to kill the messenger. That's why I sent Cards," L.B. added with a slow smile. "He's just off the DL, so I figured she'd take it easy on him."

"That's why you're chief."

Gull swung by the barracks to grab a Coke, considered, and though he thought it the lamest form of camouflage outside a Groucho mustache, he grabbed caps and sunglasses.

On the way to the loft, he pulled out his phone, called Lucas.

Since most of the unit was doing PT or still at breakfast, he found only a handful working in the loft along with Rowan. She inspected, gore by gore, a canopy hanging in the tower.

"Busy," she said shortly.

He tipped the Coke from side to side. "You know you're jonesing by now."

"Very busy." Using tweezers, she removed some pine needles lodged in the cloth.

"Fine, I'll drink it." He popped the top. "L.B. wants you in Ops if we catch a fire."

She jerked around. "He's not grounding me."

"I didn't say that. You're third load, so unless we catch a holocaust, you're probably not going to jump on the first call. You're a qualified assistant Ops manager, aren't you?"

She grabbed the Coke from him, gulped some down. "Yeah." She shoved it back at him, returned to her inspection. "Thanks for letting me know."

"No problem. About this situation."

"I don't want or need to be reassured, protected, advised or—"

"Jesus, shut up." He shook his head at the ceiling towering above, took another drink.

"*You* shut up."

He had to grin. "I'm rubber; you're glue. You really want to sink that low? I don't think Brakeman's your problem."

"I'm not worried about him. I can take care of myself, and I'm not stupid. I've got plenty to keep me busy, here, in manufacturing, in the gym when I'm not out on a fire."

Meticulously she removed a twig, marked a small, one-inch tear for repair before she lowered the apex to examine higher areas.

"Last night, Brakeman eluded two cops by pushing his full-size pickup across his backyard, cutting a fence, pushing it across another yard until he reached the road. He loaded up everything he'd need to live in the wild. That tells me he's not stupid, either."

"So he's not stupid. Points for him."

"But he leaves weapons, *twice*, so they're easily found. A handgun properly registered to him, a rifle that has his name on it. That's pretty damn stupid."

"You're back to thinking he didn't do any of this."

"I'm back to that. I'd rather not be, because this way, we've got nothing. We don't know who or why. Not really. On the other hand, I'm also thinking it's unlikely anyone's going to be using you or the base for target practice. Unlikely isn't enough, but it's comforting."

"Because it would be stupid for somebody else to shoot at me, when Brakeman's on the run and the cops know what weapons he's got with him."

No, she wasn't stupid, she reminded herself, but she'd been too angry to think clearly. Gull, it seemed, didn't have the same problem.

"But if it's not him, Gull, why is somebody working so hard to make it look like him?"

"Because he's an asshole? Because he's plausible? Because they want to see him go down? Maybe all three. But the point is, you've got to be smart—and you are—but I don't think you have to sweat this."

She nodded, inspected the apex bridle cords, then the vent hoods.

"I wasn't sweating it. I'm pissed off."

"Your subconscious sweats it, then."

"All right, all right." She inspected the top of each slot, then the anti-inversion net. There she marked a line of broken stitching.

Gull waited her out until she'd attached the inspection tag to the riser.

"I guess I have to call my father. Word travels, and he'll get worried."

"I talked to him before I came up. We went over it."

"He came by? Why didn't he—"

"I called him."

She faced him with one quick pivot. "You did what? What do you mean calling my father about all this before I—"

"It's called male bonding. You'll never get it. I believe women are as capable as men, deserve equal pay—and that one day, should be sooner than later, in my opinion, the right woman can and should be leader of the free world. But you can't understand the male bonding rituals any more than men can understand why the vast majority of women are obsessed with shoes and other footwear."

"I'm not obsessed with shoes, so don't try to make this something cultural or—or gender-based."

"You have three pairs of jump boots. Two is enough. You have four pairs of running shoes. Again, two's plenty."

"I'm breaking in a third pair of jump boots before the first pair gets tossed so I don't get boot-bit. And I have four pairs of running shoes because . . . you're trying to distract me from the point."

"Yes, but I'm not done. You also have hiking boots—two pairs—three pairs of sandals and three of really sexy heels. And this is just on base. God knows what you've got in your closet at home."

"You've been counting my shoes? Talk about obsessed."

"I'm just observant. Lucas wants you to call him when you get a chance. Leave him a text or voice message if he's in the air, and he'll come by to see you tonight. He likes knowing I've got your back. You'd have mine, wouldn't you?" he asked before she could snap at him.

So she sighed. "Yes. You defeat me with your reason and your diatribe over shoes. Over which I am *not* obsessed."

"You also have a good dozen pairs of earrings, none of which you wear routinely. But we can discuss that another time."

"Oh, go away. Go study something."

"You could give me a rigging lesson. I want to work on getting certified."

"Maybe. Come back in an hour, and we'll—"

When the siren sounded she stepped back. "I guess not. I'm switching to Ops."

"I'll walk you over. Here."

He handed her her cap and sunglasses, then put on his own while she frowned at them.

"What is this?"

"A disguise." He grinned at her. "Dobie wants you to wear them. Let's give him a break, or he might order fake mustaches and clown noses off the Internet."

She rolled her eyes, but put them on. "And what, this makes us look like twins? Where are your tits?"

"You're wearing them, and may I say they look spectacular on you."

"I can't disagree with that. Still, everybody should stop worrying about Rowan and do their jobs."

By four P.M., she was jumping fire, doing hers.

23

July burned. Hot and dry, the wild ignited, inflamed by lightning strikes, negligence, an errant spark bellowed by a gust of wind.

For eighteen straight days and nights Zulies jumped and fought fire. In Montana, in Idaho, Colorado, California, the Dakotas, New Mexico. Bodies shed weight, lived with pain, exhaustion, injury, battling in canyons, on ridges, in forests.

The constant war left little time to think about what lived outside the fire. The manhunt for Leo Brakeman heading into its third week hardly mattered when the enemy shot firebrands the size of cannonballs or swept on turbulent winds over barriers so effortfully created.

Along with her crew, Rowan rushed up the side of Mount Blackmore, like a battalion charging into hell. Beside her another tree torched off, spewing embers like flaming confetti. They felled burning trees on the charge, sawed and cut the low-hanging branches the fire could climb like snakes.

Can't let her climb, Rowan thought as they hacked and dug. Can't let her crown.

Can't let her win.

So they fought their way up the burning mountain, sweat running in salty rivers in the scorched air.

When Gull climbed up the line to her position, she pulled down her bandanna to pour water down her aching throat.

"The line's holding." He jerked a thumb over his shoulder. "A couple of spots jumped it, but we pissed them out. Gibbons is going to leave a couple down there to scout for more, and send the rest up to you."

"Good deal." She took another drink, scanning and counting yellow shirts and helmets through the smoke. On the left the world glowed, eerie orange with an occasional spurt of flame that picked out a hardened, weary face, tossed it into sharp relief.

In that moment, she loved them, loved them all with a near religious fervor. Every ass and elbow, she thought, every blister and burn.

Her eyes lit when she looked at Gull. "Best job ever."

"If you don't mind starving, sweating and eating smoke."

Grinning, she shouldered her Pulaski. "Who would? Head on up. We're still making line here so—" She broke off, grabbed his arm.

It spun out of the orange wall, whipped by the wind. The funnel of flame whirled and danced, spinning a hundred feet into the air. In seconds, screaming like a banshee, it uprooted two trees.

"Fire devil. *Run!*" She pointed toward the front of the line as its wind blasted the furnace heat in her face. She grabbed her radio, watching the flaming column's spin as she shouted to the crew, "Go up, go up! *Move* your asses. Gibbons, fire devil, south flank. Stay *clear.*"

It roared toward the line, a tornadic gold light as gorgeous as it was terrifying, spewing flame, hurling fiery debris. The air exploded with the call of it, with its lung-searing heat. She watched Matt go down, saw Gull haul him up, take his weight. Keeping her eye on the fire devil, she shifted, got her shoulder under Matt's other arm.

"Just my ankle. I'm okay."

"Keep moving! Keep moving!"

It snaked toward them, undulating. They'd never outrun it,

she thought, not with Matt stumbling and limping between them. Behind Matt's back, Gull's hand gripped her elbow, and in acknowledgment, she did the same.

This is it. Even thinking it she pushed up the ridge. No time for emergency gear, for the shelters.

"There!" Gull jerked her, with Matt between them, to the right, and another five precious feet. He shoved her under the enormous boulder first, then Matt, before crawling under behind them.

"Here we go," Gull breathed, and stared into Rowan's eyes while the world erupted.

Rock exploded and rained down like bullets. Through smoke black as pitch, Rowan saw a blazing tree crash and vomit out a flood of flame and sparks.

"Short, shallow breaths, Matt." She gripped his hand, squeezed hard. "Just like in a shake and bake."

"Is this what Jim felt?" Tears and sweat rolled down his face. "Is this what he felt?"

"Short and shallow," she repeated. "Through your bandanna, just like in a shelter."

For an instant, another, the heat built to such mad intensity she wondered if they'd all just torch like a tree. She worked her other hand free, found Gull's. And held on.

Then the screaming wind silenced.

"It's cooling. We're okay. We're okay?" she repeated, in a question this time.

"What can you see?" Gull asked her.

"The smoke's starting to thin, a little. We've got a lot of spots. Spots, no wall, no devil." She shifted as much as she could. "Get behind me, Matt, so I can look out." She angled beside Gull, cautiously eased her head out to look out, up. "It didn't crown, didn't roll the wall. Just spots. Jesus, Gull, your jacket's smoking." She beat at it with her hands as he worked to shrug out of it. "Are you burned?" she demanded. "Did it get you?"

"I don't think so." He crab-walked back. "The ground's still hot. Watch yourselves."

Rowan crawled out, reaching for her radio. On it Gibbons shouted her name.

"It's Ro, Gull, Matt. We're good. We're clear. Is everybody all right? Is everybody accounted for?"

"We are now." Relief flooded his voice. "Where the hell are you?"

She stood, scanned the area to give him the best coordinates. "Matt's bunged up his ankle. Gull and I can handle these spots, but we dumped most of the gear on the run so . . . Never mind," she said as she heard the shouts, saw the yellow shirts through the smoke. "Cavalry's coming this way."

Dobie came on the run with Trigger right behind him. "Jesus Christ, why don't you just give us all heart attacks and get it over with?"

He grabbed Gull, slapped his back. "What the hell happened to you?"

"A little dance with the devil. Better put out those spots before we end up having to run again."

Trigger crouched beside Matt, held out a scorched and mangled helmet. "Found your brainbucket, snookie. You're a lucky bastard." He put Matt in a headlock, a sign of relief and affection. "A lucky son of a bitch. Have a souvenir."

He set the helmet beside Matt before hurrying over to help Dobie with the spot fires.

"Let's check that ankle out." Rowan knelt to undo his boot.

"I thought we were finished. I would've been finished if you and Gull hadn't gotten me in there. You saved my life. You could've lost yours trying."

She probed gently at his swollen ankle. "We're Zulies. When one of us goes down, we pick them up. I don't think it's broken. Just sprained bad enough to earn you a short vacation."

She looked up, smiled at him as she started to wrap it. "Lucky bastard."

Though he protested, they medevaced Matt out, while the rest of the crew beat the fire back, finally killing it in the early hours of the morning. Mop-up took another full day of digging, beating, dousing.

"You volunteered to stay back, confirm the put-out," Rowan told Gull.

"I've got to quit all this volunteering."

"With me. The rest are packing out."

"That's not such a bad deal."

"We've got MREs, a cool mountain spring, in which the beer fairy has snugged a six-pack."

"And people say she doesn't exist."

"What do people know? I wanted to see this one through, all the way, and take a breath, I guess. So you're good with it?"

"What do you think?"

"Then let's take a hike, start doing a check before the sun goes down."

They moved through the burnout at an easy pace, looking for smoke and smolder.

"I wanted to wait until it was over—all the way—before I said anything about it," Rowan began. "I didn't think we were going to make it back there against the fire devil. If you hadn't spotted those boulders, reacted fast, we'd have all ended up like Matt's now-famous helmet."

"I don't plan on losing you. Anyway, if you'd been on my side, you'd've seen the boulders."

"I like to think so. It was beautiful," she said after a moment, and with reverence. "It might be crazy to say that, think that, about something that really wants to kill you, but it was beautiful. That spinning column of fire, like something from another world. In a way, I guess it is."

"Once you see one, it changes things because you know you can't beat it. You run and hide and you pray, and if you live through it, for a while, all the bullshit in real life doesn't mean dick."

"For a while. I guess that's why I wanted to stay out, stick with it a little longer. There's a lot of bullshit waiting out there. Leo Brakeman's still out there. He's no fire devil, but he's still out there."

She blew out a breath. "Every time we get a call, I wonder if we're going to stumble over another body. His, someone else's. Because he's out there. And if he didn't start those fires, whoever did is out there, too."

"It's been three weeks. That's a long time between."

"But it doesn't feel over and done."

"No. It doesn't feel over and done."

"That's the bullshit waiting." She gestured. "Why don't you

take that direction, I'll take this one. We'll cover more ground, then meet back at camp." She checked her watch. "Say six-thirty."

"In time for cocktails and hors d'oeuvres."

SHE BEAT HIM BACK to the clearing by the bubbling stream. The campsite, a hive the night before of very tired, very grungy bees, held quiet as a church now, and shimmered in the rays of evening sun. She stowed her gear, checked on the six-pack of beer and the six-pack of Coke she'd asked L.B. to drop.

She'd rather have that, she realized, in this remote spot on the mountain than a bottle of the finest champagne in the fanciest restaurant in Montana.

In anywhere.

She went back for her PG bag and her little bottles of liquid soap and shampoo.

Alone in the sunlight, she pulled off her boots, socks, stripped off the tired work clothes. The stream barely hit her knees, but the cool rush of the water felt like heaven. She sat down, let it bubble over her skin as she looked up to the rise of trees, the spread of sky.

She took time washing, as another woman might in a hot, fragrant bubble bath, enjoying the cool, the clean, the way the water rushed away with the froth she made.

Drawing her knees up, she wrapped her arms around them, laid her cheek on her knees, closed her eyes.

She opened them again as a shadow fell over her, and smiled lazily up at Gull. Until she saw the camera.

"You did not take my picture like this. Am I going to have to break that thing?"

"It's for my private collection. You're a fantasy, Rowan. Goddess of the brook. How's the water?"

"Cold."

He, as she did, pulled off his boots. "I could use some cold."

"You're late. It's got to be close to seven."

"I had a little detour."

"Did you find fresh spots?"

"No, all clear. But I found these." He picked up a water bottle filled with wildflowers.

"You know you're not supposed to pick flowers up here." But she couldn't stop the smile.

"Since we save them, I figured the mountain could spare a few. Yeah, it's pretty damn cold," he said as he stepped into the water. "Feels great."

She pulled out the bottle of soap she'd shoehorned between rocks, tossed it to him. "Help yourself. It feels like we're the only two people in the world. I wouldn't want to be the only two people in the world for long—who'd do the cooking?—but it's nice for right now."

"I heard birds in the black. They're already coming back, at least to see what the hell happened. And in the green, across the meadow where I got the flowers, I saw a herd of elk. We may be the only people here, but life rolls on."

"I'm going to get dressed before I freeze." She stood, water sliding down her body, sun glinting to turn it to tiny diamonds.

"Wow," Gull said.

"For that, and the bottle of wildflowers, I guess you've earned a beer." She got out, shivering now, rubbing her skin to warm and dry it. "We've got spaghetti and meat sauce, fruit cups, crackers and cheese spread and pound cake for dinner."

"Right now I could eat cardboard and be happy, so that sounds amazing."

"I'll get the campfire going," she told him as she dressed. "And you get the beer when you get out. I guess cocktails and hors d'oeuvres will consist of— Holy shit."

"That I don't want to eat, even now."

"Don't move. Or do—*really* fast."

"Why?"

"Life rolls along, including the big-ass bear on the other bank."

"Oh, fuck me." Gull turned slowly, watched the big-ass bear lumber up toward the stream.

"This may be your fantasy come true, but I really think you should get out of the water."

"Crap. Throw something at him," Gull suggested as he stayed low, edging through the water.

"Like what, harsh words? Shit, shit, he's looking at us."

"Get one of the Pulaskis. I'm damned if I'm going to be eaten by a bear when I'm naked."

"I'm sure it's a more pleasant experience dressed. He's not going to eat us. They eat berries and fish. Get out of the water so he doesn't think you're a really big fish."

Gull pulled himself out, stood dripping, eyeing the bear and being eyed. "Retreat. Slowly. He's probably just screwing with us, and he'll go away, but in case."

Even as Rowan reached down for the gear, the bear turned its back on them. It squatted, shat, then lumbered away the way it came.

"Well, I guess he showed us what he thinks of us." Overcome, Rowan sat on the ground, roared with laughter. "A real man would go after him, make him pay for that insult—so I could then tend your wounds."

"Too bad, you're stuck with me." Gull scooped both hands through his dripping hair. "Christ, I want that beer."

As far as Gull was concerned, ready-to-eat pasta and beer by a crackling campfire in the remote mountain wilderness scored as romantic as candlelight and fine wine in crystal. And beat the traditional trappings on the fun scale by a mile.

She'd relaxed for the first time in weeks, he thought, basking in the aftermath of a job well done and the solitude of what they'd preserved.

"Does your family do the camping thing?" she asked him.

"Not so much. My aunt's more the is-there-room-service? type. I used to go with some buddies. We'd head up the coast—road trip, you know? Pick a spot. I always figured to head east, take on the Appalachian Trail, but between this and the arcade, I haven't pulled that one off."

"That'd be a good one. We mostly stuck to Montana, for recreation. There's so much here anyway. My dad would work it out so he'd have two consecutive days off every summer, and take me. We'd never know when he'd get them, so it was always spur-of-the-moment."

"That made it cooler," Gull commented, and she just beamed at him.

"It really did. It didn't occur to me until after I'd joined the unit that wilderness camping on his days off probably wouldn't have been his first choice. I imagine he could've used that room service."

"Kids come first, right? The universal parental code."

"I guess it should be. I was thinking about Dolly and her father earlier, and the way they'd tear into each other. Was it their fractured dynamic that made her the way she was, or did the way she was fracture the dynamic?"

"Things are hardly ever all one way or the other."

"More a blend," she agreed. "A little from each column. Don't you wonder what aimed her at Latterly? There are plenty of unmarried men she could've hooked up with. And he was, what, about fifteen years older and not what you'd call studly."

"Maybe he was a maniac in bed."

"Yeah, still waters and so on, but you've got to get into bed to find that out. A married guy with three kids. A God guy. If she'd really planned on reeling him in toward the 'I do's,' didn't she consider what her life would be like? A preacher's wife, and stepmother of three? She'd have hated it."

"It might just have been a matter of proving something. Married God guy, father of three. And she thinks, I could get him if I wanted."

"I don't get that kind of thinking," she stated. "For a one-night stand, I can see it. You've got an itch, you scope out the talent in the bar, rope one out of the herd to scratch it. I don't see wrecking a family for another notch on the bedpost."

"Because you're thinking like you." Gull opened the last two beers. "The older-man thing. He'd probably be inclined to indulge her, and be really grateful that a woman her age, with her looks, wanted to sleep with him. It's a pretty good recipe for infatuation on both sides."

She angled her head. "You know, you're right. A guy a little bored in his marriage, a needy young single mother. There's a recipe. Of course, for all we know Latterly might've been a hound dog boning half the women in his congregation, and Dolly was just the latest."

"If so, the cops'll find out, if they haven't already. Sex is never off the radar."

"Maybe they'll have this thing wrapped up when we get

back." She broke off a piece of pound cake. "Nobody talks about it much, but it's on everybody's mind. L.B.'s especially because he's got to think about everybody, evaluate everybody, worry about everybody."

"Yeah, he's handling a lot. He has a smooth way of juggling."

"My rookie season, we had Bootstrap. He was okay, ran things pretty smooth, but you could tell, even a rook could tell, his head was already halfway into retirement. He had this cabin up in Washington State, and that's where he wanted to be. Everybody knew it was his last season. He kept a distance, if you know what I mean, with the rookies especially."

Gull nodded, sampled pound cake. Ambrosia. "He didn't want to get close. Didn't want to make any more personal bonds."

"I think that was a good part of it. Then L.B. took over. You know how he is. He's the boss, but he's one of us. Everybody knows if you need to bitch or whine or let off steam, you can go to him."

"Here's to L.B."

"Bet your ass." She tipped her head as they clinked beer cans. "I like having sex with you."

Those cat eyes gleamed in the firelight. "That's a non-sequitur I can get behind."

"Seriously. It occurs to me that the season's half over, and I've never had another one like it. Murder, arson, mayhem, and I'm having sex regularly."

"Let's hope the last element is the only one that spills over into the second half."

"Absolutely. The thing is, Gulliver, while I really like sex with you, I also realize that if we stopped having sex—"

"Bite your tongue."

"If we did," she said with a laugh, "I'd still like sitting around the fire with you, and talking about whatever."

"Same here. Only I want the sex."

"Handy for both of us. What makes it better, over and above the regular, is you don't secretly wish I'd be something else. Less tied up with the job, more inclined to fancy underwear."

He pulled out a cigar, lit it. Blew out a long stream. "I like fancy underwear. Just for the record."

"It doesn't bother you that I had a hand in training you, and I might be the one giving you orders on a fire."

She took the cigar when he offered it, enjoyed the tang. "Because you know who you are, and that matters. I can't push you around, and that matters, too. And there's this thing I didn't think mattered because it never did. But it does when it's mixed in with the rest. When it's blended, like we said before. You bring me flowers in a bottle."

"I think of you," he said simply.

She pulled on the cigar again, giving her emotions time to settle, then passed it back to him. "I know, and that's another new element for the season. And here's one more. I guess the thing is, Gull, I'm in care with you, too."

He reached out for her hand. "I know. But it's nice to hear you say it."

"Know-it-all." Still holding his hand, she tipped her head back, looked at the star-swept sky. "It'd be nice to just stay here a couple of days. No worries, no wondering."

"We'll come back, after the season's over."

She couldn't see that far. Next month, she thought, next year? As distant as the stars. As murky as smoke. Always better, to her way of thinking, to concentrate on the right now.

TOWARD DAWN, Gull slipped through a dream of swimming under a waterfall. He dove deep into the blue crystal of the pool where sunbeams washed the gilded bottom in shimmering streaks. Overhead water struck water in a steady, muted drumbeat while Rowan, skin as gold and sparkling as the sand, eyes as clear and cool as the pool, swam toward him.

Their arms entwined, their mouths met, and his pulse beat like the drumming water.

As he lay against her, his hand lazily stroking along her hip, he thought himself dreaming still. He drifted toward the surface, in the dream and out of the dream, and the water drummed on.

It echoed in the confines of the tent when he opened his eyes. Smiling in the dark, he gave Rowan a little shake.

"Hey, do you hear that?"

"What?" Her tone, sleepy and annoyed, matched the nudge

back she gave him. "What?" she repeated, more lucidly. "Is it the bear? Is it back?"

"No. Listen."

"I don't want . . . It's rain." She shoved him with more force as she pushed to sit up. "It's raining!"

She crawled to the front of the tent, opened the flap. "Oh, yeah, baby! Rain, rain, don't go away. Do you *hear* that?"

"Yeah, but I'm a little distracted by the view right this minute."

He caught the glint of her eyes as she glanced over her shoulder, grinned. Then she was out of the tent and letting out a long, wild cheer.

What the hell, he thought, and climbed out after her.

She threw her arms up, lifted her face. "This isn't a storm, or a quick summer shower. This is what my grandfather likes to call a soaker. And about damn time."

She pumped her fists, her hips, high stepped. "Give it up, Gulliver! Dance! Dance to honor the god of rain!"

So he danced with her, naked, in the rainy gloom of dawn, then dragged her back in the tent to honor the rain gods his way.

The steady, soaking rain watered the thirsty earth, and made for a wet pack-out. Rowan held on to the cheer with every step of every mile.

"Maybe it's a sign," she said as rain slid off their ponchos, dripped off the bills of their caps. "Maybe it's one of those turning points, and means the worst of the crap's behind us."

Gull figured it was a lot to expect from one good rain in a dry summer—but he never argued against hope.

24

Rowan refused to let the news that Leo Brakeman remained at large discourage her, and instead opted for Gull's glass half full of no further arson fires or connected murders in almost a month.

Maybe the cops would never find him, never solve those crimes. It didn't, and wouldn't, change her life.

While she and Gull packed out, a twelve-man team jumped a fire in Shoshone, putting the two of them back on the jump list as soon as they'd checked in.

That was her life, she thought as she unpacked and re-organized her gear. Training, preparing, doing, then cleaning up to go again.

Besides, when she studied the big picture, she couldn't complain. As the season edged toward August, she'd had no injuries, had managed to maintain a good, fighting weight by losing only about ten pounds, and had justified L.B.'s faith in her by proving herself a solid fire boss on the line. Most important, she'd had a part in saving countless acres of wildland.

The fact she'd managed to accomplish that *and* build what

she had to admit had become an actual relationship was cause to celebrate, not a reason to niggle with the downsides.

She decided to do just that with something sweet and indulgent from the cookhouse.

She found Marg out harvesting herbs in the cool, damp air.

"We brought the rain down with us," Rowan told her. "It followed us all the way in. Didn't stop until we flew over Missoula."

"It's the first time I haven't had to water the garden in weeks. Ground soaked it right up, though. We're going to need more. Brought out the damn gnats, too." Marg swatted at them as she lifted her basket. She spritzed a little of her homemade bug repellant on her hands, patted her face with it and sweetened the air with eucalyptus and pennyroyal. "I guess you're looking for some food."

"Anything with a lot of sugar."

"I can fix you up." Marg cocked her head. "You look pretty damn good for a woman who hiked a few hours in the rain."

"I feel pretty damn good, and I think that's why."

"It wouldn't have anything to do with a certain good-looking, green-eyed jumper?"

"Well, he was hiking with me. It didn't hurt."

"It's a little bright spot for me." Inside, Marg set her herb basket on the counter. "Watching the romances. Yours, your father's."

"I don't know if it's . . . My father's?"

"I ran into Lucas and his lady friend at the fireworks, and again a couple days ago at the nursery. She was helping him pick out some plants."

"Plants? You're talking about my father? Lucas black-thumb Tripp?"

"One and the same." As she spoke, Marg cut a huge slice of Black Forest cake. "Ella's helping him put in a flower bed. A little one to start. He was looking at arbors."

"Arbors? You mean the . . ." Rowan drew an arch with her forefingers. "Come on. Dad's gardening skills start and stop with mowing the lawn."

"Things change." She set the cake and a tall glass of milk in front of Rowan. "As they should or we'd all just stand in the same place. It's good to see him lit up about something that doesn't involve a parachute or an engine. You ought to be happy about that, Rowan, especially since there's a lot of lights dimming around here right now."

"I just don't know, that's all. What's wrong with standing in the same place if it's a good place?"

"Even a good place gets to be a rut, especially if you're standing in it alone. Honey, alone and lonely share the same root. Eat your cake."

"I don't see how Dad could be lonely. He's always got so much going on. He has so many friends."

"And nobody there when he turns off the lights—until recently. If you can't see how much happier he is since Ella, then you're not paying attention."

Rowan searched around for a response, then noticed Marg's face when the cook turned away to wash her herbs in the sink. Obviously she hadn't been paying attention here, Rowan realized, or she'd have seen the sadness.

"What's wrong, Marg?"

"Oh, just tough times. Tougher for some. I know you'd probably be fine if Leo Brakeman wasn't seen or heard from again. And I don't blame you a bit for it. But it's beating down on Irene."

"If he comes back, or they find him, he'll probably go to prison. I don't know if that's better for her."

"Knowing's always better. In the meantime, she had to take on another job, as her pay from the school isn't enough to cover the bills. Especially since she leveraged the house for his bail. And taking on the work, she can't see to the baby."

"Can't her family help her through it?"

"Not enough, I guess. It's the money, but it's also the time, the energy, the wherewithal. The last time I saw her, she looked worn to the nub. She's ready to give up, and I don't know how much longer she can hold out."

"I'm sorry, Marg. Really. We could take up a collection. I guess it wouldn't be more than a finger in the dike for a bit, but the baby's Jim's. Everybody'd do what they could."

"Honestly, Ro, I don't think she'd accept it. On top of it all, that woman's shamed down to the root of her soul. What her husband and her daughter did here, that weighs on her. I don't think she could take money from us. I've known Irene since we were girls, and she could hardly look at me. That breaks my heart."

Rowan rose, cut another, smaller slice of cake, poured another glass of milk. "You sit down. Eat some cake. We'll fix it," she added. "There's always a way to fix something if you keep at it long enough."

"I like to think so, but I don't know how much long enough Irene's got left."

WHEN ELLA CAME BACK DOWNSTAIRS, Irene continued to sit on the couch, shoulders slumped, eyes downcast. Deliberately Ella fixed an easy smile on her face.

"She's down. I swear that's the sweetest baby, Irene. Just so sunny and bright." She didn't mention the time she'd spent folding and putting away the laundry in the basket by the crib, or the disarray she'd noticed in Irene's usually tidy home.

"She makes me want more grandbabies," Ella went on, determinedly cheerful. "I'm going to go make us some tea."

"The kitchen's a mess. I don't know if I even have any tea. I didn't make it to the store."

"I'll go find out."

Dishes were piled in the sink of the little kitchen Ella always found cozy and charming. The near-empty cupboards, the sparsely filled refrigerator, clearly needed restocking.

That, at least, she could do.

She found a box of tea bags, filled the kettle. As she began filling the dishwasher, Irene shuffled in.

"I'm too tired to even be ashamed of the state of my own kitchen, or to see you doing my dishes."

"There's nothing to be ashamed of, and you'd insult our friendship if you were."

"I used to have pride in my home, but it's not really my home now. It's the bank's. It's just a place to live now, until it's not."

"Don't talk like that. You're going to get through this. You're just worn out. Why don't you let me take the baby for a day or two, give yourself a chance to catch your breath? You know I'd love it. Then we could sit down, and if you'd let me, we could go over your financial situation, see if there's anything—"

She broke off when she turned to see tears rolling down Irene's face. "Oh, I'm sorry. I'm sorry." Abandoning the dishes, she hurried over to wrap Irene in her arms.

"I can't do it, Ella. I just can't. I've got no fight left. No heart."

"You're just so tired."

"I am. I am tired. The baby's teething, and when she's fretful in the night, I lie there wishing she'd just stop. Just be quiet, give me some peace. I'm passing her off to anybody who'll take her for a few hours while I work, and even with the extra work, I'm not going to make the house payments, unless I let something else go."

"Let me help you."

"Help me what? Pay my bills, raise my grandchild, keep my house?" Even the hard words held no life. "For how long, Ella? Until Leo gets back, if he comes back? Until he gets out of prison, if he goes to prison?"

"With whatever you need to get you through this, Irene."

"I know you mean well, but I don't see getting through. I wanted to believe him. He's my husband, and I wanted to believe him when he told me he didn't do any of it."

With nothing to say, Ella kept silent while Irene looked around the room.

"Now he's left me like this, left me alone, and taking money I need out of the ATM on the way gone. What do I believe now?"

"Sit down here at the table. Tea's a small thing, but it's something."

Irene sat, looked out the window at the yard she'd once loved to putter in. The yard her husband had used to escape, to run from her.

"I know what people are saying, even though it doesn't come out of their mouths in my hearing. Leo killed Reverend Latterly, and if he killed him, he must've killed Dolly. His own flesh and blood."

"People say and think a lot of hard things, Irene."

The bones in Irene's face stood out too harshly under skin aged a decade in two short months. "I'm one of them now.

I may not be ready to say it, but I think it. I think how he and Dolly used to fight, shouting at each other, saying awful things. Still . . . he loved her. I know that."

She stared down at the tea Ella put in front of her. "Maybe loved her too much. Maybe more than I did. So it cut more, the things she'd do and say. It cut him more than me. Love can turn, can't it? It can turn into something dark in a minute's time."

"I don't know the answers there. But I do know that you can't find them in despair. I think the best thing for you now is to concentrate on the baby and yourself, to do what you have to do to make the best life you can make for the two of you, until you have those answers."

"That's what I'm doing. I called Mrs. Brayner this morning before I went into work. Shiloh's other grandmother. She and her husband are going to drive out from Nebraska, and they'll take Shiloh back with them."

"Oh, Irene."

"It's what's best for her." She swiped a tear away. "That precious baby deserves better than I can give her now. She's the innocent in all this, the only one of us who truly is. She deserves better than me leaving her with friends and neighbors most of the day, better than me barely able to take care of her when I'm here. Not being sure how long I can keep a roof over her head, much less buy her clothes or pay the baby doctor."

Her voice cracked, and she lifted the tea, sipped a little. "I've prayed on this, and I talked with Reverend Meece about it. He is kind, Ella, like you told me."

"He and his church could help you," Ella began, but Irene shook her head.

"I know in my heart I can't give Shiloh a good life the way things are, and I can't keep her, knowing she has family who can. I can't keep her wondering if her grandpa's the reason she doesn't have her mother."

Ella reached over, linked her hands with Irene's. "I know this isn't a decision you've come to lightly. I know how much you love that child. Is there anything I can do? Anything?"

"You didn't say it was the wrong decision, or selfish, or weak. That helps." She took a breath, drank a little more tea.

"I think they're good people. And she said—Kate, her name's Kate. Kate said they'd stay in Missoula a couple days or so, to give Shiloh time to get used to them. And how we'd all work together so Shiloh could have all of us in her life. I . . . I said how they could have all the baby stuff, her crib and all, and Kate, she said no, didn't I want to keep that? Didn't I want it so when we fixed it so Shiloh could come see me, it would all be ready for her?"

Ella squeezed Irene's hands tighter as tears plopped into the tea. "They do sound like good people, don't they?"

"I believe they are. I'm content they are. Still, I feel like another part of me's dying. I don't know how much is left."

HER CONVERSATION WITH MARG had Rowan's wheels turning. The time had come, she decided, for a serious sit-down with her father. Since she wanted to have that sit-down off base, she walked over to L.B.'s office.

She saw Matt step out. "Hi. Is he in there?"

"Yeah, I just asked him for a couple days at the end of the week." His face exploded into a grin she'd rarely seen on his face since Jim's accident. "My parents are driving in."

"That's great. They get to see you, and Jim's baby."

"Even more. They're taking Shiloh home with them."

"They got custody? That's so fast. I didn't think it worked so fast."

"They didn't get a lawyer. They were talking about maybe, but they didn't get one yet. Mrs. Brakeman called my ma this morning and said she needed—wanted—them to have Shiloh."

"Oh." Not enough long enough, Rowan thought, and felt a pang of sympathy. "That's great for your family, Matt. Really. It's got to be awfully rough on Mrs. Brakeman."

"Yeah, and I'm sorry for her. She's a good woman. I guess she proved it by doing this, thinking of Shiloh first. They're going to spend a couple days, you know, give everybody a chance to adjust and all that. I figured I could help out. Shiloh knows me, so that should make it easier. It's like I'm standing in for Jim."

"I guess it is. It's a lot, for everybody."

"The way Brakeman ran?" The light in his face died into something dark. "He's a coward. He doesn't deserve to even see that baby again, if you ask me. Mrs. Brakeman's probably going to lose her house because of him."

"It doesn't seem right," Rowan agreed, "for one person to lose so much."

"She could move to Nebraska if she wanted, and be closer to Shiloh. She ought to, and I hope she does. I don't see how there's anything here for her now anyway. She oughta go on and move to Nebraska so the baby has both her grans. Anyway, I've got to go call my folks, let them know I got the time off."

One family's tragedy, another family's celebration, Rowan supposed as Matt rushed off. The world could be a harsh place. She gave L.B.'s door a tap, poked her head in.

"Got another minute for somebody looking for time off?"

"Jesus, maybe we should just blow and piss on the next fire."

"An interesting new strategy, but I'm only looking for a few hours."

"When?"

"Pretty much now. I wanted to hook up with my father."

"Suddenly everybody wants family reunions." Then he shrugged. "A night off's okay. We've got smoke over in Payette, and up in Alaska. The Denali area's getting hammered with dry lightning. Yellowstone's on first attack on another. You should count on jumping tomorrow."

"I'll be ready." She started to back out before he changed his mind, then hesitated. "I guess Matt told you why he wanted the time."

"Yeah." L.B. rubbed his eyes. "It's hard to know what to think. I guess it's the best thing when it comes down to it, but it sure feels like kicking a woman in the teeth when she's already taken a couple hard shots in the gut."

"Still no word on Leo?"

"Nothing, as far as I know. Fucker. It makes me sick he could do all this. I went hunting with the bastard, even went on a big trip up to Canada with him and some other guys once."

"Did you tell the cops all the places you knew he liked to go?"

"Every one, and I didn't feel a single pang of guilt. Fucker," he repeated, with relish. "Irene's a decent woman. She doesn't deserve this. You'd better go while the going's good. If we get a call from Alaska, we'll be rolling tonight."

"I'm already gone." As she left, Rowan pulled out her phone and opted to text, hoping that would make her plans a fait accompli.

Got a couple hours. Meet you at the house. I'm cooking!
Really want to talk to you.

Now she had to hope he had something in the house she could actually cook. She stopped by the barracks, grabbed her keys, then stepped into the open doorway of Gull's quarters.

"I cleared a few hours so I can go over and see my father."

Gull shifted his laptop aside. "Okay."

"There are some things I want to air out with him. One-on-one." She jingled her car keys. "We've got potential situations out in Yellowstone, down in Wyoming, up in Alaska. We could be up before morning. I won't be gone very long."

"Are you waiting to see if I'm going to complain because you're going off base without me?"

"Maybe I was wondering if you would."

"I'm not built that way. Just FYI, I wouldn't mind maybe having dinner with you and your father sometime, maybe when things slow down."

"So noted. See you when I get back." She jingled her keys again. "Hey, I just remembered, my car's low on gas. Maybe I can borrow yours?"

"You know where the base pumps are."

"Had to try."

She'd talk him into letting her drive it before the end of the season, she promised herself as she headed out to her much less sexy Dodge. She just had to outline the right attack plan.

The minute she drove off the base, something shifted inside her. As much as she loved what she did, she felt just a bit lighter driving down the open road. Alone, away from the pressure, the intensity, the dramas, even the interaction.

Maybe, for the moment, she realized, especially the interaction. A little time to reconnect with Rowan, she thought, then in turn for Rowan to reconnect with her father.

She could admit to the contrary aspect of the feeling. If L.B. had insisted she take time off, had pulled her off the jump list, she'd have fought him tooth and nail. Asking for the little crack in the window was more a little gift to herself, and one where she chose the wrapping and the contents.

Maybe, too, it hit just close enough to the camping trips her father had always carved out during the season—this one evening together, her making dinner in the house they shared half the year. Just the two of them, sitting at the table with some decent grub and some good conversation.

Too much had happened, too many things that kept running around inside her head. So much of the summer boomeranged on her, making her think of her mother, and all those hard feelings. She'd shaken off most of them, but there remained a thin and sticky layer she'd never been able to peel away.

She liked to think that layer helped make her tougher, stronger—and she believed it—but she'd started to wonder if it had hardened into a shield as well.

Did she use it as an excuse, an escape? If she did, was that smart, or just stupid?

Something to think about in this short time alone, and again in the company of the single person in the world who knew her through and through, and loved her anyway.

When she pulled up in front of the house, the simple white two-story with the wide covered porch—the porch she'd helped her father build when she was fourteen—she just sat and stared.

The slope of lawn showed the brittleness of the dry summer, even in the patches of shade from the big old maple on the east corner.

But skirting that porch, on either side of the short steps, an area of flowers sprang out of a deep brown blanket of mulch. Baskets hung from decorative brackets off the flanking posts and spilled out a tangle of red and white flowers and green trailing vines.

"I'm looking at it," she said aloud as she got out of the car, "but I still can't quite believe it."

She remembered summers during her youth when her grandmother had done pots and planters, and even dug in a little vegetable garden in the back. How she'd cursed the deer and rabbits for mowing them down, every single season.

She remembered, too, her father's rep for killing even the hardiest of houseplants. Now he'd planted—she didn't know what half of them were, but the beds hit hot, rich notes with a lot of deep reds and purples, with some white accents.

And she had to admit they added a nice touch, just as she had to admit the creativity of the layout hadn't come from the nongardening brain of Iron Man Tripp.

She mulled it over as she let herself into the house.

Here, too, the difference struck.

Flowers? Since when did her father have flowers sitting around the house? And candles—fat white columns that smelled, when she sniffed them, faintly of vanilla. Plus, he'd gotten a new rug in the living room, a pattern of bold-colored blocks that spread over a floor that had certainly been polished. And looked pretty good, she had to admit, but still . . .

Hands on hips, she did a turn around the living room until her jaw nearly landed on her toes. Glossy magazines fanned on the old coffee table. Home and garden magazines, and since when had her father . . . ?

Stupid question, she admitted. Since Ella.

A little leery of what she'd find next, she started toward the kitchen, poked into her father's home office. Bamboo shades in spicy tones replaced the beige curtains.

Ugly curtains, she remembered.

But the powder room was a revelation. No generic liquid soap sat on the sink, no tan towels on the rack. Instead, a shiny and sleek chrome dispenser shot a spurt of lemon-scented liquid into her hand. Dazed, she washed, then dried her hands on one of the fluffy navy hand towels layered on the rack with washcloths in cranberry.

He'd added a bowl of potpourri—*potpourri*—and a framed print of a mountain meadow on a freshly painted wall that matched the washcloths.

Her father had cranberry walls in the powder room. She might never get over it.

Dazed, she continued on to the kitchen, and there stood blinking.

Clean and efficient had always been the Tripp watchwords. Apparently fuss had been added to them since she'd last stood in the room.

A long oval dish she thought might be bamboo and had never seen before held a selection of fresh fruit. Herbs grew in small red clay pots on the windowsill over the sink. An iron wine rack—a filled wine rack, she noted—graced the top of the refrigerator. He'd replaced the worn cushions on the stools at the breakfast counter, and she was pretty damn sure the glossy magazines in the living room would call that color pumpkin.

In the dining area, two place mats—bamboo again—lay ready with cloth napkins rolled in rings beside them. If that didn't beat all, the pot of white daisies and the tea lights in amber dishes sure rang the bell.

She considered going upstairs, decided she needed a drink first, and a little time to absorb the shocks already dealt. A little time, like maybe a year, she thought as she opened the refrigerator.

Okay, there was beer, that at least was constant. But what the hell, since he had an open bottle of white, plugged with a fancy topper, she'd go with that.

She sipped, forced to give it high marks as she explored supplies.

She felt more at home and less like an intruder as she got down to it, setting out chicken breasts to soften, scrubbing potatoes. Maybe she shook her head as she spotted the deck chairs out the kitchen window. He painted them every other year, she knew, but never before in chili pepper red.

By the time she heard him come in, she had dinner simmering in the big skillet. She poured a second glass of wine.

At least he looked the same.

"Smells good." He folded her in, held her hard. "Best surprise of the day."

"I've had a few of them myself. I poured you this." She offered him the second glass. "Since you're the wine buff now."

He grinned, toasted her. "Pretty good stuff. Have we got time to sit outside awhile?"

"Yeah. That'd be good. You've been busy around here," she commented as they walked out onto the deck.

"Fixing things up a little. What do you think?"

"It's colorful."

"A few steps out of my comfort zone." He sat in one of the hot-colored deck chairs, sighed happily.

"Dad, you planted flowers. That's acres outside your zone."

"And I haven't killed them yet. Soaker hose."

"Sorry?"

"I put in a soaker hose. Keeps them from getting thirsty."

Wine, soaker hoses, cranberry walls. Who was this guy?

But when he looked at her, laid his hand over hers, she saw him. She knew him. "What's on your mind, baby?"

"A lot. Bunches."

"Lay it on me."

She did just that.

"I feel like I can't get a handle on things, or keep a handle on. This morning, I thought I did, then it started slipping again. I've been having the dreams about Jim again, only worse. But with everything that's gone on this season, how am I supposed to put that aside anyway? Everything Dolly did, then what happened to her. Add on her crazy father. And the thing is, if he did what they say he did, if he killed her, the preacher, started the fires—and he probably did—why am I more pissed off and disgusted that he ran, left his wife twisting in the wind? And I know the answer," she said, pushing back to her feet.

"I know the answer, and *that* pisses me off. My mother ditching us doesn't define my life. I sure as hell don't want it to define me. I'm smarter than that, damn it."

"You always have been," he said when she turned to him.

"I'm tangled up with Gull so I'm not sure I'm thinking straight. Really, where can that go? And why am I even thinking that because why would I want it to go anywhere? And you, you're planting flowers and drinking wine, and you have potpourri."

He had to smile. "It smells nicer than those plug-in jobs."

"It has berries, and little white flowers in it. While that's screwing with my head, Dolly's mother's giving the baby to the Brayners because she can't handle it all by herself. It's probably the best thing, it's probably the right thing, but it makes me feel sick and sad, which pisses me off all over again because I *know* I'm projecting, and I *know* the situation with that baby isn't the same as with me.

"I may be jumping fire in Alaska tomorrow, and I'm stuck on pumpkin-colored cushions, a baby I've never even seen and a guy who's talking about being with me after the season. How the hell did this happen?"

Lucas nodded slowly, drank a little wine. "That is a lot. Let's see if we can sift through it. I don't like hearing you're having those nightmares again, but I can't say I'm surprised. The pressure of any season wears on you, and this hasn't been just any season. You're probably not the only one having hard dreams."

"I hadn't thought about that."

"Have you talked to L.B.?"

"Not about that. Piling my stress on his doesn't work for anybody. That's why I pile it on you."

"I can tell you what we talked about before, after it happened. We all live with the risks, and train body and mind to minimize them. When a jumper has a mental lapse, sometimes he gets lucky. Sometimes he doesn't. Jim didn't, and that's a tragedy. It's a hard blow for his family, and like his kin, the crew's his family."

"I've never lost anybody before. She doesn't count," she said, referring to her mother. "Not the same way."

"I know it. You want to save him, to go back to that jump and save him. And you can't, baby. I think when you've really settled your mind on that, the dreams will stop."

He got up, put an arm around her shoulders. "I don't know if you'll really be able to settle your mind until this business with Leo is resolved. It's in your face, so it's in your head. Dolly tried to put the blame for what happened to Jim on you, and it looks like her telling him she was pregnant right before a jump contributed to his mental lapse. Then Leo came at you about Jim, about Dolly—and the cops think he's the one responsible for her murder. Time to use your head, Ro." He kissed the top of it. "And stop letting the people most responsible lay the weight on you. Feeling sorry for Irene Brakeman, that's just human. Maybe you and me tend to be a little more human than most on that score. Ella's over there right now helping her get through it, and I feel better knowing that."

"I guess it's good that she—Mrs. Brakeman—has somebody."

"I had your grandparents, and I leaned on them pretty hard. I had my friends, my work. Most of all I had you. When somebody walks out, it leaves a hole in you. Some people fill it up, the good and the bad, and get on that way. Some people leave it open, maybe long enough to heal, maybe too long, picking at it now and then so it doesn't heal all the way. I hate knowing it as much as you, but I think we've been like the last."

"I don't even think about it, most of the time."

"Neither do I. Most of the time. Now you've got this guy, who'd be the first one you've ever mentioned to me as giving you trouble. And that makes me wonder if you've got feelings for him you've managed to avoid up till now. Are you in love with him?"

"How does anybody answer that?" she demanded. "How does anyone know? Are you in love with this Ella?"

"Yes."

Stunned, Rowan stepped back. "Just like that? You can just . . . poof, I'm in love."

"She filled the hole, baby. I don't know how to explain it to you. I never knew how to talk about this kind of thing, and maybe that's where I fell down with you. But she filled that hole I never let all the way heal, because if I did, there could be another. But I'd rather take that chance than not have her. I wish you'd get to know her. She . . ."

He lifted his hands as if to grab something just out of reach. "She's funny and smart, and has a way of speaking her mind that's honest instead of hurtful. She can do damn near anything. You should see her on a dive. I swear she's a joy to watch. She could give Marg a run for her money in the kitchen, and don't repeat that or I'll call you a liar. She knows about wine and books and flowers. She has her own toolbox and knows how to use it. She's got great kids and they've got kids. She listens when you talk to her. She'll try anything.

"She makes me feel . . . She makes me feel."

There it was, Rowan realized. If there'd been an image in the dictionary for the definition of "in love," it would be her father's face.

"I have to get dinner on the table." She turned away to the door, then turned back to see him looking after her, that light dimmed. "Are you, more or less, asking for my blessing?"

"I guess. More or less."

"Anybody who makes you this happy—and who talked you into getting rid of those ugly curtains in your office—is good with me. You can tell me more about her while we eat."

"Ro. That means more than I can say."

"You don't have heart-shaped pillows on your bed now, do you?"

"No. Why?"

"Because that's going to be my line in the sand. Anything else I think I can adjust to. Oh, and none of those crocheted things over spare toilet paper. That's definitely a deal breaker."

"I'll take notes."

"Good idea because I probably have a few more." She walked to the stove, pleased that light had turned back on full.

25

Feeling sociable, Gull plopped down in the lounge with his book. That way he could ease out of the story from time to time, tune in on conversations, the ball game running on TV and the progress of the poker game he wasn't yet interested in joining.

Or he could just let all of it hum at the edges of his mind like white noise.

With the idea he might be called up at any time, he opted for a ginger ale and a bag of chips to snack him through the next chapter or two.

"Afraid of losing your paycheck?" Dobie called out from the poker table.

"Terrified."

"Out?" An outraged Trigger lurched out of his chair at a call on second. "That runner was safe by a mile. Out my ass! Did you see that?" he demanded.

He hadn't, but Gull's mood hit both agreeable and sociable. "Damn right. The ump's an asshole."

"He oughta have his eyes popped out if he can't use them better than that. Where's the ball to your chain tonight?"

Amused, Gull turned a page. "Ditched me for another man."

"Women. They're worse than umps. Can't live with them, can't beat them with a brick."

"Hey." Janis discarded two cards at the poker table. "Having tits doesn't mean I can't hear, buddy."

"Aw, you're not a woman. You're a jumper."

"I'm a jumper with tits."

"Unless you're going to toss them in the pot," Cards told her, "the bet's five to you."

"They're worth a lot more than five."

Better than white noise, Gull decided, and likely better than his book.

Across the room, Yangtree—with an ice bag on his knee—and Southern played an intense, nearly silent game of chess. Earbuds in, Libby ticked her head back and forth like a metronome to her MP3 while she worked a crossword puzzle.

A lot of sociable going around, he mused. About half the jumpers on base gathered, some in groups, some solo, more than a few sprawled on the floor, attention glued to the Cardinals v. Phillies matchup on-screen.

Waiting mode, he decided. Everybody knew the siren could sound anytime, sending them north, east, south, west, where there would be camaraderie but little leisure. No time to insult umpires or figure out 32 Across. Instead of raking in the pot, as Cards did now with relish, they'd rake through smoldering embers and ash.

He watched Trigger throw up his hands in triumph as the runner scored, saw Yangtree take Southern's bishop and Dobie toss in chips to raise the bet, causing Stovic to fold on a grunt of disgust.

"What's a five-letter word for boredom?" Libby asked the room.

"TV ads," Trigger volunteered. "Ought to be outlawed."

"Boredom, not boring. Besides, some of them are funny."

"Not funny enough."

"Ennui," Gull told her.

"Damn it, I knew that."

"He can spout off all those pussy words," Dobie commented.

Gull only smiled. He definitely didn't feel ennui. Contentment, he thought, best described his current state. He'd be ready to roll if and when the call came, but for now knew the contentment of lounging with friends, enjoying the cross talk and bullshit while he waited for his woman to come home.

He'd found his place. He didn't know, not for certain, when he'd first understood that. Maybe the first time he'd seen Rowan. Maybe his first jump. Maybe that night at the bar when he'd kicked some ass.

Maybe looking over a meadow of wild lupine.

It didn't matter when.

He'd liked his hotshot work, and the people he'd worked with. Or most of them. He'd learned to combine patience, action and endurance, learned to love the fight—the violence, the brutality, the science. But what he found here dug deeper, and deep kindled an irresistible love and passion.

He knew he'd sprawl out in the lounge, listening to cross talk and bullshit season after season, as long as he was able.

He knew, he thought as Rowan came in, he'd wait for her to come home whenever she went away.

"Man, they let anybody in the country club these days." She dropped down beside Gull, shot a hand into the chip bag. "Score?"

"Tied," Trigger told her, "one to one due to seriously blind ump. Top of the fifth."

She stole Gull's ginger ale, found it empty. "What, were you waiting for me to get back, fetch you a refill?"

"Caught me."

She pushed up, got a Coke. "You'll drink this and like it." She downed some first, then passed it to him.

"Thanks. And how's the ball to my chain?"

"*What* did you call me?"

"He said it." Gull narked on Trigger without remorse.

"Skinny Texas bastard." She angled her head to read the cover of the book Gull set aside. "*Ethan Frome*? If you've been reading that, I'm surprised I didn't find you lapsed into a coma drooling down your chin."

He gave the Coke back to her. "I thought I'd like it better now, being older, wiser, more erudite. But it's just as blindingly boring as it was when I was twenty. Thank God you're back, or I might have been paralyzed with ennui."

"Get you."

"It was a crossword answer a while ago. How's your dad?"

"He's in love."

"With the hot redhead."

Rowan's eyebrows beetled. "I wish you wouldn't call her the hot redhead."

"I call them like I see them. How's by you?"

"I had to get by the flower beds he's planted, the flowers in vases, candles, the potpourri in the powder room—"

"Mother of God! Potpourri in the powder room. We need to get a posse together *ASAP*, go get him. He can be deprogrammed. Don't lose hope."

Since he'd stretched his legs across her lap, she twisted his toe. Hard. "He's got all this color in the place all of a sudden. Or all of an Ella. I told myself it was fussy, she'd pushed all this fussy stuff on him. But it's not. It's style, with an edge of charm. She brought color to the beige and bone and brown. It makes him happy. She makes him happy. She filled the hole he couldn't let heal—that's what he said. And I realized something, that she was right that day we saw her in town. Ice cream day. She said that if I made him choose between her and me, she didn't stand a chance. And if I'd done that, I'd be just enough like my mother to make myself sick. Either/or, pal, you can't have both."

"But you're not."

"No. I'm not. I have to get used to it—to her, but she's put a light in him so I think I'm going to be a fan."

"You're a stand-up gal, Swede."

"If she screws him up, I'll peel the skin off her ass with a dull razor blade."

"Fair's fair."

"And then some. I need to walk off the not-too-shabby skillet cuisine I prepared, then I'm going to turn in."

"Wait a minute. You cooked?"

"I have a full dozen entrées in my repertoire. Four of them are variations on the classic grilled cheese sandwich."

"A whole new side of you to explore while we walk. I want my shoes."

Gibbons came in as Gull tossed the Edith Wharton onto the table for someone else.

"You might want to wrap up that card game. Everybody's

on standby. It's not official, but it looks like we'll roll two loads to Fairbanks tonight, or maybe straight to the fire. L.B.'s working out some details. And it's looking like Bighorn might need some help come tomorrow."

"Just when my luck's starting to turn," Dobie complained.

"New shoes for baby," Cards reminded him.

"I rake another couple pots in, I can buy the new shoes without eating smoke."

"Anybody on the first and second loads might want to check their gear while they've got a chance," Gibbons added.

"I've never been to Alaska," Gull commented.

"It's an experience." Rowan shoved his feet off her lap.

"I'm all about them."

SHE STUFFED more energy bars into her PG bag, and after a short debate added two cans of Coke. She'd rather haul the weight than do without. She changed from the off-duty clothes she'd worn to her father's, and was just buckling her belt when the siren sang out.

Along with the others, she ran to the ready room to suit up.

The minute she stepped onto the plane, she staked her claim, arranging her gear and stretching out with her head on her chute. She intended to sleep through the flight.

"What's it like?" Gull poked her with the toe of his boot.

"Big."

"Really? I hear it's cold and dark in the winter, too. Can that be true?"

She let the vibration of the engines lull her as other jumpers settled in. "Plenty of daylight this time of year. It's not the trees as much there to worry about on the jump. It's the water. They've got a lot of it, and you don't want to miss the spot and land in it. A lot of water, a lot of land, mountains. Not a lot of people, that's an advantage."

She shifted, found a more comfortable position. "The Alaskan smoke jumpers know their stuff. It's been dry up there this season, too, so they're probably spread pretty thin, probably feeling that midseason fatigue."

She opened her eyes to look at him. "It's beautiful. The snow that never melts off those huge peaks, the lakes and rivers, the glow of the midnight sun. They've also got mosquitoes the size of your fist and bears big as an armored truck. But in the fire, it's pretty much the same. Kill the bitch; stay alive. Everybody comes back."

She closed her eyes. "Get some sleep. You're going to need it."

She slept like a rock; woke stiff as a board. And grateful they put down at Fairbanks, giving the crew time to loosen up, fuel up, and the bosses time to cement a strategy.

With nearly four hundred acres involved, and the wind kicking flare-ups, they'd need solid communication with the Alaskan team. She managed to scrounge up a cold soda, preserving the two in her bag, before they performed a last buddy check and loaded.

"You're right," Gull said when they flew southwest out of Fairbanks. "It's beautiful. Not far off midnight, either, local time, and bright as afternoon."

"Don't get enchanted. You'll lose focus. And she'll eat you alive."

He had to change his angle to get his first glimpse of the fire, shift his balance as the plane hit turbulence and began to buck.

"Just another maw of hell. I'm focused," he added when she sent him a hard look.

He saw the white peaks of the mountain through the billows of smoke. Denali, the sacred, with the wild to her north and east burning bright.

He continued to study and absorb as she moved to the rear to confer with Yangtree, and with Cards, who worked as spotter. Others lined the windows now, looking down on what they'd come to fight.

"We're going to try for a clearing in some birch, east side. The Alaska crew used it for their jump spot. Cards is going to throw some streamers, see how they fly."

"Jesus, did you see that?" somebody asked.

"Looks like a blowup," Gull said.

"It's well west of the target jump spot. Everybody stay chilly," she called out. "Settle in, settle down. Stay in your heads."

"Guard your reserves!" Cards pulled in the door.

Gull watched the streamers fly, adjusted with the bank and bounce of the plane. The wind dragged the stench and haze of smoke inside, a small taste of what would come.

Rowan got in the door, shot him a last grin. She propelled herself out, with Stovic seconds behind her.

When it came his turn, he evened his breathing, listened to Cards tell him about the drag. He fixed the clearing in his head and, at the slap on his shoulder, flew.

Gorgeous. He could think it while the wind whipped him. The staggering white peaks, the impossibly deep blue in glints and curls of water, the high green of summer, and all of it in sharp contrast with the wicked blacks, reds, oranges of the fire.

His chute ballooned open, turning fall into glide, and he shot Gibbons, his jump partner, a thumbs-up.

He caught some hard air that tried to push him south, and he fought it, pushing back through the smoke that rolled over him. It caught him again, gave him a good, hard tug. Again he saw that deep dreamy blue through the haze. And he thought no way, goddamn it, no way he'd end up hitting the water after Rowan had warned him.

He bore down on the toggles, saw and accepted he'd miss the jump spot, adjusted again.

He winged through the birch, cursing. He didn't land in the water, but it was a near thing, as his momentum on landing nearly sent him rolling into it anyway.

Mildly annoyed, he gathered his chute as Rowan and Yangtree came running.

"I thought for sure you'd be in the drink."

"Hit some bad air."

"Me too. I nearly got frogged. Be grateful you're not wet or limping."

"Tore up my canopy some."

"I bet." Then she grinned as she had before jumping into space. "What a ride!"

Once all jumpers were on the ground, Yangtree called a briefing with Rowan and Gibbons while the others dealt with the paracargo.

"They thought they could catch it, had forty jumpers on it, and for the first two days, it looked like they had it. Then it

turned on them. A series of blowups, some equipment problems, a couple injuries."

"The usual clusterfuck," Gibbons suggested.

"You got it. I'll be coordinating with the Alaska division
boss, the BLM and USFS guys. I'm going to take me a copter
ride, get a better look at things, but for right now."

He picked up a stick, drew a rough map in the dirt. "Gibbons, take a crew and start working the left flank. They've got
a Cat line across here. That's where you'll tie in with the
Alaska crew. You've got a water source here for the pumpers.
Swede, you take the right, work it up, burn it out, drown it."

"Take it by the tail," she said, following his dirt map.
"Starve the belly."

"Show 'em what Zulies can do. We catch her good, shake
her by the tail and push up to the head." He checked the time.
"Should reach the head in fifteen, sixteen hours if we haul our
asses."

They discussed strategy, details, directions, crouched in
the stand of birch, while on the jump site the crew unpacked
chain saws, boxes of fusees, pumpers and hose.

Gibbons leaped up, waved his Pulaski toward the sky.
"Let's do it!" he shouted.

"Ten men each." Yangtree clapped his hands together like
a team captain before the big game. "Get humping, Zulies."

They got humping.

As planned, Rowan and her team used fusees to set burn-
outs between the raging right flank and the service road, sawing snags and widening the scratch line as they moved north
from the jump spot.

If the dragon tried to swing east to cross the roads, move
on to homesteads and cabins, she'd go hungry before she got
there. They worked through what was left of the night, into the
day with the flank crackling and snarling, vomiting out firebrands the wind took in arches to the dry tundra.

"Chow time," she announced. "I'm going to scout through
the burn, see if I can find how close Gibbons's crew is."

Dobie pulled a smashed sandwich out of his bag, looked up
at the towering columns of smoke and flame. "Biggest I've
ever seen."

"She's a romper," Rowan agreed, "but you know what they

say about Alaska. Everything's bigger. Fuel up. We've got a long way to go."

She couldn't give them long to rest, she thought as she headed out. Timing and momentum were as vital tools as Pulaski and saw because Dobie hadn't been wrong. This was one big mother, bigger, she'd concluded, than anticipated and, she'd already estimated by the staggered formation of her own line, wider in the body.

Pine tar and pitch tanged in the air, soured by the stench of smoke that rose like gray ribbons from the peat floor of the once, she imagined, pristine forest. Now mangled, blackened trees lay like fallen soldiers on a lost battlefield.

She could hear no sound of saw, no shout of man through the voice of the fire. Gibbons wasn't as close as she'd hoped, and she couldn't afford to scout farther.

She ate a banana and an energy bar on the quickstep hike back to her men. Gull gulped down Gatorade as he walked to her.

"What's the word, boss?"

"We're shaking her tail, as ordered, but she's got a damn long one. We'll be hard-pressed to meet Yangtree's ETA. We've got a water source coming up. It should be about a hundred yards, and a little to the west. We'll put the baby hoses on her, pump it up and douse her like Dorothy doused the Wicked Witch."

She took his Gatorade, chugged some down. "She's burning hot, Gull. Some desk jockey waited too long to call in more troops, and now she's riding this wind. If she rides it hard enough, she can get behind us. We've got to bust our humps, get to the water, hose her down and back."

"Busting humps is what we do."

Still, it took brutal, backbreaking time to reach the rushing mountain stream, while the fire fought to advance, while it threw brands like a school-yard bully throws rocks, its roar a constant barrage of taunts and threats.

"Dobie, Chainsaw, beat out those spots! Libby, Trigger, Southern, snags and brush. The rest of you, get those pumps set up, lay the hose."

She grabbed one of the pumps, connected the fuel can line to the pump, vented it. Moving fast, sweat dripping, she attached the foot valve, checked the gasket, tightened it with a spanner wrench from her tool bag.

Beat it back here, she thought, had to, or they'd be forced to backtrack and round east, giving up hundreds of acres, risk letting the fire snake behind them and drive them farther away from the head, from Gibbons. From victory.

She set the wye valve on the discharge side of the pump, began to hand-tighten it. And found it simply circled like a drain.

"Come on, come on." She fixed it on again, blaming her rush, but when she got the same result, examined the valve closely.

"Jesus Christ. Jesus, it's stripped. The wye valve's threads are stripped on this pump."

Gull looked over from where he worked. "I've got the same deal here."

"I'm good," Janis called out on the third pump. "It's priming."

"Get it warmed up, get it going."

But one pump wouldn't do the job, she thought. Might as well try a goddamn piss bag.

"We're screwed." She slapped a fist on the useless pump.

Gull caught her eye. "No way two stripped valves end up on the pumps by accident."

"Can't worry about that now. We'll hold her with one as long as we can, use the time to saw and dig a line. We'll double back to that old Cat line we crossed, then retreat east. Goddamn it, give up all that ground. There's no time to get more pumps or manpower in here. Maybe if I had some damn duct tape we could jerry-rig them."

"Duct tape. Hold on." He straightened, ran to where Dobie shoveled dirt over a dying spot fire.

Rowan watched in amazement as he ran back with a roll of duct tape. "For Dobie it's like his Tabasco. He doesn't leave home without it."

"It could work, or work long enough."

They worked together, placing the faulty valve, wrapping it tight and snug to the discharge. She added another insurance layer, continued the setup.

"Fingers crossed," she said to Gull, and began to stroke the primer. "She's priming," she mumbled as water squirted out of the holes. "Come on, keep going. Duct tape heals all wounds. Keep those fingers crossed."

She closed the valve to the primer, opened it to the collapsible hose.

"It's going to work."

"It *is* working," she corrected, and flicked the switch to start and warm the engine. "Trigger, on the pump! Let's get the other one going," she said to Gull.

"Not two of them," Gull repeated while they worked.

"No, not two of them. Somebody majorly fucked up or—"

"Deliberately."

She let the word hang when she met his eyes. "Let's get it running. We'll deal with that when we get out of this mess."

They beat it back, held the ground, laying a wet line with hoses, hot shoveling embers right back in the fire's gullet. But Rowan's satisfaction was tempered with a simmering rage. Accident or deliberate, carelessness or sabotage, she'd put her crew at risk because she'd trusted the equipment.

When they reached Yangtree's proposed rendezvous time, they were still over a half mile south of the head with fourteen hours' bitter labor on their backs. She deployed most of the crew north, sending two back to check the burnout, and once again cut across the burn.

She took the time to calm, to radio back to Ops with a report of the faulty equipment and the progress. But this time when she crossed the dead land, she heard the buzz of saws.

Encouraged, she followed the sound until she came to Gibbons's line.

"Did I call this a clusterfuck?" He paused long enough to swipe his forearm over his brow. "What's the next step up from that?"

"Whatever this is. We've run into everything but Bigfoot on this. I had two pumps with stripped wye valves."

"I had three messed-up chain saws. Two with dead spark plugs, one with a frayed starter cord that snapped first pull. We had to—" He stopped, and his face reflected the shock and suspicion in hers. "What the fuck, Ro?"

"We need to brief on this, but I've got to get back to my

crew. We'll be lucky to make the head in another three hours the way it's going."

"How far east are you now?"

"A little more than a third of a mile. We're tightening her up. We'll talk about this when we camp. We may catch her tonight, but we're not going to kill her."

"The crew's going to need rest. We'll see how it goes. Check back in—if we don't tie up before—around ten, let's say."

"You'll hear from me."

She caught up with her men, following the sound of saws as she had with Gibbons, found them sawing line through black spruce.

They'd been actively fighting for nearly eighteen hours. She could see the exhaustion, the hollow eyes, slack jaws.

She laid a hand on Libby's arm, waited until the woman took out her earplugs. "Extended break. An hour. Nappie time. Pass it up the line."

"Praise Jesus."

"I'm going to recon toward the head, see what we have in store for us."

"Whatever it is, I'll kick its ass, if I have my nappie time."

She signaled to Gull. "I'm going to recon the head. You could come with me, but you'd miss an hour's downtime."

"I'd rather walk through the wilderness with my woman."

"Then let's go."

They walked through the spruce while around them jumpers dumped their tools, dropped down on the ground or sprawled on rocks.

"Gibbons had three defective chain saws—two dead spark plugs, one bad starter cord."

"I'd say that makes it officially sabotage."

"That's unofficial until the review, but, yeah, that's what it was."

"Cards was spotter. That puts him as loadmaster."

"Load being the operative word," she reminded him. "He wouldn't check every valve and spark plug. He just makes sure everything gets loaded on, and loaded right."

"Yeah, that's true enough. Look, I like Cards. I don't want

to point fingers at anybody, but this kind of thing? It has to be one of us."

She didn't want to hear it. "A lot of people could get to the equipment. Support staff, mechanics, pilots, cleaning crews. It's not just who the hell—it's why the hell."

"Another good point."

Because she felt shaky, she took out one of her precious Cokes for a shot of caffeine and sugar, and used it to make yet another energy bar more palatable.

"We wouldn't have been trapped," she added. "We had time to take an escape route, get to a safe zone. If we hadn't fixed the hoses and held that line, we'd have gotten out okay."

"But," he prompted.

"Yeah, but if the situation had been different, if we'd gotten in a fix and needed the hoses to get out, some of us could've been hurt, or worse."

"So the why could be one, wanting to screw around, cause trouble. Two, wanting to give fire an advantage. Or three, wanting somebody to get hurt or worse."

"I don't like any of those options." Each one of them made her sick. "But the way this summer's been going, I'm afraid it might be three. L.B.'s ordering a full inspection of all equipment, right down to boot snaps." She pulled off her gloves to rub her tired eyes.

"I don't want to waste the energy being pissed about it," she told him, "not until we demob anyway. God, Gull. Look at her burn."

They stopped a moment, stood staring at the searing wall.

She'd fought fire on more than one front before. She knew how.

But she'd never fought two enemies in the same war.

26

Ella studied Lucas across the pretty breakfast table she'd set up on the deck. She'd gone to a little trouble—crepes and shirred eggs on her best china, fat mixed berries in pretty glass bowls, mimosas in tall, crystal flutes, and one of her Nikko Blue hydrangeas sunk into a low, square glass vase for a centerpiece.

She liked to go to the trouble now and again, and Lucas usually showed such appreciation. Even for cold cereal and a mug of black coffee, she thought, he always thanked her for the trouble.

But this morning he said little, and only toyed with the food she'd so carefully prepared.

She wondered if he was regretting taking the day off to be with her, to go poking around the Missoula Antique Mall. Her idea, she reminded herself, and really, did any man enjoy the prospect of spending the day shopping?

"You know, it occurs to me you might like to do something else today. Lucas," she said when he didn't respond.

"What?" His gaze lifted from his plate. "I'm sorry."

"If you could do anything, what would you want to do today?"

"Honestly. I'd be up in Alaska with Rowan."

"You're really worried about her." She reached over for his hand. "I know you must worry every time, but this seems more. Is it more?"

"I talked to L.B. while you were fixing breakfast. He thought I should know— No, she's fine. They're fine," he said when her fingers jerked in his. "But the fire's tougher and bigger than they thought. You get that," he added with a shrug. "The thing that's got me worried is it turns out they jumped with several pieces of defective equipment, tools."

"Aren't those kinds of things inspected and maintained? That shouldn't happen."

"Yeah, they're checked and tested. Ella, they think these tools may have been tampered with."

"You mean . . . Well, God, Lucas, no wonder you're worried. What happens now?"

"They'll examine the equipment, investigate, review. L.B.'s already ordered a complete inspection of everything on base."

"That's good, but it doesn't help Rowan or the rest of them on the fire."

"When you're on a fire, you've got to depend on yourself, your crew and, by God, on your equipment. It could've gone south on my girl."

"But she's all right? You're sure?"

"Yeah. They worked nearly twenty-four hours before making camp. She's getting some sleep now. They'll hit it early today; they'll have the light. They dropped them more equipment, and they're sending in another load of jumpers, more hotshots. They're sending in another tanker, and . . ." He trailed off, smiled a little, waved his hand. "Enough fire talk."

She shook her head. "No. You talk it through. I want you to be able to talk it through with me."

"What they had was your basic clusterfuck. Delays in calling in more men and equipment, erratic winds and a hundred percent active perimeter. Fire makes its own weather," he continued, and pleased her when talking relaxed him enough to have him cutting into a crepe. "This one kicked up a storm, kept bumping the line—that means it spots and rolls, delays containment. Blowups, eighty-foot flames across the head."

"Oh, my God."

"She's impressive," he said, and amazed Ella by smiling.

"You really do wish you were there." She narrowed her eyes, pointed at him. "And not just for Rowan."

"I guess it never goes away, all the way away. Bottom line is they've made good progress. They're going to have a hell of a day ahead of them, but they'll have her crying uncle by tonight."

"You know what you should do—the next best thing to flying yourself to Alaska and jumping out over Rowan's campsite? You should go on over to the base."

"They don't need me over there."

"You may have retired, but you're still Iron Man Tripp. I bet they could use your expertise and experience. And you'd feel closer to Rowan and to the action."

"We had plans for the day," he reminded her.

"Lucas, don't you know me better by now?"

He looked at her, then took her hand to his lips. "I guess I do. I guess you know me, too."

"I like to think so."

"I wonder how you'd feel . . . I'd like to ask if I could move in here with you. If I could live with you."

It took a minute for her brain to catch up. "You—you want to live together? Here?"

"I know you've got everything you want here, and we've only been seeing each other a few months. Maybe you need to—"

"Yes."

"Yes?"

"I mean, I'll have everything I want here when you are. So, yes, absolutely yes." Delighted by his blank stare, she laughed. "How soon can you pack?"

He let out a breath, then picked up the mimosa, drank deep. "I thought you'd say no, or that we should wait awhile more."

"Then you shouldn't have asked. Now you're stuck."

"Stuck with a beautiful woman who knows me and wants me around anyway. For the life of me, I can't figure out what I did right." He set the glass back down. "I did this backward because first I should've said—I should've said, I love you, Ella. I love you."

"Lucas." She got up, went around the table to sit in his lap.

Took his face in her hands. "I love you." She kissed him, sinking in. "I'm so happy my son wanted me to jump out of a plane." She sighed as she laid her cheek against his. "I'm so happy."

WHEN HE LEFT, she adjusted her plans for the day. She had to make room for a man. For her man. Closet space, drawer space. Space for manly things. The house she'd made completely her own would become a blend, picking up pieces of him, shades of him.

It amazed her how much she wanted that, how very much she wanted to see what those shades would be once blended.

She needed to make a list, she realized, of what should be done. He'd want some office space, she decided as she took out a notebook and pen to write it down. Then she tapped the pen on the table, calculating which area might work best.

"Oh, who can think!" Laughing, she tossed down the pen to dance around the kitchen.

She had to call her kids and tell them. But she'd wait until she'd settled down a little so they didn't think she'd gone giddy as a teenager on prom night.

But she felt like one.

When the phone rang, she boogied to it, then sobered when she saw Irene's readout.

She took two quiet breaths. "Hello."

"Ella, Ella, can you come? Leo. Leo called."

"Slow down," she urged when Irene rushed over the words. "Leo called you?"

"He turned himself in. He's at the police station, and he wants to talk to me. They let him call me, and he said he's not saying anything about anything until he talks to me. I don't know what to do."

"Don't do anything. I'll be right over."

She grabbed her cell phone out of the charger, snagged her purse on the run. On the way out the door, she called Lucas.

"I'm on my way over to Irene's. Leo's turned himself in."

"Where?" Lucas demanded. "Where is he?"

"He called her from the police station." She slammed her car door, shifted the phone to yank on her seat belt. "He says he won't talk to anyone until he talks to her. I'm going with her."

"Don't you go near him, Ella."

"I won't, but I don't want her to go alone. I'll call you as soon as I'm back."

She closed the phone, tossed it in her purse as she reversed down the drive.

WAKING TO THE VIEW of the Alaska Range and Denali lifted the spirits. As she stood in camp, Rowan felt the mountain was on their side.

The crews had worked their hearts out, had the burns and bruises, the aches and pains to prove it. They hadn't slayed the dragon, not yet, but they'd sure as hell wounded it. And today, she had a good, strong feeling, today they'd plunge the sword right through its heart.

She knew the crew was banged up, strung out, but they'd gotten a solid four hours' sleep and even now filled their bellies. With more equipment, more men, an additional fire engine and two bulldozers, she believed they could be flying home by that evening, and leave the final beat-down and mopping up to Alaska.

Sleep, she decided, the mother of optimism.

She pulled out her radio when it signaled. "Ro at base camp, go ahead."

"L.B., Ops. I've got somebody here who wants to talk to you."

"How's my girl?"

"Hey, Dad. A-OK. Just standing here thinking and looking at a big-ass mountain. Wish you were here. Over."

"Copy that. It's good to hear your voice. Heard you had some trouble yesterday. Over."

"Nothing we couldn't handle with some bubble gum and duct tape. We softened her up yesterday." She watched the cloud buildup over the park, and puffs of smoke twining up from islands of green. We're coming for you, she thought. "Today, we'll kick her ass. Over."

"That's a roger. Ro, I've got something you should know," he began, and told her about Leo.

When she'd finished the radio call, Rowan walked over, sat down by Gull.

"Hell of a view," he commented. "Libby's in love. She's talking about moving up here. Ditching us for the Alaska unit."

"People fall for the mountain. Gull, Leo turned himself in this morning. He's in custody."

He studied her, then drank more coffee. "Then it's a damn good day."

"I guess it is." She heaved out a breath. "Yeah, I guess it is. Let's make it better and kill this dragon dead."

"I hear that," he said, and leaned over to kiss her.

IT SHOOK IRENE to the core to walk into the room and see Leo shackled to the single table. He'd lost weight, and his hair, thinner, straggly, hung over the collar of the bright orange prison suit. He hadn't shaved for God knew how long, she thought, and the beard had grown in shockingly gray around his gaunt face.

He looked wild. He looked like a criminal.

He looked like a stranger.

Had it only been a month since she'd seen him?

"Irene." His voice broke on her name, and the shackles rattled obscenely in her ears when he reached out.

She had to look away for a moment, compose herself.

The room seemed airless, and much too bright. She saw the reflection in the wide mirror—two-way glass, she thought. She watched *Law & Order*, and she knew how it worked.

But the reflection stunned her. Who was that woman, that old, bony woman with dingy hair scraped back from her haggard face?

It's me, she thought. I'm a stranger, too.

We're not who we were. We're not who we're supposed to be.

Were they watching behind that glass? Of course they were. Watching, judging, condemning.

The idea struck what little pride she had left, kindled it. She straightened her shoulders, firmed her chin and looked into her husband's eyes. She walked to the table, sat, but refused to take the hands he held out to her.

"You left me."

"I'm sorry. I thought it'd be better for you. They were looking to arrest me, Irene, for *murder*. I thought if I was gone, you'd be better off, and they'd find the real killer so I could come back."

"Where did you go?"

"I went up in the mountains. I kept moving. I had the radio, so I kept listening for word they'd arrested somebody. But they didn't. Somebody did this to me, Reenie. I just—"

"To you? To you, Leo? I signed my name with yours, putting up our home for your bail. You left, and now I'm going to lose my home because even taking another job isn't enough to meet the payments."

Pain, and she judged it sincere, cut across his face. "I didn't think about that until I'd already gone. I wasn't thinking straight. I just thought you and the baby would do better if I left. I didn't think—"

"You didn't think I'd be alone with no idea where my husband was, if he was dead or alive? You didn't think I'd have a baby to tend to, bills to pay, questions to answer, and all this right after I put my daughter's bones in the ground?"

"Our daughter, Reenie." Under the beard his cheeks reddened as he pounded his fist on the table. "And they think I killed my own girl. That I broke her neck, then burned her like trash in a barrel. Is that what you think? Is it?"

"I stopped thinking, Leo." She heard her own voice, thought it as dull as her hair, her face. "I had to, just to get from one day to the next, one chore to the next, one bill to the next. I lost my child, my husband, my faith. I'm going to lose my home, and my grandchild."

"I've been living like an animal," he began. Then stopped, squinted at her. "What are you talking about? They can't take Shiloh away."

"I don't know if they can or not. But I know I can't raise her right on my own without a good home to give her, or enough time. The Brayners will be here tomorrow, and they're taking her home to Nebraska."

"No." That stranger's face lit with fury. "Irene, no. Goddamn it, you listen to me now."

"Don't you swear at me." The slap in her voice had his head

snapping back. "I'm going to do what's right by that baby, Leo, and this is what's best. You've got no say in it. You left us."

"You're doing this to punish me."

She sat back. Funny, she realized, she didn't feel so tired now, so worn, so full of grief. No, she felt stronger, surer, clearer of mind than she had since they'd come to tell her Dolly was dead.

"Punish you? Look at yourself, Leo. Even if I had a mind to punish you, and I just don't, you've already done plenty of it on your own. You say you lived like an animal—well, that was your choice."

"I did it for you!"

"Maybe you believe that. Maybe you need to. I don't care. There's an innocent baby in all this, and she comes first. And for the first time in my life I'm putting myself next. Ahead of you, Leo. Ahead of every-damn-body else."

Something stirred in her. Not rage, she thought. She was sick of rage, and sick of despair. Maybe, just maybe, what stirred in her was faith—in herself.

"I'm going to do what I have to do for me. I have some thinking to do about that, but I'll be leaving, most likely to move closer to Shiloh. I'll take my half of whatever's left once this is said and done, and leave you yours."

He jerked back as if she'd slapped him. "You're going to leave me like this, when I'm locked up, when I need my wife to stand with me?"

"You need," she repeated, and shook her head. "You're going to have to get used to your needs being down the line. After Shiloh's and after mine. I'd've stood with you, Leo. I'd've done my duty as your wife and stuck by you, whatever it took and for however long. But you changed that when you proved you wouldn't do the same for me."

"Now you listen to me, Irene. You listen to me. Somebody took that rifle, took that gun, right out of my house. They did that to ruin me."

"I hope for the sake of your soul that's true. But you and Dolly made our house a battlefield, and neither one of you cared enough about me to stop the war. She left me without a second thought, and when we took her back, because that's what a parent does for a child, she lied and schemed just like always. And you fought and clawed at each other, just like always. With me in the middle, just like always."

God help her, Irene thought. She'd mourn her child for the rest of her life, but she wouldn't mourn the war.

"Now she's gone, and my faith's so broken I don't even have the comfort of believing it was God's will. I don't have that. You left me alone in the dark when I most needed a strong hand to hold on to.

"I don't know what you've done or haven't done, but I know that much. I know I can't depend on you to give me that strong hand, so I have to start depending on me. It's past time I did."

She got to her feet. "You should call your lawyer. He's what you need now."

"I know you're upset. I know you're mad at me, and I guess you've got a right to be. But please, don't leave me here alone, Irene. I'm begging you."

She tried, one last time, to reach down inside herself for love, or at least for pity. But found nothing.

"I'll come back when I can, and I'll bring you what they say I'm allowed to bring. Now I've got to go to work. I can't afford to take any more time off today. If I can find it in me to pray again, I'll pray for you."

L.B. HAILED MATT as Matt came back from his run.

"Have you got your PT in for the day?"

"Yeah. I was going to grab a shower and some breakfast. Have you got something you want me to do?"

"We could use some help restocking gear and equipment as it gets inspected. The crew got in from Wyoming while you were out."

"I saw the plane overhead. Man, L.B., did they have trouble, too?"

"Another bad pumper."

"Well, shit."

"We've got mechanics going over every inch of the rest of them, the saws and so on. We're unpacking all the chutes, and

I've got master riggers going over them. Iron Man's here, so he's helping with that."

"Jesus Christ, L.B., you don't think somebody messed with the chutes?"

"Are you willing to risk it?"

Matt pulled off his cap, scrubbed a hand over his hair. "I guess not. Who the hell would do something like this?"

"We're damn sure going to find out. Iron Man had news. Leo Brakeman turned himself in this morning."

"He's back? In Missoula? The cops have him?"

"That's exactly right. It makes me wonder how long he's been around these parts."

"And he could've done this. Screwed with us like this." Matt looked away, stared off, shaking his head. "Threatening Ro, shooting at her, for God's sake. Now messing with equipment. We never did anything to him or his. Never did a damn thing, and he can't say the same."

"Right now, we take care of our own, so grab that shower and some chow, then report to the ready room."

"Okay. Listen, if you need me back on the jump list—"

"We'll leave you off for now."

"I appreciate it, a lot. My parents should be in late this afternoon. I'm going to let them know I might have to cut it short. I don't want you having to shuffle somebody into my spot with the other crap on your plate, too. You call me in if you need me."

"Copy that." He gave Matt a slap on the shoulder.

He headed back into Operations. He had twenty-one men in Alaska, and didn't expect to see them back until the next day, soonest. Another load barely touched down, and a fire in California where they might need some Zulies before it was said and done. Dry conditions predicted for the next two weeks.

He'd be damned if he'd send the first load up without being sure, absolutely sure, every strap, every buckle, every fucking zipper and switch passed the most rigorous inspection.

He thought of Jim, felt the familiar heartsickness. Accidents couldn't be controlled, but he could and would control this human-generated bullshit.

AT THE END of a very long day, Lieutenant Quinniock drove out to the base. He wanted to go home, see his wife and kids, have dinner with them the way men who weren't cops did.

Most of all he wanted to be done with Leo Brakeman.

The man was a stone wall, wouldn't give an inch.

Every pass he or DiCicco had taken at him—together or separately—met with the same result.

Zero.

Brakeman just sat there, arms folded, eyes hard, jaw tight under that scruffy man-of-the-mountain beard. He'd lost ten pounds, gained ten years, and still wouldn't budge from his I'm-being-framed routine.

Now he demanded—through his lawyer, as he'd stopped talking altogether—a polygraph. So they'd have to go through that dance and shuffle.

Quinniock suspected if the polygraph results indicated Brakeman was a lying sack of shit who couldn't tell the truth over the size of his own dick, he'd claim the polygraph framed him.

They had circumstantial evidence aplenty. They had motive, means, opportunity and the fact that he'd run. What they didn't have was a confession.

The DA didn't want to charge Leo Brakeman, former All-State tackle, a Missoula native, with no priors and deep ties to the community, with the murder of his own daughter without a confession.

And since every goddamn bit of that evidence tied Dolly's murder with Latterly's, they couldn't charge him with that, either.

Need a break, Quinniock thought. Need a little off-the-clock before going back the next day to beat his head against the DA's. But first he had to see what the hell Michael Little Bear wanted.

Once on base, he aimed directly for Little Bear's office.

"You looking for L.B.?"

Quinniock stopped, nodded at the man who hailed him. "That's right."

"He just walked over to the loft. Do you know where that is?"

"Yeah, thanks."

He changed direction. It struck him how quiet the base seemed. None of the crew training outside or hustling from building to building, though he had seen a couple of them hauling ass down one of the service roads in a jeep. Either a test or a joyride, he decided.

When he made his way to the loft, passed what he knew they called the ready room, he saw why.

Here the hive of activity buzzed. Men and a handful of women worked on tools, taking them apart or putting them back together. Others pulled equipment off shelves or replaced it.

Routine inspection? he wondered, considered the organized chaos as he entered the loft.

There he saw chutes spread on counters, being unpacked or meticulously repacked. More hung in the tower waiting to be inspected or already tagged for repair or repacking.

He spotted Little Bear standing beside Lucas Tripp at one of the counters.

"Iron Man." Quinniock offered a hand with genuine pleasure. "Have they talked you back on the team?"

"Just helping out for the day. How's it going, Lieutenant?"

"I've had better days, and I've had worse. You wanted to talk to me?" he said to L.B.

"Yeah. Where's the tree cop?"

"Seeing to some tree cop business. Did you want her here?"

"Not especially. I have crews in Alaska, and another just back this morning from Wyoming."

"I heard about the fires in Alaska, threatening Denali Park. What's the status?"

"They hope to have it contained within a few hours. It's been a long, hard haul and my people jumped that fire with defective equipment."

"Is that what this is about?" Quinniock took another look around the loft. "You're running an equipment inspection?"

"What this is about is the fact that the equipment was tampered with. Stripped valves in pumpers, and one of them went into Wyoming. Chain saws with burned-out spark plugs and a frayed starter cord."

"I don't want to tell you your business, but all of that sounds like it could easily be simple wear and tear, something that got overlooked during the height of a busy season."

L.B.'s face went hard as stone. "We don't overlook a damn thing. Equipment comes in from a fire, it's gone over, checked out and checked off before it goes back in rotation. The same valve stripped on three pumpers, and two in the load that went to Denali?"

"Okay, that's a stretch."

"You're damn right. We're inspecting everything, and we've already found two more defective saws, and four piss bags with the nozzles clogged with putty. We're not careless; we can't afford to be. We don't overlook."

"All right."

"We have to inspect every chute, drogue, reserve. And thank God so far none of the ones we've gone over show any signs of tampering. Do you know how long it takes to repack a single chute?"

"About forty-five minutes. I've taken the tour. All right," Quinniock repeated, and took out his notebook. "You have a list of who checked off the equipment?"

"Sure I do, and I've gone over it. I'll give you the names, and the names of the mechanics who did any of the repairs or cleaning. It doesn't fall on one person."

"Are any of your crew dealing with more than the usual stress?"

"My people in Alaska who had to jerry-rig pumpers with duct tape, goddamn it, or lose their ground."

As he also sent men out into the field, bore the weight of those decisions, Quinniock understood the simmering rage. He kept his own tone brisk. "Have you had to discipline anyone, remove anyone from active?"

"No, and no. Do you think one of the crew did this? These people don't know when they'll have to jump or where or into what conditions until they do. Why in the hell would somebody do this when they might be the one with a starter cord snapping off in their hands, or scrambling with a useless pump with a fire bearing down on him?"

"Your support staff, your mechanics, your pilots and so on don't jump."

"And Leo Brakeman walked into your house this morning. He's already shot up mine, and isn't shy about starting fires. Tampering with the equipment here takes a little mechanical know-how."

"And he has more than a little." Quinniock blew out a breath. "I'll look into it. If it was him, I can promise you he's going to be sitting just where he's sitting for some time to come."

"His wife's leaving him," Lucas put in. He'd finished packing the chute, tagged it, then turned to address Quinniock. "She's giving the baby to the Brayners, the father's parents. They're coming in from Nebraska. She's making arrangements to turn the house over, to sell whatever she can sell, cash out whatever she can cash out. She's thinking about moving out near the Brayners so she can be near the baby, help out, watch her grow up."

"You're well informed."

"My . . ." Did a sixty-year-old man have a girlfriend? he wondered. "The woman I'm involved with is a close friend of Irene's."

"Ella Frazier. I'm well informed, too," Quinniock added. "I met her at the funeral."

"She's helping Irene as much as she can. Irene told Leo all this when she went to see him this morning."

Quinniock passed a weary hand over his face. "That explains why he shut down."

"It seems to me he's got nothing left to lose now."

"He wants to take a polygraph, but that could be the lawyer's idea. He's sticking with the same story, and the more we twist it up, the harder he bears down. Maybe tossing this tampering at him will shake him. I want the timelines, when each piece was last used, last inspected, by whom in both cases if you can get that for me. I have to make a call first."

He flipped out his phone, called the sergeant on duty and ordered a suicide watch on Leo Brakeman.

27

The plane touched down in Missoula shortly after ten A.M. They'd hit very rocky air over Canada, with hail flying like bullets while the plane rode the roller coaster of the storm.

Half the crew landed queasy or downright sick.

Since she'd slept the entire flight, Rowan calculated she felt nearly three-quarters human. Human enough to take a year-long shower, and eat like a starving horse.

As she and Gull walked to the barracks, she spotted L.B. with Cards, supervising the off-loading. She suspected L.B. had been waging his own war while they had waged theirs.

She didn't want to think about either battle for a little while.

She dropped down to sit on the bed in her quarters, remove her boots. "I want lots and lots of sex."

"You really are the woman of my dreams."

"First round, wet shower sex, after we scrape off a few layers of the Alaskan tundra, then a short and satisfying lunch break." She unbuckled her belt, dropped her pants. "Then a second round of make-the-mattress-sing sex."

"I feel a tear of gratitude and awe forming in the corner of my eye. Don't think less of me."

God, the man just tickled every inch of her. And, she decided, even with the scruff on his face, his hair matted, twanged her lust chords.

"Then a quickie just to top things off before I start my reports. I'll have to brief with L.B. at some point, and squeeze in daily PT, after which there must be more food."

"There must."

"Then I believe it's going to be a time for relax-into-a-nap sex."

"I can write up an agenda on this, just so we don't miss anything."

"It's all here." She tapped her temple. "So . . ." She strolled naked into the bathroom. "Let's get this party started."

Rowan considered the first round a knockout. Now that she felt a hundred percent human, and with Gull shaving off the scruff in her bathroom, she went out to dress.

She picked up the note someone must have shoved under her door in the last forty minutes.

FULL BRIEFING ALL CREW
OPS
THIRTEEN HUNDRED

"Oh, well. Round two's going to have to be postponed." She held the note up for Gull to read.

"Maybe he has some answers."

"Or maybe he's just got a whole lot of questions. Either way, we'd better scramble if we're going to get any food before thirteen hundred."

"Marg might know something."

"I'm thinking the same."

Since Marg liked him well enough, Gull went with Rowan to the kitchen.

Probably not the best timing, he realized as they walked into the heat and the rush. Marg, Lynn and the new cook—Shelley, he remembered—turned, hauled, chopped and scooped with a creative symmetry that made him think of a culinary Cirque du Soleil.

"Hey." Lynn filled a tub with some sort of pasta medley. "Shelley, we need more rolls, and the chicken salad's getting low."

"I'm all over it!"

"Bring the barbecue pan back when you come," Marg told Lynn while she swiped a cloth over her heat-flushed face. "They'll be ready for it by then. I know how they suck this stuff down.

"Briefing at one o'clock," she muttered, and wagged a spoon at Rowan. "Right in the middle of things, so they all storm this place before noon like Henry the Fifth stormed, wherever the hell that was."

"I could chop something," Rowan volunteered.

"Just stay clear. Once we get this second round of barbecue out to them, they'll hold awhile."

"You were right." Lynn bustled back in with a near-empty pan. Together, she and Marg filled it.

"This tops everything off but the dessert buffet. Shelley and I can get that."

"Good girl." Marg flipped out two plates, tossed the open rolls on them, dumped barbecue on the bottom, scooped the pasta medley beside it, added a serving of summer squash. Then pointed at Gull. "Get three beers and bring 'em out to my table. Take this." She shoved one of the plates at Rowan before grabbing up flatware setups.

She sailed outside and, after setting the plate and setups down, pressed her hands to her lower back. "God."

"Sit down, Marg."

"I need to stretch this out some first. Go on and eat."

"Aren't you going to?"

Marg just waved a hand in the negative. "That's what I'm after," she said, taking the beer Gull held out to her. "I've got the AC set to arctic blast, but by the time we're into the middle of the lunch shift, it's like Nairobi. Eat. And don't bolt it down."

Gull lifted the sloppy sandwich, got in the first bite. Warm, tangy, with the pork melting into sauce and the combination melding into something like spiced bliss.

"Marg, what'll it take for you to come and live with me?"

"A lot of sex."

"I'm good for that," he said over another bite, pointing to Rowan for verification. "I'm good for that."

"Everybody's got to be good for something," Rowan commented. "What's the word, Marg?"

"L.B.'s on a tear, that's for certain. You don't see that man get up a head of steam often. It's why he's good at the job. But he's been puffing it out the last couple days. He had every chute, every pack, every jumpsuit gone over. He'd have used microscopes on them if he could have. Every piece of equipment, every tool, every damn thing. He's having the jeeps gone over, the Rolligons, the planes."

She took a long, slow sip of beer, set it aside, then surprised Gull by lowering smoothly into a yoga down dog. "God, that feels better. He called Quinniock out here."

"He wants a police investigation?" Rowan asked.

"He's made up his mind Leo managed to do this. He may be right." She walked her feet up to a forward fold, hung there a moment, then straightened. "Irene's leaving him. She's already packing up. The Brayners are taking the baby tomorrow, and I don't think she plans to be far behind. She's going to move into your daddy's place for a couple weeks, until she clears up her business."

"She's moving in with Dad?"

"No, into the house. He offered it to her. He'll be in Ella's."

"Oh."

"Don't give me that WTF look. Talk to your father about it. Meanwhile, I hear they have Leo on suicide watch and he's clammed up tight. He wants to take a lie detector test. I think they're going to do that today or tomorrow.

"That's about it. I've got to get back."

Gull waited a moment, then scooped up some pasta. "All that, and I bet the only thing you're thinking is your father's going to be living with the hot redhead."

"Shut up. Besides, he's just doing a favor for Mrs. Brakeman."

"Yeah, I bet it's a real sacrifice. You know what I'm thinking?"

Deliberately she stared up at the sky. "I don't care."

"Yes, you do. I'm thinking, the way this is working out, I'll move in with you. You're going to have the room, then I can be closer to Marg and get this barbecue on a regular basis."

"I don't think this is something to joke about."

"Babe, I never joke about barbecue." He licked some off

his thumb. "I wonder how a Fun World would go over in Missoula."

Rowan tried to squeeze out some stress by pinching the bridge of her nose. "I'm losing my appetite."

"Too bad. Can I have the rest of your sandwich?"

The snort of laughter snuck up on her. "Damn it. Every time I should be annoyed with you, you manage to slide around it. And no." With a smirk, she stuffed the rest of her sandwich into her mouth.

"Just for that I'm going to get some pie. And I'm not bringing you any."

"You don't have time." She tapped her watch. "Briefing."

"I'll take it to go."

He didn't get her any pie, but he did bring her a slab of chocolate cake. They ate dessert out of their palms on the way to Ops.

Jumpers poured out of the woodwork, heading in from the training field and track, striding out of the barracks, filing in from the loft. A grim-faced Cards, shoulders hunched, hands deep in his pockets, turned out of the ready room.

Rowan nudged Gull's arm with her elbow and shifted direction to intersect.

"You look like somebody stole your last deck," she commented.

"Do you think I didn't do my job? Didn't pay attention to what I load?"

"I know you did. You do."

"That equipment was inspected and checked. I've got the goddamn paperwork. I checked the goddamn manifest."

"Are you taking heat on this?" Rowan demanded.

"It's got to go up the chain, something like this, and when shit goes up the chain, the hook drops on somebody. What're we supposed to do, check every valve, nozzle, cord and strap before we load it, when every damn thing's been checked before it goes into rotation? Are we supposed to start everything up before we put it on the damn plane?

"Fuck it. Just fuck it. I don't know why I do this damn job anyway."

He stalked off, leaving Rowan looking after him with a

handful of cake crumbs and smeared icing. "He shouldn't take a knock for this. This is nobody's fault except whoever messed up the equipment."

"He's right about the way things drop back down the chain. Even if they pin it on Brakeman, on anybody, Cards could take a hit."

"It's not right. L.B. will go to bat for him. It's bad enough, what we've been dealing with, without one of us getting dinged for it." She stared down at her chocolate-smeared hand. "Hell."

"Here." Gull dug a couple of wet naps out of his pocket. "Some problems have easy solutions."

"He's a damn fine jumper." She swiped at the chocolate. "As good a spotter as they come. He can be annoying with the card games and tricks, but he puts a lot into this job. More than most of us."

Gull could have pointed out that putting more than most into it meant Cards had regular and easy access to all the equipment, and that as spotter he hadn't jumped the Alaska fire.

No point in it, he decided. Her attachment there ran deep.

"He'll be all right."

They went into the building where people milled and muttered.

He saw Yangtree sitting, rubbing his knee, and Dobie leaning against a wall, eyes closed in a standing-up power nap. Libby played around with her iPhone while Gibbons sat with a hip hitched on a counter, his nose in a book.

Some drank coffee, some huddled in conversations, talking fire, sports, women—the three top categories—or speculating about the briefing to come. Some zoned out, sitting on the floor, backs braced against the wall or a desk.

Every one of them had dropped weight since the start of the season, and plenty of them, like Yangtree, nursed aching knees. The smoke jumper's Achilles' heel. Strained shoulders, pulled hamstrings, burns, bruises. Some of the men had given up shaving, sporting beards in a variety of styles.

Every one of them understood true exhaustion, real hunger, intense fear. And every one of them would suit up if the siren called. Some would fight hurt, but they'd fight all the same.

He'd never known people so stubbornly resilient or so willing to put body, mind and life on the line, day after day.

And more, to love it.

"L.B. hasn't started." Matt maneuvered in beside him. "I thought I'd be late."

"Not yet. I didn't expect to see you for a couple more days."

"I'm just in for this. L.B. wanted all of us, unless we caught a fire. What's the word?"

"As far as I know they're still inspecting. They found a few more pieces of equipment tampered with."

"Son of a bitch."

"Did your parents get in all right?" Rowan asked him.

"Yeah. They're over visiting with Shiloh. We're going to take her out for a couple hours later, so she gets used to being with us. She's already taken to my ma."

"How's Mrs. Brakeman doing?"

He lifted his shoulders, stared toward the Ops desk. "She's being real decent about it. It shows how much she loves the baby." He let out a little sigh. "She and my ma had a good cry together. L.B.'s getting ready to start."

"All right, settle down," L.B. called out. "I've got some things to say, so pay attention. Everybody knows about the equipment failures on the jumps in Alaska and Wyoming. I want to tell you all that we're continuing a full inspection, any equipment or gear not yet inspected and passed doesn't go out. I called in a couple extra master riggers to help reinspect, clear, repack every chute on this base. I don't want anybody worrying about the safety of their gear."

He paused a moment.

"We've got a good system of checks on this base, and nobody cuts corners. Everyone here knows it's not just important, it's fucking *essential* that every jumper have confidence the gear and equipment needed to jump and attack will be safe, meet the highest standards and be in good working order. That didn't happen on these jumps, and I take responsibility."

He hard-eyed the protests until they died off.

"I've been in touch with the Management Council so they're aware of what we're dealing with. The local police and the USFS are also aware and conducting their own investigations."

"They know damn well Leo Brakeman did this," somebody shouted out and started everybody else up again.

"He shouldn't have been able to." L.B. roared it over the rise of chatter, smashing it like a boot heel on an anthill. "He shouldn't have been able to get to us the way he did. The fact he's locked up is all fine and good, but we're going to be a lot more security-conscious around here. We're going to do spot checks, regular patrols. If I could suspend the tours, I would, but since that's not an option, two staff members will go with each group.

"Until the investigations and reviews are complete, and we know who and how, we're not taking any chances."

He stopped again, took a breath. "And I'm recommending everybody toss a roll of duct tape into their PG bags."

That got a laugh, succeeding in lowering the tension.

"I want you to know I've got your backs, on base, in the air and on a fire. I've posted a new jump list and a rotation of assignments. If you don't like it, come see me in my office so I can kick your ass. Anybody's got any questions, suggestions, public bitching, now's the time."

"Can we get the feds to pay for the duct tape?" Dobie asked, and earned hoots and applause.

Gull sent his friend an appreciative look. The right attitude, he thought. Keep it cocky, keep it steady, maintain unity.

Whether the sabotage had been an inside or outside job, unity equaled strength.

He had questions, but not the sort he wanted to ask here.

"I've got something I need to work on," he told Rowan over the cross talk. "Catch up with you later."

He noted her disapproving frown, but slipped out and walked straight to his quarters. There, he booted up his laptop and got to work.

He shut down, passcoding his work when the siren sounded. He wasn't on the first or second loads, but he ran to the ready room to assist those who were. He loaded gear on speed racks, hefted already packed and strapped paracargo onto the electric cart.

He listened, and he observed.

With Rowan and Dobie, he watched the plane rise into the wide blue cup of the sky.

"It's good L.B. got that briefing in before the call." Rowan shaded her eyes from the sun with the flat of her hand. "The sky looks a little dicey to the east."

"Might be jumping ourselves before long."

Hearing the eagerness in his voice, Rowan angled her body toward Dobie. "You've got jump fever. The best thing for you is to go sleep it off."

"I got me an assignment. I'm on PC," he said, using the shorthand for paracargo. "Packing and strapping in the loadmaster's room. You, too, pal," he told Gull. "Swede pulled the loft."

"Yeah, I saw that, and that anybody on the Alaska jump could take a two-hour break first. But what the hell." He leaned over, kissed Rowan. "We'll get back to our agenda later."

"Count on it."

"I don't see how it's right and fair you got a woman right on base," Dobie said as they walked toward the loadmaster's room together. "The rest of us have to hunt one up, if we're lucky and get a turn at a bar."

"Life's just full of not right and not fair. Otherwise I'd be stretched out on a white sand beach with that woman, drinking postcoital mai tais."

"Postcoital." Dobie snickered like a twelve-year-old. "You beat all, Gull. Beat all and back again."

SINCE HE DIDN'T FIND her in her quarters, Gull assumed he'd finished up his duties before her, and went back to his room to continue on his project.

He sat on the bed, left the door open in a casual, nothing-to-see-here mode.

People walked by now and then, but for the most part his section stayed quiet.

Since he'd left his window open as well, he caught snippets of conversation as people wandered outside. A small group not on the jump list made plans to go into town. Somebody muttered to himself about women as the shimmering afternoon light dimmed.

He took a moment to shift to look out, and saw Rowan had

been right about the eastern sky. Clouds gathered now, sailing in like warships.

A storm waiting to happen, he thought, toying with getting his run in before it did, then decided to wait for Rowan.

She and the first grumble of thunder arrived at the same time.

"Lightning strikes all over hell and back," she told him, and flopped on the bed. "I ran up to check the radar. Tornadoes whipping things up in South Dakota."

She circled her neck, rubbing hard at the back of her left shoulder as she spoke.

"We'll probably have to run on the damn treadmill. I hate that."

He pressed his fingers where she rubbed. "Jesus, Rowan, you got concrete in here."

"Don't I know it. I haven't had a chance to work it out today. I need that run, some yoga . . . or that." She sighed when he shifted and dug his fingers and thumbs into the knotted muscles.

"We'll do our run after the storm's over," he said. "Use the track."

Lightning struck, a flash and burn, and the wind rattled the blinds at his window. But no rain followed.

"When things slow down, we'll hit L.B. up for a night off and get a fancy hotel suite. One with a jet tub in the bathroom. We'll soak in it half the night."

"Mmm." She sighed her way into the image he painted. "Room service with fat, juicy steaks, and a great big bed to play on. Sleeping with somebody who has money and doesn't mind spending it has advantages."

"If you've got money and mind spending it, you can't be having much fun."

"I like that attitude. Are you e-mailing back home?"

"No, something else. You're not going to like it."

"If you're e-mailing your pregnant wife to ask about your two adorable children and frisky puppy, I'm not going to like it." She angled around. "That's the kind of tone you used. Like you were going to tell me something that meant I had to punch you in the face."

"My wife's not pregnant, and we have a cat." He gave her shoulders a last squeeze, then got up to close the door.

"You didn't do that because we're going to continue our planned agenda from this morning."

"No. It's the tampering, Rowan. Brakeman thinking of it, then pulling it off—all while eluding the cops. That's just not working for me."

"He knows this area better than most. He's a mechanic, and he has a grudge against us. It works for me."

On the surface, he thought, but you only had to scratch off a layer.

"Why tamper with some of the equipment?" Gull began working off his mental list. "He doesn't know how we roll here, or in a fire. Not all the ins and outs."

"His daughter worked here three seasons," Rowan pointed out. "She had a working knowledge of how we roll, and he's spent time on base."

"If he wanted to hurt us, there are more direct ways. He had weapons; he could've used them. Sure, he could've known or found out where the equipment is," Gull conceded, "and he could've gotten to it. This stretch of the season, most of us would sleep through a bomb blast. We'd hear the siren, the same way a mother hears her baby crying in the night even when she's exhausted. We're tuned, but otherwise, we're out for the count.

"This was subtle, and sneaky, and it was the kind of thing, it seems to me, you'd know to do if you knew just how broken equipment could impact a crew on a fire. Because you've been there."

He was right, Rowan thought. She didn't like it. "You're actually saying one of us did this?"

"I'm saying one of us could have done it, because we know how to access the equipment, how to screw it up and how it could impact an attack."

"How stupid would that be since you could be the one impacted?"

"There's that. Let's take that first. Who didn't jump either fire?"

He toggled his screen back to the document he'd worked on.

"You're right; I don't like it one damn bit. And first, Yangtree jumped with us."

"He spent nearly the entire jump coordinating, doing flyovers."

"That's crap. And L.B.? Seriously?"

"He didn't jump. Cards worked as spotter, so he didn't jump. Neither did any of these. That's over twenty, with six of them off the list altogether for personal reasons or injuries."

"Yangtree's been jumping thirty *years*. What, suddenly he decides to find out what'll happen if he screws up equipment? Cards has ten years in, and L.B. more than a dozen. And—"

"Look, I know how you feel about them. They're friends—they're family. I feel the same."

"In my world people don't make up a suspect list of friends and family."

"How often in your world has your equipment been sabotaged?" He laid a hand on her knee to soften the words. "Look, it's more with you because you've been with them a long time. But I trained with a lot of the names on this list, and you know going through that makes a tight bond."

"I don't even know why you're doing this."

"Because, damn it, Rowan, if it wasn't Brakeman, then we can do our patrols, our rechecks and spot checks, but . . . If you wanted to get in the ready room, the loadmaster's room, any damn place on base tonight and mess something up, could you?"

She didn't speak for a moment. "Yeah. I could. Why would I? Why would any of us?"

"That's another deal entirely. Before that, there's the possibility, if it's one of us, it *is* somebody who jumped, who knew they were high on the list. Who wanted to be there, be part of it. We're in a stressful line of work. People snap, or go too far. The firefighter who starts fires, then risks himself and his crew to put it out. It happens."

"I know it happens."

He hit another key, took her to another page.

"I divided the crews, the way we were that day."

"You're missing some names."

"I think we can eliminate ourselves."

"Dobie's not here."

"He had the duct tape."

"Yeah, that was real handy."

"He always carries . . . Okay, you're right." It burned his belly and his conscience, but he added Dobie's name. "I should add us because you wished for the damn tape, and I remembered he'd have it."

"What's our motive?"

"Maybe I want to scare you off the job so you'll stay home and cook me a hot dinner every night."

"As if. But I mean the question. What's any motive?"

"Okay, let's roll with that. Yangtree." He toggled back again. "He's talking about giving it up. His knees are shot. Thirty years, like you said. He's given this more than half his life, and now he knows he can't keep it up. The younger and stronger are moving in. That's a pisser."

"He's not like that." She snapped it out—knee-jerk—then subsided when Gull only looked at her. "All right. This is bogus, but all right."

"Cards? He's had a bad-luck season. Injuries, illness. It wears. The woman he wanted to marry dumped him. Last summer, when he was spotter, Jim Brayner died."

"That wasn't—"

"His fault. I agree. It wasn't yours, either, Rowan, but you have nightmares."

"Okay. Okay. I get it. We could walk down your lists and find a plausible motive for everyone. That doesn't make it true. And if it's such a good theory, the cops would've thought of it."

"What makes you think they haven't?"

That stopped her. "That's a really ugly thought. The idea they're looking at us, investigating us, scraping away to hunt for weaknesses, secrets. That they're doing what we're doing here, only more."

"It is ugly, but I'd rather take a hard look than ignore what might be right here with us."

"I want it to be Brakeman."

"Me too."

"But if it's not," she said before he could, "we have to think of the safety of the unit. It's not L.B."

He started to argue, then backed off. "What's your reasoning?"

"He worked hard for his position, and he takes a lot of pride in it. He loves the unit and he also loves its rep. Anything that damages or threatens that reflects on him. He could've closed ranks and kept this internal, but he opened it up. He's the one shining the light on it when he knows he may pay consequences."

Good points, Gull decided. Every one a good point. "I'll agree with that."

"And it's not Dobie. He's too damn good-natured under it all. And he loves what he's doing. He loves it all. Mostly he loves you. He'd never do anything that put you at risk."

"Thanks."

"I didn't say that for you."

"I know." But it soothed both his belly and his conscience. "Thanks anyway."

She looked out the window where lightning flashed, and thunder echoed over the gloom-shrouded peaks. "The wind's pushing the rain south. We just can't catch a break."

"We don't have to do this now. We can let it alone, hit the gym."

"I'm not a weak sister. Let's work it through. I'll tell you why it's not Janis."

"All right." He took her hand, disconcerting her by bringing it briefly to his lips. "I'm listening."

"Thanks for meeting me."

"No problem. I still run here some days, so I got a mile or so in. I have to figure this has to do with Rowan since you didn't want to talk to me on base."

"With her, with everybody. Nobody knows the players better than you, Lucas. The staff and crew, the Brakemans, the cops. Maybe not the rookies as much as the long-timers, but I'm betting you've got some insight there, as they jump with your daughter."

Lucas cocked an eyebrow at that, but Gull just shrugged.

"You'd size them up, ask some questions, get some answers."

"I know you're fast on your feet, had a good rep with the hotshots, and L.B. considers you a solid asset to the crew. You don't mind a fight, like fast cars, have a head for business and good taste in women."

"We've got the last in common. Let me ask you straight out, does Leo Brakeman have the brains, the canniness, let's say, the aptitude to do all that's being laid down here? Forget motive and opportunity and all that cop shit." Gull shrugged it off. "Is he the man for this?"

Lucas said nothing for a moment, only nodding his head as if affirming his own thoughts. "He's not stupid, and he's a damn good mechanic. Starting from the back, yeah, he could've figured how to disable equipment without it showing until it was too late. Killing Latterly . . ."

Lucas stuck his hands in his pockets, looked away at the mountains. "I'd see him going after the son of a bitch once he found out Latterly was messing with his daughter. I'd see him beating the man bloody for it, especially considering Irene's connection to the church. It's harder to see Leo putting a bullet in him, but not impossible to see."

He sighed once. "No, not impossible. He'd be capable of shooting up the base. Aiming for anybody, I don't think so. But if he had, he wouldn't have missed. And that's one I've thought long and hard on since he'd have had Rowan in the crosshairs.

"Dolly? They kept at each other like rottweilers over the same bone. He's got a temper, that's no secret, and it's no secret she caused him a lot of shame and disappointment."

"But?"

"Yeah, but. The only way I can see him killing her is an accident. I don't know if I'm putting myself into it, or if that's a fact, but it's how I see it. I guess what I'm saying is I can see him doing any of those things, in the heat. He's got a short fuse, burns hot. But it burns out."

"You've been giving all of this some long, hard thought."

"Rowan's in the middle of it."

"Exactly. Hot temper. Hot and physical." And, Gull thought, straight down the line of his own take on it. "Latterly and the tampering. Those were cold and calculated."

"You're thinking some of this, maybe all of it, comes from somebody who works on base. Maybe even one of your own."

He thought of the men and women he'd trained with, the ones he fought with. "I haven't wanted to think it."

"Neither have I, but I started asking myself these same questions after L.B. told me about the tampering. After I settled down some. We've skirted around it, but I'm pretty sure L.B.'s asking himself the same."

"Are you leaning in any particular direction?"

"I worked with some of these people. You know as well as I that's not like sharing an office or a watercooler. I can't see anyone I know the way I know those men and women in this kind of light. And I don't know if that's because of what we were—still are—to each other or because it's just God's truth."

He waited a beat, watching Gull's face carefully. "You haven't told Rowan your line of thinking?"

"I did."

Approval and a little humor curved Lucas's lips. "We can add you've got balls to what I know about you."

"I'm not going behind her back." He thought of where he stood right now, and with whom. And grinned. "Much. Anyway, I made a spreadsheet. I like spreadsheets," he said when Lucas let out a surprised laugh. "They're efficient and orderly. She doesn't want to think it could be true, but she listened."

"If she listened, and didn't kick the balls I know you have up past your eyes for suggesting it, it must be serious between the two of you."

"I'm in love with her. She's in love with me, too. She just hasn't figured it out yet."

"Well." Lucas studied Gull's face for a long moment. "Well," he repeated, and sighed a second time. "She's got a hard view of relationships and their staying power. That's my fault."

"I don't think so. I think it's circumstances. And she may have a hard head and a guarded heart, but she's not closed up. She's too smart, too self-aware, not to mention a bred-in-the-bone risk-taker to deny herself what she wants once she's decided she wants it. She'll figure out she wants me."

"Cocky bastard, aren't you? I like you."

"That's a good thing, because if you didn't, she'd give me the boot. Then she'd be sad and sorry the rest of her life."

At Lucas's quick, helpless laugh, Gull glanced at his watch. "I've got to start heading back."

"I'll walk back with you. I run here off and on," he reminded Gull. "And I have something I need to tell Rowan, face-to-face."

"If it's that you're moving in with Ella, she heard."

"Hell." Lucas scrubbed a hand over the back of his neck as they walked. "I should've known it'd bounce through the base once I so much as thought about doing it. You'd think with everything going on, my personal life wouldn't make the cut."

"Well?" Lucas jabbed an elbow in Gull's ribs. "How'd she take it?"

"It knocked her back some. She'll get used to it because she loves you, she respects Ella, and she's not an idiot. Anyway, before we get back—and I'd as soon, unless she asks directly, Rowan assume we ran into each other on the road."

"Probably for the best."

"Generally I don't mind pissing her off, but she's got a lot on her plate. So, before we get back, I wanted to ask if I can e-mail you the spreadsheet."

"Jesus Christ. A spreadsheet."

"I've listed names in multiple categories, along with general data, then my take on each. Rowan's take. Adding yours might help narrow the field."

"Send me the damn spreadsheet." Lucas rattled off his e-mail address. "Want me to write it down?"

"No, I've got it."

"Even if Brakeman didn't do all this—or any of it, for that

matter—as long as he's behind bars it should end. You can't frame him if you do any of this crap when the cops know exactly where he is twenty-four/seven. I guess the question we should ask is, who's got this kind of grudge against Leo?"

Lucas lifted his eyebrows when Gull said nothing. "You're thinking something else?"

"I think it could be that, just exactly that. But I also think Brakeman, with his temper, his history with Dolly, makes a pretty good patsy. And I know whoever's responsible for this is one sick son of a bitch. I don't think sick sons of bitches stop just because it's smart."

"I wish you hadn't said that and made me think the same. Fear the same. If I could I'd make Rowan take the rest of the season off, get the hell away from this."

"I won't let anything happen to her." Gull looked Lucas dead in the eye. "I know that's a stupid and too usual a thing to say, but I won't. She can handle just about anything that comes at her. What she can't, I will."

"I'm going to hold you to that. Now, you might want to make yourself scarce while I go talk to her. Not too scarce," Lucas added. "It's likely she'll need to take out how she feels about my new living arrangements on somebody after I'm gone. It might as well be you."

ROWAN FINISHED HER REPORTS, rechecked the attached list of paracargo she'd requested and received the second day of the attack. All in order, she decided.

Once she'd turned it over to L.B., she could get the hell outside for a while, and then . . .

"It's open," she called out at the two-tap knock on her door. "Hey." Her face brightened as she rose to greet her father. "Great timing. I just finished my reports. Got your run in?"

"I thought I'd take it this way, get a twofer and see my girl."

"I tell you what, I'll dig out a cold drink from the cooler, trade you for glancing over my work here."

"If you've got any 7UP, you've got a deal."

"I always keep my best guy's favorite in stock," she reminded him as he braced his hands on her desk, scanning the work on her laptop.

"Thorough and to the point," he said after a moment. "Are you bucking for L.B.'s job?"

"Oh, that's a big hell no. I don't mind spending the time on reports, but if I had to deal with all the paperwork, personalities, politics and bullshit L.B. does, I'd just shoot myself and get it over with. You could've done it," she added. "Gotten in a couple more years."

"If I'm going to do administrative crap, it's going to be *my* administrative crap."

"Yeah, I guess that's where I got it. Do you want to walk over to the lounge? Or maybe the cookhouse? I imagine Marg has some pie we could talk her out of."

"I don't really have enough time. Ella's picking me up in a little bit."

"Oh."

"I wanted to see you, talk to you about some things."

"I heard Irene Brakeman's letting her house go, and she's probably moving to Nebraska. That you're letting her use your house until she's got it all dealt with. That was good of you, Dad. It has to be hard for her, being alone in the house, with all the memories. Added on to knowing it's not really hers anymore."

"She's moving in tomorrow. I need to pack up a few more things I'll need with me now. Ella's been helping her do the same—pack up what she'll need—and pack up what she wants to take with her when she goes."

"It's a big step she's taking. A lot of big steps. Leaving Missoula, leaving her husband, her friends, her job."

"I think she needs it. She looks better than she has since this all started. Once she decided what she needed to do for herself, for the baby, I think it took some of the weight off."

He took a long, slow drink. "Speaking of decisions, big ones. I won't be moving back into the house. I'm going to live with Ella."

"Jesus, are you going to marry her?"

He didn't choke, but he swallowed hard. "One step at a time, but I think that one's right down the road."

"I'm just getting used to you dating her, now you're moving in together."

"I love her, Rowan. We love each other."

"Okay, I guess I'm going to sit down for a minute." She chose the side of the bed. "Her place?"

"She's got a great place. A lot of room, her gardens. She's done it up just the way she wants it. Her house means a lot to her. Ours?" He let his shoulders lift and fall. "Half the year or more it's just where I sleep most nights."

"Well." She didn't know what she felt because there was too much to feel. "I guess if I'd known that would be our last dinner in the house together, I'd've . . . I don't know, done something more important than skillet chicken."

"I'm not selling the house, Ro." He sat beside her, laid a hand on her knee. "Unless you don't want it. I figured you'd take it over. We can get somebody to cut the grass and all that during the season."

"Maybe I can think about that awhile."

"As long as you want."

"Big changes," she managed. "You know how it takes me a while to navigate changes."

"Whenever you got sick as a kid, we had to dig out the same pajamas."

"The blue puppies."

"Yeah, the blue ones with puppies. When you outgrew them there was hell to pay."

"You cut them up and made me a little pillow out of the fabric. And it was okay again. Crap, Dad, you look so happy." Her eyes stung as she reached for his face. "And I didn't even notice you weren't."

"I wasn't unhappy, baby."

"You're happier now. She's not the only one who loves you," she told him, and kissed his cheeks. "So consider I've got my blue puppy pillow, and it's okay."

"Okay enough that you'll take some time when you have it to get to know her?"

"Yeah. Gull thinks she's hot."

Lucas's eyebrows winged up. "So do I, but he'd better not get any ideas."

"I'm running interference there."

"You've had some changes yourself since he came along."

"Apparently. This is the damnedest season. Gull's got it

into his head that somebody on base might be responsible for what's been going on, instead of Brakeman."

"Does he?"

"Yeah, and in his Gull way he's got all the data and suppositions organized in a file. I think it's whacked, but then I start wondering, once he's done laying it out. Then I go about my business and decide it's whacked again. Until he points out this and that. I end up not sure what to think. I hate not knowing what to think."

Gently, he skimmed a hand over her crown of hair. "Maybe the best thing to do is keep your eyes, your ears and your mind open."

"The first two are easy. It's the last that's hard. Everybody's edgy and trying to pretend they aren't. We've jumped nearly twice as many fires as we did by this time last season, and the success rate's good, injuries not too bad. But outside of that? This season's FUBAR, and we're all feeling it."

"Do me a favor. Stick close to the hotshot, as much as you can. Do it for me," he added before she could speak. "Not because I think you can't take care of yourself, but because I'll worry less if I know somebody's got your back."

"Well, he's hard to shake off anyway."

"Good." He patted her leg. "Walk me out."

She got up with him, chewing over everything they'd talked about while they walked outside. "Is it different with her, with Ella, than it was with my mother? Not the circumstances, or rate of maturity, or any of that. I mean . . ." She tapped a fist on her heart. "I'm okay with however you answer. I'd just like to know."

He took a moment, and she knew he sought out the words.

"I was dazzled by your mother. Maybe a little overwhelmed, a lot excited. When she told me she was pregnant, I loved her. And I think it was because I loved what was inside her, what we'd started without meaning to. Sometimes I wonder if she knew that, even before I did. That would've been hurtful. I cared about her, Rowan, and I did my best by her. But you were why.

"I can say Ella dazzled me, overwhelmed me, excited me. But it's different. I know what I didn't feel for your mother because I feel it now, for Ella."

"What is it you're supposed to feel?" she demanded. "I can never figure it out."

He cleared his throat. "Maybe you should ask another woman about this kind of thing."

"I'm asking you."

"Ah, hell." Now he shuffled his feet, the big man, the Iron Man. "I'm not going to talk about sex. I did that with you once already, and that was scarier than any fire I ever jumped."

"And embarrassing for both of us. I'm not asking about sex, Dad. I know about sex. You tell me you love her, and I can see it all over you. I can see it, but I don't know how it feels—how it's supposed to feel."

"There's a lot that goes around it. Trust and respect and—" He cleared his throat again. "Attraction. But the center's a reflection of all of those things, all your strengths and weaknesses, hopes and dreams. They catch fire there, in the center. Maybe it blazes, maybe it simmers, smolders, but there's the heat and the light, all those colors, and what's around it feeds it.

"Fire doesn't only destroy, Rowan. Sometimes it creates. The best of it creates, and when love's a fire, whether it's bright or a steady glow, hot or warm, it creates. It makes you better than you were without it."

He stopped, colored a little. "I don't know how to explain it."

"It's the first time anyone ever explained it so I could understand it. Dad." She took his hands, looked into his eyes. "I'm really happy for you. I mean it, all the way through. Really happy for you."

"That means more than I can tell you." He drew her in, held her tight as Ella drove up. "You were my first love," he whispered in Rowan's ear. "You always will be."

She knew it, but now let go enough to accept he could love someone else, too. She nodded as Ella stepped out of the car.

"Hi."

"Hi." Ella smiled at Lucas. "Am I late?"

"Right on time." Keeping his hand in Rowan's, he leaned down, kissed Ella. "How'd it go with Irene?"

"Packing up, organizing, deciding over the contents of a house a woman's lived in for twenty-five years is a monumental project—and you know I love projects. It's helping her,

I think, the work, the planning. Helping her get through the now."

"Did Jim's parents . . ." Rowan trailed off.

"They're leaving this afternoon. I met them, and they're lovely people. Kate's asked Irene to come stay with them if and when she goes to Nebraska. To stay until she finds a place of her own. I don't think she will, but the offer touched her."

"Don't be sad," Lucas said, sliding an arm around Ella's shoulders as her eyes filled.

"I can't figure out what I am." She blinked the tears back. "But I called my son, asked him to bring the kids over later. I know how I feel after a few hours with my grandchildren. Happy and exhausted."

Grandchildren, Rowan thought. She'd forgotten. Did that make her father kind of an unofficial grandfather? What did he think about *that*? How did he—

"Oh, hell, I forgot I need to run something by L.B. Two minutes," he promised Ella, and loped off.

"So," Ella began, "are we okay?"

"We're okay. It's . . . strange, but we're okay. I guess you've told your son and daughter."

"Yes. My daughter's thrilled, which may be partially due to hormones as she's pregnant and that was just great news."

Another one? she thought. "Congratulations."

"Thanks. My son's . . . a little embarrassed right now, I think, at the distinct possibility Lucas and I do more than jigsaw puzzles and watch TV together."

"He shouldn't be embarrassed that you guys play gin rummy now and then."

Ella let out an appreciative laugh. "He'll get over it. I'd like to have you over for dinner, all the kids, when you can manage it. Nothing formal, just a family meal."

"Sounds good." Or manageable, she decided, which had the potential for good. "You should know, straight off, I don't need a mother."

"Oh, of course you do. Everyone does. A woman who'll listen, take your side, tell the truth—or not, as you need it. A woman you can count on, no matter what, and who'll love you no matter how much you screw up. But since you've already got that in Marg, I'm happy to settle for being your friend."

"We can see how that goes."

The siren shrilled.

"Hell. I'm up."

"Oh, God! You have to go. You have to— Can I watch? Lucas told me how this part works, but I'd like to see it."

"Fine with me. But you have to run." Without waiting, Rowan tore toward the ready room.

She breezed by Cards, so he kicked it to keep pace.

"What's the word?" she asked.

"Laborious. Got one up in Flathead, tearing down the canyon. That's all I know."

"Are you spotting?"

"Jumping."

They rushed into the controlled chaos of the ready room, grabbing gear out of lockers. Rowan pulled on her jumpsuit, checked pockets, zippers, snaps, secured her gloves, her letdown rope. She shoved her feet into her boots and caught sight of Matt doing the same.

"How'd you get back on the list?"

"Just my luck. I checked back in twenty minutes ago." He shook his head, then snagged his chute and reserve off the speed rack. "I guess the fire god decided I'd had enough time off."

Rowan secured her chutes, her PG bag. "See you on the ship," she told him, and tucked her helmet under her arm.

She shuffled toward the door, surprised to see Gull, already suited up, standing with her father and Ella.

"That was quick."

"I was in the loadmaster's room when the siren went off. Handy. Are you set?"

"Always." Rowan tapped her fingers to her forehead, flashed her father a grin. "See you later."

"See you later." He echoed the good-bye they'd given each other all her life.

"I asked if it was allowed, and since it is, I'm going to say stay safe."

Rowan nodded at Ella. "I plan on it. Let's roll, rook."

"I know you told me it all moves fast," Ella said as Rowan walked with Gull toward the waiting plane, "but I didn't realize just how fast. There's no time to think. The siren goes off, and they go from drinking coffee or packing boxes to flying to a fire, in minutes."

"It's a routine, like getting dressed in the morning. Only on fast forward. And they're always thinking. Kick some ass," he told Yangtree.

"Kicking ass, taking names. And counting the days. Catch you on the flip side, buddy."

He spoke to others as they waddled toward the plane, some he'd worked with, others who seemed as young as saplings to him. He slipped his hand in Ella's as the plane's door closed.

One of them might be a killer.

"They'll be fine." She squeezed his fingers. "And back soon."

"Yeah." Still, he felt the comfort of having her hand in his as he watched the plane taxi, rev, then rise.

AFTER THE BRIEFING IN FLIGHT, Rowan huddled with Yangtree and Trigger over maps and strategy.

Gull plugged his MP3 in, slid on his sunglasses. The music cut the engine noise, left his mind free to think. Behind the shaded glasses, he scanned the faces, the body language of the other jumpers.

Maybe it felt wrong, this suspicion, but he'd rather suffer a few pangs of guilt than suffer the consequences of more sabotage.

Cards and Dobie passed some time with liar's poker while Gibbons read a tattered paperback copy of *Cat's Cradle*. Libby huddled with Matt, patting his knee in one of her there-there gestures. The spotter got up from his seat behind the cockpit to pick his way through to confer with Yangtree.

When the call came out for buddy checks, Gull walked back himself to perform the ritual with Rowan.

"Yangtree's dumping us," Rowan told him.

Yangtree shook his head with a smile. "I'm going to work for Iron Man the first of the year. I'm going to take the fall off, buy myself a house, get my other knee fixed, do some fishing. I'll have a lot more fishing time without having to ride herd over the bunch of you every summer."

"You're giving up this life of travel, glamour and romance?" Gull asked him.

"I've had all the glamour I want, and might just find some romance when I'm not eating smoke."

"Maybe you should take up knitting while you're at it," Trigger suggested.

"I might just. I can knit you a real pretty sling since you like keeping your ass in one." He climbed over men and gear for another consult with the spotter and pilot.

"He's barely fifty." Trigger folded gum into his mouth. "Hell, I'm going to be fifty one of these days. What's he want to quit for?"

"I think he's just tired, and his knee's killing him." Rowan glanced forward. "He'll probably change his mind after he gets it fixed."

Once again, the spotter moved to the door. "Guard your reserves!"

Hot summer air, scorched with smoke, blasted in through the opening. Rowan repositioned to get a look out the window, at the blaze crowning through the tops of thick pines and firs. Red balls of ignited gases boomed up like antiaircraft fire.

"She's fast," Rowan said, "and getting a nice lift from the wind through the canyon. We're going to hit some serious crosswinds on the way down."

The first set of streamers confirmed her estimate.

"Do you see the jump spot?" she asked Gull. "There, that gap, at eight o'clock. You'll want to come in from the south, avoid doing a face-plant in the rock face. You're second man, third stick, so—"

"No. First man, second stick." He shrugged when she frowned at him, knowing Lucas had asked L.B. to switch him to her jump partner. "I guess L.B. shuffled things when he put Matt back on."

"Okay, I'll catch the drift behind you." She nodded out the window at the next set of streamers. "Looks like we've got three hundred yards."

He studied the streamers himself, and the towers of smoke, glinting silver at the fire's crown, mottled black at its base.

On final, Trigger snapped the chin strap of his helmet,

pulled down his mesh face mask before reaching for the overhead cable to waddle his way toward the door. Matt, second man, followed.

Rowan studied the fire, the ground, then the flight. Canopies billowed in the black and the blue as the plane came around for its second pass.

"We're ready," Gull answered at the spotter's call. With Rowan behind him, he got in the door, braced to the roar of wind and fire. The slap on his shoulder sent him out, diving through it, buffeted by it. He found the horizon, steadied himself as the drogue stabilized him, as the main put the brakes on to a glide.

He found Rowan, watched her canopy billow, watched the sun arrow through the smoke for an instant to illuminate her face.

Then he had a fight on his hands as the crosswinds tried to push him into a spin. A gust whipped up, blew him uncomfortably close to the cliff face. He compensated, then overcompensated as the wind yanked, tugged.

He drifted wide of the jump spot, adjusted, then let the wind take him, so he landed neat and soft on the edge of the gap.

He rolled, watched Rowan land three yards to his left.

"That was some fancy maneuvering up there," she called out to him.

"It worked."

Gathering their chutes, they joined Matt and Trigger at the edge of the jump spot. "Third stick's coming down," Trigger commented. "And shit, Cards is going into the trees. He can't buy luck this season."

Rowan clearly heard Cards curse as the wind flipped him into the pines.

"Come on, Matt, let's go make sure he ain't broke nothing important."

Since she could still hear Cards cursing, meaning he hadn't been knocked unconscious, she kept her eyes on the sky.

"Yangtree and Libby," she said as the plane positioned for the next pass. "Janis and Gibbons." She rattled off the remaining jumpers. "When they're all on the ground, I want you to take charge of the paracargo."

She put her hands on her hips, watching the next person hurtle out of the plane. Yangtree, she thought. He'd instruct, and he'd keep jumping out of planes. But doing free falls with sports groups and tourists was a far cry from . . .

"His drogue. His drogue hasn't opened." She ran forward, shouting for the others on the ground. "Drogue in tow! Jesus, Jesus, cut away! Cut away. Pull the reserve. Come on, Yangtree, for Christ's sake."

Gull's belly roiled, his heart hammered as he watched his friend, his family, tumble through the sky and smoke. Others shouted now, Trigger all but screaming into his radio.

The reserve opened with a jerky shudder, caught air—but too late, Gull realized. Yangtree's fall barely slowed as he crashed into the trees.

29

She ran, bursting through brush, leaping fallen logs, rocks, whatever lay in her path. Gull winged past her; her own fear raced with her. With her emotions in pandemonium, she ordered herself to think, to act.

His reserve had deployed at the last minute. There was a chance, always a chance. She slowed as she reached Cards, face bloody, shimmying down a lodgepole pine with his let-down rope.

"Are you hurt bad?"

"No. No. Go! Jesus, go."

Matt stumbled through the forest behind her, his cheeks gray, eyes dull. "Stay with Cards. Make sure he's okay."

She didn't wait for an answer, just kept running.

When she heard Gull's shout, she angled left, dry pine needles crunching under her feet like thin bones.

She caught sight of the reserve, a tattered mangle of white draped in the branches high overhead. And the blood, dripping like a leaky faucet, splatting on the forest floor.

Caught in the gnarled branches seventy feet above, Yangtree's limp body dangled. A two-foot spur jutted through his side, the point of it piercing through like a pin through a moth.

Gull, spurs snapped on, climbed. Rowan dumped her gear, snapped on her own and started up after him.

Broken, she could see he'd been broken—his leg, his arm and likely more. But broken didn't mean dead.

"Can you get to him? Is he alive?"

"I'll get to him." Gull climbed over, then used his rope to ease himself onto the branch, testing the weight as he went. He reached out to unsnap the helmet, laid his fingers on Yangtree's throat.

"He's got a pulse—weak, thready. Multiple fractures. Deep gash on his right thigh, but it missed the femur. The puncture wound—" He cursed as he moved closer. "This goddamn spur's holding him onto the branch like a railroad spike. I can't maneuver to stabilize him from here."

"We secure him with the ropes." Rowan leaned out as far as she could, trying to assess the situation for herself. "Cut the branch, bring him down with it."

"It's not going to take my weight and a saw." He crawled back. "It cracked some at the base. I don't know if it'll hold for you."

"Let's find out."

"Dobie or Libby. It would hold one of them."

"I'm up here, they're not. He's losing a lot of blood. Let me see what I can do. Get me more rope, a saw, a first-aid kit."

"How bad?" Trigger called up. "How bad is it?"

"He's breathing."

"Thank Christ. I've got a medevac team coming. Is he conscious?"

"No. Fill him in, okay?" She and Gull switched positions. "We need rope, first-aid kit, a chain saw. Gull's heading down."

Rowan leaned back in her harness, stripped off her shirt, cut strips and pads with her pocketknife. Tying herself off, she scooted out onto the branch. It would hold, she vowed, because she damn well needed it to.

"Yangtree, can you hear me?" She began to field-dress the jagged gash in his thigh. "You hold on, goddamn it. We'll get you out of this."

She used what rope she had, wrapped it around his waist, then shimmied back to secure it. Gull was there, handing her more.

"I'm going to secure it to the branch just above, get it under his arms." She watched Trigger and Matt scaling the neighboring tree, nodded as she saw the plan.

"Get another over to them, and we lower him down in a vee after I cut away the harness, saw off the branch."

Fear sweat dripped into her eyes as she worked, and, forced to shift the shattered leg, she prayed Yangtree stayed unconscious until they'd finished. She padded the wound around the spur as best she could, used her belt to strap him even more securely to the branch.

Then she hesitated. If it didn't work, she might kill him. But his pulse was growing weaker, and left no choice.

"I'm going to release his harness. Get ready."

Once she'd freed him from the ruined chute, she reached back for the saw. "It's going to work," she said to Gull.

"Medevac's no more than ten minutes out."

She planted her feet, yanked the starter cord. The buzz sent a tremor through her. She saw Trigger and Matt brace to take the weight, knew Gull and Dobie did the same behind her.

Trusting the rope, for him, for herself, she inched out onto the branch to set the blade into bark and wood as close to Yangtree's body as she dared.

"Hold him steady!" she shouted. "Don't let him drop."

She cut clean, felt the branch shimmy from the shock. Then Yangtree hung suspended, the spur and the lever of branch fixed in his side like a corkscrew. His body swayed as they lowered him slowly, hand over hand, to where Libby and Stovic waited to take his weight.

"We've got him! We've got him! Oh, Jesus." Stovic's voice trembled. "Jesus, he's a mess."

But breathing, Rowan thought, as she heard the clatter of the chopper. He just had to keep breathing.

IT CUT HER in two, standing on safe ground, watching as the copter lifted off with her friend. Shattered, she thought, as the wind from the blades whipped over her. His arms, his legs, and God knew what else—and there was nothing more she could do.

She shouted into her radio, updating base, realigning strategy while Cards, battered face in his hands, sat on the ground. Trigger watched the copter, then slowly turned to her. Everything she felt—the shock, the grief, the stupefying rage—was reflected on his face.

"Paracargo," she began, and Gull squeezed her arm.

"I've got that. I've got it," he repeated when she just stared at him. "Dobie, Matt, give me a hand?"

Pull it together, Rowan ordered herself. "Trig." She took a breath, then walked over to draw in the dirt. "She's moving northeast, gaining steam. I need you," she said quietly when he just stood, shaking his head.

"Give me a sec, okay? Just a goddamn fucking second."

Crouched, she laid a hand on his boot. "We've got to slay this dragon, then get back to Yangtree. The delay." Rowan had to stop, steady her voice. "The fire's taken advantage. She's burning hot, Trig. They've dumped some mud on her head, but she caught some wind, jumped this ridge line, and she's climbing fast."

"Okay." He swiped the back of his hand under his nose, crouched with her. "I can take the left flank, cut line with five, hold her in."

"Take seven. L.B.'s sending us another crew, and I'll pull from that. You got a water source here." She drew an X in the dirt. "So take pumper and hose. I'll get a crew heading up the right, and do some scouting."

When he reached for her hand, she linked fingers. "We're going to kill her," he said. "Then we're going to find out what the hell happened."

"Damn right we are."

They talked Cat lines, safe spots, two possible fire camps.

When he'd culled out his seven, gathered the gear, Rowan turned to the rest. "Cards, I need you to stay here and—"

"Fuck that, Swede." His snarl had blood leaking from his split lip. "I'm not hanging back."

"I'm not asking you to hang back. I need you to wait for the next load, take half and start up the left flank after Trigger. Send the rest to me. I need Gibbons on my crew, and Janis.

And make it clear they're going to bust their asses. I need you to take charge of this," she said before he could speak. "And Trigger's going to need you on the line."

She turned away when he nodded. "Gull, Dobie, Libby, Stovic. Tool up."

No time to waste. No time to think beyond the fire. Everything else had to stay locked outside.

They dug and cut, with every strike of Pulaski or buzz of blade echoing to Rowan like vengeance. And the fire reared and snapped.

"I need you to take charge here until Gibbons makes it in," she told Gull. "He just checked in. Everybody hit the jump spot safely. I'm going to work my way toward the head, get a better sense of her. If you tie in with the Cat line before I get back, let me know."

"Okay."

"You've got a water source about fifty yards up, this same course. You're going to end up with a crooked line, and Gibbons is going to be coming double time, but if you get there before he meets up, get Stovic and Libby on the hose. Any change in the wind or—"

"I've got it, Rowan. Go do what you need to do; we'll work it from here. Just stay in touch."

"Don't let them think about it. Keep them focused. I'll be back."

She set off fast, moving through the trees, up the rough incline, and vanished in smoke.

All she heard was the fire, the muttering glee of it. It crackled over the dry timber, lapped at molten pine resin, chewed through leaves, twigs littering the ground. She dodged a firebrand as she climbed, beat out the spot.

She thought of bodies charred to the bone.

When she crested the ridge she stopped to check her bearings. She could see the red-orange fury, gobbling up fuel. They'd given her a head start, she thought; they'd had no choice. The dragon ran strong and free.

She called in to request retardant drops, and received a brief, unsatisfying report on Yangtree.

They were working on him.

She felt the change in the wind, just a flutter, and saw the fire grab its tail to ride. A cut to the west now, still north of Trigger's crew, she noted, but moving toward them.

She circled around, contacting him by radio.

"She's shifting, curling back toward you."

"We've got a Cat line here, a good, wide one. I don't think she can jump it. Escape route due south."

"They're bringing mud. I just called to tell them to dump a load west, down your flank. Stay clear."

"Roger that. Cards just got here with reinforcements. We're going to hold this line, Swede."

"After the mud drops, I'm going to get an air report. I want to take four from your team, same from mine, get them up to the head. Squeeze it. But if she jumps the road, get gone."

"Bet your ass. And watch yours."

As she worked her way through the fire, she coordinated with Gibbons, with base, kept her ears and eyes peeled for the tankers. She cut east, eyes smarting with smoke, then jumped back, skidding onto her back as a burning limb thick as a man's thigh crashed to the ground in front of her.

It caught fresh fuel on the forest floor, ignited with a whoosh to claw at the soles of her boots before she scrambled clear.

"Widowmaker," she shouted to Gibbons. "I'm good, but I'm going to be busy for a minute."

She beat at the fresh flames, chopping at the ground to smother what she could with dirt. She heard the thunder of a tanker, muttered curses as she fought her small, personal war.

"I'm clear." Shoveling, stomping, she signaled Gibbons, then the tanker pilot. "I'm clear."

And ran.

The thick pink rain fell, smothering flame, billowing smoke, thudding onto the ground, the trees, with heavy splats. She sprinted for shelter as globs of it struck her helmet, her jacket. A volley of firebrands sent her on a zigzagging dash for higher, clearer ground.

She heard the telltale roar at her back, felt the ground shimmy under her feet. Following instinct, she leaped through the undulating curtain of fire, all but heard it slam shut behind her before the blowup burst. Rocks skidded under her feet as she pushed herself up an incline above the hungry, murderous blaze.

"I'm clear." She shouted it as her radio popped with voices. "Had a little detour."

She wheezed in a breath, wheezed one out. "Give me a minute to orient."

A wall of fire, solid as steel, cut off her route back to her team.

She pulled out her compass to confirm direction, accepted that her hand shook lightly.

Cut across to Trigger's line, she calculated, regroup, then circle down and around to her own.

She relayed her plan, then took a moment to hydrate and settle her nerves.

Back on the line, Gull looked straight into Gibbons's eyes. "Is she hurt?"

"She says no. She's playing it down, but I think she had a close one." He swiped at sweat. "She's cutting over to Trig, then she'll circle around back to us. The mud knocked it back some on their flank, and they're working the pumps up toward the head. They're in good position."

He shook his head. "We can't say the same. The wind's whipping her up this way. Elf, take Gull, Stovic and Dobie and get these pumps up there. Follow the Cat line. Start drowning her. I'll send you up four more as soon as we get the men."

"Spot!" Libby shouted, and two of the team leaped to action.

"We're getting hammered over here," Gibbons told Trigger over the radio. "Can you spare anybody?"

"Give you two. That'll be three when Swede gets around."

"Tell them to hump it!"

GULL MANNED the hose and swore the force of water only made the fire dance. The wind chose sides, blew flames into massive walls.

"L.B.'s sending in another load, and pulling in jumpers from Idaho," Janis told him.

"Did Rowan make it to Trigger?"

"Rowan changed tactics. She's doubling back to Gibbons. We've got to catch this thing here, catch her here, or fall back." She yanked out her radio. "Gibbons, we need help up here."

"I'm waiting on Matt and Cards from Trigger's line. And the Swede. Fresh jumpers coming. ETA's thirty."

"Thirty's no good. I need more hands or we're pulling back."

"Your call, Elf. I'll get locations and come back. If you've got to move, move."

"Goddamn it, goddamn it. Stovic, get those snags. If she crowns, we're screwed." As water arced and sizzled, she looked over at Gull. "We can't hold her for thirty without more hands."

Something stirred in his gut. "Rowan, Cards and Matt should've gotten through by now. Radio her, get her location."

"Gibbons is—"

"Radio her, Janis," he interrupted. "This has been going south since the jump."

And maybe it wasn't just nature they fought.

He listened to her try to raise Rowan once, twice, a third time. And with each nonresponse his blood ran colder.

She tried Matt, then Cards, then answered swiftly when Gibbons hailed her.

"I can't reach any of them on the radio," Gibbons told her. "I'm going to send somebody in to their last known location."

But Janis had her eye on Gull. "Negative. Gull's going. He's the fastest we've got. Send me somebody. We're going to try to hold it."

"Libby's heading up now. I'll get more mud, call in another Cat. If you have to retreat, head southwest."

"Copy that. Find her," she said to Gull.

"Count on it." He turned to Dobie. "Hold it as long as you can."

"As long as you need," Dobie vowed, and took the hose.

He ran, using his compass and the map in his head to gauge direction. She'd been forced west, then south before she'd angled toward the left flank. He tried to judge her speed, her most probable route before she'd reversed to head east again to assist the right flank.

She'd have met up with Matt and Cards if possible, he calculated, but she wouldn't have wasted time waiting for them or changing from the best route back, not when her team needed help.

A spot burst to his left, flames snaking from ground to tree. He ignored the instinct to deal with it, kept running.

But she wouldn't have, he thought. She'd have fought the fire as she went, and doing so shifted her direction at any time.

And if another enemy had crossed her path, she wouldn't have recognized him. She would see a fellow soldier, a friend. Someone trusted, even loved.

He jumped a narrow stream, pushing himself through the heat and smoke and growing fear.

She was smart, and strong, and canny. She'd fight, he reminded himself—maybe more fiercely when the enemy had disguised himself as friend.

He forced himself to stop, check his compass, reorient. And to listen, listen, for another under the growling voice of the fire.

North, he decided. Northeast from here, and prayed he was right. A tree crashed, spewing out a whirlwind of sparks that stung his exposed skin like bees.

The next sound he heard came sharper, more deadly. He raced toward the echo of the gunshot, even as his heart leaped as if struck by the bullet.

30

When she could, Rowan moved at a steady jog. She'd bruised her hip avoiding the widowmaker, but the pain barely registered—just a dull, distant ache.

They were losing the war, she thought, had been losing it since Yangtree's chute failed to open.

Everything felt off, felt wrong, felt out of balance.

The wind continued to rise, to shift and stir, adding to the fire's speed and potency. Here and there, small, sly dust devils danced on it. The air remained dry enough to crack like a twig.

She'd never made it to Trigger's crew to judge the progress or lack of it for herself, to check that flank, sense just what the fire was thinking, plotting. No, she thought now, not when she'd heard the urgency in Gibbons's voice. No choice but to reverse.

She'd cut north, through the fire, to carve off a little distance, and calculating her path might cross with Matt and Cards.

Spots sprang up so fast and often, she began to feel like she was playing a deadly game of Whac-A-Mole.

She gulped down water on the run, splashed more on her

sweaty face. And resisted the constant urge to call in to base, again, for a report on Yangtree.

Better to believe he was alive and fighting. To believe it and make it true.

Under that remained the nagging fear that it hadn't been an accident but sabotage.

How many others harbored that same fear? she wondered. How did they bear down and focus with that clawing at the mind? How could she when she kept going over every minute and move in the ready room, on the flight, on the jump sequence?

Had something been off even then? Should she have seen it?

Later, she ordered herself, relive it later. Right now, just live.

With her stamina flagging, she pulled an energy bar out of her bag, started to tear the wrapper.

She dropped it, ran, when she heard the scream.

Smoke blinded her, disoriented her. She forced herself to stop, close her eyes. Think.

Due north. Yes, north, she decided, and sprinted forward.

She spotted the radio smoldering and sparking on the ground, and the blood smeared on the ground at the base of a snag that burned like a candle. Nearby a full engulfed branch snaked fire over the ground.

Alarmed for her friends, she cupped her hands to her mouth, started to shout. Then dropped them again with sickness countering fear. She saw the blood trail, heading east, and followed it as she slowly drew her radio out of her belt.

Because she knew now, and somewhere inside her she wondered if she'd always known—or at least wondered. But loyalty hadn't allowed it, she admitted. It simply hadn't allowed her to cross the line—except in dreams.

Now with her heart heavy with grief, she prepared to cross the line.

Before she could flick on her radio, he was there, just there, a lit fusee in his hand, and his eyes full of misery. He heaved it when he saw her, setting off his tiny bomb. A black spruce went off like a Roman candle.

"I don't want to hurt you. Not you."

"Why would you hurt me?" She met those sad eyes. "We're friends."

"I don't want to." Matt pulled the gun out of his belt. "But I will. Throw away the radio."

"Matt—" She jolted a little when Gibbons spoke her name through the radio.

"If you answer it, I'll shoot you. I'll be sorry for it, but I'll do what has to be done. I'm doing what has to be done."

"Where's Cards?"

"Throw the radio away, Rowan. Throw it!" he snapped. "Or I'll use this. I'll put a bullet in your leg, then let the fire decide."

"Okay. All right." She opened her hand, let it drop, but he shook his head.

"Kick it away. Don't test me."

"I'm not. I won't." She heard Janis's voice now as she kicked it aside. "We've got to get out of here, Matt. The place is coming apart. It's not safe."

She struggled to keep her eyes level with his, but she'd seen the Pulaski hooked in his belt, and the blood gleaming on the pick.

Cards.

"I never wanted it to be you. It wasn't your fault. And you came to the funeral. You sat with my mother."

"What happened to Jim wasn't anyone's fault."

"Dolly got him worked up, got him all twisted around. Got us both all twisted around so the last things we said to each other were ugly things. And Cards was his spotter. He should've seen Jim wasn't right to jump. You *know* that's so."

"Where's Cards?"

"He got away from me. Maybe the fire's got him. It's about fate anyway. I should've shot him to be sure of it, but it's about fate and destiny. Luck, maybe. I don't decide. Dolly fell. I didn't kill her; she fell."

"I believe you, Matt. We need to head north, then we can talk when—"

"I gave her money, you know, for the baby. But she wanted more. I was just going to talk to her, have it out with her when I went by her house. And she was just driving off, without the baby. She was a bad mother."

"I know." Calm, agreeable, understanding. "Matt, who'd know better than me about that? About Shiloh being better off now? I'm on your side."

"She went to that motel. She was a tramp. I saw him, the preacher, come to the door to let her in. My brother's dead, and she's balling that preacher in a motel room. I wanted to go in, but I was afraid of what I might do. I waited, and she came out and drove away."

She heard another tree torch off. "Matt—"

"She got that flat tire. That was fate, wasn't it? She was surprised to see me—guilt all over her—when I pulled in behind her. I told her to pull off onto the service road. I was going to have it out with her. But the things she said . . . If she hadn't been screwing around, hadn't been a liar, a cheat, a selfish bitch, I wouldn't have pushed her that way. She was just going to up and leave that baby. Did you know? What kind of mother does that?"

"We have to move," she told him, keeping her tone calm but firm. "I want you to tell me everything, Matt. I want to listen, but we're going to be cut off if we don't move."

"Shiloh's . . . may be my baby."

He wiped his free hand over his mouth as Rowan stared at him. "It was just one time, when I was so lonely and missing Annie so much, and drinking a little. It was just one time."

"I understand." It made her sick inside, for all of them. "I get lonely, too."

"You *don't*! She told me it was mine, and she told Jim it was his. Then she said it was mine, maybe, because she *knew* he didn't want a baby, didn't want her. She *knew* I'd do what I had to do, and I'd have to tell Annie. And we fought about it right before the siren went off, me and Jim. He was on the list. I wasn't. He's dead. I'm not."

"It's not your fault."

"What do you know about it! I told him to go to hell, and he did. This is hell. I was just going to fix Cards so he couldn't jump because that's what he loves most. Like I loved my brother. Put something in his food, trip him up. And I was just going to get the baby from Dolly, have her for my ma. That was the right thing. But she fell, and I had to do something, didn't I?"

"Yes."

"I sent her to hell. That's when I knew I had to do what needed doing. I had to get the baby for my ma, so I had to get Leo out of the way. Make him pay, too. He was always giving Jim grief, never had a good thing to say."

"So you got his rifle out of his gun safe, and you shot at me. You shot at me and Gull."

"Not at you. I wasn't going to hurt you. Dolly told Jim the combination, and he told me. It was like he was showing me what to do. Leo had to pay, and he did. I got the baby for my ma. Jim would've wanted that."

"Okay." Firebrands flew like missiles. "You were getting justice for Jim, and doing what you could for your family. And I'll listen to you, do whatever you want, just tell me. But not here. The wind's changed. Matt, for God's sake, we're going to be trapped in this if we don't move."

Those sad eyes never wavered. "It's up to fate, like I said. Up to fate who got the bad pumps and saws, who got the bad chute."

"You played Russian roulette with our chutes?" She regretted it immediately, but the fury just bubbled out. "Yangtree never did anything to you. He might die."

"I could've gotten the doctored one just as easy as him. It was a fair deal. In the end, Ro, it was all of us killed Jim. All of us doing what we do, getting him to do it, too. And everybody had the same chance. I didn't want it to be you, even though I saw how you looked at me when I said how we'd get a lawyer over the baby, how my ma was going to raise her. I saw how everybody looked at me because I was alive, and Jim wasn't."

She couldn't outrun a bullet, Rowan thought as her heart kicked in her chest. Before much longer, she wouldn't be able to outrun the fire.

She could hear the whoosh and the roar as it built, as it rolled toward them.

"We need to go, so you can be there for the baby, Matt. She needs a father."

"She has my parents. They'll be good to her." Fire glowed red and gold on his sweat-sheened face. His eyes had gone from sad to mad. "I broke it off with Annie last night. I've got nothing for her. And I knew when I got in the door today, it had to be the last time. One way or the other. I thought it would be me, going like Jim did. The fire's all I got left."

"You have the baby."

"Jim's dead. I see him dead when I look at her. I see him burning. It's just the fire now. I liked it. Not the killing, but the fire, making it, watching it, seeing what it did. I liked making it more than I ever did fighting it. Maybe I'll like hell."

"I'm not ready to go there." She rolled to the balls of her feet.

A tree fell with a shrieking crash, shaking the ground when it landed less than a yard away. Rowan sprang to her right, dug in to run blind. She heard the crack of the gunshot, her spine snapping tight as she braced for a bullet in the back.

She heard a whine, like an angry hornet wing by her ear, then jagged left again as a firebrand burst at her feet.

If Matt didn't kill her, the fire would.

She preferred the fire, and like a moth, flew toward the flames.

For a moment, they wrapped around her, a fiery embrace that stole her breath. The scream shrieked inside her head, escaping in a wild call of fear and triumph as she burst free. Momentum pitched her forward, had her skidding onto the heels of her hands and her knees. Her pack weighed like lead as she struggled up again, hacking out smoke. Around her, the forest burned in a merry cavalcade with a deep, guttural roar as mad as the man who pursued her.

At the snap of another gunshot, she fled deeper into the belly of the beast.

She heard him coming, even over the bellow of the fire. The thud of his footsteps sounded closer than she wanted to believe. She scanned smoke and flame.

Fight or flight.

She was done with flight, finished letting him drive her like cattle to the slaughter. With the burn towering around her, she planted her feet, yanked out her Pulaski. Gripping it in both hands, she set for fight.

He might kill her. Hell, he probably would. But she'd damn well do some damage first.

For herself, for Yangtree. Even, she thought, for poor, pathetic Dolly.

"You'll bleed," she told herself. "You'll bleed before I'm done."

She saw the yellow shirt through the haze of smoke, then the silhouette coming fast.

Deliberately she panted air in and out, pumping adrenaline. She had an instant, maybe two, to decide whether to hurl her weapon, hope for a solid strike, or to charge swinging.

Charge. Better to keep the ax in her hands than risk a miss.

She sucked in more filthy air, cocked the Pulaski over her shoulder, gritting her teeth as she judged the timing.

Coming fast, she thought again—then her arms trembled. Coming really fast. Oh, God.

"Gull." She choked out his name as he tore through the smoke.

She ran toward him, felt his hands close tight around her shoulders. Nothing, she realized, no caress, no embrace, had ever felt so glorious.

"Matt."

"I got that."

"He's got a gun."

"Yeah, I got that, too. Are you hurt?" He scanned her face when she shook her head, as if verifying for himself. "Can you run?"

"What do you take me for?"

"Then we run because Matt's not our only problem."

She started to agree, then stiffened. "Wait. Do you hear that?"

"You're the one with ears like a . . . Yeah. Now I do."

"He's coming. That way," she added, pointing. "It sounds like he's crying."

"I feel real bad for him. Best shot's south, I think."

"If we can reach the black. But if we can, so can he."

"I sure as hell hope so. That's where we'll take him down. Run now; talk later."

"Don't hold up for me," she began.

"Oh, bullshit." He grabbed her hand, yanked her into a run. She bore down. She'd be damned if he held back because she couldn't keep pace. It didn't matter if her lungs burned, if her legs ached, if the sweat ran into her eyes like acid.

She ran through a world gone mad with violence, stunning in its kaleidoscope lights of red and orange and molten blue. She flung herself through fetid smoke, leaping or dodging burning branches, hurdling burning spots that snapped over the ground like bear traps.

If they could get into the black, they'd fight. They'd find a way.

She risked a glance at Gull. Sweat poured down his soot-smeared face. Somewhere along the run he'd lost his helmet, and his hair was gray with ash.

But his eyes, she thought as she pushed, pushed, pushed herself on. Clear, focused, determined. Eyes that didn't lie, she thought. Eyes she could trust.

Did trust.

They'd make it.

Something exploded behind them.

Breath snagging, she looked back to see an orange column of smoke climb toward the sky. Even as she watched, it brightened.

"Gull."

He only nodded. He'd seen it as well.

No time to talk, to plan, even to think. The ground shook; the wind whipped. With its roaring breath, the fire blew brands, coals, burning pinecones that burst like grenades.

Blue-orange flames clawed up on their left, hissing like snakes. A snag burst in its coils, showered them with embers. The smoke thickened like cotton with the firefly swirl of sparks flooding through it.

A fountain of yellow flame spewed up in front of them, forcing them to angle away from the ferocious heat. Gull grunted when a burning branch hit his back, but didn't break stride as they flung themselves up an incline.

Rocks avalanched under their boots, and still the hellhound fire pursued. Came the roar, that long, throaty war cry, as the blowup thundered toward them.

A fire devil swirled out of the smoke to dance.

Nowhere to run.

"Shake and bake." Gull yanked the bandanna around Rowan's throat over her mouth, did the same with his own.

It screamed, Rowan thought as she tore the protective case off her fire shelter, shook it out. Or Matt screamed, but a madman with a gun had become the least of their problems.

She stepped on the bottom corners of the foil, grabbed the tops to stretch it over her back. Mirroring her moves, Gull sent her a last look and shot her a grin that seared straight into her heart.

"See you later," he said.

"See you later."

They flopped forward, cocooned.

Working quickly, Rowan dug a hole for her face, down to the cooler air. Eyes shut, she took short, shallow breaths into the bandanna. Even one breath of the super-heated gases that blew outside her shelter would scorch her lungs, poison her.

The fire hit, a freight train of sound, a tidal wave of heat. Wind tore at the shelter, tried to lift and launch it like a sail. Sparks shimmered around her, but she kept her eyes closed.

And saw her father, frying fish over a campfire, the flames dancing in his eyes as he laughed with her. Saw herself spreading her arms under his on her first tandem jump. Saw him open his as she ran to him after he'd come back from a fire.

Saw him, his face lit now by an inner flame as he told her about Ella.

See you later, she thought as the impossible heat built.

She saw Gull, cocky grin and swagger, pouring a helmet of water over her head. Saw him tip back a beer, cool as you please, then fight off a pack of bullies as ferocious as a fire devil.

Felt him yank her into his arms. Turn to her in the dark. Fight with her in the light. Run with her. Run to her.

He'd come through fire for her.

The fear speared into her belly. She'd been afraid before, but she realized most of it was because she damn well wasn't ready to die. Now she feared for him.

So close, she thought while the fire screamed, crashed, burst. And yet completely separate. Nothing to do for each other now but wait. Wait.

See you later.

She held on. Thought of Yangtree, of Jim. Of Matt.

Cards—God, Cards. Had Matt killed him, too?

She wanted to see him again, see all of them again. She wanted to tell her father she loved him, just one more time. To tell Ella she was glad her father had found someone to make him happy.

She wanted to joke with Trigger, rag on Cards, sit in the kitchen with Marg. To be with all of them, her family.

But more, she realized, even more, she wanted to look into Gull's eyes again, and watch that grin flash over his face.

She wanted to tell him . . . everything.

Why the hell hadn't she? Why had she been so stubborn or stupid or—face it—afraid?

If he didn't make it through this so she could, she'd kick his ass.

Dizzy, she realized, sick. Too much heat. Can't pass out. Won't pass out. As she regulated her breathing again, she realized something else.

Quiet.

She heard the fire, but the distant snarl and song. The ground held steady under her body, and the jet-plane thunder had passed.

She was alive. Still alive.

She reached out, laid a hand on her shelter. Still hot to the touch, she thought. But she could wait. She could be patient.

And if she lived, he'd damn well better live, too.

"Rowan."

Tears smarted her already stinging eyes at his voice, rough and ragged. "Still here."

"How's it going there?"

"Five-by-five. You?"

"The same. It's cooling down a little."

"Don't get out yet, rook."

"I know the drill. I'm calling base. Anything you want me to pass on?"

"Have L.B. tell my dad I'm A-OK. I don't know about Cards. There was blood. They need to look for him. And for Matt."

She closed her eyes again, let herself drift, passing the next hour thinking of swimming in a moonlit lagoon, drinking straight from a garden hose, making snow angels—naked snow angels, with Gull.

"Cards made it back," he called out. "They had to medevac him. He lost a lot of blood."

"He's alive."

Alone in her shelter, she allowed herself tears.

When her shelter cooled to the touch, she called to Gull. "Coming out."

She eased her head out into the smoky air, looked over at Gull. She imagined they both looked like a couple of sweaty, parboiled turtles climbing out of their shells.

"Hello, gorgeous."

She laughed. It hurt her throat, but she laughed. "Hey, handsome."

They crawled to each other over the blackened, ash-covered ground. She found his lips with hers, her belly quivering with a wrecked combination of laughter and tears.

"I was going to be so pissed off at you if you died."

"Glad we avoided that." He touched her face. "Heck of a ride."

"Oh, yeah." She lowered her forehead to his. "He might still be alive."

"I know. We'd better figure out where we are, then we'll worry about where he is."

She took out her compass, checking their bearings as she drank what water she had left in her bottle. "If we head east, we'll backtrack over some of the area, plus it's the best course for the camp. We need water."

"I'll call it in."

Though her legs still weren't steady, Rowan got to her feet to examine the shelters.

"Inner skin's melted," she told Gull. "We hit over sixteen hundred degrees. I'd say we topped a good one-eighty inside."

"My candy bar's melted, and that's a crying shame." He reached for her hand. "Want to take a walk in the woods?"

"Love to."

They walked through the black with ash still swirling.

Training outweighed exhaustion, and had them smothering smoldering spots.

"You came for me."

Gull glanced up. "Sure I did. You'd have done the same."

"I would have. But I thought I was dead—not going down easy, but dead all the same. And you came for me. It counts. A lot."

"Is there a scoreboard? Am I winning?"

"Gull." She didn't laugh this time, not when everything she felt rose up in her raw throat. "I need to tell you—" She broke off, grabbed his arm. "I heard something." She closed her eyes, concentrated. Pointed.

She looked in his eyes again. Toward or away? He nodded, and they moved toward the sound.

They found him, curled behind a huddle of rocks. They'd protected him a little. But not nearly enough.

His eyes, filled with blood, stared up from his ruined face. She thought of her dream of Jim, of his brother. The fire had turned them into mirror images.

He moaned again, tried to speak. His body shook violently as his breath came in rapid pants. Raw, blistered burns scored the left side of his body, the most exposed, where the fire had scorched the protective clothing away.

He'd nearly made it out, Rowan noted. Another fifty yards, and he might've been clear. Had he thought he could make it, left his life to fate rather than shake out his shelter?

Gull handed her the radio. "Call it in," he told her, then crouched. He took one of Matt's ruined hands carefully in his.

He had that in him, Rowan thought. He had that compassion for a man suffering toward death, even though the man was a murderer.

"Base, this is Swede. We found Matt."

His eyes tracked to hers when she said his name. Could he still think? she wondered. Could he still reason?

For an instant she saw sorrow in them. Then they fixed as the panting breaths cut off.

"He didn't make it," she said, steady as she handed the radio back to Gull.

Steady until she sat on the ground beside a man who'd been a friend, and wept for him.

SHE WANTED TO STAY and fight, termed it a matter of pride and honor to be in on the kill. She rehydrated, refueled, replaced lost and damaged equipment. Then complained all the way when ordered to copter out.

"We're not injured," she pointed out.

"You sound like a frog," Gull observed as he took his seat in the chopper. "A sexy one, but a frog."

"So we ate some smoke. So what?"

"You lost most of your eyebrows."

Stunned, she pressed her fingers above her eyes. "Shit! Why didn't you tell me?"

"It's a look. They've got it on the run," he added, scanning down as they lifted off.

"That's the *point*. That bitch tried to kill us. We should be in on the takedown."

"Don't worry, babe." He reached over to pat her knee. "There'll be other fires that try to kill us."

"Don't try to smooth it over. L.B.'s letting the cops push us around. What the hell difference does it make when we give them a statement? Matt's dead." She turned her face, stared out at the sky. "I guess most of him, the best of him, died last year when Jim did. You held his hand so he didn't die alone."

Though Gull said nothing, she clearly felt his discomfort so turned to him again. "That counts a lot, too. You're really racking them up today."

"People have a choice when life takes a slice out of them. He made the wrong one. A lot of wrong ones."

"You didn't. We didn't," Rowan corrected. "Good for us."

"Don't cry anymore. It kills me."

"My eyes are watering, that's all. From all the smoke."

He figured it couldn't hurt for both of them to pretend that was it. But he took her hand. "I want a beer. I want a giant, ice-cold bottle of beer. And shower sex."

The idea made her smile. "I want eyebrows."

"Well, you're not getting mine." He tipped his head back, closed his eyes.

She watched out the window, the roll of land, the rise of

mountain. Home—she was going home. But the meaning had changed, deepened. Time to man up and tell him.

"I need to say some things to you," she began. "I don't know how you're going to feel about it, but it is what it is. So . . ."

She shifted back, narrowed her eyes.

No point baring her soul to a man who was sound asleep.

It could wait, she decided, and watched the sun lower toward the western peaks.

SHE SAW HER FATHER running toward the pad, and L.B., and the flying tangle of Ella's hair as she rushed after them.

Marg sprinting out of the cookhouse. Lynn stopping to bury her face in her apron. Mechanics, jumpers not cleared for the list pouring out of hangars, the tower, the barracks.

The cop and the fed standing together in their snappy suits just outside Ops.

She gave Gull an elbow poke. "We've got a welcoming committee."

She climbed out the second the chopper touched ground, then ran hunched over under the blades to jump into her father's arms.

"There's my baby. There's my girl."

"A-OK." She breathed him in, squeezed hard. And, seeing Ella over his shoulder, seeing the roll of tears, held out a hand. "It's nice to see you."

Ella gripped her hand, pressed it to her cheek, then wrapped her arms as best she could around both Lucas and Rowan.

"Don't go anywhere," Lucas murmured, then, setting Rowan down, walked over to Gull. "You took care of our girl."

"That's the job. But mostly she took care of herself."

Lucas pulled him into a bear hug. "Keep it up."

They both looked over when Rowan let out a shout, broke from Marg and ran toward the man slowly walking toward the pad.

"I told that son of a bitch he could only check out of the hospital if he stayed in bed." L.B. shook his head at Cards.

"Yangtree?" Gull asked.

"Fifty-fifty. They didn't expect him to make it this far, so I'm putting my money on him. Got a cold one for you."

"Let's not keep it waiting."

"Do you want me to tell the cops to back off until you and Rowan settle in?"

"We might as well get it done and over. She needs it finished. I guess I do, too."

"He just started talking crazy," Cards told Rowan. "About me letting Jim die, about Dolly. And he said . . . he said Dolly called Vicki, and told her we'd been screwing around. Hinted to her the baby was mine, for God's sake. That it was his idea."

"You can fix it with her."

"I'm going to try. But . . . Ro, he came at me. Jesus." He touched his shoulder where the pick had dug in. "Matt came at me. I knocked him back, or down. I told the cops it's like this crazy reel inside my head. I ran. He was coming after me. I think he was, then he wasn't. I just kept running. Got all screwed around until I found the saw line. I followed it."

"Good thinking."

"I don't know how he could've done what he did, Ro. I worked right beside him. All of us did. Yangtree . . ." His eyes watered up. "Then to come after you, to die like he did. I can't get my head around it."

"You're worn out. Go on and lie down. I'll come in and see you later."

"I loved the fucker."

"We all did," Rowan said, as Cards walked back into the barracks.

Gull stepped up. "Unless you want to do it otherwise, we can talk with the cops now. Marg's throwing on some steaks."

"There is a God."

"We can get it done while we eat."

They took seats at one of the picnic tables.

"First, I want to say it's good to see both of you back here, safe." Quinniock folded his hands on the table. "It doesn't do much good, but you should know after some digging, a little pressure, Agent DiCicco learned earlier today that Matthew Brayner ended his engagement a short time ago, cut off communication with his fiancée. Also, that he quit his job."

"I also learned a few days ago that he has a number of

trophies and awards. Marksmanship. There are several people in your unit who have sharpshooter experience."

Rowan nodded at DiCicco. "You've been investigating all of us."

"That's my job. We arrived here to question him about the same time he assaulted your associate," DiCicco continued. "We were able to convince Mr. Little Bear to let us search Brayner's quarters. He kept a journal. It's all there. What he did, how, why."

"He was grieving," Rowan said.

"Yes."

She looked at Quinniock. "He blamed himself, at the bottom of it, for what happened to Jim. For being weak, sleeping with Dolly, for fighting with his brother before that jump. He couldn't live with that, so he had to blame Cards, Dolly, all of us."

"Very likely."

"But it was more." She looked at Gull now. "He fell in love with the fire. Found a kind of purpose in it, and that justified the rest. He said he left it up to fate, but he lied to himself. He gave it all to the fire, turning what he loved and had trained to do into a punishment. Maybe he thought he could burn away the guilt and the grief, but he never did. He died, grieving for everything he'd lost."

"It would help," DiCicco told her, "if you could tell us exactly what happened, what was said and done."

"Yeah, I can do that. Then I'm never talking about it again, because he paid for all of it. There's nothing more to wring out of him, and no changing anything that happened."

She went through it like a fire report. Precisely, briefly, pausing only to lean into Marg's side when the cook set down still sizzling steaks.

She ate while Gull did the same from his perspective.

"You knew it was Matt when you caught up with me," Rowan interrupted.

"Cards has had nothing but shit for luck all season. Cards was Jim's spotter. You have to respect the streak, good or bad, but when you break it down it seemed like maybe it wasn't a matter of bad luck. Then Matt couldn't bring himself to look at Yangtree once we got him down.

"You were too busy to notice," he added, "but Matt was the only one who couldn't. When Janis said none of the three of you answered the radio, it was point A to B."

He looked back over at DiCicco. "That's it. There's nothing more to tell you."

"I'll do whatever I can to close this without bothering you again," DiCicco said to Rowan. "And I'm pulling for your friend, for Yangtree."

"Thanks. What happens with Leo Brakeman?"

"He's cleared of the murders, and as Brayner detailed the shooting at the base in his journal, how he had the combination for the safe—from Jim through Dolly—he's clear of those charges. Regardless, he jumped bail, but given the circumstances, we're recommending leniency there."

"Matt didn't kill him," Rowan murmured, "but he shattered his life. He did it so he could get the baby for his mother."

Quinniock rose. "A smart man would head to Nebraska and work to put his life back together. That'll be up to Brakeman. Despite the circumstances, it was a pleasure meeting both of you. Thank you for your service."

"I'll say the same."

Rowan chewed over a bite of steak as they walked away. "That was kind of weird at the end."

"Just at the end?"

She laughed. "You know what I mean. I need to spend some time with my father. You could get in on that."

"Sure. Is that before or after shower sex?"

"After, for a variety of reasons. Right now, I need a walk. Moon's rising."

"So it is." He got up, reached for her hand.

It would probably be more appropriate, she thought, if they got cleaned up first, if she waited until the base slept and they were alone.

Then again, covered with soot, smelling of smoke and sweat? Wasn't that who they were?

"I did a lot of thinking in the shake and bake," she began as they strolled toward the training field.

"Not much else to do in there."

"I thought about my father. The two of us at little moments. About him and Ella. I'm only going to admit this once, but you were right about my first reaction to them, and the reasons for it. I'm done with that."

"You don't have to say it again, but maybe you could write it down, for my files."

"Shut up." She hip-bumped him. "I thought about Jim and Matt, about all the guys. Yangtree."

"He's going to make it. I'd put money on it."

"I believe that because he's a tough bastard, and because there's been enough loss this season. I thought about you."

"I hoped I was in there somewhere."

"Little moments. And when you narrow it, look at them really close, they can turn out to be key." She stopped, faced him. "So. I want to get married."

"To me?"

"No, to Timothy Olyphant, but I'm settling for you."

"Okay."

"That's it?"

"I'm still dealing with Timothy Olyphant, so give me a minute. I think I'm better-looking."

"You would."

"No, seriously. I've got better hair. But anyway." He swooped her in, right up to her toes. The kiss wasn't casual or lighthearted, but raw and deep and real. "I was going to take you on another picnic and ask you. This is better."

"I like picnics. We could—"

He laid his hands on either side of her face. "I love you. I love everything about you. Your voice, your laugh. Your eyebrows when they grow back. Your face, your body, your hard head and your cautious heart. I want to spend the rest of my life looking at you, listening to you, working with you, just being with you. Rowan of the purple lupines."

"Wow." He'd literally taken her breath away. "You're really good at this."

"I've been saving up."

"I didn't want to fall for anybody. It's so messy. I'm so happy it was you. I'm so happy to love you, Gulliver. So happy to know I'll have a life with you, a home, a family with you." She pressed her lips to his. "But I want a bigger bed."

"Big as you want."

"Where are we going to put it? After the season, I mean."

"I've been thinking about that."

Naturally, she thought. "Have you?"

"First, I think I should get my pilot's license. We'll be doing a lot of zipping between Montana and California."

He took her hand and, as she'd once seen her father do with Ella, gave their linked arms a playful swing.

"Maybe we'll find a place between, but I'm fine setting down here most of the year."

She cocked her head. "Because Missoula needs a family fun center?"

He grinned, kissing her knuckles as they walked again. "I've been doing some research on that."

"I really do love you," she told him. "It's kind of astonishing."

"I'm a hell of a catch. Really better than Olyphant. Where we dig in, that's just details. We'll work them out."

She stopped and, trusting them both, linked her arms around his neck. "We'll work them out," she repeated.

"Hey!" L.B. shouted across the field. "Thought you'd want to know, they've got her contained. They caught her, and they're taking her down."

"Go Zulies," Gull called back.

She grinned at him. More good news, she thought. They'd go in soon, give their own good news to her father, to their family.

But for now, she'd caught her own fire and wanted to walk awhile sharing the warmth of it, just with him, under the rising moon.

Keep reading for an excerpt from
the first novel in the Bride Quartet
by Nora Roberts

VISION IN WHITE

Now available from Berkley Books

PROLOGUE

By the time she was eight, Mackensie Elliot had been married fourteen times. She'd married each of her three best friends—as both bride and groom—her best friend's brother (under his protest), two dogs, three cats, and a rabbit.

She'd served at countless other weddings as maid of honor, bridesmaid, groomsman, best man, and officiant.

Though the dissolutions were invariably amicable, none of the marriages lasted beyond an afternoon. The transitory aspect of marriage came as no surprise to Mac, as her own parents boasted two each—so far.

Wedding Day wasn't her favorite game, but she kind of liked being the priest or the reverend or the justice of the peace. Or, after attending her father's second wife's nephew's bar mitzvah, the rabbi.

Plus, she enjoyed the cupcakes or fancy cookies and fizzy lemonade always served at the reception.

It was Parker's favorite game, and Wedding Day always took place on the Brown Estate, with its expansive gardens, pretty groves, and silvery pond. In the cold Connecticut winters, the ceremony might take place in front of one of the roaring fires inside the big house.

They had simple weddings and elaborate affairs. Royal weddings, star-crossed elopements, circus themes, and pirate ships. All ideas were seriously considered and voted upon, and no theme or costume too outrageous.

Still, with fourteen marriages under her belt, Mac grew a bit weary of Wedding Day.

Until she experienced her seminal moment.

For her eighth birthday Mackensie's charming and mostly absent father sent her a Nikon camera. She'd never expressed any interest in photography, and initially pushed it away with the other odd gifts he'd given or sent since the divorce. But Mac's mother told her mother, and Grandma muttered and complained about "feckless, useless Geoffrey Elliot" and the inappropriate gift of an adult camera for a young girl who'd be better off with a Barbie doll.

As she habitually disagreed with her grandmother on principle, Mac's interest in the camera piqued. To annoy Grandma—who was visiting for the summer instead of being in her retirement community in Scottsdale, where Mac strongly believed she belonged—Mac hauled the Nikon around with her. She toyed with it, experimented. She took pictures of her room, of her feet, of her friends. Shots that were blurry and dark, or fuzzy and washed out. With her lack of success, and her mother's impending divorce from her stepfather, Mac's interest in the Nikon began to wane. Even years later she couldn't say what prompted her to bring it along to Parker's that pretty summer afternoon for Wedding Day.

Every detail of the traditional garden wedding had been planned. Emmaline as the bride and Laurel as groom would exchange their vows beneath the rose arbor. Emma would wear the lace veil and train Parker's mother had made out of an old tablecloth, while Harold, Parker's aging and affable golden retriever, walked her down the garden path to give her away.

A selection of Barbies, Kens, and Cabbage Patch Kids, along with a variety of stuffed animals lined the path as guests.

"It's a very private ceremony," Parker relayed as she fussed with Emma's veil. "With a small patio reception to follow. Now, where's the best man?"

Laurel, her knee recently skinned, shoved through a trio of

hydrangeas. "He ran away, and went up a tree after a squirrel. I can't get him to come down."

Parker rolled her eyes. "I'll get him. You're not supposed to see the bride before the wedding. It's bad luck. Mac, you need to fix Emma's veil and get her bouquet. Laurel and I'll get Mr. Fish out of the tree."

"I'd rather go swimming," Mac said as she gave Emma's veil an absent tug.

"We can go after I get married."

"I guess. Aren't you tired of getting married?"

"Oh, I don't mind. And it smells so good out here. Everything's so pretty."

Mac gave Emma the clutch of dandelions and wild violets they were allowed to pick. "You look pretty."

It was invariably true. Emma's dark, shiny hair tumbled under the white lace. Her eyes sparkled a deep, deep brown as she sniffed the weed bouquet. She was tanned, sort of all golden, Mac thought, and scowled at her own milk white skin.

The curse of a redhead, her mother said, as she got her carroty hair from her father. At eight, Mac was tall for her age and skinny as a stick, with teeth already trapped in hated braces.

She thought that, beside her, Emmaline looked like a gypsy princess.

Parker and Laurel came back, giggling with the feline best man clutched in Parker's arms. "Everybody has to take their places." Parker poured the cat into Laurel's arms. "Mac, you need to get dressed! Emma—"

"I don't want to be maid of honor." Mac looked at the poofy Cinderella dress draped over a garden bench. "That thing's scratchy, and it's hot. Why can't Mr. Fish be maid of honor, and I'll be best man?"

"Because it's already planned. Everybody's nervous before a wedding." Parker flipped back her long brown pigtails, then picked up the dress to inspect it for tears or stains. Satisfied, she pushed it at Mac. "It's okay. It's going to be a beautiful ceremony, with true love and happy ever after."

"My mother says happy ever after's a bunch of bull."

There was a moment of silence after Mac's statement. The unspoken word *divorce* seemed to hang in the air.

"I don't think it has to be." Her eyes full of sympathy, Parker reached out, ran her hand along Mac's bare arm.

"I don't want to wear the dress. I don't want to be a bridesmaid. I—"

"Okay. That's okay. We can have a pretend maid of honor. Maybe you could take pictures."

Mac looked down at the camera she'd forgotten hung around her neck. "They never come out right."

"Maybe they will this time. It'll be fun. You can be the official wedding photographer."

"Take one of me and Mr. Fish," Laurel insisted, and pushed her face and the cat's together. "Take one, Mac!"

With little enthusiasm, Mac lifted the camera, pressed the shutter.

"We should've thought of this before! You can take formal portraits of the bride and groom, and more pictures during the ceremony." Busy with the new idea, Parker hung the Cinderella costume on the hydrangea bush. "It'll be good, it'll be fun. You need to go down the path with the bride and Harold. Try to take some good ones. I'll wait, then start the music. Let's go!"

There would be cupcakes and lemonade, Mac reminded herself. And swimming later, and fun. It didn't matter if the pictures were stupid, didn't matter that her grandmother was right and she was too young for the camera.

It didn't matter that her mother was getting divorced again, or that her stepfather, who'd been okay, had already moved out.

It didn't matter that happy ever after was bull, because it was all pretend anyway.

She tried to take pictures of Emma and the obliging Harold, imagined getting the film back and seeing the blurry figures and smudges of her thumb, like always.

When the music started she felt bad that she hadn't put on the scratchy dress and given Emma a maid of honor, just because her mother and grandmother had put her in a bad mood. So she circled around to stand to the side and tried harder to take a nice picture of Harold walking Emma down the garden path.

It looked different through the lens, she thought, the way

she could focus on Emma's face—the way the veil lay over her hair. And the way the sun shined through the lace was pretty.

She took more pictures as Parker began the "Dearly Beloved" as the Reverend Whistledown, as Emma and Laurel took hands and Harold curled up to sleep and snore at their feet.

She noticed how bright Laurel's hair was, how the sun caught the edges of it beneath the tall black hat she wore as groom. How Mr. Fish's whiskers twitched as he yawned.

When it happened, it happened as much inside Mac as out. Her three friends were grouped under the lush white curve of the arbor, a triangle of pretty young girls. Some instinct had Mac shifting her position, just slightly, tilting the camera just a bit. She didn't know it as composition, only that it looked nicer through the lens.

And the blue butterfly fluttered across her range of vision to land on the head of a butter yellow dandelion in Emma's bouquet. The surprise and pleasure struck the three faces in that triangle under the white roses almost as one.

Mac pressed the shutter.

She knew, *knew*, the photograph wouldn't be blurry and dark or fuzzy and washed out. Her thumb wouldn't be blocking the lens. She knew exactly what the picture would look like, knew her grandmother had been wrong after all.

Maybe happy ever after was bull, but she knew she wanted to take more pictures of moments that *were* happy. Because then they were ever after.

1

On January first, Mac rolled over to smack her alarm clock, and ended up facedown on the floor of her studio.

"Shit. Happy New Year."

She lay, groggy and baffled, until she remembered she'd never made it upstairs into bed—and the alarm was from her computer, set to wake her at noon.

She pushed herself up to stagger to the kitchen and the coffeemaker.

Why did people want to get married on New Year's Eve? Why would they make a formal ritual out of a holiday designed for marathon drinking and probably inappropriate sex? And they just had to drag family and friends into it, not to mention wedding photographers.

Of course, when the reception had finally ended at two a.m., she could've gone to bed like a sane person instead of uploading the shots, reviewing them—spending nearly three more hours on the Hines-Myers wedding photos.

But, boy, she'd gotten some good ones. A few great ones.

Or they were all crap and she'd judged them in a euphoric blur.

No, they were good shots.

She added three spoons of sugar to the black coffee and drank it while standing at the window, looking out at the snow blanketing the gardens and lawns of the Brown Estate.

They'd done a good job on the wedding, she thought. And maybe Bob Hines and Vicky Myers would take a clue from that and do a good job on the marriage.

Either way, the memories of the day wouldn't fade. The moments, big and small, were captured. She'd refine them, finesse them, print them. Bob and Vicky could revisit the day through those images next week or sixty years from next week.

That, she thought, was as potent as sweet, black coffee on a cold winter day.

Opening a cupboard, she pulled out a box of Pop-Tarts and, eating one where she stood, went over her schedule for the day.

Clay-McFearson (Rod and Alison) wedding at six. Which meant the bride and her party would arrive by three, groom and his by four. That gave her until two for the pre-event summit meeting at the main house.

Time enough to shower, dress, go over her notes, check and recheck her equipment. Her last check of the day's weather called for sunny skies, high of thirty-two. She should be able to get some nice preparation shots using natural light and maybe talk Alison—if she was game—into a bridal portrait on the balcony with the snow in the background.

Mother of the bride, Mac remembered—Dorothy (call me Dottie)—was on the pushy and demanding side, but she'd be dealt with. If Mac couldn't handle her personally, God knew Parker would. Parker could and did handle anyone and anything.

Parker's drive and determination had turned Vows into one of the top wedding and event planning companies in the state in a five-year period. It had turned the tragedy of her parents' deaths into hope, and the gorgeous Victorian home and the stunning grounds of the Brown Estate into a thriving and unique business.

And, Mac thought as she swallowed the last of the Pop-Tart, she herself was one of the reasons.

She moved through the studio toward the stairs to her upstairs bed and bath, stopped at one of her favorite photos.

The glowing, ecstatic bride with her face lifted, her arms stretched, palms up, caught in a shower of pink rose petals.

Cover of *Today's Bride*, Mac thought. Because I'm just that good.

In her thick socks, flannel pants, and sweatshirt she climbed the stairs to transform herself from tired, pj-clad, Pop-Tart addict into sophisticated wedding photojournalist.

She ignored her unmade bed—why make it when you were just going to mess it up again?—and the bedroom clutter. The hot shower worked with the sugar and caffeine to clear out any remaining cobwebs so she could put her mind seriously to today's job.

She had a bride who was interested in trying the creative, a passive-aggressive MOB who thought she knew best, a groom so dazzling in love he'd do anything to make his bride happy. And both her B and G were seriously photogenic.

The last fact made the job both pleasure and challenge. Just how could she give her clients a photo journey of their day that was spectacular, and uniquely theirs?

Bride's colors, she thought, flipping through her mental files as she washed her short, shaggy crop of red hair. Silver and gold. Elegant, glamorous.

She'd had a look at the flowers and the cake—both getting their finishing touches today—the favors and linens, attendants' wardrobes, headdresses. She had a copy of the playlist from the band with the first dance, mother-son, father-daughter dances highlighted.

So, she thought, for the next several hours, her world would revolve around Rod and Alison.

She chose her suit, her jewelry, her makeup with nearly the same care as she chose her equipment. Loaded, she went out to make the short trek from the pool house that held her studio and little apartment to the main house.

The snow sparkled, crushed diamonds over ermine, and the air was cold and clean as mountain ice. She definitely had to get some outside shots, daylight and evening. Winter wedding, white wedding, snow on the ground, ice glistening on the trees, just dripping from the denuded willows over the pond. And there the fanciful old Victorian with its myriad rooflines, the arched and porthole windows, rising and spreading, soft blue against the hard shell of sky. Its terraces and generous portico heralded the season with their festoons of lights and greenery.

She studied it as she often did as she walked the shoveled paths. She loved the lines of it, the angles of it, with its subtle touches of pale yellow, creamy white picked out in that soft, subtle blue.

It had been as much home to her as her own growing up. Often more so, she admitted, as her own had run on her mother's capricious whims. Parker's parents had been warm, welcoming, loving and—Mac thought now—steady. They'd given her a calm port in the storm of her own childhood.

She'd grieved as much as her friend at their loss nearly seven years before.

Now the Brown Estate was her home. Her business. Her life. And a good one on every level. What could be better than doing something you loved, and doing it with the best friends you'd ever had?

She went in through the mudroom to hang up her outdoor gear, then circled around to peek into Laurel's domain.

Her friend and partner stood on a step stool, meticulously adding silver calla lilies to the five tiers of a wedding cake. Each flower bloomed at the base of a gold acanthus leaf to glimmering, elegant effect.

"That's a winner, McBane."

Laurel's hand was steady as a surgeon's as she added the next lily. Her sunny hair was twisted at the back of her head into a messy knot that somehow suited the angular triangle of her face. As she worked, her eyes, bright as bluebells, held narrowed concentration.

"I'm so glad she went for the lily centerpiece instead of the bride and groom topper. It makes this design. Wait until we get to the Ballroom and add it."

Mac pulled out a camera. "It's a good shot for the website. Okay?"

"Sure. Get any sleep?"

"Didn't hit until about five, but I stayed down till noon. You?"

"Down by two thirty. Up at seven to finish the groom's cake, the desserts—and this. I'm so damn glad we have two weeks before the next wedding." She glanced over. "Don't tell Parker I said that."

"She's up, I assume."

"She's been in here twice. She's probably been everywhere twice. I think I heard Emma come in. They may be up in the office by now."

"I'm heading up. Are you coming?"

"Ten minutes. I'll be on time."

"On time is late in Parker's world." Mac grinned. "I'll try to distract her."

"Just tell her some things can't be rushed. And that the MOB's going to get so many compliments on this cake she'll stay off our backs."

"That one could work."

Mac started out, winding through to check the entrance foyer and the massive Drawing Room where the ceremony itself would take place. Emmaline and her elves had already been at work, she noted, undressing from the last wedding, redressing for the new. Every bride had her own vision, and this one wanted lots of gold and silver ribbon and swag as opposed to the lavender and cream voile of New Year's Eve.

The fire was set in the drawing room and would be lit before the guests began to arrive. White-draped chairs sparkling with silver bows formed row after row. Emma had already dressed the mantel with gold candles in silver holders, and the bride's favorite white calla lilies massed in tall, thin glass vases.

Mac circled the room, considered angles, lighting, composition—and made more notes as she walked out and took the stairs to the third floor.

As she expected, she found Parker in the conference room of their office, surrounded by her laptop, BlackBerry, folders, cell phone, and headset. Her dense brown hair hung in a long tail—sleek and simple. It worked with the suit—a quiet dove gray—that would blend in and complement the bride's colors.

Parker missed no tricks.

She didn't look up but circled a finger in the air as she continued to work on the laptop. Knowing the signal, Mac crossed to the coffee counter and filled mugs for both of them. She sat, laid down her own file, opened her own notebook.

Parker sat back, smiled, and picked up her mug. "It's going to be a good one."

"No doubt."

"Roads are clear, weather's good. The bride's up, had breakfast and a massage. The groom's had a workout and a swim. Caterers are on schedule. All attendants are accounted for." She checked her watch. "Where are Emma and Laurel?"

"Laurel's putting the finishing touches on the cake, which is stupendous. I haven't seen Emma, but she's started dressing the event areas. Pretty. I want some outdoor shots. Before and after."

"Don't keep the bride outside for too long before. We don't want her red-nosed and sniffling."

"You may have to keep the MOB off my back."

"Already noted."

Emma rushed in, a Diet Coke in one hand, a file in the other. "Tink's hungover and a no-show, so I'm one short. Let's keep this brief, okay?" She dropped down at the table. Her curling black hair bounced over the shoulders of her sweatshirt. "The Bride's Suite and the Drawing Room are dressed. Foyer and stairway, nearly finished. The bouquets, corsages, and boutonnieres checked. We've started on the Grand Hall and the Ballroom. I need to get back to that."

"Flower girl?"

"White rose pomander, silver and gold ribbon. I have her halo—roses and baby's breath—ready for the hairdresser. It's adorable. Mac, I need some pictures of the arrangements if you can fit it in. If not, I'll get them."

"I'll take care of it."

"Thanks. The MOB—"

"I'm on it," Parker said.

"I need to—" Emma broke off as Laurel walked in.

"I'm not late," Laurel announced.

"Tink's a no-show," Parker told her. "Emma's short."

"I can fill in. I'll need to set the centerpiece of the cake and arrange the desserts, but I've got time now."

"Let's go over the timetable."

"Wait." Emma lifted her can of Diet Coke. "Toast first. Happy New Year to us, to four amazing, stupendous, and very hot women. Best pals ever."

"Also smart and kick-ass." Laurel raised her bottle of water. "To pals and partners."

"To us. Friendship and brains in four parts," Mac added, "and the sheer coolness of the whole we've made with Vows."

"And to 2009." Parker lifted her coffee mug. "The amazing, stupendous, hot, smart, kick-ass best pals are going to have their best year ever."

"Damn right." Mac clinked her mug to the rest. "To Wedding Day, then, now, and always."

"Then, now, and always," Parker repeated. "And now. Timetable?"

"I'm on the bride," Mac began, "from her arrival, switch to groom at his. Candids during dressing event, posed as applies. Formal portraits in and out. I'll get the shots of the cake, the arrangements now, do my setup. All family and wedding party shots separate prior to the ceremony. Post-ceremony I should only need forty-five minutes for the family shots, full wedding party, and the bride and groom."

"Floral dressing in bride and groom suites complete by three. Floral dressing in foyer, Parlor, staircase, Grand Hall, and Ballroom by five." Parker glanced at Emma.

"We'll be done."

"Videographer arrives at five thirty. Guest arrivals from five thirty to six. Wedding musicians—string quartet—to begin at five forty. The band will be set up in the Ballroom by six thirty. MOG, attended by son, escorted at five fifty, MOB, escorted by son-in-law, directly after. Groom and groomsmen in place at six." Parker read off the schedule. "FOB, bride, and party in place at six. Descent and procession. Ceremony duration twenty-three minutes, recession, family moments. Guests escorted to Grand Hall at six twenty-five."

"Bar opens," Laurel said, "music, passed food."

"Six twenty-five to seven ten, photographs. Announcement of family, wedding party, and the new Mr. and Mrs. seven fifteen."

"Dinner, toasts," Emma continued. "We've got it, Parks."

"I want to make sure we move to the Ballroom and have the first dance by eight fifteen," Parker continued. "The bride especially wants her grandmother there for the first dance, and after the father-daughter, mother-son dance, for her father and his mother to dance. She's ninety, and may fade early. If we can have the cake cutting at nine thirty, the grandmother should make that, too."

"She's a sweetheart," Mac put in. "I got some nice shots of her and Alison at the rehearsal. I've got it in my notes to get some of them today. Personally, I think she'll stay for the whole deal."

"I hope she does. Cake and desserts served while dancing continues. Bouquet toss at ten fifteen."

"Tossing bouquet is set," Emma added.

"Garter toss, dancing continues. Last dance at ten fifty, bubble blowing, bride and groom depart. Event end, eleven." Parker checked her watch again. "Let's get it done. Emma and Laurel need to change. Everyone remember their headsets."

Parker's phone vibrated, and she glanced at the readout. "MOB. Again. Fourth call this morning."

"Have fun with that," Mac said, and escaped.

She scouted room by room, staying out of the way of Emma and her crew as they swarmed over the house with flowers, ribbons, voile. She took shots of Laurel's cake, Emma's arrangements, framed others in her head.

It was a routine she never allowed to become routine. She knew once it became rote, she'd miss shots, opportunities, bog down on fresh angles and ideas. And whenever she felt herself dulling, she thought of a blue butterfly landing on a dandelion.

The air smelled of roses and lilies and rang with voices and footfalls. Light streamed through the tall windows in lovely beams and shafts, and glittered on the gold and silver ribbons.

"Headset, Mac!" Parker rushed down the main staircase. "The bride's arriving."

As Parker hurried down to meet the bride, Mac jogged up. She swung out on the front terrace, ignoring the cold as the white limo sailed down the drive. As it eased to a stop she shifted her angle, set, and waited.

Maid of honor, mother of the bride. "Move, move, just a little," she muttered. Alison stepped out. The bride wore jeans, Uggs, a battered suede jacket, and a bright red scarf. Mac zoomed in, changed stops. "Hey! Alison!"

The bride looked up. Surprise turned to amused delight,

and to Mac's pleasure, Alison threw up both arms, tossed back her head, and laughed.

And there, Mac thought as she caught the moment, was the beginning of the journey.

Within ten minutes, the Bride's Suite—once Parker's own bedroom—bustled with people and confusion. Two hairdressers plied their tools and talents, curling, straightening, styling, while others wielded paints and pots.

Utterly female, Mac thought as she moved through the room unobtrusively, the scents, the motions, the sounds. The bride remained the focus—no nerves on this one, Mac determined. Alison was confident, beaming, and currently chattering like a magpie.

The MOB, however, was a different story.

"But you have such beautiful hair! Don't you think you should leave it down? At least some of it. Maybe—"

"An updo suits the headdress better. Relax, Mom."

"It's too warm in here. I think it's too warm in here. And Mandy should take a quick nap. She's going to act up, I just know it."

"She'll be fine." Alison glanced toward the flower girl.

"I really think—"

"Ladies!" Parker wheeled in a cart of champagne, with a pretty fruit and cheese tray. "The men are on their way. Alison, your hair's gorgeous. Absolutely regal." She poured a flute, offered it to the bride.

"I really don't think she should drink before the ceremony. She barely ate today, and—"

"Oh, Mrs. McFearson, I'm so glad you're dressed and ready. You look fabulous. If I could just steal you for a few minutes? I'd love for you to take a look at the Drawing Room before the ceremony. We want to make sure it's perfect, don't we? I'll have her back in no time." Parker pushed champagne into the MOB's hand, and steered her out of the room.

Alison said, "Whew!" and laughed.

For the next hour, Mac split herself between the Bride's and Groom's suites. Between perfume and tulle, cuff links and cummerbunds. She eased back into the bride's domain, circled around the attendants as they dressed and helped one another dress. And found Alison alone, standing in front of her wedding dress.

It was all there, Mac thought as she quietly framed the shot. The wonder, the joy—with just that tiny tug of sorrow. She snapped the image as Alison reached out to brush her fingers over the sparkle of the bodice.

Decisive moment, Mac knew, when everything the woman felt reflected on her face.

Then it passed, and Alison glanced over.

"I didn't expect to feel this way. I'm so happy. I'm so in love with Rod, so ready to marry him. But there's this little clutch right here." She rubbed her fingers just above her heart. "It's not nerves."

"Sadness. Just a touch. One phase of your life ends today. You're allowed to be sad to say good-bye. I know what you need. Wait here."

A moment later, Mac led Alison's grandmother over. And once again stepped back.

Youth and age, she thought. Beginnings and endings, connections and constancy. And, love.

She snapped the embrace, but that wasn't it. She snapped the glitter of tears, and still, no. Then Alison lowered her forehead to her grandmother's, and even as her lips curved, a single tear slid down her cheek while the dress glowed and glittered behind them.

Perfect. The blue butterfly.

She took candids of the ritual while the bride dressed, then the formal portraits with exquisite natural light. As she'd expected, Alison was game to brave the cold on the terrace.

And Mac ignored Parker's voice through her headset as she rushed to the Groom's Suite to repeat the process with Rod.

She passed Parker in the hallway as she strode back to the bride. "I need the groom and party downstairs, Mac. We're running two minutes behind."

"Oh my God!" Mac said in mock horror and ducked into the Bride's Suite.

"Guests are seated," Parker announced in her ear moments later. "Groom and groomsmen taking position. Emma, gather the bridal party."

"On it."

Mac slipped out to take her stand at the bottom of the stairs as Emma organized the bridesmaids.

"Party ready. Cue the music."

"Cuing music," Parker said, "start the procession."

The flower girl would clearly be fine without the nap, Mac decided as the child nearly danced her way down the staircase. She paused like a vet at Laurel's signal, then continued at a dignified pace in her fairy dress across the foyer, into the enormous Parlor, and down the aisle formed by the chairs.

The attendants followed, shimmering silver, and at last, the maid of honor in gold.

Mac crouched to aim up as the bride and her father stood at the top of the stairs, holding hands. As the bride's music swelled, he lifted his daughter's hand to his lips, then to his cheek.

Even as she took the shot, Mac's eyes stung.

Where was her own father? she wondered. Jamaica? Switzerland? Cairo?

She pushed the thought and the ache that came with it aside, and did her job.

Using Emma's candlelight, she captured joy and tears. The memories. And stayed invisible and separate.

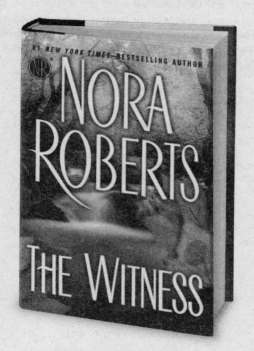

Finally!
Classic Nora Roberts novels
available as eBooks for the first time!

Nora Roberts' popular characters—the O'Hurleys, the Donovans, and the Cordinas—are going digital for the very first time. Now, with just a few clicks, readers can experience the engaging family dynamics, the powerful friendships, and the thrilling passion that Nora brings to life in her bestselling novels.

The O'Hurleys
THE LAST HONEST WOMAN
DANCE TO THE PIPER
SKIN DEEP
WITHOUT A TRACE

The Donovan Legacy
CAPTIVATED
ENTRANCED
CHARMED
ENCHANTED

Cordina's Royal Family
AFFAIRE ROYALE
COMMAND PERFORMANCE
THE PLAYBOY PRINCE
CORDINA'S CROWN JEWEL

Look for a new selection of classic Nora Roberts titles available throughout 2012!

noraroberts.com
facebook.com/noraroberts
penguin.com/intermix

M1012AS0112

Praise for #1 *New York Times* bestselling author
JENNIFER WEINER

All Fall Down

"Weiner's skill is in the specifics. There's no doubt she knows how to deliver a certain kind of story, and well."

—*The New York Times Book Review*

"Weiner, who is a master at creating realistic characters, is at her best here. Readers will be nodding their heads in sympathy as Allison struggles to balance being a mother, a daughter, and a wife while desperately just wanting to be herself."

—*Booklist* (starred review)

"Unputdownable . . . Well-drawn characters, lively prose, and [a] sharp sense of humor. Like the best of Weiner's work, it's comfort food in book form."

—*Entertainment Weekly*

"Pitch-perfect . . . Weiner's portrayal of rehab is sharp, sad, and mordantly funny. . . . Allison is a memorable character wise-cracking her way through despair."

—*The Philadelphia Inquirer*

"An absolutely heartbreaking read that will leave readers haunted. Great for book clubs or for anyone trying to understand a loved one's addiction."

—*Library Journal* (starred review)

"Darkly witty . . . Weiner's latest delivers the well-observed humor her fans love."

—*People*

"Weiner fans will be happy to find this as one of her best works. For those who aren't familiar with her, *All Fall Down* is a great place to start."

—*Boston Herald*

"Weiner creates relatable heroines with everyday worries, such as losing weight or finding a mate. Add her clever pop-culture references, girlfriend conversations over goblets of wine, and her trademark self-deprecating humor and you have sure-to-please novels that hook you in and never let go."

—*USA Today*

"Reading one of Jennifer Weiner's contemporary novels of manners is a bit like biting into an apple. The experience is full of flavor, more crisp than juicy, and refreshingly tart."

—*The Baltimore Sun*

"Weiner's sly portrayal of family, entitlement, and recovery culture is a romp—with an edge."

—*Good Housekeeping*

"Dark humor and a surprise twist."

—*People StyleWatch*

"The everymom heroine in this novel becomes a hard-core pill addict—and it's impossible to look away."

—*Glamour*

"Best known for her sense of humor, in Weiner's raw new novel she proves she is equally as fluent in poignancy. A searing, no-holds-barred look at an ordinary woman whose life spirals out of control."

—Jodi Picoult, #1 *New York Times* bestselling author

All Fall Down

A NOVEL

JENNIFER WEINER

WASHINGTON SQUARE PRESS
New York   London   Toronto   Sydney   New Delhi

WASHINGTON SQUARE PRESS
An Imprint of Simon & Schuster, Inc.
1230 Avenue of the Americas
New York, NY 10020

First Washington Square Press trade paperback edition April 2015

WASHINGTON SQUARE PRESS and colophon are trademarks of Simon & Schuster, Inc.

For information about special discounts for bulk purchases, please contact Simon & Schuster Special Sales at 1-866-506-1949 or business@simonandschuster.com.

The Simon & Schuster Speakers Bureau can bring authors to your live event. For more information or to book an event contact the Simon & Schuster Speakers Bureau at 1-866-248-3049 or visit our website at www.simonspeakers.com.

Permissions acknowledgments appear on page 385.

Manufactured in the United States of America

10   9   8

The Library of Congress has cataloged the hardcover edition as follows:

Weiner, Jennifer.
    All fall down: a novel / Jennifer Weiner.—First Atria Books hardcover edition.
        pages   cm
    1. Women drug addicts—Rehabilitation—Fiction.   2. Self-realization in women—Fiction.   3. Domestic fiction.   I. Title.
PS3573.E3935A78   2014
813'.6—dc23   2014009100

ISBN 978-1-4516-1778-8
ISBN 978-1-4516-1779-5 (pbk)
ISBN 978-1-4516-1780-1 (ebook)

For my readers . . . who have come with me this far

Vera said: "Why do you feel you have to turn everything into a story?" So I told her why:

Because if I tell the story, I control the version.

Because if I tell the story, I can make you laugh, and I would rather have you laugh at me than feel sorry for me.

Because if I tell the story, it doesn't hurt as much.

Because if I tell the story, I can get on with it.

—FROM *HEARTBURN* BY NORA EPHRON

PART ONE

~

Down the
Rabbit Hole

ONE

Do you generally use alcohol or drugs more than once a week?

I hesitated with my hand over the page. I'd picked up the magazine to read the "How to Dress Right for Your Shape" story advertised on the cover, but it had opened to a quiz that asked "Has Your Drinking or Drug Use Become a Problem?" and something had made me stop. Maybe it was the black-and-white photograph of a woman in profile, bending sadly over her wineglass, or maybe the statistic beside it that said that prescription painkiller overdose was now the leading cause of accidental death of women in America, surpassing even car crashes. I had a pen in my hand—I'd been using it to fill out the stack of forms for Eloise's five-year-old well-child checkup—and, almost without thinking, I made an X in the box for "Yes."

I crossed my legs and looked around Dr. McCarthy's waiting area, suddenly worried that someone had seen what I'd written. Of course, no one was paying any attention to my little corner of the couch. Sleet ticked at the panes of the oversized windows; a radiator clunked in the corner. The lamplit room, on the third floor of an office building at the corner of Ninth and Chestnut, with a volunteer in a striped pinny at a knee-high table reading *Amelia Bedelia* to kids sitting in miniature chairs, felt cozy, a respite from the miserable winter weather. Three years ago my husband, Dave, my daughter, and I had moved out of Center City and into a house in Haverford that I refused to call a McMansion, even though that's exactly what it was, but I loved Ellie's pediatrician so much that I'd never even tried to find a suburban replacement. So here we were, more than half a year late for Ellie's checkup, in the office where I'd been taking her since she was just a week old. We'd parked in the lot on Ninth Street and trekked through the February slush to get here, Ellie stepping delicately over the piles of crusted, dirty snow and the ankle-deep, icy puddles at the corners, complaining that her feet were getting wet and her socks were getting splashy. I'd lured her on with the promise of a treat at Federal Donuts when her checkup was over.

Ellie tugged at my sleeve. "How much longer?"

"Honey, I really can't say. The doctors need to take care of the sick kids first, and you, Miss Lucky, are not sick."

She stuck out her lower lip in a cartoonish pout. "It isn't FAIR. We made an APPOINTMENT."

"True. But remember when you had that bad sore throat? Dr. McCarthy saw you right away. Even before the kids who had appointments."

She narrowed her eyes and nibbled at her lip before dropping her voice to a stage whisper that was slightly more hushed than your average yell. "I am having an idea. Maybe we could tell the nurse lady that I have a sore throat now!"

I shook my head. "Nah, we don't lie. Bad karma."

Ellie considered this. "I hate karmel." She smoothed her skirt and wandered off toward the toy basket. I recrossed my legs and checked out the crowd.

The room was predictably full. There were first-time mothers from Queen Village and Society Hill, who wore their babies wrapped in yards of organic cotton hand-dyed and woven by indigenous Peruvian craftswomen who were paid a living wage. The moms from the Section 8 housing pushed secondhand strollers and fed their infants from plastic bottles, as opposed to ostentatiously breast-feeding or slipping the baby a few ounces of organic formula in a BPA-free bottle with a silicone-free nipple hidden under a prettily patterned, adorably named nursing cover-up (I'd worn one called the Hooter Hider).

On the days when you use drugs or alcohol, do you usually have three drinks/doses or more?

Define "dose." One Percocet, from the bottle I got after I had my wisdom teeth pulled? Two Vicodin, prescribed for a herniated disc I suffered in a step class at the gym? I'd never taken more than two of anything, except the day after my father had been diagnosed with Alzheimer's and my mother had set up a temporary fortress in our guest room. Could three pills count as a single dose? I decided not to answer.

Do you use drugs or alcohol to "unwind" or "relax"?

Hello. That's what they're there for. And was that so bad, really? How many times had I heard my husband say "I need to go for a run," or my best friend, Janet, say "I need a glass of wine"? What I did was no different. It was, actually, better. A run was time-consuming and sweaty and hard on the joints, and wine could stain.

"Mommy?"

"Hang on, sweetie," I said, as my iPhone rang in my purse. "Just one minute."

"You ALWAYS say that. You ALWAYS say just one minute and it ALWAYS takes you for HOURS."

"Shh," I whispered, before hurrying toward the door, where I could keep an eye on her while I talked. "Hi, Sarah."

"Allison," said Sarah, in the gruff, all-business tone that surprised people, given her petite frame, sleek black bob, and freck-led button nose. "Did the fact-checker call?"

"Not today." The *Wall Street Journal* was in the midst of its every-six-months rediscovery that women were online. They were doing a piece on women who blog, and Ladiesroom.com, the website that I wrote for and Sarah ran, was to be featured. I was alternately giddy at the thought of how the publicity would raise Ladiesroom's profile and nauseous at the notion of my picture in print.

"She just read my quotes back to me," said Sarah. "They sounded great. I've really got a good feeling about this!"

"Me too," I lied. I was optimistic about the piece . . . at least some of the time.

"Mom-MEE."

My daughter was standing about six inches from my face, brown eyes brimming, lower lip quivering. "Gotta go," I told Sarah. "We're at the doctor's."

"Oh, God. Is everything okay?"

"As okay as it ever is!" I said, striving to inject good cheer into my tone before I slipped the phone back into my purse. Sarah, technically my boss, was twenty-seven and childless. She knew I was a mother—that was, after all, why she'd hired me, to give readers live, from-the-trenches reports on married-with-children life. But I tried to be a model employee, always available to talk through edits or help brainstorm a headline, even if Ellie was with me. I also tried to be a model mother, making Ellie feel like she was the center of my universe, that I was entirely present for her, even when I was on the phone, debating, say, the use of "strident" versus "emphatic," or arguing about which picture of Hillary Clinton to use to illustrate another will-she-or-won't-she-run story. It was a lot of juggling and quick switching and keeping my smile in place. "Sorry, honey. What do you need?"

"I'm FIRSTY," she said, in the same tone of voice an old-school Broadway actress might use to announce her imminent demise.

I pointed at the water fountain on the other side of the room. "Look, there's a water fountain!"

"But that is where the SICK kids are." A tear rolled down my daughter's pillowy cheek.

"Ellie. Don't be such a drama queen. Just go get a drink. You'll be fine."

"Can I check what is in your purse?" she wheedled. Before I could answer, she'd plunged both hands into my bag and deftly removed my bottle of Vitaminwater.

"Ellie, that's—" Before I got the word "Mommy's" out of my mouth, she'd twisted off the cap and started gulping.

Our eyes met. Mine were undoubtedly beseeching, hers sparkled with mischief and satisfaction. I considered my options. I could punish her, tell her no screens and no *SpongeBob* tonight, then endure—and force everyone else in the room to endure—the inevitable screaming meltdown. I could ignore what she'd done, reinforcing the notion that bad behavior got her exactly what she wanted. I could take her outside and talk to her there, but then the receptionist would, of course, call us when we were in the hall, which meant I'd get the pleasure of a tantrum on top of another half-hour wait.

"We will discuss this in the car. Do you understand me?" I maintained the steady eye contact that the latest parenting book I'd read had recommended, my body language and tone letting her know that I was in charge, and hoped the other mothers weren't taking in this scene and laughing. Ellie took another defiant swig, then let a mouthful of zero-calorie lemon-flavored drink dribble back into the bottle, which she handed back to me.

"Ellie! Backwash!"

She giggled. "Here, Mommy, you can have the rest," she said, and skipped across the waiting room with my iPhone flashing in her hand. Lately she'd become addicted to a game called Style Queen, the object of which was to earn points to purchase accessories and makeup for a cartoon avatar who was all long hair and high heels. The more accessories you won for your avatar—shoes, hats, scarves, a makeup kit—the more levels of the game you could access. With each level, Ellie had explained to me, with many heaved sighs and eye rolls, you could get a new boyfriend.

"What about jobs?" I had asked. "Does Style Queen work? To get money for all that makeup, and her skirts and everything?"

Ellie frowned, then raised her chubby thumb and two fingers. "She can be an actress or a model or a singer." Before I could ask follow-up questions, or try to use this as a teachable moment in which I would emphasize the importance of education and hard work and remind her that the way you looked was never ever the most important thing about you, my daughter had dashed off, leaving me to contemplate how we'd gone from *The Feminine Mystique* and *Free to Be . . . You and Me* to this in just one generation.

The magazine was still open to the quiz on the couch beside me. I grabbed it, bending my head to avoid the scrutiny of the übermommy two seats down whose adorable newborn was cradled against her body in a pristine Moby Wrap; the one who was not wearing linty black leggings from Target and whose eyebrows had enjoyed the recent attention of tweezers.

Do you sometimes take more than the amount prescribed? Yes. Not always, but sometimes. I'd take one pill and then, ten or fifteen or twenty minutes later, if I wasn't feeling the lift, the slow unwinding of the tight girdle of muscles around my neck and shoulders I'd expected, I'd take another.

Have you gotten intoxicated on alcohol or drugs more than two times in the past year? (You're intoxicated if you use so much that you can't function safely or normally or if other people think that you can't function safely or normally.)

This was a tricky one. With painkillers, you did not slur or get sloppy. Your child would not come home from school and find Mommy passed out in a puddle of her own vomit (or anyone else's). A couple of Vicodin and I could function just fine. The worst things that had happened were the few times Dave had accused me of being out of it. "Are you okay?" he'd ask, squinting at my face like we'd just met, or apologizing for being so boring that I couldn't muster five minutes of attention to hear about his day as a City Hall reporter at the *Philadelphia Examiner*. Never mind that his anecdotes tended to be long and specific and depend on the listener's deep interest in the inner workings of Philadelphia's government. Some days, I had that interest. Other days, all I wanted was peace, quiet, and an episode of *Love It or List It*. But I'd been occasionally bored and disinterested even before my use of Vicodin and Percocet had ramped up, over the past two years, from a once-in-a-while thing to a few-days-a-week thing to a more-days-than-not thing. It wasn't as if one single catastrophe had turned me into a daily pill popper as much as the accumulated stress of a mostly successful, extremely busy life. Ellie had been born, then I'd quit my job, then we'd moved to the suburbs, leaving my neighborhood and friends behind, and then my dad had been diagnosed. Not one thing, but dozens of them, piling up against one another until the pills became less a luxury than a necessity for getting myself through the day and falling asleep at night.

I checked "No" as Ellie skipped back over. "Mommy, is it almost our turn? This is taking for HOURS."

I reached into my purse. "You can watch *Les Miz*," I said. She handed me the phone and had the iPad out of my hands before I could blink.

"That's so cute," said the mother who'd just joined me on the couch. "She watches musicals? God, my two, if it's not animated, forget it."

I let myself bask in the all-too-rare praise: Ellie's passion for Broadway musicals was one of the things I loved best about her, because I loved musicals, too. When she was little, and tormented by colic and eczema, and she hardly ever slept, I would drive around in my little blue Honda, with Ellie strapped into her car seat and cast recordings from *Guys and Dolls* and *Rent* and *West Side Story* and *Urinetown* playing. "Ocher!" she'd yelled from the backseat when she was about two years old. "I WANT THE OCHER!" It had taken me ten minutes to figure out that she was trying to say "overture," and I'd told the story for years. *Isn't she funny. Isn't she precocious. Isn't she sweet*, people would say . . . until Ellie turned four, then five, and she was funny and precocious and sweet but also increasingly temperamental, as moody as a diva with killer PMS. *Sensitive* was what Dr. McCarthy told us.

Extremely sensitive, said Dr. Singh, the therapist we'd taken her to visit after her preschool teacher reported that Ellie spent recess sitting in a corner of the playground with her fingers plugged into her ears, clearly pained by the shouts and clatter of her classmates. "Too loud!" she'd protest, wincing as we got close to a playground. "Too messy!" she'd whine when I'd try to lure her outdoors, into a game of catch or hide-and-seek, or ply her with finger paints and fresh pads of paper. Movies "made too much noise," sunshine was "too bright," foods that were not apples, string cheese, or plain white bread, toasted and buttered and minus its crust, were rejected for "tasting angry," and glue and glitter gave her "itchy fingers." For Eloise Larson Weiss, the world was a painful, scary, sticky place where the volume was always turned up to eleven. Dave and I had read all the books, from *The Highly Sensitive Child* to *Raising Your Spirited Child*. We'd learned about how to avoid overstimulation, how to help Ellie through transitions, how to talk to her teachers about making accommodations for her. We'd done our best to reframe our thinking, to recognize that Ellie was suffering and not just making trouble, but it was hard. Instead of remembering that Ellie was wired differently than other kids, that she cried and threw tantrums because she was uncomfortable or anxious or stressed, I sometimes found myself thinking of her as just bratty, or going out of her way to be difficult.

The woman beside me nodded at her son, who seemed to be about eight. He had a Band-Aid on his forehead, and he was making loud rumbling noises as he hunched over a handheld video game. "A little girl would have been so nice. I've got to bribe Braden to get him in the tub."

"Oh, that's not just a boy thing. Ellie won't go near a tub unless it's got one of those bath bombs. Which are eight bucks a pop."

The woman pursed her lips. I felt my face heat up. Eight-dollar bath bombs were an indulgence for a grown-up. For a five-year-old, they were ridiculous, especially given that our mortgage payments in Haverford were so much higher than they'd been in Philadelphia, and that instead of a raise last year, Dave and everyone else at the *Examiner* had gotten a two-week unpaid furlough. When we'd filed our taxes the year before, we'd both been surprised—and, in Dave's case, mortified—to learn that I was earning more with my blog than he was as a reporter. This, of course, had not been part of our plan. Dave was supposed to be the successful one . . . and, up until recently, he had been.

Three years ago, Dave had written a series about inner-city poverty, about kids who got their only balanced meals at school and parents who found it less expensive to stay at home, on welfare, than to look for work; about social services stretched too thin and heroic teachers and volunteers trying to turn kids' lives around. The series had won prizes and the attention of a few literary agents, one of whom had gotten him a book deal and a hefty advance. Dave had taken the chunk of money he'd received when he'd signed the contract and driven off to Haverford, a town he'd fallen in love with when the newspaper's food critic had taken him there one night for dinner. Haverford was lovely, with leafy trees and manicured lawns. The schools were excellent, the commute was reasonable, and it all fit into my husband's vision of what our lives would one day be.

Unfortunately, Dave didn't discuss this vision with me until one giddy afternoon when he'd hired a Realtor, found a house, and made an offer. Then, and only then, did he usher me to the car and drive me out past the airport, off the highway, and into the center of town. The sun had been setting, gilding the trees and rooftops, and the crisp autumnal air was full of the sounds of children playing a rowdy game of tag. When he pulled up in front of a Colonial-style house with a FOR SALE sign on the lawn, I could hear the voices of children playing in the cul-de-sac, and smell barbecuing steaks. "You'll love it," he'd said, racing me through the kitchen (gleaming, all stainless steel appliances, granite countertops, and tile floors), past the mudroom and the powder room, up the stairs to the master bedroom. There we had kissed and kissed until the Realtor cleared his throat twice, then knocked on the door and told us we needed to respond to the seller's offer within the hour.

"Yes?" Dave asked. His eyes were shining; his whole face was lit up. I'd never seen him so boyish, or so happy, and it would have been heartless to tell him anything except what he wanted to hear.

"Yes."

I hadn't thought it through. There wasn't time. I didn't realize that I was signing up not just for a new house and a new town but, really, for an entirely new life, one where, with Dave's encouragement, I'd be home with a baby instead of joining him on the train every morning, heading into the city to work. Dave wanted me to be more like his own mother, who'd gladly given up her career as a lawyer when the first of her three boys was born, swapping briefs and depositions for carpools and class-mom duties. He wanted a traditional stay-at-home mother, a wife who'd do the shopping and the cooking, who'd be available to sign for packages and pick up the dry cleaning and, generally, make his life not only possible but easy. The problem was, he'd never told me what he wanted, which meant I never got to think about whether it was what I wanted, too.

Maybe it would have worked if the world hadn't decided it had no great use for newspapers . . . or if the blog I wrote as a hobby hadn't become a job, turning our financial arrangement on its head, so that I became the primary breadwinner and Dave's salary ended up going for extras like private school and vacations and summer camp. Maybe our lives would have gone more smoothly if I hadn't found the house so big, so daunting, if it didn't carry, at least to my nose, the whiff of bad luck. "The sellers are very motivated," our agent told me, and Dave and I quickly figured out why: the husband, a political consultant, had been arrested for embezzling campaign contributions, which he used to fund his gambling habit . . . and, *Examiner* readers eventually learned, his mistress.

Dave and I had both grown up in decent-sized places in the suburbs, but the Haverford house had rooms upon rooms, some of which seemed to have no discernible function. There was a kitchen, and then beside it a smaller, second kitchen, with a sink and a granite island, that the Realtor ID'd as a butler's pantry. "We don't have a butler," I told Dave. "And if we did, I wouldn't give him his own pantry!" The main kitchen was big enough to eat in, with a dining room adjoining it, plus a living room, a den, and a home office with floor-to-ceiling bookshelves. Upstairs there were no fewer than five bedrooms and five full bathrooms. There was the master suite, and something called a "princess suite" that came with its own dressing room. The basement was partially finished, with space for a home gym, and out back a screened-in porch overlooked the gentle slope of the lawn.

"Can we afford this?" I'd asked. It turned out, between Dave's advance and the embezzler's desperation, that we could. We could buy it, but we couldn't fill it. Every piece of furniture we owned, including the folding card table I'd used as a desk and the futon from Dave's college dorm, barely filled a quarter of the space, and it all looked wrong. The table that had fit perfectly in our Philadelphia row house was dwarfed by the soaring ceilings and spaciousness of the Haverford dining room. The love seat where we'd snuggled in Center City became dollhouse-sized in the burbs. Our queen-sized bed looked like a crouton floating in a giant bowl of soup in the master bedroom, and our combined wardrobes barely filled a third of the shelves and hanging space in the spacious walk-in closet.

Overwhelmed, out of a job, and with a baby to care for, I'd wander the rooms, making lists of what we needed. I'd buy stacks of magazines, clip pictures, or browse Pinterest, making boards of sofas I loved, dining-room tables I thought could work, pretty wallpaper, and gorgeous rugs. I would go to the paint store and come home with strips of colors; I'd download computer programs that let me move furniture around imaginary rooms. But when it came time to actually buy something—the dining-room table we obviously needed, beds for the empty guest rooms, towels to stock the shelves in the guest bathrooms—I would go into vapor lock. I'd never considered myself indecisive or suffered from fear of commitment, but somehow the thought *That bed you are buying will be your bed for the rest of your life* would make me hang up the phone or close the laptop before I could even get the first digits of my card number out.

Four months after Dave had signed his advance, another book came out, this one based on a series that had run in one of the New York City papers, about a homeless little girl and the constellation of grown-ups—parents, teachers, caseworkers, politicians—who touched her life. The series had gotten over a million clicks, but the book failed to attract more than a thousand readers its first month on sale. Dave's publisher had gotten nervous—if a book about the poor in New York City didn't sell, what were the prospects for a book about the poor in Philadelphia? They'd exercised their option to kill the contract. Dave didn't have to give back the money they'd paid him on signing, but there would be no more cash forthcoming. His agent had tried but had been unable to get another publisher to pick up the project. Poverty just wasn't sexy. Not with so many readers struggling to manage their own finances and hang on to their own jobs.

Dave's agent had encouraged him to capitalize on the momentum and come up with another idea—"They all love your voice!" she'd said—but, so far, Dave was holding on to the notion that he could find a way to get paid for the writing he'd already done, instead of having to start all over again. So he'd stayed at the paper, and when Sarah had approached me about publishing my blog on her website, saying yes was the obvious choice. Once I started working, I had no more time to fuss with furniture. Just finding clean clothes in the morning and something for us all to eat at night was challenge enough. So the house stayed empty, unfinished, with wires sticking out from walls because I hadn't picked lighting fixtures, and three empty bedrooms with their walls painted an unassuming beige. In the absence of dressers and armoires, we kept our clothes in laundry baskets and Tupperware bins, and, in addition to the couch and the love seat, there were folding canvas camp chairs in the living room, a temporary measure that had now lasted more than two years—about as long as Dave's bad mood.

I remembered the sulk that had followed the *Examiner*'s edict that every story run online with a button next to the byline so that readers could "Like" the reporter on Facebook.

"It's not even asking them to like the stories," he'd complained. "It's asking them to like me." He hadn't even smiled when I'd said, "Well, I like you," and embraced him, sliding my hands from his shoulder blades down to the small of his back, then cupping his bottom and kissing his cheek. Ellie was engrossed in an episode of *Yo Gabba Gabba!*; the chicken had another thirty minutes in the oven. "Want to take a shower?" I'd whispered. Two years ago, he'd have had my clothes off and the water on in under a minute. That night, he'd just sighed and asked, "Do you have any idea how degrading it is to be treated like a product?"

It wasn't as though I couldn't sympathize. I'd worked at the *Examiner* myself, as a web designer, before Ellie was born. I believed in newspapers' mission, the importance of their role as a watchdog, holding the powerful accountable, comforting the afflicted and afflicting the comfortable. But it wasn't my fault that newspapers in general and the *Examiner* in particular were failing. I hadn't changed the world so that everything was available online immediately if not sooner, and not even our grandparents waited for the morning paper to tell them what was what. I hadn't rearranged things so that "if it bleeds, it leads" had become almost quaint. These days, the *Examiner*'s home page featured photographs of the Hot Singles Mingle party that desperate editors had thrown, or of the Critical Mass Naked Nine, where participants had biked, nude, down ten miles of Broad Street (coverage of that event, with the pictures artfully blurred, had become the most-read story of the year, easily topping coverage both of the election and of the corrupt city councilman who'd been arrested for tax fraud after a six-hour standoff that ended after he'd climbed to the top of City Hall and threatened to jump unless he was provided with a plane, a million dollars in unmarked bills, and two dozen cannoli from Potito's). "A 'Like' button is not the end of the world," I'd said, after it became clear that a sexy shower was not in my future. Then I'd gone back to my iPad, and he'd gone back to watching the game . . . except when I looked up I found him scowling at me as if I'd just tossed my device at his head.

"What?" I asked, startled.

"Nothing," he said. Then he jumped up from the sofa, rolled his shoulders, shook out his arms, and cracked a few knuckles, loudly, like he was getting ready to enter a boxing ring. "It's nothing."

I'd tried to talk to him about what was wrong, hoping he'd realize that, as the one who'd gotten us into this mess—or at least this big house, this big life, with the snooty private-school parents and the shocking property-tax bills—he had an obligation to help figure out how we were going to make it work. Over breakfast the week after the "Like" button rant, while Ellie dawdled at the sink, washing and rewashing her hands until every trace of syrup was gone, I'd quietly suggested couples therapy, telling him that lots of my friends were going (lie, but I did know at least one couple who had gone), and adding that the combined stress of a new town, a sensitive child, and a wife who'd gone from working twenty hours a week to what was supposed to be forty but was closer to sixty would put any couple on edge. His lip had curled. "You think I'm crazy?"

"Of course you're not crazy," I'd whispered back. "But it's been crazy for both of us, and I just think . . ."

He got up from the table and stood there for a moment in his blue nylon running shorts and a T-shirt from a 10K he'd completed last fall. Dave was tall, broad-shouldered, and slim-hipped, with thick black hair, deep-set brown eyes, and a receding hairline he disguised by wearing baseball caps whenever he could. When we'd first started dating we would walk holding hands, and I'd try to catch glimpses of the two of us reflected in windows or bus-shelter glass, knowing how good we looked together. Dave was quiet, brooding, with a kind of stillness that made me want nothing more than to hear him laugh, and a goofy sense of humor you'd never guess he had just by looking at him. *Still waters run deep*, I'd thought. Later, I learned that silence did not necessarily guarantee depth. If you interrupted my husband in the middle of one of his quiet times, asked him what he was thinking about, and got him to tell you, some of the time the answer would concern the latest scandal at City Hall, or his attempts to confirm rumors about a congressional aide who'd forged his boss's signature. Other times, the answer would involve his ongoing attempt to rank his five favorite 76ers.

Still, there was no one I wanted to be with more than Dave.

He knew me better than anyone, knew what kind of movies I liked, my favorite dishes at my favorite restaurants, how my mood could instantly be improved by the presence of a Le Bus brownie or a rerun of *Face/Off* on cable. Dave would talk me into jogging, knowing how good I'd feel when I was done, or he'd take Ellie out for doughnuts on a Saturday morning, letting me sleep until ten after a late night working.

He could be considerate, loving, and sweet. The morning I suggested therapy, he was none of those things. He went stalking down to the basement without a word of farewell. A minute later, the treadmill whirred to life. Dave was training for his first marathon, a goal I'd encouraged before I realized that the long runs each weekend meant I wouldn't see him for four or five hours at a time on a Saturday or Sunday, and would have the pleasure of Ellie all to myself. While the treadmill churned away in the basement, I got to my feet, sighing, as the weight of the day settled around my shoulders.

"Ellie," I said. Ellie was still standing at the sink, dreamily rubbing liquid soap into her hands. "You need to clear your plate and your glass."

"But they're too HEAVY! And the plate is all STICKY! And maybe it will DROP!" she complained, still in her Ariel nightgown, dragging her bare feet along the terra-cotta tiled floor until finally I snapped, "Ellie, just give me the plate and stop making such a production!"

Inevitably, she'd started to cry, dashing upstairs to her room, leaving soapy handprints along the banister. I loaded the dishwasher, wiped down the counters, and swept the kitchen floor. I put the milk and juice and butter back in the fridge and the flour and sugar back in the pantry. Then, before I went to Ellie to apologize and tell her that we should both try to use our inside voices, I'd taken a pill, my second Vicodin since I'd gotten up. The day had stretched endlessly before me—weepy daughter, angry husband, piles of laundry, messy bedroom, a blog post to write, and probably dozens of angry commenters lined up to tell me I was a no-talent hack and a fat, stupid whore. *I need this,* I thought, letting the bitterness dissolve on my tongue. It had been, I remembered, not even nine a.m.

Have you ever felt like you should cut down on your drinking or drug use?

Feeling suddenly queasy, I lifted my head and looked around the waiting room again to see if anyone had noticed that I was taking this quiz seriously. Did I think about cutting down? Sure. Sometimes. More and more often I had the nagging feeling that things were getting out of control. Then I'd think, *Oh, please.* I had prescriptions for everything I took (and if Doctor A didn't know what Doctor B was giving me, well, that wasn't necessarily a problem—if it was, pharmacies would be set up to flag it, right?). The pills helped me manage everything I needed to manage.

Have other people criticized your drinking or drug use, or been annoyed by it?

I checked "No," fast and emphatically, trying not to think about how nobody criticized my use because nobody knew about it. Dave knew I had a prescription for Vicodin—he'd been there the night I'd come hobbling home from the gym—but he had no idea how many times I'd gotten that prescription refilled, telling my doctor that I was doing my physical-therapy-prescribed exercises religiously (I wasn't), but that I still needed something for the pain. Dave didn't know how easy it was, if you were a woman with health insurance and an education, a woman who spoke and dressed and presented herself a certain way. Good manners and good grammar, in addition to an MRI that showed bulging discs or an X-ray with impacted molars, could get you pretty much anything you wanted. With refills. Pain was impossible to see, hard to quantify, and I knew the words to use, the gestures to make, how to sit and stand as if every breath was agony. It was my little secret, and I intended to keep it that way.

"Eloise Weiss?" I looked up. A nurse stood in the doorway with Ellie's chart in his hands.

Startled, I half jumped to my feet, and felt my back give a warning twinge, as if to remind me how I'd gotten into this mess. I wanted a pill. I'd had only one, that morning, six hours ago, and I wanted something, a dam against the rising anxiety about whether my marriage was foundering and if I was a good parent and when I'd find the time to finish the blog post that was due at six o'clock. I wanted to feel good, centered and calm and happy, able to appreciate what I had—my sunny kitchen, with orchids blooming on the windowsill; Ellie's bedroom, for which I'd finally found the perfect pink chandelier. I wanted to slip into my medicated bubble, where I was safe, where I was happy, where nothing could hurt me. *As soon as this is over,* I told myself, and imagined sitting behind the wheel once the doctor had let us go and swallowing a white oval-shaped pill while Ellie fussed with her seat belt. With that picture firmly in mind, I reached out my hand for my daughter.

"No shots," she said, her lower lip already starting to tremble. "I don't think so."

"No SHOTS! You SAID! You PROMISED!" Heads turned in judgment, mothers probably thinking, *Thank God mine's not like that.* Ellie crossed her arms over her chest and stood there, forty-three pounds of fury in a flowered Hanna Andersson dress, matching socks and cardigan, and zip-up leopard-print high-top sneakers. Her fine brown hair hung in braided pigtails, tied with purple elastic bands, and she had a stretchy flowered headband wrapped, hippie-style, around her forehead.

The nurse gave me a smile that was both sympathetic and weary, as I half walked, half dragged my daughter off to the scales and blood-pressure cuffs. Eloise whined and balked and winced as she was weighed and measured. The nurse took her blood pressure and temperature. Then the two of us were left to wait in an exam room. "Put this on," the nurse said, handing Ellie a cotton gown. Ellie pinched the gown between two fingertips. "It will ITCH," she said, and started to cry.

"Come on," I said, taking the gown, with its rough texture and offending tags, in my hand. "I bet if you just get your dress off, you'll be okay."

Still sniffling, Ellie bent gracefully at the waist—she'd gotten her ease in the physical world from her father, who ran and ice-skated and, unlike me, did not inhabit a universe where the furniture seemed to reposition itself just so I could trip over or bang into it. I watched as she eased each zipper on her high-tops down, slid her foot out of her right shoe, pulled off her pink sock, and laid it carefully on top of the sneaker. Off came the left shoe. Off came the left sock. I sat down in the plastic chair as Ellie moved on to her cardigan. I had never mistreated her while under the influence. I'd never yelled (well, not scary-yelling), or been rough, or told her that she needed to put on her goddamn clothes this century, because we couldn't be late for school again, because I couldn't sit through another lecture about Your Responsibilities to Stonefield: A Learning Community (calling it just a "school," I supposed, would have failed to justify its outrageous tuition). It was the opposite. The pills calmed me down. They gave me a sense of peace. When I swallowed them, I felt like I could accomplish anything, whether it was writing a post about the rising costs of fertility treatments or getting my daughter to school on time.

"Mom-MEE." I looked at Ellie. Glory be, she'd gotten all the way down to her Disney Princess underpants. I held open the gown. She made a face. "Just try it," I said. Finally, with the hauteur of a high-fashion model being forced to don polyester, she slipped her arms through the sleeves and permitted me to knot the ties in the back while she pinched the fabric between her fingertips, holding it ostentatiously away from her body, making sure the tag wouldn't touch her. She retrieved my iPad and cued up *Les Miz*. I went back to my quiz. *Have you ever used more than you could afford?* Hardly. My doctors would write me prescriptions. My copay was fifteen dollars a bottle. But it was true that the bottles were no longer lasting as long as they were supposed to, and I spent what was beginning to feel like a lot of time figuring out how many pills I had left and which doctor I hadn't called in a while and whether the pharmacist was looking at me strangely because I was picking up yet another bottle of Vicodin.

Have you ever planned not to use that day but done it anyway?

Yes. I had thought about stopping. I had tried, a few times, and managed, for a few days . . . but during the last few not-today days, it was as if my brain and body had disconnected at some critical juncture. I'd be standing in my closet, in my T-shirt or the workout clothes I'd put on in the hope that wearing them would make me more inclined to exercise, thinking *No*, while watching my body from the outside, watching my hands uncap the bottle, watching my fingers select a pill.

Have you ever not been able to stop when you planned to?

"Mommy?" Ellie sat on the examining table, legs crossed, gown spread neatly in her lap. "Are you mad?" she asked. Her lower lip was quivering. She looked like she was on the verge of tears. Then again, Eloise frequently appeared to be on the verge of tears. When she was a baby, a slammed car door or the telephone ringing could jolt her out of her nap and into a full-fledged shrieking meltdown. In her stroller, she'd cringe at street noises; a telephone ringing, a taxi honking. Even the unexpected rustling of tree branches overhead could make her flinch.

"No, honey. Why?"

"Your face looks all scrunchy."

I made myself smile. I held out my arms and, after a moment's hesitation, Ellie hopped off the table and sat on my lap, folding her upper body against mine. I breathed in her little-girl smell—a bit like cotton candy, like graham crackers and library books—and pressed my cheek against her soft hair, thinking that even though she was high-strung and thin-skinned, Ellie was also smart and funny and undeniably lovely, and that I would do whatever I could to maximize her chances of being happy. I wouldn't be like my own mother, a circa 1978 party girl who hadn't realized that the party was over, a woman who'd slapped three coats of quick-drying lacquer over herself at twenty-six—teased hair, cat-eye black liquid liner, a slick, lipglossed pout, and splashes of Giorgio perfume—and gotten so involved in her tennis group, her morning walk buddies, her mah-jongg ladies, her husband and his health that she had little time for, or interest in, her only child. I knew my mother loved me—at least, she said so—but when I was a girl at the dinner table, or out in the driveway, where I'd amuse myself by hitting a tennis ball against the side of the garage, my mother would look up from her inspection of her fingernails or her *People* magazine and gaze at me as if I were a guest at a hotel who should have checked out weeks before and was somehow, inexplicably, still hanging around.

When I was almost eight years old, my parents asked me

what I wanted for my birthday. I'd been thinking about it for weeks and I knew exactly how to answer. I wanted my mother, who was usually asleep when I left for school, to take me out to breakfast at Peterman's, the local diner that sat in the center of a traffic circle at the intersection of two busy highways in Cherry Hill. Everyone went there: it was where kids would get ice cream cones after school, where families would go for a dinner of charcoal-grilled burgers for Dad and dry tuna on iceberg lettuce for Mom and a platter of chicken wings, onion rings, and French fries with ranch and honey-mustard dipping sauces for the kids. One of my classmates, Kelly Goldring, had breakfast there with her mother every Wednesday. "She calls it Girls' Day," Kelly recounted at a Girl Scout meeting, taking care to roll her eyes to show how dopey she found the weekly breakfasts, but I could tell from her tone, and how she looked when she talked about splitting the Hungry Lady special with her mom and still having home fries left over to take in her lunch, that the breakfasts were just what Mrs. Goldring intended—special. I imagined Kelly and her mom in one of the booths for two. Mrs. Goldring would be in a dress and high heels, with a floppy silk bow tie around her neck, and Kelly, who usually wore jeans and a T-shirt, would wear a skirt that showed off her scabby knees. I pictured the waitress, hip cocked, pad in hand, asking "What can I get you gals?" As I imagined my own trip to the diner, my mother would order a fruit cup, and I'd get eggs and bacon. The eggs would be fluffy, the bacon would be crisp, and my mother, fortified by fruit and strong coffee, would ask about my teacher, my classes, and my Girl Scout troop and actually listen to my answers.

That was what I wanted: not a new bike or an Atari, not cassettes of Sting or Genesis, not *Trixie Belden* books. Just breakfast with my mom; the two of us, in a booth, alone for the forty-five minutes it would take us to eat the breakfast special.

I should have suspected that things wouldn't go the way I'd hoped when my mother came down to the kitchen the morning of my birthday looking wan with one eye made up and mascaraed, and the other pale and untouched. "Come on," she'd said, her Philadelphia accent thicker than normal, her voice raspy. Her hand trembled as she reached for her keys, and she winced when I opened the door to make sure the cab was waiting out front. I rarely saw my mom out of bed before nine, and I never saw her without her makeup completely applied. That morning her face was pale, and she seemed a little shaky, as if the sunshine on her skin was painful and the floor was rolling underneath her feet.

This, I reasoned, had to do with the Accident, the one my mother had gotten into when I was four years old. I didn't know many details—only that she had been driving, that it had been raining, and that she'd hit a slick patch on the road and actually flipped the car over. She'd spent six weeks away, first in the hospital, having metal pins put into her shoulder, then in a rehab place. She still had scars—a faint slash on her left cheek, surgical incisions on her upper arm. Then there were what my father portentously referred to as "the scars you can't see." My mom had never driven since that night. She would jump at the sound of a slammed door or a car backfiring; she couldn't watch car chases or car crashes in the movies or on TV. A few times a month, she'd skip her tennis game and I'd come home from school to find her up in her bedroom with the lights down low, suffering from a migraine.

The morning of my birthday, my mother slid into the backseat beside me. I could smell Giorgio perfume and toothpaste and, underneath that, the stale smell of sleep.

The cab pulled up in front of the restaurant. My mother reached into the pocket of her jacket and handed me a ten-dollar bill. "That's enough, right?" I stared, openmouthed, at the money. My mom looked puzzled, her penciled-in eyebrows drawn together.

"I thought you'd eat with me," I finally said.

"Oh!" Before she turned her head toward the window, I caught an expression of surprise and, I thought, of shame on her face. "Oh, honey. I'm so sorry. When you said 'I want you to take me to Peterman's,' I thought . . ." She waved one hand as if shooing away the idea that a daughter would want to share a birthday breakfast with her mom. "Since I knew I'd be getting up early, I set up a doubles game." She looked at her watch. "I have to run and get changed . . . Mitzie and Ellen are probably there already."

"Oh, that's okay," I said. Already I could feel tears pricking the backs of my eyelids, burning my throat, but I knew better than to cry. *Don't upset your mother,* my father would say.

"Is ten dollars enough?"

How was I supposed to know? I had no idea . . . but I nodded anyhow. "Have a good day, then. Happy birthday!" She gave me a kiss and a cheery little wave before I got out of the cab and closed the door gently behind me.

I hadn't braved the restaurant. It wasn't Wednesday, but I could still imagine sitting at the counter and seeing Kelly and her mom in a booth. I didn't even know whether an eight-year-old could be in a restaurant and order by herself—I could read the menu, of course, but I was too shy to talk to a waitress, and shaky about the mechanics of asking for a check and leaving a tip. I went to the bakery counter instead, where I ordered by pointing at the case—two glazed doughnuts, two chocolate, a jelly, and a Boston cream. There was a path through the woods that led from downtown to my school, and in those days a kid—

even a girl—could walk through the woods alone, without her parents worrying that she'd get kidnapped or molested. I walked underneath the shade, kicking pine needles and gobbling my breakfast, devouring the doughnuts in huge, breathless mouthfuls, cramming down my sadness, trying to remember what my mom had said—that she loved me—instead of the way she'd made me feel. By Language Arts, I was sick to my stomach, and my mother had to take a cab to come get me. In the nurse's office, still in her tennis whites, she'd been impatient, rolling her eyes as I checked my backpack for my books, but in the backseat of the taxi her pout had vanished, and she looked almost kind.

She had on a tennis skirt and a blue nylon warmup jacket with white stripes. Her legs were tan and her thighs barely spread out as she sat, whereas my legs, in black tights underneath my best red-and-green kilt, were probably blobbed out all over the seat.

"I guess breakfast didn't agree with you," she said. She reached into her tote bag for her thermos and a towel, giving me a sip and then gently wiping my forehead, then my mouth.

In Ellie's doctor's office, I sighed, remembering how special I'd felt that my mother had shared her special blue thermos, how I'd never have dreamed of grabbing it out of her bag, let alone backwashing, when Ellie's doctor came striding into the room.

"Hello, Miss Eloise!" Dr. McCarthy wore a blue linen shirt that matched his eyes, white pants, and a pressed white doctor's coat with his name stitched on it in blue. Ellie sprang out of my arms and stood, trembling, at the doorway, poised for escape. I gathered her up and set her onto the crinkly white paper on the table, ignoring my back's protests. The doctor, with a closely trimmed white goatee and a stethoscope looped rakishly around his neck, walked over to the table and gravely offered Ellie his hand.

"Eloise," he said. "How is the Plaza?"

She giggled, pressing one hand against her mouth to protect her single loose tooth. Now that she had a handsome man's attention, she was all sweetness and cheer as she sat on the edge of the examination table, legs crossed, poised enough to be on *Meet the Press.* "We went for tea for my birthday."

"Did you now?" While they chatted about her birthday tea, the white gloves she'd worn, the turtle she had, of course, named Skipperdee, and how her computer game was "very sophisticating," he maneuvered deftly through the exam, peering into her eyes and ears, listening to her chest and lungs, checking her reflexes.

"So, Miss Ellie," he said. "Anything bothering you?"

She tapped her forefinger against her lips. "Hmm."

"Any trouble sleeping? Or using the bathroom?"

She shook her head.

"How about food? Are you getting lots of good, healthy stuff?"

She brightened. "I like cucumber sandwiches!"

"Who doesn't like a good cucumber sandwich?" He turned to me, beaming. "She's perfect, Allison. I vote you keep her." Then he lowered his voice and took my arm. "Let's talk outside for just a minute."

My heart stuttered. Had he seen the quiz I'd been working on? Had I done, or said, something to give myself away?

I handed Ellie the iPad and walked out into the hallway as a young woman, one of the medical students who assisted in the office, stepped in to keep an eye on the patient. "Do you like Broadway musicals?" I heard my daughter ask, as Dr. McCarthy steered me toward the window at the end of the hallway.

"I just wanted to hear how you were doing. Any questions? Any concerns?"

I tried to keep from making too much noise as I exhaled the breath I'd been holding. Maybe I'd picked Dr. McCarthy for shallow reasons—he was the first pediatrician we'd met with who hadn't called me "Mom"—but he'd turned out to be a perfect choice. He listened when I talked, he never rushed me out of his office or dismissed any of my ridiculous new-parent questions as silly, and he provided a necessary balance between me, who was prone to panic, and Dave, who was the kind of guy who'd wrap duct tape around a broken leg and call it a job.

Dr. McCarthy put Ellie's folder down on top of the radiator. "How's the eczema?"

"We're still using the cream, and we're seeing Dr. Howard again next month." Skin conditions, I'd learned, were one of the treats that went along with the sensitive child—that, and food allergies.

"And is school okay?" He paged through Ellie's chart. "How was the adjustment from preschool to kindergarten?"

I grimaced, remembering the first day of school and Ellie clinging to my leg, weeping as if I were sending her into exile instead of a six-hour day at the highly regarded (and very expensive) Stonefield: A Learning Community. (In my head, I carried out an invisible rebellion by thinking of it as just the Stonefield School.) "She had a rough few weeks to start with. She's doing fine now . . ." "Fine" was, perhaps, an exaggeration, but at least Ellie wasn't weeping and doing her barnacle leg-lock at every drop-off. "She's reading, which is great."

He looked at her chart again. "How about the bad dreams?"

"They've gotten better. She still doesn't like loud noises." Or movies in theaters, or any place—like the paint-your-own-pottery shop or the library at storytime—where more than two or three people might be talking at once. I sighed. "It's like she feels everything more than other kids."

"And maybe she does," he replied. "Like I said, though, most kids do grow out of it. By the time she's ten she'll be begging you for drum lessons."

"It's so hard," I said. Then I shut my mouth. I hated how I sounded when I complained about Ellie, knowing that there were women who wanted to get pregnant and couldn't, that there were children in the world with real, serious problems that went far beyond reacting badly to loud noises and the occasional rash. There were single mothers, women with far less money and far fewer resources than I had. Who was I, with my big house and my great job, to complain about anything?

Dr. McCarthy put his hand on my forearm and looked at me with such kindness that I found myself, absurdly, almost crying.

"So tell me. What are you doing to take care of yourself?"

I thought for a split second about lying, giving him some story about actually attending yoga classes instead of just paying for them, or how I was taking Pilates, when, in fact, all I had was a gift certificate from two birthdays ago languishing in my dresser drawer. Instead I said, "Nothing, really. There just isn't time."

He adjusted his stethoscope. "You've got to make time. It's important. You know how they tell you on planes, in case of an emergency, the adults should put their oxygen masks on first? You're not going to be any good to anyone if you're not taking care of yourself." His blue eyes, behind his glasses, looked so gentle, and his posture was relaxed, as if he had nowhere to go and nothing more pressing to do than stand there all afternoon and listen to my silly first-world problems. "Do you want to talk to someone?" I didn't answer. I didn't want to talk to someone. I wanted to talk to him. I wanted to go to his office—it was small but cozy, with cluttered bookshelves, and a desk stacked high with charts, and a comfortably worn leather couch against the wall. He'd offer me a seat and a cup of tea, and ask me what was wrong, what was really wrong, and I would tell him: about Dave, about Ellie, about my dad, about my mom. About the pills. I'd tuck myself under a blanket and take a nap while the volunteers kept Ellie amused in the waiting room and Dr. McCarthy came up with a plan for how to fix me.

Instead, I swallowed hard. "I'm okay," I said, in a slightly hoarse voice, and I gave him a smile, the same one I'd given my mother on my way out of the taxi on my eighth birthday.

"Are you sure? I know how hard this part can be. Even if you can find twenty minutes a day to go for a walk, or just sit quietly . . ."

Twenty minutes. It didn't sound like much. Not until I started thinking about work, and how time-consuming writing five blog posts a week turned out to be, and how on top of my paying job I'd volunteered to redesign the website for Stonefield's annual silent auction. There were the mortgage payments, which still felt like an astonishing sum to part with each month, and the *Examiner,* where it was rumored there'd be another round of layoffs soon. There was the laundry that never got folded, the workouts that went undone, the organic vegetables that would rot and liquefy in the fridge because, after eight hours at my desk and another two hours of being screamed at by my daughter because she couldn't find the one specific teddy bear she wanted among the half-dozen teddy bears she owned, I couldn't handle finding a recipe and preparing a meal and washing the dishes when I was done. We lived on grab-and-heat meals from Wegmans, Chinese takeout, frozen pizzas, and, if I was feeling particularly guilty on a Sunday afternoon, some kind of casserole, for which I'd double the recipe and freeze a batch.

Dr. McCarthy tucked Ellie's folder under his arm and looked down at the magazine in my hand. "Are you reading one of those

'How to Be Better in Bed' things?" he asked. I gave a weak smile and closed the magazine so he couldn't see what I was really reading. This was craziness. I didn't have a problem. I couldn't.

He glanced over my head, at the clock on the wall. From behind the exam-room door, I could hear Ellie and the medical student singing "Castle on a Cloud." "Nobody shouts or talks too loud . . . Not in my castle on a cloud."

I gave him another smile. He gave my arm a final squeeze. "Take care of yourself," he said, and then he was gone.

I pushed the magazine into the depths of my purse. I got Ellie into her clothes, smoothing out the seam of her socks, buttoning her dress, re-braiding her hair. I held her hand when we crossed the street, paid for parking, and then, before I drove southwest to Federal Donuts for the hot chocolate I'd promised my daughter, I reached for the Altoids tin in my purse.

No, I thought, and remembered the quiz. *Have you ever planned not to use that day but done it anyway?* What excuse did I have for taking pills?

Maybe my mother had been cold and inattentive . . . but it had been the 1970s, before "parent" became a verb, when mothers routinely stuck their toddlers in playpens while they mixed themselves a martini or lit a Virginia Slim. So I had a big house in the burbs. Wasn't that what every woman was supposed to want? I had a job I was good at, a job I liked, even if it felt sometimes like the stress was unbearable; I had a lovely daughter, and, really, was being a little sensitive such a big deal? I was fine, I thought. Everything was fine. But even as I was thinking it, my fingers were opening the little box, locating the chalky white oval, and delivering it, like Communion, to the waiting space beneath my tongue. I heard the pill cracking between my teeth as I chewed, winced as the familiar bitterness flooded my mouth, and imagined as I started the car that I could feel the chemical sweetness untying my knotted muscles, slowing my heartbeat, silencing the endless monkey-chatter of my mind, letting my lungs expand enough for a deep breath.

At the corner of Sixth and Chestnut, I saw a woman on the sidewalk. Her face was red. Her feet bulged out of laceless sneakers, and there was a paper cup in her hands. Puckered lips worked against toothless gums. Her hands were dirty and swollen, her body wrapped in layers of sweaters and topped with a stained down coat. Behind her stood a shopping cart filled with trash bags. A little dog was perched on the topmost bag, curled up in a threadbare blue sweater.

Ellie slowly read each word of her sign out loud. " 'Homeless. Need help. God bless.' Mommy, what is 'homeless'?"

"It means she doesn't have a place to live." I was glad Dave wasn't in the car. I could imagine his response: *It means she doesn't want to work to take care of herself, and thinks it's someone else's job to pay for what she needs.* I'd known my husband was more conservative than I was when I married him, but, in the ten years since, it seemed like he'd decided that anything that went wrong in his life or anyone else's was the liberals' fault.

Ellie considered this. "Maybe she could live in our guest room."

I bit back my immediate reply, which was, *No, honey, your daddy lives there.* That had been true for at least the past six weeks. Maybe longer. I didn't want to think about it. Instead I said, "She probably needs a special kind of help, not just a place to stay."

"What kind of help?"

Blessedly, the light turned green. I pulled into traffic and drove to the doughnut shop, feeling the glow of the narcotic envelop me and hold me tight. Leaving the shop, I caught a glimpse of myself in the window, and compared what I saw—a white woman of medium height, in a tan camel-hair trench coat, new-this-season walnut leather riding boots, straightened hair lying smoothly over her shoulders—with the woman on the corner. *A little makeup*, I thought, in the expansive, embracing manner I tended to think in when I had a pill or two in me, *and I could even be pretty.* And even if I wasn't, I thought, as I drove us back home, as Ellie sang along to Carly Rae Jepsen and the city where I'd been so happy slipped away in my rearview mirror, I was a world away from the woman we'd seen. That woman—she was what addiction looked like. Not me. Not me.

TWO

My alarm cheeped at six-fifteen. Without opening my eyes, I crab-walked my hand across the bedside table, located my throbbing phone, and swiped it into silence. Then I held still, flat on my back, listening to Ellie snore beside me as I fought the same mental battle I fought every morning: Exercise or sleep?

I should exercise, I told myself. The day after Ellie's doctor's appointment the fact-checker had called me and said the story about Ladiesroom would show up today on the *Wall Street Journal*'s website, and would be in the printed paper tomorrow. I'd told Dave it was coming, but we'd barely discussed it. I didn't want him to think I was bragging, or that I was drawing a distinction between us—Dave, who wrote stories, and me, who had somehow become one of the written-about. Dave hadn't noticed my nerves, how I'd picked at my dinner and been awake most of the night, worrying that the picture would be terrible and that the world, and everyone I knew in it, would wake up and bear witness to precisely how many chins I actually had.

Lying underneath the down comforter, I touched my hips, feeling the spread, then moved my hands up to the jiggly flesh of my belly. My waistline had been the only thing that kept me from resembling a teapot in profile, but, unfortunately, it had never really reappeared in the months, then years, after Ellie's birth. I'd always told myself that I'd get around to losing the baby weight when things calmed down, but that had never happened, and the baby was now almost six.

I could see Ellie's eyes moving underneath her lavender eyelids, and then Dave, with his pillow in his hands, dressed in pajamas that he wore buttoned to his chin, creeping into the room. Quickly, I shut my eyes so he'd think I was still asleep and we wouldn't have to talk. It had been like this for longer than I liked to think about—every night he'd sleep in the guest room, and every morning he'd come tiptoeing back to the marital bed, the reverse of a teenage boy sneaking out through his beloved's window. The idea was that when Ellie woke up and came to greet us, she'd see a happy couple, not two people who communicated mostly through texts about picking up milk and putting out the recycling. The good news was, Ellie generally showed up in the middle of the night, half-asleep and not in a position to notice anything.

Dave settled himself on the far side of the bed, arranging his pillows just so. I turned on my side, remembering how it had been when we'd first moved in together, how his first act after waking would be to spoon me, his chest tight against my back, his legs cupping mine, how he'd scratch his deliciously stubbled cheeks against the back of my neck and whisper that it couldn't be morning, it was still early, we didn't have to move, not yet. These days, he was more likely to open his eyes and fling himself, facedown, to the carpet for a quick set of planks and push-ups before his run.

I opened my eyes and considered the clothes I'd left folded on the dresser: Lululemon yoga pants and an Athleta tank top in a pretty shade of pink, with my sneakers and a running bra and a pristine pair of white ankle socks beside them. All good, except

I'd laid out the shoes and the clothes on Sunday night, and it was now Thursday morning, and all I'd done with the cute outfit was admire it from the safe remove of my bed.

Five more minutes, I decided, then reached for my cell phone, scanning my e-mail. As usual, Sarah had been up for hours. "Pos col?" she'd asked—Sarah-ese for "possible column"—in a message sent an hour earlier that linked to the Twitter feed of a prominent comic-book creator. When asked how to write strong female characters, he'd answered, "Be sure not to give them weenies." "So transwomen are out?" one of his followers had shot back, touching off a lengthy debate about biology and genitals and who qualified as female. Among her "pos col" contenders, Sarah had also included an update on the trial of the celebrity chef being sued by her (male) assistant for sexual harassment, and a profile of the showrunner of an Emmy Award–winning soap opera.

I considered clicking over to the *Journal,* but decided to wait. The story probably wasn't up yet. I'd get in a workout—maybe thirty minutes on the treadmill, instead of the forty-five I'd been shooting for, but still, better than nothing—and then, with endorphins pumping through my body, giving me a lovely post-exercise high, I'd read the story. And look at the picture. If it was terrible, I'd use it as motivation. I'd print it out, tape it to the refrigerator and to the treadmill. It would be my "Before" shot. All the moms in the carpool lane would tell me how fantastic I looked, how together I had it, after three months, or six months, or however long it took me to lose twenty pounds and maybe get some Botox.

Eloise muttered in her sleep, then rolled over and opened her eyes.

"Good morning, beautiful," I said.

She yawned, eyelashes fluttering, arms stretching over her head. "Mommy, there's somefing I need to tell you."

"What's that?" Maybe I wasn't objective, but Ellie was a gorgeous child. She had light-brown hair that curled in glossy ringlets, big brown eyes that tipped up at the corners and gave her a playful, secretive look, and the kind of porcelain skin that is the exclusive property of infants and children. A perfectly symmetrical spray of freckles ornamented her nose, her lips were naturally pink and curved into a Cupid's bow, and she already showed signs of inheriting my husband's lanky, long-limbed frame.

My daughter was delicious in the morning, I thought, as she nuzzled up next to me, and I kissed her cheek.

"What is it, sweetie?" I whispered.

"I peed in the bed," Ellie whispered back.

"Oh, Christ." Dave rolled himself onto the floor and leapt to his feet, with his hair sticking up in tufts on his head and the head of his penis wagging through the slit of his pajama bottoms as he examined himself for dampness.

"Dave!" I hissed, and jerked my chin toward the offending area. He tucked himself into his pajamas and stalked off toward the bathroom, while I pushed myself out of bed (twenty minutes on the treadmill? I'd still have time for that, right?) and yanked back the duvet. Ellie lay in a slowly widening stain. Her nightgown was soaked. So were the sheets underneath it, and probably the bed underneath that. I'd been meaning to find a waterproof mattress cover, but, like most of my well-intentioned domestic chores, it had been postponed and postponed again and eventually forgotten.

"Oh, God," I breathed.

"I'm SORRY!" Ellie wailed, and began to cry.

"It's okay, baby. Don't worry. These things happen." *About once a week,* I thought. "Ugh," I groaned before I could stop myself. I knew you weren't supposed to embarrass kids for having accidents. I'd read a million child-care books when I was pregnant, which was a good thing, because I barely had a spare ten seconds to read my horoscope now that I had a child, and I knew that shaming them over bodily functions was a bad idea, but seriously?

I scooped her into my arms, ignoring the clammy wetness and the smell. I wished that I'd kept her in overnight diapers, but Ellie would lift her nose and say, "Those are for BABIES," every time I'd offered. "Honey, can you strip the bed?" I called, just as I heard the sound of the shower turning on. *Of course,* I thought. Because letting me wash her off in our bathroom would make it too easy, and helping with the mess would have been too kind. I carried her down the hall.

"NO! NO SHOWER! DON'T WANNA!"

"Ellie," I said, looking her in the eye, "we have to get you clean."

"USE WIPIES!"

Wipies were not going to cut it, I thought as I unstuck her nightgown from her belly and tugged it off over her head, then peeled off her underwear and left them in a crumpled heap on the bathroom floor. Ellie looked at them and started to cry harder. "Princess Jasmine is ALL WET!"

"It's okay, sweetie. We'll put her in the washing machine, and she'll be good as new."

Ellie was unconsoled. "I PEED ON PRINCESS JASMINE!" she sobbed. Never mind that she'd also probably soaked our mattress. Our expensive, less-than-a-year-old, pillowtop mattress.

I cannot take this. The thought rose in my head. It was instantly chased by a second thought. *I know what would make it better.*

"Stay right here, honey," I said, and trotted back to the bedroom. I yanked back the top sheet, the fitted sheet, and the mattress pad. Sure enough, the mattress was soaked . . . and, before I knew it, the bottle was in my hands. *Take one pill every four to six hours as needed for pain.* I popped the lid, shook one pill into my hand, debated for a moment, then added a second, noticing as I did that the bottle was getting light. I'd taken one at five o'clock the night before, after Ellie had thrown a fit because the TiVo had deleted her favorite episode of *Team Umizoomi,* and then another one at midnight, when I couldn't fall asleep.

In the bathroom, I scooped a mouthful of water from the sink and swallowed. Immediately, even before the pills were down my throat, I felt a sense of calm come over me, a certainty that I could handle this crisis and whatever others emerged before seven a.m. *All will be well,* the pills sang as they descended. *All will be well, and all will be well, and all manner of things will be well.*

"Here we go," I said to Ellie. I pulled off my own evening finery—an XXL T-shirt from Franklin & Marshall College and a pair of cotton Hanes Her Way boy shorts, which I'd bought because they covered more real estate than briefs or bikinis. Maybe I could count this as a workout, I thought as I lifted my shrieking daughter and stepped under the spray.

"Too hot! TOO HOT!" Ellie flailed her arms. One fist clipped me underneath my eye. I yelped, then gripped her arms tightly.

"Hold still," I said. With one hand, I kept her immobilized. With the other, I reached for the Princess body wash, wishing I'd added a third pill, wondering if I would have a chance to see the article before I had to take Ellie to school.

Dave stuck his head into the bathroom. "Did you pick up the dry cleaning?" he yelled over the drumming of the water. I could picture his face, the tightness around his mouth, the expression of disappointment he'd have in place even before I disappointed him.

"Oh, shit."

Ellie blinked at me through the water. "Mommy, that's a bad word."

"Mommy knows." I raised my voice. "Honey, I'm sorry."

He didn't sigh or complain, even though I knew he wanted to do both. "I guess I'll get it. Do you want me to pick you up for tonight?" he asked, in a tone of exaggerated patience and goodwill.

"What's tonight?" The second the words were out of my mouth, I remembered what "tonight" was—Dave's birthday dinner. I'd made reservations at his favorite restaurant, invited two other couples, picked out and picked up the wine, and ordered the fancy heart monitor he'd asked for, and wrapped it myself.

"It's Daddy's birthday," Ellie said pertly.

"I know that, honey." I raised my voice so Dave could hear. "I'm sorry. Senior moment." I was six months older than Dave. In better, pre-baby times, we'd joked about it. He'd call me his "old lady," or install a flashlight app on my phone so I could read the menu in dimly lit restaurants. Lately, though, the jokes had taken on an unpleasant edge. "I can meet you at Cochon."

"Fine." He didn't exactly slam the bathroom door, but he wasn't particularly gentle when he closed it, either. I sighed, flipped open the body wash—pink and sparkly, with a cloying scent somewhere between apple blossom and air freshener—and squirted a handful into my palm. I washed Ellie's hair and body, trying to ignore her kicks and shrieks of "THAT HURTS!" and "IT TICKLES!" and "NOW YOU GOT IT IN MY EYES!"

and then washed myself off. I bundled her into a towel, wrapped another towel around my midsection, then scooped her sodden clothes and the soaked bath mat off the floor and tossed them toward the washing machine on my way to Ellie's bedroom.

I gave Ellie a fresh pair of panties and dumped detergent into the machine. When I turned around, Ellie was still naked, her belly sticking out adorably, frowning at the panties.

"These are not Princess Jasmine."

"I know, honey. They're . . ." I squinted at the underwear. "Meredith? From *Brave*?"

"Not Mere-DITH, Meri-DA."

"Right. Her."

"Meridas are for Fridays!"

"Well, you're going to have to wear Merida today. Or else you can try . . ." I pawed through the laundry basket, producing a pair with a grinning cartoon monkey on the back. "Who is this? Paul Frank?"

"I HATE Paul Frank. Only BOYS like Paul Frank."

"Ellie. We're late. Pick one."

She chewed her thumbnail thoughtfully, before extending her index finger at the first pair. "Eenie . . . meenie . . . miney . . . moe."

"We don't have time for this."

"Catch . . . a . . . tiger . . . by . . . the . . . toe."

"Ellie." I bent down so I could look her in the eye. "I didn't want to tell you this, because I didn't want to scare you, but the truth is, there is actually a very dangerous monster living in your closet, and he only eats girls without underpants."

She smiled indulgently. "You are FIBBING."

"Maybe I am," I said, tightening my towel, "and maybe I'm not. But if I were you, I'd put on my underwear."

Back in my bedroom, the wet sheets and comforter were still

on the floor. Sighing, I picked them up, ran them to the laundry room, and tried to pull up the *Journal* on my phone. It was seven o'clock, which gave me thirty minutes to get myself and Ellie dressed, fed, and out the door, and no time at all for a workout. I pulled on my panties and a bra, a pair of leggings, and a dress that was basically an oversized long-sleeved gray tee shirt, and went back to Ellie's room.

She stared at me, gimlet-eyed, hip cocked, a bored supermodel in a pair of panties with a monkey on the butt. I took the requisite three dresses out of her closet, holding their hangers as I made each one speak. "Hi, Ellie," I said in my squeaky pretending-to-be-a-dress voice as I wiggled one of the choices in front of her. "I am beautiful purple!"

"Well, I have a tutu!" I squeaked next, shoving the second dress in front of the first one.

"But I am the favorite!" I said, in the persona of dress number three, a yellow-and-orange tie-dyed number that I'd picked up at a craft fair in Vermont, where Dave and I had gone for Columbus Day weekend two Octobers ago. We'd run a race together—well, Dave had run the 10K, and I'd started off the 5K at an ambitious trot, which had slowed to a stroll, the better to enjoy the foliage and the smell of smoke in the air. When no one was looking. I'd tucked ten dollars into my running bra, and when I was sure I was the last person in the race I'd stopped at a stand and bought a cider doughnut. We'd spent the night in a gorgeous old inn, and slept in a four-poster bed set so far off the floor that there was a miniature set of stairs on each side. Dinner had been in a restaurant built in a former gristmill, at a table overlooking a stream—roast duck in a dark cherry sauce, a bottle of red wine so rich and smooth that even I, who enjoyed things like piña coladas, knew it was something special. There'd been cream puffs with chocolate sauce and glasses of port for dessert.

The innkeepers had lit a fire in the fireplace in our bedroom, and left out a box of chocolates and a bottle of Champagne. I remember climbing into that high bed, and Dave saying, "Let's do it like we're Pilgrims."

"What's that mean?"

He gathered me into his arms, kissed my forehead, then each cheek, then my lips, slowly and lingeringly. "You lie there and don't make any noise, like you're just trying to endure it."

"So, the usual."

"Oh, you," he said, flashing his white teeth in a grin, sliding his hand up the white lace-trimmed nightgown that I'd bought for the occasion. We made love, and then slept for fourteen hours, our longest stretch since Ellie had joined us, and then we ordered room-service waffles and sausage for breakfast, and made love again. We spent the rest of the day walking around the quaint little town, holding hands, buying maple candies and painted wooden birdhouse.

This had been before the *Examiner*'s first layoffs, before everyone who'd been eligible for the buyout had been persuaded—or, in some cases, strongly encouraged—to take the money and go. Now, instead of three reporters covering City Hall, there was just one, just Dave. Instead of leaving the house at nine, he left at eight, then seven-thirty, and I rarely saw him home before eight o'clock at night. On weekends he'd be either hunched over his computer or pounding out miles around Kelly Drive. When we were first married, we'd had sex three or four times a week. Post-baby, that dwindled to three or four times a month . . . and that was a good month. Sometimes it felt as if I'd gone to the hospital, given birth, then lifted my head five years later to find that my husband and I were barely speaking, and that sex with him was at the very end of a very long to-do list, instead of something that I actively wanted and missed.

Part of me thought this was normal. Certainly I'd read and overheard plenty about post-baby bed death. I knew that the passion of the early years didn't last over the length of the union, but lately I'd started to wonder: If we weren't talking, what was he not telling me? And who might he be talking to? The truth was, I wasn't sure I wanted to know the answers, or his secrets, any more than I wanted him to know mine.

"Mommy? Oh, Mommmm-eeee." Ellie was wiggling her fingers in front of my face, then trying hard and, so far, without success, to snap them.

"Sorry," I said.

She pointed at the dresses. "Make them fight!"

"Pick me!" I squeaked, shaking one of the dresses so it looked like it was having a seizure. "No, me!" Using both of my hands and skills that would have impressed a puppeteer, I maneuvered the dresses, making them wrestle and punch. Finally, Ellie pointed at the tie-dyed dress. "I will wear she to school this morning, and she"—an imperious nod toward the purple one—"when I get home for my snack."

"In your face! IN YOUR FACE!" I chanted, making the winning dress taunt the other two as the losers hung their hanger heads. I found red tights and located one of Ellie's favored lace-up leopard-print high-top sneakers under her bed, and the other one in the bathroom. "Wait here," I said, and trotted into the bedroom for my shoes. It was 7:18. I pulled my wet hair away from my face and secured it with a plastic clip, grabbed my phone, and clicked on the link that read—ugh—LETTING IT ALL HANG OUT, IN CYBERSPACE: A NEW GENERATION OF WOMEN WRITERS SHARE (AND SHARE) ON THE INTERNET.

Typical, I thought, and shook my head. It was an old reporter's trick—call your subject and say, "I'm so interested in what you do!" Of course, "interested in" could mean anything from "impressed with" to "disgusted by." Judging from that headline, I strongly suspected the latter.

"Breakfast!" I called. Ellie slouched down the stairs in slow motion, like she was dragging herself through reduced Nutella. I grabbed a box of Whole Foods' pricy, organic version of Honey Nut Cheerios from the pantry, and scooped coffee into the filter. The phone began to buzz against my breast.

"Hello?"

"Did you just call?" Janet asked.

"Nope. I must have boob-dialed you."

"I feel so special," she said. "Did you see the story?"

"Just the headline."

"Well, the article's adorable, and the picture looks great."

"Really?" Part of me felt relieved. Another part knew that Janet would tell me I looked cute even if the picture made me look like a manatee in a dress.

"Yeah, it's . . . CONOR, PUT THAT DOWN!" I winced, poured water into the coffeemaker, and shook cereal into Ellie's preferred Disney Princess bowl.

Ellie pouted. "I WANT FROOT LOOPS!"

Of course she did. Needless to say, I'd never fed her a Froot Loop in my life—all of her food was low in fat, high in fiber, hormone-free, made with whole grains and without high-fructose corn syrup, with, of course, its name correctly spelled. Dave's mother, the Indomitable Doreen, had hosted her for a weekend, during which Ellie had discovered the wonders of highly pro-cessed sugary breakfast treats. "I only gave it to her once!" Do-reen had told me, her voice laced with indignation, even though I'd asked in my least confrontational tone and hastened to reas-sure her that it was no big deal. Clearly, once had been enough.

"I'll send you the link!" Janet said. I slid the coffeepot out from underneath the filter and replaced it with my aluminum travel mug. "Let me know if you need me to—DYLAN, WHERE'S YOUR JACKET?"

"I'll see you tonight," I said. Janet had three kids, five-year-old twins Dylan and Conor and a nine-going-on-nineteen-year-old daughter named Maya, whose pretty face seemed frozen in a sneer and who already regarded her mother as a hopeless embarrassment. Janet and I had met in the Haverford Reserve park when Ellie was two and I was still attempting (when we could still afford for me to attempt) the life of a nonworking stay-at-home mom. I'd gone to the park to kill the half hour between Little People's Music and Tumblin' Tots. Janet was standing in front of a bench with her hands over her eyes, a short, medium-sized woman with light-brown hair in a ponytail, Dansko clogs, and a gorgeous belted white cashmere coat that I correctly identified as a relic of her life as a career lady (no mother of small children would ever buy anything white). "Okay, ready?" she'd called.

Her boys nodded. They were dressed identically, in blue jeans and red-and-blue-striped shirts. Over a glass of wine, the first time we met for drinks, Janet told me that the boys shared a single wardrobe. After her third glass, she confided that she was convinced she'd mixed them up on the way home from the hospital, and that the boy she and Barry were calling Dylan was actually Conor, and vice versa.

"One . . . two . . . three . . ." she began. The boys had dashed away and hid as Janet counted slowly to twenty. When they were gone, she'd looked around, sat down on the bench, and picked up her latte and an issue of *The New Yorker*. I watched for a minute, waiting until she'd turned a page. Then I cleared my throat.

"Um . . . aren't you going to look for them?"

"Well, sure. Eventually." She closed her magazine and looked at me. She had a heart-shaped face, olive skin, and a friendly expression. She wasn't beautiful—her eyes were a little too close together, her nose too big for her face—but she had a welcoming look, the kind of expression that invited conversation. She smiled as she watched me finish daubing Ellie's cheeks with sunscreen, then start swabbing the bench with a sterilizing wipe.

"Your first?" Janet asked.

"However did you guess?" My stroller was parked in front of me. Hanging from the handlebars were recycled-plastic tote bags filled with fruits and vegetables that I would cook and cut up for the nutritious lunch Ellie would eat two bites of, then push around her plate. Tubes of sunscreen and Purell were tucked into the stroller's mesh pocket, along with BPA-free containers of snacks and juice, and a copy of *The Happiest Toddler on the Block*—which I already suspected my daughter would never be—stuck out from the top of my pink-and-green paisley silk Petunia Pickle Bottom diaper bag.

"All that effort," Janet said, and shook her head. "I did all of that with my first. Sunscreen, hand sanitizer, organic everything, baby playgroup . . ."

I nodded. Ellie and I were enrolled in a playgroup that met at the JCC one afternoon each week. Eight moms sat in a circle, complaining, while our kids splashed in the sink, and played with clay and blocks, and dumped oats and eggs and honey into a bowl, which they'd stir with eight plastic spoons while singing "Do You Know the Muffin Man"—or "Do You Know the Muffin Lady," because God forbid the program send the message that girls could not be perfectly adequate and professionally compensated makers of tasty baked treats. For this fun, we paid a hundred bucks a session. What did moms who lacked the cash do? Suffer silently? Watch soap operas? Drink?

"Tumbling class?" Janet asked.

"Check." Ellie and I attended once a week.

"Music Together?" She was smiling, a wide, slightly lopsided grin. I liked her for her teeth—a little too big, crooked on the bottom. Most of the women I met in the various groups and lessons and Teeny Yogini classes had blindingly white veneers or teeth that had been bleached an irradiated white so bright it was almost blue. My theory was that, having given up high-powered jobs to become mothers in their thirties, they now divided all the time and energy that would have gone to their careers between their children and their appearance. I'd gotten the first part of the mandate, quitting my job at the *Examiner* at Dave's urging and making sure that Ellie's every waking hour was full of enriching activities, her meals were wholesome, and her screen time was restricted, and reading to her for one half hour for every ten minutes I let her play on my iPad.

As for my looks, I kept up with my hair color, mostly because I'd started turning gray when I was thirty. However, my closet was not filled with the flattering, expensive, classic garments that the other mommies at Mommy and Me wore. Nor did I have the requisite taut and flab-free body to carry those pricy ensembles. I was always meaning to go to Pilates or CrossFit or Baby Boot Camp, so I could quit slopping around in Old Navy yoga pants or one of the super-forgiving sweater dresses I'd found on clearance at Ann Taylor to go with the inevitable Dansko clogs, the clumsy, clown-sized footwear of the hard-charging stay-at-home suburban mom.

"Since I'm coming clean, we also do Art Experience," I confessed.

"What a cutie," she said, bending down to inspect Ellie, who gave her a sunny grin, the kind of smile she'd never give me. "I'll bet she's never had high-fructose corn syrup in her life."

"Actually . . ." I'd never told anyone this—not Dave, not any of the mothers at the JCC or on the PhillyParent message board, not even my own mother, who wouldn't have understood why it was a big deal—but something about Janet invited confidence. I lowered my voice and looked around, feeling like a con on the prison yard. "I gave her a McNugget."

Janet gave me a look of exaggerated horror, with one hand— unmanicured nails, major diamond ring—pressed to her lips. "You did not."

"I did!" I felt giddy, like I'd finally found someone who thought mommy culture was just as crazy as I did. "On a plane trip! She wouldn't stop screaming in the terminal, so I bought a Happy Meal." I paused, then thought, *What the hell?* "She had fries, too."

"Whatever it takes, that's my motto," said Janet. "Flying with kids is the worst. When we went to visit my in-laws in San Diego last Christmas, I bought my oldest an iPad, and brought mine and my husband's so I wouldn't have to listen to them fight about who got to watch what three iPads. My husband thought I was crazy. Of course, he got upgraded to first class. I told him he could either give me his seat or suck it up."

"So did he suck?"

"He sucked," she confirmed. "Like he was going to give up the big seat to come back and run the zoo. Thank God I had half a Vicodin left over from when I had my wisdom teeth out."

"Mmm." On that beautiful, long-ago morning, I hadn't had any painkillers since my post-C-section Percocet had run out, but I remembered loving the way they'd made me happy, loose-limbed, and relaxed. A kindred spirit, I thought, looking at Janet—someone with my sarcastic sense of humor and my by-any-means-necessary tactics for getting kids to behave.

That had been three years ago, and now Janet and I talked or texted every day and saw each other at least twice a week. We'd pile the kids in her SUV and go to one of the indoor play spaces or museums. In the summer, we'd take the kids to the rooftop pool in the high-rise in Bryn Mawr where her parents had a condo. In the winter, we'd go to the Cherry Hill JCC, and sometimes meet my parents at a pizza parlor for dinner. Eloise adored Maya, who was happy to have a miniature acolyte follow her around and worshipfully repeat everything she said, and I was happy that Ellie had a big-girl friend, even if it meant that sometimes she'd come home singing "I'm Sexy and I Know It," or tell me seriously that "nobody listens to Justin Bieber anymore." She and the boys mostly ignored one another, which was fine with me. If Ellie had favored one over the other it would have meant I'd finally have to figure out how to tell them apart.

Back in the kitchen, I stowed my phone, picked up my mug of coffee, and grabbed Ellie's lunchbox from the counter. The instant I felt its weight—or, rather, its lack of weight—in my hand, I realized I'd forgotten to pack her lunch the night before. "Crap," I muttered, and then looked at Ellie, who was busy taking her shoes off. "Ellie, don't you dare!" I yanked the refrigerator door open, grabbed a squeezable yogurt, a juice box, a cheese stick, a handful of grapes, and a takeout container of white rice from when we'd ordered in Chinese food that weekend. I'd probably get a sweetly worded e-mail from her teachers reminding me that Stonefield had gone green and the Parent-Teacher Collective had agreed that parents should do their best to pack lunches that would create as little waste as possible, but whatever. At least she didn't have any tree-nut products. For that, your kid could be suspended.

It was 7:41. "Honey, come on." Sighing, in just socks, Ellie began a slow lope toward the door. I grabbed her jacket, then saw that her hair was still wet, already matted around her neck. Steeling myself, I set down the mug and the lunchbox, sprinted back upstairs, and grabbed the detangling spray, a wide-tooth comb, and a Hello Kitty headband.

Ellie saw me coming and reacted the way a death-row prisoner might to an armed guard on the day of her execution. "Nooooo!" she shrieked, and ducked underneath the table.

"Ellie," I said, keeping my voice reasonable, "I can't let you go to school like that."

"But it HURTS!"

"I'll do it as fast as I can."

"But that will hurt MORE!"

"Ellie, I need you to come out of there." Nothing. "I'm going to count to three, and if you're not in your chair by the time I say 'three' . . ." I lowered my voice, even though Dave was gone. "No *Bachelor* on Monday." Obviously, I knew that a cheesy reality dating show was not ideal viewing for a kindergartner. But the show was my guilty pleasure, and Dave usually worked late on Mondays, so rather than wrestle Ellie into bed and have her sneak into my bedroom half a dozen times with requests for glasses of water and additional spritzes of "monster spray" (Febreze, after I'd scraped the label off the container), thus risking an interruption of the most dramatic rose ceremony ever, I let her watch with me.

Moaning like a gut-shot prisoner, she dragged herself out from under the table and slowly climbed up into her chair. I squirted the strawberry-scented detangling spray, then took a deep breath and, as gently as I could, tugged the comb from her crown to the nape of her neck.

"Ow! OWWWW! STOBBIT!"

"Hold still," I said, through gritted teeth, as Ellie squirmed and wailed and accused me of trying to kill her. "Ellie, you need to hold still."

"But it HUUUUURTS!" she said. Tears were streaming down her face, soaking her collar. "STOBBIT! It is PAINFUL! You are MURDERING ME!"

"Ellie, if you'd stop screaming and hold still it wouldn't hurt that much!" Sweating, breathing hard, I pulled the comb through her hair. *Good enough,* I decided, and used the headband to push the ringlets out of her eyes. Then I scooped her up under my arm; snatched up her jacket; half set, half tossed her into her car seat; and, finally, got her to school.

cause I'd failed to plug it in the night before, and then started hunting the living room for Dave's. I knew that Sarah was probably right. I'd been in journalism long enough to know that anonymous quotes usually came from disgruntled underlings too chicken to sign their names to their critiques. But I was the one who'd written about—how did the *Journal* put it?—"the politics of marriage and motherhood," and whatever the piece said was sure to sting.

I had started on the marriage-and-motherhood beat by accident with a post on my personal read-only-by-my-friends blog called "Fifty Shades of Meh." I'd written it after buying *Fifty Shades of Grey* to spice up what Dave and I half-jokingly called our "grown-up time," and had written a meditation on how the sex wasn't the sexiest part of the book. "Dear publishers: I will tell you why every woman with a ring on her finger and a car seat in her SUV is devouring this book like the candy she won't let herself eat," I had written. "It's not the fantasy of an impossibly handsome guy who can give you an orgasm just by stroking your nipples. It is, instead, the fantasy of a guy who can give you everything. Hapless, clueless, barely able to remain upright without assistance, Ana Steele is that unlikeliest of creatures, a college student who doesn't have an e-mail address, a computer, or a clue. Turns out she doesn't need any of those things. Here is dominant Christian Grey, and he'll give her that computer, plus an iPad, a Beamer, a job, and an identity, sexual and otherwise. No more worrying about what to wear—Christian buys her clothes. No more stress about how to be in the bedroom—Christian makes those decisions. For women who do too much—which includes, dear publishers, pretty much all the women who have enough disposable income to buy your books—this is the ultimate fantasy: not a man who will make you come, but a man who will make agency unnecessary, a man who will choose your adventure for you."

I'd put the post up at noon. By dinnertime, it had been linked to, retweeted, and read more than anything else I'd ever written. The next morning, an e-mail from someone named Sarah Lai arrived. She was launching a new website and wanted to talk to me about being a regular contributor. "I write about sex," she told me. "Don't be alarmed when you Google me." So I'd Googled her and read her posts on pony play and next-generation vibrators on my way to New York City.

I'd walked into the Greek restaurant in Midtown where we'd decided to meet for lunch expecting a leather-clad vixen, a kitten with a whip, in teetering stripper heels and a latex bodysuit. Sarah Lai looked like a schoolgirl, in a white button-down shirt with a round collar tucked into a pleated gray skirt. Black tights and conservative flat black boots completed her ensemble. "I know, I know," she'd said, laughing, when I told her she wasn't what I expected. "What can I say? The quiet ones surprise you." She set down the wedge of pita she was using to scoop hummus into her mouth and said, "So how'd you know your husband was The One?"

I looked at her, surprised. I'd figured she'd want to know how I got started with my blog, where I found my inspiration, which writers I admired, what other blogs I read. What I saw on her face, underneath the tough-girl pose of a cynic in the city, was unguarded curiosity . . . and hope. She was twenty-six, maybe old enough to have a serious boyfriend of her own, and wonder, as I had at her age, whether he was a keeper or just a guy who'd keep her happy through the holidays.

"On our first date, I wasn't even sure I wanted to see him again," I told her, picturing Dave across the table at the Chinatown restaurant where we'd walked after work. "He was handsome, but really serious. He scared me a little. I thought he was a lot smarter than I was—I still think that, sometimes—and he was, you know, completely focused on his work." We'd talked about his current project, about the mayoral candidate he admired and the three others running for the office he thought were stupid or corrupt, and then he'd told me the story that had won my heart forever, his dream of the Me So Shopping Center.

"The what?" Sarah's expression was rapt, her eyes wide. She'd done everything but pull out a notebook to take notes.

"You're probably too young to remember the movie *Full Metal Jacket,* but there's a scene where this Vietnamese prostitute says, 'Me so horny'? It was the title of a rap song." I was convinced Sarah had no idea what I was talking about, but she nodded anyhow. "Dave's big idea was to have a bunch of shops. Like, Me So Horny would be the town brothel, and Me So Hungry would be the diner, and there'd be a psychiatrist's office called Me So Sad, and a clothing shop . . ."

"Me So Naked?" Sarah guessed.

"It was either that or Me So Cold. And the doctor's office, Me So Sick, and the cleaning service, Me So Messy." I was laughing as I remembered the increasingly silly ideas we'd come up with, how I'd contrived to touch Dave's hand and wrist as I'd laughed. "And that was it. He was already losing his hair, and I could see that sometimes he'd bore me, but I thought, we'll always have Me So. He'll always make me laugh."

Sarah nodded. I had the sense of clearing some invisible hurdle, passing a quiz I hadn't known I'd taken. Sarah had moved to New York from Ohio, had gotten a job in a coffee shop and given herself a year to make it as a writer. When we met, she'd started making a decent amount of money from the ads on her blog. Her dream was to start a bigger, more comprehensive, less sex-centric site. "Fashion, food, magazines, marriage, children, all that," she'd rattled off, before giving the waiter our order—

moussaka, grilled lamb, stuffed grape leaves, and more warm pita. "I'll write about sex, of course, but I'll need someone to cover marriage and motherhood." Throughout the lunch we discussed design and ad buys, ideas, headlines, and titles. By the time dessert arrived, Sarah suggested I give the column a shot and try to write a few blog posts.

"Are you sure you don't want someone with more experience?" I'd asked. I'd never thought of myself as a writer. Dave was the writer; I was a graphics-and-images girl. But we could certainly use the extra money. And the truth was that staying at home with a baby—now a toddler—did not fulfill me the way working at the paper once had. With work, there was a sense of completion. You'd start to lay out a page, or create graphics, or embed just the right video clip in an article about the city's failing schools, and eventually, after editing and feedback and sometimes starting over again, you'd be done. With motherhood and marriage there was no finish line, no hour or day or year when you got to say you were through. Life just went on and on, endless and formless, with no performance evaluation, no raises or feedback or two weeks' vacation. I thought that maybe working for money again could give me back that sense of satisfaction I'd once gotten from a job well done . . . or even just done.

"How is this website going to be different from the women's websites that are already out there?" I had asked. Sarah, who'd clearly been waiting for that question, launched into her answer, about tone and content and reader engagement. I nibbled a stuffed grape leaf and thought about how lucky I was—how without my even trying, a solution for my worries had landed, like a gift-wrapped box dropped out of a window, right in my lap.

Ladiesroom.com had launched six weeks after my interview,

finding its niche in the online world—and its advertisers—faster than either of us could have expected. Four months after its launch, the site was acquired by Foley Media, a bigger company looking to expand its brand. I was working harder than I had at the *Examiner,* pulling my first all-nighters since college, powering through the next day on espresso and a twenty-minute nap, engaging each day with the people who commented on my posts. And now the *Wall Street Journal* had decided we were, in a sense, newsworthy.

"Call me when you've read it," Sarah said. I made some kind of affirmative noise and then turned on Dave's laptop and found the story. I scrolled through their recap of our success, the quotes that captured Sarah's and my funny banter, and the claims from critics who questioned our experience and asked whether our motives were self-promotional. Beneath the words LIVING OUT LOUD, I found my photograph. "Oh, God," I groaned. I'd worn a pink jersey dress and nude heels, and Sarah and I had posed on Sarah's desk, in front of her floor-to-ceiling windows that overlooked Bryant Park. When the shot had been set up, I'd thought we looked nice. Seeing the picture now, all I could think was Before and After. Way, Way Before and After. Worst of all, the caption underneath read "SEXY MAMAS: Mom-bloggers Allison Weiss and Sarah Lai at play in Manhattan." Never mind that I hardly looked sexy, and Sarah wasn't a mom.

Ah, well. At least we looked reasonably professional. The photographer, who'd clearly been expecting the online version of *Girls Gone Wild,* had been disappointed to find ladies in business clothes, one of whom was almost forty, with nary a tattoo in sight (Sarah had a few—"just not," as she put it, "where the judge can see them"). He had not-so-subtly pushed me toward the edge or the back of the shots, while trying to get Sarah to bend over her desk, or to stand with her hands on her knees and wave her bottom in front of her laptop—"so it's, you know, sex and the Internet." When she refused, and also politely turned down his offer to shoot her posing with a whip, he'd asked us to have an edible-body-paint fight (thanks but no thanks). Finally, he asked if we would at least stand side by side. "And can you kind of touch each other?"

We'd declined but agreed to play catch with the Egg, a vibrator designed to look like a retro kitchen timer that Sarah had reviewed in her monthly sex-toy roundup.

I turned away from the laptop and slipped my finger into my bag, found my tin, put the pills I knew I'd be needing—two Percocet, courtesy of my dentist, who was still prescribing them for the wisdom teeth he'd taken out six months ago—underneath my tongue. Then I called Sarah.

"It's great!" I said. I'd meant to sound cheery, but I thought I sounded closer to hysterical.

"I told you it was NBD," Sarah answered. I took a deep breath.

"I guess I'm just worried about what Dave's going to think."

"Ah." Sarah's boyfriend, an architect ten years her senior, was unswervingly supportive and, as far as I knew, completely unthreatened by a girlfriend who wrote about threesomes and bestiality for a living.

"But it'll be fine," I reassured her. "Hey, I should get going on my post. Call you later?" We hung up and I scrolled, idly, to the bottom of the *Journal*'s story, where twenty-three comments had already appeared.

I clicked, and began to read. *LOL the one in the pink looks like Jabba the Hutt. No wonder she needs sex toys!* "But I'm not the sex-toy writer," I said, as if my computer could hear me. I shook my head and kept reading. *I'd hit that* . . . the second commenter had written, followed by three blank lines that I scrolled past to read, . . . *with a brick, so I could get to the hot one.* The third left behind the topic of my looks to consider my credentials. *This is why the terrorists hate us,* added commenter number four.

I closed my eyes. I told myself it did not matter what a bunch of strangers who, clearly, could hardly read and who would never meet me had to say. I told myself that it was ridiculous to get upset by comments on the Internet . . . It wasn't as if the people could reach through the screen to actually hurt me. It wasn't as if I was real to them; I was a name, a picture, a thing: Feminism, or Women Today. I told myself that I looked just fine and that the people who'd written those hateful things were probably idiots who played video games in their parents' basement, putting down their joysticks only long enough to spew a little hate online and then masturbate bitterly.

Dave's computer gave a soft chime, the same noise my laptop made when an e-mail arrived. Reflexively, I toggled to the e-mail screen and double-tapped the link that would let me read the incoming missive. Which turned out to be for Dave, from one LMcintyre@phila.gov. *Happy birthday!*

Okay, I thought. Totally benign. Except that when another e-mail arrived, I clicked it open again, almost without thinking. This one was from Dave, asking, *We still on for lunch?*

Absolutely, wrote back L. McIntyre. I ran through lists of male names that began with "L." Larry. Luke. Lawton. Lonnie. Then I scrolled to the next line. *I wouldn't miss it!*

Hmm. Possibly still innocuous. Dave's reply, *See you soon,* was also perfectly proper. But, in addition to his usual e-mail signature—*David Weiss, Reporter*—he'd used an emoji, a winking yellow smiley face, the kind that subliterate fourteen-year-old girls would text to their crushes, the kind Dave and I rolled our eyes at and had vowed to never use. "We're word people," Dave had said, and even though I was more of a picture person myself, I'd agreed with him that these silly symbols were the height of the ridiculous, turning adult conversations into puppet shows and ruining the English language. Except, if I could believe what I was seeing, here was my husband, using emojis, with someone named L. McIntyre.

Don't do it, a voice in my brain mourned. The computer chimed again, and here was L's reply, another smiley-face emoji, only hers had lipstick and long eyelashes.

"Oh, you have got to be kidding me!" I cried.

First things first. I pulled my hair into a ponytail and literally rolled up my sleeves. I'd never acquired the ninja-level Googling skills that *Examiner* reporters took for granted, but I didn't need them. A quick search revealed that L. McIntyre was Lindsay McIntyre, and she was an assistant United States attorney, and she had gone to UPenn and law school at Temple and she looked—I would ask Janet to confirm this—like a younger, paler, mousier version of me. We both had shoulder-length hair, and similar features, only my face was rounder and her complexion was lighter. But there was a definite resemblance. Except she was single. And young.

It was just after ten o'clock in the morning, but it felt like my wet-the-bed wake-up call had happened to a different person, possibly a century ago. I was considering another pill but decided that I didn't have the luxury. No matter what was going on with my husband, I had work to do.

I sat in front of the laptop. I opened a new window and typed a single word: *Exposed.* The word seemed to expand and contract, throbbing like an infected tooth at the top of the page. *I think my husband is having an affair,* I wrote, then, as if typing them might make it real, I erased the words, then wrapped my arms around my shoulders, sitting in front of the computer and rocking. I thought about calling Sarah and asking for a sick day, but I knew that, today of all days, with traffic probably at an all-time high, there was no way I could afford to go dark.

I squeezed my eyes shut, hearing the percussion of my fingers coming down harder than they had to on the keys as I typed: *Hey, commenters, I'm sorry. I'm sorry my disgusting, blobbity body (which is, after all, no bigger than the average American woman's, but who's counting) offends you. I'm sorry I was foolish enough to pose for a photograph, and let that photograph appear in the world, instead of hiding behind an avatar of an actress or insisting on being airbrushed into acceptability. I'm sorry my mere existence has forced you to actually consider the reality of a woman who is neither a model nor an actress and does not feel compelled to starve herself, or binge and purge, or spend hours engaged in rigorous workouts so that she scrapes into "acceptable" territory and can thus be seen in public.*

I'm sorry I'm not skinny. I'm sorry I haven't had my fat sucked, my face plumped, my nose bobbed, my skin peeled, and my brows plucked. I'm sorry that I forced you into the unwelcome realization that MOST WOMEN DO NOT LOOK LIKE THE WOMEN YOU SEE ON TV. I'm sorry that even the women you see on TV don't look like the women you see on TV, because they've been lit and made up, strapped into Spanx and posed just so.

I'm sorry that, evidently, you are living with terrorists who have the ability to force you to read stories you're not interested in reading. That must be terrible! I, personally, can click or flip away from something that doesn't hold my attention, or interest me, or line up with a worldview that I want affirmed. Whereas you, poor, unfortunate soul, are required to read every loathsome syllable written by some uncredentialed housewife. How sad your life must be!

They'll never print this, I decided. So I saved it, logged off, and then sat there, my heart beating too hard, wishing I was somewhere else, or someone else.

I told myself I wouldn't look at Dave's e-mail again, and I

didn't. I also told myself I wouldn't read any more comments on the *Journal* story, but of course I found myself refreshing obsessively, watching the tally grow higher, feeling each insult and cruel remark burn itself into my brain. *FEMINAZZI,* read one. Angry and a shitty speller. Excellent. I wondered whether Dave had seen the piece, whether he was reading the comments, how he might feel, watching the world consider his wife and find her wanting.

Just before noon, my phone buzzed, flashing my mother's number. Since the day she'd called me and said, "Daddy got lost on the way to the JCC this morning," we'd talked every day, even if most of those "talks" consisted of my mother sobbing softly while I sat there and squirmed.

I picked up the phone. "Hi, Mom."

"Are you okay?" she asked. For a crazy instant, I thought that somehow she knew about L. McIntyre and that she was calling to comfort me. Which was, of course, insane on two fronts: my mother had no idea what was going on in my private life, and if she did, she wouldn't have any idea of how to help, and she wouldn't even try.

"Am I okay with what? Did something happen?" Did I sound awful? I must, I decided, if every caller's first question was whether or not I was all right.

"Oh, no. But I saw the story."

"Don't read the comments," I said. As soon as the words were out of my mouth, I realized that if she hadn't already, my telling her not to look was a guarantee that she would.

"It's been quite a morning," said my mother. "Sharon Young picked me up for yoga, and she had the story up on her phone." She paused. I braced myself.

"Slow news day," I murmured.

"I told her that probably not many people read it. I told her that Dave's the real writer, and you just do it for fun."

"For shits and giggles," I said.

"What?"

"You're right. I only do it for fun," I said, marveling, as I often did, at my mother's passive-aggressive genius, the way she could minimize and dismiss any of my achievements, all under the guise of doing it for my own good.

Having dispensed with the subject of her problematically opinionated daughter, my mom moved on to a new one. "Daddy has an appointment at the urologist's tomorrow."

By "Daddy," she meant her husband, my father, not her own . . . and I thought the visit was next week. Had I gotten it wrong, maybe entering the date incorrectly after taking a few too many pills?

My mom lowered her voice. "He had an accident this morning, so I called to see if they could fit him in."

I cringed, feeling ashamed for my father and sorry for my mom, that she now had to see her husband, the man she'd loved and lived with for almost forty years, shamefaced, with sodden PJ's clinging to his skinny legs. "There's a lot of that going around," I said.

"What?"

"Nothing."

My mother started to cry. "I'm sorry," she said, the way she always apologized for her tears. "It's just so hard to watch this happening to him."

"I know, Mom." It was horrible for me, too, seeing the slackness of his mouth, the eyes that had once missed nothing swimming, befuddled, behind his bifocals.

"He was so embarrassed," said my mother. "It was just awful."

"I can imagine," I said, knowing that as hard a time as Eloise had given me, coaxing a seventy-year-old man in the grip of early Alzheimer's out of his clothes and into the shower would be exponentially more difficult, especially for my five-foot, ninety-five-pound mother.

"I need you to take him to the doctor's."

"When's the appointment?"

"Nine." She sniffled. Her Philadelphia accent stretched the syllable into *noine*. "That was the earliest they could see him."

"Okay," I said. "I'll make it work."

My mother hung up. Without remembering reaching for it, I found a pill bottle in my hand and two more pills in my mouth. Crunching and swallowing, I waited for the familiar, comforting sweetness to suffuse me, that sunny, elevating sensation that everything would be all right, but it was slow in arriving. My heart was still pounding, and my head was starting to ache along with it, and I was so overwhelmed and so unhappy that I wanted to hurl my phone against the wall. *My husband is cheating. Or at least he's flirting. My father is dying. My mother is falling apart. And I'm not sure what to do about any of it.*

Instead of throwing the phone, I punched in one of my speed-dial numbers. The receptionist at my primary-care physician's office put me through to Dr. Andi.

"The famous Allison Weiss!" she said. "I was drinking my smoothie this morning, and there you were!"

"There I was," I repeated, in a dull, leaden voice.

"Ooh, you don't sound good." It was one of the many things I liked about Dr. Hollings—she could take one look or one listen and know something was up. "Back go out again?"

My life, I thought. *My life went out.* "You got it. This morning. I crawled up to bed and I've been here ever since. I took a Vicodin, but, honestly, it's not doing much, and I can't stay in bed all day. I've got a million things to do, and it's Dave's birthday dinner tonight."

"Well, God forbid you miss that!"

"I know, right?"

There was a pause. Maybe she was pulling my chart, or checking something in a book. "Okay, let's see. We called in a refill, what, three weeks ago? I don't normally recommend doing this because of the acetaminophen—it's not great for your liver—but if you're really struggling, you can double down on the Vicodin."

"I tried that," I confessed. "I know I wasn't supposed to, but . . ." I let her hear the quaver in my voice, the one that had nothing to do with my discs and everything to do with L. McIntyre, my dad, and the article. "I'm really not doing so well here."

She clicked her tongue against the roof of her mouth, thinking. "Okay. I can call you in a scrip for OxyContin. It's a lot stronger, so be careful with it until you see how you react. I don't want you driving . . ."

"No worries. I can take a cab tonight."

"Good. Check in with me in a few days. Feel better!"

"Thanks," I said.

An hour later, the pharmacy had my prescription ready. I zipped through the drive-in window to pick it up and tucked the paper bag into my purse, but at the first traffic light I hit I found myself opening first the bag, then the bottle inside it.

The OxyContin pills were slightly smaller than Altoids, and also white. "Take one every three hours for pain." *Pain*, I thought, and quickly swallowed one, wincing at the bitterness.

By the time I got home, I was finally beginning to feel some relief. I floated up the stairs and drifted into the bathroom for a proper shower, not one with Princess Bath Soap. As I lathered my hair I sang "I'm Gonna Wash That Man Right Outa My Hair" under my breath. Why had it taken me so long to find OxyContin? It was lovely. Blissful. Heaven.

L. McIntyre. Maybe she was just a work friend who'd become more like a work wife. I felt the knot between my shoulder blades loosen incrementally as I thought of those words. I knew what a work wife was. I'd been one myself, back when I was at the *Examiner*. My work husband's name was Eric Stengel. He was a photographer, and very discreetly gay, my friend and ally, my partner-in-crime and my lunch buddy. We talked about everything—MTV series, the spin classes that were just popping up in Philadelphia, the mysteries of men's hearts, our shared obsession with the movie *Almost Famous*. We never saw each other outside of the newsroom hours, but every Monday morning I'd pick up cappuccinos for both of us and a single muffin to split, and we'd spend our first hour of the workweek at his desk, debriefing each other about our weekends. We had lunch together at Viet Nam at least once a week. In warm weather, we'd buy fruit salads from the vending truck on Callowhill, and sit outside and talk about Liev Schreiber and Jake Gyllenhaal and the mysterious appeal of Ryan Gosling (Eric got him; I didn't). I was there to talk Eric out of having his name legally changed to Edward ("It has nothing to do with *Twilight;* it's just that Eric's such a nerd name," he'd said). He'd been there to convince me that Dave wasn't cheating after I'd found an inscribed book of Pablo Neruda poetry, dated two weeks after we'd started seeing each other, under Dave's bed. "He's not going to marry someone who reads Neruda," Eric had told me. "Cummings, maybe. Auden, Larkin, those guys, I could see it. But Neruda? Nuh-uh."

"He's so mysterious," I'd moaned—back then, when I thought I had things to complain about. "How am I supposed to know if he's cheating?"

Eric had lifted one finger. "Is he working late?"

I shook my head. Some nights, he was even home before I was.

Eric continued the questions. Was Dave finding excuses

to go out, alone, on the weekends? Had he joined a new gym, started wearing a new cologne, bought himself a new wardrobe or a new car? No, and no, and no again.

"Finally," Eric had said, performing a fingertip drumroll on his desk, "are you two still making the beast with two backs?"

I'd giggled and said, "All the time." It had been true, then . . . and it was true now that at least one of us wanted an active sex life. At least once a week I'd get into bed and feel my husband's hand brush the side of my breast, or my thigh, marital shorthand for *You wanna?* The trouble was, I didn't. Ever. At the end of a day, especially after I'd taken a pill or three to deal with the emotional obstacle course of getting Ellie to bed, the absolute only thing I wanted to do was curl on my side with my cheek against the soft white pillowcase, close my eyes, and let sleep take me. Sex felt like an invasion. Things weren't as bad as they had been the first few months after Ellie was born, when Dave's touch had actively revolted me, when, more than once, I'd shuddered in dismay if he tried for a kiss, but they hadn't improved all that much. I hadn't worried about it, either. Judging from the women's magazines I read, and the stories I'd hear on the playground or in the school pickup lane, our story wasn't especially original. When we'd first started dating, and during the first year and a half of our marriage, we'd done it in the bed, in the shower, on the kitchen table, and, a few times late at night, in various corners of the newsroom. By the time I left the paper, there was one editor's desk I couldn't look at without blushing. Dave had a great body. Better than that, he had an amazing imagination, and the two of us would pretend all kinds of crazy stuff. He'd be a reclusive dot-com genius who'd made ten million dollars at nineteen but had never slept with a woman, and I'd be the high-priced hooker he hired to teach him about women. He'd be the quarterback for the Eagles, and I'd be the rookie sportswriter he invited up to his apartment for an in-depth interview. He'd be a BMW salesman, and I'd be a woman who'd do anything to get a break on the price of the new sedan.

The last time we'd attempted any role-playing had been months ago. It had not gone well. "How about we're both virgins, and we've just gotten married in an arranged marriage, and it's our first night together?" he'd suggested, one leg slung over both of mine, his erection growing against my thigh.

I'd stifled a yawn. I wasn't bored, just tired. "Were there elephants at our wedding?"

"Boy, you really weren't paying much attention," Dave said.

Focus, I told myself. Maybe I wasn't a hundred percent into it, but for the sake of the greater good, I could, as they said, take one for the team. "Okay. You're Ramesh, and I'm Surya. What's your job?"

"I'm a chemical engineer."

"What, you don't own a Dunkin' Donuts?"

He'd propped himself up on his elbow, glaring at me. "Jeez, Allie."

"I was kidding!" I said, thinking, sadly, that there was a time, not long ago, when I wouldn't have had to explain that it was a joke.

"Fine." He flopped onto his back, removing his leg from mine. His erection was wilting. I placed one hand gently on his chest, on top of his T-shirt. "Can I touch you?" I whispered, in character as an inexperienced bride.

"Yes," he whispered back. Slowly, I began stroking his pectoral muscles, feeling his nipples getting stiff against my palm. I tweaked one gently, hearing him suck in his breath. "Just like mine!" I said, delighted. "Will you kiss me?" I whispered.

He nibbled at my neck, nipped at my earlobe, pressed his lips gently against mine. I shut my eyes, lost in the sensation of his tongue dipping into my mouth, gently prodding my own tongue, as one hand slid up the leg of my pajamas. "Actually," he breathed in my ear, "I lied. I have been with a woman before."

I drew back, feigning shock. "When was this?"

In the darkness, he looked ashamed. "Well. You know I'm an engineer. But I also play the sitar in my uncle's restaurant on the Lower East Side on Saturday nights. And you know how ladies love musicians."

"So you didn't save yourself for me?" On behalf of the imaginary Surya, I was feeling legitimately angry. "Where did you take your groupie?"

"We did it . . ." He stifled a yawn. "In the back of my uncle's minivan."

"You couldn't even spring for a hotel room?" Unbelievable. Why did Dave have to be cheap, even in fantasies?

He flopped on his back. "You know what? Let's forget it."

And that had been the end of that. The truth was, in the past year, I could count the times we'd had sex on two hands . . . and I'd probably have fingers left over.

Tonight, I promised. It was, after all, his birthday. I would force all thoughts of L. McIntyre and the jerks from the comments out of my head. I would pull on my flimsiest, most tight-fitting T-shirt, and the drawstring bottoms Dave liked best. I'd light candles by the side of the bed; I'd sing "Happy Birthday to You" Marilyn Monroe style; I would do all the things he liked, just the way he liked them, and we would come back to each other and be a team, a partnership, again.

FOUR

I spent almost an hour in a pilled-up haze, styling my hair, applying my makeup, squeezing myself into a dress with a built-in belt that made it seem like I still had a shape. Even the five minutes it took me to wrestle myself into my Spanx weren't so terrible.

"Oh, you look beautiful!" our sitter, Katrina, said as I came down the stairs, while Eloise narrowed her eyes. I was carrying my pair of Jimmy Choos, one of the few surviving relics from my single-lady days, in one hand.

"When will you be BACK?"

"Not too late. It's a school night."

"Why aren't you taking me?" Her lower lip quivered. "I want to go out to dinner!"

"No, you don't. This place only has fish," I lied. Ellie's face crumpled. "I'll bring you a dessert," I promised . . . and then, before her pique could swell into a full-blown tantrum, I brushed a kiss on her forehead and trotted out to the car, feeling a pang of guilt at my broken promise about not driving. Dave would drive us home, I told myself . . . and, at this point, sad to say, I had enough of a tolerance that even the new medication didn't seem to be hitting me too hard. It was just making me feel unguard-edly wonderful, like life was a delicious lark, full of possibilities, all of them good. So what if a few online meanies had jerky things to say about me? Tonight was my husband's birthday. We would celebrate with our friends, share a delicious meal, fall asleep in each other's arms, and wake up in the morning once more, one hundred percent, a couple.

Cochon was a tiny BYOB in our old neighborhood, one of our longtime favorites. With its black-and-white-checked floors, café tables, and framed Art Deco posters on pumpkin-colored walls, it looked Parisian . . . or as Parisian as you could get in Philadelphia. As I pulled my Prius to the curb, I saw David waiting inside by the hostess stand with his phone pressed to his ear. My heart started hammering. I wondered if he was chat-ting with L. McIntyre, and made myself promise that I wouldn't bring anything up until we were alone and, preferably, after I'd spoken to Janet. No dropping the bomb, and no drinking, I told myself sternly as I struggled to parallel park, a skill I'd lost al-most entirely since our move to the burbs.

As I backed into the curb for the second time, I watched Dave through the window. He turned his back to end his call and put the phone back in his pocket. While he walked outside, I extricated myself from the driver's seat. It took a little while, given that my undergarments made it hard for me to breathe and my gorgeous shoes were half a size smaller than what I usually wore now. *Damn clogs,* I thought.

"Happy birthday," I said once I reached him, and handed off the bag containing six bottles of wine to the hostess.

Dave's hands were in his pockets, his stylish canvas messen-ger bag—the one I'd had made for his last birthday—was slung over his shoulder, and his jaw was already bluish, even though he'd shaved that morning. In his best blue suit, he was so hand-some, I thought, feeling a wave of nostalgia, and sadness. I knew all of his quirks and failings, his hairy hands and short, stubby fingers, his toes oddly shaped, the nails so thick he needed spe-cial clippers to cut them. I knew the sound he made when he ground his teeth, deep in sleep; how he'd sometimes skim the first paragraphs of a story or chapters of a book and then claim he'd read it; the name of the boy at his high school who'd stolen his backpack and thrown it into the girls' locker room; and how he cried every time he read *The World According to Garp*. I knew him so well, and I loved him so much. Why had I pushed him away that last time in bed, and the time before that, and the time before that? What woman wouldn't want him? What was wrong with me?

Dave, meanwhile, was looking me over carefully. "Did you get the party started early?" he asked. He took one hand out of his pocket and rubbed it against his cheek, checking to see if he was due for a shave. "You look a little loopy."

"I'm fine," I said, and did my best not to teeter in my heels. A little loopy, I thought, was better than looking like my heart was breaking. I grabbed his arm, which he hadn't offered, and let him walk me the few steps to the empty table, trying to act casual as I brought my head close to his shoulder and inhaled, hoping I wouldn't smell unfamiliar perfume. The new pills made my body feel loose and springy, warmed from the inside, but I didn't think there was a chemical yet invented that could have quelled my insecurity, or convinced me, in that moment, that my husband loved me still.

A waiter, touchingly young, in a crisp white shirt, black pants, and an apron that looped behind his neck and fell to his ankles, pulled out my chair. "Something to drink?"

"Let's open the white," said Dave, before I could announce, virtuously, that I would just have water. Before I knew it, there was a glass in my hand. "Mmm," I hummed, taking a sip, enjoying the wine's tart bite. Show him you love him, I thought, and tried to give the birthday boy a seductive look, lowering my eyebrows and pouting my lips.

Dave frowned at me. "Are you sure you're okay?"

"I'm fine. Why?"

"Because you look like you're half asleep."

So much for seduction. Dave got to his feet as Janet and Barry came through the door, followed by Dan and Marie. I adored Janet's husband, who was round and bearded, a professor in Penn's history department, smart about pop culture and FDR's legacy, and madly in love with his wife. He and Dave weren't really friends—they tolerated each other because Janet and I and the kids spent so much time together, but they didn't have much in common. Still, they gave each other a manly hug and back slap, and Barry's "Happy birthday, buddy" sounded perfectly sincere.

"My man," said Dan, thumping Dave between his shoulders hard enough to dislocate something. "How'd this happen? How'd we get so goddamned old?" As much as I liked Barry, I disliked Dan. Dan managed a consortium of parking garages that stretched from Center City to the Northeast and did what I thought was extortionate business, charging someone (me, for example) eighteen dollars for half an hour's worth of time spent at Twentieth and Chestnut so she (I) could run into the Shake Shack for a cheeseburger and a milkshake. He and Dave had been fraternity brothers at Rutgers, and Dan was the kind of guy I could picture sitting on his frat house's balcony, watching girls as they walked along the quad and holding up cards rating them from one to ten; the kind of guy who took it as a personal affront when a woman larger than his all-but-anorexic wife had the nerve to show herself in public.

Said wife, Marie, gave Dave a peck on the cheek and mustered a weak smile for me. Marie was the kind of lady the Dans of the world ended up with: eight years younger than her husband, slim of hip and large of bosom. The hair that fell halfway down her back was thickened by extensions, human hair glued to her own locks, then double-processed until it was a streaky blonde. "Two thousand dollars," she'd once told me, raking her bony fingers through her tresses, "but it's worth it, don't you think?" Marie worked as an interior designer, although in my head, the word "work" came with air quotes. She had a degree in theater and had built sets for student and community-theater productions before she'd landed Dan. Now she spent her time redecorating her girlfriends' beach houses. She'd drive down the Atlantic City Expressway to Ventnor or Margate or Avalon with her Mercedes SUV stuffed full of swatch books, fabrics and trims and fringes, squares of wallpaper and samples of paint. Marie had offered to give me a consultation about our place after we'd bought it, and I'd been putting her off as gracefully as I could, knowing that eventually, for the sake of Dave and Dan's friendship, Marie and her swatches would be a regular fixture in my life, and that I, too, would end up with shelves full of objets d'art, at least one statement mirror, one red-painted wall, and prints that had been chosen because they matched the furniture.

"Should we open up the Beaujolais?" asked Barry, who'd helped me choose the wine. Dan had another glass of white. Marie pulled a Skinnygirl margarita packet out of her purse and gave it to the waiter. "Did you get a lot of feedback from the story?" asked Janet, after our waitress distributed menus and ran down the specials.

I eased my feet out of my shoes, wondering where to start as I recalled some of the choicest comments—*Fat load* and *Feminazzi* and *This is why alpha men marry women from other countries.* "I need another drink," I announced. I said it without thinking about it, and certainly without thinking about the quiz I'd taken in the doctor's office, or the pills I'd been downing all day. Nobody looked shocked. In fact, nobody seemed to hear me.

"I thought the story came out great," said Barry. I glanced to my left, where Dave was sitting, and wondered if he'd heard. If he knew about the story, he hadn't said anything to me yet.

"The comments were a real treat." As if by magic, my wineglass was full again. I lifted it and sipped.

"Oh, God, do not tell me you actually read the comments!" Janet cried. "Please. How many times have I told you? You lose brain cells every time you read one."

"I know," I said, nibbling at an olive. Certainly I did know how bad online comments were—I'd read enough of them, in stories about celebrities and politicians. But why me? Who was I hurting? Why even bother going after me?

"Seems like it's been good for business," Barry offered. "Your post today got a ton of hits."

I managed a faint smile. I'd written a new version of my apology—*sorry for offending you, sorry for the nerve of showing up unairbrushed, unretouched, looking like your mom or your sister or maybe even you.*

"You read it?" I was touched.

"I read everything Janet tells me to read." He leaned across the table to brush a kiss on Janet's cheek.

"As if," she said, coloring prettily. Janet had confided once that Barry believed she was seriously out of his league, all because the guy she'd dated before him had been a professional athlete. "Never mind that he was a benchwarmer for the Eagles who got cut after three games, and that we only went out once," Janet said. That single date had been enough to convince Barry that Janet was a prize above rubies. He treated her with a kind of reverence that might have been funny, if he hadn't taken it so seriously. Janet never drove the car when they were together, never pumped gas, never lifted anything heavier than a five-pound bag of flour, and Barry never questioned her spending—on pricy shoes, on designer handbags, on a cleaning lady who came five days a week, meaning that the only housework Janet was responsible for was hand-washing her own bras, a task she refused to entrust to anyone else.

"He loves me more than I love him," she'd told me one morning while our kids splashed in her parents' pool and we ate the bagels we'd bought, still warm, on South Street.

"Really?" I'd asked.

"I think, in every couple, there's one who loves the other one more. In our case it's Barry." She looked at me from behind her fashionably gigantic sunglasses. "How about Allison and Dave? What's the history?"

I hadn't answered right away. Dave and I had met when we were both in our late twenties. He'd been newly hired at the *Examiner*, where I'd worked since I'd graduated from Franklin & Marshall with a degree in graphic design. I'd always loved drawing and painting. When I was a teenager, every artist I discovered became my favorite for a few days or weeks or months. I fell in love with Monet's dreamy pastel gardens, Modigliani's attenuated lines, the muscular swirls of van Gogh's stars, the way a Kandinsky or a Klimt could echo inside me like a piece of music or the taste of something delicious.

I loved looking at art. I loved painting. But I'd been realistic about the world and my own talents, and susceptible to my father's influence. "It's good to have a skill you can depend on," he'd told me during one drive into the city, where I was taking a figure study class at Moore College. My parents supported my dreams, but only up to a point. They'd paid for classes, for paints and canvas; they'd attended all my student shows and even sent me to art camp for two summers, where I had a chance to blow glass and try printmaking and animation, but they let me know, explicitly and in more subtle ways, that most artists couldn't make a living at art, and that they had no intention of supporting me once I was an adult.

Graphic design was a way to indulge my love of color and proportion, my desire to make something beautiful, or at least functional, to see a project through from start to finish, and still have a more or less guaranteed paycheck.

So I'd gone to Franklin & Marshall and studied art and art history, supplementing my courses in drawing and sculpture with summer courses in video and layout and graphic design. The *Examiner* had come to a recruiting session on campus; I'd dropped off my résumé, then gone to the city for an interview, then gotten hired, at a salary that was higher than anything I had the right to expect. At twenty-two, with an apartment in Old City, I'd been the pretty young thing, with a wardrobe from H&M and the French Connection and a few good pieces from Saks, a gym membership, a freezer full of Lean Cuisine, and a panini press that I used to make eggs in the morning and sandwiches at night.

After almost six years on the job, I'd met Dave. He had graduated summa from Rutgers and started his career at a small paper in a New York City suburb in New Jersey, where he'd covered five local school districts. After his second year there, he'd exposed how a school superintendent and the head of the school board were colluding to raise the superintendent's salary. By his third year, he'd won a statewide prize for his stories about how the Democratic Party was paying homeless men and women to fill out absentee ballots. Then, at the *Examiner*, I'd been tapped to design graphics for his series about the mayor's race, fitting together the text elements with pictures and, online, with video.

"Hey, thanks," he'd said, bending over in front of my oversized screen as I'd shown him my first draft. "That's really great." Unlike most of the other, dressed-down reporters, he wore a crisp, ironed shirt and a tie. He smelled good, when I was close enough to notice, and I'd already appreciated his slender-hipped, broad-shouldered body and imagined myself folded against the solidity of his chest. He'd smiled at me—white teeth, beard-shadowed cheeks. "Can I buy you a snack item?" He'd walked me out into the hall to the vending machine, where I'd selected a bag of pretzels and he'd bought himself a bottled water, and we sat in the empty stairwell, exchanging first names, then work histories. The conversation flowed naturally into an invitation to meet at a bar the next night. Drinks became dinner at Percy Street Barbecue, where we sat over plates of ribs and Mason jars of spiked lemonade, talking about our parents, our schools, which bones we'd broken (his leg, my wrist), and our shared love of Dire Straits and Warren Zevon. We'd both been startled when our waiter had cruised by our table to announce that it was last call. We'd talked from six o'clock that night until two in the morning.

Within a week, we were a couple. I imagined he'd only get more successful as time went by. Neither of us believed that newspapers were going anywhere or that, eventually, my funny, dashed-off blog posts would be more valuable than his ability to wrest a great (or damning) quote out of a politician or a criminal, to write fast on deadline, to think of witty headlines and slyly funny photo captions, or to bide his time for months, filing Freedom of Information Act requests, gathering documents, hunting down sources, doing the kind of reporting the *Examiner* ended up not being able to afford anymore. He would be the breadwinner, I would be the homemaker . . . only now, as I looked at him, with his eyes the same shade as Ellie's and the circles that had been underneath them since her birth, I marveled at how everything had changed, and wondered if our marriage could survive it.

"Ma'am?" I blinked. The waitress stared down at me, pen and pad in hand. Somehow, my wineglass was empty. I'd had an oyster—Dan had ordered two dozen of them—and a single slice of bread, but nothing else.

"Oh . . . um . . ." I fumbled for my menu, doing the quickstep between what I wanted (scalloped potatoes and slow-roasted pork shoulder) and what I should allow myself (steamed asparagus, grilled salmon). I settled on the stuffed pork chop.

"Very good," she said, and vanished. I turned back to Janet, who was gossiping with Dave and Barry about whether the pretty twenty-four-year-old pre-K teacher with the tattoos we could sometimes glimpse under the sleeves of her vintage blouses had actually worn nipple rings to Parents' Night.

The food arrived. I used my heavy steak knife to slice into the glistening meat. A puddle of juice pooled underneath the pork chop. I squeezed my eyes shut and made myself nibble a tiny sliver.

"Not hungry?" Janet asked. She'd ordered the pork shoulder

dish with a lot of garlic—per its name, Cochon was heavy on the pig—and the smell was making me queasy.

"I think I already drank my calories," I said. The truth was, I hadn't been hungry much lately, a strange situation for a girl who'd always loved her food. Nothing looked good, and the effort of purchasing groceries, preparing a meal, setting the table, and washing the dishes seemed monumental. I'd heat up organic chicken nuggets for Eloise and keep the freezer stocked with Trader Joe's heat-and-eat meals that Dave could prepare on the nights I was stuck at my computer, writing or editing or interacting with Ladiesroom's readers. For myself, I'd grab a yogurt or a bowl of cereal. The irony of the Internet comments was that I was thinner now than I'd been in years, but I didn't look good, and I knew it. My complexion had taken on a grayish undertone; my flesh—even if there wasn't as much as usual—seemed to sag and hang.

Janet touched my arm. I looked up, startled. We were good friends, but neither of us was the touchy-feely type. "Are you okay?" she asked quietly.

I bent my head. "I'm scared," I said quietly.

"Of what?" Janet asked, looking worried. "What's wrong?"

"Hey, honey, can we get that Pinot down here?" Dan asked. I reached out and managed only to knock the bottle onto the floor. There were gasps, a flurry of fast motion, Skinny Marie thrusting herself away from the spill like it was toxic. A waiter and a waitress hurried over with rags. "I'm sorry," I whispered. Nobody appeared to hear me. "Oh, this'll never come out of silk," Marie was fretting, and Janet was asking, "Could you bring us some club soda, please?" and Barry was patting Marie's back, saying "No big deal," and, from the other side of the table, Dave was looking at me with his eyes narrowed and his lips compressed.

"It was an accident," I said. My voice came out too loud, almost a shout.

"It's okay." Dave sounded cool. "It happens." Which, of course, was what we said to Ellie when she wet the bed.

Eventually, the tablecloth got changed and the worst of the damage was mopped up. Marie had returned from the ladies' room, where she'd fled with a carafe of club soda and an offended look on her face, and I'd apologized half a dozen times, my face hot as a griddle, wilting underneath my husband's disapproval. I'd just tried to restart the conversation, asking Janet and Barry about the twins' hockey season, a topic guaranteed to take up at least ten minutes of their time, when I heard Marie's high-pitched voice from the opposite side of the table.

"Did you all hear about that Everleigh Connor?" she asked. I looked up to see Dave pouring the last bit of the last bottle of red into his glass. Everleigh Connor was a reality-TV star who'd launched her career on one of those shows about the private lives of rich people—she'd been the teenage daughter of one of the face-lifted fortysomething moms who were the ostensible stars of the show. Then she'd appeared in a sex tape—she put out some statement about how the tape was a private memento she and her boyfriend had made that had been stolen from a safe in her house, but it was obvious that the tape had been made with a hired porn star, not a boyfriend, and that she, her mother, and their PR firm had managed every step of its release. From there, Everleigh had gotten and dumped a boyfriend in the NFL, landed a small role on a network drama, and had most recently become the Las Vegas bride of an eighteen-year-old pop star.

"What happened?" I asked . . . Did my voice sound the tiniest bit slurry?

Marie smiled. "You didn't hear? OMG. It's all over Twitter!"

"What?" There. It was impossible to slur on words of one syllable. To reward myself for sounding coherent, I had another sip of wine.

"She's pregnant," said Dave, directly to me.

"They're saying that she basically forced Alex to put a ring on it," said Barry.

Janet rolled her eyes. "My husband the twelve-year-old girl. 'Put a ring on it,' Bar? Really?"

I looked down the table at my husband. He looked back at me, his eyes meeting mine, one eyebrow lifted, like he was daring me to say something.

I felt as if I'd been slapped, having him give me that look, when I wasn't the one sending dozens of chatty, flirty e-mails to someone who was not my spouse. I raised my chin, suddenly furious . . . and sober. Or at least it felt that way. "Honey, you should tell everyone about your big story. The one about the casino." For months, Dave had been tracking down rumors about which consortium would be the next to put a casino in Philadelphia, about where they'd buy, what they'd build, which neighborhood could brace for the boom and the nuisance of dozens of buses loaded with slot-machine-playing, quarter-toting retirees and well-lubricated frat boys rolling through its streets each day.

"Seriously, Dave-O, give me a tip," said Dan. "We build a parking lot in the right place, we're golden."

"Dave's got all the best sources," I said, my tongue loose and reckless. "Who's that woman in the mayor's office you're always talking with? Lindy someone?"

From across the table I thought I saw my husband flinch, and saw hurt in his hooded eyes.

"She's a wonderful source, isn't she?" I asked. "What's the word . . . 'forthcoming'? Is that it? You're the word guy, right?"

Janet was looking worried. Barry was, too. I got myself away from the table in a series of small steps: pushing my palms against the edge, unlocking my knees, levering myself upright, making my way carefully around my chair, squinting through the dimly lit restaurant past groups of laughing, red-faced men with empty bottles lining their tables, until I found the bathroom, a spacious stall for just one, thank God. I locked the door and, without turning on the lights, sat on the toilet and rested my cheek against the cool stainless steel of the toilet-paper dispenser, feeling stunned and empty and furious.

There was a gentle tap at the door. "Allie?" Janet said, her voice a whisper. "Are you okay?"

"I'm fine," I told her. "Just a little too much wine. I'll be right out." My heart was thudding; my temples were pounding. My purse was in my hands. My hands were in my purse. My new little friends were in their bottle. I shook one of them out into my palm, craving the comfort they would give me, the easing-toward-sleep feeling that would take away the scalding hurt, the shame of the way Dave had looked at me.

Nobody knew this—not Janet, not my parents, not anyone—but after Dave and I had been dating for a little over a year, my period, typically regular, had failed to arrive. I was on the pill, and I'd always remembered to take it, but I knew, from my tender breasts to the way I woke up nauseated by the smell of coffee, what had happened. I'd freaked out and gone to Dave in a panic, watching his face turn pale and his lips tighten until they were almost invisible as I'd laid out the options: I could have the baby and place it for adoption. I could have the baby and raise it myself. Or we could get married.

By then, we'd been seeing each other exclusively for months. The Pablo Neruda girl was gone—or, at least, I'd never seen evidence of another female in his apartment, or on his phone (which I had guiltily checked once). We'd been saying "I love you" and talking, casually, about which neighborhoods we liked, whether we preferred condos in the new high-rises in Washington Square West or a row house in Society Hill or Bella Vista. There had been no explicit promises, we were spending three or four nights a week at my place but not yet living together, we had not plighted our troth nor promised our future, and I would never have tried to trick Dave, or trap him by getting knocked up accidentally on purpose. Still, I'd been confident that, in light of the reality of our situation, he would do the thing he'd been planning on doing, albeit on a somewhat expedited schedule.

Instead of looking happy, though, Dave had pinched the bridge of his nose between finger and thumb and looked everywhere but at me after I'd laid out the news.

"You wouldn't get an abortion?" he had asked. We were in my walk-up apartment on Arch Street, Dave on my denim-covered couch, me in the armchair I'd inherited from my mother and had slipcovered in a pricy French toile I'd found on Fabric Row. My cute little living room, perfect for two, was in no way big enough for three. Even the thought of dragging a stroller up three flights of stairs left me exhausted. My eat-in kitchen would be just a kitchen if I had to add a high chair; my bathroom had a luxurious shower, with extra showerheads poking out of the walls, but no bathtub. It was all entirely unsuitable for a baby.

"I don't know," I said slowly. I was certainly pro-choice in my beliefs—I'd gotten my well-woman checkups and my contraception at Planned Parenthood since I was an undergraduate, and I'd been supporting them with regular, if modest, donations since I'd gotten my job—but in my mind, it was a baby, Dave's and mine, and I could no more consider aborting it than I could hurting myself, or hurting him.

The silence stretched out until I heard Dave give a slow sigh. "Well, then," he said, "let's get hitched." It was not, needless to say, the proposal of my dreams . . . but Dave was the man of my dreams, and, surely, the life we would build together would be the stuff I had dreamed about, the life I had always wanted, a partnership with a man I adored and admired. I flung my arms around his neck and kissed him and said, "Yes."

Four weeks later, with a hastily purchased one-karat princess-cut diamond ring on my finger and the memory of the Indomitable Doreen's stiff smile and my mother's insulting exuberance at our meet-the-parents-slash-engagement party still crisp and bright in my mind, I'd gone to my obstetrician and learned, during the ultrasound, that there was an egg sac, but no heartbeat. No baby. My body, it seemed, had ended the pregnancy before it really started. He gave me four pills; I went home and took them, then endured the worst cramps and bleeding of my life while Dave fetched me hot-water bottles and shots of brandy. Half-drunk, with my fifth industrial-strength sanitary napkin stuck into my high-waisted cotton briefs, I'd said, "We don't have to go through with it now, if you don't want to. I won't hold you to anything. You're free."

"Don't be crazy," Dave had said. He'd been so tender as he helped me into the shower. He washed my hair, soaped my body with my favorite vanilla-scented body wash, and then smoothed lotion on my arms and legs before bundling me into a warm towel, putting me into my pajamas, and tucking me into bed. I'd hung my future on that night. Whenever I'd had doubts, whenever he seemed quiet, or moody, or distant, I remembered the smell of vanilla and brandy, and how gentle he'd been, how kind, how he hadn't considered, even for a minute, the possibility that he could be rid of me.

"Allison?" Janet's voice was worried. "Tell me you're okay or I'm going to get a manager and have them unlock the door."

"I'm fine. I'm okay," I rasped. *I'm fine*, I told myself, even as a voice inside whispered, softly but firmly, that I was a world away from fine, that I was not okay at all.

FIVE

I splashed water on my face, freshened my lipstick, and crammed my feet back into my shoes. With Janet's help, I found the waiters, gave them instructions, and led the crowd in "Happy Birthday" after the cake I'd ordered from Isgro's, with buttercream icing and a flaming crown of candles, was brought to the table. I clapped when Dave blew out all the candles, without letting myself wonder what he might have wished for, and used my fork to push bits of cake and frosting around my plate. I laughed at the jokes, raised my glass in a toast, and discreetly managed the payment of the check. I kissed Dan and Marie goodbye, let Barry hug me, and whispered, "I'm okay. I promise," after Janet pulled me into a hug and said, "You know I'm here if you want to talk about anything."

The ride home was silent, as if we'd both tacitly agreed not to fight until we were back at the house. I paid Katrina, Dave drove to her dorm, and I crept past Ellie's bedroom and into my own, shucking off my dress and my painful undergarments, then pulling on a T-shirt that dated back to the 1990s and was where sexy went to die. I had planned on feigning sleep by the time Dave returned from the drop-off, but he turned on the lights and waited at the door until I sat up.

"Happy birthday," I said, blinking at him. In my dreams I'd been in the bathtub, with Dave kneeling beside me, rubbing a warm washcloth against my shoulders, telling me that he loved me.

"What was that about?" he demanded.

I could have been coy, asking what he was talking about. Instead, I said, "Why don't you tell me?"

He stared in my direction, hands jammed in the pockets of his suit pants, jaw jutting.

"Come on," I sighed. "L. McIntyre? Lindsay? Linds? The one you e-mail with all day long?"

I watched as one of his hands went to his cheek and started rubbing. When he finally managed to speak, his voice was strangled. "It's not like that."

"Oh? Then what's it like?"

"We talk," he said, sounding indignant. Somehow, I didn't think he was lying. I knew how he looked when he lied, how he'd rock from his heels to his toes, how his voice would rise. There was no shifting and no squeaking. Just Dave, looking wretched. "She's a friend."

I didn't reply, or let my face show my relief.

"This hasn't been easy for me." Dave's eyes were wide, his face arranged in his little-boy-wants-a-cookie expression, the one that usually made me feel sympathetic.

"Which part?" I asked, hearing the edge in my voice.

"Living here," Dave said.

"What do you mean?" I was honestly bewildered. "You were the one who wanted to move. You were the one who complained all the time about us being in a starter house, and how you didn't want to raise Ellie in the city." I would have been happy to stay. I loved our little house, with its spiral staircase, the fireplace in the kitchen that contractors had uncovered when they'd installed our new dishwasher, the French doors that opened onto a narrow brick walkway, and a niche that was the perfect size for a grill and a hanging basket of impatiens that I'd set on the ground when we cooked.

Without a word, Dave turned, walked into the bathroom, and shut the door. I could hear water running, could picture him squeezing more toothpaste than he needed from the center of the tube, then leaving the tube uncapped and spit and toothpaste drips inside the sink, because buying the toothpaste and cleaning the sink were my jobs. That was the deal we'd made, the terms we'd both agreed on, before everything had changed.

Not fair, I thought, and was suddenly so angry that I jumped out of bed and knocked—pounded—on the door. "Do you think I'm happy like this? Doing everything?" I asked. "I'm the one who's paying the mortgage. I'm the one who takes care of Ellie. I'm the one who's in charge of her schedule, and our social life, and keeping the house clean and making sure the car gets inspected. Don't you think I get tired? That maybe I'd like someone to talk to? Someone to take me to lunch?"

His voice came through the door, maddeningly calm. "You seem to be doing just fine by yourself."

My fingers curled into fists. "So, what? I should complain more, so you know that I'm unhappy? Well, consider this an official update: I'm unhappy."

"Keep your voice down," Dave hissed as he opened the door. In his white T-shirt and boxer shorts, with his hair combed away from his forehead, exposing the growing wings of skin on his temples, he had a narrow, aquiline appeal, and I knew that if we were to split, it would take him approximately ten minutes to replace me. "You just don't seem very interested in hearing from me."

"I'm just . . . I'm overwhelmed. It's all too much. I need you to help me." I meant to sound sincere, but I thought I'd only managed sullen. Reaching out, I let my fingertips brush his forearm, feeling the soft hair, the warm skin, remembering that I used to spend hours dreaming of when he would touch me again, happy weekends when we barely got out of bed, delighting in each other's bodies.

"I'm busy, too." He went to the bed, pulled off a blanket and two pillows, and stood, facing me, with the bedding bundled in his arms. "I'm basically doing the work of three people now. And blogging and answering e-mail, and doing those goddamn live chats." He rubbed at his cheek again. "I'll help you as much as I can, but full-time is full-time."

"I can't keep doing all of this," I said. There were tears on my cheeks. I scrubbed them away. "I can't. There's my work, my dad, my mom, and everything with Ellie, and the house, and it's all just too much, Dave."

He tilted his head, skewering me with his gaze. "Just a thought here, but do you think maybe the pills are part of the problem?"

My breath froze in my throat. My hands turned to ice. I couldn't move. Had he guessed the extent of it, how many pills I was taking, how many different doctors were prescribing how many different things, and how I'd come to depend on medication to get through my days? "What are you talking about?" I asked.

He looked at me for a long moment. I felt myself cringing, wondering what he'd say . . . but instead of confronting me with what he knew or what he'd guessed, he said, "I need to get some sleep."

"David . . ." He turned toward the door. I followed him into the guest room, reaching for him and not quite touching his shirt. "I'm sor—," I started to say, then stopped when I realized that I didn't know what I was apologizing for. Was I sorry that I wasn't the one he wanted to talk to, to share his life with? Was I sorry I was taking so many pills, or just sorry that I'd gotten caught?

"Do you think we should go to counseling?" I asked, hating how timid I sounded. "Maybe we just need to sit down with someone and figure it all out."

He shrugged, pulling back the covers on the guest-room bed. There was a phone charger plugged into the wall and a stack of *Sports Illustrated* and *ESPN: The Magazine* on the floor beside the bed, where I'd meant to put a table. He had more or less moved in here, and somehow I'd let it happen.

"Look, I'm sorry if I seem a little spacey, but things have been so stressful," I said. "Did you see what people were saying about me in the comments on that story?" I tried to sound like I was joking, like it didn't really bother me. "Jesus, who's reading the paper these days? A bunch of sixteen-year-old virgins stockpiling guns in their parents' basements?" I wanted to tell him how much the comments hurt me, and how much I wanted him to need me, to want me in his life, the way my own parents had not. I wanted to tell him why I needed the pills, and maybe even ask him for help . . . because, honestly, it was starting to scare me, how many of them I took, and how I couldn't imagine getting through a day without them.

"What an encouraging thought," he said. "Given that newspaper readers are my employers."

I pressed my lips together. I wanted to cry. I wanted to scream. I wanted to take pills until I couldn't feel anything anymore. I wanted to hate him, wanted to be angry enough to throw something heavy and sharp at his face, but I wasn't. Maybe because I loved him . . . or maybe it wasn't love so much as knowledge, or time, something weedy and unlovely and impossible to kill; the cockroach of emotions, a feeling that could survive even nuclear war. We had spent the past ten years of our lives together, and now every place I went, every song I heard, all of my familiar phrases and jokes, Ellie's bedtime ritual (three kisses on her forehead and a quick spritz of monster spray), all of it I'd seen or heard or experienced or created with my husband. At our favorite restaurants I knew what he'd order, and then what I'd convince him to order by saying *I just want a few bites,* after which I would end up devouring it. I knew which pump he'd pull up to at the gas station, which glaze he liked on the chicken at Federal Donuts, and how he'd always forget his mother's birthday and have to spend a hundred dollars on flowers at the last minute unless I reminded him to get her a gift. I was myself, but, I realized as I looked at his silhouette, I was also half of a marriage. How could I live a life where the person who'd built and experienced and created it alongside me, the person who'd seen me in a hundred different moods, at my highest, at my lowest, in the middle of a C-section with my uterus laid out on my belly, was gone?

With stiff jerks of his arms, Dave pulled the decorative pillows off the guest-room bed and tossed them on the floor. "I'm going to sleep," he announced.

"Wait," I said. He didn't answer, just lay on the bed, on his side, knees drawn up toward his chest, hands folded. He might as well have donned a sandwich board reading CLOSED. "Dave." He didn't answer. I stood there, wringing my hands, and then I stepped back out into the hallway and closed the door. After the miscarriage, he was the one who'd handled the business of telling both sets of parents that there would still be a wedding but there wouldn't be a baby. I'd never asked what he'd said, and all he told me was, "There's nothing for you to worry about. Just concentrate on getting better." He'd never made me feel like I'd trapped him, and, if his parents had decided I was a gold digger and told him this was his chance to slip free of the handcuffs and make a better choice, he'd never let me hear about it.

I walked back to the master bedroom, remembering when Ellie was six weeks old and barely sleeping two hours at a time and Dave had found, on his own, a little cottage at Bethany Beach. "Maybe the sound of the water will calm her down," he'd said, and I'd been so frayed, so exhausted, shuffling through my days like a zombie in need of a shower, that I'd agreed, thinking that anything had to be better than the nights of screams we'd endured. Dave had packed for all three of us, considerately choosing only my most comfortable leggings and sweatpants, nothing with an actual waistband or buttons or zippers, because my scar was still tender and my actual waist was still buried under rolls of water weight and pregnancy bloat. He'd picked out onesies and tiny cotton pants for Ellie, as well as the dye-and-scent-free detergent we washed her stuff in; he'd packed my breast pump and bottles and nipples and pacifiers, rattles and board books and burp cloths and diaper cream and the dozens of items, big and small, that the baby required. He had loaded up the little Honda, slotting the Pack 'n Play and the suitcases, the bassinet and the jogging stroller into the trunk as if expertly engineering a game of Tetris.

In the cottage, a pair of sunwashed rooms plus a galley kitchen, he'd instructed me to nap on the daybed on the porch while Ellie, who'd fallen asleep after a hundred miles of wailing, slept in her car seat beside me, and he made the beds and set up the Pack 'n Play. He'd held the baby while I swam. The cottage was on the bay, and there was a little island, just a clump of trees and shrubs and wild blackberries, maybe a quarter of a mile out. I'd done the crawl all the way there, then breast-stroked back, feeling my heart beating hard, the muscles of my chest and shoulders working, and then I'd flipped on my back and let the salt water buoy me and the waves rock me. "Don't worry, I've got her," he said after I'd rinsed off in the outdoor shower and had nursed Ellie on the porch. He clipped her into the jogging stroller and trotted off to town, returning an hour later with cartons full of shrimp and fries, clams and coleslaw— a feast, exactly what I was craving. "I've got her," he said again that night, and I'd collapsed onto the crisp sheets just after seven, falling almost instantly into the deepest sleep I could remember.

When I woke up to the rosy glow of the sunrise, it was just after five in the morning. Ellie had slept through the night— there she was, blinking calmly from the center of the bed, where Dave had put her. He was on her other side in his familiar po-sition, curled up with his knees pulled toward his chest, in his T-shirt and his boxers, dark hair sticking up in unruly cowlicks, breathing deeply, not quite snoring as he slept. I could hear the sound of the waves through the window, and of Ellie smacking her lips while she wiggled her fingers in the air and stared as if they were the best movie she'd ever seen. *Now we are three,* I thought. That thought filled me with such unalloyed delight that it took my breath away. This was what it meant to be a family; all three of us, so close. This was what I'd worked for and wanted since I was a little girl.

Now my husband was taking some other woman to lunch. He thought that I was spacey. No, actually, he thought I was a junkie. Worse, he was discontented with his life, our life, in a way I couldn't understand and, thus, couldn't fix. Had we ever

SIX

"Allison?"

"Yes, Mom?" I called toward the car's speakers as I steered, one-handed, into the parking lot of BouncyTime, where the birthday party for a classmate of Ellie's named (I was almost positive) Jayden was starting in ten minutes. It was a miserable April day, gray-skied and windy, with a dispirited rain slopping down.

"Are you almost here?" she asked in a quivering voice.

Dave sat next to me, stiff and silent as one of those inflatable man-shaped balloons that drivers in California buy so they can use the high-occupancy-vehicle lanes. It had been several weeks since his birthday dinner, but we hadn't talked about anything more substantive than whether we were running out of milk or if I'd remembered to make the car insurance payment. I took my pills, he, presumably, found comfort in conversation with L. McIntyre, and we tried to be polite to each other, especially in front of our daughter. Said daughter was in the backseat, chatting with her friend Hank.

"If you are going to put something in your nose," I heard Ellie announce, "it should not be a Barbie shoe."

"Okay," Hank snuffled. Hank was a pale and narrow-faced

little boy with a ring of whitish crust around his eyes and mouth. He was going on six, the same as my daughter, but thanks to his allergies to eggs, wheat, dairy, shellfish, and pet dander, he was the size of a three-year-old and he sniffled nonstop.

How did Ellie even know what a Barbie doll was? I wondered as I maneuvered into a parking spot between a Jaguar and a minivan. I wasn't sure, but I bet that I had Dave's mother, the Indomitable Doreen, to thank. Doreen scoffed at my "notions," as she called them, about organic food, gender-neutral toys, and limiting Eloise's TV time. Doreen was tall, broad-shouldered, and slim, with the same fair complexion that her sons had inherited and the same cropped dark hair, although I suspected she dyed it. Doreen had raised three boys and had been waiting for years to have a girl child to dote upon. Whenever Doreen got my daughter alone, she'd let her gorge on ice cream and candy. They would stay up all night in Doreen's silk-sheeted king-sized bed, playing Casino and watching *Gilligan's Island* and God only knew what else. "Lighten up," Doreen would tell me, sometimes with a good-natured (but still painful) sock on the shoulder, when I politely reminded her that Ellie did better when she kept to her bedtime schedule, or mentioned that Dave and I gave her an allowance for doing her chores, and that when she slipped our daughter twenty bucks it tended to undermine our authority. "Calm down, or you're going to make yourself crazy!"

I knew that my mother-in-law meant well. She'd never talked about whether she'd missed the job she gave up once her sons were born, but I wondered if she had, and if she saw how I had struggled, first as a full-time stay-at-home mother and now as a stay-at-home mom with a part-time (inching ever closer to full-time) job. I could have asked, but the truth was, things hadn't been great between us since I learned that she'd read my birth plan out loud to her book club. In retrospect, the plan might have been a little excessive—it was eight pages long and spelled out everything from the music I wanted to how I didn't want any external interventions, including an epidural, and had gone on, at length, about the necessity for a "peaceful birthing environment"—but that did not mean I wanted the six members of Words and Wine laughing at me over copies of Sue Monk Kidd's latest.

In the backseat, Ellie was regaling Hank with the story of the dead squirrel she'd seen at the corner of South Street during one of our visits to the city. "Its middle was all crumpled, and there was BLOOD on its BOTTOM," she said, as Hank mouth-breathed in horror.

"Hey, El, I'm not sure that's appropriate," I said.

Ellie paused, gnawing at her lower lip. Then she turned to Hank and said, in such a perfect lady-at-a-cocktail-party tone that both Dave and I smiled, "And what are your plans for the weekend?"

I put the car in park and waited until Hank said, "I don't know."

" 'Plans for the weekend' just means what you are going to do," Ellie explained. "Like, you could say, 'Watch *Sam & Cat*,' or maybe 'Put all your nail polishes into teams.' "

"I don't have nail polishes," Hank said wistfully.

The phone rang again. I ignored it, thinking that at least, unlike my mother, Doreen didn't need instructions for the most basic tasks—calling the oil company to have the tank refilled, remembering to change the car's windshield wipers instead of just, as she'd once done, buying a new car. If my father had still been himself, I would have asked how he dealt with her, even though I suspected the answer probably involved sex.

If I'd had time I would have helped more, but in the six weeks since the *Journal* story had run, traffic to Ladiesroom.com had increased by more than two hundred percent, and Sarah had started hinting that I should think about writing not just five times a week but every day. I'd also gotten a few queries from other outlets—some websites, two in-print magazines, and a cable TV shout-show—asking if I'd want to write or blog or dispense online or on-the-air commentary. So far, I'd turned them all down, but I suspected that if Sarah learned about the offers she'd encourage me to take them, knowing it would only help build Ladiesroom's brand.

Ideally, Dave would have taken over Ellie duties a few nights a week, and maybe even spared an hour each week for counseling, but Dave, bless his heart, had declined both of those requests and instead signed up for another marathon. I'd tried not to read too deeply into the symbolism, about how he'd be spending hours each week literally running away from his wife and his daughter, and I'd assiduously avoided Googling L. McIntyre's name to see if she, too, would be participating in the race, thus avoiding the need to imagine the two of them logging training runs along the Schuylkill, trotting side by side along the tree-canopied paths of the Wissahickon. Instead of complaining, I'd bumped my housekeeper up to two days a week, hired a backup sitter who could work nights and weekends, and enrolled Ellie in after-school activities every day but Thursday—tumbling, swimming, Clay Club, even a class on "iPad mastery." It was heartbreaking, but the more she was out of the house, the more smoothly things ran inside of it. She'd even found a new best friend. Hank did most of the same activities she did—his mom was a urologist who worked full-time. Ellie had all but adopted Hank, who was even more sensitive and high-strung than she was, and appointed herself as his unofficial advisor and life coach.

"If you need to go to the potty, just ask me," I heard her saying as she unhitched herself from her booster seat, then reached
over to help Hank with his buckles. "I've been to probably a billion parties here before."

I helped Ellie out of the car, handed Dave the birthday boy's
gift, and then stood with him in the parking lot, feeling as if
we'd been shoved onstage without a script. Normally, we would
have kissed before I drove away—just a little peck, a quick brush,
enough for me to get a whiff of his scent, which I still found
intoxicating, and then we'd separate. Instead, Dave gave me a
half wave and a "See ya" before shepherding the kids through
the front doors. Part of me wanted to run after him and hug
him, taking strength from even an instant of physical connection. Another part of me felt like giving him the finger. Since
the birthday-night fight, Dave had barely touched me, and he'd
continued to spend his nights in the guest bedroom. I imagined
him under the covers, curled on his side with that goddamned
BlackBerry pressed against his ear, talking to his work wife,
L. McIntyre, while his real wife was alone in bed down the hall,
staring up into the darkness, sometimes crying, until the narcotics allowed her to fall asleep.

I sat behind the wheel as the doors closed behind Dave and
Hank and Ellie, feeling hollow underneath the euphoria the
pills guaranteed. At least I still had that—a guaranteed pick-
me-up at the start of the day; a comfort at the end. With a pill
or two (or three, or four) coursing through my bloodstream, I
felt calm, energetic, in control, as if I could manage work and
being a good mother and a good daughter, keeping the house
running and the refrigerator stocked and even performing the

occasional stint as a chaperone during a Stonefield trip to the Art Museum.

The bad news was that Dr. Andi was being far stingier with the Oxy handouts than she'd been with the Vicodin. "You want to be careful with this stuff," she'd said the first time I called for another prescription. "It's seriously addictive."

"Oh, I will be," I promised. I could keep that promise easily because, during one of my daily rounds of the gossip websites that I wasted too much time on, I'd come across a story I at first assumed had to be fake. "Introducing Penny Lane: the Top Secret Website Where You Can Buy Any Drug You Want." *No way,* I'd thought, but the story at least made the site sound legitimate as it described a kind of Amazon.com for illegal substances. You had to use anonymizing software to get to the site, and use encryption to register. Once you'd cleared those hurdles, you could, allegedly, order anything you wanted—anything from pot to Viagra to painkillers to heroin. You'd send the vendors your real name and address—encrypted, of course—and payment via a new kind of online-only currency, and the vendors would send you the goods.

I figured it had to be a scam . . . but what did I have to lose? Other than some money. And my freedom, I assumed, if you could be jailed for trying to buy prescription drugs on the Internet, but that was a risk I decided I was willing to take. I spent about ten seconds wondering if anyone would recognize my name, then decided that the overlap between illegal drug dealers and Ladiesroom.com readers was probably tiny. Downloading the software took less than a minute; learning how to use it took maybe five minutes more. The hard part was figuring out how to trade dollars for the e-coins the site used instead of cash. It took me the better part of another week to register the bank account I'd established for my own personal use, an account at a different bank from the one Dave and I used. I'd then had to register with yet another website to send my e-currency to my account at Penny Lane. Once I'd picked a screen name ("HarleyQueen," a play on the name of one of the sexy lady villains in *Batman*) and loaded a thousand dollars' worth of cash into my account, I started wandering through the virtual aisles, amazed at what was for sale. Hallucinogens. Amphetamines. Dissociatives, whatever they were. Viagra and Cialis, Ecstasy and Special K and crystal meth. I'd clicked on "Opiods," and there was everything—your Percocet, your Vicodin, your Tylenol with codeine. With my mouth open in disbelief, I put twenty Oxy-Contin pills into my cart, then browsed around, pricing Vicodin from India and wondering, again, whether this could possibly be legitimate.

I figured that I'd be sent fakes, if the vendors bothered sending anything at all. Then the first delivery arrived. The pills were in a tiny plastic bag that had been encased in a layer of bubble wrap and folded and tucked into an Altoids tin. They looked exactly like the ones I'd been prescribed and, according to Pillfinder.com, they appeared to be exactly what I'd paid for. Cautiously, I slipped one underneath my tongue, waiting for the familiar bitterness. It arrived right on schedule, but, still, I was seized with dread. What if it was a clever fake? What if I'd taken poison? What if Ellie came home and found me convulsing on the kitchen floor? But ten minutes later I was dreamy-eyed and practically floating around the kitchen. Since then, my use had ramped up slightly (or maybe "considerably" would be more accurate) . . . but if I could get as many pills as I wanted whenever I wanted them, if I could afford my vices, and if the whole transaction felt as risky as ordering a bra from Victoria's Secret, what did it matter?

At a stoplight, I punched in my mother's number. "Daddy

just woke up," she said. "He thinks he needs to get dressed to go to the airport. I've been telling him and telling him . . ."

"Okay, Mom."

". . . but he won't listen. I didn't get any sleep last night. He kept shaking me, or turning on his phone and shining it in my eyes. At three a.m. he started packing his suitcase . . ."

"I'm ten minutes away," I said, mentally canceling the pit stop I'd planned at Starbucks (or, if I was being honest, at McDonald's). I'd spent so much time trying to coax a few bites of cereal into Eloise's mouth that I hadn't had time for my own breakfast. I deserved a hash brown. Hash brown, singular, I told myself, and definitely no sausage biscuit.

"Ronnie!" I could hear my dad yelling. "Where's the cab?"

"Put him on the phone with me," I told her, figuring it couldn't hurt.

A minute later, my father was growling "Who's this?" into my ear.

"Daddy, it's Allison. Mom says you need a ride?" I hadn't been sure whether it was a good idea to play along with someone suffering from early-stage Alzheimer's and dementia—which my mother, God love her, pronounced *dee-men-she-ah*—but Dad's doctor said it was all right to indulge him up to a point. "A therapeutic lie" was what he'd called it. Translation: whatever worked.

"Allison," said my father. I held my breath. Last Saturday, when I'd sent Eloise to Hank's house for a playdate and invited my parents over for brunch, he'd known who I was, but sometimes he thought I was his sister and called me Joyce. I knew that the day was coming when he wouldn't know me at all, but I prayed it hadn't come yet, not so much for my sake, but for my mother's.

My parents had met when my mom was eighteen-year-old

Ronnie Feldman, with an adorable pout and soft brown eyes, a cute little figure and shiny black hair, and my dad was twenty-eight, a college graduate who'd served for two years as an information officer in the army, stationed in Korea, and was finishing up his MBA at Penn. She'd been a CIT at the summer camp he'd attended, and he was back for a ten-year reunion. She was still in high school, still riding her ten-speed with a wire basket embellished with plastic flowers between the handlebars and buying her clothes in the children's department. Little Ronnie, who'd dotted the "i" of her name with a heart, who'd never lived on her own, never paid a bill, and never held a job outside of being a not-quite counselor at Camp Wah-Na-Wee-Naw in the Poconos; Little Ronnie with her tanned legs and pert chin and the ponytail she tied in red-and-white ribbons—camp colors, of course—had married him two summers later, going straight from her parents' house to the apartment my dad had rented, where she played house until I came along and it stopped being a game. There had always been a man to take care of her, first her own father, then mine. My mother never had any reasons to master the fundamentals of adulthood—balancing a checkbook, registering a car, buying a house. My dad had taken care of everything. Pretty Little Head, or PLH, was what Dave and I called my mom in happier times, when we'd still had a private language of jokes with each other, as in "Don't worry your pretty little head about a thing."

"Are you all packed?" my father asked.

So he thought I was coming on this imaginary trip. "All packed and ready to go."

"I'm proud of you," he said, his voice thick, the way it got after he'd had the second of his two pre-dinner martinis. "I hope you'll have fun in college. Blow off some steam! Put down the paints and go to some parties! Meet some nice boys! College isn't just for book learning, you know."

So he thought he was taking me to college. At a red light, I took a deep breath, remembering that trip, how we'd stopped for milkshakes and he'd given me a pained and heartbreakingly sweet speech about how college boys would want certain things, and how, at parties, I shouldn't ever put my drink down lest some knave try to "slip me a mickey," and how I should be careful about what I wore. "I know that's not a very modern thing to say," my dad had told me, and I'd been so embarrassed when he used the phrase "it's just their nature" that I'd spent the next ten minutes hiding in the bathroom.

I stepped on the gas and tried not to think about what it would be like when the time came to drive him to an assisted-living facility, or a nursing home, or whatever he'd end up requiring. No milkshakes; no speeches about how he should avoid the divorcées with hungry eyes; no joking or resigned tenderness about how this was just what happened: little birds left the nest. It was all wrong, I thought, remembering how impressive my dad had looked offering my new roommate his hand, and how he'd helped me make my bed. I cleared my throat so he wouldn't be able to tell that I was crying. "I'm just grabbing some coffee, and then I'll be ready to go."

"Sounds good, princess." He sounded jovial, hearty, so completely himself. I thought, not for the first time, that maybe it would have been better if he'd just died, a thunderclap heart attack, an artery bursting in his brain, a peaceful exit in the middle of the night, in his own bed, after his favorite meal, with my mom beside him. We'd have mourned, then moved on. This was a slow-motion catastrophe, death by a thousand cuts.

"Why don't you watch CNBC?" I said, forcing cheeriness into my voice. "Check your stocks. Let Mom take a shower. I'll be there as soon as I can." His love of CNBC was one of the things he'd retained, even as he slipped further and further down the rabbit hole. In my parents' house, the television in the den was always on, at a volume just slightly less than deafening, tuned to the financial news so my dad could keep an eye on his portfolio, which was, in fact, being managed by his former protégé, a man named Don Ettlinger, who worked in Center City and who remembered me from when I was a girl.

"Okay, then. I'll see you when I see you." There was a thumping sound as he set the phone down—sometimes he'd get confused, then angry, when he went to hang up the phone and discovered that cell phones had no cradles, just chargers. I clenched my hands on the steering wheel. When I was fourteen, after my complexion had calmed down and the rest of my features had caught up with my nose, a boy asked me out to a movie. His mother drove us there. We spent the next two hours palm to sticky palm, eyes on the screen, each, undoubtedly, waiting for the other to make a move. My father picked us up and drove us home. In the kitchen, where my mother had left a plate of cookies, he'd looked sternly down at all five feet three inches of Marc Schwartzbaum. "You two are behaving yourself, correct?" he asked, in a voice that seemed deeper than usual, and Marc, gulping, had bobbed a nervous nod.

"Excellent," Dad said. "Because I'll be watching." With that, according to the plan I'd begged my parents to approve, Marc and I went down to our finished basement, where there was a wide-screen TV, a Ping-Pong table, and an air hockey game where the puck glowed in the dark, requiring that the lights be turned off. I'd flicked the switches and plugged in the machine, and after a few minutes, Marc and I had retired to the couch for what I even then recognized was inept and unsatisfying fumbling when, suddenly, my father's voice came booming out of the ceiling, sounding, for all the world, like God. "I'LL BE WATCHING," he intoned. Marc, shrieking like a girl, sprang into the air, hit his back on the arm of the couch, and tumbled to the floor in a groaning, tumescent heap. I started laughing, and every time I came close to collecting myself to the point where I'd be able to comfort my paramour, I'd hear my dad's voice again, coming through the house-wide speaker system he'd installed last year so my mother could hear James Taylor and Simon & Garfunkle wherever she went. "I'LL BE WATCHING." Marc had never asked me out again. I didn't mind. It had been worth it.

In the driveway of the modern four-bedroom house in Cherry Hill where I'd grown up—a model of late-eighties chic, all angled hardwood and glass—I sat for a moment, taking deep breaths. I pictured a deserted beach, with white sand and lace-edged waves lapping at the shore. That was good. Then I slipped my hand into my purse and curled my fingers around the Altoids tin that contained ten magical pills. That was even better. I put one in my mouth and stepped out of the car.

The instant my feet touched the driveway the front door popped open. My mom opened her mouth, undoubtedly prepared to launch into her catalog of woe, and then shut it, slowly, as she considered my outfit. "You know," she said, "in my day you'd have to put on your face to even open your front door to get the paper."

"Aren't I lucky that times have changed," I said lightly, wishing I'd taken two pills. I looked down at myself: black leggings, a gray-and-black wool tunic that could have benefitted from a trip to the dry cleaner's, black patent-leather clogs. No makeup, true, and my hair was in an untidy bun, but it at least had been recently washed. My mother, meanwhile, had lost her bounce, the ponytailed girlishness that had kept my father in thrall for all those years. Her skin, normally tanned and glowing, had a crepey, wrinkled pallor, suggesting that she'd been spending most of her waking hours indoors. The polish on her fingernails was chipped, and her ring, a rock the size of a marble that my father had purchased (at her insistence, I suspected) for their thirtieth anniversary, hung loosely from her finger. She was, as always, tiny. Never in her life had she topped a hundred pounds—"except," she liked to say, in a just-short-of-accusatory tone, "when I was pregnant with you." She had on the same Four Seasons bathrobe she'd been wearing last Saturday, only there was a stain I hoped was ketchup on one sleeve, and a smear of something yellow on the lapel. Her trembling hands were pressed together—my mother's hands had shaken for as long as I could remember. I think I'd been told it was related somehow to the Accident. When I hugged her, I breathed in her familiar scent, something fruity and sweet with top notes of Giorgio and Listerine. Her tiny feet were bare, with chipped coral polish on the toenails and purple veins circling her ankles. In the morning sun, I could see the outline of her skull through her thinning hair.

"Sidney!" she yelled, over the sound of financial news. "I'M GOING TO TAKE A SHOWER!"

My father called back something I couldn't hear. My mother walked up the stairs, head bent, moving slowly, as if every step hurt. I draped my coat over a chair at the breakfast bar. I guessed Brenda, the last cleaning lady the agency sent, hadn't worked out any better than Maria, or Dot, or Phyllis, or whoever had preceded Phyllis. When my dad had gotten his diagnosis, I'd offered to pay for a cleaning lady–slash–helper to come five days a week. But Blanca, who'd worked for my parents forever, coming every Tuesday and Thursday to wash the floors, vacuum the carpets, run a load of laundry, and wipe down the countertops with bleach, had other families to tend to and couldn't quit on them.

I'd found an agency and explained what I needed—someone to do the housework, to help with the laundry, to take my mother to the grocery store and the dry cleaner's and to run whatever other errands she might have, someone with a decent personality and a driver's license. The agency had sent over an entire football team's worth of women, but my mom had a complaint about each one of them. Maria the First had insisted on being paid in cash, not by check, and my mother refused to "make a special trip to the bank, just for her." The second Maria drove a Dodge that was missing one of its front hubcaps. Exit Maria the Second. "There's no way," my mother had sniffed, "that I'm driving around in that . . . vehicle." Dot had either refused to iron the sheets or done it badly. Phyllis, my mom claimed, had stolen a pair of Judith Leiber earrings right out of her jewelry box. (My suspicion was that if I looked hard enough, I'd find those earrings somewhere—my mother was a notorious loser of things, from keys to credit cards to jewelry—but it was easier to call the agency again than to have the fight.)

That morning, the kitchen table was covered with salad-bar take-out containers, a glass with an orange juice puddle coagulating at the bottom, a collection of prescription bottles, and crumpled sections of the newspaper. I started to straighten the mess, then gave up and went to the den to find my father.

He was sitting on the couch in a crisp white shirt with monogrammed cuffs, suspenders, and pin-striped navy pants. His suit jacket, still on its hanger, was waiting on the doorknob. I swallowed hard. He looked just the way he had the morning he'd driven me to Lancaster for college, the way he'd looked every morning of my girlhood, when he'd slipped into my bedroom, smelling of Old Spice and the grapefruit he ate for breakfast. "With your shield or on it," he would say, which is what

Spartan fathers would say to their sons before sending them off to war.

Maybe he'd have been a little gentler, more inclined to treat me like a little girl instead of a son or a successor, if I'd looked more like my mom . . . but I'd inherited my face and figure from my dad's mother, Grandma Sadie, who was tall, especially for a woman back then, and busty. I'd learned to modulate my voice (Grandma Sadie's honk could silence an entire supermarket), and, after an embarrassingly minor amount of begging, I'd gotten my nose done the summer between high school and college. (My father had said, "You look fine!" My mom had asked if I wanted to get a breast reduction, too.)

My mother was Sadie's opposite, tiny and soft-voiced and sweet. Unlike my grandma, who drove the car and signed the checks and made all of her household's big decisions, my mother was utterly dependent on my dad. He hired Blanca so she wouldn't have to clean; he hired a car service so she wouldn't have to drive after the Accident. When they entertained more than one other couple, he'd hire a catering company to cook and clean. If it had been possible to pay someone to go through pregnancy and labor for her, so she wouldn't have to suffer even an instant of pain, he would have done that, too.

Until now, she had drifted through life like a queen who had only a few ceremonial duties to discharge. She didn't work, or take care of me or the house. What she did was amuse my dad. She would gossip and dance and play card games and tennis and golf; she'd listen to his stories and laugh at his jokes and use her long, painted fingernails to scratch at the back of his neck. Her biggest fear, voiced daily, was that she would outlive him and be left all alone in a world she couldn't begin to handle, so it wasn't surprising that she became a world-class hypochondriac by proxy. If my father sniffled, she'd schedule a doctor's appointment to make sure it wasn't pneumonia. If he had indigestion, she'd want him to go to the emergency room to make sure it really was the tomato sauce and not his heart. She'd stand by the front door in the morning, refusing to let him leave until he'd put sunscreen on his hands, face, and bald spot (his own father had died of melanoma), and in the evening she'd bring him a glass of red wine (okayed because of the healthful tannins). Instead of nuts, he'd take his drink with a little green glass dish filled with vitamins, supplements, fish-oil capsules—whatever she'd read about in *Prevention* or *Reader's Digest* that week.

We would have dinner, the two of them would retire to the den, and I'd go to my bedroom and shut the door, doing my homework or listening to music or drawing in my sketchbook.

I wasn't the most popular girl in my school, but I wasn't a total embarrassment either. In high school, I was moderately popular, with a circle of reliable friends and, from the time I was sixteen on, a boyfriend, or at least someone to make out with at the movies. I worked hard on my looks, keeping a food journal all the way through college that recounted everything that went into my mouth and every minute of exercise I'd done. (Recently I'd found stacks of notebooks in my childhood room's desk drawers describing cottage-cheese lunches and apple-and-peanut-butter snacks. Why had I saved them? Had I imagined wanting to reread them someday?)

In the den, my father was bent over, pulling on his white orthopedic walking shoes, the ones that closed with Velcro straps. I turned away, my chest aching. My father had always been fastidious about his clothing. He'd loved his heavy silk ties from Hermès, the navy blue and charcoal gray Hickey Freeman suits he wore to work. Once a year, he and I would make a trip to

Boyd's, an old-fashioned clothing store on Chestnut Street in Philadelphia, where the clerks would greet my father by name. I'd sit on a velvet love seat with a cup of hot chocolate and an almond biscotti from the store's café, and watch as my father and Charles, the salesman who always helped him, discussed summer-weight wool and American versus European cuts and whether he was getting a lot of use out of the sports jacket he'd bought the year before. My dad would ask about Charles's sons; Charles would ask me about school and sports and if I had a boyfriend. Then my dad would disappear into the changing room with one suit over his arm and two or three more hanging from a hook on the door, and he'd emerge, with the pants bagging around his ankles, for more discussion with Charles, before turning to me.

"What do you think, Allie-cat? How's the old man look?"

I would narrow my eyes and nibble my cookie. "I like the gray suit the best," I would say. Or, "I bet that navy pinstripe would look nice with the silver tie I got you for Father's Day."

"She's got quite an eye," Charles would say—the same every year.

"She's an artist," my dad would say, his tone managing to convey both pride and skepticism.

Eventually, a tailor would be summoned, and my dad would stand in front of the three-way mirror while the stooped old man with a mouthful of pins and a nub of chalk between his fingers marked and pinned. Then my father would change back into his weekend wear—khakis and leather boat shoes and a collared shirt—and he would take me out to a dim sum lunch. We'd order thin-skinned soup dumplings, filled with rich golden broth and pork studded with ginger, and scallion pancakes, crispy around the edges, meltingly soft in the middle, fluffy white pork buns and cups of jasmine tea, and then we'd walk to the Reading Terminal for a Bassetts ice-cream cone for dessert.

My father got up. Ignoring the gray nylon Windbreaker my mother had left hanging over one of the kitchen chairs—an old man's jacket, if ever there was one—he took his trench coat off the hanger in the closet, put it on, and followed me out the door.

"Remember when we used to go to Boyd's for your suits?" I said as I pulled into the street.

"I'm not brain-dead," he said, staring out his window. "Of course I remember."

"Do you think Charles still works there?" In all the years we'd shopped at Boyd's, Charles, a handsome, bald African-American man who always matched his pocket square to his tie, had never seemed to age.

"I have no idea," said my father. "I haven't needed a new suit just lately, you know."

We rode toward Philadelphia listening to NPR, not talking. My plan was to get him lunch at Honey's Sit 'n Eat, a Jewish soul-food diner where they served waffles and fried chicken and all kinds of sandwiches. "Where's your girl?" asked my father, as we pulled off the highway at South Street. I tried to remember whether he'd called Ellie "your girl" before, or if this was new and meant he'd forgotten her name.

"She's with Dave at a birthday party." Although Dave was never around as much as I'd hoped he would be, when he was with Ellie, he was a wonderful dad. The two of them adored each other, in exactly the way I'd always hoped my dad would adore me. Ellie would slip her little hand sweetly in his, beaming up at him, or pat the pockets of his jacket, searching for treats, when he came home from the *Examiner*. "Hello, princess," he would say, and hoist her in his arms, tossing her once, twice, three times gently up toward the ceiling as she shrieked in delight.

I found a parking spot on the street, fed the meter, and followed my father into the restaurant, where we were seated at a table overlooking South Street: the fancy gym, the fancier pet shop, the moms piloting oversized strollers, hooded and tented against the rain.

"I love the fried chicken. And the brisket's great. Or if you want breakfast, they serve all their egg dishes with potato latkes . . ." I was chattering, I realized, the same way I did with Ellie, trying to keep the conversational ball in the air without any help from my partner.

My father shrugged, then stared down at the menu. Was he depressed? It wouldn't be surprising if that were the case . . . but could he take antidepressants, with the Aricept for his dementia and the other meds he took for his blood pressure? Was there even a point in treating depression in someone who was losing touch with reality?

By the time the waitress had filled us in on the specials and we'd placed our orders—a brisket club sandwich for my father, a grilled cheese with bacon and avocado for me—I was exhausted.

"Tell me the story of the night I was born." Asking someone with memory loss to tell you a story, to remember something on cue, was risky . . . but this was one of my father's favorites, one I'd heard him tell dozens of times, including but not limited to each of my birthdays. Maybe he would talk for a while, and I could sit quietly, catching my breath, maybe sneaking a pill in the ladies' room before we left.

He took a bite of his sandwich, dabbed at his lips, and began the way he always did: "It was a dark and stormy night." I smiled as he went on. "It was three days after your mother's due date.

We lived on the fourth floor of an old Victorian at Thirty-Eighth and Clark. I was a starving graduate student, and she was . . ." He paused, his eyes losing focus, his features softening, his face flushed, looking younger than he had in years, more like the father I remembered, as I mouthed the next five words along with him. "Your mother was so pretty." We smiled at each other, then he continued. "When she started having contractions, we weren't worried. First babies can take a while, and we were maybe ten blocks from the hospital. Her bag was packed, and I'd memorized the numbers for two different cab companies. She had one contraction and then, ten minutes later, another one. Then one more five minutes after that, then one two minutes after that . . ." He used his hands as he told the story—how my mother's labor progressed faster than they had expected, how by the time they got down to the street to wait for the cab, rain was lashing the streets and the wind was bending the trees practically in half, and the mayor and the governor were on the radio, telling people to stay inside, to stay home unless they absolutely had to leave. "I was ninety percent sure you were going to be born in the back of a taxicab," my father said.

He got every detail, every nuance of the story right—the way the cab smelled of incense and curry, the driver's unflappable calm, how he'd left my mother's little plaid suitcase on the sidewalk in front of our house in his haste to get my mom in the cab, and how one of the neighbors had retrieved it when the rain stopped, dried each item of clothing, and brought it over the next day.

"Did you want more kids?" I asked him. All these years of wondering, and I'd finally gotten up the nerve to ask. He waited until the waiter had cleared our plates and taken our orders for two cups of coffee and one slice of buttermilk chocolate cake, and patted his lips with his napkin again before saying, "It wasn't meant to be. We had you, and then your mother had her trouble . . ."

"What trouble?" I asked, half my mind on his answer, the other half on my sandwich. He probably meant the Accident. That was the only trouble I'd ever heard about.

He pushed the salt and pepper shakers across the table like chess pieces and did not answer.

"Was I a hard baby?" I asked. Had I been like Ellie, shrieky and picky and inclined toward misery? Again, no answer from Dad. I knew, of course, how overwhelming a baby could be, and I suspected that in addition to feeling like a newborn's demands were more than she could handle, my mother had also felt isolated. It couldn't have been easy, I thought, and pictured Little Ronnie, her flawless skin suddenly mottled with stretch marks, her beauty sleep disrupted, all alone in the apartment and, eventually, in the big house my father had bought her. Who had she gone to with her questions and concerns? I'd had friends, a pricy lactation consultant, and the leader of the playgroup I attended, who had a degree in early childhood development. I'd had Janet, and my own mom, and even the Indomitable Doreen. My mother had no one. Her own mother had died before I was born, and as a teenage bride and young mother, she hadn't yet formed bonds with the types of women I'd come to know. She had only my father . . . and that might have been lonely.

I pictured her now, back in Cherry Hill. Was she trying to clean up the mess in the kitchen? Was she paging through old photo albums, the way she had the last time I'd spent the day with her, looking at pictures of cousins I couldn't remember and uncles I'd never met? Was she remembering my father, dashing and young and invulnerable, and wishing that she'd been the one to get sick instead of him?

"Excuse me," I said. The bathroom at Honey's had a rustic wooden bench to set a purse or a diaper bag on. The walls were hung with framed magazine ads from the 1920s advertising nerve tonics and hair-restoring creams, and a mirror in a flaking gold frame.

I looked at my reflection. My face looked thinner, and the circles under my eyes seemed to have deepened over the past few weeks. I'd lost a few more pounds—with the pills, I'd found myself occasionally sleeping through meals—but I didn't look fit or healthy, just weary and depleted. Even on my best days, I was no Little Ronnie, with her bright eyes and long, thick hair, the kind of girl a man would want to tuck in his pocket and keep safe forever.

Turning away from the mirror, I reached into my purse. I crunched up two pills, washed them down with a scoop of water from the sink, and walked back to the table. I'd had an idea of how to give my mother some extra time, and make the day go by. "Hey," I said to my father, "do you want to go see Ellie?"

As soon as I walked into BouncyTime, I knew that bringing my dad there had been a mistake. Raucous music boomed from overhead speakers. The singer fought against the roar of the blowers that kept the climbing and bouncing structures inflated. Kids dashed around the room, screaming, racing up the giant slide, hurling inflatable beach balls at one another's heads, or shooting foam missiles out of air cannons. A clutch of mothers stood in a circle, in the Haverford uniform of 7 For All Mankind jeans and a cashmere crewneck, or Lululemon yoga pants and a breathable wicking top in a complementary color. Along the wall, a smaller group of dads had gathered, heads down, tapping away at their screens, looking up occasionally to cries of "Daddy, look at me!" or, more often, "Daddy, take a video!" I found Dave with two other men, one a lawyer, one who ran a dental insurance business.

"Hey," said the lawyer. "It's the Sexy Mama from the *Wall Street Journal*."

"That's me," I said, pasting a look of fake cheer on my face. "Have you guys met my dad?" I let Dave handle the introductions while I looked around for Ellie. She wasn't in the bouncy castle with the girls, or waiting in line for the air cannons with the boys. Eventually I found Hank, sitting glumly on one of the benches with an ice pack clutched to his forehead. He pointed out Ellie huddled against a wall, with her skirt smoothed over her lap, playing with what appeared to be the iPod I'd lost the week before.

I walked over, trying not to look angry. "Ellie, is that my iPod?"

She looked up. "You're not supposedta BE HERE!"

"Well, hello to you, too." I sat down on the floor beside her and held out my hand. "You know the rules. You don't just take other people's things. You need to ask first." She threw the iPod at me. It hit me just above my left eyebrow and fell to the floor.

"Ellie! What was that for?"

"Jade and Summer and Willow all have THEIR OWN iPODS!" She widened her eyes into a look suggesting she could barely bring herself to contemplate such unfairness.

"Ellie, we do not throw things," I said, struggling not to yell. Ellie ignored me.

"And they're the new touch ones, not STUPID TINY BABY ONES like YOU HAVE!"

"We don't throw," I repeated. "And you shouldn't have taken Mommy's things without permission."

Ellie stuck out her lower lip. "I didn't even WANT TO COME to this STUPID BABY PARTY! Why can't everyone just LEAVE ME ALONE!"

I sighed as she started to cry. Maybe—probably—this place was just too bright and noisy for Eloise. As if to confirm my thought, she leaned against me, resting her head on my shoulder. "I'm sorry I taked your thing and threw it at your head."

"It's okay," I told her. "Just next time, ask first."

At the sound of sniffling, I looked up to see Hank. "Will you do the slide?" he asked.

Ellie shook her head. "Too scary," she proclaimed.

"What if we went down together?" I asked. "You could sit on my lap."

Ellie narrowed her eyes, judging the steep angle of the slide, watching the kids zip down, hands raised, mouths open, squealing with glee. Most slid on their own, but a few made the descent seated on parents' laps.

"You want to try it?"

She sighed, as though she was granting me an enormous favor. "Oooh-kay."

"How about you, Hank?"

He shook his head. "I'm allergic to burlap."

But of course. I got to my feet—not half as gracefully as one of the yoga moms would have managed—and held out my hand. Ellie and I were walking toward the line at the back of the slide when Dave intercepted us.

"Hey, Al. You want to check on your dad?"

"What's wrong?" I peered toward the benches where I'd left him, and saw him sitting there, staring into space the same way he stared at CNBC.

"He seems kind of uncomfortable."

I gave him a patient, beatific Mary Poppins kind of smile, and hoped I didn't look drugged. "Ellie and I are going to try the slide. Just sit with him. I'll be there in two minutes."

"I don't wanna," Ellie said as soon as she realized she'd have to climb a ladder built into the back of the slide to get to the top.

"Honey, I'll be right here. Just put your hands like this . . ." I bent down and lifted, putting her feet on the bottom rung and her hands on the one above it. "Now just take a step . . ."

"I don't WANT TO DO THIS. I'm SCARED!"

"Hurry up!" shouted the little boy—Hayden? Holden?— behind us. I scooped Ellie into one arm and hauled us both up the ladder.

"Come on! You'll love it! I used to love slides when I was a little girl!"

"I WILL NOT LOVE SLIDES!" said Ellie, but she let me carry her to the top of the slide. Red-faced, panting, with sweat dribbling down my back, I grabbed a sack, marveling at the lack of progress—in these days of satellite radios and wireless Internet, why were kids still sliding on actual burlap sacks? I hoisted Ellie in my arms and got us in position.

"One . . . two . . . three!"

I kicked off with my heels. I could hear my daughter screaming—from fear or delight, I wasn't sure. Nor was there time to figure it out, because the instant we got to the bottom of the slide, someone grabbed my shoulders and started shaking me.

"What are you doing with my daughter?"

I tried to wriggle away, but my father's hands were clamped down tight, his fingers curling into the flesh of my upper arms. His shirt was untucked, his tie had been yanked askew, and the

Velcro closure of one of his shoes had come undone and was flapping.

"How could you be so irresponsible?" he asked.

"Dad. *Dad!* It's me, Allison!"

"You put her down right this minute, Ronnie! Don't you ever, *ever* do that again!"

Oh, God. Eloise was wailing as another mother-child duo came hurtling down the slide and slammed into my back, knocking Ellie out of my arms and onto the floor . . . where, unsurprisingly, she started to scream.

"Ohmygod, I'm so sorry!" said the mother.

"How could you be so irresponsible!" my father was shouting.

"Ellie's mommy is in trou-ble," sang the little boy as I finally managed to wrench myself free. Ellie, weeping, limped dramatically over to Dave. Everyone in the place was staring at us, moms and dads and kids.

"Um, ma'am? Excuse me?" A teenage girl in a BouncyTime T-shirt tapped my shoulder. "You can't stay here. There are other people waiting to use the slide."

"Believe me, I am trying to leave," I told her. I took my father by the elbow and steered him away from the slide and over to the metal bench against the wall.

"Dad," I said, trying to keep my voice low and calm as, beside me, Dave attempted to soothe Ellie. "Listen to me. I'm your daughter. I'm Allison. That was Ellie, your granddaughter, and she's fine . . . that slide was perfectly safe . . ."

"Why was Grandpa YELLING at me?" Ellie wailed. She lifted the hem of her skirt and blotted her tears.

"Ew, gross!" a little boy said. My eyes followed his pointing finger. Oh, God.

"I think your dad had an accident," Dave said. His voice was quiet, but not quiet enough. I figured Ellie would be revolted, but instead she slipped her hand into my father's hand and pulled him toward the door.

"Don't worry, Pop-Pop," she stage-whispered. "Sometimes that happens to me, too."

Ellie and Dave arranged to ride home with Hank's mother. I got my dad back into the car, slipping a towel from the trunk onto his seat, and concentrated on getting him back home as fast as I could.

"Dad, are you okay?" I asked. "Do you need anything?"

He didn't answer . . . he just lifted his chin and turned his face away from me. As soon as we were moving I rolled down my window, holding my breath and hoping he wouldn't notice. When I heard what sounded like a choked sob from the passenger seat, I kept both hands on the wheel and my eyes straight ahead. *Get through this,* I told myself. *Get through this, and there will be happy pills at the end.*

We arrived to find my mother asleep on the couch, curled up in her housecoat with her bare feet tucked around each other, the same way Ellie arranged her feet when she slept. "Do you want me to . . ." I asked my dad, then let my voice trail off and cut my eyes toward the stairs. My father ignored me, pressing his lips together as he made his way past me. I waited until I heard the water running in the bathroom before I let myself collapse at the kitchen table. The room was still a mess, the sink piled with dirty dishes, the counters greasy and streaked, the flowers I'd brought the previous weekend dying in a vase of scummy water. I emptied the vase, loaded the dishwasher, sprayed and wiped down the counters, and took out the trash. I pulled a package of turkey thighs past their expiration date out of the refrigerator, along with a bag of softened zucchini and three dessicated lemons, and threw them all away. I dumped sour milk down the drain, wiped off the refrigerator shelves, and boiled water for a pot of tea, which I placed on a tray with a napkin and a plate of cookies.

I knocked on the bedroom door. "Dad?" No answer. I eased the door open. He was curled on his side, his fist propped underneath his chin, mouth open, sleeping. With his forehead smooth and his eyes closed he looked like a little boy, a boy who'd played until he was exhausted and had fallen asleep on his parents' bed. I set down the tray, then picked up my dad's wet pants using my thumb and forefinger and carried them to the washing machine, which was already full of damp, moldy-smelling clothes. I ran the machine again, adding more detergent. Then I slipped back into my parents' bedroom. Half-empty water glasses, crumpled tissues, and discarded newspapers covered the bedside tables. Dirty clothes were heaped on the floor; magazines and newspapers were stacked in the corners. I stepped over a tangle of ties and a dozen discarded shoes and opened the bathroom door. The room was still steamy from the shower. Wet towels were piled in the tub, and a few more lined the floor. Hot water was pouring into the sink, and my father's razor rested against an uncapped bottle of shaving cream. I turned off the water, capped the cream, and opened the medicine chest. My hands moved expertly over the bottles, fingertips just brushing the tops long enough to distinguish between over-the-counter and prescription stuff. I pulled down propranolol, diltiazem, and various other medications for high blood pressure and diabetes before I got to the good stuff. Vicodin 10/325. "Take as needed for pain." Tramadol. And—bingo—OxyContin. Without pausing, without thinking, I uncapped the bottles and emptied half of each one into my hands.

What are you doing? a part of my brain cried as I crunched three of the pills, then bent down to gather the dirty towels, pick up the soap off the shower floor, pull a wad of hair out of the drain, and sweep discarded Q-tips and Kleenexes into the wastebasket. *You're stealing medicine from your father, your sick father. Have you really sunk so low?*

It appeared that I had. *I need this,* I told myself as I moved through the bedroom, gathering armloads of clothing and piling them into garbage bags, and then loading the bags into the trunk of my car to take home to wash and fold. *I need this.*

PART TWO

~

All Fall Down

SEVEN

"Welcome to Eastwood." The woman who met me on the front lawn of the Eastwood Assisted Living Facility had her silver-gray hair in a neat bob, a high, sweet voice, and a cool, brisk handshake. She wore khakis, a sweater, and a nametag with KATHLEEN YOUNG written on it, and she led me through the doors with a bounce in her step, like a former high-school jock who'd stayed on campus to teach phys ed. "Let me show you around!"

Her bubbly, energetic manner only made the handful of residents—a man in a wheelchair by the door, hands shaking as he held up the *Examiner;* a woman in a pink-and-white bathrobe, using a walker to make her slow way toward the art room—look even older and sadder. I tried to picture my father here, my smart, strong, competent father in a bathrobe, requiring the kind of care a place like this could give him. It hurt, but it was a distant kind of pain. The pills let me consider his future without feeling it too deeply. It was almost like watching a movie about someone else's sorrows—*now her father can't remember his granddaughter's name; now he's having temper tantrums; now he's having accidents, and wandering away from home, and crying—* and knowing they were painful without feeling them acutely.

Narcotics were like a warm, fuzzy comforter, a layer of defense between me and the world.

"Follow me, please," said Kathleen, bounding down the hallway on the balls of her feet. I grappled with a brief but fierce desire to go sprinting back to my car, to burn rubber out of the parking lot and never see this place again . . . only what good would that do? My mother was unlikely to take this on. Someone had to step up and do what was required.

In the foyer I braced myself for the smell of urine, of industrial cleansers and canned chicken soup that I remembered from my dad's last hospital stay, but Eastwood's green-carpeted corridors smelled pleasantly of cedar and spice. There was a basket of scented pinecones on top of the front desk, behind which two women in headsets were busy typing. Behind them was an oversized whiteboard, the kind I remembered from Ellie's preschool, with sentences left open-ended, so the kids and teachers could fill in the blanks. *Today is MONDAY,* read the top line. *It is APRIL 7th. The weather is . . .* Instead of the word "sunny," someone had affixed a decal of an affably beaming sun. *Our SPECIAL ACTIVITIES are BINGO in the Recreation Parlor, and a TRIP TO THE CAMDEN AQUARIUM.* I felt a tug at my sleeve, and heard a whispered "Help me." I looked down. While Kathleen was deep in conversation with one of the head-setted ladies behind the desk, a tiny, curled shrimp of a woman had wheeled up beside me and grabbed my sleeve.

"What's wrong?" I asked.

The woman gave a very teenager-y eye roll. Fine white hair floated around her pink scalp in an Einsteinian nimbus. Her frail torso was wrapped in an oversized pink cardigan, and she wore pink velour pants and a pair of white knitted slippers beneath it. Her veined hand trembled, but her eyes, behind enormous glasses, were sharp, and I was relieved to see a full set of teeth (or realistic-looking dentures) when she started talking.

"This place is what's wrong," she murmured, speaking out of the side of her mouth, like a prisoner in the yard who didn't want the guards to overhear. "The steak is tough. The pudding's bland. They've been promising me for weeks to order my gluten-free crumpets, and . . ." She lifted her hands in the air, palms up, a mute appeal to the God of gluten-free crumpets. "Also, my kids never visit."

"I'm sorry," I stammered, then squatted, my face close to hers. She extended one of her gnarled paws toward me.

"Lois Lefkowitz. Formerly of sunny Florida, until I broke my hip and my kids moved me back here."

I shook her hand gently. "I'm Allison Weiss." I shot a glance at the counter, making sure the brisk Ms. Young was still occupied, before I whispered, "Is it really that bad here?"

She patted my hand and shook her head.

"What's not to like?" she asked. "I don't have to cook, I don't have to clean, I don't have to shop, and I don't have to listen to Murray go on about his fantasy football team. I read . . ." She tapped the e-reader in her lap. "With this thing, every book is a large-print book. I go to the museum, I go to the symphony, and the beauty shop's open once a week for a wash and set." She patted her wisps of white hair, then put one gnarled paw on my shoulder. "Mother or father?"

"My dad."

"Memory loss or just can't get around?"

"He's got Alzheimer's."

"Oh, sweetie. I'm sorry." Pat, pat, pat went the wrinkled little hand. It felt surprisingly nice. Both of my grandmothers were long gone—my mother's mother had died of breast cancer before

I was born, and my father's mother, Grandma Sadie, had gone to Heaven's screened-in porch when I was in college. I liked to imagine her sometimes, sitting in a rocking chair, listening to the Sox and yelling at my grandfather. "They'll take good care of him here."

My throat felt thick as I swallowed. "You think so?"

"I see things. I watch. They'll make sure he's safe. Do you have children?"

"A little girl."

"Pictures?"

I pulled my phone out of my purse. Ellie, in her favorite maxidress, was my wallpaper. In the picture, she stood on the beach in a broad-brimmed sun hat, with waves foaming at her feet. My new friend peered at the screen, then sighed. "It goes so fast," she told me. "One minute you're putting diaper cream on their tushies, the next thing you know, you're walking them down the aisle. Then they're putting you in a place like this." She sighed again, and I thought I saw the glimmer of moisture on one seamed cheek. "And you sit here and wonder where the time went, and how you never wanted to live long enough that someone should be changing your diapers." Another sigh. "Still. I wouldn't have missed a day of it." She poked at my phone. "You got Candy Crush on here?"

"Oh. No. Sorry."

Kathleen Young was heading toward us, her pleasant smile still in place, but I noticed the creases around her eyes had deepened.

"Mrs. Lefkowitz, you're not scaring away prospectives, are you?"

My new friend gave Ms. Young a sunny smile. "You mean I shouldn't tell them about the rats in the showers?"

"She's kidding," said Ms. Young. Mrs. Lefkowitz gave me another smile of surpassing sweetness.

"I hope I'll see you again," she said. "And that pretty little girl!"

"Nice to meet you," I said, and gave her little paw another squeeze.

"Right this way," said Kathleen Young. "This is the Manor," she said, walking at a swift clip past opened doors with nameplates on them. "Our residents who require the most care stay here. This," she said, opening a door, "is a typical double room."

I stepped inside. The room wasn't large, with most of the space taken up by adjustable hospital beds with side rails that could be raised or dropped. There were two oak dressers; two bookcases; two armchairs, one on each side of the room, each upholstered in blue plastic, dyed and patterned to make it look like cloth. The bathroom had all of the stainless steel rails you'd expect, with a metal-and-plastic chair in the oversized walk-in shower cubicle, and grippy mats on the floor. Back in the room, I let my fingertips drift along the armrest of one chair and tried not to wince at the feeling of plastic. Would my dad see the difference between the furniture in his house and this stuff? How could he not? Noticing my expression, Kathleen said, "Of course, our residents are welcome to bring their own furniture. Most do. We find it helps with their sense of dislocation." I nodded, mentally erasing the hospital bed, the cheap bureau and bookcase, and the plasticized armchair, and replacing them with things from my parents' home. Better.

"Are there single rooms available?"

"Of course. They're significantly more expensive . . ."

"That shouldn't be a problem," I said, and watched Kathleen's pupils expand. Years ago my father, in a tacit admission that my mother was equipped to handle precisely nothing that his golden years might entail, had bought himself a life-insurance policy and all kinds of disability and extended-care policies, too. There was money to pay for everything he'd need, and to pay for the help my mother might eventually require, now that my father was unable to arrange her days. "Tell me about the, uh, level of care." I'd done all kinds of research about the questions I was supposed to ask, even if the answers were all on the website. As Kathleen recited statistics about physician's assistants, physicians on call, and nurse-practitioners, LPNs, and nurse's aides, and how it was a goal at Eastwood to encourage as much independence as was feasible and safe, I thought of when I was twelve, and my father had taken me to New York City.

The whole thing was an accident. He'd gotten the tickets for *South Pacific* as my mother's birthday present. For weeks, she'd gone around playing the cast recording, singing "Younger than Springtime," making appointments for a haircut and color, trying on and returning different dresses. I had come home on the Friday afternoon of their proposed trip and found her sick in bed. Some kind of twenty-four-hour bug, I'd thought, remembering the sounds of retching, murmuring behind closed doors, my dad asking if she wanted a doctor and my mother, shrill and weepy, saying she'd be fine, just fine, she just needed to sleep. My father had emerged tight-lipped, visibly unhappy. He'd already paid for the tickets, made plans for dinner, reserved the hotel room. If there'd been time he would have found a way to cancel the whole thing. Instead, he'd mustered up a smile and said, "How'd you like to go to the Big Apple with your dear old dad?"

At twelve, I was not looking good. My breasts and my nose had both sprouted to what would become their adult dimensions, with the rest of my body and my face lagging behind. I had braces, with rubber bands to pull my upper jaw back into alignment with my lower jaw, and my oily skin, in spite of all the Clearasil and the benzoyl-peroxide-soaked scrubbie pads, was routinely spattered with pimples. I was wearing my hair with bangs, figuring the more of my troubled complexion I could hide, the better, and my oversized button-down shirts, paired with pants pegged at the ankles and flowy everywhere else, did nothing to minimize my size. But on that night, due to some miracle of luck and timing, my skin was clear, my hair was be- having, and I looked like a girl any father would be happy to escort to a show.

"Try my silver dress," my mother had croaked from her bed. It was meant to be knee-length. On me, it was a hip-skimming tunic. Paired with plain black leggings and my mom's black leather boots, it made me look almost like a grown-up, sophisti- cated and smart. She swept my bangs back with one of the wide cotton bands she wore to yoga, then blow-dried and straightened my hair and let me wear a little lipstick, red, which made my skin look olive instead of sallow. "Nice," she whispered with a smile, before turning on her side and falling noisily asleep. My father had been dressed in his newest suit and the tie my mom had gotten him for his birthday. His eyes widened in appreciation as I came down the stairs, with my mother's good black winter coat draped over one arm. "Those boys don't know what they're missing," he'd blurted, and then instantly looked ashamed, but I carried that compliment close, like a jeweled locket, something wonderful and rare. He had held the car door open for me, re- galed me with stories of the brain-dead interns from Penn's and Temple's graduate schools who descended on his office every summer, and how one of them had gotten so drunk at the man- aging partner's Fourth of July party that he'd vomited in the hot tub. Exiting the car, paying the parking-lot attendant, holding his arm out to hail a taxi, or holding a door open and saying "After you," he'd looked so handsome, tall and assured in his camel-hair topcoat, his shoes polished to a high gloss, the Rolex my mother had bought him for his fiftieth birthday gleaming on his wrist. In the theater, he kept one hand lightly between my shoulder blades as he steered us toward our seats, and in the restaurant, the pride in his tone was unmistakable as he introduced me to the maître d' and the waiter, who both seemed to know him, as "my daughter, Allison."

I could remember everything from that night—the look of the theater, lit like a temple in the frosty Manhattan night, the smell of perfume and silk and fur in the air, the rustle of programs as the audience settled into the seats, the plaintive voice of the lead actor, lamenting about how paradise had once nearly been his. I remembered how women's eyes had turned toward my father, the approving looks they gave him, how I'd felt about the way he belonged in their company, tall and smart and successful. I could name everything we'd eaten at the little French bistro on Fifty-Sixth Street, and could conjure up the taste of lobster bisque laced with sherry, profiteroles drizzled in dark chocolate, the single sip each of white wine and red wine and after-dinner port he'd let me have. Half-asleep in the taxi's backseat as it cut through the traffic, humming the overture to myself, I had thought that I would never feel more content, more beloved, more beautiful.

Today is MONDAY, read the sign in the dining room, where tables for four were draped in pink cloths and set at wide intervals, the better to steer wheelchairs around them. On a shelf were dozens of paperbacks by Lee Child, Vince Flynn, Brad Thor. Was there some kind of law that men who wrote military thrillers had to have two-syllable names where the first and the last sounded interchangeable? There were romances for the ladies—your Nora Roberts, your Danielle Steel—and board games in worn boxes, some with their sagging edges reinforced with duct tape, the same games I played with Ellie: Sorry! and Parcheesi and Monopoly and Battleship. *Our next meal will be DINNER,* read the whiteboard at the front of the room. *Tonight we are having CREAM OF MUSHROOM SOUP, LONDON BROIL, MASHED POTATOES, and GREEN BEANS. Oh, Dad,* I mourned, and wondered how my mother would survive, seeing her beloved husband in a place like this.

Kathleen interrupted my reverie, giving me a glossy "Welcome to Eastwood" folder and a big smile. "If you're ready, we can go back to my office. There's some preliminary paperwork you can fill out, and then, once our finance department has had a look, they'll be in touch. Did you bring your father's tax returns?"

"I'm sorry," I said. The insides of my eyelids were stinging, and I was already blinking back tears. "I think I'm going to have to take care of that another time."

"Are you all right?" Kathleen's tone was not unsympathetic. She must have seen this dozens, if not hundreds of times— spouses and children who thought they were ready flipping out and running when it came time to sign the forms, to write the checks, to make it real. I managed a nod, and then hurried past the front desk, through the doors, out to the parking lot, and into my car. *One dream in my heart,* I heard in my head, and brushed my sleeve against my cheeks to wipe away the tears. *One love to be living for . . . One love to be living for . . . This nearly was mine.*

EIGHT

"Allison Weiss?" The girl waiting at the door was tiny, with a nose the size of a pencil eraser and feet so small I bet she had to shop in the children's department. It was May, the weather springtime-perfect. The scents of flowers, cut grass, and freshly turned earth wafted on a warm breeze (I could see a gardener digging the beds adjacent to the parking lot), and the sky outside the television studio was a perfect turquoise, dotted with cotton-ball clouds.

I smiled at the young woman with the warmth and goodwill that only the pure of heart, or the people who've recently swallowed a bunch of OxyContin, can muster. "I'm Allison Weiss. Are you Beatrice?" I had gotten the call the night before, from a woman who'd introduced herself as Kim Caster, a producer for *The News on Nine,* the local evening newscast. "Did you hear about that mess in Akron?" she had asked.

"I did." The mess in Akron was the kind of story that had become depressingly familiar since every teenager in America, it seemed, had been issued an iPhone. On a fine spring weekend, a fifteen-year-old girl had gone to a party. She'd gotten drunk. Four different boys, all football teammates, had taken advantage of her. Then, just to add to the fun, they'd posted photographs of their deeds on Instagram and video on YouTube. Within the next twenty-four hours, almost every kid who attended the town's high school saw what had happened. The girl had tried to kill herself after a few of the most lurid shots ended up on her Facebook page. The boys had been arrested . . . but their defenders spread the word that the girl had come dressed provocatively with a vibrator in her purse and had texted her friends that she was looking for action.

"As someone who writes a lot about sex and relationships—and, of course, as a mother yourself—what are your thoughts?"

"I don't think owning a vibrator, or even having one with you, is a standing invitation for guys to do whatever they want," I'd said. "A girl can wear a short skirt and not be asking for it. She can even get drunk and have the right not to be raped. It's never the victim's fault."

"Mmm-hmm . . . uh-huh . . . great . . . great," said the producer. "And what about the argument that it wasn't really a gang rape because some of it involved only digital penetration?"

I'd rolled my eyes. A columnist at no less an institution than the *Washington Post* had made that very point on the op-ed page last week, and the *Examiner* had reprinted his column. In our better days, I might have given Dave some grief about it, but these days Dave and I were barely speaking. It felt as if we were trapped in the world's longest staring contest, neither of us willing to blink and bring up the topic of L. McIntyre, or Dave's ever-lengthening stay in the guest room, or the pills. "There's no 'only' when it comes to rape," I said. "I don't think it matters whether it's a penis or a finger. Anything you don't want inside you shouldn't be there."

The producer had seemed impressed enough with my answers to invite me to come on the air for the channel's Sunday-morning *Newsmakers on Nine* show, where local folks gave their opinions on the issues of the day. I'd spent an hour on my makeup and allotted myself fifteen minutes to just sit quietly and catch my breath after wrestling myself into many layers of compressing undergarments, and now here I was. I'd calibrated my dosage carefully; just two pills, enough to take the edge off, to let me push through the sorrow that threatened to keep me pinned to the bed in despair.

"Follow me, please," said Beatrice, whose hair bounced as she walked. "We'll go right to makeup."

"That bad, huh?"

Beatrice stopped mid-stride and turned and studied me carefully.

"That was a joke! Don't answer!" I said.

"Oh. Okay."

Kids these days, I thought, as Beatrice waved a plastic card at an electronic eye and glass barriers parted.

"Makeup" turned out to be a closet-sized room with two beauty-salon chairs, a mirror that covered one wall, and a table stocked with a department store's worth of pots and tubs and containers of eye shadow and foundation and fake eyelashes arrayed like amputated spiders' legs. One chair was empty. In the other sat a middle-aged white guy with short, sandy hair, bland features, a wedding ring on his left hand, and a class ring with a gaudy red stone on his right. The makeup artist introduced herself as Cindy, handed me a smock, and went back to patting foundation on the man's face.

I sat down in the empty chair. "Hey, that's my brand!" I said to the man, who did not smile. "Hi, I'm Allison Weiss. Are you on the panel, too?"

Without meeting my eyes, he gave a stiff nod. "I am." His small brown eyes were sunk back into the flesh of his oddly rectangular head, like raisins in dough that had risen around them. "You must be the sex worker."

I laughed. I couldn't help it. "Sex worker? Who do you think would hire me?" When the man didn't answer, I realized that he wasn't kidding. "I'm not a sex worker. I'm a blogger." Realizing that might not sound any different to the uninitiated, I said, "I write about marriage and motherhood on a website called Ladiesroom.com." Which, I thought with a sinking heart, also sounded vaguely pornographic. I mustered a smile. "Trust me, I'm about as far from a porn star as you could be."

"We're all set," said the makeup lady, giving the man's nose a final dusting. He stood up and unsnapped his smock, revealing the plain black shirt and white clerical collar underneath. Oops.

"Good God," I said. The makeup lady giggled. The pills did not make me slurry or sloppy, but they did lower my inhibitions. On them, I'd say whatever was on my mind, and think it over later. Usually it wasn't a problem. This might turn out to be an exception. I bit my lip and wondered if it had been a good idea to take anything before leaving for the studio. This, of course, led me to wonder if the shipment I was expecting that day would show up, and whether I had enough to get through the weekend if it didn't. I wondered, as I walked down the hall, who Penny Lane's vendors were, the druggy Oz behind the Internet's green curtain. Were they cancer patients willing to sell their meds and suffer in order to pay off their bills and leave their kids cash? Scummy thieves who robbed cancer patients, then sold their pills for cash? Kids who worked in drugstores, sneaking out five or ten pills at a time, or people getting them from doctors without ethics, or maybe even actual doctors?

Never mind. "Did you do your own makeup?" Cindy asked,

cupping my chin in her hand and turning my face first left, then right.

"My friend helped." Janet and Maya had come over that morning, lugging a light-up mirror and bags of makeup. Maya had actually been excited enough to speak directly to her mother while they debated brown versus black eyeliner and whether my brows required additional plucking.

"Not bad," Cindy said.

"Just please don't make me look too slutty," I said, as she began filling in my lashes with a brush dipped in brown powder. "Slutty would not do." With that in mind, I'd worn a pencil skirt and pumps with a not-too-high heel, a fuchsia cardigan with a pale-pink T-shirt underneath, and a single strand of pearls. I was going for "mildly sexy librarian," and I'd already solemnly vowed to refrain from looking at any and all online commentary on my outfit, my figure, or what I had to say.

"Good luck," Dave had told me as I'd gathered my car keys and my purse. He sounded friendlier than he had in weeks, and, almost without thinking, I'd turned my face up toward his for a good-luck kiss. Maybe he'd just intended to brush my lips with his, but I'd stumbled, as a result either of the heels or of the Penny Lane pills, and we'd ended up with his arms around me, the length of my body pressed against his, close enough to feel the heat of him through the cotton and denim, to smell his scent of shampoo and warm, clean skin. I'd opened my mouth and he'd settled one hand at the small of my back, tilting me against him, the better to feel his thickening erection, the other at the base of my neck so he could keep my head in place while he kissed me, lingeringly, thoroughly . . .

"EWWW!"

We sprang apart. I stumbled again—this time, it was definitely the heels—and staggered backward, praying that my skirt wouldn't rip. "Ellie, what's wrong?" I'd asked. Ellie, predictably, had started to cry.

"I don't like KISSING. It is DISGUSTING."

"Not when mommies and daddies do it!"

"That," my daughter proclaimed, chin lifted, "is the MOST DISGUSTING OF ALL!"

"Well all righty, then," I'd muttered, as Dave helped me to my feet. I could still barely believe what had happened, and wondered what had prompted it. Had he realized that, deep down, he really loved me . . . or, my mind whispered, had L. turned him down, telling him to go home to his wife unless he was ready to leave her?

"Later," he'd whispered, and I'd sailed out the door, resolved not to think too hard about it, buoyed by this unexpected show of affection, by lust, and by the confidence that only a dose of narcotics could give me. Maybe everything was going to be fine. Maybe I'd go home and we'd make love (in my fantasy, Ellie had been whisked away, possibly by the Indomitable Doreen). Dave would tell me that he loved me, that he'd always loved me, and, more than that, that he was proud of me. He would tell me he was grateful that I'd kept us going during hard times. Then he'd tell me that he'd come up with another book idea, that his agent loved it, that the publisher loved it, that they'd given him another advance even bigger than the first one, and that L. McIntyre had been transferred to Butte, Montana.

"No slutty," said Cindy. Working quickly, she touched up my foundation, patted concealer underneath my eyes, glued a few falsies into my lashes, and ran a flat iron over my hair. "Put on more lipstick and lipgloss right before they start," she said, handing me tubes of both. Beatrice and her clipboard were waiting in the hallway.

"I'll take you to the greenroom. You've got about ten minutes."

"Who else is on this segment?" I asked as we walked.

Her heels clipped briskly against the tiled floor. "Let's see. It's you, Father Ryan of the Christian League of Decency, and, um, a parenting person. She's a child psy . . . psychologist? Psychiatrist?" She frowned at her clipboard as if she were disappointed it wasn't volunteering the answer. "A child something."

"Great. Can I ask you a quick question?" Without giving her time to mull it over, I said, "You guys know I'm not a sex worker, right?" The line between her eyebrows reappeared as Beatrice looked from her clipboard to my face, then down at her clipboard again. "So you're not a sex worker."

I shook my head.

"But you work in the sex industry?"

"No, no I don't. Really, the most accurate thing you could say is that I work for a website that sometimes addresses women's sexuality." *Sarah*, I thought. Sarah was Ladiesroom's go-to sex-positive person, but she wasn't here because this was Philadelphia, and I was the local girl.

She scribbled something on her clipboard. "Got it."

I was unconvinced. But I said, "Okay, great," and followed her pointing finger into another closet-sized room. This was the greenroom—painted, I noticed, an unremarkable beige. It had a conference-style table, a big flat-screen TV set to Channel 9, and a cart with three cans of Diet Coke, a bucket full of water I assumed had once been ice, and a black plastic tray covered in crumbs and two barely ripe strawberries. Father Ryan sat at one end of the table, with his Bible open and his head bent. At the other end sat a tiny, dark-haired woman in a red suit talking into a Bluetooth headset. "Mmm-hmm. That's right. Have Dolly pick up the sushi on her way in. The flowers come at five and the caterers start at six. Right—oh, hang on." She jabbed at her phone with one fingertip. "Hello, this is Dr. Carol Bendinger, how can I help you?"

I took one of the cans of Diet Coke and found a seat. When neither of my fellow panelists acknowledged me, I pulled out a copy of my morning blog post and highlighted the points I wanted to make. *Being sexually active is not an invitation to rapists,* I'd written. True. *The fact that a teenage girl chooses to have sex with someone doesn't mean she's willing to sleep with everyone.* Also true. But rape wasn't sex. Should I be making more of a distinction between a girl using her vibrator with her boyfriend (or girlfriend, I reminded myself) and what the boys at the party had done to her?

I rummaged oh-so-casually in my purse until I found the Altoids tin. Flipping it open, I counted two, four, six, eight, ten pills. I'd taken those two pills less than an hour ago, but I was already starting to feel the familiar anxiety working its way through my body, nibbling at my knees, making them feel as if they were filled with air instead of flesh and blood and bone, and my brain was revving too quickly, flooding with thoughts of Ellie and Dave and Sarah and Ladiesroom and whether I really needed to start writing seven times a week and how I was going to get two hundred plastic eggs filled with school-approved treats before the Celebration of Spring on Monday afternoon. There was the mortgage that needed paying. The roof that needed replacing. The second car we needed to buy, and Ellie's tuition, and summer camp, and had I ever made her a dentist appointment? I couldn't remember.

"Panelists?" Beatrice and her clipboard were back. "We're going to mic you, and then get you seated during the commercial break."

I held still while a big, bearded man with delicate fingers

clipped a microphone to my sweater collar and looked me up and down before hanging a small black box with an on/off toggle switch to the back of my skirt's waistband. The Decent Christian got his clipped to the back of his belt. The parenting expert, evidently a TV veteran, produced her own microphone from her pocket. Then we were led onto the set that I'd seen a thousand times from my own kitchen and living room—the curving desk where the sports guy and the weather girl would banter with the anchorman, a map of Pennsylvania off to one side. The three of us were positioned on a raised platform, in armchairs grouped around a coffee table with a neat stack of books and a vase of flowers on top of it. As soon as the commercial break began, the Sunday anchor, a gorgeous woman named LaDonna Cole, came and took the seat across from us.

"Pretend we're all just sitting around talking," she instructed as a woman with a blow-dryer in a leather holster around her waist sprayed something onto LaDonna's hair and another lady brushed powder onto her cheeks. "Interrupt each other! Jump in if you've got something to say! Keep it lively, 'kay?" She gave us a twinkling smile. I studied her face anxiously. She was wearing a ton of makeup, even though, as far as I could tell, her skin was flawless. Should I be wearing more?

"In three . . . two . . . one." The bearded man behind the camera pointed two fingers toward LaDonna, who flashed her dazzling teeth again. "Good morning. I'm LaDonna Cole. It's the case that's on every paper's front page, and all over social media. It happened in Akron, last Friday night, and almost everyone knows the details. A fifteen-year-old girl goes to a party hosted by an eighteen-year-old classmate, whose parents are away. There's drinking. The girl passes out. Her ex-boyfriend, who's seventeen, tells her friends that he'll take her home. Instead, according to the girl's testimony, he and three of his friends carry her down the street, to one of the friends' basements, and sexually assault her, posting pictures and video of the assault to popular social media sites. And that's where things get complicated." Photographs flashed on the screen behind LaDonna's head to illustrate her talking points—yearbook pictures of the accused, candids from the football field. "The ex-boyfriend, a popular athlete, says that she did, in fact, consent to their activities. He claims he had no idea that his friends were recording them. The other boys also posted pictures of a vibrator the girl allegedly had in her purse. The case has sparked vigorous debate," said LaDonna, angling her body expertly to face a second camera. "Does the young woman have any responsibility for what allegedly happened that night? Is this a case of rape or, as some have said, a case of a girl who woke up with regrets the morning after? We're joined this morning by Father David Ryan of the Christian League of Decency, Dr. Carol Bendinger, child psychologist and author of *Online and On Guard: Keeping Our Kids Safe in a Wired World,* and Allison Weiss, a popular blogger whose column at Ladiesroom.com deals with sexuality, marriage, and motherhood."

Okay, I thought. *Not bad.*

"Father Ryan, let's start with you."

"Of course, what happened last Friday is a tragedy, for all the young people involved—the young woman and the young men," Father Ryan intoned. "None of them will emerge from this unscathed. The young woman's had her reputation ruined, and the young men are now facing the possibility of prison time, and of having to be registered as sex offenders for the rest of their lives."

"And you think that's wrong," LaDonna prompted.

"I think it's a tragedy, and I think that the young woman has to shoulder some of the blame."

"Why is it her fault?" I asked. All three of their heads turned toward me, and, out of the corner of my eye, I caught the camera's motion. "She went to a party and drank. So did the boys. We've got a lot of he-said/she-said about whether she consented to sex. But the pictures aren't ambiguous. The pictures don't lie. And what the pictures show is a group of boys assaulting a girl who is clearly unconscious, a girl who is in no position to say yes or no or anything at all."

"The pictures also show how she was dressed," Father Ryan said smoothly. "You can't go to a party wearing little more than underwear and not realize that you've put yourself in danger."

"So she deserves to be raped for wearing a short skirt, and the boys who did it, and the ones who took pictures of their buddies, they don't deserve to be punished at all?" I was surprised to find how furious I was, how easily I could imagine my own daughter wearing the wrong thing, downing a drink that was stronger than she'd known, letting the wrong guys walk her home. "What kind of fine, upstanding citizens go to a party and take pictures of one of their buddies having sex, and then put those shots online?"

"Those boys were provoked," Father Ryan said.

"So she was asking for it?" I could feel my anger . . . but I could feel it from a distance, from behind the protective, warm bubble of the drugs, the invisible armor that let me be brave.

"It might be a pleasant fantasy to imagine that women can dress any way they want to and nothing bad will happen," said Father Ryan. "But we live in the real world. Teenage boys, teenage boys who've been drinking . . ."

". . . know that stealing is wrong. They know that arson is wrong. Yet these boys managed to get drunk without helping themselves to anyone's wallets or setting the house on fire. It's ridiculous to give them a free pass for sexual misconduct, to think that everything they know about what's right and fair and legal goes out the window because they've had a bunch of beer and they see a girl in a short skirt."

"Let's hear from Dr. Bendinger," said LaDonna. Her widened eyes suggested that she might have gotten a more lively conversation than she'd envisioned.

Dr. Bendinger said the case illustrated how social media raised the stakes of all of our actions; how no matter what you did, it would dwell online, forever.

"And is that fair?" asked LaDonna.

Father Ryan shook his head. "This was a youthful indiscretion," he said.

"This was a rape," I replied.

He shook his head again, looking annoyed, like I was a mosquito who wouldn't quit buzzing. "A young girl goes to a party in a short skirt and a tank top. She gets drunk. She's announcing her intentions to have sex. She's got a vibrator in her purse . . ."

"None of which meant it was okay for four guys to carry her down to the basement and rape her."

"So you don't have a problem with a fifteen-year-old having a vibrator?" asked LaDonna.

"I do not," I said. "I think it's better for a young woman to use a vibrator in a loving, committed, monogamous relationship, or to use it all by herself, in no relationship at all, than for her to participate in hookup culture, where she's there to service a guy, where he gets off and she gets nothing." Was I allowed to say "get off" on TV? Never mind. The pills were lifting me, buoying me, making me feel invincible, effortlessly witty, even cute. "Maybe vibrators are actually keeping girls out of trouble," I said. "Maybe every girl should get one along with her driver's license. A chicken in every pot and a vibrator in every purse!"

I said. Father Ryan looked horrified. I, on the other hand, felt great.

"With that, I'm afraid we're out of time," said LaDonna Cole, who looked more than slightly relieved. "Father Ryan, Dr. Bendinger, Ms. Weiss, thank you so much for joining us." When the camera was off, we all shook hands; then, still glowing with triumph, I sailed out of the building and into my car. My phone was buzzing, flashing Sarah's picture on the screen.

"Hi!"

"A chicken in every pot and a vibrator in every purse?" She sounded somewhere between bemused and grossed out. "Dude. You have got to write that and get it up ASAP."

"ASAP," I repeated, and giggled. Oh, but I felt good! And a few more pills—two, maybe even three, why not?—would only make me feel better. I could surf this delicious, happy wave all the way home. I could write my next blog post, make love with my husband and fall asleep in the warmth of his arms, and then I'd get up, go to the grocery store, and buy the ingredients for his favorite coq au vin for dinner. While it was simmering, I'd call Skinny Marie and give her carte blanche and a blank check. My house would finally have furniture. My life would finally be okay.

"Six hundred words. Quick as you can." Then Sarah paused. This was uncharacteristic. Sarah was usually full speed ahead, without as much as an "um" to disrupt the staccato rhythms of her thoughts. "This is kind of awkward, but I need to ask you something."

"Ask away!" I said. Just like that, the delicious wave of joy collapsed underneath me, leaving me splayed on an icy shore. Suddenly I was terrified. *She knows,* I thought. Maybe I'd accidentally typed my work address at Penny Lane, and they'd delivered a package of Percocet or Oxy to the office?

Sarah cleared her throat. Then, before I could beg her to put me out of my agony, she said, "There's some money missing from the petty cash account."

"Oh!" Ladiesroom maintained the account Sarah had mentioned, a few thousand dollars that all writers and editors above a certain level could access if they wanted to, for example, pay for membership to a sex club without using their own credit card or having to wait for the expense reports to wend their way through the accounting department (which had been, we guessed, outsourced to some country where women would work for a dollar an hour).

On Wednesday afternoon, sitting idly at my computer, I'd realized, with an unpleasant jolt, that at my current rate of consumption I would run out of pills by Sunday. Purchasing drugs online was a tedious affair that involved buying Internet currency on one site, then moving those coins to Penny Lane . . . and I saw, as my heartbeat sped up, that the checking account I used to fund my illicit activities was almost empty. I could transfer money in from a household account, or get a cash advance from one of my credit cards, then make a deposit . . . but what if Dave decided to look?

Unable to think of a solution, feeling desperate and trapped, I'd taken a thousand dollars out of the petty cash account, moved it to my personal checking account, and then used it on Penny Lane. I'd planned on replacing the cash first thing Monday, as soon as I got paid, and hoped that nobody would notice.

Except, of course, somebody had.

"Oh my God, I'm so sorry!" I said, apologizing to buy time while I tried to come up with some kind of plausible explanation. "I meant to tell you. What happened was, I got caught short on my property taxes. I had no idea how high they'd be out here—I mean, obviously, I did know, at least at some point, but I must have repressed it. So my accountant called me last Wednesday and was, like, you need to pay this before the end of the workday, so I just moved the money, and I was going to e-mail you about it, and of course I was going to pay it back as soon as I got my paycheck Monday morning, but it must have totally slipped my mind. It was a really stupid thing to do, and I am so, so sorry . . ."

I made myself shut my mouth. In the silence that followed, I imagined the cops showing up, Ellie watching as they snapped on the handcuffs and led me away. Sarah had every right to accuse me of stealing. Petty cash was for work-related expenses, not property taxes. She could turn me in to the cops, or to Ladiesroom's bosses. Worse than that, she could demand to know why I really needed the money. My tale of property-tax woe sounded flimsy even to my own ears.

Instead of asking more questions, though, Sarah said, "Okay. I figured it was probably something like that. It wasn't like you were trying to be sneaky about it . . . I mean, you didn't exactly try to cover your tracks."

I felt like my internal organs were turning to soup, like my bones were caving in. I was shaking all over, sweating at my hairline and underneath my arms, struggling to keep my voice steady as I repeated how sorry I was, how stupid I'd been, how of course I would put the money back immediately if not sooner and how I would never ever ever do anything that dumb again.

"It's okay." Sarah sounded a little stiff. My eyes prickled with tears; my cheeks burned with humiliation. Did Sarah have any idea what was really going on? Had I lost her respect and her trust? "Just get home and get to writing. 'A chicken in every pot and a vibrator in every purse.' I wonder if we can get T-shirts made?"

On that happy note, I apologized some more, then unclenched one sweat-slicked hand from the steering wheel and shoved it into my purse. I didn't have enough pills to calm myself down, to erase what I'd done and make it okay. When I was wound up like this, four or five or even six pills could barely take the edge off. But I had to do something to slow my racing heartbeat, to get rid of the sick, sinking feeling in my gut, the shame that had taken up residence in my bones . . . and this was the only thing I knew. "I'll call you as soon as I'm done writing," I said, and slipped my medicine under my tongue.

I paid close attention to the speed limit and kept a safe distance between my front bumper and the car ahead of me. I'd never been the most mindful of drivers even in my pre-pill era, and a fistful of Oxy did not do much to improve one's concentration. More than once since I'd found Penny Lane, I had pulled out of our driveway with my coffee mug on top of the car or driven away from a gas station with the gas cap still dangling. I put on music, practiced yoga breathing, and tried to tell myself that everything was fine, that I'd dodged the petty-cash bullet, and that, as soon as I finished my blogging, Dave and I could pick up where we'd left off.

That thought should have been enough to keep me occupied. When we first fell in love, we had a fantastic sex life. We were spontaneous, but we would also plan elaborate surprises for each other, scavenger hunts and carefully thought-out gifts and getaways. Even when we didn't have a lot of money, we had always managed to delight each other on special occasions and, sometimes, just on regular Friday nights.

For our first anniversary, I'd done an Alice in Wonderland–style adventure. I had propped a stoppered glass vial filled with Dave's favorite Scotch on the kitchen table, with a card reading DRINK ME and an arrow pointing down the hallway. A trail of roses led to the bedroom. After contemplating and rejecting the idea of lying on the bed naked, except for some cute lace panties with a card reading EAT ME affixed to the waistband, I'd instead left those words on a card with a single chocolate-dipped strawberry beside it. On the flip side of the EAT ME card was another clue, telling Dave to go "where I like to get wet." This led him to the Lombard Swim Club, where we'd splurged on a membership for the summer. The girl behind the desk had given him an *Amazing Race*–style envelope with a handmade crossword puzzle, which had sent him to the Boathouse Row Bar in the Rittenhouse Hotel, where I'd been waiting with cocktails and a reservation at a restored Victorian bed-and-breakfast in Avalon down on the Jersey Shore, where we would run in a race together the next morning.

Maybe I should plan something like that again, I thought as I swung the car onto our street. True, I hadn't been running much these days, but it wasn't as if I'd been sitting around doing absolutely nothing. (*You run after drugs,* my mind whispered. *You run to the bank. You run to the pharmacy.* I told it to shut up.) A few weeks of training and I'd be able to run at least the better part of a 5K. I'd find a race somewhere pretty, not too far away, get Doreen to take Eloise for the night or maybe even the weekend, buy a bottle of good Champagne for when we were through . . .

A blue Lexus was parked in our driveway, with Pennsylvania plates and an Obama bumper sticker. Hmm. I grabbed my purse, got out of my car, and walked in through the garage, hearing the sound of singing coming from the kitchen. Ellie was standing on a chair, performing what I recognized as her *Legally Blonde* medley. " 'Honey, whatcha crying at? You're not losin' him to that.' "

"A star is born," Dave said to a woman sitting at the table. Ellie was in full Ellie gear, with a tutu around her waist and a tiara on her head, a fake feather boa wrapped around her neck, and my high heels on her feet. Dave was wearing jeans and a Rutgers T-shirt, his hair still wet from the shower. The woman at the table looked as comfortable as if she lived there . . . or as if Dave had called some casting agency and asked for a slightly younger, significantly hotter version of me. Her jeans were crisp, dark, and low-rise, tucked into knee-high leather riding boots. Her fuchsia T-shirt had just enough Lycra for it to hug her torso in a flattering line, with a boatneck showing off her collarbones and pale, freckled skin. Her blonde hair was drawn into a sleek ponytail that looked casual but must have taken at least twenty minutes of fussing and a few different products to achieve, and she wore subtle makeup—light foundation, a little tinted lip-gloss, mascara and pencil to darken her brows and her lashes. L. McIntyre, I presumed.

"Hello," I said, and dropped my purse on the counter. I rested my left hand on Dave's shoulder, wedding and engagement bands on proud display, and extended my right. "I'm Allison."

"Lindsay is a work friend of Daddy's," Ellie explained.

"She came by to drop off some documents," Dave added. I thought I could feel him flushing.

"Wasn't that nice," I said. "Do you live out this way?"

"Old City," L. answered. "I'm Lindsay McIntyre." She had one of those cool, limp handshakes, with no grip at all. I moved her fingers up and down once, then let go.

"Dave, can you come give me a hand for a moment?" My voice was sugar-cookie sweet. His expression was unreadable as he followed me through the kitchen and into the mudroom.

"What is going on here?" I hissed. "You're bringing your girlfriend over for playdates?"

He raked his fingers through his damp hair. "Allison, she isn't my girlfriend. I'm married. You don't get to have girlfriends if you're married."

"Glad we're on the same page with that. So what is she doing in my house?"

"*Your* house?" Dave repeated. Underneath the TV makeup, I felt my cheeks get hot.

"Our house. Why is she in our house, at our kitchen table, singing show tunes with our daughter?"

"She's doing exactly what I said. She was dropping off some information I needed for a story I'm working on. It's part of the election series," he added, his tone suggesting I was supposed to know what that was. Since I didn't, I said, "And she just decided to hang out and do a number?"

"She and Ellie seemed to be getting along."

How nice for you, I wanted to say, *that you can audition my replacement before I'm even gone.* Cut it out, I told myself. Maybe this was completely innocent. Maybe the pills were making me paranoid.

My phone buzzed in my purse. Sarah, terse as ever, was texting me. *ETA?* she'd written. Shit.

"I need to write something. Can you keep Ellie amused for an hour?"

"I actually need to get to the office. I've had her all morning," he said.

While I was goofing off, I thought. Instead, I walked wordlessly into the kitchen, where Ellie was wrapping up her finale.

"I should get going," L. said, after Ellie, who'd moved on to *The Sound of Music,* hit the last notes of "So Long, Farewell." She got to her feet, straightening her shirt and giving her hair a pat. It was astonishing, really. A few subtle changes in features and hair color and she could have been me, ten years ago.

"Can we go to the zoo?" Ellie wheedled after L. and Dave had departed.

"I'm sorry, honey. Mommy has to blog." On the couch,

my laptop open, Ellie bribed into compliance with a bag of jelly beans and the remote control, I thought of what Lindsay McIntyre had seen when she stopped by. The kitchen, at least, had furniture. There was a cheerful jumble of family pictures on the refrigerator. One wall had been painted with blackboard paint and turned into a calendar, with "Clay Club" and "Daddy's 10K" and "Stonefield Pajama Party" written in colorful chalk. There were apples in a yellow-and-blue ceramic bowl, the orchid that I hadn't managed to kill in a clay pot on the windowsill. You would never see my kitchen and guess how many milligrams of narcotics I required to drag myself through the day. You would never look at my living room and know how much I'd cried reading comments on one of my blog posts, or looking at the online banking site and fretting about the increased frequency with which I was moving money to my secret account or the widening gap between what I put in each month and Dave's contributions. You'd check out the big house with its princess suite, the princess herself, her brown hair for once neatly combed, and imagine that we had a happy life. *Nothing to see here,* you would think. *Everything is fine.*

NINE

In all my years of working at the *Examiner* and then for Ladiesroom, I'd never had anything come close to going viral. When I'd organized the slide show of nude cyclists that ran with the paper's coverage of Philadelphia's annual Naked Critical Mass ride, the pictures had gotten a tremendous number of hits, but that had all been local attention. Nothing I'd done, and certainly nothing I'd said, had ever gained national traction. Maybe it was a slow news week, or maybe it had to do with prudish, hypocritical America's fascination with anything related to women and sex, but by Sunday night the "vibrator in every purse" sound bite was racking up hits on YouTube (I'd smartened up enough to know not to watch the clip or even glance at the comments). On Monday morning, a nationally syndicated conservative radio host spent ten minutes frothing into his microphone, incensed at the notion that the writers and editors of Ladiesroom—"a pack of pornography purveyors," as he put it—wanted the government to equip innocent teenage girls with vibrators. Where he got the idea that we were asking for government money, I wasn't sure, but I welcomed the attention. Every hyperbolic, spittle-flecked "THIS is what liberals WANT!" harangue got Ladiesroom.com another ten thousand hits. More hits meant more attention, and more money. Money: Our corporate masters offered a generous bonus for pieces that topped fifty thousand views. I stuck the cash directly into my Naughty Account, knowing I'd need drugs to get through the backlash, the inevitable dissection of my looks and politics and sex life, or lack of same. I was planning on cutting back . . . just not now. There was even a bit on *The Daily Show*, with Jon Stewart smirking as he repeated my line: "A chicken in every pot and a vibrator in every purse! Just make sure you don't get them mixed up," he said as the screen behind him showed a picture of a Hitachi Magic Wand in a Dutch oven. My inbox overflowed with e-mailed condemnations and praise, which I quickly gave up trying to answer. A "thank you for reading my work" would suffice, whether the reader was telling me that I was a genius and a hero and an inspiration to girls everywhere, or a fat ugly whore bent on making men obsolete.

I tried to distract myself by writing something new. "A Mother's Guide to the Online World" was the idea I'd been playing with, a series of tips and how-tos for protecting girls on the Internet and in real life. Nothing scared me more than the idea of Ellie as a teenager, among peers who accepted as normal things like girls texting topless shots of themselves to boys they liked, or boys filming sexual activity and then making the video available to their buddies. She was too young for even the most preliminary conversation—only six months ago I'd stumbled through a speech about where babies came from—but I thought if I could come up with a list of what to do and what to say, maybe I'd be prepared for when she was eight or nine or ten or twelve and the conversation was no longer theoretical.

"Mommy, come visit with me!" Ellie would say, banging on my locked bedroom door in the days and weeks after my TV debut.

"Mommy's working right now," I would call back, telepathically begging her babysitter to come upstairs and whisk her away. Katrina, bless her heart, meant well, but she would usually come with some elaborate craft or cooking project that would take a while to arrange, leaving Ellie free to wander the house, or bang on my door, while her sitter laid out pages of origami paper or baked gingerbread for a gingerbread house.

Dave, meanwhile, had gone back to being tight-lipped and silent, his face unreadable and his body rigid as he passed me in the kitchen or the halls. I was afraid to try to grill him about L. McIntyre. I wanted to know the truth . . . but I suspected that the truth would burst my opiated bubble, revealing the unhappy realities that even four or five Oxys couldn't mask—that my marriage was a sham, that my happiness was an illusion, that even though the pieces were in place and everything seemed okay, underneath the veneer of good looks and good manners, the three of us were falling apart.

Or, at least, I was.

Two weekends after my television triumph, the guilt got to me. I woke up early, chewed up sixty milligrams of OxyContin, took a shower, and announced, over a breakfast I'd cooked myself, that I was putting everything on hold and taking Ellie on a girls' day outing.

"Great," Dave said. He even managed to smile. Ten minutes after I'd made my announcement, he had his running shoes in his hand, his high-tech lap-and-pace-counting watch on his wrist, and his body covered in various wicking and cooling fabrics made from recycled bamboo. "Bye," he called, closing the door behind him. Ellie gave me a syrup-sticky smile. "Can we go to my museum? And the Shake Shack? And the zoo? And to sing-along *Sound of Music*?"

"Sing-along *Sound of Music* was a special treat. How about you pick two of the other things?" I said pleasantly. Meanwhile, I was performing a mental inventory of how many little Oxys I had left, and how I'd space them out to get me through until noon the next day, when my next batch would come in the mail. *You're taking too many,* a voice in my head scolded. I stacked dishes in the sink, then rinsed them and put them in the dishwasher, and told the voice to shut up. *How much money did you spend last month?* the voice persisted. *Four thousand dollars? Five?* I can afford it, I thought uneasily, shoving aside the memory of the petty cash I'd borrowed, or how worried I was that Dave would take a hard look at our joint checking account. *As long as I stay on top of things, as long as I'm careful, I'll be fine.*

After lengthy deliberations, Ellie decided on the zoo, and burgers for lunch. For two hours, we admired the elephants, held our noses in the monkey house, screamed "Ew!" at the naked mole rats, and sat on a bench eating soft-serve pretzels in the sunshine. I let her have everything she wanted—a pedal through the pond on the swan boats, a pony ride, and a trip on the miniature train that circled the zoo. She got her face painted to look like a leopard (a pink-and-white-spotted leopard) and bought friendship bracelets and a souvenir keychain and widened her eyes in disbelief when, at the Shake Shack, I said she could have both cheese fries and a milkshake, when usually I made her choose one or the other.

The cashier gave Ellie a buzzer—by far, one of the highlights of the Shack. "It'll go off when your food's ready."

"I KNOW it! I KNOW it will!" Using two hands, Ellie carried the buzzer to our table and set it reverently in the center after cleaning the surface with an antibacterial wipe from my purse. "Now, don't freak out," she instructed the buzzer.

"Okay. I won't. I won't freak out," I answered, in character as Wa, which is what we'd named the Shake Shack's buzzers, for the *wah-wah-wah* sound they made.

"Just be CALM, Wa," she said, giggling.

"I'm gonna. I-I'm gonna be calm," I stammered, in Wa's trembling, not-at-all-calm voice.

"Just say, 'Your food is ready,' in a NORMAL voice. Don't LOSE YOUR BUSINESS," Ellie said, her eyes sparkling with mirth.

"I got it. I got it. No freaking out. No losing my business. No . . ." Ellie was already starting to giggle as the buzzer lit up and started to hum. "WA! WA! WA! Yourfoodisready!" I said. "Wa! Wa! WAWAWAI'MFREAKINGOUTHEREWA!"

"Wa, calm down! It's just a burger!" Ellie gave the buzzer an affectionate pat as I continued to narrate its breakdown. An older woman sitting at the counter watched the proceedings. On our way back with our tray, she tapped my shoulder.

"Excuse me. I just want to say how much I'm enjoying watching you and your daughter."

"Oh, thank you!" I said, touched almost to tears.

"So many parents, you see them on their phones, barely looking at their kids. You're giving your daughter memories she'll have forever."

Now I was tearing up, thinking about what the woman would never see—the times I had been on my phone or my laptop or napping when Ellie wanted my company.

"That's really nice of you to say," I said, just as—irony!—my phone rang. I gave the woman an apologetic smile. "Hello? Mom?"

For a minute, all I could hear was the sound of her crying. "He f-f-fell . . . out of bed . . . I tried to pick him up and then he p-p-pushed me . . ."

I sat down in my chair. "Okay, Mom. Take a deep breath. Is Daddy there?"

"He left! He ran away!" Another burst of sobbing. "I tried to stop him, but he pushed me down and he ran out the door. He's got bare feet, or maybe just his slippers. I couldn't s-s-stop him . . ."

"Okay." My head spun. Ellie, for once, was sitting quietly, maybe appreciating the seriousness of the situation, staring at me wide-eyed over the lid of her milkshake. "Do you know where he went?"

"No," she sobbed. "By the time I got to the door he was gone."

"Okay. I think you need to get off the phone with me and call the police."

"What do I say?" she wailed.

"Tell them what you told me. Tell them that Daddy has Alzheimer's, and that he was confused and that he's . . ." Run away from home? Wandered off? Gone for a walk in his bare feet? "Just tell them what happened. I'm in Center City, I'm going to put Ellie in the car right now. We'll be there as soon as we can." Even as I was talking, I was packing up my purse, handing Ellie a wipe for her face, rummaging for my parking stub and a twenty-dollar bill.

"Good luck," the woman who'd praised my parenting said as I hustled Ellie out the door, across the street, into the car, and, as fast as I could legally manage it, over the Ben Franklin Bridge and into New Jersey.

There were three police cars at my parents' house when I arrived, one in the driveway and another two parked at the curb in front of the house. On my way over, I'd had a two-minute conversation with Dave, telling him what had happened.

"What can I do?" he'd asked, and I'd found myself almost in tears, melting at the kindness in his voice.

"Just sit tight . . . Actually, you know what? Can you call . . ." What was the woman's name? I pulled to the side of the road and rummaged through my wallet until I found the business card I'd tucked in there for this very moment. "Kathleen Young. She's at Eastwood—you know, the assisted-living place out here?"

"Kathleen Young," Dave said, and repeated the phone number after I read it.

"If she's not working on the weekend, ask for whoever's handling intake. I went there a few weeks ago, just to check it out, so they know me, and they'll at least know my dad's name and his situation. If you tell them what's going on, maybe they'll have a bed for him, or they'll be able to find us someplace that does."

"Got it," said Dave. "Call when you can."

I parked on the street behind one of the cruisers, grabbed Ellie, and raced into the house. My mother was on the couch with an officer in uniform on each side of her. My father, in sweatpants, his bare feet grimy and one big toe bleeding, was sitting in an armchair, his face completely blank. He was missing his glasses, and his hair hadn't been combed.

"Oh, Dad," I said. I put Ellie down and half sat, half collapsed on the couch next to his armchair. He didn't move, didn't acknowledge me, just kept staring into the middle of the room as my mother, bracketed by cops, cried into a fistful of tissue. "What happened?" I asked the room. My mother continued to cry. My dad continued to stare. Finally, one of the cops, who introduced himself as Officer Findlay, said that they'd found my father two blocks away from the house, walking toward the elementary school in his bare feet. "He appeared disoriented, but he didn't give us a hard time."

"Climbed right in the backseat and let us take him home," said the second officer. "Your mother was explaining your dad's situation . . ."

"We should call his doctor," I said to my mom. I hoped, foolishly, that she'd say she'd already done so—that she'd done something. Of course she hadn't. She just sat there, mutely, shaking with sobs.

"I'm going to call," I told the police officers.

I got Ellie situated in front of the television set, handing her the remote and watching her eyes widen as if I'd given her a key to the city, and went upstairs to my dad's study to try to reach his physician. Of course an answering service picked up. I left my name and number and a brief version of the story. Then I called Dave.

"They have a bed available," he reported. "But it'll have to be paid out of pocket until you finish giving them your dad's insurance information. They'll need a copy of your parents' tax returns, too. I'm going to e-mail you all that information," Dave said, in his full-on brisk-and-businessy reporter mode. "There's an Emily Gavin you'll be talking to—she's handling intake over the weekend. They e-mailed a packing list that I can forward along . . ." While Dave kept talking, I let my eyes slip shut.

"Do you think . . ." I swallowed hard. Here was the part I hadn't quite figured out, the puzzle piece I'd never managed to snap into place. "Honey, would it be okay if my mom stayed with us for a while?"

I'd expected objection, at least a pained sigh. But Dave's voice was gentle when he said, "Of course it's fine."

I started to cry. "I love you," I said as the call waiting beeped to let me know that someone from my dad's doctor's practice was calling.

"Love you, too," said Dave.

I sniffled. How long had it been since I'd felt that certainty, that unshakable belief that Dave had my back? And did he know that I had his? Would he come to me in a crisis, or just try to get through it on his own . . . or, worse, would he turn to L. McIntyre, with her understated makeup and sleek ponytail, and ask her to help?

My father's doctor was calling from a movie-theater lobby. "Count yourself lucky that no one got hurt," he said. "Now, clearly, Dad's ready for a higher level of care."

I agreed that Dad was.

"You picked out a place?" He'd given my mother and me a list of possibilities the same day he gave us my father's diagnosis.

"Eastwood has a bed for him."

"Good. They're good people. Don't forget to bring two forms of ID when you go. Pack all his medication—they'll probably let him take his own meds for the first night, then they'll have their doctors call in new scrips for everything, just so they know exactly what he's taking, and when, and how much." I half paid attention as he explained the process of getting my dad situated—what to pack, whom to call—as I tried to figure out how I would actually get my father to Eastwood. Could I leave Ellie with my mother while I drove my father there? What if he got confused, or even violent, or refused to get in my car, or refused to get out of it when he saw where we were? Maybe I'd wait for Dave to make the trip from Philadelphia and have him come along. That would work. I thanked the doctor, got off the phone, closed the study door quietly . . . but before I went downstairs, I detoured into the bathroom that had been mine when I was a girl. The seat was up, the hand towels were askew, and something white—toothpaste, I hoped—was crusted on the cold-water handle at the sink. I ignored it all, shoved my hand deep into my bag, retrieved my Altoids tin, and piled two, then four, then six pills into my mouth.

TEN

Maybe my dad had been belligerent in the morning, but by the time the cops departed, all the fight had gone out of him. He sat quietly in front of the television with a glass of juice and a plate of cheese and crackers while I went upstairs to start packing. "Mom, you want to help?" I asked, pulling a suitcase out of the guest-room closet. There was only silence from downstairs.

No matter. I began emptying the drawers, consulting the packing list Dave had e-mailed. Undershirts and underwear, jeans and khakis, pullover tops ("We find our clients do best in familiar, comfortable clothing without clasps, zippers, buttons, or buckles," the list read). I packed up his phone and its charger, wondering if he'd need it. I added a stack of books, biographies of Winston Churchill and FDR, a copy of *Wolf Hall*, which I knew he'd read and loved. Toothbrush, toothpaste, shaving cream, soap . . . I put in everything I thought he'd need. When I heard Dave arrive, I went downstairs and found my mom next to my father on the couch. I knelt down and took one of her hands between both of mine.

"Dave and I are going to take Daddy to Eastwood. You can wait here with Ellie, and we'll be back as soon as he's settled."

I put my arm around her, feeling like someone had just handed me a script, and I was reading the lines and playing the part of the Good Daughter. "Try not to worry. They'll take good care of Daddy. He's going to be safe."

She didn't answer, but I felt her body shaking. After a minute, she bent forward, briefly resting her body against mine. Her lips were pressed together, her tiny hands clenched in fists. She rocked, and rocked, and I heard a faint whistling noise coming from between her pursed lips, a wretched, keening sound.

The side of her face was already swelling—she'd bounced into the dresser when my dad had pushed her that morning. I found an ice pack in the freezer, wrapped it in a dish towel, then pressed it against her cheek, and murmured nonsense: *Don't worry* and *He'll be fine* and even *He's going to a better place.* Dave was the one who got my father into the backseat and the suitcase into the trunk. He drove, and I cried, and my father sat, silently, with his seat belt on and his hands folded neatly in his lap.

Three hours later, he was relatively settled in a double room, with a framed picture of my mom on his nightstand and his favorite afghan draped across the bed and a social worker, whose job was to help him transition through his first few days, introducing him to his temporary roommate. *Today is SUNDAY,* read a whiteboard on the door. *The next meal is DINNER. We are having ROAST TURKEY, SWEET POTATOES, and SALAD. After dinner, you can watch "SISTER ACT" in the Media Room, or play HEARTS in the Recreation Room. Tomorrow morning is ART THERAPY at nine a.m.*

I looked at the board, then looked away, as Dave, maybe guessing at what I was feeling, took my hand. "It's the right thing to do," he told me, and I nodded, feeling hollow and sad.

Back at my parents' house, Ellie and my mother were where I'd left them, on the sofa, with the TV switched from CNBC to

Nickelodeon and a cheese sandwich, missing two bites, in front of them.

"I made SANDWIDGES," Ellie announced.

"I can tell." The sandwich was decorated with no fewer than six frilly toothpicks, and there was a neat pile of gherkins, Ellie's preferred pickle, beside it.

"Come on, Mom," I said, and took my mother's cool, slack hands. Then I raised my voice, trying for cheer. "Hey, Ellie, guess what? Grandma's going to be visiting with us for a while!"

"Yay!" said Ellie. Wordlessly, soundlessly, my mother got to her feet and climbed the stairs, with Ellie and I trailing behind her. For a minute, she stood in front of the unmade bed, with one pillow still bearing the impression of my dad's head. Then, as I watched, she took the pillow in her arms and hugged it.

"I love him so much," she said. She wasn't crying, and that was scarier, even, than the keening she'd been doing before. Her voice was quiet and matter-of-fact, and she shook off my hand when I tried to touch her shoulder. "You have no idea . . . How will I live without him?"

"You'll still see him," I said, trying to sound encouraging and hold back my own tears. "He needs you." I paused. "I need you," I added, trying not to notice how strange those words sounded. Had I ever told my mother I needed her? Had it ever been true? "And Ellie needs her grandmother."

We packed a bag for her, with what I guessed was a week's worth of clothes, and loaded another bag with her cosmetics, her blow-dryer and curling iron, the pots and bottles and canisters of sprays and gels and powders she used every day. While I zipped up the bags, I explained to her that Eastwood was convenient to both of us. I told her that I'd visited a number of places (true, if online visits counted) and had settled on this one as the best of the bunch. I described the attractive facilities, the comfortable room, the doctors on staff, and the trips Dad could take. On the drive back to Haverford, she sat in silence with her hands folded in her lap, watching the trees flash past, as if she were a corpse that no one had gotten around to burying yet.

"Why isn't Grandma TALKING?" Ellie demanded from her booster.

Before I could answer, my mother said, "Grandma is sad," in a rusty, tear-clogged voice. I waited for her to elaborate. When she didn't, Ellie said, "Sometimes I am sad, too."

"Everyone gets sad sometimes," I said, and left it at that. I was thinking, of course, of my pills. Instead of lifting me out of the misery of the moment, they had left me there, shaky and wired and miserable, thinking, *If I just take one more* or *Maybe if I took two.* Since I'd gotten the call at the Shake Shack, I had swallowed . . . how many? I didn't want to think about it. I was afraid the number might have entered double digits . . . and even I knew that was way, way too many.

I'll cut back, I promised myself as I swung the car into my driveway. Now that my father was somewhere safe, now that things weren't quite so crazy with work, I could start tapering off. But, as the days went by, as the media furor over the vibrator-in-every-purse remark died down and my dad settled in to the routines of Eastwood, the tapering never began. I would start each day with the best of intentions. Then Ellie would have a tantrum after she realized we'd run out of her preferred breakfast cereal, or I would find my mother slumped at the kitchen table, still in her bathrobe, waiting, along with my five-year-old, to be fed, and I'd have to coax her to eat a few bites, to put on her clothes, to please get in the car because if you don't, we're going to be late for Daddy's appointment with the gerontologist, and I would think, *Tomorrow. I'll start cutting back tomorrow. I just need to get through today.*

• • •

When she wasn't at Eastwood visiting my dad, my mom spent her days in the guest room, with the door shut, doing what, I didn't know. When Ellie came home she'd emerge—pale and quiet, but at least upright and clothed—and the two of them would spend the afternoon together. My mom was teaching Ellie to play Hearts, a game she and my father used to play together on the beach. She was also teaching Ellie how to apply makeup—which didn't thrill me, but it wasn't a battle I was going to fight. From my computer, behind the bedroom door, I'd brace myself for shrieks of "NO," and "DON'T WANT TO," and, inevitably, "YOU ARE MURDERING ME WITH THE COMB!" But Ellie rarely complained. After dinner, I'd find them cuddled together in the oversized armchair slipcovered in toile, a relic of my single-girl apartment, flipping through *Vogue*, discussing whether or not a dress's neckline flattered the model who wore it.

One morning, after shuttling yet another thousand dollars from my secret checking account to the account I'd set up at Penny Lane, I started adding up what all the pills had cost me. I stopped when I hit ten thousand dollars, feeling dizzy, feeling terrified. The truth was, I had probably spent much more than that, and I was equally sure that if I tried to stop, cold turkey, I'd get sick. Already I'd noticed that if I went more than four or five hours between doses, I would start sweating. My skin would break out in goose bumps; my stomach would twist with nausea. I'd feel dizzy and weak, panicked and desperate until I had my hands on whatever tin or bottle I was using, until the pills were in my mouth, under my tongue, being crunched into nothingness.

Just for now, I told myself. Just until my parents' house sells, just until I figure out what to do about my mom, just until my father settles in. Another six weeks—two months, tops. Then

I'd do it. I'd figure out how many pills I was taking each day, and cut down by a few every day, slowly, gently, until I was back to zero. I'd have a long-postponed confrontation with Dave. I'd ask the questions that scared me the most: *Are you in or are you out? Do you love me? Can we work on this? Is there anything left to save?* Whatever he told me, whatever answers he gave, I would work with them. I would be the woman I knew I could be: good at my job, a good mother to my daughter, a good wife, if Dave still wanted me. Just not right now. For now, I needed the pills.

ELEVEN

"How's your dad?"

I sighed, taking a seat at Janet's kitchen counter, next to a stack of catalogs and what appeared to be a half-assembled diorama of a Colonial kitchen. It was three-fifteen on a balmy, sweetly scented May afternoon, and I'd just arrived at her house, half a mile from my own, with perfectly pruned rosebushes lining the walkway from the street to the front door. We'd passed the living room and the den, both decorator-perfect, and ended up in the kitchen, where Janet was thawing a pot of beef stew on the stove and had the wineglasses out on the counter.

"Half a glass," I said, as she started to pour from a lovely bottle of Malbec. We'd already agreed that I would fetch the kids from Enrichment, the after-school program that Stonefield: A Learning Community offered between the hours of three and six for working parents. I would, therefore, drink responsibly. Of course, Janet had no idea that I'd helped myself to a handful of my dad's Vicodin in the car, and that there were more pills in my purse and in my pocket.

"And thanks for asking. My dad's adjusting." Sipping my wine, I told Janet about how, the day after his arrival, my father had switched from silent to belligerent, throwing things and shouting at the attendants to show him another room, that he'd reserved a suite, goddamnit, and if there wasn't a suite he at least wanted a better view. As best I could figure, he thought he was in a hotel, on a business trip. He'd unpacked, hanging his shirts and pants in the closet, and if he'd noticed the lack of ties and jackets, or that the only shoes I'd sent with him were sneakers, he hadn't said anything. Eastwood had assigned seating at mealtimes, and his case manager, a young woman named Nancy Yanoff, reported that my father was eating and seemed to be enjoying the company of the other residents at his table. Meanwhile, I was scrambling to get my parents' house on the market, to finish filling out the thick sheaf of forms the long-term care required, and to figure out a long-term plan for my mom.

God bless narcotics. The pills gave me the energy and confidence to get through the day. They lulled me to sleep at night. They made it possible for me to have an uncomfortable conversation with my husband about how long my mom could stay. Dave was still being generous, still speaking to me kindly, but I sensed that his patience had a limit, and that in a month or two I'd find myself approaching it.

For now, though, he'd moved his belongings back to the master bedroom. I'd hastily ordered a dresser, two bedside tables, lamps, and an area rug for the guest room that had previously contained only a bed. Most nights I'd fall asleep before Dave did. Sometimes, if he woke me up with the bathroom light, I'd take my book and go to Ellie's bedroom, lying beside my daughter in the queen-sized bed we'd been smart to purchase, telling her that Daddy was snoring again when she woke up and was surprised to see she had company. "But all things considered, it's not too bad," I told my friend.

Janet looked at me sidewise, skepticism all over her face. "How is it going with Little Ronnie?"

"Okay, here's the shocker. She's actually functioning. She helps take care of Ellie in the afternoons." It was true that my mother still had the annoying habit of wandering down to the kitchen for breakfast, lunch, and dinner with the expectation that someone (not her) would put a hot, balanced meal on the table, and clean up afterward. She would leave her dirty clothes piled in the hamper with the unspoken assumption that they would be washed and put away, and she would announce that she had an appointment here or there instead of requesting a ride . . . but she was spending a few hours each day with Ellie. "And Ellie's actually calmed down a little. I think, in a weird way, she feels responsible for her grandmother."

Janet nodded, sipped her wine, and said, "Maybe I could rent your mother. My three need to get the memo that they're responsible for more than just wiping themselves." She made a face, flashing her crooked teeth. "And one of the boys isn't even doing that so well. I don't know which one—I buy them identical undies, and it's not really the kind of thing you want to, you know, investigate thoroughly . . ."

I smiled, imagining my friend with a pair of lab tweezers and a fingerprinting kit, gingerly tugging a pair of skidmarked Transformers underpants out of an inside-out pair of little boy's jeans.

"And did I tell you that Maya is now a vegan? And the boys won't eat vegan food—which I can't really blame them for— so I'm now cooking two meals a night? What happened?" she asked. Her cheeks were flushed, eyes narrowed, ponytail askew. "I mean, really. I was Phi Beta Kappa. I was most likely to succeed. I billed more hours than any other associate my first three years out of law school. And now I spend my days driving my kids to hockey practice and swim club and choir rehearsal, and my afternoons making lasagna with tofu cheese, and my nights folding their underwear and checking their homework and spraying the insides of hockey skates with Lysol. I don't even know who I am anymore."

She poured wine almost to the top of her glass and took a healthy swallow. "Do you know what I think when I wake up in the morning?" Without waiting for an answer, she said, "I count how many hours there are until I can have a glass of wine. There's something wrong with me, if that's all I'm looking forward to. If I have this . . ."—she gestured, hands spread to indicate the room, the house, the neighborhood—"this life, these kids, this house, this husband, and I love him, I swear I do, but most days the only thing that's giving me any pleasure, the only thing I'm looking forward to at all is my goddamn glass of wine. That's a problem, isn't it?"

"I don't know," I said, and started reflexively straightening the stack of catalogs on the counter. Pottery Barn. J.Crew. L.L.Bean. Lands' End. Ballard Designs. Garnet Hill. Saks. Nordstrom. Restoration Hardware. Sundance. All the same ones I got and kept in a basket in the powder room, to leaf through late at night. If Janet was counting the hours until her five o'clock drink, I was in way worse shape than she was. I wasn't waiting until five anymore. Or even noon. My days began with pills—I would wake up sad and shaky and overwhelmed and I'd need a little pop of something just to get out of bed—and I kept a steady dose of opiates in my bloodstream all day long. More and more, my mind returned to that quiz in the doctor's office, and I found myself wondering: What would happen if I tried to cut back and I couldn't?

You can stop, my mind said soothingly. *But you don't have to. Not right now.* Which sounded good . . . except what if I couldn't?

What if I was really and truly addicted, just like the actresses in the tabloids, or the homeless people I avoided while they begged at the intersections and on the sidewalks of Center City? What if that was me? Late at night, with Dave snoring away and Ellie and my mother asleep down the hall, I'd lie awake, the bitterness of the pills still on my tongue and my laptop making the tops of my thighs sweat, Googling rehabs, reading articles about drugs and alcohol, taking quizzes and reading blogs and newspaper stories about mommies who drank and celebrities who'd ended up addicted to painkillers or Xanax. With my Oxy or Percocet still pulsing in my head, I would point and click my way down the tunnel as midnight slipped into the small hours of the morning.

"I think you're a great mother," I told Janet. "You're doing an amazing job. And you know this isn't going to last. You'll blink and they'll be in college."

"College," she repeated. She lifted her glass and seemed surprised to find it almost empty. "I was going to have this big life. Barry and I were supposed to have adventures. I was going to be a prosecutor, then a judge, and then maybe I'd teach law. I used to dream about that. And now . . ." Her lips curled, her face twisting into an expression of deep disgust. "Allison, I'm a *housewife*. When I go online, I'm researching cereal coupons, or trying to figure out if my kid's ADHD medicine is going to interact with his asthma stuff. The last thing I read for pleasure was *Wonder,* which was great but was written for ten-year-olds, and the only reason I even read that was because it was lying around the living room because Maya had to read it for school. I have all these clothes . . ."

As discreetly as I could, I snuck a look at the clock on my phone, wondering if my mail had been delivered yet and if the pills I'd ordered from Penny Lane had arrived. They came in regular Express Mail envelopes, but I couldn't risk Dave's intercepting one of them. I didn't want the first real conversation we had in forever to be about why I was illegally purchasing prescription medication on the Internet.

I slipped my hand into my pocket, touching my tin. At this point, I could guess just by its weight how many pills it contained. Ten, I estimated. Surely ten pills would last me until tomorrow, if they had to? Maybe I could excuse myself, tell Janet I had to make a call, and see if one of my doctors would phone in another prescription, just to tide me over.

"All these clothes," she repeated. "Skirts and suits and jackets. High heels. All that stuff, just hanging there."

"You'll wear them again," I told her. I knew Janet's plan had been to start working part-time the previous fall, when the boys started kindergarten. But then Conor had gotten his ADHD diagnosis, and Janet had spent what felt like an entire year at some doctor's or therapist's office every day after school. As soon as Conor had been stabilized with the right combination of medicine and tutoring and a psychologist to teach him cognitive behavioral strategies for managing his disorder (translation: how to keep from screaming and throwing things when he got frustrated), Dylan had started acting out, getting in fights at school, yelling at his teachers, hiding in the bathroom when recess was over. This, of course, meant therapy for him, too. Somewhere in there, Maya had stopped speaking to her mother. When Janet had described her attempts to give Maya the "your changing body" talk, and how Maya had literally thrown the helpful *Care & Keeping of You* book into the hallway so hard it had left a dent in the paint, Barry and I had laughed, Barry so hard there were tears glistening in his beard, but I could tell that Janet was heartbroken at her daughter's silent treatment.

"Five years from now you'll be running the attorney general's office, and you'll be too important to take my calls," I told her.

"Ha." It was a very bleak "Ha." I wanted to reassure her that we'd get through this time, that in three or five or eight years things would come around right and we would find ourselves again the smart, vital women we'd once been . . . but who was I to talk?

"OMG," Janet said, looking at the clock. Somehow, it was five-thirty. "Are you okay to drive? Are you sure?"

"I'm good." I'd had only a single glass of wine. At least, as far as she knew.

"Want me to come with you?"

"That's okay. I'll have the boys back here by six-fifteen."

She nodded. Then she hugged me, with her wineglass still in her hand. "You're my best friend," she said, and, briefly, rested her head on my shoulder. I gave her a squeeze, located my purse, got behind the wheel, and pulled out of Janet's driveway. My heart lurched as I heard a car honking and the word "ASS-HOLE!" float down the street. *Shit,* I thought, realizing how close I'd come to backing into the side of someone's BMW. Oh, well. The other car had probably been speeding. I hoped Janet hadn't seen it as I put the car in drive and proceeded toward Stonefield, coming to a full stop at each stop sign, keeping as-siduously to the speed limit. Where had that BMW even come from?

I pulled up at a red light, with my eyelids feeling as heavy as if someone had coated them with wet sand. I kept my foot on the brake and let my eyes slip shut, feeling the warmth of the pills surging through my veins, that intoxicating sense of everything being right with the universe. My head swung forward. I could feel my hair against my cheeks . . .

Someone behind me was honking. I bolted upright, opening my eyes. "Jesus, cool your jets!" I hit the gas and was jerked backward as my car leapt through the intersection. Why was everyone in such a goddamn rush? What happened to manners? I squinted into the rearview mirror, trying to make out the face behind the wheel of the car that had honked, wondering if it was anyone I knew . . . and then, in an instant, the sign for Stonefield was looming up on my right. I stomped on the brakes, hit the turn signal, and heard the squeal of rubber on the road as I made the turn, cutting off the car in my right-hand lane. My heart thudded as I hit the brakes. There were two cars in front of me, and I could see Janet's twins waiting, in their baseball caps and matching backpacks, along with Eloise, in the Lilly Pulitzer sundress she'd picked out herself. I put the car in park, grabbed the key fob, and hopped out of my seat. The heel of my shoe must have caught on the floor mat, because instead of the graceful exit I'd planned on, I tripped and went down hard on the pavement, landing on my hands and knees.

"Ow!" I yelled. My palms were stinging, dotted with beads of blood, and my pants were torn at the knee. I wondered if anyone had seen me. I looked around, swallowing hard as I spotted Mrs. Dale, one of the teachers in Ellie's class, standing at the curb with a clipboard in her hand. Just my luck. Miss Reckord, the other teacher, was a sweet-faced, dumpling-shaped twenty-five-year-old with rosy cheeks and a whispery voice. The little boys all nursed crushes on her, and the girls fought to sit on her lap at story time, where they could finger her dangly earrings. Mrs. Dale was a different story. Thin-lipped, broad-shouldered, and flat-chested, with hair the color and consistency of a Brillo pad and skin as pale as yogurt, Mrs. Dale—who had, as far as I knew, no first name that was ever used by anyone in the Stonefield community—had been bringing five-year-olds to heel for more than thirty years. Mrs. Dale was not impressed with your special little snowflake. She did not believe in affirmations or unearned compliments to boost a kid's self-esteem, or the unspoken Stonefield philosophy that every child was a winner. She believed in children keeping their hands to themselves, not running in the hallways, and coloring inside the lines. She took zero shit off of anyone, and she never, ever smiled.

I waved at her, surreptitiously sliding my bleeding palms into my pockets. "Sorry I'm late! Come on, everyone!" I opened the rear passenger side door, scooping Eloise up by her armpits and hoisting her into her seat.

Mrs. Dale was watching me. "Did you get my messages about the board meeting?"

Oof. I'd gotten several calls from the school over the past few days—maybe even the past few weeks—but I'd hit "Ignore" and let them go straight to voicemail. I was busy. I was tired. I had a job, unlike half the mothers of kids in Ellie's class. Why didn't the school ever call them?

"Sorry. I've been running around like crazy. New project . . ."

"MOMMY, I'm BLOODY!" Eloise shrieked. I looked at her and, sure enough, my bloody palm had left a red smear on her pink-and-green dress.

Mrs. Dale stepped closer. "Mrs. Weiss? Are you all right?"

"What? Oh, yeah. Just ripped my pants, no big deal. I'm such a klutz. Don't ever stand near me in a Zumba class." I followed her gaze down to my palms. Blushing, I grabbed a baby wipe from the box in the backseat and cleaned my hands, then fumbled with the buckle of the seat belt, tugging it hard against Ellie's chest.

"Ow, Mommy, that HURTS!"

"Sorry, sorry," I said. I could feel it now, the pills and the wine, surging through me with each heartbeat, singing their imperative: *Sleep. Now.* I finally clicked the buckle shut. "We'll be at Janet's in ten minutes. I'll give you a *Despicable Me* Band-Aid."

"I HATE *Despicable Me!*"

"Sure you do," I muttered. She'd loved it last week. "Dylan? Conor? You guys okay?" The boys nodded. One of them had a handheld video game. The other had an iPod, with the buds stuck in his ears. I pulled the rear door shut, turned, and felt Mrs. Dale's hand close around my hand. Around my key fob.

"Why don't you come in and have a cup of coffee?"

"Oh, that's so nice of you, but I really . . . I have to . . . Janet's got dinner on the table, and Ellie's going to freak out if I don't get her cleaned up."

"We can wash her dress in the nurse's office. We've got Band-Aids there, and snacks if the boys are hungry."

"That's very kind." I could hear my pulse thumping in my ears. "But I really have to get these guys going."

Mrs. Dale's hand stayed in place. "Have you been drinking?" she asked, stepping close, eyes narrowed, nostrils flaring, like she was trying to smell my breath.

I stiffened, feeling the flesh of my back break out in goose bumps, almost swooning in terror. *Busted.* I was busted. I'd get arrested. I'd lose my license. Dave would find out. Everyone would know.

I pulled myself up straight, trying to look and sound as sober as I could. "Janet and I had a glass of wine, but that was over an hour ago. I'm fine. Really. I swear." I said it firmly, trying to look and sound respectable and sober, hoping that Mrs. Dale would be mindful that I was, for all intents and purposes, her employer. I smoothed my hair and tried to ignore my torn pants and my bloody palms, and project a look of serenity and competence.

Mrs. Dale appeared to be unmoved. "Mrs. Weiss, I think you need to come inside."

"I'm *fine*." I yanked at the keys, pulling them out of her hand so hard that I stumbled backward, almost falling on the sidewalk.

"Listen to me." Her voice was the commanding, imperious one I'd heard on the playground, a tone that could get a few dozen unruly kindergartners to snap to attention. "As a teacher, I am a mandated reporter. If I believe that children are in danger, I have to call the Department of—"

"What are you talking about?" My voice was almost a shout. I widened my eyes to show how completely ridiculous she was being. "You think the children are in danger?" The soft comfort of the pills was gone, vanished, evaporated, as if it had never been there. My body was on high alert, heart pounding, adrenaline whipping through my bloodstream, and I could hear my voice getting higher and louder. "I had one glass of wine." Never mind the pills I'd taken beforehand. "One. Glass. I'm fine."

"I don't know what you've had, but I can't let you drive with children in your car." She put a hand—a patronizing hand—between my shoulder blades. "Come inside. Sit down. Have coffee."

Now there were three cars behind mine. I recognized Tracy Kelly, and Quinn Gamer, and a man I didn't know, and all of them were staring. Quinn had her phone in her hand, busily texting, probably telling someone—her husband, a friend—exactly what was going on; Allison Weiss, Mrs. Vibrator in Every Purse, had shown up at Stonefield wasted.

"Mommy?"

I looked inside the car, where Ellie was buckled into her

booster seat, with her thumb hooked into her mouth. Ellie hadn't sucked her thumb since she was three. "Why is everybody YELLING?"

"Okay," I said, and opened my hand. The key fob slid out from my sweaty fingers and fell onto the sidewalk with a *clink*. "Okay."

TWELVE

Mrs. Dale got the kids out of the car and drove it to the teachers' lot. She left me in her classroom, then disappeared with Ellie and the boys. I hoped she was taking them back to the Enrichment room, giving them treats, letting them play with the newest toys. I took a seat at one of the munchkin-sized desks and pulled out my phone. Janet answered on the third ring.

"Allison?"

"Hey!" I said, trying to sound upbeat and untroubled, even though fingers of cold sweat were tracing the curve of my spine and I'd noticed my hands shaking as I'd punched in her number. "Just letting you know that I'm running a little late. The traffic was a mess," I lied, knowing that Janet would believe me. "Sit tight. I'll have them home as soon as I can."

"Take your time," she said.

We hung up, and I rummaged through my purse for a bottle of water. I sipped it, looking longingly at my tin, knowing how stupid it would be to take a pill now, now of all times. My heart was still beating so hard I could feel my temples pounding, and I could feel more sweat collecting there, beading above my upper lip. Then I thought, *In for a penny, in for a pound.* The pills were my normal. They'd help me calm down. They would get me through this. And if they did, I promised God and Ellie and whatever forces or spirits might have been listening, I would stop. I would.

I slid two blue pills under my tongue just as Mrs. Dale came into the room, carrying a steaming WORLD'S BEST TEACHER mug and packets of sugar and Cremora and Sweet 'N Low.

"Thanks," I said. I dumped fake cream and sugar into the cup and sipped. Mrs. Dale sat at her desk and loaded folders into a tan leather satchel. I waited for the lecture to begin. When it didn't, I started talking.

"Listen. I appreciate what you did out there. I understand that it's your job. But, like I told you, I had one glass of wine, this afternoon with Janet Mallory. You can call her if you don't believe me."

She looked at me steadily. "Were you taking anything else?"

That's when I glimpsed my loophole. My way out. The light at the end of the tunnel, shining glorious and gold. "Oh my God," I whispered, widening my eyes, letting my jaw go slack, doing everything but slapping my forehead. "My back went out over the weekend, and I'm taking . . . God, what's it called? A muscle relaxer, and a painkiller. I totally forgot I'm not supposed to drink with them." I hung my head, my expression of shame entirely unfeigned. "Oh my God, what is wrong with me?"

Maybe I imagined it, but I thought Mrs. Dale's expression softened. So I kept going. "I'm so sorry," I whispered. "I can't believe I didn't double-check." I swallowed hard. The enormity of the situation—the trouble I could be in, the fact that I could have hurt children, mine and someone else's, or hit someone else, some stranger on the road—was covering me like a skin of ice, freezing my feet, my knees, my belly. If she reported this, I could lose my daughter. If Dave found out that I was driving under the influence . . . I shook my head, unwilling to even think about it. I couldn't let myself go there. Containment. Containment was the name of the game. "You were absolutely right to not let me drive. I'm sorry. It'll never happen again."

Mrs. Dale's expression was unreadable. Was she buying any of this? I couldn't tell.

"You were taking painkillers?" she finally asked. I started nodding almost before the last syllable was out of her mouth.

"That's right. And a muscle relaxant. My back . . ."

She looked at me for another long moment. "When my niece had a C-section," she finally said, "they gave her Percocet. Her doctor kept prescribing them for almost six months after she'd given birth, and when he cut her off, she found another doctor, a pain specialist, to write her prescriptions for Vicodin and OxyContin."

I tried not to flinch. Vicodin and Oxy. My favorites, my nearest and dearest . . . and, at that very moment, I wanted about a dozen of each. I wanted not to be there, not to have been seen by the ladies in the carpool lane, who were probably already spreading the word, not to be in that classroom that smelled like little-kid sweat and banana bread, being lectured by some old battle-ax who probably had no idea what it was like, trying to raise kids and hold a job and run a household these days.

"She took those pills for years. I believe that we all got used to it when Vicki didn't seem quite right, or when she was tired all the time. We'd ask her about what she was taking, and she'd say it was no big deal, and because she had prescriptions, because she was under a doctor's care, none of us worried. We didn't know she was borrowing pills from her friends when her prescriptions ran out, or buying them from someone she met at the gym . . . or that she'd gotten a prescription for Xanax and was trading those for her neighbor's painkillers."

"What happened?" I asked.

"What happened was, she died," Mrs. Dale said. In the quiet, empty classroom, I heard myself gasp. "On the death certificate it said respiratory failure, but she had taken about five times more pills than she should have, and she had a few glasses of wine on top of it, and she went to sleep and she didn't wake up." She looked at me, unflinching. "Her little girl found her. It was a school morning, and my niece's husband was in the shower, and Brianna went into the bedroom and tapped her mom's shoulder." I sat there, frozen, my body prickling with goose pimples, my eyes and nose stinging with unshed tears. I could picture it—a woman about my age, in a nightgown, on her back in bed, underneath the covers. The sound of running water from the bathroom, the billow of steam and the smell of soap, and a little girl in Ariel pajamas shaking the woman's shoulder gently, then more insistently, not noticing the stiff, unyielding texture of the flesh, or how cold it was, saying *Mommy, Mommy, wake up!* And in my head, the little girl was Ellie.

I swallowed hard. Oh, God. What was I going to do? I had to stop, that was clear. But what if I couldn't? Mrs. Dale was looking at me. I wanted to explain, to tell her how this had happened, how stressful my life was, between my job and my parents and my husband and his work wife and Ellie, and how sometimes I didn't like being a mother much at all—how I liked the concept, but the reality of it was killing me. I couldn't take the tears and tantrums and endless Monopoly games, the way Ellie would wander down the stairs half a dozen times after she'd been put to bed, requesting a glass of water, a story, her night-light turned on, her night-light turned off, how she'd bang on the door when I was in the shower, or even on the toilet, just trying to pee or put in a tampon, until I was ready to scream, to grab her by her little shoulders and shake her, shouting, *Just stay in bed, please! Just leave me alone and give me five minutes of peace!*

"Brianna was four," said Mrs. Dale.

"Four," I repeated. I imagined Ellie going to move-up day with only her daddy in the audience to cheer as she crossed over the bridge to first grade. I thought about her getting her period with no one to tell her what to do . . . or, worse, some bimbo of a stepmother who'd regard my daughter as competition. Her bat mitzvah . . . her first date . . . senior prom . . . college acceptance letters. All without a mother to encourage her and console her, to love her, no matter what.

I dropped my head. *No more,* I thought. *I can't do this anymore.* And right on the heels of that thought came, inevitably, another: *I need them.* I couldn't imagine leaving Ellie to face life without a mother . . . but I also couldn't imagine facing my life without a chemical buffer between me and Dave, me and my mother, me and the Internet, me and my feelings. How could I survive without that sweet river of calm wending its way through my body, easing me, untying knots from the soles of my feet to the top of my head? How could I make it through a day without knowing I had that reliable comfort waiting at the finish line?

I gave my head a little shake. This was stupid. So I had let things get a little out of hand. So I'd come to school a little loopy. Nobody had gotten hurt, right? And I wasn't going to die. I wasn't. I wasn't taking that much, and it was prescription medication, not heroin I was buying on the streets. It wasn't like I was some cracked-out junkie . . . or like I'd end up dead in bed with a mouthful of puke and a little girl to find me. I was smarter than that.

Except, a little voice inside me whispered, *wasn't Mrs. Dale's niece on the same stuff as you? And you're buying extra, and you're not taking it as prescribed. Not even close.* I told the voice to shut up, but it persisted. *Instead of taking one every four hours, you're taking four every one hour . . . and you're drinking on top of that.*

You need help.

No, I don't.

This can't go on.

I'm doing fine!

"I'm fine," I muttered, half to Mrs. Dale and half to myself . . . but, even as I said it, I could imagine a little girl shaking her mother's shoulder. Her mother's cold, stiff, dead shoulder.

"I'm not trying to scare you," said Mrs. Dale. "But I know what this looks like. And I know it can happen to anyone. The nicest people. The smartest people. My niece was so beautiful. You'd never look at her and think that she was a drug addict. She was just taking what the doctors gave her. Right until she died."

"I appreciate what you're saying, but that's not me. I don't have a problem." Never mind the surveys I'd taken, the questionnaires I'd filled out, the increasing number of pills I needed to get through the day. Never mind the promises—*not before nine, not before noon, not while I'm working, not when I'm with Eloise*—that I'd broken, one after another, every day, stretching back for months. "I don't. I just made a mistake today, and you were right to take my keys, and I swear, I swear on my daughter's life, that it'll never happen again." I took a gulp of lukewarm coffee and forced myself to ask, "Are you going to report me?"

After an interminable pause, Mrs. Dale shook her head.

"Thank you. I'm sorry. I promise . . . I swear to you," I repeated, "this will never happen again."

She gazed at me, and her eyes, behind her bifocals, looked kind. "There's no shame in asking for help if you need it," she said . . . and then she walked out, leaving me alone with my coffee, and my keys.

I waited until she was out the door before I shoved my hand

in my purse and touched the Altoids tin, then the prescription bottles, one, two, three, four. I had pills halfway to my mouth before something inside me, the little voice of reason, rose up and demanded, *What the FUCK are you doing?*

I put the pills back. I put the cap on the bottle. I put the bottle in my purse, and laid my head on top of my folded arms . . . and then, alone in the empty classroom, I started to cry.

THIRTEEN

The next morning, I didn't take a single pill. I dropped Ellie off at school, treated myself to an extra-hot latte with a double shot of espresso, and then drove to Center City, pulled on oversized sunglasses and a baseball cap and slipped through the side door of the church on Pine Street I'd found online the night before. In the basement, about twenty people, most of them men, sat in folding metal chairs. Tattered posters were thumbtacked to the walls. One read "The Twelve Steps" and the other "The Twelve Traditions." In the front of the room was a wooden desk with two more folding chairs behind it and a sculpture of the letters AA carved out of wood on top, along with a battered-looking three-ring binder and a basket. I pulled my baseball cap low, flipped my collar up, and took the seat closest to the door. The chairs began to fill, until there were almost fifty people in the room.

I looked around, dividing the attendees into categories: Aged Homeless (lots of layers of dirty clothes, and not many teeth) and Young Punks (pale, white, wormy Eminem clones in obscene T-shirts and with multiple piercings). There were old guys in Phillies jackets you'd pass on the street without a second look, and a single woman in a business suit with gold hoop earrings and leather pumps that I knew couldn't have cost less than five hundred dollars, but it was mostly a collection of people who looked nothing like me.

"This seat taken?" asked a young man—maybe a teenager—in a blue T-shirt. When I shook my head, he sat down, swiped at his nose, and gave the pimple on his chin a squeeze. "Hey," he said.

"Hey," I said back. He had a ring through his nose that made me think of Ferdinand the bull; Ferdinand, who didn't want to fight, just sit and sniff the flowers. I glanced at my phone—five minutes until this thing kicked off—and continued my appraisal. The crowd was mostly made up of men, but in the back of the room I spotted two more women, both in their fifties or sixties, looking like, as Dave's frat buddy Dan might have said, they'd been ridden hard and put away wet. One of them had unnaturally blonde hair pulled into a high ponytail that went uncomfortably with her weathered face. The other was a brunette with gaudy earrings and a phlegmy cough. The blonde wore sweatpants, the brunette, a pair of high-waisted jeans and a mock turtleneck, à la Jennifer Aniston, circa *Friends*, season one. To pass the time, I made up jobs for them. The blonde was a cashier at a gas station; the brunette waited tables at a diner. Not a hipster diner with Pabst Blue Ribbon on tap and a legitimate chef using artisanal ingredients in the kitchen, either, but a grungy place somewhere in Northeast Philadelphia, where the mashed potatoes came from a box, where truckers and cabdrivers and construction workers came to eat meatloaf and play Patsy Cline on the jukebox.

"First time?"

Oh, joy. Ferdinand was making conversation. I hoped a curt nod would appease him. It did not.

"You court-stipulated?"

I didn't know what that meant. "Excuse me?" I asked, and

then yawned. For the past twenty minutes, I hadn't been able to stop yawning. My nose was running, and my eyes were watery. Allergies, I figured. Also, I felt like I was jumping out of my skin. My toes wanted to tap; my legs wanted to bounce and kick; my torso wanted to squirm. It was all I could do to hold still.

"Didja get, like, a DUI or something?"

"Oh, no. No, nothing like that." Were all the people at this meeting here just because a judge told them they had to be?

He gave me a grin. When he smiled I saw that, in spite of the ring in his nose and the spiderweb tattooed on his neck, he was still more boy than man. Not too long ago, he'd been climbing off a school bus every afternoon, and dressing up on Halloween. Someone had kissed him when he'd fallen down, had put silver dollars under his pillow in exchange for his baby teeth, had signed his report cards and attended his parent-teacher conferences, had worried when he'd stayed out late, lying awake in the dark, waiting for the sound of his key in the front door.

An elderly man in a plaid shirt and khaki pants with a large bandage on one cheek took a seat behind the desk and rapped his knuckles on the table. "Welcome to Alcoholics Anonymous. My name is Tom, and I'm an alcoholic." At least, that was what I suspected he said. Between the way he mumbled and his thick-as-taffy Philadelphia accent, I caught maybe every third syllable.

"Hi, Tom!" the room chorused, their voices cheery, as if being an alcoholic was something awesome to celebrate.

"This is an open meeting of Alcoholics Anonymous. Anyone who wishes to attend may do so. The only requirement for membership in AA is a desire to stop drinking. I've asked a friend to read 'How It Works.'"

As Tom's friend, a rotund white-bearded man who'd introduced himself by saying "I'm Glen, and I don't drink alcohol," droned through both sides of a laminated piece of paper—

something about half-measures availing us nothing, something else about suggested steps as a program of recovery—I began plotting my escape. Aside from the business-suit woman, who was probably completing a degree in therapy or social work and observing this as part of her coursework, there was no one in the room I could imagine even having a conversation with.

"Many of us exclaimed, 'What an order! I can't go through with it,'" Glen read. I shrugged my purse onto my shoulder. Who talked like that? No one I knew. "Do not be discouraged. No one among us has been able to maintain anything like perfect adherence to these principles. We are not saints. The point is that we are willing to grow along spiritual lines. We claim spiritual progress, rather than spiritual perfection. Our description of the alcoholic, the chapter to the agnostic, and our personal adventures before and after make clear three pertinent ideas. One, That we were alcoholic and could not manage our own lives."

Not me, I thought. Except for that little slipup the day before, I was managing my own life just fine. Not to mention my daughter's life, my husband's life, and my parents' lives.

"Two," Glen continued. "That probably no human power could have relieved our alcoholism."

Wrong again. I could do this myself. I just hadn't tried. I would cut back on my own. Eighteen pills today, then sixteen pills tomorrow, and fourteen by the weekend, and ten a day by Monday . . .

"Three: That God could and would if He were sought." Everyone in the room joined in, chanting those last words: *could and would if He were sought.* At which point, I realized that I had wandered into a cult. Why hadn't anyone told me that AA was some strange turn-it-over-to-God deal? I thought it was a self-help thing, where you got together with other drunks and druggies and figured out how to solve your problem. Shows what I knew.

"Any anniversaries?" Tom asked from behind the desk, looking around the room. "Anyone here counting days?"

A young man in a blue sweatshirt and dirty work boots raised his hand. "I'm Greg, and I'm an alcoholic and an addict."

"Hi, Greg!" chorused the room.

"Today I got thirty days."

The room burst into applause. "And," Greg said on his way up to the front of the room, where Tom gave him a bear hug and what looked like a poker chip, "my parole officer says if I stay clean for ninety and I pass all my piss tests, that bitch has gotta let me see my kid."

Awesome, I thought, as the room clapped for this charming sentiment. *Greg has a kid. Greg has a parole officer. Greg just called his kid's mother a bitch.* Suddenly I needed to leave with an urgency that approached my desperate need for a pill first thing in the morning. I sidled over toward the coffee urn, thinking that I'd stay there until the group's attention was occupied, then make a break for it. Meanwhile, I pretended to be interested in the dog-eared posters framed behind smeary glass: KEEP IT SIMPLE. ONE DAY AT A TIME. THERE BUT FOR THE GRACE OF GOD.

I don't belong here, I thought. *These people aren't like me. I'm not as bad as they are; not even close. I can figure this out on my own.*

"This is a speaker meeting," said Tom. "I've asked one of my sponsees, Tyler, to speak." He pointed to his left, where a man who was maybe twenty-one, with skin the color of skim milk past its sell-by date, sat slumped in a thin, discolored T-shirt, jeans, and battered sneakers.

"Hey," he said, managing to pull himself upright. "I'm Tyler, and I'm an alcoholic and an addict."

"Hey, Tyler!"

Tyler hocked back snot and scratched his forearm. "Yeah, so. Um. Tom here's my sponsor. He's a real good guy. And he said I gotta come to a meeting and speak, so here I am. I've got . . . what is it? Fifty-seven days today."

The room applauded, with people calling out "Congratulations!" and "Way to go!" and "Keep coming back!" Tyler ducked his head modestly and delivered the next part of his speech directly into his sternum.

"I know I'm s'posed to be sharing my experience, strength, and hope, but I'm mostly gonna be sharing hope, because . . ." He gave a self-deprecating chuckle. "I don't really have much experience with this whole not-using thing."

With that, Tyler launched into his tale. Mom was an alcoholic, Dad was a heroin addict. They'd leave him alone in the house for days at a time while they were "out partyin'." Tyler had his first drink at eleven, stealing a pint of his grandfather's vodka and drinking the whole thing. "And, from then on, I guess it was just one big party." I dumped powdered creamer into a styrofoam cup and listened. "I'd drink vodka before school, sneak a few beers during lunch, smoke a joint in the parking lot before I came home. And that was ninth grade." By tenth grade he was smoking meth; by the time he was expelled in the eleventh grade, he was sneaking out of the house in the middle of the night to hitchhike to Kensington, where he'd started to shoot heroin. Finally, his parents performed an intervention. No word on whether they'd cleaned up their own acts or were just sober enough to notice that their son was in trouble.

"They said I had to move out or go to rehab. This was after I, uh, stole my mom's engagement ring and pawned it, 'cause I was all strung out, you know, and I, like, needed to score, and

I didn't care what it took. Didn't care who I hurt. That was me when I was using."

As quietly as I could, I tossed my coffee cup into the trash can and slipped out the door. *This isn't for me,* I thought. I didn't do meth, I didn't shoot heroin, and God knows I never stole anything from anyone. I didn't even smoke!

I walked briskly back to my car. Anyone who saw me would think I was a regular stay-at-home mom on her way to pick up some essential, forgotten ingredient—a dozen eggs, a cup of sugar—before her kids came home from school. Which I was, I decided. I wasn't an addict, like the people in that room. I was a working mother under an inordinate amount of stress due to her job, her marriage, and a father in crisis; a woman who had, quite naturally, turned to an available remedy to help her manage her days.

"I'm fine," I said. And then, to prove it, I bought a dozen eggs and a bag of brown sugar at the grocery store, and had fresh chocolate-chip cookies waiting when Eloise came home.

FOURTEEN

"Mommy!"

I blinked, rolling onto my side, running through my own internal whiteboard. Today is TUESDAY. It is five-fifteen. The next meal is DINNER, and you'd better start cooking. I heard, then saw, the doorknob of my bedroom turning back and forth.

"Mommy's resting!" I called, and closed my eyes again. I'd been working flat out from five in the morning until it was time to take Ellie to school, and then from the moment I'd gotten back home until one. I'd decided to take a nap, and, after three Oxys failed to do the trick, I'd chewed up two more, then shut my eyes, and it was like I'd been punched hard in the head. I hadn't just fallen asleep, I thought, trying to get my legs moving. I'd been knocked out, plunged into unconsciousness.

My phone was blinking. There were three new e-mails and a pair of texts from Sarah. *CALL ME BACK*, read the memo line. *R U okay?* read the second. *U sounded weird.*

Oh, God. I had no memory of speaking to Sarah. What had I said? What had I done? Panic surged through me. I pushed myself out of bed, pressed the phone to my ear, dialed Sarah's number, and hurried to the bathroom so I could pee and talk at the same time.

I got her voicemail. "Hey, Sarah, it's Allison. Um. Sorry if I sounded a little out of it." I wiped and flushed, feeling frantic and sick and disgusted with myself, wondering how to gracefully ask what I'd said. "Call me back—I'm fine now!"

I opened the bedroom door and almost bumped into my mother. As always, she had her face on—foundation and eyeliner and a gooey lipgloss pout. A studded black leather belt showed off her tinier-than-ever waist, and her French manicure looked just-that-afternoon fresh, but her expression was worried as she twisted her hands and looked me over. "Allison, are you okay?" she asked.

"Fine!" I edged past her, down the stairs. Had I remembered to defrost the chicken? Was there a vegetable I could cook to go with it? And—oh, God—had I said something to my mother after I'd taken all that Oxy?

"You seem . . ." She followed me down the stairs, impressively managing to keep pace with my half trot, even though I was barefoot and she was in heels. "You seem like you're not doing well."

"I'm okay!" I pulled a box of rice out of the pantry, along with a can of hearts of palm. The chicken was still half-frozen in the fridge. I put it in the microwave. "Really. Just, you know, lots of stuff with work . . . and I'm worried about Daddy." Normally, changing the subject to my father would be enough to start the waterworks, but my mother was looking at me with an unfamiliar intensity, narrowing her eyes as she studied my face.

"You know," she said, "if you needed to take a break . . . if you and Dave wanted to go away somewhere, I'd be happy to stay with Ellie."

I blinked. Was this my mother? My mother, who could barely take care of herself?

"That's really generous of you. But I'm fine. Like I said, just a little overwhelmed right now." My mind was running on its typical three tracks. There was dinner to be prepared. There was work to be considered—I'd filed my blog post, but I still had to throw some red meat to the commenters, whom I'd been neglecting. And, as always, there were the pills to count, and count again. Did I have enough? Were there more on the way? Had I sent money to my Penny Lane account?

I shook my head. Ellie and my mother both watched me as I cracked eggs, shook breadcrumbs into a bowl, set the table, and preheated the oven.

"Ellie, let's go play cards," said my mom. They filed into the living room.

Everything's cool, I told myself, vowing to apologize to Sarah in person and to be more present—or at least more awake—for Ellie. *I am fine.*

I heard the garage door creaking upward. "Daddy, Daddy, Daddy!" Ellie chanted, sprinting toward the door. I wasn't expecting Dave for dinner. Hadn't he told me that he had some dinner thing to go to, some bash one of the big unions was throwing that he needed to attend? Or had that been the night before?

"Ellie, help me set the table," I called. I could hear Dave's low voice mixing with Ellie's bright chatter, and then the two of them came into the kitchen with Ellie's feet balanced on Dave's shoes, clutching his hands and giggling as he walked.

"How was your day?" he asked.

"Fine! Busy!" I bent to check on the chicken.

"Mommy was sleeping," Ellie announced.

"Mommy was tired," I said, feeling grateful that Dave

couldn't see my face. I hadn't told him about my run-in with Mrs. Dale. Ellie hadn't, either. At least not yet. I knew better than to tell her not to say anything—that, of course, would guarantee that she'd go running to Dave with the whole story, about how Mommy fell down and Mommy got her dress all bloody and Mommy got put in a time-out by a teacher. My hope was that her typical five-year-old attention span would save me, and that events from the other day would be, to Ellie, as distant as things that had happened years ago.

"Do you know Mommy snores when she sleeps?" Ellie inquired.

"I do not!" I was smiling so hard that my cheeks ached as I cracked ice cubes into a pitcher, then gave the hearts of palm a squeeze of lime juice, a drizzle of olive oil, and a sprinkling of salt.

"You do too. And you DROOL. There was a whole PUDDLE underneath your face."

"Tough day at the office," I said, and turned to get the milk out of the refrigerator. When I shut the refrigerator door, Dave and my mother were looking at each other.

"What?" I said. Neither adult answered.

"What?" I said again, trying to sound happy, trying to look happy, trying to pretend I hadn't spent the past five hours passed out in a puddle of my own saliva.

"Are you sure you're all right?" my mother finally ventured.

"I'm all right," I said. Smile still in place, voice still untroubled. Dinner in the oven. Blog post filed. At least, I thought I'd filed it. I would cut Ellie's chicken, then I'd run upstairs just to double-check. And have another pill. "Everything's good."

My mom and Dave exchanged a look. "Hey, Ellie, how about you and Grandma go out for sushi so Mommy and Daddy can talk," Dave said.

"Sushi, sushi!" chanted Ellie, grabbing my mother's hand and towing her toward the door.

"Do you need a ride?" I asked.

"We'll get a cab!" called my mother. The door swung shut behind them.

"Let's sit down in the dining room," Dave said. I felt my knees start to quiver as I followed him there. The dining room was low on my list of priorities, which meant the only furniture in it was the table and six cheap IKEA chairs. The walls were bare, covered in an unattractive greenish-blue wallpaper that I'd planned on removing as soon as I had the time and then the money.

"What is it?" I said, trying to sound casual and unconcerned.

"Sit down," Dave said.

I curled my fingers around the back of a chair. "Not until you tell me what's wrong."

He sighed. Typical Dave. He could never come right out and say something. There had to be a few moments of prefatory sighing and throat-clearing first. "You and I need to talk."

"Okay," I said slowly, buying time. The news began to register in my body. My chest felt heavy, and my knees had that airy, trembly feeling. Was he going to ask me for a divorce? My heart stopped beating as Dave reached into his work bag and pulled out a FedEx envelope. From Penny Lane. *Shit,* I thought. *Oh, shit, shit, shit.*

"What is this?" He hadn't opened it. And the return address probably said something banal about Computer Parts or eBay Services. Maybe there was a chance I could talk my way out of this.

"It's a SIM card for my cell phone." I widened my eyes. "Terrifying, I know."

"You're telling me that if I open this envelope I'm not going to find drugs?"

My heart was thudding so hard I was surprised Dave couldn't hear it. "Oh, Jesus, Dave. What are you, McGruff the Crime Dog? You think I'm"—I curled my fingers into sarcastic air quotes, rolling my eyes at the very notion—"doing drugs?"

He lifted the envelope and shook it. I braced myself for the sound of rattling, praying that the package had come from one of the vendors who was liberal with the bubble wrap. No rattle. *Thank you, God.* But Dave wasn't giving up.

"Why don't you open the envelope and show me what's inside."

Maybe it was the smug look on his face, or the accusation in his tone. Whatever it was, it infuriated me. "Because I don't fucking have to!" I yelled. "Because I didn't sign up to play show and tell! Because you're my husband, not Inspector Javert!"

A wave of dizziness swept from the base of my spine to the crown of my head. There was a ringing in my ears, a high-pitched chime. My mouth was dry. My palms were icy. I wanted a pill. I needed a pill. Just the thought of them, crunching between my teeth, that familiar bitterness flooding my mouth, helped me relax the tiniest bit.

Dave continued to stare at me. I thought about that day at Stonefield, and how, a few hours ago, I'd called Sarah but had no idea what I'd said. I thought about the money I was spending, the naps I was taking, the sleepless nights, my racing heart. *This needs to stop,* said a voice in my head. *It can be over right now. This can be the end.*

"I don't—" I blurted. I made myself shut my mouth, take a seat, look him straight in the eye when I spoke. "Okay. I will tell you the truth. I have been buying stuff online. But it's prescription medication. You know I've got herniated discs."

Dave reached into his work bag. From the inside pocket he pulled out a Ziploc bag full of empty prescription bottles. He reached in again and pulled out a sheaf of papers. I squinted until I could see what they were—printouts from Penny Lane, detailing every purchase I'd made.

Closing my eyes, I turned my face toward the wall.

"I called Janet last night," Dave said into the silence. "I told her I was worried about you. I asked if she'd seen anything alarming—if you were late dropping Ellie off, or picking her up."

"I have never been late," I said. That, at least, was pretty much the truth.

"And then," he continued doggedly, "I called the school."

Oh, shit. "Dave . . ."

"Mrs. Dale called me back. She said you seemed like you were—the word she used was 'impaired'—when you came to get the kids a few days ago. She said you told her you were drinking. That you'd had a glass of wine with a prescription medication, and you'd forgotten that you weren't supposed to."

I tried to interrupt. "Dave, listen . . ."

"You were going to drive drunk with Ellie in the car!" He started yelling, his face red, a vein throbbing in the center of his forehead, tears in his eyes. "What if she died? What if you died? What the fuck is the matter with you?"

I started to cry. "I don't know. Maybe I don't like having a husband who won't even talk to me anymore. Maybe I'm sick of being the one who does everything around here."

He glared at me, unmoved by my tears. "Don't make this my fault, Allison."

"You don't know." My voice cracked on the last word. "You

have no idea what it's like. Dealing with Ellie. Dealing with my parents. My work . . ."

"Maybe not," he said coolly. "Maybe I don't know. But I think there are people in the world who manage to do all of those things without becoming drug addicts."

"I am not a drug addict!" And fuck that bitch Mrs. Dale for ratting me out. I mentally tore up the check I'd been planning to send to the Annual Giving campaign. I'd take myself shopping instead. "Okay. Obviously I shouldn't have been drinking on top of the medication. I was tired, and I made a mistake. I'm not perfect."

"You aren't yourself. I don't know any other way to say it. And everyone's noticed. Me, your mom, Ellie . . ." He reached across the table, but I pulled my hand away before he could touch me. "If you want to get some help, I'll support you as best I can."

My laugh was high and shrill. "Help? What, like rehab? You think I need to go to rehab? You think I'm Lindsay Lohan now?"

"I don't know what you need. But I know you're taking more of those pills than you should be. I'm worried about you . . . and, quite frankly, I'm worried about you taking care of Ellie."

I thought I'd been scared before, that day at Stonefield, when Mrs. Dale hadn't let me drive. I was wrong. That wasn't anything. This was real fear. This was true terror. And the best defense was a good offense. My father used to say that all the time. I drew myself up straight, grateful that I was wearing makeup, that I'd washed my hair that morning, that my clothes were clean. "Are you suggesting that I'm an unfit mother?"

Dave shook his head. "I'm saying that I'm worried about you, and I'm worried about Ellie when she's with you. You need to take this seriously, Allison. People die from what you're doing."

"Okay! So fine! I'll quit!" I made a show of extracting a bottle of Vicodin from my purse, uncapping it, and pouring the pills down the drain. I had a small secret stash, of course—a mints tin stuffed in my purse, a dozen Oxys in the bottom of my tampon box, a few Percocet in the glove compartment.

I turned on my heel and made what might have been a grand exit if my hip hadn't caught the side of the table. I stumbled, and would have fallen if I hadn't grabbed the wall. Dave was right behind me, holding my gaze, glaring at me, with no trace of goodwill or humor or love in his expression.

"I don't want to have to spy on you," he said. "But I will do whatever I have to do to keep Ellie safe."

"Ellie," I said, with all the dignity I could muster, "is perfectly safe. I would never, ever do anything to put her at risk." Except, of course, the thing I'd done a few days ago.

"If you want help, I am here for you."

I rolled my eyes. "Great. See if you can send me to the place the guy from *Friends* went. They have Pilates."

"Allison."

"I promise," I roared, before he could get off another adult-sounding, well-meaning warning. "I promise I promise I promise." And I kept my promise all the way up the stairs, down the hall, and into the bathroom, where I fished pills out of the tampon box where I'd hidden them, and swallowed them, one, two, three.

FIFTEEN

I was too upset to sleep that night. I sat in the living room with my laptop, pounding out a blog post called "Husbands Just Don't Understand," while Ronnie slept in the guest bedroom and Dave snored away down the hall. I burned through work I'd been putting off, spending ninety minutes engaging with the comments section and coming up with story ideas for one of the magazines that had been e-mailing in the wake of my "vibrator in every purse" comment. Every time I felt my brain edging toward the words *Dave knows what I've been doing* or *I'm going to lose my family* or even just *I want to stop and I can't,* I would march myself into the bathroom and take another pill. By six a.m., I was wild-eyed, smelling of acrid sweat, feeling both sluggish and frantic. And, somehow, the unthinkable had happened. I was out of pills.

"Can you take Ellie to school?" I rasped through the bathroom door. Rats' teeth of panic were nibbling at my heart. Dave sounded disgustingly collected.

"Sure. No problem."

I went to the computer and logged on to Penny Lane, to make sure I hadn't placed an order and then forgotten about it. No. There was only the stuff that Dave had intercepted. Prior to that was an order for sixty pills that had arrived two days ago, and every last one of them was gone. I stared at the screen, feeling my jaw drop as I did the math. Thirty pills in less than a day and a half? That couldn't be right. Except I could remember the package arriving, and how fast I'd gotten the envelope open and transferred the pills into my mints tin, how before I'd even gotten inside the house I had four of those babies inside me.

"Fuck," I whispered. I went to the bedroom and began to go through my usual hiding places: my tampon box, the second drawer of my bedside table, the zippered pockets inside the different purses I'd used that month. There was nothing. I couldn't even find a piece of a broken pill to tide me over. Everything was gone.

I sat down on the bed, heart thumping, palms and temples greasy with cold sweat. I picked up my phone and scrolled through the names of my doctors. *Called her last week . . . called him on Monday . . . haven't called her in so long she'll probably ask questions about why I need painkillers now.*

Think, I told myself fiercely as I heard the garage door open and the car pull out of the driveway. Maybe there was stuff left in my father's medicine cabinet . . . except I knew that there wasn't. I'd cleared it all out before the Realtor had come for a final walkthrough. Did my mom have anything? And did I want to risk trying to get her out of the house so I could check?

Forty minutes after Dave's departure, still in my pajama bottoms and the Wonder Woman T-shirt I'd worn while I worked, I sat on the examination table of a strip-mall clinic where a cab had dropped me off, talking to a doctor with a heavy accent and bags under his eyes.

"You hurt the back when?"

"Two years ago." I was shivering, sweating, and having a hard time keeping my legs still. My knees wanted to kick, my feet wanted to tap, my body itched all over, and my fingers wanted to dig into my skin and start clawing. *Withdrawal*, I thought bleakly. A loop of every movie I'd ever seen in which a junkie kicked his or her habit had set itself on "repeat" in my mind. I was terrified of the agony I suspected was awaiting me . . . and I was furious at myself, furious that I'd let this happen, not stayed on top of what I had and what I needed. All those weeks—months, even—of promising myself I'd cut back, just not today, when in fact my use had increased and increased, my tolerance building until I needed four, or five, or even six little OxyContin to feel the transporting euphoria that a single Vicodin had once given me . . . and now here I was with nothing.

"You take how much of the painkiller?"

"I don't know. A lot. Maybe ten pills a day," I lied.

"Of the thirty milligrams?"

"Yes." Ten was a good day, and Oxys weren't the only thing I was taking, but never mind. He'd give me something—I didn't even care what. Then I'd get on top of this. I'd slow my roll, start being prudent. No more pills first thing in the morning, no more pills in the middle of the night. Three or four days—a week, tops—and I'd have this under control.

"Every day, you take them?"

I nodded, launching into the story I'd already told the intake nurse. "And, like I said, I'm going to see my regular doctor, only she's out sick, and I'm leaving for vacation this afternoon, and if you could just give me maybe ten pills, just so I can get through the plane trip . . ."

He leaned back against the exam room's sink, taking me in. His name was Dr. Desgupta, and his eyes, behind heavy brown plastic frames, were not unkind.

"Every day, you're taking these pills," he said again.

I bent my head and prayed. *Please, God, just let him give me enough to get through the day and I'll stop, I'll get help, I'll do something, I swear I will.*

"And is it because the back hurts? Or is it because you need them, because you are getting sick without them?"

I didn't answer. I wrapped my arms around myself and concentrated, as hard as I could, on not throwing up. "Sick," I finally said. "I've never tried to stop, and I think . . . I mean, I'm not feeling so great already."

"There is medication. Suboxone." I lifted my head. "An opiate agonist-antagonist. It blocks your receptors, so you can't take the heroin, or the Vicodin, or the OxyContin. Whatever narcotic you were taking. But it gives you some of the effects of an opiate, too. Not enough so you get, you know, the high, but enough that you feel okay."

I nodded. This sounded like an acceptable solution. I could take this Suboxone stuff and stop hurting, and then take a day to sort myself out. I'd get more pills, either online or from doctors, enough so that this would never happen again. I would contact a lawyer, and a child psychologist, which Ellie would undoubtedly require. I would taper myself off the pills, maybe try more of those meetings, or get myself a therapist, or start running again. But all I wanted, at that moment, was something to take, something to swallow or smoke or snort. Something that would ease my panic, slow my heartbeat, let me feel okay again.

"Here." Dr. Desgupta had finally pulled out his prescription pad. "I will write for seven days. The medicine is a film; you dissolve it under your tongue." He ripped off the page. I snatched it out of his hand. "How long ago was last dose of OxyContin?"

I tried to remember what time it had been when I'd chewed

up the last of my pills, and tried not to remember licking the
inside of the jewelry box where I'd found the final two Vicodin.
If you were ever wondering whether you had a problem or not,
the taste of jewelry-box felt was answer enough. "Four in the
morning?"

He looked at the clock, calculating. He had big brown
eyes, a bald head with a few strands of black hair carefully arranged on top, and a soft, accented voice. "Take first one at
noon. You should be started in the withdrawal by then. Feeling
like you have the flu. Sweaty, hands shaking . . . you feel like
that, you take first one."

"Thank you," I said faintly, and was up and out of the chair,
the prescription in one hand and my cell phone in the other,
before he could tell me goodbye.

I could remember the rest of the day only in snatches. I remembered my cab ride from the doc-in-a-box to the drive-through
lane of the pharmacy. *The flu*, the doctor had told me . . . except
this was to the flu like a pack of rabid pit bulls was to a Chi-
huahua. I was running with foul-smelling sweat and shaking
so hard that my teeth were chattering. My skin was covered in
goose pimples; whatever I'd eaten the day before churned un-
happily in my belly. I remembered the pharmacist telling me
that the medicine wasn't covered by my insurance without prior
approval, and insisting, over and over, that I didn't care, that it
didn't matter, that I'd pay out of pocket and worry about reim-
bursement later.

Back at home, I speed-read the instructions, then tore open
one of the packets and let the yellow film dissolve into sour slime
under my tongue. I locked the bedroom door and lay on my bed,
where I endured six hours of the worst hell I could imagine. My

entire body twitched and burned. My legs kicked and flailed uncontrollably. I couldn't hold still, couldn't get comfortable. My skin felt like it was host to hundreds of thousands of fiery ants wearing boots made of poison-tipped needles. I scratched and clawed, but I couldn't make them go away. The first time I threw up, I made it to the toilet, and, from there, I managed to send my mother and Dave a text explaining that I was sick and that, between the two of them, they'd have to handle Ellie and her obligations. The second time, I made it to the sink. The third time, I couldn't even make it out of bed. I was freezing cold, so I'd tried to get under the covers, but the kicking—kicking! I was actually kicking!—had disarranged everything, had loosened the fitted sheets and the mattress cover. I writhed on the bed, trying to moan into the pillow, praying that the Suboxone would start its work, that I'd feel better, that Ellie wouldn't see or hear this.

My mother knocked at the door. "Allison? Allison, are you okay?"

"Flu," I called back, in a voice that didn't sound like mine. I'd gotten myself wrapped in a blanket and was sitting, hunched over and moaning, in the old glider chair I'd used to nurse Ellie. I was burning up, my hair glued to my cheeks in matted clumps, making high, whining noises. I moaned and rocked, moaned and rocked, as the minutes dragged by. At six o'clock I couldn't stand it any longer. I found the phone, crawled into bed, and managed to dial the clinic and tell the receptionist that it was an emergency and that I needed Dr. Desgupta.

"Yes, hello?" he answered.

I told him my name. My voice was a high, wavering whisper. I didn't sound like myself; I sounded like Ellie when she woke up sick in the middle of the night. "There's something wrong . . . I'm really sick . . ."

"You are having the nausea and the diarrhea?"

"Yes," I whispered. I was crying, on top of everything else. "I'm cold . . . I can't stop shaking . . . everything hurts . . . I feel like I'm going to die . . ."

"Twenty-four hours," he said calmly. "The Suboxone is kicking the opiates off your receptors. But in a day or two you will be well again."

A day or two? I wasn't sure I could take another twenty minutes of this agony. "I can't do this," I said. My voice was sounding less like human conversation than like a cat's yowl. "Please, you have to help me . . . I think I need to go to a hospital . . ."

"I am thinking," the doctor said calmly, "that maybe you need to be in a rehab bed." He trilled the "r" of "rehab," making it sound like something wonderful and exotic.

"No rehab," I said. "I'm not an addict. Please. I'm not. I'm just really, really sick."

"You go to one of these places, they will help you," he explained. "There is no need to stay for the twenty-eight days unless you like. But you need to be watched until you are well."

Rehab. I started crying even harder, because I suspected that he was right. Maybe I didn't need rehab, but I needed to be somewhere with nurses and doctors and medicine and machines. The pain was intolerable. I could barely speak; I couldn't keep my legs still. I actually wanted to die. Death would be an improvement over this.

The doorknob turned. Shaking and sick, I felt the weight of Ellie's body as she crawled beside me. "Mommy?" she whispered. With her tiny hands she patted my hair, then my forehead. "Mommy, do you need true love's kiss?"

I made some noise, thinking that I'd never hated myself as much as I did at that moment. Then my mother was there. "Oh my God." Somehow, she kept her voice calm as she said, "Ellie, go to your room. Let me help your mommy."

I opened my eye. "Mom." She bent down and hugged me hard. I whispered Dr. Desgupta's name, then handed her the phone, and shut my eyes again as I heard her say, "Yes, I'm Allison Weiss's mother, and she's very, very ill."

Curled on my side, I rocked and rocked. Faintly, as if I were listening through a paper tube, I could hear my mother's voice, her questions and answers. *Opiate addiction . . . Suboxone . . . Precipitated withdrawal . . . Which facility would you recommend?*

"No rehab!" I moaned, and grabbed at my mother's sleeve.

"Yes, rehab," she said, and pulled herself away. She wasn't falling apart or weeping. There were no snail tracks of mascara on her cheeks, no trembling hands or whimpered complaints about how she could not go on. It was funny, I thought. All it took for my mother to actually be a mother was a little withdrawal. "You're sick, honey. You're sick, but I'm going to help you get better."

I shut my eyes. Later I remembered voices in the bedroom, a stethoscope against my chest, my mother's voice, then Dave's, reciting from the Penny Lane invoice a list of what I'd been taking, how many, and for how long. *We see a lot of this,* someone—a paramedic—had said. More than you'd expect. Happens to the nicest people. *The nicest people,* I thought. That was me. Then they lifted me onto a gurney, and I felt the sting of a needle in my arm, and when I opened my eyes again I was in a hospital bed, feeling as if every bone in my body had been smashed, then clumsily reset.

"Where am I? What happened?" I whispered. Dave stood there in a Blind Melon T-shirt and jeans, looking at me. I hurt all over. My body felt like a skinned knee, flayed and bloody, like a single, stinging nerve ending . . . and I was more ashamed than I had ever been in my life. I couldn't deal with this. Not now. Not until someone gave me something for the pain.

"You're in the hospital. You had something called precipitated withdrawal." Dave had come to the doorway, but had not
taken a single step inside the room, like he'd committed to stopping by, but not staying, at a party whose guests he had no interest in knowing. "It's what happens when you've been taking lots
of opiates for a long time, and then something kicks them off
your system."

"FYI, it's not a lot of fun," I whispered. Dave didn't smile.

"There're two days left of school." Dave was doing his reasonable, just-the-facts thing, the one I recognized from telephone
conversations with his editor. "Your mom and I can manage
Ellie. Then she can do day camp at Stonefield."

"My mom can barely manage herself," I said.

"You need to go somewhere," he said.

"You mean rehab." Dave did not deny it. "Look," I said, into
the silence. "Obviously, buying pills online was a bad idea. I
know I was taking way more than I should have. I'm under a
lot of stress. I've been making some bad decisions. But look, it's
been . . . " I looked around for a clock, then took my best guess.
"What, twenty-four hours since I had anything, right?" Without
waiting for him to confirm, I plowed on. "So I should be fine.
Maybe I just need some rest. Fluids. Then I can come home, and
I'll be okay. I just won't take any more pills."

Could I do it? I wondered, even as I made my case. Maybe,
twenty-four hours later, I'd be physically free, but I knew that if
I was home alone I'd be on the computer or the phone, getting
more.

You're an addict.

No I'm not.

You can't stop.

Yes I can.

And in that moment, in that bed, what I'd done, what I'd

let myself become, hit me hard. I had endangered my daughter. Janet's boys. Myself. Even though no one had gotten hurt—*yet,* my mind whispered; *no one has gotten hurt yet*—the truth was that if I kept going this way, Ellie might grow up with an absence far worse than what I endured. She would have the same hole in her heart that I had, the same questions that tormented me—why wasn't I good enough for my own mother to love?

"It's just twenty-eight days," Dave said.

"What about my dad?" I managed. "What about Ellie?"

"Your father's in a safe place. Your mom can take care of herself, and I can take care of Eloise."

"And what if I don't go?"

Dave didn't answer. He just looked at me steadily. "I hope you'll do the right thing," he finally said. "Because I need to do whatever it takes to make sure that Ellie is safe."

Panic was blooming inside me, pushing the air out of my lungs, as I sorted out what that could mean. I imagined Dave moving out, and taking Ellie with him. I pictured my husband in his good navy blue suit, standing in front of a judge, all the evidence—the envelopes from Penny Lane, bank statements and receipts, copies of all the prescriptions I'd accumulated from all the different doctors. *Your honor, my wife is not capable of caring for a small child.* Or, worse, what if I came home from the hospital and found that the locks had been changed?

"Allison. Be reasonable." His voice was as gentle as it had been on the phone the day we'd moved my dad to Eastwood. "Is this how you want to live your life? Is this the kind of mom you want to be?"

I opened my mouth to tell him, once again, that things were all right, that they were almost entirely okay; that yes, obviously, there'd been some slips, that things had gotten out of hand, but they were by no means completely off the rails or—what was the word they kept using in that meeting?—unmanageable. My life was not unmanageable. I could manage it just fine.

But before I could say that, I thought about how I'd been spending my days. Waking up in the morning, my very first thoughts were not of my daughter or my husband, not of my job or my friends or my plans for the day, but of how many pills I had left, and whether it was enough, and how I was going to get more. The time I spent chasing them, the energy, the money, the mental resources . . . and the truth was, at that point I was barely feeling the euphoria they'd once provided. A year ago, one or two Vicodin could make me feel great. These days, four or five Oxys—the medicine they gave to cancer patients, for God's sake, cancer patients who were dying—were barely enough to get me feeling normal. Was this how I wanted to live?

But how could I leave? How could I walk away from everything—my home, my work, my father, my daughter? There was no way. I could just go home and fix this on my own. I could do better. I could get it under control, cut back, be more reasonable. Except, even as I began to outline a plan in my head, I was suspecting a different truth. My "off" switch was broken, possibly forever. Having just one pill felt about as likely as taking just one breath.

I looked up at my husband. "I suppose you've already found a place to ship me?"

He nodded. "It's in New Jersey. It's very highly rated. And my insurance will pay for twenty-eight days."

Twenty-eight days, I thought. *I could do anything for twenty-eight days.*

"Okay," I said quietly, thinking, *This has to end somehow, somewhere, and maybe this is as good an ending as any.* "Okay."

PART THREE

—

Checking In

SIXTEEN

When I was a girl, every summer my parents and I would spend a week in Avalon, at the Jersey Shore. Every summer we'd rented the same little cottage a block away from the beach and set up camp there. Now that I was a mother myself, I would have called it a relocation instead of a vacation, but back then it was like being transported to the land of fairy tales. Every day I'd swim in the ocean, and at night I'd fall asleep listening to the sound of the waves through my open window instead of the hum of our house's central air, looking at the little bedroom that was mine by the glow of moonlight on water instead of my Snow White night-light. The last night, we'd go to the boardwalk in Wildwood, gorge ourselves on sweet grilled sausages and cotton candy, play the carnival games, ride the Ferris wheel and the roller coaster.

In the mornings, we'd eat cold cereal and toast, then pack up a cooler of sodas and snacks and walk the single block between our cottage and the beach. My mother would spread out a pink-and-white-striped blanket; my father would rock the stem of our umbrella back and forth, digging it into the sand, and then swoop me into his arms and carry me, screeching with half-pretend terror, out into the waves.

Every year, I was allowed to buy a single souvenir. The summer I was eight years old, I'd saved a few dollars of tooth fairy and allowance money, augmented by the quarters I'd cadged from the sofa cushions and the dollar bills from the lint filter in the dryer. My plan was to go to the store by myself, buy a pair of Jersey Shore snow globes, and give them to my parents for Chanukah.

I waited until my mother was dozing, facedown on her beach towel, her back and legs gleaming with Hawaiian Tropic lotion, and my dad was settled into his folding chair with the *Examiner* before I took my shovel and pail as camouflage and walked down the beach, toward a spot where, beneath the disinterested gaze of a teenage babysitter, a half-dozen kids were at work making sand mermaids, with long, wavy strands of seaweed mermaids hair and seashell bikinis. "Stay where we can see you," my father called as I walked off, and I told him that I would. I waited until he'd opened the Business section before double-checking to make sure I had my change purse and walking from the beach to the sidewalk, then to the corner, looking both ways before I crossed the street.

The store where we shopped every year was a high-ceilinged, barnlike room where the sunshine streamed in through skylights. It was full of bins of lacquered seashells and preserved starfish, penny candy and wrapped pieces of taffy. Behind a glass case were glossy slabs of fudge and caramel-dipped apples. Next to the cash register were racks of postcards, some featuring pretty girls in bikinis, with "See the Sights at the Jersey Shore" written underneath them. That morning, though, it was cloudy outside, and the store looked dim and empty. The cash register was abandoned; there weren't any teenage clerks in their red pinnies, restocking shelves or telling shoppers where they could find inflatable floats or swim diapers. Instead of a sparkling treasure

trove, the merchandise—marked-down T-shirts, foam beer co-
zies, "Jersey Shore" shot glasses, skimpy beach towels—looked
dingy and cheap. The postcard rack squeaked when I spun it, and
I noticed a card I hadn't seen before. It had a picture of a very
heavy woman in a red one-piece bathing suit not unlike my own.
"The Jersey Shore's Good, but the Food Is Great!" read the words
printed over the sand. I stared, not quite understanding the joke
but knowing that the woman in the bathing suit was the brunt
of it, and wondering under what circumstances she'd posed for
the picture. Had she just been lying there, sunning herself, when
a man with a camera came by and tricked her, saying, *You're so
pretty, let me take your picture*? Or had she been aware the picture
was going to be used for a joke? And if that was the case, why
had she allowed it, knowing that people would laugh at her?

I readjusted my grasp on my change purse, gave the metal
rack a final spin, and was heading off to find the snow globes
when a man grabbed me by the shoulder and spun me around.

"Did you see?" he demanded. I blinked up at him. He wore
a baseball shirt with the buttons open over his bare chest, cutoff
denim shorts, and leather sandals. His eyes looked wild and his
teeth were stained brown, and the smell of liquor coming off of
him was so thick it was almost visible, like the cloud surround-
ing Pig-Pen in the *Peanuts* comic strip. As I stared, the man
shook my shoulder again. "Did you see?"

I shook my head. I hadn't seen anything, but even if I had,
I would have denied it. There was something wrong with this
man; even a little kid like me could tell. I couldn't remember ever
being so scared. Worse than the waves of liquor smell that rolled
off him was the feeling of not-rightness. His pupils were too
big; his hand was holding me way too hard. A squeak escaped
my lips as tears spilled onto my cheeks. I wished I'd never come
here, never snuck away from my parents. I wished they would

come rescue me, right this minute. As we stood there, with his fingers still curled into the flesh of my shoulder, a woman, barefoot in a bikini top and a short denim skirt, with the kind of bleached-blonde hair my mother would have dismissed with a curled lip and the word "cheap," came around the corner. She had a red plastic shopping basket over one forearm, empty except for a canister of Pringles, and a tattoo of what looked like a heart visible above the bra cup of her swimsuit.

"You're scaring her, Kenny," the woman said, and knelt down beside me. She had a southern accent and a sweet, high voice, but she, too, smelled like booze when she breathed. "What's your name, pretty girl? You want some fudge?"

"No, thank you," I whispered, as wild-eyed Kenny repeated, in a droning whine, "She saw us."

"She didn't see a thing." The woman's eyes looked like spinning pinwheels, her pupils tiny pinpricks of black in the blue of her irises. "How about a lollipop, pretty little miss?"

"I have to go now," I whispered, and ran past them, out the door. I knew which way the beach was—there was only one street to cross, then I'd be there—but, somehow, I must have gone the wrong way, because when I stopped running I couldn't see the water, and the street was completely unfamiliar. BAR AND GRILLE, read one sign. I heard the sound of an American flag, hanging at the corner, snapping in the breeze. There were people on the street, but not tourists, not people like me and my parents, in swimsuits and sun hats, carrying coolers and portable radios and folding chairs. All I saw were a few men dressed like Kenny, men with dark glasses and bent heads and a palpable aura of strangeness, of *off-ness,* around them, going in and out of the BAR AND GRILLE. I stood on the corner in my pink rubber flip-flops and my white terry-cloth cover-up. I'd dropped my change purse at some point during my flight.

Eventually, a man in a blue bathing suit, with a coating of white zinc on his nose, found me standing on the street corner, crying. "Little girl, are you lost?" I'd told him my name and that I lived in Cherry Hill but was staying in Avalon, and he'd walked me back to the beach, just two blocks away, where I found my parents at the lifeguard station. "Where did you go?" my mother asked, her voice shaking as she scooped me into her arms. My father gave me a lecture about staying where I could see them and not ever, ever scaring my mother like that. "You know how sensitive she is," he'd said, and I'd nodded, crying wordlessly, meaning to explain that I'd wanted to go shopping, to get presents, to surprise them, but I never caught my breath enough to form the words, and they never asked where I'd gone, or why. They'd taken me back to the blanket and given me lemonade. My sobs tapered off into hiccups, and, eventually, I'd fallen asleep in the wedge of shade under our umbrella, and had to be woken up so they could walk me back to the cottage for lunch. By the afternoon, I'd all but forgotten about my adventure . . . but as I got older, I'd remembered, and I would spend hours trying to figure out what the couple, he with the baseball shirt, she with the shopping basket and the southern accent, had been doing that they'd worried I had seen. Had they robbed the place? Shoplifted a bottle? Were they paranoid because of something they'd smoked or swallowed, jumping at shadows, scaring little girls for no reason? I never knew . . . but the sense of that morning had never left me, the idea that everything could change with just one wrong turn. There was a parallel universe that ran alongside the normal world, and if you went through the wrong door, or turned left instead of right, ran up the street instead of down it, you could accidentally push the curtain aside and end up in that other place, where everything was different and everything was wrong.

That was how I felt, waking up that first morning in a single bed in a small, dingy room at Meadowcrest. "Oh, shit, not here," I'd said when Dave had pulled off the road and I'd seen the signs that read MEADOWCREST: PUTTING FAMILIES FIRST. There were at least half a dozen billboards with the same slogan along I-95 on the way from Center City to the airport, with a picture of a white guy with a superhero's jawline holding a beaming toddler in his arms. Dave and I had joked about it, wondering if the guy had been told he'd be posing for an ad for beer or Cialis, and the ribbing his buddies must have given him when he'd turned out to be the face of addiction.

Tight-lipped, without smiling, Dave had said, "They had a bed."

"I want to go to Malibu. Seriously. If I'm going to do this, I might as well do it right." I still felt awful—sick and weak and nauseous, and gutted from the shame—but I had lifted my chin, trying to look imperious with my ratty hair and my dirty clothes and Ellie's Princess Jasmine fleece blanket wrapped around my shoulders. "Take me to the place where Liza Minnelli's on the board of directors."

Dave said nothing to me as he pulled the car up to the guard's stand. "Allison Weiss. She's checking in."

"I'm checking in!" I sang, trying to remember the lyrics of the *Simpsons* rehab anthem. "No more pot or Demerol. No more drugs or alcohol! No more stinking fun at all . . . !" I glanced sideways, wondering if Dave remembered how, when we'd started dating, we'd call each other and watch *The Simpsons* together, him in his apartment, me in mine, and how we'd speculate, during commercials, about whether the severely nerdy bow-tied weather guy on the NBC station got laid nonstop.

He parked the car, took my duffel bag out of the backseat, and walked me inside, where a woman behind a receptionist's desk led us to the comfortable, well-appointed waiting room, with leather couches and baskets of hundred-calorie snack packs and a wide-screen TV.

They'd been showing *Jeopardy!* The categories were World History, English Literature, Ends in "Y," Famous Faces, and—ha—Potent Potables. Curled on the couch in my Jasmine blanket, I answered every question right. "Do I really need to be here?" I'd asked Dave.

"Yes, Allie," said Dave, sounding distant and tired. "You do." I could see wrinkles at the corners of his eyes and a few grayish patches in the beard that had grown in since that morning, and the cuff of one pant leg was tucked into his sock. How must these last few days have been for him? I wondered, before deciding it was better not to think about it.

I'd tried to tell him that I felt much better, that, clearly, I'd had some kind of bad reaction to Suboxone, but now I was fine and, as *Jeopardy!* indicated, clearheaded, that it would be all right for him to take me home, and I remembered him not-too-gently removing (*prying* might have been a better word) my fingers from his forearms and delivering me into the care of a short, bald male nurse who'd hummed Lady Gaga's "The Edge of Glory" while he'd taken my blood and medical history, before handing me a plastic pee cup and directing me to the bathroom. "Gotta pat you down," he'd said when I came out, handing me a robe and telling me to take everything off. "And we're gonna do the old squat-and-cough." I stared at him until I realized he was serious. Then, shaking my head in disbelief, I squatted. And coughed.

Once my exam was done, I'd joined Dave in a cubicle, where a young woman with doughy features and too much blue eyeliner sat behind a computer and asked me embarrassing questions. When I didn't answer, or couldn't, Dave stepped in. "I think she's been abusing painkillers for about a year," he'd said, and,

"Yes, she has prescriptions, but she's also been buying things on-line," and, finally, most terrifyingly, "Yes, I'll pay out of pocket for what insurance doesn't cover." I'd grabbed his sleeve again and leaned close, whispering, "Dave . . ."

He'd pulled his arm away and given me a look that could only be called cold. "You need to get yourself together," he'd said. "If not for your own sake, then for Ellie's."

So here I was. I looked around, running my hands down my body. My jeans felt greasy; the waistband had slipped down my hips, the way it did when I'd worn them for too long without a wash. My clogs, resting by the side of the bed, were stained with something I didn't want to examine too closely. My T-shirt smelled bad, and there was a smear of the same offensive some-thing on its sleeve. I had clean clothes in the duffel Dave had packed, but I'd last seen it on the other side of the receptionist's desk. "We'll just hang on to it up here until one of the staffers has time to search it, 'kay?" she'd said.

"Good morning, Meadowcrest!" a voice blared from the ceil-ing. I bolted upright with my heart thudding in my chest. I still felt weak, and sick, and I ached all over. I wasn't sure whether that was related to precipitated withdrawal, or how much was the result of the phenobarbital they were giving me to get me through the worst of the lingering withdrawal symptoms.

"It is now seven a.m.," said the ceiling. "Ladies, please head down to get your morning meds. Breakfast will begin at seven-thirty. Gentlemen, you'll eat at eight o'clock. Room inspections will commence at nine. Riiiiiise and shiiiine!"

I collapsed on my back. My head hit the pillow with a crack-ling sound. Investigation revealed that both the pillow and the mattress were thin, sad-looking affairs encased in crinkly, stained plastic. Lovely.

Swinging my feet onto the floor, I took my first good look at my room: a narrow, cell-like space with a bed, a desk, a scarred wooden wardrobe, and a tattered poster reading ONE DAY AT A TIME stuck to the wall with a scrap of Scotch tape. My duffel bag, which now had a construction-paper label bearing the words ALLISON W. and SEARCHED attached to one strap with a garbage bag twist-tie, sat on the floor beside me.

I took one shuffling step, then two, then crossed the room to the door, where a man in a khaki uniform was pushing a mop. "Excuse me," I said.

He looked at me blankly.

"Is there someone here I can talk to?"

The blank look continued.

"I'm not supposed to be here," I said, enunciating each word clearly. "I need to talk to someone so I can go home."

The man—a janitor, I guessed—shrugged and cocked his thumb toward the opposite end of the hall. There was a desk with no one behind it. A few people—teenagers, mostly—were milling in the hall, wearing pajama bottoms and slippers and sweatshirts, making quiet conversation. I stood there until they saw me. "Excuse me," I said. "Is there anyone who works here who can help me?"

"They come in at eight o'clock," said one of the shufflers in slippers. I went back to my room, where, for lack of anything better to do, I unzipped the duffel bag and inspected its contents. Dave hadn't even let me go home from the hospital long enough to pack. He was probably worried that I'd use the opportunity to run, when all I wanted to do was say goodbye to Ellie and my mom. A look in the mirror in my hospital room had convinced me to wait. If Ellie had seen me looking so sick, she'd probably have been even more worried. I hoped Dave would tell her I'd gone away on a last-minute trip to New York.

I made the bed, smoothing the thin, pilled brown comforter

before I started going through the bag. There were six pairs of tennis socks, two pairs of lace panties that I had bought before Eloise's birth and not tried to squeeze myself into since, a single sports bra, a pair of jeans, two long-sleeved T-shirts, and a pair of black velvet leggings that I recognized as the bottom half of a long-ago Catwoman Halloween costume. I stopped rummaging after that. It was just too depressing. Why had Dave packed, and not Janet or even my mom? Was there anything like a toothbrush and deodorant in here? How had he managed to pack everything I'd needed that weekend when Ellie was a newborn, but get it so wrong this time?

Maybe he was scared, I thought. Five years ago, he'd been packing for a romantic retreat, a family honeymoon by the beach. This time, he'd been shipping a drug addict to rehab. Big difference.

Someone was knocking on the other side of my bathroom door. "Come in," I called. My voice was weak and croaky. A girl who didn't look much older than fourteen stuck her head into my room and looked around.

"We share the bathroom and you gotta keep it clean and everything off the floor," she said. "Or else we'll both get demerits."

Demerits? "Okay," I said, and forced myself to stand on legs that felt as though something large and angry had been chewing on them all night long.

"I'm going to brush my teeth. Do you need to use the bathroom?"

I shook my head, although I wasn't sure what I needed, other than my pills. I cast a sideways glance at my purse. Maybe there was a stash I'd missed, or even some dust in the Altoids tin that could help.

"I'm Allison," I said.

"Hi," said the girl as she followed my gaze. "Forget it," she said. "They search everything that comes in." She had shimmering blonde hair hanging to the small of her back, a small, foxy face, pale eyes, and vivid purple bruises running up and down her bare arms.

"I'm Aubrey," she said, and tugged at the strap of her tank top. She was dressed like she was ready to go clubbing, or at least the way I imagined girls on their way to clubs would dress. Her jeans were tight enough to preclude circulation, her black boots had high heels, her top was made of some thin silvery fabric, which she had matched with silver eye shadow and, if I wasn't mistaken, false eyelashes that were also dusted with glitter.

"Listen," I said, trying not to sound as desperate as I felt. "Who do I talk to about getting out of here?"

Aubrey snickered.

"No, seriously. I think this is a mistake."

"Sure," said Aubrey, in the same indulgent tone I used to jolly Eloise out of her bad moods.

"Please. There must be, like, a counselor, or a supervisor. Someone I can talk to."

"Yeah, you'd think so," Aubrey said. "For what this place costs, there should be. But there's nobody, like, official, until lunchtime. Hey, it could be worse," she said, after seeing the look on my face. "My last place, there were, like, six girls to a room, in bunk beds. At least here you've got your own space. So why are you here?" she asked.

"Because my husband's an asshole," I said.

She smiled, then quickly pressed her lips together, covering her discolored teeth. "You better not let the RCs hear you say that," she said. "They'll say you're in denial. That until you're ready to admit you have a problem, you won't ever get better."

"What if I don't have a problem?"

She lifted her narrow shoulders in a shrug. "I dunno. Honestly, I've never seen anyone in rehab who didn't have a problem. And I've been in rehab a lot."

Yay, you, I thought.

"What were you taking?" she asked. When I didn't answer, she said, "C'mon, you must have been taking something."

"Oh. Um. Painkillers. Prescription painkillers." The "prescription" suddenly struck me as important, a way of announcing to this girl that I wasn't scoring crack on the streets, that I might be a junkie, but I was a reputable junkie.

"Percs?" she asked, smoothing her hair. "Vics? Oxys?"

"All of the above," I said ruefully.

"Yeah. That's how I started." She looked over my shoulder, out the window, which revealed an unlovely view of a waterlogged field. "You know how it goes. One day you're snorting a Perc before history class, the next day you're down in Kensington, and some guy named D-Block is sticking a needle in your arm."

"Ah," I said. Meanwhile, I was thinking, *D-Block?* There was no D-Block in my story. Or Kensington. Or needles.

"You court-stipulated?" she asked, without much interest. She'd moved on from her hair and the window and was now checking her eye makeup in a mirror she'd pulled out of her pocket.

I shook my head.

"Did you fail a random?"

I tried to make sense of the question. "I don't know what that means."

"Like, a random drug test at work. A lot of the older ladies are here for that." She gave me a look that was not unsympathetic. "No offense."

"Oh, none taken." I wasn't sure whether her "no offense" applied to my age or to the assumption that I'd gotten in trouble at work. "No, I work for myself, so no drug tests or anything."

"Lose your license? DUI?"

I shook my head. "How about you?" I said, like we'd just been introduced at a cocktail party and she'd just tapped the conversational ball over to my side of the net. "Are you working, or in school?"

"I waitressed." It took her a minute to remember how conversation happened. "What do you do?"

"I'm a journalist," I said, which sounded like more of a real job than "blogger."

"Huh." She tugged at her hair. "Did you have to go to college for that?"

"Um. Well, I did. But I guess, technically, you don't have to. You just need to have something to say." I had to remind myself that I was here to get help for myself, not to rescue anyone else, or save all the little broken birds. *You are not coming out of here with an intern,* I told myself. I didn't plan on staying long enough to learn names, let alone collect résumés.

"Good morning, Meadowcrest!" the intercom said again. Aubrey rolled her eyes and shot her middle finger at the ceiling. "Ladies, it's about that time. Morning meds, breakfast, and inspections. Riiiise and shiiine!"

There was another knock. "Are you the new girl?" an older woman asked. She had curly white hair and wore black polyester slacks, white orthopedic sneakers with pristine laces, and a red cardigan with shiny cut-glass buttons. Reading glasses dangled from a beaded chain against her sizable bosom. She wore a gold watch, a gold wedding band, a gold cross hanging on a necklace, and another necklace with little ceramic figurines in the shapes of boys and girls, probably intended to represent her grandchildren.

"Hello," she said, offering me her hand to shake. "I'm Mary. I'm an alcoholic."

Aubrey rolled her eyes. "You don't have to say that, like, everywhere you go, Mare," she said. "Only in meetings."

"I'm trying to get used to it," Mary said.

"Hi," I said, and tried to think of a polite follow-up. "So, how long have you two been here?"

"Three days," said Aubrey.

"Four for me," said Mary. "We're the new kids on the block." She looked at Aubrey anxiously. "Did I get that right? New kids on the block?"

Aubrey made a face. "Like, how should I know? They're oldies."

"Well," said Mary, looking flustered. "Do you want some help with your room?"

"Fuck," Aubrey said. I followed her gaze past the bathroom to what must have been her bedroom, a narrow space the twin of mine. Based on its appearance, Aubrey had had a seizure in the middle of the night and flung everything she possessed to its four corners.

"I'll help," said Mary. I decided to join in, thus avoiding demerits, whatever they turned out to be. I wouldn't be staying here long, but that didn't mean I wanted to make a bad impression. Bending down, I began to gather up girl things: ninety-nine-cent nail polish, Victoria's Secret panties, a black eyeliner pencil, a paperback copy of *The Big Book of Alcoholics Anonymous*, a packet of Xeroxed pages labeled RELAPSE PREVENTION, a piece of posterboard with MY TIMELINE OF ABUSE written on top, a blouse, a pair of inside-out jeans, a single Ugg boot, and a half-empty package of peanut butter cookies.

"Do you know where we are, exactly? Like, what town?" I'd been so sick and so out of it on the ride down, I'd barely noticed exactly where we were heading.

"Buttfuck, New Jersey," Aubrey said, shoving books and papers under her bed. "I mean, I guess it's got a name, but I have no fucking clue what it's called. All rehabs are, like, in the middle of fucking nowhere. So you can't cop."

I took my armload of stuff and deposited it gently at the bottom of her freestanding wardrobe. "How many times have you done this?"

She kept her smirk in place while she answered, but her eyes looked sad. "Six."

Six rehabs. Dear Lord.

"How about you?" I asked Mary, who shook her head.

"Oh, no, dear, this is my first time in treatment. Come on," she said. "We should get in line for meds."

Aubrey wandered toward the bathroom. In my bedroom, I put on clean jeans and a T-shirt, gave my plastic pillow a fluff, and zipped up my duffel and set it in the wardrobe. Then I followed Mary out of the bedroom and into the wide, fluorescent-lit hallway. Dozens of doors just like mine ran along each side of it, amplifying the place's resemblance to a cheap motel. We walked down the hall until we arrived at the desk I'd found earlier. There were maybe two dozen women milling around, most of them dressed, a few in pajamas and robes. Many of them held white plastic binders. "What's that?" I asked, pointing to the one Mary had in her arms.

"It's the welcome packet, and the schedule. You didn't get one?"

I shook my head no. A heavy-set woman wearing khakis and a yellow short-sleeved shirt hunched behind the computer at the desk. An engraved plastic nametag announced that she was

MARGO, and the words MEADOWCREST COTTAGE were sewn in red thread onto the right side of her chest. Her desk was a poor relation to the burnished oak desk out front, with a bouquet of flowers and a dish of hard candy. This desk was made of cheap pressboard, and, instead of blossoms or treats, there was a stack of papers with the title A LETTER FROM YOUR ADDICTION.

Dear Friend, I've come to visit once again. I love to see you suffer mentally, physically, spiritually, and socially. I want to have you restless so you can never relax. I want you jumpy and nervous and anxious. I want to make you agitated and irritable so everything and everybody makes you uncomfortable. I want you to be depressed and confused so that you can't think clearly or positively. I want to make you hate everything and everybody—especially yourself. I want you to feel guilty and remorseful for the things you have done in the past that you'll never be able to let go. I want to make you angry and hateful toward the world for the way it is and the way you are. I want you to feel sorry for yourself and blame everything but your addiction for the way things are. I want you to be deceitful and untrustworthy, and to manipulate and con as many people as possible. I want to make you fearful and paranoid for no reason at all and I want you to wake up during all hours of the night screaming for me. You know you can't sleep without me; I'm even in your dreams.

"Excuse me," I said, aiming a smile at Margo. "I'm hoping I can speak to someone about leaving."

She looked up at me. "Where's your tag?"

"Tag?"

"Tag," she repeated, pointing to my chest in a way I might have found a little forward if I hadn't been such a wreck. "When you're admitted, they give you a nametag with your welcome binder and your schedule. You need to wear it at all times."

"Right. But I'm not staying. I'm not supposed to—"

She lifted her hand. "Honey, I can't even talk to you till you've got your tag on. Check your room."

"Fine." I went back to my room as more women drifted out into the hallway. Most of them appeared to be Aubrey's age, but I saw a few thirty- and fortysomethings, and some who were even older. The young girls wore tight jeans, high heels, faces full of makeup. The women my age wore looser pants, less paint, and, inevitably, Dansko clogs. The official shoe of playgrounds, operating rooms, restaurant kitchens, and rehab. "Excuse me," said a sad, frail, hunched-over woman who looked even older than Mary, as she used a walker to make her way toward the desk. I shuddered, thinking that if I were an eighty-year-old addict, I would hope my friends and my children would leave me alone to drink and drug in peace.

Sure enough, back in my cell of a room, on top of the desk, I found a beige plastic nametag clipped to a black lanyard with my name—ALLISON W.—typed on the front. Beside it was a binder and schedule. I spared my single bed a longing glance, wishing I could just go back to sleep, then looped the tag over my neck and proceeded back down the hall.

SEVENTEEN

The scent of mass-produced food was seeping from behind the cafeteria's double doors. Even if I hadn't been so nauseous, I couldn't imagine eating anything. I felt like Persephone in the underworld—one bite, one sip, a single pomegranate seed, and I'd be stuck here forever.

I walked back to the desk and flapped my nametag at Margo, the desk drone. "I'd like to call home."

"Morning meds," she said, without looking up.

I went to the nurse's counter, stood in line for twenty minutes, swallowed what was in the little white paper cup she gave me, and then returned.

"I took my medicine," I said, showing Margo the empty cup, feeling grateful she hadn't asked to see my empty mouth, the way the nurse had. "May I please use the phone?"

"You're on a seven-day blackout," she recited without looking past my chin. "No visits, no phone calls."

"Excuse me? I don't remember agreeing to that."

Margo heaved a mighty sigh. "If you're here, then you signed a contract agreeing to follow our rules."

"May I see that contract, please?" I remembered signing my

name to all kinds of things—releases for my doctor to share my
medical history, releases for Meadowcrest to talk to my insurance company—but it seemed unlikely that I'd sign something
promising I wouldn't call home for a week. Nor did it seem reasonable that they'd expect parents with young children to go that
long between calls. Besides, could a contract be legally binding if
the person who signed it was fresh out of the ER and still going
through withdrawal?

Margo yawned without bothering to cover her mouth. "You
can ask your counselor."

"Who is my counselor?"

"You'll be assigned one after orientation."

"When's that?"

"After breakfast."

"I'm not planning on staying for breakfast." I made myself
smile and lowered my voice. "This isn't the right place for me. I
just want to go home."

"You need to discuss that with your—"

Before she could say "counselor," I pointed toward the front
of the building—the nice desk, the clean waiting room with
its wide-screen TV and baskets of snacks, the door—and said,
"What happens if I just walk out of here right now?"

That got her attention. She sat up straighter and looked at
me like she was seeing me for the first time. "If you choose to
sign yourself out AMA, you can leave after twenty-four hours,"
she recited. "We can't let you go right now. You still have detox
drugs in your system. It would be a liability."

"Even if I have someone pick me up? And I go right to a
hospital or something?" A hospital sounded good. I'd get a private room, and I'd bring my own bedding, of course. I pictured
an IV in my arm, delivering whatever drugs would make this

process more bearable. Then maybe I'd take myself to a spa for a few days. Fresh air, long hikes, nothing stronger than aspirin and iced tea. That was the ticket.

"Twenty-four hours. That's the rule."

"Okay." I could endure anything for twenty-four hours. I'd been in labor that long, having Eloise. I went back down the hall and found Mary and Aubrey waiting in line.

"Where'd you cop?" I heard a statuesque brunette, who could have been a model except for her acne-ravaged complexion, ask a petite blonde girl in a see-through top. I didn't hear the girl's answer, but the brunette gave a squeal. "Ohmygod, no way! Who was your dealer?"

The petite girl gave a shrug. "He just said to call him Money." She must have noticed me staring, because she turned toward me, eyes narrowed. "You work here?"

"Me? No, I . . ." Now there were a few young girls staring at me.

"Booze?" asked the tall brunette.

"Pills," I said, deciding to keep it short and sweet.

"Yeah," the brunette said wistfully. "That's how I started." I was beginning to get the impression that pills were how everyone started, and that when you couldn't afford or find the pills anymore, you moved on to heroin.

"Come on," said Aubrey, as the herd of girls and women began moving down the hall. "Breakfast."

I bypassed the limp slices of French toast and greasy discs of sausage in stainless steel pans on steam tables, with jugs of flavored corn syrup masquerading as maple, and made a mug of tea. The room was chilly and cavernous, a high-school cafeteria from hell with unflattering lights, worn linoleum, and aged inspirational posters, including the inevitable kitten-on-a-branch "Hang In There!" thumbtacked to walls painted a washed-out yellow. Six long plastic-topped tables with bolted-on benches took up most of the room's space. Each one was adorned with a tiny ceramic vase of plastic flowers—someone's sad attempt at making the place look pretty. The air smelled like the ghosts of a thousand departed high-school cafeteria lunches—steamed burgers and stale French fries, cut-up iceberg lettuce birthed from a bag and served with preservative-laden croutons hard enough to crack a tooth. I sat at the end of a table, numb and aching for my pills, listening as the conversation between the tall, dark-haired girl and the petite blonde continued.

". . . parents found my works underneath my mattress and, like, hired an interventionist . . ."

"You had an intervention? That is so cool! Shit, my mom said she was taking me to the movies, and then she dropped me off here . . ."

I sipped my tea and watched the clock. I would say as little as possible for as long as I could. I'd sit through their orientation and endure the mandatory twenty-four hours. Then I'd find a supervisor, explain the situation, and get Dave or Janet or someone to come pick me up.

I didn't belong here. I wasn't like these women. I didn't have any DUIs that needed to be expunged, a judge hadn't ordered me to stay, and I hadn't flunked a drug test at work. Nobody named D-Block had ever stuck a needle in my arm, and I wasn't sure I could find Kensington even with my GPS. *Heroin*, I thought, and shuddered. These girls had done IV drugs, and probably worse things to get the drugs. All I'd done was swallow a few too many pills, all of which (except the ones I'd ordered online) had been legitimately prescribed. I didn't belong here, and all I needed to do was figure out how quickly I could leave. My daughter needed me. So did my readers. How on earth had I let Dave convince me, even for a minute, that I could just check out of all of my responsibilities to come to a place like this?

"What's your damage?" asked the girl next to me. She was in her twenties, broad-shouldered and solid, with no makeup on her pale skin and long brown hair piled on top of her head in a messy bun. She wore gray sweatpants and an Eagles jersey and a nametag that read LENA.

"Excuse me?"

"Your stuff. Your drug of choice," she explained in a flat, nasal voice, as Mary sat down across from me.

"Pills. But I don't really . . . I mean, I don't think that I'm . . ." I shut my mouth and tried again. "I'm not actually planning on staying. I don't think this is the right place for me."

The Eagles-jersey girl and Mary both gave me knowing smiles. "That's what I said," Mary told us. With her blue eyes and white curls, her rounded hips and sagging bosom, she looked like Mrs. Claus. Possibly like Mrs. Claus after a rough weekend, during which she'd discovered naughty pictures of the elves on Santa's hard drive. "I used to put my gin in a water bottle. Because that was *classy*." A Boston accent turned the word to *clah-see*. I sipped my tea as the other girls and women nodded. "So I came down here with my bottle of Dasani, thinking I had everyone fooled."

"I wasn't fooling anyone," said Lena. "I came straight from the hospital. They Narcanned me."

"Excuse me?" I asked.

"I OD'd. I almost died. They had to give me Narcan—it's a shot that, like, brings you back to life. I woke up and ripped the IVs out of my arm and, like, ran out the door. I had my stash in my bra," she said.

"Ah." *Stash in bra,* I thought. Add that to the list of things I didn't do and did not completely understand. Was *stash* different from *works?*

"But they caught me—of course." Lena used her hands when she talked, big, broad, sweeping motions. When she wasn't gesturing, she was smoothing her ponytail like a pet. "I was in jail for six weeks, and then I was on work release, but I fucked that up and got loaded, and my PO busted me . . ." PO. Work release. Jail. Gin in water bottles. Drinking before the third hour of the *Today* show. I looked around, again noting the doors, wondering what would really happen if I just got up, collected my purse and duffel bag, and walked out. Of course, I didn't know exactly where I was. That was a problem. Nor did I have any money—I remembered that they'd taken my wallet and my phone when they'd taken my bag. I rested my throbbing temples in my palms and forced myself to breathe slowly, trying to keep that jumping-out-of-my-skin feeling at bay.

A buzzer sounded. The girls and women stood, trays in hand, and marched to a stainless steel window cut into the wall. I picked up my own empty tray and got in line, depositing my silverware in a bin full of detergent, pushing my mug through the slot, from which a plastic-gloved, hair-netted dishwasher grabbed it. "Come on," said Aubrey, and I followed the crowd out the door.

EIGHTEEN

At nine o'clock that morning, I was sitting on a couch covered in a shiny and decidedly unnatural fabric in a room called the Ladies' Lounge, and a thumb-shaped, red-faced man was yelling at me.

"All addicts are selfish," he said. He was, like the famed little teapot, short and stout. His cheap acrylic sweater was a red that matched his face. His blue slacks bunched alarmingly at his crotch, the cuffs so short they displayed his argyle socks and an expanse of hairy white shin. His tassled loafers were scuffed. On his sweater was pinned a nametag reading DARNTON. He looked at us accusingly. There were three of us in orientation: me, and Aubrey, and Mary, who'd been crying quietly since she'd walked through the door.

"All addicts are selfish," Darnton repeated, and raised his caterpillar-thick eyebrows, daring us to disagree. When no one did, he opened the blue-covered paperback in his hand and began reading. I wondered idly whether he was starting where he'd left off with the last group; whether he just worked his way right through *The Big Book*, regardless of who was listening. "The first requirement is that we be convinced that any life run on self-will can hardly be a success." I blinked. My hands hurt and were trembling. My head was still throbbing. I wanted to lie down, curled beneath a blanket, soothed and calmed by my pills.

"Why are you here?" Darnton asked Aubrey.

She shrugged. "'Cause my parents found my works."

"Do you want to stop using?"

Another shrug. "I guess."

"You guess," Darnton repeated, his voice rich with sarcasm. Was mocking addicts really an effective way to get them to change? Before I could come to any conclusions, Darnton turned on Mary. "How about you?"

"I was drinking too much," she whispered in a quavering voice. "I did terrible things."

Darnton appeared just as interested in Mary's self-flagellation as he did in Aubrey's nonchalance. "And you?"

I forced myself to sit up straight. "I was taking painkillers."

"And you were taking painkillers because . . . ?" the thumb persisted.

"Because I was in pain," I said. Duh. Never mind that the pain was spiritual instead of physical. The thumb did not need to know that. I turned my eyes toward the wall, where two posters were hanging. STEP ONE, I read. *We admitted that we were powerless over alcohol and that our lives had become unmanageable,* then tuned back into the jerky little man lecturing us about our "character defects," hectoring us about what he kept calling "the brain disease of addiction," a disease that, he claimed, was rooted in self-centeredness.

"If anything, I was using the pills because I was trying to do too much for other people," I interrupted. "My father's got Alzheimer's, so I've been helping him and my mother. I take care of my daughter. And I write for a women's website."

Darnton's eyebrows were practically at his hairline . . . or where his hairline must have been at some point. "Oh, a writer," he said. He probably thought I was lying. Given my scratched hands, my pallor, my ratty hair and attire, my vague smell of puke—and, of course, the fact that I was in rehab—I couldn't blame him.

"Yes, I'm a writer," I said. "And my life was not unmanageable. Everyone else's life was unmanageable."

The thumb opened his book again and kept reading. "Selfishness—self-centeredness! That, we think, is the root of our trouble. Driven by a hundred forms of fear, self-delusion, self-seeking, and self-pity—"

"I volunteered," I said, hearing my voice quiver. I swallowed hard. No way was I going to cry in front of this hectoring little jerk. "I ran my house. I took care of my daughter. I took care of my parents. I helped out at my daughter's school . . ."

He lifted his eyebrows again. "Doing everything, were we?"

"So either I'm selfish or I'm a martyr?"

The man shrugged. "Your best thinking got you here. Think about that." He returned to his reading. "The alcoholic is an extreme example of self-will run riot, though he usually doesn't think so." He paused to give me a significant look.

"I'm not a 'he,' " I said. I'd been acquainted with *The Big Book* for only twenty minutes, but I could already tell that it needed a gender update.

"Above everything, we alcoholics must be rid of this selfishness. We must, or it kills us!" He set the book down and looked us over. Aubrey appeared to be asleep, and Mary was crying quietly into her hands.

"You think your life is fine," he said to me. *Better than yours,* I thought unkindly, imagining the existence that went with his outfit—a vinyl-sided house in some unremarkable suburb, a ten-year-old shoebox of a car with spent shocks, waiting for his tax refund to arrive so he could pay down the interest on his credit card. A little man with a little mind and a handful of slogans he'd repeat, no matter who was in the room with him or what their problems were.

"I bet when you go home, and you're looking at things with sober eyes, you're going to think differently." When I didn't answer, he said, "Before I got sober, I'd been building shelves in my kitchen. I thought they were beautiful. I thought I really knew what I was doing. When I came home, I saw that those shelves were a disaster. They were crooked. The cabinet doors didn't shut. I'd kicked a hole in the wall when I got frustrated."

"Sorry to hear that," I said, even though I wasn't. I couldn't have cared less about this man with his bad haircut and cheap clothes. Besides, my house looked fine. No holes in my walls, no crooked cabinets. I had Henry the handyman on speed dial.

"You were taking care of your parents," said the little man.

"My father has early-stage Alzheimer's."

Mary finally stopped crying long enough to look up. "Me, too! I mean, not me. My husband."

Darnton lifted a hand, silencing Mary. "And your daughter," the little man continued.

"My daughter. My business. My husband. My house."

"Did you ever think that you were . . ."—he hooked his fingers into scare quotes—" 'helping' all those people so you could control them?"

Suddenly I was so tired I could barely speak, and I was craving a pill so badly I could cry. How was I going to live the rest of my life, in a world overrun with idiots like this one, without the promise of any comfort at the end of the day? "I was helping them because they needed help."

"I'm selfish," said Aubrey, in a whisper. Her heavily shadowed eyelids were cast down, and she worried a cuticle as she spoke. "I stole from my parents. I stole from my grandma."

"What about you?" the man asked Mary.

"I don't think I was," she said hesitantly. "My drinking didn't get bad until after my daughter had her babies. She had triplets, because of the in vitro, so I'd drive from Maryland to Long Island once a week, and spend three days with her, and then drive down to New Jersey for the weekends to help my son. He's single, and he only sees his two on the weekends. That's why I drank, I think. I'd be so wound up after all that driving, and the kids, that I just couldn't turn myself off. So I'd have a gin and tonic—that was what my husband and I always drank, gin and tonics—and when that didn't do it, I'd have two, and then . . ." Tears spilled over the reddened rims of her eyes. "I got a DUI," she whispered. One hand wandered to the hem of her sweatshirt and tugged at it as she spoke. "I rear-ended someone with my grandbabies in the car. I wasn't planning on driving, but my son got stuck at work, and I was the only one who could get the kids. I should have said no, made up some reason why I couldn't drive them, but I was so ashamed. So ashamed," she repeated, then started to cry again.

Great, I thought. *An angry thumb, a drunk granny, and a thief.* What was wrong with this picture? The fact that I was in it.

"Excuse me," I said politely, and walked to the door.

Darnton glared at me. "Orientation's until ten-fifteen. Then you have Equine."

"Equine? Yeah, no," I said. "I need to speak to someone now." I exited the room. Margo, the woman from the breakfast hour, had been replaced by another young woman in the same outfit. This one had a mustache, faint but discernible. *The Big Book* was open on her computer keyboard. Underneath it, I could see *People* magazine—"*The Bachelor*'s Women Tell All!"

"Oh my God," I said. "I'm going to miss the Fantasy Suites."

The woman flashed a quick smile. She wore a pin, instead of a nametag on a lanyard around her neck, which read WANDA. "Yeah, sorry. No TV for you guys, just recovery-related movies."

"How will I live," I wondered, "if I don't know whether he picks Kelly S. or Kelly D.?" As I spoke, I remembered all the episodes I'd watched with Ellie snuggled on the bed beside me, a bowl of popcorn between us, her head on my shoulder as she slipped into sleep. Normal. (Sort of.) Happy. God, what had happened to take me away from that and bring me here?

The woman lowered her voice. "Can you actually tell them apart?"

"One's a hairdresser, and the other one's a former NBA dancer," I said.

"Okay, but they look exactly the same."

"All the women on that show look exactly the same." I could talk about this forever and had, in fact, written several well-received blog posts on the homogeneity of *The Bachelor*'s ladies.

"Tell you what," said the woman. "I can't sneak in a DVD. But I'll tell you who got roses."

"Deal," I said, feeling incrementally relieved that not everyone in this place was a monster. Just then, a new Meadowcrest employee cruised into view. Wanda shoved her *People* magazine out of sight, as the new woman—middle-aged, blonde hair in a bob, tired blue eyes behind wire-rimmed glasses—looked me over.

"Hi there," I said, sounding professional and polite. "Can you help me find my counselor?"

"Who is it?"

"Well, I'm hoping you can help me with that. I actually don't have a name yet. I just finished orientation." As far as I was concerned, that was true.

"Normally, you aren't assigned a counselor until your third or fourth day."

"Can I use the phone?"

"If you just came, you're on your seven-day blackout. You need to get permission to use the phone from your counselor."

"But you just told me I don't have a counselor." This conversation was beginning to feel like a tired Abbott and Costello routine.

"Then," said the woman, her voice smug, "you'll just have to be patient, won't you?"

"I don't think you understand," I said. "This is a mistake. I don't need to be in rehab. I'm not a drug addict. I was taking painkillers that were prescribed to me by a doctor. Now I'm fine, and I want to go home."

"You can sign yourself out AMA—that's 'against medical advice'—but your counselor needs to sign your paperwork."

"But I don't have a counselor!"

She stared at me for a minute. I stared right back, my feet planted firmly.

"Hold on," she finally grumbled. Bending over the telephone, she muttered something I couldn't catch. A minute later, a very large woman with lank brown hair, pale skin, and pale, bulging eyes came waddling around the corner. Her khaki pants swished with each step; her lanyard flapped and flopped against the lolloping rolls of her flesh.

"Allison? I'm Michelle. I understand that there's a problem?" Her voice was high and singsongy. She sounded a lot like Miss Katie, who taught kindergarten at Stonefield.

I followed her into a closet-sized office dominated by a desk. A fan clipped to the doorframe pushed the air around, along with the smell of microwaved pizza. The Twelve Steps hung on the wall. Michelle settled herself into her chair, which squeaked in protest. "Why don't you tell me what's going on?"

I explained it all: the heroin addicts at breakfast, the condescending little man at orientation, how I understood that I was having problems managing my medication—"but not, you know, rehab-level problems."

Michelle turned to her computer, tapped briefly on the keyboard, and then turned to stare at me with her bulgy eyes. "You were taking six hundred milligrams of OxyContin a day?"

I shrugged, trying not to squirm. "Only on really bad days. Normally it wasn't that many," I lied.

She picked up a cheap plastic pen and tapped it against her desk. "My guess, Allison, is that the pills were a way for you to self-medicate. To remove yourself from painful situations without actually going anywhere."

It sounded reasonable, but I wouldn't let myself nod or give any other indication that she might be right.

"So I think . . ." She raised a hand, as if I'd tried to interrupt her. "No, just hear me out. I think that you really do need to be here."

"Maybe I do need help," I said. "But I don't think this is the place for me. No offense, but I think I'm here because my husband thought I'd change my mind before he got me in the car. I bet he found this place in five minutes on the Internet. I didn't leave him time for lots of research. And I think there are probably places that might be a better fit. Where the"—I searched for an institutional-sounding word—"population might be more like me."

An alarmed expression flitted across Michelle's face. It was quickly replaced by the tranquil look she'd been wearing since our conversation began. "Why do you feel that way?"

"Well, for starters, I'm old enough to be most of the other girls' mother."

"That's not true," she said. "There are quite a few women your age or older."

"I'll give you 'a few,' but not 'quite a few,'" I said. "Unless you're hiding them somewhere. Besides, these girls were doing street drugs."

"And you weren't?"

I shook my head. "No. I had prescriptions." Except for the ones I ordered online, but never mind that.

"Do you think that makes you different from the rest of the ladies here?"

I hesitated, sensing a trap. "Yes," I finally said. "I do think I'm different."

"Do you think you're better?" I didn't answer. "*I* think," said Michelle, "that what I'm hearing is your disease talking. You know, addiction is the only disease that tells you that you don't have a disease."

"I'm not sure I actually believe that addiction is a disease," I said, but Michelle was on a roll.

"Your *disease* is telling you that you don't belong here. Your *disease* is saying that you didn't even have a problem, or that if you did, it wasn't that bad. Your *disease* is saying, 'I can handle this. I'll do it on my own. I can cut back. I don't need the Twelve Steps, and I definitely don't need rehab.'" I was quiet. This, of course, was exactly what I'd been thinking.

"But your best thinking is what got you here. Think about that for a minute." This, of course, was exactly what Darnton had told me. Another trite slogan, one they probably recited to every patient who was giving them trouble.

"I'd like to speak to my husband and my mom. I need to know how my daughter is doing."

"Your counselor can help you to arrange that."

"But I don't have a counselor!" I closed my mouth. I was shouting again. "Look, you don't understand," I said, and knotted my fingers together so my hands would stop shaking. "I didn't have time to make any arrangements for my daughter or my mom. My father just moved into an assisted-living facility, and my mom moved in with us."

"Well, then," said Michelle, with a simper, "it sounds like your husband will have plenty of help at home."

Under other circumstances, I would have laughed. "If my mother was a normal person, that would be true," I told her. "But my mother's basically another child. She doesn't drive, and even if she did, she doesn't know Ellie's schedule, and Ellie won't be her priority. She'll be worried about my dad." I was getting overwhelmed just thinking about the mess I'd left behind, the assignments I hadn't completed, the comments I hadn't approved, the dentist's appointment I hadn't made for Ellie, the checkup that I'd postponed for myself, the visit from the roofers that I'd never gotten around to scheduling. "I can't stay here," I told Michelle. "It's impossible. There are too many things I need to take care of."

She nodded. "So many of us women feel like we're the ones holding up the world. Like it's all going to fall down without us."

"I can't speak for anyone else, but in my case, that's actually true," I offered. Michelle appeared not to hear.

"Acceptance is hard," she said.

I frowned. "Acceptance of what?"

"Why don't you tell me, Allison? What are you having a hard time accepting?"

I tried not to roll my eyes. "For starters, that you won't let me talk to my daughter and explain why I'm not home. I don't think that's an unreasonable request. Please," I said. Maybe it was withdrawal, the exhaustion of what my body had been through over the past few days, but I was too tired and too sad to keep arguing. "I just want to talk to someone at my home."

Michelle swiped her mouse back and forth, peered at her computer screen, and then spent a minute typing. "The head of our counseling department has an opening at noon. His name is Nicholas."

"Thank you. I appreciate your help." There. I could be reasonable, I could be polite . . . and I was feeling encouraged.

"For now, though, I need you to go join your group."

"Thank you," I said again, thinking that I was on my way. It had taken me three hours to orchestrate even the promise of a phone call home. By day's end, I was confident I'd be able to talk my way out of here and get myself home.

NINETEEN

I walked out the door and onto the sidewalk. The fresh air felt good on my face after the recirculated staleness I'd been breathing inside. I was halfway across the lawn before I heard someone yelling. "Hey," he called. "You can't walk there! Hey!"

I turned and saw a young man in khakis. "That's the men's path."

I looked around to make sure he was talking to me, then down at what seemed to be gender-neutral pavement. "Excuse me?"

"Men and women have to walk on separate paths. Yours is here." He pointed. I shrugged and started across the grass. "No!" he hollered. "You have to go back and start at the beginning! No walking across the grass!"

I stopped and stared at him. "Is this like Simon Says?"

" 'Half-measures availed us nothing!' "

"Excuse me?"

"From *The Big Book*. You can't take shortcuts."

Whatever. I went back to the door, got on the proper path, and found Aubrey and Mary standing in the middle of a fenced-in oval, staring uneasily at a big horse with a brown coat and a sandy mane, which was ignoring them as it nibbled on a clump of grass. I waved at them, then ducked through the fence and was crossing the muddy ground when a woman in a cowboy hat held up her hand.

"I think you missed the entrance."

Shit. I sighed, went back through the fence, walked the long way around the ring, and pushed open the gate. "What's up?"

The woman in the cowboy hat didn't answer. Aubrey, whose glittery eyeshadow and high-heeled boots looked strange in the June sunshine, said, "We're supposed to put this on that." *This* was a tangle of leather straps and metal buckles. *That* was the horse.

"Why?"

"This is equine therapy," Mary explained.

"How's it supposed to help us?"

"Well, I'm not exactly sure, dear."

Aubrey handed me the straps and buckles. It was some kind of harness. At least that was my best guess. My experience with horses was limited to taking Ellie on pony rides at the zoo. "Excuse me," I asked the woman in the cowboy hat. "Can you tell me what the point of this is?"

She didn't answer. "I don't think they're allowed to talk to us," Mary said.

"This is ridiculous," I muttered. Aubrey shifted from foot to foot, rubbing her arms with her palms. "Do you have any idea what this has to do with anything?"

Aubrey shrugged, shaking her head. "Maybe it's about working as a team? Or building confidence or something? I don't know. Half the shit in rehab doesn't have anything to do with anything, and the other half's so boring you could die. Just wait till Ed McGreavey does the 'Find Your Purpose' lecture."

"You didn't like that?" Mary asked. "Oh, I've heard that it's very inspiring."

Aubrey began finger-combing her hair. "Yeah, I thought so, too, like, the first time I heard it. But after you've heard it, like, three or four times, and you've seen Big Ed cry at the exact same part . . ."

"When he talks about how his brother broke his leg when they were heli-skiing?"

"You know it."

I looked at the harness, then looked at the horse. "So we just have to get the harness on the horse somehow?"

"And," said Aubrey, "we have to be touching each other while we do it."

"Huh?"

"Like a conga line," Mary explained, and put her hands on my hips.

"Okay." With Mary holding my hips and Aubrey holding hers, we inched across the ring and approached the horse. It lifted its head and gave us the equine equivalent of a raspberry. Aubrey squealed, and Mary flinched backward.

"He's more afraid of us than we are of him," I said. I found a vaguely loop-shaped opening in the complicated mess of straps and pushed it over the horse's head. Then I tied the remaining dangling straps in a bow. "There. Done."

Mary was frowning. "That doesn't look right."

"They said it had to be on. They didn't say it had to be pretty." I pulled on the straps. The horse didn't move. I yanked harder. "Come on, you." Finally, reluctantly, the horse lifted one foot, then another.

"It's moving!" Aubrey cheered.

"We did it!" Mary cried. The stone-faced woman in the cowboy hat said nothing as she watched our progress. We were almost done with our second lap when a golf cart zipped up to the fence and a kid in khakis called my name. "Allison W.?"

I handed the reins to Mary and caught a ride in the cart, which dropped me at a single-story building that looked like it was made of wood but turned out to be covered in vinyl siding. The couch in the waiting room looked like leather, but wasn't, and the Twelve Steps framed and hung on the wall were simplified: *I Can't*, read Step One. *God Can*, said Step Two. *Let Him*, Step Three advised. *God again*, I thought, and collapsed onto the couch. The God thing was going to be a problem. I'd been raised Jewish, with a vague notion of God as a wrathful old guy with a long white beard who was big on testing and tormenting His followers: casting Adam and Eve out of the garden, punishing poor Job, drowning Egyptian soldiers. Was that God—a God I wasn't even sure I believed in—actually supposed to keep me from taking too much OxyContin? Especially when He let kindergartners get shot in their classrooms and young mothers die of cancer and millions of people suffer and die because of their skin color or religion?

There were no magazines I recognized in the waiting area, just battered copies of something called *Grapevine*, which appeared to be a cross between *True Confessions* and *MAD*, only for drunks. In the hallway outside, I saw a constant flow of people, men and women, alone and in groups, slouchy dudes with shifty eyes, pretty girls in jeans so tight I wondered if they were actually leggings with pockets painted on. Finally, a door flew open and a willowy African-American man in a linen suit smiled at me.

"Allison W.?"

I nodded, getting to my feet and breathing deeply as another wave of dizziness swept over my body.

"Come on in."

His office was by far the nicest place I'd seen at Meadowcrest. There was a plush Oriental rug on the floor. The walls were painted a pretty celery green, the carved and polished wooden desk looked like a genuine antique, and the chair behind it was leather. The obligatory copy of the Twelve Steps hung on the wall—did they buy them in bulk?—but at least his had a pretty gold-leaf frame.

Nicholas took my hand. "It's nice to meet you," he said. Maybe it was the way he actually appeared to be seeing me when he looked my way, or maybe it was that my gaydar was pinging, but Nicholas reminded me of Dr. McCarthy in Philadelphia. Dr. McCarthy, in whose office I'd taken that quiz, Dr. McCarthy, who'd asked me so kindly what I was doing to take care of myself. How different would things be if I'd told him then what was going on, or even if I'd just stopped it all right there, before I'd learned about ordering pills on the Internet?

I took the chair on the other side of his desk and looked at a picture in a silver frame. There was Nicholas and an older white guy, both of them in tuxedoes, each with one hand on the shoulder of a pretty dark-haired girl in what looked like a flower girl's dress.

He saw me looking. "Our wedding," he said.

"Is that your daughter? She's beautiful."

"My goddaughter, Gia," he said. "You've got a little girl, right?" There was, no surprise, a folder open on his desk, with my name typed on the tab.

"Eloise," I said, feeling my heart beating, hearing her name catch in my throat.

"From the book?"

"From the book," I confirmed. *Ellie*, I thought, remembering her funny, imperious gestures, the way she would yell every fifth word, or complain that whatever I was doing was taking for HOURS, or come home crying because "everyone else in kindergarten has loosed a tooth but me."

Nicholas sat down, flipped open the first page of my folder, and ran his finger from top to bottom.

"So, painkillers."

"That's right."

"Why?"

"I beg your pardon?"

He crossed his legs, folded his hands in his lap, and looked at me steadily. "Why were you taking so many painkillers? Were you in pain?"

"I guess that's how it started. I hurt my back at the gym."

"So you were taking them for back pain?"

I shook my head. "Just . . . pain. Pain in general. Or to unwind at the end of the day. I thought it was sort of the same as having a glass of wine at night. Except I never really liked wine. And I did love pills. I loved how they made me feel."

He lifted one arched eyebrow. "Twenty pills," said Nicholas, "is more than one glass of wine."

Blushing, I said, "Well, obviously, things got a little out of hand. But not, you know, rehab-level out of hand. That's why I asked to see you. I really don't think I need to be here."

Nicholas flipped to another page in the folder. Then another one. "I had a conversation with your husband while you were in Equine," he began.

I felt as if I'd swallowed a stone, but I kept my voice calm. "Oh?"

"He was able to fill me in on a little more of what's been going on in your life."

My lungs expanded enough for me to take a deep breath. "So you know about my father being sick?" That was good news, I told myself. If he knew about my dad, and maybe even about Ellie, if he had any sense of my job, and what it was like to get torn apart in public, maybe he'd understand why pills were so seductive . . . and he'd know that someone who was managing that kind of life, keeping all those balls in the air, was clearly not someone who required this kind of facility.

"He told me about your father, yes. And the incident at your daughter's school?" His voice lifted, turning the sentence into a question.

I winced, feeling my face go pale at the memory. "That was awful. I had a glass of wine with a friend after I'd taken my medication." I congratulated myself for the use of the phrase "my medication," even though I knew the pills I took had been bought online rather than prescribed.

"I'm sure you know that David is very concerned. About your safety, and also your daughter's."

"That was a terrible day. What happened—what I did—it was awful. But I would never do anything like that again." My sinuses were burning, my eyes brimming with unshed tears. "I love my daughter. I'd never hurt her."

"Sometimes, in our addiction, we do things we'd never, ever do if we were sober." His voice was low and soothing, like the world's best yoga teacher. "David also said there was an incident with your business? The misappropriation of some funds?"

I sat up straight. How did Dave even know about that? "Th-that was a clerical error," I stammered. "I was just being careless. It was the end of a week from hell; I was trying to get my parents' financial stuff over to our accountant so they could admit him at the assisted-living place . . ." I shut my mouth. The thing with Ellie had been a mistake. The thing with the money—another mistake. The word "unmanageable" was floating around in my head with dismaying persistence. I pushed it away. I was managing. I was managing fine.

"Have any authorities been involved?" asked Nicholas. "The police? The Department of Youth and Family Services?" I shook my head. "Teachers are mandated reporters, and normally, in a case like that, they'd be obligated to tell someone at DYFS what was going on." He gave me a serious look. "You're very lucky that no one got hurt . . . and that you still have custody of your daughter."

I felt sick as I nodded numbly, accepting the reality of how badly I'd fucked up. They could have taken Ellie away. I could have gone to jail.

"You're an intelligent woman," said Nicholas. "I think that if you're here, if you agreed to come here, even if there were extenuating circumstances, probably a part of you thinks you need to be here."

I opened my mouth to say *No way*. Then I made myself think. *An intelligent woman*, Nicholas had said. What would an intelligent woman do under these circumstances? Would she resist; would she fight; would she argue and continue to insist that she didn't have a problem and that she didn't belong? Or would she fake compliance? Would she nod and agree, march to meetings and activities with the rest of the zombies, eat the crappy cafeteria food and drink the Kool-Aid? If I did all that, if I toed the line and recited the slogans and—I glanced at the poster on Nicholas's wall—made a searching and fearless moral inventory of myself, I could probably get out of here in a week. Two weeks, tops.

"You know what?" I said. "Maybe you're right. Maybe there was a part of me that knew it was time to stop. I was concerned about how many I was taking. I was concerned that I needed to keep taking more and more to feel the same way. Then I was worried about having to take them just to feel normal, and always worrying about whether I had enough, and if I was going to run out, and which doctor I could call to get more. And I didn't . . ." I swallowed hard around the lump in my throat, letting Nicholas hear the catch in my voice. "I didn't want to be all spaced out around my daughter. She deserves a mom who's there for her."

"Had you made attempts to stop before?" Nicholas's voice was so calm, so quiet. Did learning to talk that way require special training?

I shook my head, thinking about that afternoon at Stonefield, Mrs. Dale wrestling the car keys away from me, telling me that I wasn't safe to drive my own daughter, and how I'd sworn to myself that I would quit, or at least stop taking so much. I thought about that terrible AA meeting the next morning, and how by noon that day I'd been right back in the bathroom, staring at my face in the mirror as I shook pills into my hand. In spite of my best intentions, and the very real threat of being exposed or shamed or worse, I hadn't even been able to make it halfway through one day without a pill.

Nicholas pushed a box of tissues across the desk. "What are you feeling?"

"I don't know," I said, and swiped at my face. "I'm not feeling well."

"That's completely understandable. You're still going through withdrawal."

"I feel so stupid," I blurted. "I've never been in trouble my whole life, you know? I've been successful. I'm good at my job. I have a beautiful little girl. I had everything I wanted. And now . . ." *Now I'm a drug addict.* The words rose in my head. I shoved them away. I wasn't. I *wasn't.* I was just having a little problem. I was *experiencing technical difficulties,* like they said on TV.

"I'm worried about being here," I said. I figured this was exactly what someone who'd come to a place like this would say. It also happened to be the truth. "My mom is staying with us, but, really, she's not going to be much help. My husband works full-time, and I'm the only one who can write my blog posts. There's not, like, a substitute I can call in."

"You're going to be surprised at how people step up," said Nicholas.

I shook my head, brushing tears off my cheeks. I made myself take a deep, slow breath. What was the stupid slogan I'd seen on the church basement wall? "One Day at a Time." I would get through this place, one day at a time. I would fake contrition, pretend acceptance, act like I bought every bit of the Higher Power hooey, and sort out the rest of it when I was back home. I sniffled, wiped my face again, and gave Nicholas a brave look. "I don't suppose you have massages here," I said, feeling the tiredness, the sickness of withdrawal, the sadness that had colored everything gray settle inside me.

"Every other week, we have someone come in." He leaned forward to match my posture and kept his voice low. "I can't promise you it's going to rival what you'd get at Adolf Biecker." I suppressed a smile. Somehow he'd landed on my favorite Philadelphia salon, the one I never told my mother I patronized, because she operated on the assumption that anyone named Adolf was a Nazi.

"And in our common room, you'll find any number of board games." He smiled, then made a show of looking around, making sure we were alone. "You haven't lived until you've played Jenga with someone having DTs. We're talking guaranteed victory."

I smiled in spite of myself. Then I remembered my mission. "I want to make a phone call," I said. "Michelle said I needed permission from my counselor, but I don't have one yet, and I need to tell my daughter . . ." I felt the lump swelling in my throat again, remembering how I must have looked in the throes of withdrawal. "I want to tell her that I miss her, and that I'm thinking about her. I want her to know I'm okay."

"I don't think that should be a problem," he said, and scribbled something on the back of a business card. "You can use the phones behind the main desk back in Residential. And you have my permission to skip drum circle, if you're still feeling woozy."

Drum circle? "I am," I said, grateful that not everyone here was a robot who'd treat me like a junkie. "Two other things. I'm supposed to be on TV next week." I tried to sound casual, as if I were the kind of woman who was on TV so regularly that mentioning it was akin to saying that I was the snack mom for that weekend's six-and-under soccer game. The *Newsmakers on Nine* people, perhaps unsurprisingly, had asked me back, this time to talk about abstinence-only sex ed in public schools. "And my daughter's birthday party is on the fourteenth, and I can't miss it." That, I decided, would be my endgame. I'd be out of here in time for Ellie's birthday party. I would meet her at BouncyTime, where she'd asked to have her party (in hindsight, she had decided the giant slide was the most fun she'd ever had in her entire life), and then, when the party was over, I'd load the trunk of the Prius with presents and leftover pizza, and we'd drive back home.

Nicholas steepled his fingers and rested his chin on top of them. "That," he said, "might be a problem."

"I can skip the TV thing," I said, eager to show that I was a reasonable woman, able to compromise. "But I can't miss Ellie's birthday."

"Normally, twenty-eight days is twenty-eight days. It's your time to focus on yourself." When he saw the look on my face, his voice softened. "Your daughter is going to have other birthdays. She probably won't even remember you weren't at this one."

I gave him a thin smile. "You don't know my daughter."

"Well, I won't tell you we've never made exceptions." He turned to his computer, tapped at the keyboard. "It looks like you're going to be in Bernice's group. Why don't you mention it to her, see what she says."

"Okay. When will I meet her?"

"Monday."

Monday? I blinked in disbelief. Today was Thursday, and I wasn't seeing a therapist until Monday? I filed that factoid away for the letter to the director of Meadowcrest that I was already composing in my head.

"All I'd suggest is that you keep an open mind," Nicholas said. "I know you're not in the best place physically to process a lot of new information, but just listen as much as you can."

I got up, with the card in my hands . . . and then, before I could stop myself, I blurted the question that had kept me awake for months. "What if this doesn't work? What if I can't stop?"

"Honesty, willingness, and open-mindedness," said Nicholas. "You're being honest already, telling me what's scaring you. Are you willing to try? And keep an open mind about twelve-step fellowships?"

I looked out the window—gathering clouds, trees stretching their budding branches toward the sky, shadows flickering across the grounds. Girls strolled along the path, carrying what I now knew were copies of *The Big Book*, and they didn't look like drunks and junkies, just regular people, leading ordinary lives.

Across the desk, Nicholas was still looking at me, waiting for my answer. "I don't think I believe in God," I finally said.

He smiled. "How cheesy would it sound if I told you that God believes in you?"

For what seemed like the first time since I'd landed in this dump, I smiled. "Pretty cheesy."

"For a lot of beginners, their Higher Power is the group itself—it's the other people working toward the same goal, supporting your sobriety."

I pointed out the window at a guy I'd glimpsed from the waiting room. He had pierced ears and a tattooed neck, and wore a baseball cap pulled low over his brow. His sweatshirt hung midway down his thighs, his jeans sagged off his hips, and his enormous, unlaced basketball shoes looked big as boats. "Does he get to be my Higher Power?"

Nicholas followed my finger. "Maybe not him specifically." He squeezed my shoulder. "Lunchtime," he said. "Hang in there. I know this part is hard. Just try to keep an open mind. Try to listen."

I nodded as if I was listening, as if I believed every word he'd told me, and walked back across the campus, taking care to stay on the women's path. Inside Residential, all the women were lined up again, in front of a window from which a small, plump, dark-skinned woman with bobbed black hair and big, round glasses was dispensing medications.

"Boy, did you miss all the fun," said Mary. "We had to figure out a way to get the horse to jump over a puddle."

"Fucking bullshit," Aubrey muttered. "How is leading around a horse on a rope supposed to help me not shoot dope?"

"You are a poet!" said Mary. "I bet you didn't know it!"

Aubrey snorted, then gazed down balefully at her mud-caked feet. "These fucking boots are ruined." In front of the window, a woman gulped her pills, then opened her mouth wide and waggled her tongue at the nurse.

"How desperate do you have to be," I wondered, "to convince someone to save their saliva-coated pill for you?"

"Just wait," Aubrey said. "When you've only slept for two hours a night six days in a row, you'll give anything for that pill." She banged a boot heel against the wall, sending a shower of flaked dirt onto the carpet.

"Aubrey F., that's a demerit," called the teenage boy behind

TWENTY

"So listen," said Aubrey, after we'd gathered our chicken fingers, Tater Tots, and canned corn and taken a seat at one of the long cafeteria tables. "Do you think..." She twirled a lock of hair around her finger.

"No," Mary said immediately. She was cutting her chicken fingers into cubes, dipping each cube into ranch dressing, and then popping them in her mouth, one after another.

"But he's in rehab, too!" Aubrey stabbed an entire chicken strip, doused it in ketchup, and held it aloft on her fork as she nibbled. "If I think he's not gonna stay sober, doesn't that mean that I'm not gonna make it, either?"

"I'm not saying you can't give him a chance," said Mary. "Remember what they said back in the Cold War? 'Trust but verify'?"

Aubrey dunked her chicken back into the ketchup slick. "Like I remember the Cold War."

Mary turned to me, the light glinting off her glasses as the chain swung against her bosom. "Aubrey's boyfriend is in rehab, too. She's trying to decide whether to see him again when she's done here." Over the younger woman's head, Mary mouthed the words *Bad idea.*

I looked at Aubrey's bruised arms. "This would be the guy who did that to you?"

Aubrey gave a shamefaced nod.

"Oh, Aubrey. Why would you even think of going back to someone who hurt you like that?"

She mumbled something I couldn't hear.

"What?"

She raised her head. "We've got a kid," she said defiantly. "A little boy." She flipped her white plastic binder so I could see a snapshot of a toddler centered in the plastic cover, a beaming toddler with fine blond hair and two bottom teeth and a slick of drool on his ruddy red chin.

I felt my heart clench. This child, who couldn't possibly be a day over eighteen, had a baby? She'd had a baby with a drug addict who beat her?

Mary reached for her hands across the table. "What kind of life is that for Cody?" she asked. "Do you want him to grow up thinking that men push women around? Choke them? Hit them?"

"It only happens when he's high," Aubrey protested.

"But you told us he's high all the time," Mary said.

"Well, but maybe if he goes to rehab and takes it seriously this time . . ."

"Who's got the baby now?" I asked.

"Justin's mom. That's who we were living with. Me and Justin and Cody."

A recovery coach—I'd learned that's what the khaki-clad teenagers who seemed to be running Meadowcrest were called—tapped Aubrey's shoulder. "They need you in Detox," he said. Aubrey cleared her tray. We watched her go.

"I'll pray for her," Mary said, and touched the gold cross around her neck before returning to her chicken. "Not that I'm judging," she said, "but I'm not sure Aubrey has the equipment she needs to make better choices."

Another recovery coach, a girl with elfin features and delicate, pointed ears exposed by a cropped haircut, tapped my shoulder. "Allison W.? There's a phone free, if you want to make your call."

I hurried out of the cafeteria, clutching the card Nicholas had given me, the bright, coppery taste of pennies and fear in my mouth as I dialed.

"Hi, Mom. It's Allison."

"Oh, Allie . . ." She sounded—big surprise—like she was going to cry. "Hold on," she said, before the sobs could start. "Ellie's been wanting to talk to you."

I waited, sweating, my heart beating too hard, my lips creased into a smile, thinking that if I looked happy, even fake-happy, I would sound happy, too. Finally, I heard heavy breathing in my ear.

"Mommy? Daddy says you are in the HOSPITAL!"

My insides seemed to collapse at the sound of her voice, everything under my skin turning to dust. *Keep it together,* I told myself. At least "hospital" was better than "rehab," even if it wasn't as good as "business trip," which was what I'd been hoping for. "Hi, honey. I'm in a kind of hospital. It's a kind of place where mommies go to rest and get better."

"Why do you need to REST? You sleep all the TIME. You are always taking a NAP and I have to be QUIET." She paused, and then her voice was grave. "Are you sick?"

"Not sick like that time you had an earache, or when Daddy had the flu. It's a different kind of sick. So I'm just going to stay here until I'm all better and the doctors say I can come home."

"How many days?" Ellie demanded.

"I'm not sure, El. But I'm going to try very hard to be there for your party, and I'll be able to talk to you on the phone, and I can send you letters."

"Can you send me a present? Or some candy or a pop?"

I smiled. Maybe it was good that she didn't seem shattered— or, really, fazed in the slightest. Or maybe this was just her typical compensation, the way she'd try to make my father, and Hank, and now me, feel better about our screwups.

My job, I decided, was not to scare her. Let her think Mommy had some version of an earache or the flu, something that wasn't fatal and that the doctors knew how to fix.

"What dress are you wearing?" I asked.

"New Maxi." New Maxi was a pink-and-white-patterned maxi dress, not to be confused with Old Maxi, which I'd bought her at the Gap last summer. "Grandma does NOT make my dresses FIGHT. She says they're supposed to all get along. But I ask you, where's the fun in THAT?" Ellie demanded.

I smiled and made a noise somewhere between laughter and a sob, then sneezed three times in a row. "Not much fun at all, really."

"But she said we could get a pedicure. AND that I could get a JEWEL on my toes."

"Well, aren't you lucky?"

"Grandma is AWESOME," Ellie said . . . which was news to me. "And she let me have noodles for two nights!" The recovery coach tapped my shoulder and, when I looked up, pointed at her watch.

"I love you and I miss you," I said. "You are my favorite."

"I KNOW I am," she trumpeted. "I KNOW I am your favorite!"

"Is Daddy there?" I asked.

Ellie sounded indignant. "Daddy is at WORK. It's the middle of the DAYTIME."

"I will call you when I can, and I'm going to write you a letter as soon as we say goodbye. Listen to Grandma and Daddy, and eat your growing foods, and make your bed in the morning, and floss your teeth."

"I have to go now. *Sam & Cat* is on!" There was a thump, the muffled sound of voices, and then my mom was on the line.

"How . . . how are you doing?"

"As well as I can, I guess."

"Don't worry about anything. Everything here is going well."

"Really?" I'd braced myself for a litany of complaints, bracketed by *When will you be home?* and laced with plenty of implied *How could you*s, but my mother sounded . . . cheerful? Could that be?

"You just take care of yourself. Everything's under control. We've got . . ." There was a brief pause. "Let's see, gymnastics today, is that right?"

"TUMBLING!" Ellie shouted in the background.

"And then Sadie's birthday party on Saturday, and Chloe's birthday party on Sunday . . ."

"I have presents for them in the downstairs closet."

"Yes. We found them, and we made cards. You just take care of yourself . . ." Almost imperceptibly, I heard her voice thicken. "We'll see you when we can."

"Thanks, Mom. Thanks for everything." I hung up the phone and sat there, teary-eyed and sneezing, as the recovery coach tapped my shoulder and, on the other side of the desk, a guy with tears tattooed on his cheeks shouted for Seroquel.

"You know, there's a seven-day blackout," said Miss Timex. "You won't be talking to anybody again until that's over."

I didn't answer. I'd already decided that the khaki brigade wasn't worth wasting my breath on. Nicholas would be my go-to guy.

"You need to join your group," she told me as I walked past the desk.

"Nicholas said I could lie down if I wanted."

She narrowed her eyes. "Are you not feeling well?"

"I feel awful," I said, and followed her as, sighing heavily, she walked me down the hall and unlocked the room where I'd woken up that morning.

I hung the handful of items that needed hangers in the gouged and battered freestanding wardrobe. Then I pulled a sheet of paper from the notebook I'd been issued and wrote Ellie a note. *What do you call a grasshopper with a broken leg? Unhoppy! I love you and miss you and will see you soon.* I drew a heart, a dozen *X*'s and *O*'s, then wrote *MOM*.

After I'd emptied my duffel bag, I went through my purse. My plan had been to curl up with a novel and try to make the time go by, but my e-reader, like my wallet and phone, was gone. I marched back out to the desk.

"Nothing but recovery-related reading," said Wanda, my *People* magazine–loving friend. She looked left and right before mouthing the word *Sorry*.

"Is there a library?"

"You can buy approved reading materials in the gift shop. But it's only open on Monday, Tuesday, and Friday mornings, and I think maybe Sunday afternoons."

That figured. I remembered a *New York Times* story about rehabs from a few years ago. Most of them were private businesses, some were run by families, and all of them were for-profit . . . and the profits they turned were jaw-dropping. It wasn't enough that they were milking patients and insurance companies for upwards of a thousand dollars a day so we could eat crappy cafeteria food, sleep in rooms that made Harry Potter's under-the-staircase setup look like a Four Seasons suite, and be lectured about our selfishness by old men in polyester. We also had to pay what were undoubtedly inflated prices for recovery-related literature.

"You can read *The Big Book*," she said, and handed me a copy of a squat paperback with a dark-blue cover. No words, no title on the cover, just the embossed AA logo.

I carried it back to my room, lay on the bed, and began reading, starting at the beginning, then flipping randomly. *The Big Book* was first published in 1939, and it didn't take me long to realize that it was in desperate need of an update. The prose was windy, the sentences convoluted, the slang hopelessly dated (I snickered at a reference to "whoopee parties," whatever those were). Worse, the working assumption, in spite of a footnote stating otherwise, seemed to be that all boozers were men. There was a blog post in that, for sure; maybe a whole series of them. If the Twelve Steps were the order of the day, and they were still geared toward middle-class, middle-aged white guys, how were women (not to mention non-white people, or gay people) expected to get better?

I kept reading. From what I could tell, in order to get sober the AA way, you had to have some kind of spiritual awakening . . . or, as the gassy prose of "The Doctor's Opinion" put it, "one feels that something more than human power is needed to produce the essential psychic change." So you got sober by finding God. And if you weren't a believer? I flipped to the chapter called "We Agnostics," and found that AA preached that if you didn't believe, you were lying to yourself, "for deep down in every man, woman, and child is the fundamental idea of God. It may be obscured by calamity, by pomp, by worship of other things, but in some form or other it is always there."

So my choices were God and nothing. I shut the book, feeling frustrated. A few minutes later, Aubrey stuck her head through my doorway. "We need to go to Share."

I consulted my binder and made my way to the art therapy room. Three round tables had been pushed to the walls and two dozen folding chairs were arranged in a semicircle, with women seated in most of them. I took a seat between Mary and Aubrey.

"Good afternoon, Meadowcrest!" called the middle-aged woman sitting behind a desk at the center of the semicircle. A moderator, I figured, except she wasn't wearing khaki. Her laminated nametag hung on a pink cord, instead of a plain black one. Her name, according to her tag, was Gabrielle.

"Good afternoon!" the group called back.

"Is this anyone's first community meeting?"

After Mary looked at me pointedly, I raised my hand. "Hi, I'm Allison." When this was met with silence, I muttered, "Pills."

"Hi, Allison!" the room chorused.

"Welcome," said Gabrielle, who then began reading from the binder. "Here at Meadowcrest, we are a community." *Just like Stonefield,* I thought. *And probably just as expensive.* "Is there any feedback?" Silence. "Responses to yesterday's kudos and callouts?" More silence. "Okay, then. Today we're going to hear from Aubrey. Aubrey, are you ready to share?"

Aubrey crossed her skinny legs, tucked stray locks of dyed hair behind her small ears, and licked her lips. "Hi, um, I'm Aubrey, and I'm an addict."

"Hi, Aubrey!"

She lifted one little hand in a half wave. "Hi. Um, okay. So I was born in Philadelphia in 1994 . . ."

Oh, God. In 1994 I'd been in college.

"My parents were both alcoholics," Aubrey continued, twirling a strand of blonde hair around one finger. "They split up when I was two, and I lived with my mom and my stepdad." She took a deep breath, pulling her knees to her chest. "I guess the first time he started abusing me, I was five. I remember he came into my bed, and at first he was just snuggling me. I liked that part. He said I was his special girl, and that he loved me more than he loved Mommy, that I was prettier, only we couldn't tell Mommy; it had to be our secret."

I started to cry as Aubrey went into the details of what happened for the first time the year she turned six, and kept happening until she was fourteen and moved out of the house and in with a boyfriend of her own, who was twenty-two and living in his parents' basement. How at first pot and vodka made the pain of what was happening go away, and how pills were even better, and how heroin was even better than that.

By the time Aubrey moved from snorting dope to shooting it, I was crying so hard it felt like something had ruptured inside me. Tears sheeted my face as her boyfriend turned abusive, as she moved in with her estranged father, who stole her money and her drugs, as she got pregnant and delivered an addicted baby when she was only seventeen.

Lurid and awful as it was, Aubrey's story turned out to be dismayingly typical as my week crawled by. During every "Share" session, twice each day, a woman would talk about how her addiction had happened. Typically, the stories involved abuse, neglect, unplanned pregnancies, dropping out of school, and running away from home. There were boyfriends who hit; there were parents who looked the other way. Instead of being the exception, rape and molestation were the rule.

My mom's new husband. My sister's boyfriend. The babysitter (female). The big boy with the swimming pool who lived at the end of our street. I listened, crying, knowing how badly these girls had been damaged, and how pathetic my own story sounded. What would happen when it was my turn to share? Could I say that the stress of motherhood, writing blog posts, coping with a faltering marriage, and aging parents, parents who maybe weren't the greatest but had never hit me and certainly had never molested me, had driven me to pills? They'd laugh at me. I would laugh at me.

On my third day at Meadowcrest, a woman named Shannon told her story. Shannon was different from the other girls. She was older, for one thing, almost thirty as opposed to half-past teenager, and she was educated—she talked about her college graduation, and made a reference to graduate school. She'd lived in Brooklyn, had wanted to be a writer, had loved pills in college and had discovered, in the real world, that heroin was cheaper and could make her feel even better.

"Eventually, it turned me into someone I didn't recognize," Shannon told the room, in her quiet, cultured voice. "You know that part in *The Big Book* where it talks about the real alcoholic?" Shannon flipped open her own blue-covered paperback and read. " 'Here is the fellow who has been puzzling you, especially in his lack of control. He does absurd, incredible, tragic things while drinking.' Or, if you're in the rooms"—"the rooms," I'd learned, was a shorthand term for AA meetings—"you'll hear someone talking about how they paid for their seat, and 'paid' stands for 'pitiful acts of incomprehensible destruction.' "

Shannon sucked in a breath and scrubbed her hands along her thighs. "That was me. I did things that were incomprehensible. I stole from my parents. I stole from my great-aunt, who was dying. I went to visit her and stole jewelry right out of her bedroom, and medication from her bedside table."

In my folding chair, I felt my body flush, remembering the pills I'd taken from my dad. Shannon continued, her voice a monotone. "I slept with guys who could give me heroin. I sold everything I had—artwork my friends had made for me, jewelry I'd inherited—for drugs." Her lips curved into a bitter smile. "You know how they say an alcoholic will steal your wallet, but an addict will steal your wallet, then lie about it and help you look for it the next day? I can't tell you the lies I told, or the stuff I stole, or the things I did to myself in my active addiction. And you know the scariest part?" Her voice was rising. "After everything I've done, everything I've been through, I don't know if I can stop. I don't know if I want to. I'm not even sure that when I get out of here I'm not going to be right back on that corner. Because nothing ever—ever—made me feel as good as heroin did. And I'm not sure I want to live the whole rest of my life without that feeling."

The entire room seemed to sigh. I found that I was nodding in spite of myself. I looked around, waiting for a counselor who would say "One day at a time," or tell us to "play the tape" of how our pleasures had turned on us, or remind Shannon it wasn't for the rest of her life, just right now, this minute, this hour, this day, that she had friends, that there were people who loved her and wanted her to get well . . . but there were never any counselors in Share. *Nobody here but us chickies,* Mary had said when I'd asked her.

"The last time I went home, there was one navy-blue dress in my closet, and a pair of shoes. My parents had gotten rid of the rest of my stuff—my desk, my books, my clothes, all the posters I used to have on the walls. There was just that one dress. My mom told me, 'That's the dress we're going to bury you in.' "

Nobody spoke. Shannon rubbed her palms on her jeans again, then looked up. Her shoulder-length hair was in a ponytail, and if it wasn't for her pockmarked complexion and the deep circles beneath her tear-reddened eyes, you would have no way of guessing that she was a junkie. She looked like any other young woman, dressed down, like she could be a teacher or a bank teller or a web designer. Just like me. And now she was trapped. The thing that had once been a pleasure, a treat, was now a necessity, as vital as air and water. *I don't know if I can stop. I don't know if I want to.* Just like me . . . because, honestly, I wasn't sure I could stop. And I knew what all of that meant: that I wasn't just a lady who'd taken a few too many pills and developed a pesky little physical dependence. It meant I was an addict—the same as Mary and her DUI, and Aubrey and her six trips through rehab, and Marissa, who'd lost her front tooth and custody of her kid after she and her boyfriend had gotten into a fistfight over the last bag of dope.

Hello, I'm Allison, and I'm an addict.

I shook my head. It wasn't true. I wasn't an addict. I was just . . . it was only . . . Aubrey was staring at me. "You okay?" she asked. Her eyes were wide and clear, rimmed with sparkly silver liner and heavily mascara'd lashes. The bruises on her arms had started to fade. She was still way too thin, but she looked better.

"I'm fine," I whispered, even as a shudder wracked my shoulders. My skin bristled with goose bumps. My stomach lurched. I hadn't let myself think much about the future, or anything besides getting through each day, keeping my head down, not attracting attention, doing what was necessary until I could go home. All this time, I'd been telling myself I wasn't an addict, that I didn't need to be here, and that as soon as I could I'd go home and go back to my pills, only I'd be more careful. Now every question I'd been asked, every slogan they'd repeated, every phrase I'd glimpsed on a poster or heard in passing was coming at me, like dozens of poison-tipped arrows ripping through the sky. *Who is an addict?* began the chapter of the same name in the Narcotics Anonymous Basic Text. *Most of us do not have to think twice about this question. We know! Our whole life and thinking was centered in drugs in one form or another—the getting and using and finding ways and means to get more. We lived to use and used to live.*

That wasn't me, I thought, as Shannon pulled a crumpled sheet of paper out of her back pocket, a list like the one they made all of us write, a list of what we had that was good in our lives besides drugs. "My parents still love me," she read in a quivering voice that made her sound like she was twelve instead of thirty. "I can still write, I think. I'm not HIV-positive. I don't have hep C."

I shuddered. *Not me*, I thought again . . . but the words from the Basic Text wouldn't stop playing. *Very simply, an addict is a man or woman whose life is controlled by drugs. We are people in the grip of a continuing and progressive illness whose ends are always the same: jails, institutions, and death.* I shook my head, so hard that Aubrey and Mary both looked up. *No. Not me. Not me.*

TWENTY-ONE

R ehab time, it turned out, was like dog years. Every hour felt like a day. The weekdays were bad, but Saturdays and Sundays were almost impossible. The handful of counselors went home, along with the more senior and experienced recovery coaches, leaving the youngest and greenest to tend the farm. The inmates were running the asylum, in some cases almost literally. One of the RCs casually confided that, not six months prior, she, too, had been a Meadowcrest patient.

On Saturday and Sunday, our hours were filled with busywork and bullshit activities that seemed to have nothing to do with recovery and everything to do with keeping a bunch of junkies occupied. By Sunday, I was sitting through my tenth—or was it my twelfth?—Share, so inured to the recitations of abuse, neglect, and damage that I'd started subbing in my favorite fictional characters. *Hi, my name is Daenerys Targaryen, and I'm an addict (Hi, Dany!). I guess you could say it all started when my brother married me off to Khal Drogo, a vicious Dothraki warlord, when I was just thirteen. I started drinking after my husband killed my brother by pouring molten gold on his head. For a while, it was social. I'd have a drink before dinner with my bloodriders, maybe two if we'd had a rough day, but after Mirri Maz Duur murdered my husband, it turned into an all-day-long thing* . . . After Share came Meditation, where we'd spread yoga mats on the cafeteria floor and spend forty minutes dozing to the sounds of Enya on one of the RCs' iPods, and Activity, which mostly consisted of pickup basketball games for the guys and walking around the track for the ladies, and Free Time, where we could play board games or read *The Big Book* or write letters home. I had bought a bunch of cards at the gift shop, and on Sunday had spent an hour writing notes to Ellie and to Janet. "Greetings from rehab!" I'd begun, hoping Janet would get the joke, imagining that at some unspecified point in the future, we would be able to laugh about this.

I had spent twenty minutes gnawing on my pen cap, trying to decide what I could possibly say to my mother, or to Dave. I'd finally settled on a few generic lines for both of them. *Thank you for taking care of Ellie. I'm doing much better. Miss you. See you soon.*

That left me with the rest of the afternoon to kill. I'd eaten a salad for lunch, then gone outside with Aubrey and Shannon. There was a volleyball net, but the guys had taken over the court, and we weren't allowed to use the ropes course. "Some insurance thing," Aubrey had explained as we walked around the track and she pointed out the rusted zipline and the storage shed where, two summers ago, one of the girls from the women's residential program had gotten in trouble for having sex with one of the men.

"I can't even imagine wanting to have sex in here," I said. Aubrey moaned, rolled her eyes, and launched into a familiar monologue about how bad she missed Justin and, specifically, the things Justin would do to her. "I think it's, like, closing back up," she said, and I told her I was pretty sure that was medically impossible, then sneezed, one, two, three times in a row, so hard it was almost painful. Shannon grinned at me.

"You're dope-sneezing!"

"What?"

Aubrey lowered her voice. "When you do a lot of downers, your systems all slow down. Like, were you really constipated?"

I tried to remember and couldn't.

"And probably you, like, never sneezed at all when you were on dope," Aubrey continued. "So now, you're Sneezy!"

"Good to know," I said. Already, I could hear the way living around all these young women had changed my vocabulary. *It's a clip,* they'd say when they meant it was a situation, or *It's about to go off* when trouble was starting. Aubrey and a few of her friends had started calling me A-Dub. Occasionally, I would make them laugh by saying something in my best middle-aged-white-lady vocabulary and voice, and then throw my fingers in the air and say, straight-faced, "I'm gangsta." It was like suddenly having a pack of little sisters. Drug-addicted, lying, stealing, occasionally homeless, swapping-sex-for-money little sisters, but sisters nevertheless. When I was growing up I had begged my parents for a sister, imagining a cute little Cabbage Patch Kid that lived and breathed, that I could dress up and teach to swim and ride a bike. No sibling had been forthcoming. My requests had been met with pained smiles from my mother and a strangely stern talking-to from my dad. *You're hurting your mother's feelings,* he told me in a voice that had made me cry. I had been maybe eight or nine years old. I wondered if there'd been some kind of medical issue, a reason why I was an only child that went beyond my mother's selfishness or the way raising me seemed not like a fulfillment but like an interruption.

I walked, and wondered what Ellie was doing on this sunny, sweet-scented morning. Was someone making her pancakes and letting her sprinkle chocolate chips onto each one? Was my mother reminding her to brush her teeth, because sometimes she'd just put water on the toothbrush and lie? Were her friends asking where I'd gone, and did she know what to tell them?

On Monday, I finally met with my therapist. She was a middle-aged black woman who wore a jewel-toned pantsuit, sensible heels, glasses, and a highlighted bob that could have been a wig. There were six of us in Bernice's group: me, Aubrey, Shannon, Mary, Lena, and the other Oxy addict, Marissa, who had a daughter Eloise's age. Lena was gay, and flirtatious: night after night during the in-house AA or NA meetings, I'd watch the various Ashleys and Brittanys fight over who got to sit in her lap. Lena would unbraid their hair and whisper into their ears; she'd plant delicate kisses along their cheeks while the RCs pretended not to notice.

"Miz Lena," said Bernice, flipping through a clipboard. We'd already signed in, rating our moods on a scale of one to ten. We had circled the cartoon face that best represented our current emotional state, and rated the chances, on a one-to-ten scale, of using again if we were sent home that day. I answered honestly. My mood was a one. My emotional state was a frowny-face. If I went home that day, the chances that I would use were one hundred percent. Under the question "Are you experiencing any medical issues?" I wrote about my insomnia—just as Aubrey had predicted, they'd cut off my Trazodone and I was down to two hours of sleep a night. I mentioned the night sweats that soaked my shirts, my lack of appetite, and the way my hair was coming out in handfuls. I checked "yes" for anxiety and depression, "no" for a question about whether I had "kudos or callouts" for other residents. Then I remembered that whoever was reading these forms would decide whether I could attend my television appearance, and Ellie's birthday party, and that I hadn't provided the answers of a sane, sober woman happily on her way to a drug-free life. I hastily revised my responses, upgrading my mood and downgrading the chances that I'd use again, rewriting and erasing until Bernice collected the forms.

Lena yanked at the strings of her hooded sweatshirt. "Whatever they said," she began, in her low, raspy voice, "it's a total exaggeration."

Bernice raised an eyebrow. "How do you know 'they' were saying anything about you? What do you think you did wrong?"

More squirming and string-yanking. "I guess maybe I wasn't so respectful during the AA meeting last night."

I rolled my eyes. Lena had sat in the back row with an Ashley in her lap as the speaker detailed his rock bottom, which involved leaping from the twelfth-story balcony of his New York City apartment to a neighboring balcony because he was pretty sure his neighbor had left her door unlocked and he wanted to see if she had any goodies in her bathroom cabinet. "I didn't even care that I could have fallen and died," he said. "I just wanted something so bad."

Bernice turned to me. "New girl. Allison. What are you here for?"

"Pills." I should have saved time and just put it on my name-tag. ALLISON W.—PILLS.

"Huh. What'd you think of Miss Lena's performance last night?"

I sighed. I didn't want to get on Lena's bad side. From what I'd heard, she could be vindictive. She'd let a girl drop to the art therapy room floor during trust falls after the girl had ratted out one of Lena's friends for sneaking in loose cigarettes in her Bumpit.

"Come on," said Bernice. "This is a program of total honesty."

"I think Lena could have been a little more respectful."

Lena pulled her sweatshirt hood up over her head and muttered something.

"What was that?" asked Bernice. "Share with the group, please."

"I said you'd treat this like a joke, too, if you'd been through it five times."

Five times. When I'd first arrived I'd been shocked to hear numbers like that. Now it just made me sad. Repeat offenders, I had learned, were the rule, not the exception. If you were an addict, there was rehab, and if rehab didn't work, there was more rehab. Some of the rehabs were different—one girl, a Xanax addict, had been through aversion therapy, where she'd get a shock while looking at a picture of her drug of choice—but most of them were the same. They followed the Twelve Steps; they relied on a Higher Power to bring the "still sick and suffering" to sobriety; they were programs of total abstinence, which meant you could never have so much as a sip of beer or a glass of wine, even if your problem had been prescription pills or crack cocaine. If rehab didn't work, they'd send you back again . . . and I was learning that rehab hardly ever took the first time, and that most of the women had been through the process more than once.

Bernice was staring at me, her eyes sharp behind the thick lenses of her glasses. She looked like someone they'd cast as a mom in a TV commercial, the one who'd have to be convinced that the heat-and-eat spaghetti sauce was as good as what her own mother used to make. "How'd you feel, watching Miss Lena at the meeting last night? No. Scratch that. Let's back up. How do you feel about being here in general?"

I shrugged. "Fine, I guess."

The group groaned . . . then, as I watched in astonishment, everyone stood and did ten jumping jacks.

"You can't say 'fine.' Or 'good,' " Marissa explained. "Bernie thinks they're meaningless."

"Tell me how you really feel," said Bernice.

"Okay. Um. Well. I knew I needed help." After nearly a week in here, I knew that was Rehab 101. You had to start by admitting you had a problem, or they'd badger you and break you down, pushing and pushing until you blurted the worst thing you'd ever done in the worst moment of what they insisted you call your active addiction.

"How come?" she asked, tilting her head, watching me closely. "You get a DUI? Fail a drug test?"

"No, no, nothing like that." I swallowed hard, knowing what was coming, as Bernice looked down at her notes.

"Says here you got in some trouble at your daughter's school."

"That's right." No point in lying. "I went to pick up my daughter and my friend's kids at their school, and I'd had some pills. I thought I was fine—" Aubrey nudged me, whispering, *"No 'fine's."* "Sorry. I thought I was okay to drive," I amended. "I know what I can handle, when I'm okay and when I'm not—but my friend and I had been drinking, and even though I'd only had one glass . . ."

"On top of the painkillers," Bernice said.

I nodded. "Right. Wine and painkillers. The teacher in charge of the carpool line took my keys away."

"So you signed yourself in?"

"Um." I swallowed hard, wondering, again, exactly what these people knew, and how much I'd told them when I'd arrived. "I—my husband and I—there was . . . I guess I'd call it kind of an intervention. He found out what I was doing, and he told me I needed to get some help, and I agreed."

Bernice looked at my file again. "Walk us through exactly what happened before you came here."

I cringed at the memories—the sickness of withdrawal, the doc-in-the-box, the ill-fated Suboxone, Ellie finding me in bed, sick and covered in vomit. Ellie seeing me on my hands and knees, ass in the air, face pressed into the carpet, desperate for one more crumb of Oxy.

"Allison?" Bernice was looking at me. Her expression was not unkind. "Little secret. Whatever you did, whatever you're remembering that's making you look like you just ate a lemon, believe me. Believe me. Someone in here's done worse, or seen worse."

I shook my head. I couldn't speak. What kind of mother would let herself get so out of control, fall down so far, that her daughter would witness such a scene? I sat there, breathing, until I was able to speak again.

"My husband found out what I'd been doing. About buying the pills online," I began. I told them about the night I'd spent awake, my laptop heating my thighs, gobbling pills one after another until they were all gone. Heads nodded as I described how frantic, how terrified, how awful I'd felt, knowing I'd come to the end of my stash, with no idea how to get more. I told them about taking a cab to the doctor's office in the strip mall, where, as Bernice put it, "you found some quack to give you Suboxone." Her penciled-in eyebrows ascended. "Because replacing one drug with another is a great idea and nothing could possibly go wrong there, am I right?"

I didn't answer. I'd already figured out that Meadowcrest took a dim view of Suboxone. There were rehabs that would use other opiates to help addicts through withdrawal, but I hadn't landed at one of them.

"So here you sit."

"Here I sit," I repeated, and wondered, again, what was happening at home. How was Ellie getting to sleep each night, without me to read her three books and sing her three songs, and give the ritual spritz of monster spray? How was she getting dressed, without me to make her sundresses fight? Had Sarah posted anything on Ladiesroom explaining my absence, or had she found a substitute mom-and-marriage columnist? How was

Dave managing with my mother? Was she getting to Eastwood to see my dad? Had he gotten any worse? I pictured Dave having a long lunch with his work wife, at a cozy table for two at the pub near the paper, my husband pouring out his heart as L. McIntyre listened sympathetically, nodding and making comforting noises while she mentally decorated my still-empty house, the one that would be her blank canvas once I'd been dispensed with and she'd moved in.

"What's going on with the husband?" asked Bernice. I felt my eyes widen. *Can they read our minds?*

"I think he's got a girlfriend. When I left he had a work wife. I'm thinking she probably got a promotion. But listen," I said, suddenly desperate to turn the focus from me to someone else, anyone else. "It's okay. Dave's a good dad, and he's got my mom there to help. I'm sure everything's—"

"No fine!" the room chorused. I shut my mouth. Bernice's gold bracelets glinted as she wrote in her pad.

"So are you two . . . estranged? Separated?"

"I don't know what we are," I admitted. "I can't get him to talk to me. He wouldn't do counseling."

"Did he know about the drugs?" asked Bernice.

I shook my head automatically before I remembered the envelope he'd intercepted; the receipts he'd brandished, the toneless recital in front of the girl in the cubicle the day I'd arrived, with Dave giving dismayingly accurate estimates of how much and how long. "He knew." I wiped my eyes. I'd cried more in less than a week in rehab than I had in the previous ten years of my life, and it wasn't like I had a particularly gut-wrenching story to weep over. "I don't know. We used to be in love, and then we had Ellie, and it was like we turned into just two people running a day care. He was the one who wanted us to live in the suburbs. He went out there and bought a house without my even seeing it. He was going to write a book, so he had this chunk of money. Then the book contract got canceled, and I started earning more, so I was the one picking up the slack there, but it was never part of the plan, you know? The plan was, I'd stay home with the baby, he'd be the breadwinner. Only he wasn't winning a ton of bread, and my daughter turned out to be kind of hard to deal with sometimes, and now I just feel so unhappy . . ." I buried my face in my hands. "I don't understand it. I have everything I want, everything I was supposed to want, so why am I so sad?"

"So you used." the counselor's voice was gentle.

I nodded. "Yeah."

"And did it work?"

I nodded, still with my face buried in my hands. "For a while, it felt good. It smoothed out all the rough edges. It made me feel like I could get through my days. But then I was doing so much of it, and spending so much on it, and worrying all the time about where I was going to get more. And I could have hurt my daughter." I lifted my head. My nose was running; my eyes felt red and raw. I looked at Bernice, her calm face, her kind eyes.

"Allison," she told me, "you can do this. You are going to be okay."

"Really?" I sniffled.

"Really really. If you want it. If you'll do the work. It'll probably be the hardest thing you've ever done in your life. But people do come back. I wouldn't be here if I didn't see it. I wouldn't be doing this work if I didn't see miracles every day."

I tasted the word "miracle." More God stuff. But whatever. Just waking up every morning and thinking that my life would be all right without pills, that I could manage work and my parents and Ellie . . . that would be enough.

"Allison W.?" A khaki-bot teenager stood in the doorway. "Michelle wants to see you."

"Go on," said Bernice.

"See you tomorrow?" I asked hopefully.

She shook her head. "I was gonna wait until the end of group to tell y'all, but today's my last day here."

Unhappy murmurs rippled through the circle. I sank back in my seat, stunned and angry. I finally had a therapist, a therapist I liked, and she was leaving after my first session? "Where are you going?" asked Shannon.

"I'll be doing outpatient, over in Cherry Hill." She smiled. "So I might see some of you on the other side."

"Wait," I protested. "You can't leave! I just got here!"

She gave me another smile, although this one seemed more professional than kind. Of course she couldn't let herself get attached to women she would know for only four weeks, or, in my case, forty-five minutes. "I'm sure they'll find someone great to replace me."

There didn't seem to be time to discuss it. So I shuffled down the hallway behind the recovery coach, yawning enormously. The night before, I'd dropped off at ten and woken up just after midnight, wide-awake and drenched in sweat. I'd taken a shower, put on fresh clothes, and put myself back to bed, trying to get some more sleep, but it hadn't happened. My thoughts chased one another until I was so frantic and sad that I was sobbing into my pillow, thinking about getting divorced, and what it would do to Ellie, and what single motherhood would do to me. "Can't you give me Ambien?" I'd asked the desk drone after four hours of that misery. "I have a prescription."

"Ambien? In here?" the RC on duty, the one everyone called Ninja Noreen for her habit of sneaking into bedrooms and shining her flashlight directly into their eyes during the hourly bed checks, actually snorted at the thought.

"Okay, then something that's approved for in here."

"Most alcoholics and opiate users have disrupted sleep. We don't believe in sleep aids. You're going to just have to ride this out. Eventually, your body's clock will reset itself." They gave me melatonin, a natural sleep aid, which didn't do a thing, and a CD of ocean sounds to listen to, which was just as ineffective. I was starting to feel like I was going crazy . . . and nobody seemed to care. *Dear Ellie,* I would write in the middle of another sleepless night, with my notebook on my lap and a towel next to me to wipe away the sweat and the inevitable tears. *I miss you so much. I can't wait to see you. Are you making lots of treats with Grandma? Are you playing lots of Monopoly and Sorry?* I would write to her about baking and board games, telling her, over and over, that I missed her and I loved her, all the while wondering how this had happened, trying to find an answer to the only question that mattered: *How does a suburban lady who's pushing middle age end up in rehab? How did this happen to me?*

TWENTY-TWO

"I understand you have a television appearance scheduled for Thursday?" Michelle began.

"That's right." I'd made an appointment with Michelle to discuss a visit to *Newsmakers on Nine,* even though I was was half hoping she would tell me I couldn't do it. I felt so exhausted and on edge that I wasn't sure I'd make any sense on the air. I also looked lousy. My skin was pale, my face felt drawn, my lips, even my eyelids, were chapped and peeling, and there were huge dark circles under my eyes and a good inch of dark roots showing at the crown of my dyed-and-highlighted head. If I'd harbored thoughts of emerging from rehab tanned and rested and ready to take on the world, those notions had quickly been dispelled. I wouldn't be all right in twenty-eight days, or six months, or even a year. On my last day of orientation they'd shown us a video called *The Brain Disease of Addiction,* from which I'd learned that I could look forward to a year to eighteen months of no sleep and mood swings and depression and generally feeling awful. How could I live through that? I was sure the video wasn't meant to discourage, but I was also sure I wasn't the only woman who came out of it thinking, *Eighteen months? That won't be happening. Sobriety's not for me.*

"Well, Allison, the team's been discussing it, and here is what we can offer." Michelle picked up a pen between two pudgy fingers. "Being out on your own would most likely be too stressful for you at this stage of your recovery." I felt myself exhale. "However, we can have a sober coach accompany you to the program."

I held up my hand. "Excuse me? A sober coach?" I thought those were jokes, invented by the tabloids and stand-up comedians.

She nodded. "Someone who can make sure there's no opportunity for a slip."

"Who would this sober coach be? And what kind of training would a sober coach have?"

Michelle's jowls flushed. "Obviously, Allison, we would send you with someone who has a lot of good clean time under her belt."

"But not a therapist," I surmised. "Look, some of the RCs are terrific, but some of them might as well be stocking shelves at Wawa for all they care. And none of them have degrees. In anything."

Michelle plowed on. "We can arrange transportation to the show and have a sober coach accompany you and then bring you back here."

"Would this cost anything extra?" I knew, from hearing other girls talk, that Meadowcrest cost a thousand dollars a day, and anything extra, from a thirty-minute massage to a family session, cost extra.

"The cost would come to . . ." She scanned the sheet of paper. "Three thousand dollars."

I stared at her, too shocked to laugh. "Are you fucking kidding me?"

"There's no need for profanity," Michelle said primly.

"Three thousand fucking dollars? Yes, there fucking is!"

Michelle gave me a smile as fake as a porn star's chest. "Why don't you think about it, Allison?"

I sighed. "I'll need to call my editor to cancel."

"Are you eligible for phone passes?"

I had no idea. "Of course I am."

Michelle scribbled out a pass.

"Just so you know," I said, "my daughter's birthday party is on Saturday. I am going to be there."

Even before I'd finished saying "birthday party," Michelle was shaking her head.

"I'm sorry, Allison, but the rules are, you need to have had at least six sessions with your counselor before you're eligible for a day pass. By this Saturday, you'll only have had three."

"But that's not my fault! You guys didn't even assign me a counselor until I'd been here almost a week!"

Michelle pursed her lips into a simper. "As you know, Allison, we've been having some staffing issues."

"Then don't you think you need to adjust the rules to reflect that? You can't require someone to have a certain number of sessions, and then have so few counselors on staff that it's impossible to hit that number. And I've done everything else!" My hands were shaking as I fumbled for the evidence. "Look, here's my time line of addiction." I pulled it out of my binder and brandished it in her face. Michelle gave it a skeptical look.

"That's it, Allison? Just one page?"

"I didn't use anything until I was in my thirties. Sorry. Late bloomer. But look . . ." I pointed at the page. "I've attended every Share and all the in-house AA meetings since I've been here. I went to a guest lecture on Sunday, and I'm volunteering in the soup kitchen on Wednesday." And wouldn't that be fun. "Listen," I said, realizing that my speeches were getting me nowhere.

"It's my daughter. She's turning six. She isn't going to understand why I can't be there."

"Children are more resilient than we give them credit for. I bet your daughter will surprise you." Michelle looked pleased when she'd shot down my TV appearance. Now she looked positively delighted, as if she could barely contain her glee. I could imagine my hands wrapping around her flabby neck, my fingers sinking into the folds of flesh as I squeezed. I made myself stop, and take a breath, and refocus.

"Michelle. Please. I'm asking you as a mother. As a fellow human being. Please don't punish my daughter because I'm an addict. Please let me go to her party."

"The rules are the rules, Allison, and you didn't do what you needed to in order to get your pass."

"But you didn't give me a chance! Aren't you listening to me? Because of your staffing issues there was absolutely no way I could have met your requirements."

"I understand that I'm hearing your disease talking. I'm hearing it say, 'I want what I want, and I want it right now.' Which is how addicts live their lives. Everything has to be now, now, now." I was shaking my head, trying to protest, but Michelle kept talking. "We think there's always going to be someone there to clean up our messes, cover for us, call the boss or the professor, make excuses."

"I never asked anyone to cover for me. I cleaned up my own messes. I never . . ." Oh, this was impossible. Didn't she understand that I wasn't one of those addicts who slept all day and got high all night? Didn't she realize that, far from making my life unmanageable, the pills were the only thing that gave me even a prayer of a shot at managing?

Michelle kept talking. "In sobriety, we don't make excuses,

and we don't make other people cover for us. We live life on life's terms. We take responsibility for our own actions, and our own failures. This was your failure, Allison, and you need to own it."

Tears were spilling down my cheeks. I'd heard the phrase "seeing red" all my life but never known it was a thing that really happened. As I sat there, a red shadow had descended over my world. My heart thumped in my ears, as loud as one of those person-sized drums you see in marching bands. It took everything I had not to lunge across the desk and hit her.

"I am going to my daughter's party. I told her I'd be there, and I'm going."

"Allison—"

"No. We're done chatting. We're through."

Still shaking with rage, I got up, closed the door, went back to my room, and lay on my bed. *Okay,* I told myself. *Think.* Maybe I could sneak out the night before the party, climb out of my bedroom window and start walking. Only where? I wasn't sure where I was, how far away from Philadelphia, whether there were buses or trains. Even if I waited until daylight, I wouldn't know where to go, or even how long it would take to get there.

I rolled from side to side and wondered what Ellie was doing. When we'd bought the Haverford house, we'd made only one improvement: in Ellie's room, instead of the standard double-hung windows, I'd had the contractor install a deep, cushioned window seat with built-in bookshelves on either side. It had turned out even better than I'd hoped. The cushions were detachable, and the lid of the seat lifted up for storage. Since Ellie had been too little to read, we'd repurposed the seat as a stage, hanging gold-tassled curtains that Ellie could open with a flourish, building a ticket box out of a shoebox and construction paper and glitter. At night, Ellie's collection of Beanie Babies and stuffed bears would perform a Broadway revue, singing everything from expurgated selections from *The Book of Mormon* and *Urinetown* to *Bye Bye Birdie* and *The Sound of Music* . . .

I sat up straight, remembering *The Sound of Music*. Hadn't that musical featured a talent show—a show within a show—and hadn't the von Trapps used the show as cover when they made their escape?

There were talent shows in rehab. I knew that from the Sandra-Bullock-gets-sober film, *28 Days,* which they'd shown us. Could that be the answer? Suggest a show, come up with an act, convince Dave that I'd gotten a day pass . . . well. I'd figure out the specifics later, but for now, I could at least see a glimmer of possibility.

TWENTY-THREE

The next day at breakfast, I brought it up, as casually as I could. "You guys all know *The Sound of Music*, right?"

Blank looks from around the table. "Is it like *American Idol*?" ventured one of the Ashleys.

"No. Well, actually, you know what? There is a talent competition. See, there's this big family, and the mother has died, so the father hires a governess."

The Ashley made a face. "You can't hire a governess. They have to be elected."

"No, no, not a governor. A governess. It's a fancy way of saying babysitter. So anyhow, she takes care of the kids, and the father starts to fall in love with her . . ."

Aubrey immediately launched into a pornographic soundtrack, thrusting her hips as she sang, "Bow chicka bow-wow . . ."

"Cut it out!" I said sternly. "This is a classic!" I remembered Christopher Plummer and Julie Andrews dancing on the veranda, his arms around her tiny waist, her eyes gazing up at him like he was the God she'd failed to find in the convent. "So they fall in love, and the kids, who've never gotten more than ten minutes of their father's time, start to straighten up and fly right.

There's, like, six kids, and one of them's a sixteen-year-old, and she's in love with the messenger boy . . ."

"The messenger boy!" Lena snickered. "She needs a man with a real job." She shook her head. "Ridin' around on his bus pass, probably. Fuck that shit."

"Anyhow. The Nazis organize this big talent show, and the Von Trapp Family Singers enter . . ."

"Wait, wait. That's their name? That's a terrible name."

"Well, this was a long time ago," I said. "Cut them some slack. So who's into it?"

I looked around the circle. The Ashley was peeling strips of pink polish off of her fingernails. Aubrey was scribbling in her notebook—probably a list of everything she intended to do when they let her go. We all had versions of that list. The women my age wrote about the luxuries we missed, the foods we wanted to eat, the clothes we'd neglected to pack, taking a shower in which the water would not emerge in a lukewarm trickle, reading books where every single story did not involve an identical arc of despair and recovery, or watching made-for-TV movies that did not involve some C-list actor in the grip of either DTs or a divine revelation. The young girls, as far as I could tell, all wanted drugs and sex, typically in that order, often from the same person.

I sat up straight and breathed in from my diaphragm, trying to remember back to high-school choir. "Raindrops on roses and whiskers on kittens . . . Bright copper kettles and warm woolen mittens . . . Brown paper packages tied up with strings . . ."

"These are a few of my favorite things!" sang Shannon. She was looking better than she had during Share. Her skin didn't look as dull, and her hair was shiny. "I used to watch it with my parents. It's cute!"

"It's corny," said Lena.

"But we could change it!" I said. "Like . . ." I thought for a minute. "Dealers on corners and elbows with track marks. Cop cars and dive bars and—"

"Blow jobs in state parks," said Mary, who immediately clapped her hands over her mouth and giggled.

"Silver-white Beamers, got repo'd last spring. These are a few of my favorite things!" I sang. "When the dog bites! When the cops call! When I'm feeling sad . . . I simply remember my favorite pills, and then I won't feel so bad."

Everyone applauded. Mary frowned. "Do you think it glamorizes drug use?"

"Maybe we should do a song about how bad it is," Shannon offered. "Like, do you guys know *Avenue Q*? There's this song called 'Mix Tape.'" She straightened her shoulders and began to sing in a low, pleasant alto. "'He likes me. I think he likes me. But does he like me, like me, like I like him? Will we be friends, or something more? I think he's interested, but I'm not sure . . .'"

She thought for a minute, and then sang, "Piss test. Just failed my piss test. I didn't know I'd have one . . . but then I did! And I smoked crack. And had some beers. And now I'm sitting here . . . all full of fear!"

Lena's nose wrinkled. "I dunno. Does everything have to be, like, a musical? What about a Beyoncé video?"

"Sure," I said, even though my knowledge of Beyoncé videos was limited to the one where she pranced around in a leotard and waved her hand to flash her ring.

"And what about the girls who can't sing?" asked Mary.

"We could do skits. Like a parody of *Are You Smarter Than a Fifth Grader?*"

Aubrey looked impressed. "You know that show?"

I frowned. "Dude. I'm old, not dead." I forked my fingers, fake-gangsta-style. "I'm A-Dub, bitch!"

"I'm ancient," said Mary, who did not sound upset, as she began to sing. "Gonna take a sentimental gurney . . . Gonna set my heart at ease . . . Gonna ride that gurney down to detox . . . Hope they don't have bedbugs or fleas . . ."

"Oh, my God, we need to do one about Ed McGreavey!" I said as I joined in the other girls' applause. "Do you guys know *Les Miz*?"

"It's about French revolutionaries," said Shannon. "And there's a love triangle . . ."

"And this horrible innkeeper, who puts cat meat in the stew, and overcharges for everything, and steals from the patrons."

"Does he have fake hair?" asked the Ashley.

"Probably. He's a revolting human being who takes advantage of the needy," said Shannon.

"That's our boy," said Lena, who'd spent more time with Ed than the rest of us combined.

"Master of the house!" I sang. My voice wasn't as strong as Shannon's, but at least I could carry a tune. "Quick to catch your eye! Never wants a passerby to pass him by. Servant to the poor! Butler to the great! Hypocrite and toady and inebriate!" I set down my pen, considering. "Wow. We don't even really need to change it."

"What's an inebriate?" asked one of the girls.

"A drunk."

"Didn't Ed do meth?" asked Aubrey.

I shrugged, but Lena was nodding. "Oh, yeah. He came back here weighing eighty pounds and missing all his teeth. He shows a picture at the lecture."

"Not the one about finding your purpose?" I'd seen that already, and I was certain that if a shot of Ed weighing eighty pounds and minus teeth had been on offer, I'd have remembered it.

"No, no, he does another one. It's called 'Finding Your Bottom,' " said an Ashley.

I burst out laughing. Mary was laughing, too. "What?" Lena asked.

" 'Finding Your Bottom'?" Aubrey asked. "My grandmother always used to say that someone was so stupid he couldn't find his own ass with both hands and a flashlight."

"How did Ed find his bottom?" Shannon asked. "Where did Ed find his bottom?"

"He was in San Francisco, giving blow jobs for drug money," said Lena.

"As one does," I murmured, and thought, again, how different I was from the drunks and druggies who populated this establishment, and how every anecdote, every personal revelation, every Share, was just another argument in favor of my not being here. *Stick it out,* I told myself.

"Hey," I said. "Did you guys see the movie *Pitch Perfect*? or *Mamma Mia*? Think there's anything there? Or, wait! Here's one for Michelle: If you change your mind, I'm the first in line . . . I'm the one you'll see . . . No one gets around me!"

"Gonna make some rules to break, have you pee in my cup," sang a Xanax addict named Samantha, who'd wandered over to our table, drawn by the singing. "Gonna turn my flashlight on, gonna wake you up."

"I think," said a girl named Rebecca, who was so quiet that the most I'd heard her do was announce her name in Share, "that we should do a skit about applying to work here. Like, 'Do you have a heartbeat?' "

"Have you been to college?" asked Mary. "No? Do you know what college is?"

"This is never going to happen," said Lena.

"Why not?" I asked.

"Because!" She rolled her eyes. "Do you honestly think they're going to sit here and let us make fun of them? They're stupid, but they're not complete idiots."

"So we don't tell them," I said. "We'll just spread the word quietly. We'll tell everyone that we're holding a talent show in the cafeteria during Meditation after lunch on Saturday." And then, I thought, when the staffers inevitably got wind of what was going on and hurried to shut it down, I'd stroll out to the parking lot, cool as Captain von Trapp facing down the Nazis, and let Dave drive me to Ellie's party.

TWENTY-FOUR

"Are you feeling all right?" my new therapist, Kirsten, asked. I nodded, even though I could barely breathe, and I hadn't been able to eat even a bite of pineapple or a single strawberry for breakfast. Three days ago, she'd asked me who to invite for my family session, the sit-down all the inmates had to endure before Meadowcrest released them from its clutches. I'd put Dave's name and my mother's on the list. "Do you want me to get in touch?" Kirsten had asked, and I'd nodded, knowing I wouldn't be able to handle it if Dave turned me down. Which he did. "He didn't say why," Kirsten reported. She was Bernice's opposite in almost every way—tall and young and white and willowy, with thin silver rings on her fingers and pencil skirts and sensible heels that were supposed to make her look grown-up but instead made her look like a teenager who was trying too hard. "Don't read too much into it. It doesn't mean he doesn't want to be involved in your treatment."

"Or my life," I'd murmured, and spent the next two nights of sleeplessness fretting that he'd have divorce papers ready for me as soon as I set foot out of Meadowcrest.

"All it means is that he can't attend today's session."

But why wouldn't he make it a priority, canceling whatever other interviews or conferences he had planned? What could be more important than helping me?

My mother had agreed to come. At the appointed hour, I'd gotten up and gotten dressed, letting Aubrey help with my hair and makeup. Shannon lent me a cashmere cardigan, and a belt to keep my jeans up—in spite of the starchy food, I'd actually lost weight, mostly because I was too distraught to eat. Mary pulled out her rosary beads and told me she'd be in chapel, praying for me, and even Lena muttered a gruff "Good luck."

I sat in a chair in Kirsten's office, legs crossed, trying not to shake visibly as the door opened and my mother, impeccable in the St. John knit suit that I recognized as the one she'd worn to her grand-niece Maddie's bat mitzvah, walked into the room. She'd gotten her hair styled and set, every trace of gray removed, and it hung in a mass of curling-iron ringlets, each one the same. She'd left it long, even after she'd turned forty, and fifty, and sixty. "Men like to see a woman take her hair down," she'd told me, even as her own hair got increasingly brittle and thin, with its shine and color coming from a bottle. Her makeup was its typical mask, the same stuff she'd probably been wearing the same way since the 1970s, liquid black eyeliner flicked up at the corner of each lid to make cat eyes, foundation blended all the way down her jawline to her neck, and her preferred Lipglass lipgloss for that lacquered, new-car finish.

But beyond the hair and makeup, there was something different—an alertness to her expression, a confidence as she moved across the room, like she knew she'd make it to the other side without requiring assistance, without bumping into anything or banging her shins on the coffee table. My whole life, my mother had been accident-prone. "Whoops," I could remember my father saying a thousand times, his hand on her elbow, guiding her away from something sharp, keeping her on her feet.

"What can I get you? Coffee? Water?" Kirsten asked.

"No, thank you," she said. From her flared nostrils, the way she held her arms tightly against her body and clutched her bag at her side, I could tell that she'd noted the smell of institutional cleaners and cheap, processed food, the RCs with their troubled complexions, the heroin girls with their piercings and tattoos. Maybe she'd even glimpsed Michelle, whose size she would regard as a personal affront. A place full of fuckups, she'd think . . . and here was her daughter among them.

"Hi, Mom." I wasn't sure if I should hug her, and she didn't make any move toward me. "How's Ellie?"

"Oh, Ellie's wonderful. She's playing at Hank's this morning." A frown creased her glossy lips. "That boy is always sticky."

"Hank has allergies."

"I'm not sure that entirely explains it. Ellie misses you . . ." My mom's voice trailed off. My eyes filled with tears.

"Why don't you have a seat," Kirsten told my mom, giving me a significant look. "And, Allison, remember. Of course you're concerned about your daughter, but we're here to focus on you."

With that, my mother lifted her chin. "How are you?" she asked.

I shrugged. "Well, given the fact that I'm in rehab, not too bad."

She flinched at the word "rehab."

"You hadn't noticed any changes in your daughter?" Kirsten asked. "Allison seemed the same to you?"

My mother doesn't notice me at all, I thought, as she took a seat and started working the clasp of her handbag, clicking it open, then shut. That wasn't particularly charitable, or entirely true—my mother noticed me; she just noticed my father much more—but I wasn't in an especially generous or honest frame of mind. This was the most embarrassing thing I could imagine; worse than the time my mom had been called to school after I'd barfed up all those doughnuts after our birthday breakfast gone wrong, or the time they'd called her in fifth grade after my best friend, Sandy Strauss, and I got in trouble for telling the new girl, a kid whose southern accent was strange to our ears and who had the improbable name Scarlett, that we'd called in to Z-100 and won tickets to a Gofios concert and that she could come with us. Where was Scarlett now? I couldn't recall her last name, but I could remember her narrow, rabbity face, her watery blue eyes that always looked like she'd just been crying.

"Allison?" I blinked to find Kirsten and my mother both looking at me. "I asked your mother if she'd noticed any changes in your behavior over the past year."

"You have to remember that my father was diagnosed around that time. I think my mom—well, all of us, really—were focused on him."

"That doesn't mean I wasn't paying attention to you," my mother said a little sharply. She turned to Kirsten. "I did notice. Especially since I started staying with Allison and Dave. Her moods were . . . a little strange. Sometimes she'd seem sleepy . . . or cheerful, but with an edge to it. Like she could go from being so happy to crying in a minute."

"I never cried," I said.

"Allison," said Kirsten, in her professionally soothing voice, "try to just listen, okay?"

I nodded. But I couldn't believe that my mother would have the nerve to come in here and try to make it sound like I was the needy one.

Kirsten turned from me to my mother. "The way your daughter's described it, she was under a tremendous amount of stress." Kirsten bent, reading from the folder she held open in her lap. "She was working a lot, and taking care of her daughter, and helping you with your husband. He has Alzheimer's, is that correct?"

My mother nodded wordlessly. Tears slid down her cheeks. Now, I thought, we'd landed on the topic that would take up the rest of the session, the rest of the day, if that was possible. My father, comma, suffering of, and mother's subsequent agony.

"Are you surprised that Allison ended up in a place like this?" Kirsten asked.

It got so quiet I could hear the clock ticking. Then, unbelievably, my mother shook her head. "No," she said in a husky whisper. "No, I wouldn't say I was surprised."

I opened my mouth, feeling shocked. I wanted to remind her what a good girl I'd been, never skipping school, always turning in my homework, getting a job three weeks after I graduated from Franklin & Marshall, never embarrassing her, never being a burden. But it seemed the shocks were just getting started. My mother asked, "It runs in families, doesn't it?"

Kirsten nodded. "We know from research that a child who has a parent with an addiction is eight times more likely to develop substance-abuse problems him- or herself."

I braced myself. I knew what was coming from listening to the other women. Next I'd hear how my mother's father had been a secret tippler, or how Grandma Sadie had gotten strung out on Mexican diet pills. My mother bent her head, crying harder. "I never meant to hurt her," she wept. "If I could be here myself . . . if I could take this pain away . . ."

Kirsten passed my mother a box of tissues, an act that was strictly forbidden during normal therapy sessions, on the grounds that being handed a box could derail someone's epiphany. *Her issue, her tissue,* the group would chant. My mother grabbed a fistful and wiped her eyes.

"What do you mean, you never meant to hurt Allison?" Kirsten asked. When my mother didn't answer, I said, "Yeah, I'd like to know what you're talking about."

"You don't remember." Her voice was dull. "Well, maybe you wouldn't. You were just four."

"Remember what? What happened when I was four?" She clicked her purse clasp open, then shut, and I remembered—of course I knew what had happened. The Accident.

"But that didn't have anything to do with me," I started to say. My mother, her eyes on Kirsten, started talking at the same time.

"I was in a car accident," she said. "I was drunk. And Allison was in the car with me."

My mouth dropped open. My mother kept talking.

"You had your seat belt on, but there were no car seats back then. When I . . . when the car . . ." She gulped. "I drove into a telephone pole. You broke your arm."

My body felt icy. "I don't remember any of this," I said, but something tickled at the back of my mind. A whining buzz, hands on my shoulder, a burning smell in the air, a man's voice saying, "Hold still, and you'll get a lolly when it's done."

My tongue felt thick as I tried to talk. "Did you get arrested?"

She shook her head. "Back then . . . back then it was different. But your father . . ." She buried her face in her hands. "He was so angry he took you away for a week."

I didn't remember that, either. "Where did we go?"

"Down the shore. It was the summertime. He must have rented a place, you know, that little cottage in Avalon where we'd go? It belonged to one of the partners at his firm. I never asked, I never knew for sure, but I think he went there. And when he came back, he told me . . . t-told me that if I ever hurt you again, if I ever did anything to put you in danger, that he'd leave me, and he would never come back. He would take you away and I'd never see either one of you again."

Puzzle pieces clicked into place in my mind. Keys slid into locks. Doors opened, revealing a different world behind them. "So you stopped driving."

She nodded.

"But you didn't stop drinking."

Her eyes welled up again. "I couldn't," she whispered. "I tried, so many times. I wanted to. For you. For your father. I wanted to be a good mother, and a good wife, but I . . ." She shook her head. I shut my eyes, remembering scenes from my girlhood. Being seven or eight years old, having a friend sleep over, and telling her to whisper when we got up the next morning. "My mom sleeps late." But she wasn't incapacitated. By ten o'clock most mornings, she was at the tennis court . . . and, if she sipped white wine and seltzer all afternoon, I never saw her sloppy, or tipsy, or heard her slur or saw her stumble.

"So you made sure Dad would never get mad at you again." *By acting like a little girl, a bubbleheaded teenager,* I thought but did not say, as my mother nodded again.

"And you stayed away from me."

She looked up, her eyes accusing. "You didn't need me!"

"What?" I looked at Kirsten, hoping she'd jump in. "What little girl doesn't need her mother?"

"You were so smart," said my mom. Her voice was almost pleading. "You could do everything by yourself. You never wanted my help getting dressed, or picking out your clothes, or with your homework. You didn't want me walking you to school." She dropped her voice to a whisper. "I felt like you were ashamed of me. Like you knew what I'd done. How stupid and reckless I'd been. You didn't want anything to do with me."

I closed my eyes, trying to imagine my mother, my beautiful, distant mother, as an alcoholic, who'd kept this secret for more than thirty-five years. How circumscribed her life must have been. No car. No friends, not real ones, because who could she trust, and how could she talk honestly to anyone? No relationship with me, and a kind of desperate, clingy, please-don't-leave-me marriage, in which other people—my dad, me—did everything because she didn't trust herself to do anything. It explained so much.

"Were you ever going to tell me?"

She didn't hesitate before shaking her head. "How could I have told you that I'd almost gotten you killed? How could you ever forgive me? But now . . ." She lifted her head, looking around. "If I'd known that you were at risk I would have said something. I would have warned you. But I never thought . . ." She shook her head again, and pressed her hands together. I saw that she was trembling, and that there was a fine mist of sweat at her temples, and above her upper lip. She must have wanted a drink so badly. I wondered what it had cost her, to get herself out of bed, and dressed, and all the way out to New Jersey, alone and sober. I wondered if she had a flask in the car, or if she'd tucked one of those airport-sized bottles into her purse, and if she was counting the minutes, the seconds, until she could slip away, into the bathroom or the backseat, to unscrew the lid with slick, shaking hands, to raise the bottle to her lips and find that relief.

"You weren't like me. You were strong. You had it all figured out."

"I don't have anything figured out," I said. "And I'm not strong."

"I wonder," Kirsten said, "if you two might have that in common. The ability to put on a show, where everything looks good from the outside."

I didn't answer. Probably, even now, my mom did look fine from the outside. Her makeup was always perfect, her clothing was impeccable, and she had a mantel full of tennis trophies to prove her athletic prowess. But inside she was a wreck, a walking-around mess. Just like me. My mother raised her head. "Allison," she said, "you need to know that I have never once been impaired around your daughter."

"Did you quit?" I asked.

She bent her head. "When your dad was diagnosed, I made myself cut back to just two glasses of wine at night," she said. "I want to help you, Allison."

"Was it hard?" I asked. Could you really go from being a full-blown alcoholic to drinking just two glasses of wine at night? Was my mom telling the truth? There was no way of knowing.

"I'll do whatever I can to help you," she said. "Only please." She was crying again, but her voice was steady. "You have to stop taking those pills. You have to try. For Ellie's sake. You can't hurt her, and you can't waste your life hiding, the way I did, pretending that things are okay, being drunk or on pills or whatever, and not being a real mother, and not really living your life." She got to her feet, crouched in front of me, and grabbed both of my hands in her icy ones. Up close, I could see what I hadn't seen, hadn't wanted to see, my whole life. It was there in the web of wrinkles around her eyes, the way her lip liner didn't strictly conform to her lips and, more than that, the faint sweet-and-sour fruity smell that exuded from her pores. I'd never given a name to that odor, any more than I'd given a name to Dave's scent, or Ellie's. People had their own smells, that was all. But now it was like I was getting blasted with it, like I'd dived head-first into a vat of cheap white wine, in which my mother had been marinating for decades.

I'd never noticed. I'd never even guessed. Even though the clues were all there, I had never put them together to come up with the inescapable conclusion. What was wrong with me, I wondered, as my mother squeezed my hands and held on hard. Was I just as selfish as she was, that she'd been sick and suffering, and I'd never seen?

"Promise me, Allison."

"I never want to be in a place like this again," I said. It was the most I could give her and not be lying.

"That's a start," Kirsten said.

TWENTY-FIVE

I staggered out of the room, a minute after my mother's departure. I hadn't remembered the Accident when I was a girl, but
I now felt like I'd been in one in that little room, like a bus had
run me over and left me flattened on the pavement.

"Drink a lot of water," Kirsten said. "Breathe. It's a lot to
take in."

I tottered along the women's path, head down lest I accidentally make eye contact with the men, and snuck a glance at the
visitor's parking lot. My mother's car and driver would be waiting. She could go out into the wide world, wherever she wanted
to go. Soon, I would have that freedom, too. Where would I go?
What would I do?

It was a sticky June day, the drone of bumblebees and lawn
mowers in the humid air that sat like a wet blanket on my limbs
and my shoulders. The sun blazed in a hazy blue-gray sky, and
the air itself looked thick with pollen that dimmed all the colors,
making it fuzzy and faint. Somewhere there were kids splashing
in swimming pools, dads underneath umbrellas, streaming the
game on their phones, moms dispensing sunscreen and sandwiches and saying *Oh, won't that hit the spot* to offers of a cold

beer or some white wine or a vodka-and-cranberry, tart and refreshing, just the thing for a hot summer day.

Behind the administration building I found a little garden, overgrown with weeds, the borders of the flower beds ragged, squirrels chittering in the dogwood tree, a splintery wooden bench in its center. I sat on the bench, staring numbly straight ahead. I felt like I'd been looking at one of those optical illusions. Examine it one way you'd see a beautiful young woman, the smooth lines of her chin and cheeks, the ripe curls of her hair. Then you'd blink or tilt your head and realize you were seeing a withered crone, her nose a tumorous hump, the young girl's hat really the old woman's rat's nest of hair. The world I had once known did not exist, had never existed. Instead of the Tale of the Childlike Mom, the Distant Dad, and the Love They Shared, I had, instead, to consider the Story of the Drunk Mother, the Dad Who Could Never Trust Her, and the daughter who was an endless source of worry for both of them.

Had I known? On some level, I must have at least guessed. All those afternoon naps in her bedroom with the shades drawn . . . and yet she'd emerge every morning in her tennis whites or her golf clothes to drink a little glass of orange juice (wheatgrass juice in the 1990s) and go off to her game. There was that ever-present tumbler full of wine and seltzer . . . but I never saw her take a sip of anything stronger. She smoked, but so did plenty of moms back then. She didn't drive, but that didn't seem worse than other parents' idiosyncrasies: Dorothy Feld's mother had weighed three hundred pounds until she got her stomach stapled; Kurt Dessange's dad wore a toupee that looked like it was made out of spray-painted pine needles.

"All those years," I said out loud. Years of lying, years of hiding. Years of her knowing she wasn't living right, that she wasn't the mother or the wife she could have been. Years of loneliness, because those kinds of secrets you couldn't tell, not to your own mother or sister or your very best girlfriend. *I don't love my husband. I'm having an affair. Sometimes I can't stand my children.* I could imagine saying these things, but *I'm a secret alcoholic? I drove drunk with my daughter in the car? I want to stop and can't?* Who could tell another soul things like that? Who would react with anything other than horror?

You're only as sick as your secrets. Another little slogan I'd picked up. Not to mention that whole fearless and searching moral inventory, where you'd list all your faults and then tell someone else exactly what you'd done wrong. "That sounds horrible," I'd told Wanda at the desk, after she'd finished her whispered recap of the previous night's *Bachelor* episode. "No, no," she'd said, with a kind of crazy glow in her eye, "it's the most liberating thing you can imagine! It makes you free!"

"Free," I croaked. My mom had never been free. She'd lived her whole life under the yoke of her secrets, with a man who probably desperately wanted her to get better but didn't know how to fix her, or how to help. So what were my chances? Where did that leave me? Was it possible that I wasn't really an addict, that I could take pills, just more carefully than I'd taken them before? Or was it like everyone in here said, that the only path the pills would put me on would end in jails, institutions, and death? *Half-measures availed us nothing,* said *The Big Book. We stood at the turning point.* Well, here I was. Which way would I turn?

One afternoon on our honeymoon in Mexico, Dave and I had gone fishing. It had been one of those perfect days: not too hot, with a crisp breeze, the sun glinting off the waves' surfaces, and the fish shoving one another out of the way for the privilege of swallowing our hooks. We'd caught half a dozen striped bass in just four hours on the water. Then, while we'd sat back (with beers, I remembered, and the tortas I'd bought in a little *panadería* on the street), the mate had set up a table and two twenty-gallon buckets of water near the back of the boat and expertly gutted each fish, stroking the blade down the center of their bellies and deftly sliding out their guts. I felt like that now, like someone had sliced me open and dumped out my insides, then stitched me back together and set me on my feet.

"So how'd it go?" Lena asked at lunch, which was manicotti, limp noodles and rubbery cheese in a meat sauce that made you sorry for the cows that had given up their lives to enter the food chain. Just the smell turned my stomach. I'd made myself a cup of tea and sat, shivering, in my customary spot between Aubrey and Mary.

"Are you all right?" asked Shannon.

"Clearly, she isn't," said Mary. "Just look at the poor girl!" She squeezed my shoulders. "Honey, what's wrong?"

"What did they say?" asked Aubrey. "Were you, like, molested by an uncle or something?"

"Oh, for heaven's sake," said Mary.

"Well, it happens," I heard Aubrey reply.

"Not that," I said, in a voice I barely recognized as my own. "It turns out that my mother's an alcoholic." I took a breath. "It explains a lot."

"You didn't know?" asked Lena.

"I feel pretty stupid," I admitted.

"Hey," said Lena, "addicts lie."

I nodded, wondering what that said about my mother, and what it said about me. She'd lied, but I'd never noticed, never tried to figure it out. I thought of that day I'd gotten lost in Avalon when I was little, how the streets and the store and the sidewalks and the sand had all looked different, completely different, like they belonged in a world I couldn't even imagine, and how the walls between this world and that one were so thin. One slip, one misplaced foot, one secret out in the open and you'd go crashing through the boundaries and find yourself in that other, unimagined world where everything was different, where everything was wrong. I made myself drink my tea, and a glass of water, and follow the group out onto the Meadowcrest lawn, where we sat in a circle and listened to a man with a flowing gray beard and a woman young enough to be his daughter who was probably his girlfriend bang on African drums and tell us that music had the power to heal. Eventually, I opened my notebook again, flipping through pages of jokes and songs that would get me to my daughter. *Eyes on the prize,* I told myself, and bent my head and began to write.

TWENTY-SIX

Three days after I came up with the concept of a talent show at our table, we had more skits and songs than we could use. The entire women's campus had caught talent-show fever. Girls who hadn't been interested in anything but reconnecting with their boyfriends or their dealers were busy writing lyrics or scraping together costumes or finding props for *The Sound of Rehab.*

As we walked to Share, two girls, Amanda and Samantha, were performing a version of a Run-D.M.C. rap called "My Addiction," instead of "My Adidas." "My addiction walked through high-school doors and danced all over coliseum floors . . . spent all my dough just blowing trees . . . we made a mean team, my addiction and me." I was learning all kinds of new words and phrases. "Blowing trees," I learned, was smoking marijuana. "On my grind" meant working. "So, when I'm at my desk, writing a blog post, that means I'm on my grind?" I asked, and both Amanda and Samantha started laughing and said, "Nah, it's a little different than that," but they wouldn't tell me how.

We were almost at the art therapy room when Michelle

popped her head out of her office. "Allison W., can I see you for a moment?"

I rolled my eyes, left the group, and took a seat on the opposite side of her desk. "Allison," she began, "I understand there's a talent show in the works."

I shrugged, saying nothing.

"You know," Michelle continued, "that any activities have to be approved by staff."

"Oh, sure," I said. Then I resumed my silence. Michelle stared at me for a moment. Then she reached into a folder and pulled out a script that, judging from the coffee stains, looked as if it had been retrieved from a cafeteria garbage can. " 'How do you solve a problem like an RC,' " she read, in a tuneless, cheerless voice. " 'How do you make them understand your world? How do you make them stay . . . and listen to what you'd say . . . when they look at you like you're a human—' "

"You know," I interrupted, "it really sounds much better when you sing it." I sat up straight and demonstrated. "Many a thing you know you'd like to tell them. Many a thing you'd hope they'd understand . . . Low bottoms and low IQs . . . they're low on empathy, too . . . with nary a prayer of ever getting canned." I bent my head to hide my smile. "You see?"

"Allison, I admire your team spirit. But you are not permitted to perform skits and songs that make fun of the staff members."

"Why?" I asked. "I mean, of course, assuming that there *is* a talent show." I arranged my face into an approximation of confusion. "And why do you think I'm the one in charge?"

"Allison, I'm not going to get into that with you. What I need you to understand—"

I cut her off before she could finish. "What I need you to understand is that, to misquote Alexander Haig, I'm not in charge here. I've got nothing to do with anything. I'm just some poor, stupid pill-head who can't figure out how many sessions with her therapist it takes to get a day pass."

Michelle narrowed her eyes, causing them to practically vanish into her doughy face. "Let me ask you something, Allison. Do you want to get better?"

"Better than what?" I muttered. *Better than you?* I thought. I was pretty sure I'd achieved that particular goal already.

"Think about it," she suggested in a sugary-sweet tone, and sent me off to Share, where I listened to a thirty-eight-year-old mother of two named Dice describe her descent from high-school cheerleader to crackhead. She'd arrived at Meadowcrest after her parents told her they could no longer care for her boys (twelve and nine), and would be putting them in foster care unless she got her act together.

I would never, I thought, as Dice described leaving her boys home alone or, worse, with strangers while she wandered the streets to cop. Her hands, with the nails bitten short and bloody, trembled as she worked to extract pictures of her sons from underneath the plastic lining of her binder. "That's Dominic Junior, my little Nicky, and that's Christopher. He eats so much I can't even believe it. Like, mixin' bowls full of cereal, gallons of milk . . . I tell him we should just get a cow, let him suck on that, 'stead of using all our money on milk . . ."

Had she ever been like me and Janet, with a husband and a house, a car in the garage and money in the bank? Had she ever had a chance at that kind of life?

"Allison?"

I glanced up. Gabrielle, she of the pink lanyard and officious-bank-lady look, was staring at me. So, I noticed, were the rest of the eighteen girls and women in the circle. "Allison, are you ready to share?"

"Um." I closed my notebook, then drummed my fingertips

on its cover. I had known this day was coming, but, of course, they never told you exactly when it would be your turn. I sat up straight, remembering how every Share began. "Well. Let's see. I was born in New Jersey, in 1974. I think I tried liquor for the first time at someone's bat mitzvah, when I was twelve or thirteen. We were sneaking glasses off the grown-ups' table. I had maybe a sip, and I hated the way it tasted, and that was that until I was sixteen. Um." I tilted my body back in my chair, looked up at the ceiling and noticed, without surprise, that it was stained. Everything in this place was worn and dirty, frayed and patched, like we didn't deserve anything better. "I got drunk at a party when I was sixteen. Vodka and peach schnapps, which was a thing back then. I hated the way it made me feel, and I didn't drink again until college . . . and even then, it was, like, a beer. Or maybe I'd have a few puffs of a joint."

"You're kidding," said a new girl whose name I didn't know. I could have gotten defensive, but instead, I just shrugged.

"Yeah, I know it sounds ridiculous, but it's the truth. I didn't like booze, I didn't like pot, and I didn't really try anything else because there wasn't much else around . . . oh, wait, I did do mushrooms one time, but they made me puke, so forget that." I shuddered. "I hate throwing up."

"Don't do heroin," said Lena, and everyone else laughed.

"So, flash forward, I'm thirty-four, I'm married, I have a kid, I throw my back out at my gym, and my doctor gives me Vicodin." I breathed, remembering. "And it was like that scene in *The Wizard of Oz* where everything goes from black-and-white to color. It was like that was the way the world was meant to feel." I could feel my body reacting to the memory, the blood rising to the surface of my skin, my heartbeat quickening. "I was calm, I was happy, I felt like I could get more things accomplished. I started writing these blog posts, and they really took off. The

pills made me brave enough to write with all those people reading. They made me patient enough to put up with my daughter,
who is gorgeous and smart but can be a handful. They made me
who I was supposed to be. I know that's not what I'm supposed
to say in here," I said, before anyone could chide me for romanti-
cizing my use or failing to "play the tape," "but I also know that
we're supposed to be honest. And that's the God's honest truth.
I loved the way I felt when I was on pills."

"So what happened?" Gabrielle prompted.

I sighed. "I just started taking too many of them. More pills,
different kinds, stronger medications, and then, eventually, I
wasn't taking them to feel good, I was taking them just to feel
normal. I was napping all the time, and I was impatient with
my daughter. I wasn't myself. I took money from a petty cash
account at work and moved it into my personal account. It wasn't
exactly embezzlement, but it wasn't exactly something I was supposed to be doing. And . . ." Here came the hard part. "I tried
to drive while I was impaired. One of the teachers saw what
was going on and took my keys away. Then my husband found
out what was going on and . . ." I shrugged. By now, my look of
contrition was so well-rehearsed that it felt almost natural on my
face. "Here I am. Just another sick person trying to get better."

For a minute, there was silence, as the ladies contemplated
my boring, bare-bones, drama-free tale. Everyone had something better—an overdose, an arrest, an intervention full of tears
and accusations. The previous week one of the women, a fifth-
grade teacher who'd also bought pills online, had talked about
being blackmailed. The person she bought from spent an afternoon on Google, figured out where she worked and to whom
she was married, and then e-mailed her to say that if she didn't
pay first five hundred, then a thousand, then three thousand
dollars, he'd tell her husband and her boss—and maybe even

the local paper—just what she'd been up to. It had gone on for months. Linda had drained her savings account and dipped into her twelve-year-old daughter's college fund before trying to kill herself. Luckily, it hadn't worked, and now she was here . . . and as for the guy who'd tortured her, Linda said with a sad smile that her counselor had helped her fill out a form on the DEA's website. "I have no idea if they caught him," she'd said. "Probably he's still out there, shaking down other housewives."

I remembered feeling almost dizzy with relief that nothing like that had ever happened to me. Now, with dozens of puzzled and accusatory faces staring at me, I almost wished something more catastrophic had landed me at Meadowcrest.

"That's it?" an Ashley or a Brittany murmured. I wondered if I should have talked about learning that my mom was an alcoholic . . . but where could I have fit that in?

"Hey, look, I'm sorry I don't have some big, dramatic story about almost dying, or almost killing someone, or getting in a car crash . . ."

"It's not that." I'd expected Gabrielle to be the one to push me for more details, more emotion, just more in general, but instead it was shiny-haired, tiny-voiced Aubrey, all scrunched up in the seat on my left, who was calling me out. "It's like you're telling your story, only it sounds like it happened to someone else." She squirmed as I looked at her, but she didn't back down. "Were you sad about it? When it was happening?"

"Of course I was sad!" I snapped. "God. Do you think I'd be here if I wasn't sad?"

"But you don't sound sad." Now one of the Brittanys had taken up the attack, only she didn't sound angry as much as puzzled. "You just sound, like, okay, this happened, then that happened, and then I started taking Percocet, and then I started taking Oxy . . ."

I wanted to say that progression was a central part of every other girl's story—first the booze, then the pills, then the powder, then the needle. So why was I being criticized for giving a version of the same tale everyone told?

"What about when your daughter would want you to play with her, and you'd tell her to go away?" Finally, Mary had decided to join the conversation. "How do you feel about that?"

"I feel incredibly ashamed. I hate myself for not being there for her." I mustered up all the sincerity I could—the hurt look, the shaky voice, the defeated posture acknowledging I'd committed the ultimate female transgression, the Sin of Bad Motherhood. "I feel awful about what I did. That's why I'm here. So I won't ever have to do those things again."

This announcement was met with unexpected silence. Aubrey fidgeted in her seat; an Amber retied her shoelaces. Gabrielle flipped to a fresh page in her notebook. Finally, she said, "I guess maybe Allison's story sounds different to us because she wasn't using for very long." She looked at me. "What was it, six months?"

"About that." Six months was as long as I'd been buying pills online. My actual abuse—or, if not abuse, the length of time my use had been problematic—was closer to two years.

"For most of us, there was that big wake-up call," Mary continued. "I got a DUI. Aubrey got arrested. People lost their relationships, or had their kids taken away. But just because Allison's got a high bottom . . ."

"Thank you," I murmured. High bottom. Was there a lovelier phrase in the English language?

"It doesn't mean she didn't have a bottom. Or that she's not in trouble. Or that she doesn't need our help."

"Thank you," I said again. As the next Share began—this one from a twenty-eight-year-old heroin addict from New Mexico who'd come to New Jersey as part of some kind of rehab exchange program—I returned my attention to the new lyrics to "One Day More." "One more day, then I'm in rehab . . . Gonna get drunk off my ass . . . I'll buy ev'ry pill and take it . . . plus Champagne and speed and grass." Would Melanie be able to pull off the role of Liesl, the besotted sixteen-going-on-seventeen-year-old, who we'd decided would be in love with crystal meth instead of Rolfe the Nazi messenger boy? I looked around the circle, realizing that I'd never know. If everything went the way I'd planned, I'd be in the car with Dave when the first song began. I felt a surprising amount of regret, as I looked at Mary, and Aubrey, and Shannon, and realized I'd never hear how their stories turned out. *Ellie,* I told myself sternly. Ellie was the one who mattered.

That night they turned the phones on, so that the women who were off the seven-day blackout could have their regular twice-a-week ten-minute phone call home. "Where am I picking you up?" asked Dave, who'd swallowed my story about having a day pass without a single question.

"You can just wait in the parking lot. I think I remember what the car looks like."

I waited for a laugh that did not come. "When do you need to be back?" He sounded like he was scheduling a dentist's appointment, not a reunion with his wife.

"Eight." Actually, I wasn't planning on coming back at all. I would attend Ellie's party, then ask Dave to take me for an early dinner, during which I would convince him that I'd gotten everything I could out of my rehab experience and was ready to come home. "Is Ellie excited?"

"She is. She and your mom have been making cupcakes, and paper chains."

"Paper chains?" I hadn't heard of such a thing since I was

Ellie's age myself, and, certainly, they hadn't been a feature of any of the birthday parties I'd attended with her.

"Yup. We decided to have the party here instead of Bouncy-Time. It's always too loud there. She gets overwhelmed. And, after Jayden's party . . ." He let his voice trail off, too polite to remind me of the disaster Jayden's party had become.

"Okay," I said slowly. I was surprised that nobody had asked me, or even told me, before making this change, but my main concern was that the party was a success, and that Ellie was happy. "So did you hire a magician? That petting zoo that Chloe had? And what about favors?" Lately, the trend was for kids to burn CDs of their own party-music mixes, and hand them out in the goody bags.

"I think there's just going to be games."

"Games?" I wondered if he meant something like laser tag.

"Party games. Charades, and pin-the-tail-on-the-donkey. Like that. Your mother's really the one running the show, and it sounds like it's under control."

Charades? Paper chains and homemade cupcakes? I wasn't sure anything was under control . . . but I tried to sound cheerful as I said, "See you Saturday."

This will work, I told myself as I got ready for bed that night. As always, I was thinking of Ellie. What had she done that day? What dress had she worn? Had she eaten her dinner, or snuck it into the toilet, the way I'd caught her doing the week before I left? Were there kids she knew at the Stonefield camp? Did she like the counselors? How was my mother handling life without my dad? And what about Dave?

I couldn't bring myself to ask him the big questions: *Do you still love me? What do you tell yourself about why I'm in here? Will we still be married when I'm out?*

I refused to let myself think about it. Instead, I brushed my teeth, put on what I knew would be the first of at least two sets of pajamas (I was still waking up at midnight, or one in the morning, having completely sweated through the first pair), and, feeling clumsy and strange, got down on my knees.

"Are you there, God?" I began. "It's me, Allison. Thank you for the beautiful sunshine today. Thank you for the inspiration about the talent show. Thank you . . ." At this part, my voice got clogged with tears. "Thank you for keeping Ellie safe. For not letting me hurt her. Thank you for another day of not using." That last part struck me as completely ridiculous—how could I possibly use, even if I wanted to, in a place like this? I said it anyhow. Then I worked myself back upright, stretched, and climbed into bed.

At ten o'clock, the lights went out. For a moment, I lay in the darkness. Then Aubrey called, from the other bedroom, "Good night, Allison."

"Good night, Aubrey," I called back.

"Good night, Mary," Shannon said.

"Good night, Shannon," said Mary.

"Good night, Ashley."

"Which one?"

Giggles, then, "Ashley C."

"Good night, Marissa."

I remembered what Nicholas had told me, about how sometimes beginners substituted the group for God.

"Good night, Ashley D."

"Good night, Lena."

Could you call this love, or a Higher Power? All of us working toward the same goal, helping one another as best we could? *Something that's bigger than you, and something that's kind and for-*

giving, I'd heard one of the meeting leaders say. *That's all your Higher Power has to be.* So could this be it?

I wasn't sure. I shut my eyes, rolled onto my side, and slipped into what had become my standard two hours' worth of sleep, followed by five hours of lying awake, sweating and crying in my narrow bed, waiting for the flashlight's glare to shine through the slit of a window, wondering how I'd gotten here and what my life would be like when I got out.

TWENTY-SEVEN

By Saturday morning, you would have thought the ladies of Meadowcrest were getting ready for a wedding . . . or an actual Broadway debut. Lena was on her bedroom floor, attempting to press a pair of pants with a curling iron. Aubrey was humming scales in the bathroom, Mary was practicing "Sentimental Gurney" in the hall, and the girls I'd dubbed the Greek Chorus were singing "Dope that's so slammin' it makes your heart flutter . . . Dealers on corners and needles in gutters . . . Wax-paper Baggies all tied up with strings . . . These were a few of my favorite things." Knowing I'd be heading home, I got Aubrey to help with my hair and makeup. She plucked my eyebrows, smoothed on concealer, and used mascara to cover my gray hairs. "Thanks for doing this," she said, unwinding the Velco curlers she'd used. "Of all the times I've been in rehab, this was the most fun." I was so touched that for one wild instant I thought about staying—directing the talent show, seeing how it all turned out. Then I thought of Ellie, gave Aubrey a hug, and said, "I'm glad I met you."

At ten o'clock, while some poor woman who'd driven in from the Pine Barrens attempted to share her experience, strength, and hope, we passed and re-passed scripts from hand to hand, making corrections, adding new jokes. By the time the announcement blared, "Ladies, please proceed to the cafeteria for afternoon Meditation," I was trembling with nerves. Sure enough, instead of the typical single, bored RC, there was Michelle . . . and Kirsten . . . and Jean and Phil, two counselors I didn't know. A half-dozen RCs were lined up by the door . . . and at the head of the line stood none other than my pal Ed McGreavey, noted heli-skier and locator of lost bottoms.

"Good morning!" he said pleasantly as we filed into the room. "Ladies," he said, as the women stared at him, then at me. "I understand you've got a performance in the works. I want to tell you, personally, how happy it makes me to see this kind of motivation!" So that was his strategy, I thought. If you can't beat 'em, join 'em . . . and act like it was your good idea all along. "We're looking forward to hearing what you've got."

I smiled as, behind me, Amanda and Samantha got into position. "Ladies and gentlemen!" I said, nodding at Ed and at the pimply RC who'd hollered at me about walking on the wrong path. "Welcome to the inaugural, one-time-only, debut performance of *The Sound of Rehab*."

Behind Amanda and Samantha, the rest of the women lined up in a half circle. Aubrey stepped to the front of the circle, twirling and twirling, before she opened her mouth and, in a very credible Julie Andrews–ish manner, began to sing, "The hills are alive . . . with the sounds of rehab . . . with songs drunks have sung . . . for a hundred years!"

I slipped to the door. "Be right back," I whispered to Mary. I was sorry to miss it, I thought as I hurried to my room, grabbed my purse, strolled past the empty desk, pushed through the double doors, and found Dave in the parking lot, behind the wheel of the Prius, right where he said he would be.

He looked at me with suspicion as I practically skipped

into the passenger's seat. "Go, go, go!" I hollered, pounding the dashboard.

"You okay?"

"I'm great! It just feels so good to be getting out of here!" I could barely breathe, or hear anything, because of the thunder of my heartbeat in my ears as we pulled past the security guard's hut, but no one said a word. The gate lifted, and we were on the road, driving toward Philadelphia. Free.

"Tell me everything," I said, adjusting the seat, and then the music, looking around for coffee or candy or anything at all from the outside world.

Dave's voice was terse, his words careful. "Ellie's been doing fine. She seems to like camp, and her swimming's gotten much better. And your mother's really stepped up to the plate. She's been driving Ellie to camp in the mornings—"

"Wait. Driving? My mom?" I felt my throat start to close again, remembering her promise, that she'd never be impaired around my daughter.

"She went out and renewed her license. Passed the test on her first try."

"Wow," I said, wondering why she hadn't told me. Dave drove us along an unfamiliar two-lane road, past a farm stand selling sweet corn and tomatoes, and a small white church. "How long's the ride home?"

"Maybe half an hour."

"That's all?"

"You don't remember?" His tone betrayed little curiosity. Dave looked good, lean and broad-shouldered as ever in his worn jeans and dark-blue collared shirt. He smelled good, too, freshly showered, the bracing scent of Dial soap filling the car.

"I wasn't in great shape at the time." I stared at him, willing him to take his eyes off the road, even for just a second, and spare me a look. When he didn't, I began talking. "Dave. I know we haven't really discussed things, and we probably won't have much of a chance today, but I want you to know how sorry I am about everything."

For a long moment, he didn't answer. "Let's just focus on Ellie," he finally said, in that maddening, almost robotic tone.

"Can't you tell me anything? Give me a hint? Because, you know, if I'm going to be single, there's a trainer who comes to Meadowcrest once a week. I gotta start working on my fitness if I'm going to be back on the market."

I saw the corners of his eyes crinkle in what wasn't quite a smile, but was at least a sign that I could still amuse him. "I made mistakes, too," he said. "I knew there was something going on for a while, and I didn't try to find out what. It was just easier to let things go."

"No, no, it wasn't your fault. It was me. I thought I could handle everything . . . that the pills were helping me handle everything . . ." I reached over the gearshift for his free hand, and he let me take it, and hold it, until we left the highway. We sat in silence until Dave parked in front of our garage.

"Mommy, Mommy, MOMMY!" Ellie shrieked once we were inside, racing into my arms, almost knocking the wind out of me. She wore a party dress with a purple sash and crinolines, her hair in a neat French braid, her feet in lace-cuffed socks and Mary Janes.

"Hi, baby girl." Oh, God, she'd gotten so much bigger. I lifted her up, burying my face in the crook of her neck, inhaling the scent of her skin. "I missed you, oh, so much."

"Why did you have to LEAVE?" She wriggled out of my arms, planted her hands on her hips, and scowled at me.

"Because I needed to get some help. Sometimes mommies need a time-out."

"Hmph." Ellie looked as if she'd heard these lines before. "Well, you're all better now, right?"

"She's getting better," said Dave. "Mommy can spend the day with you, and then I need to take her back."

Ellie's eyes filled with tears. "Why do you have to go BACK? You aren't even SICK. You look FINE."

"Remember what we talked about, Ellie?" And here was my mother. I blinked at Casual Ronnie; my mother without her lipgloss, without foundation and mascara, with her hair—I could barely believe it—pulled back in a ponytail, dressed in jeans (jeans!), with an apron (another item I'd never seen or imagined her to possess) wrapped around her waist. A pair of sneakers on her feet, where I'd only ever seen high heels or jeweled sandals, her fingernails clipped short, filed, no polish. "The doctors are taking good care of your mom, and she'll be home as soon as she's ready."

"But there is nothing WRONG with her!"

"Ellie," said Dave, "why don't you go count the apples and make sure there's enough for everyone to get one?"

Ellie gave us a darkly suspicious look before stomping off toward the dining room. "We're bobbing for apples," she called over her shoulder.

"Isn't that more of a Halloween thing?" I looked around, with a feeling of dread gathering in the pit of my stomach. There was an old-school portrait of a donkey taped to the dining-room wall, along with a metal bin full of water with a bowl full of apples beside it.

"I thought we'd play party games," my mother said.

"Party games," I repeated. It didn't sound like an awful idea, and maybe it wasn't, unless you knew that these days, in our neighborhood, a typical six-year-old's birthday party might include an outing to the local bowling alley, where the lanes were equipped with bumpers and at least some of the snacks would be gluten-free, or a scavenger hunt at the Franklin Institute in Philadelphia, followed by a make-your-own-sundae bar.

I followed Ellie into the dining room and found her sitting in the corner with an apple in her hand. "Hey, El," I said, and began to sing. " 'I did not live until today . . . how can I live when we are parted?' "

" 'Tomorrow you'll be worlds away,' " she sang, eyes wide, one hand over her heart, teenage Cosette falling in love. " 'And yet with you my world has started.' "

" 'One more day out on my own,' " I sang. " 'One more day with him not caring.' " I tried not to look at Dave, who was standing in the kitchen with his back to me as Ellie sang, " 'I was born to be with you!' " She stretched out her arms and I lifted her up, holding her against me, singing, " 'What a life I might have known.' " I tickled her ribs and she wrapped her arms around my neck, cheeks pink, a picture of delight. " 'But he never saw me there.' " I peeked over her head. Dave was watching us—maybe, I hoped, preparing to launch into the Valjean/Javert section— but before he could start a car pulled up the driveway and Hank emerged from the backseat.

"MY PARTY FRIENDS ARE HERE!" Ellie shrieked, vaulting out of my arms and hitting the ground at a sprint. I got one last whiff of her scent, a final instance of the sweetness of her skin against mine. Then she was gone.

"Happy birthday, Ellie," Hank said shyly, wiping his nose and handing my daughter an enormous, elaborately wrapped box with pink-and-white-striped wrapping paper and pink-and-silver ribbons.

"Wow," I said as Mrs. Hank smiled indulgently at her son.

She wore dark glasses, skinny jeans, and a silky sleeveless top. "Looks like someone blew his allowance."

"He's in love," Mrs. Hank affirmed, leaning over to offer her smooth cheek for the pro forma air kiss. "Meanwhile, you! You look amazing!" She eyed me up and down. I tried not to flinch under her scrutiny and wondered exactly what she was seeing. I had Aubrey's work in my favor, but my clothing options weren't great. I was wearing the best of the limited choices Dave had given me, which meant jeans that were too loose and a T-shirt that was too casual to look right underneath Shannon's cardigan. The good news was that I'd been taking every yoga class Meadowcrest offered, plus walking around the track with Shannon and Aubrey. That, and the sunshine, and the water I'd been drinking, and the absence of drugs meant that my skin was tanned and clear, and my eyes were bright.

"Amazing," Mrs. Hank repeated. I wished I could remember her first name. It was Carol, or Kara, something in that family. We'd had coffee together, and chatted at PTA meetings, with most of our conversations revolving around Hank's allergies and Ellie's sensitivities. "Are you doing a cleanse?"

"Something like that," I said.

"Allison?"

My mom called me into the kitchen, where she stood with a tray of cupcakes in her hands. Homemade. Oh, dear. Ellie had probably told her cupcakes but had failed to tell her to get them at Sweet Sue's. Their cupcakes were incredible, dense and rich, topped with swirls of icing in flavors you could never hope to duplicate at home, dulce de leche and salted caramel and panna cotta. My mother had baked treats that I bet came from a box, with frosting I was certain came from a can. I wondered how that conversation had gone, with Ellie telling my mom about the bakery and my mother somehow convincing her that baking from scratch would be better and more fun.

"Can you help me with the punch?" my mom asked.

Punch. I didn't say a word as I poured ginger ale over a block of melting sherbet in the cut-crystal punch bowl Dave and I had gotten for our wedding and, if I remembered right, had never used. My mother's transformation was astonishing. She was exuding the kind of quiet confidence I couldn't remember from my own childhood, when she'd been either brisk and brittle, rushing me out of rooms, or as giggly and giddy as a young girl, waiting for my father to come home.

"This is some affair," I said, as she arranged the cupcakes next to the punch bowl.

"Ellie and I planned it together. She helped me bake the cupcakes, and we went online and found all the party games. We downloaded the donkey!" My mother seemed very pleased with her achievement.

"That's great!" For a minute, I wanted to tell her about the talent show, and I felt a pang of unhappiness as I realized it was probably over by now.

"How are you feeling?" My mother's eyes were on the cupcakes as she waited for my answer.

"Physically, I'm okay. Mentally . . ." I sighed. I couldn't think of how to explain what I was feeling. Most days, I barely knew myself.

Mrs. Hank came breezing into the kitchen, along with a few other mothers whose names, thankfully, I knew. Holly Harper was Amelia's mom, and Susan van der Meer belonged with Sadie. "How can we help?"

My mom picked up Mason jars filled with marshmallows and penny candy and carried them into the dining room.

Mrs. Hank turned to me with a conspiratorial look on her face. "Listen," she said, "we promise we won't tell a soul." I felt the muscles in my torso clench. Somebody knew. Somebody knew, someone had found out, someone had told, and now all the moms knew exactly what was wrong with me . . . and they wanted details.

"But here's the thing," Mrs. Hank continued. "My high-school reunion's coming up, and Holly's got an—"

"Anniversary," said Holly. "And it was Jeff's big idea to go back to Hawaii. He's got this picture of me from twenty years ago in a bikini, and then he went online and actually found the goddamn thing on eBay—I should have known he was up to something when he asked what size I wore, and of course I lied, because, seriously, like I'm going to tell him the truth?"

Laughter all around. I laughed, too, and wondered how fast they'd grab their little darlings and dash out of my house if I told them what I'd been lying to my husband about.

"Just tell us," Carol/Kara whispered. "If it's a trainer . . . or one of the food-delivery things . . ."

"Oh, guys, really. I wish it was some big secret. But I just haven't been that hungry lately."

There was a beat of incredulous silence while the three of them just stared at me. Holly Harper started laughing first, and then the other two joined in.

"Oh! Good one!" said Kara/Carol. She mimed wiping tears from the smooth skin beneath her eyes. "Okay, seriously. Is it a juice fast?"

I opened my mouth to provide another jokey denial, and for a single terrifying instant I was sure that what would tumble from my lips would be the truth, the tale of what had really happened, possibly in the rhyming lyrics of one of the talent-show songs: *Vicodin, and lots of them! OxyContin, pots of them! Chewing pills up by the peck . . . Allison was bound to wreck!*

"Allison?" My knees trembled in relief as Janet came into the room, a wrapped gift box in her hands. By the time she crossed the kitchen she'd assessed the situation, setting down her gift and grabbing me in a hug. "How are you?"

"She's thin," said Susan van der Meer, in a tone just short of accusatory.

Janet kept one arm around me as she turned to face my interrogators. "Her dad's been sick," she said. "Allison and her mom had to move him into assisted living a few weeks ago."

I saw surprise on their faces, heard sympathetic murmurs. "Oh, I'm so sorry," said Susan, and Holly said, "Isn't it the worst? We went through it last year, after Jeff's mom had an aneurysm."

"Excuse me for a minute," I said. I made myself breathe until the dizziness went away, then led Janet up the stairs and down the hall to my bedroom. She closed the door behind us, then looked me up and down.

"Okay, you look . . ."

"Thin!" I said, and started making some shrill noises that approximated laughter. "I'm thin, can you believe it! What's my secret? Do you think I should tell them, or would they just fall over dead from the shock?" I sank down on the bed and put my face in my hands. "I went rogue," I confessed.

"Wait, what?" Janet ducked into my bathroom. I heard drawers and cabinets opening and closing. A minute later, she came out with her hands filled with concealer, brushes, my flat iron, and a comb.

"I don't actually have a day pass. They told me I couldn't go. It was some big red-tape nightmare. I was supposed to have a certain number of sessions with my counselor, only they didn't even assign me a counselor until I'd been there almost a week, and then she left, and they weren't going to let me leave . . ."

"Okay. Deep breath. You made it. You're here now. Want some water?"

Downstairs, I could hear the door opening, and my mother, suddenly transformed into the gracious lady of the manor, greeting Ellie's other grandmother, Doreen. If I'd stayed at Meadowcrest, if I'd gone to the talent show, then to Circle and to Share, the party would have gone off without a hitch. I wasn't indispensible. I wasn't even sure Ellie would have missed me.

"We should go downstairs."

"Here. Wait." Gently, Janet dabbed a sponge dipped in foundation on my cheeks and chin. She tapped powder onto a brush and swiped lipstick onto my lips, either undoing or redoing Aubrey's work. "When are you getting out?"

As I started to explain the logistics, there was a knock on the door.

"Allison?" called Dave. "We're going to get started."

All through the afternoon, through the games, through the cupcakes and ice cream and the inevitable gluten-free versions that the allergic and intolerant kids' mothers had sent, I felt like a fake, like this was a show someone else had written, and I'd been assigned the role of wife and mother. And, louder and louder, like something out of an Edgar Allan Poe short story, I could hear a voice whispering, *Pills*. While I negotiated the rest of the night with Dave, assuring him that I was free until eight o'clock, pleading with him to take me to Han Dynasty for dinner "so I can eat something that tastes like something" before he sent me back, I thought, *Pills*. Handing out the goody bags, packed with candy necklaces my mom and Ellie had strung and handwritten notes that read "Thank You for Coming to My Party," I thought, *Pills, pills, where am I going to find pills?*

The plan, which Dave reluctantly agreed to, was to drive Ellie to Hank's house for dinner with Hank's family. My mom would get a break, Dave would take me out for Chinese food, we'd have our talk, and then, depending on how the talk went, either he'd drive me back to Meadowcrest or I'd convince him that I could come home.

By the time Dave, Ellie, and I got to Hank's house, I could almost taste the familiar, delectable bitterness on my tongue. I got out of the car as soon as it stopped, led Ellie inside, and asked Mrs. Hank—her name, I finally remembered, was not Kara or Carol but Danielle—if I could borrow a tampon. She waved toward her staircase. "Master bathroom. Everything's in the cabinet under the sink."

Up in the bathroom, I locked the door, put a tampon in my pocket, then opened the medicine cabinet above the sink. Beside the half-used bottles of antibiotics and Advil and Tylenol PM, there were Percocet, five and ten milligrams, both with refills, and an unopened, unexpired bottle of thirty-milligram OxyContin, prescribed for Hank's father.

"Mommy!" I heard Ellie yell from downstairs.

"Hang on!" I called back, and began opening the bottles, shaking a few pills into my palms, stashing them in the pockets of my jeans.

"Mommy?" Ellie sounded like she was right outside the bathroom door. For once, she wasn't yelling.

"Just—" *Hang on*, I was about to say, when I caught sight of myself in the mirror. My eyes were enormous and frantic. My face was pale, except for two blotches of red high on my cheeks. I looked like a thief, like a junkie, like Brittany B., who'd come to Meadowcrest from jail after she and her boyfriend had robbed the local Rite-Aid . . . and all I could think of, all that I wanted, was for Eloise to go away, to go to Hank's room or the playroom or the basement or the backyard, anywhere that I could have five minutes and get myself a little peace.

What happens if you get caught? a voice in my head whispered. It seemed like a crazy thought—there had to be dozens of bottles in here, all of them (I'd checked) with refills on the labels. No way would Mrs. Hank miss a few pills, if I selected judiciously. There'd be more than enough to carry me through rehab, if I decided to return, or through my first few days home.

And then what? my mind persisted. Then I'd have to go back to my old rounds, my old sources, days of counting pills, worrying and wondering if I had enough . . . and, if I didn't, how I'd get more.

"Mommy?" Ellie sounded like she was crying. "I am sorry if I am a bother."

"What?" I sank down to the floor, my ear pressed against the door, a bottle of Percocet still in my hand.

"If that's why you went away. Because I am a bother."

It felt like a knife in my heart. "Oh, El. Oh, honey, no. You're not a bother to me. I love you! I'll . . . just give me a minute, I'll be out in a minute, and we can talk, I'll explain about everything . . ."

I put the first pill under my tongue and got that first blast of bitterness. Then it hit me. This was it: the moment they talked about in those stupid AA handouts and alluded to with those mealy-mouthed slogans, delivered with an earnestness suggesting they had been freshly minted in that moment. *Half-measures availed us nothing. We stood at the turning point. One is too many and a thousand is never enough.* It didn't matter that my turning point didn't involve turning a trick in the back of a car, or looting my parents' retirement fund, or sticking a needle in my arm. This was it. My hand in a stranger's medicine cabinet, my little girl on the other side of a locked door, needing a mother who only wanted her to go away. *Congratulations, Allison Rose Weiss. You've finally made it all the way down.*

I spat the pill out into my hand, then flushed it down the toilet. I put the pills back in the bottles. I put the bottles back in the cabinet. I sprayed about half a bottle's worth of air freshener, in case it turned out Mrs. Hank had a suspicious mind.

Outside the door, Ellie was standing with her hands in her pockets, pale-faced, in her pretty party dress, the one we'd picked out online the month before, with her sitting on my lap and me scrolling through the pages, still struggling with her "th" sound, her little finger pointing, "I will have lis one, and lat one, and lis one," and me saying, "No, honey, just pick your favorite," and her turning to me, eyes brimming, saying, "But they are ALL OF THEM MY FAVORITE."

I bent down and lifted her in my arms.

"Do you need to take a nap now?" she asked. "I will be quiet."

If anyone ever asked me what it felt like the instant my heart broke, I would tell them how I felt, hearing that.

"No. No nap. I'm okay." And I was. At least physically. Sure, I wanted the pills so bad that I was shaking. I could still taste that delectable bitterness in the back of my throat, could already feel the phantom calm and comfort as my shoulders unclenched and my heartbeat slowed, but I could get through it, minute by minute, second by second, if I had to. Even though I suspected I would remember that bliss, and crave it, for the rest of my life.

I took Ellie downstairs to play with Hank. Dave was in the kitchen, talking about the Eagles' dubious fortunes with Mr. Hank. "Honey, can I talk to you for a minute?"

I took him by the forearm, walked him out to the driveway, and told him the truth, watching my words register on his face— his wrinkled forehead, his mouth slowly falling open. "You did what?" Before I could start to explain my talent-show exit strategy again, he said, "No. You know what? Never mind." His hand was on his phone. I turned away, my eyes brimming. I wanted to ask if I got any credit for honesty, if it meant anything to him that I'd told the truth, however belatedly . . . but, before I could ask, he was connected to Meadowcrest.

"Yes . . . no, I don't know who I need to speak with . . . I thought my wife had a day pass, but now she's telling me she didn't . . . Allison W. . . . Yes, I'll hold."

While he was holding, I went back into the Hanks' house. Ellie was engrossed in a game of Wii bowling. "I'll be home soon," I whispered. She barely spared me a hug. Mrs. Hank— Danielle—was in the kitchen. "Thanks for taking her," I said. "I wonder if you could be extra nice to her for the next little while . . ."

"Are you going away again?" Danielle asked. She wasn't my friend, but, at that moment, I wished she was.

"Yes. I actually . . ." *I'm going back to rehab*, I almost said. It was right there, the words lined up all in a row, but I wasn't sure if that was oversharing, or asking for sympathy where I didn't deserve any. "A work thing," I finally concluded.

"Well, don't worry. Your mother's a rock star. And Ellie is always welcome here."

I thanked her. Dave was already behind the wheel when I got back outside. "Are they letting me come back?" I whispered.

He backed out of the driveway. "At first someone named Michelle wanted me to call a facility in Mississippi that treats dual-diagnosis patients. That's when you're an addict with mental illness."

I gave a mirthless giggle. "Does Michelle know I'm Jewish? I might be crazy, but there's no way I'm going to Mississippi."

"Eventually, they said you could come back. No guarantees about staying. Someone named Nicholas is going to be waiting for you."

Nicholas. I shut my eyes. Then I made myself open them again. "Do you want to talk about . . . anything?"

I could see his knuckles, tight on the wheel, the jut of his jaw as he ground his back teeth. "Honestly? Right now, no. I don't." We drove for a minute, me sitting there clutching my purse handles hard, Dave's face set, until he burst out, "When are you going to stop lying?"

"Now," I said immediately. "I'm done with . . . with that. With all of it. I don't want to be that kind of person. Or that kind of mom, or that kind of wife."

Dave said nothing. I didn't expect a response. I'd been honest, but, of course, what else would a liar say, except *I'm done with lying* and *I'm done with using* and *I don't want to be that way anymore*? It was classic I-got-busted talk . . . and part of accepting life on life's terms, the way they told us we had to, meant living with the knowledge that maybe he'd never be able to trust me again.

I sat in silence, the way I had during my first trip to Meadowcrest. Dave pulled up in front of the main building and sat there, the car in park, the engine still running. I'd had half an hour to think of what to say, but all I could manage was "Thank you for the ride." I got out of the car, walked past the nice-desk receptionist, back beyond the RESIDENTS ONLY PAST THIS POINT sign, to the shabby hallway with its smell of cafeteria food and disinfectant. I left my purse in my empty bedroom, looped my nametag around my neck, and took the women's path to Nicholas's office, where, as promised, he was waiting for me.

"Allison W.," he said. His voice was so kind.

I sat in front of his desk and bent my head. Then I said the words I'd already said, in Group and Share and the AA meetings, where I'd sat off to the side and scribbled lyrics in my notebook. "I think I'm really in trouble," I whispered. "I think I'm an addict. I need help."

"Okay," he said. His hand on my shoulder was gentle. "The good news is, you've come to the right place."

PART FOUR

~

The Promises

TWENTY-EIGHT

"How about these clementines?" The clerk at the Whole Foods on South Street—a white guy of maybe twenty with mild blue eyes, a wide, untroubled brow, and dreadlocks down to his waist—gave me a gentle, *Namaste* kind of smile. He spoke softly and slowly, with great deliberation. It was maddening. This guy wouldn't have lasted a day in the suburbs, but in Center City, where the Whole Foods was next to a yoga studio, infuriating slowness was the rule. "Should we leave them in the box? Or take them out of the box and put the fruit in a bag?"

"Fruit in a bag, please." I was only buying a dozen things— a turkey breast to grill for dinner, the miniature oranges that Ellie loved in her school lunches, a twenty-dollar maple-scented candle that was way too expensive but that I'd found impossible to resist—but I could already tell that I was going to be checking out for a while. *Use it as a chance to practice patience,* Bernice's voice said in my head. When I'd left Meadowcrest, I'd joined Bernice's outpatient group, and her voice had taken up residence in my brain. I tried not to sigh, and actually managed a smile as the clerk first rummaged in his drawer, then patted down his pockets, and finally called over a manager, who called over a second manager, who located a pair of scissors to snip through the netting.

"Oh, dear. It looks like a few of these are moldy," said the clerk as the miniature oranges tumbled from their wooden crate into a plastic bag.

"Mommy, I do not want MOLDY CLEMENTINES," Ellie announced.

"Do you want to get another box?" the clerk asked. Behind me, the woman with the Phil&Teds stroller and the black woolen peacoat gave a small but audible groan. *Send her peace.* That wasn't Bernice; that was the voice of my new yoga instructor, Loyal. *Peace,* I thought. Old Allison would have scoffed at the dopey sayings, at the idea that the checkout line at the supermarket offered a chance to practice anything at all (not to mention at the notion of someone named Loyal). New Allison took advice wherever she could get it—at meetings, from magazines, from Oprah's Super Soul Sundays, and from Celestial Seasonings tea bags.

"That's okay," I told the clerk. "How about just separate out the moldy ones? You can toss those, and we'll take the good ones home."

He looked at me, concern furrowing his brow. "Are you sure? You can just go get another box. It's no trouble at all."

"It's fine."

"Ooookay." Clearly, it might have been fine for me, but it was deeply troubling for him. "Now, how about the turkey? Would you like that in a separate bag?"

"Please." I held up the shopping bags I'd brought. The clerk blinked, like he'd never seen or imagined such a thing.

"So . . . use that one?"

"Oh my God," murmured the woman in the peacoat. Ellie,

meanwhile, had crouched down, the better to inspect the bees-wax lip balms.

"Mommy, is this MAKEUP?"

"Kind of. Not exactly."

"Well, can I HAVE it?"

"No, honey, we have stuff like that at home. You can use what we've got. We'll shop the closet!"

"But that will have your SPITTY STUFF ALL OVER IT!"

I squatted down, feeling my body protest. My hips creaked; my back twinged. I'd done an hour of hot yoga that morning and had a run planned for tomorrow. *How'd you do it?* they asked in AA and NA meetings, when you went up front to collect your chip—for your first twenty-four hours of sobriety, then for thirty days, sixty days, ninety days, six months, nine months, a year, and on from there. *One day at a time* was the rote answer, the line you had to say, but each time I'd collected a chip I'd made sure to say that exercise was part of my recovery. It was a chance to get completely out of my head, forty minutes when all I could do was take the next step, find the next pose, manage the next inhalation. No matter how crappy or sad I felt, how locked in my own head, in my own unhappy run of thoughts, I would force myself up and out of bed, into the clothes I'd laid out the night before, and I would make myself go through my paces like I was swallowing a dose of some noxious medicine that I knew it was critical to get down.

Some mornings Ellie would join me for a walk down Pine Street, all the way to the Delaware River, or we'd do workout routines in the basement of the row house where I'd rented an apartment back in Philadelphia. Dave had found his own place, just a few blocks away. He'd kept the fancy treadmill; I'd found one on Craigslist, along with hand weights and a step bench.

Together, Ellie and I had downloaded free fitness videos, and gotten various ten-, fifteen-, and twenty-minute workouts from magazines. We would do jump squats and mountain climbers. We'd lunge our way back and forth across the basement, and do planks and push-ups, V-sits and donkey kicks, all while playing word games. I'd start with a letter of the alphabet; Ellie would give me a classmate at her new public school whose name began with that letter . . . and then, typically, a rundown as to why she didn't like that particular kid. ("D is for Dylan, who is nice sometimes but would not let me have the window seat on the bus when we went to the art museum.")

In the grocery store, I looked Ellie in the eye. "Ellie. Remember how we talked about using a respectful inside voice?"

She pursed her lips. "Yes, except I wanted a COOKIE and you said NO COOKIE."

"I said no cookie until after dinner."

"And now I want lipstick and you are saying NO and ALL YOU EVER SAY IS NO."

"Oh, honey." I held my arms open. After a minute, Ellie let me hug her. "I know things feel hard sometimes. But there's good stuff, too."

"Ma'am?"

I straightened up. The clerk was holding my maple candle and the jug of on-sale moisturizer I'd selected. "Do you want your non-food items in a separate bag?"

"Sure," I said, and gave him a smile.

"You," said the peacoat woman, "are a saint."

I smiled at her. "Believe me, I'm not." She was maybe five years younger than I was, her hair bundled in a careless ponytail at the nape of her neck, a diamond sparkling on her left hand. I wondered, as I always did when I met strangers these days, whether she was one of them or one of us; one of the earthlings, who could take or leave a glass of wine, or a joint, or a Vicodin or an Oxy; or one of the Martians, for whom, as the Basic Text said, *one was too many and a thousand was never enough.* You never can tell, Bernice said, and, from the people in my group, I knew it was true—pass any one of them on the street, and you'd have no idea that they were drunks and druggies. Well, maybe you'd guess about Brian, who had the word THUG tattooed on the fingers of his right hand, and LIFE on the fingers of his left. But you'd never guess about Jeannie, a lawyer, who came to meetings in smart suits and leather boots, and who'd lost her license after blacking out and plowing her car into a statue of George Washington on New Year's Day. Gregory looked like your run-of-the-mill fabulous gay guy, in his gorgeous made-to-measure shirts and hand-sewn shoes. Maybe you'd think that he liked to party on weekends, but you'd never imagine that he'd done three years in prison for drug trafficking. I wondered how I looked—to the clerk, now ringing up my yogurt in slow motion, to the young mother behind me, pushing her stroller back and forth in angry little jerks. Probably no different from the rest of the earthlings, with my hair in a bun, in my workout pants and zippered black sweatshirt. I still wore my wedding ring, and Dave still wore his. We'd never discussed it, which meant I didn't know whether I was wearing the platinum band out of hope or nostalgia or just so creepy guys in the dairy aisle wouldn't ask me for help in picking out heavy cream.

"Ma'am?" After what felt like another five minutes' worth of wrangling—debit or credit? Cash back? Tens or twenties?—I gave Ellie the little bag with the candle and the moisturizer and slung the bigger one over my shoulder, along with my purse, and the two of us walked onto South Street. I'd drop her off with Dave, then go to the five-thirty meeting of what had become my home group, the AA meeting I attended every week. He'd grill the turkey, I'd make rice and asparagus to go with it when I got back, and the three of us would share dinner together before Ellie and I went home.

No big changes for the first year was what they told us at Meadowcrest, but Dave and I had had to downsize, moving to modest apartments in the city and putting the big house on the market, especially after it became clear that my job, at least for the first little while, would be staying sober, with blogging a very distant second. I had struggled with it mightily, complaining to Bernice that there was no box on the tax return that read "not taking pills."

"I hate that this is what I do," I told her and the other seven members of my outpatient group, the one I attended four mornings a week, two hours at a time. I was desperate for my world to return to the way it had been before I'd gone to rehab, before I'd started with the pills. "I want my life back. Does anyone else get that?" Fabulous Gregory had nodded. Brian had grunted. Jeannie had shrugged and said that her pre-sobriety life hadn't been all that great.

"Tell us what you mean," Bernice prompted.

"I mean," I said, "I wake up. I take Ellie to school. I get some exercise. I come here for two hours. I go to AA meetings for another hour or two, and I don't take pills, and I don't take pills, and I don't take pills." I raised my hands, empty palms held open to the ceiling. "And that's it. God, can you imagine if I had a college reunion coming up? 'What are you up to these days, Allison?' 'Well, I don't take pills.' 'And . . . that's it?' 'Yeah, it's pretty much a full-time gig.'"

"Why you so worried 'bout what other people gonna think?" Bernice could switch in and out of ghetto vernacular—or what she referred to as "the colorful patois of my youth"—with ease. When she was talking to me, she'd alternate between her brassiest round-the-way tones and her most overeducated and multisyllabic. "You really worried about what the tax man's gonna think? Or some made-up person at some college reunion you don't even have coming up?"

"I don't know," I muttered. "I just feel useless."

"Useless," said Bernice, "is better than using. And if you use . . ."

"You die," the group chanted. I hung my head. I still wasn't entirely convinced this was true, but I'd heard it enough, and seen enough evidence, to at least be open to the possibility. There would be no one more pill or just one drink for me. That way lay madness . . . or jails, institutions, and death, as the Basic Text liked to say.

The night of Ellie's birthday party, when I'd gone back to Meadowcrest, I was humbled. More than that, I was scared. In that moment, in the bathroom, I'd seen a version of my life unfolding, a path where I faked and glad-handed my way through the rest of the twenty-eight days, and then went home and picked up my addiction right where I'd put it down. Soon, of course, the pills would get too expensive, and, probably, I'd be making less money, assuming I'd be able to work at all. Maybe it would take years, maybe just months, but, eventually, I would do what all the women I'd met had done, and trade the pricy Vicodin and Percocet and Oxy for heroin, which gave you twice the high at a quarter of the cost. I pictured myself dropping Ellie off at Stonefield in the morning, then driving my Prius to the Badlands, where even a straight white lady like me could buy whatever she wanted. *Philadelphia Magazine* had done a special report on the city's ten worst drug corners and, of course, I had firsthand recommendations from the various Ashleys and Brittanys. And maybe I'd get away with it, for a little while. Or maybe I'd get into a car accident with a thousand dollars' worth of H stuffed in my bra, like one of the Meadowcrest girls. Or I'd get arrested, dragged off to jail, and left to kick on a concrete floor with nothing but Tylenol 3, like an Amber had told us all about.

Dave would divorce me—that part, of course, was nonnegotiable. Worse, I would lose Ellie. In a few years' time . . . well. *You know how they say you never see any baby pigeons?* I remembered Lena asking in group one day. *You know what else you never see's an old lady heroin addict. Or,* Shannon had added, *one with kids.*

Back in my room, my *Big Book* was still open on my desk and my clothes were still in the dresser. "Ohmygod, where *were* you?" Aubrey demanded as she stormed into my bedroom, followed by Lena, who was still wearing the mascara mustache she'd donned to appear in our play. "We were so worried," said Mary. She twisted her eyeglass chain. "The RCs wouldn't tell us anything, but they were all on their walkie-talkies, and they made us all sit in the lounge and watch *28 Days* again. They thought you ran away!"

"I did," I confessed. Sitting cross-legged on my bed, the expectant faces of the women who'd become my friends around me, I couldn't remember ever feeling so scared. Admitting you had a problem was the first step—everyone knew that—but admitting you had a problem also left you open to the possibility that maybe you couldn't fix it. "I got Dave to pick me up, and I went to Ellie's birthday party, and we dropped her off at her friend's house, and I was in the bathroom, and I looked in the medicine cabinet, and I was thinking, *Please let there be something in here,* and then . . ." Shannon took my hand in hers.

"What is wrong with me?" I cried. "What's wrong with me that I can be at my daughter's birthday party, having a perfectly nice time, and the only thing I can think about is where am I going to get pills?"

Lena made a face. Mary patted my shoulder. But it was little Aubrey who spoke up. "What's wrong with you is what's wrong with all of us," she said. "We're sick people . . ."

". . . getting better," the room chorused.

Nicholas wanted me to stay at Meadowcrest for ninety days. Horrified at the thought of being away from Ellie for so long, I'd bargained him down to sixty. I threw myself into the work, the meetings, the lectures, the role-playing assignments, the making of posters, the writing of book reports, knowing that I was safe at Meadowcrest. I couldn't get pills, even if I wanted them. The world would be a different story.

A week before my discharge, Dave came to a family session. I was so nervous that I hadn't been able to eat anything the day before. "What's the worst thing that could happen?" Kirsten asked me, but I couldn't bring myself to tell her. The worst thing was that he'd show up with papers, or a lawyer's name; that he'd tell me he didn't know if he'd ever be able to trust me again and that he didn't want to stay married. I'd gone into the meeting prepared for that, so it was actually a relief when Dave sat there, stone-faced, and ran down the list of my lies, my failings, my fuckups and betrayals—the money I'd blown on pills, the way I'd put my job, my health, and my safety at risk, and worst of all, the way I'd put Ellie in danger. "It's the lying," he'd said, in a soft, toneless voice. "That's what I can't get over. She had this whole secret life. I don't even know who she is anymore."

I didn't even try to defend myself, to point out the ways he'd let me down and made it hard to tell him the truth about how I was feeling. I'd been warned about what was known in the AA rooms as cross-talk. I couldn't argue, or bring up

L. McIntyre, or talk about how he used marathon training as an excuse to literally run away from his wife and his daughter. I couldn't do anything but sit there and stare at my hands and try not to cry when Kirsten asked if he thought our marriage was irreparably damaged and listen to him sigh and then, slowly, say, "I don't know."

After sixty days, most of the women who'd been there when I arrived had gone. Mary had left early, after her husband developed a bladder infection and her kids couldn't manage it—and him—without her. Aubrey's insurance had cut her off after twenty-eight days. When her parents and her boyfriend all declined to come get her, Meadowcrest had gotten her a bus ticket back to Center City. Lena and Marissa and Shannon had all gone and been replaced by a fresh crop of Ashleys and Brittanys and Ambers and Caitlyns. Addicts, it seemed, were a renewable resource. The world made more of us every day.

By nine o'clock on my discharge day, I was standing in the reception room with my bags neatly packed. By noon, I was in a meeting in a church on Pine Street. *Hi, my name is Allison, and I'm an addict. Hi, Allison, welcome,* the room chorused back. At three, I was in Bernice's office in Cherry Hill. Technically, it was an intake evaluation, during which she'd determine whether I was an appropriate addition to her intensive outpatient group, the just-out-of-rehab folks whose therapists had determined they were ready to live in the world again. "One thing we gon' do right this minute," she'd said, and spun her big push-button telephone around on her desk until it faced me. While she watched, I called every one of my doctors who'd ever prescribed me anything stronger than an aspirin, and told them what had happened and where I'd been.

Some of them had been brusque and businesslike about it.

Dr. Andi had practically been in tears. "Oh, God, Allison. Was this my fault? Was this going on and I didn't see it?"

"Don't blame yourself," I told her as Bernice listened on speakerphone. "I was playing you. I was good at it, too. Just . . . if I ever call you in the middle of the night and tell you I'm in agony . . ."

"Nothing!" said Dr. Andi, laughing. "Not even a hot water bottle!"

"Now go and do the next right thing," Bernice told me. I'd left her office feeling rattled and dazed. No more pills. Not unless I went back online or I found new doctors, convinced them I was in trouble, got them to give me what I needed . . . I shook my head, raised my shoulders, and quickened my pace along the street. No more. That part of my life was over. I had a daughter who needed me, I had a life to live, and I was determined to be clearheaded for all of it.

My determination lasted exactly twenty-three days. Looking back, I was trying to do too much, too fast, to have it all be normal again. Then, at ten o'clock one night, after a day of outpatient therapy and meetings and Monopoly with Ellie, I found myself thinking, *Would just one glass of wine be so bad?* Just a glass of red, like a million other women were probably sipping at that very moment, a little something to ease me, to calm me, to send me off to sleep?

I had the glass in one hand and the bottle—leftover Manischewitz from some Passover seder—in the other. Even though I'd never been a drinker, I could taste the kosher wine, sweet as syrup on my tongue, warming me, calming me as it went down.

I don't know where I found the strength—if that's what it was—to put down the bottle and pick up what people in meetings called the thousand-pound telephone. I called Sheila, a big, tall home health aide from my IOP group who'd been addicted to crack and who called me, and all the other women in the group who were under the age of fifty, baby girl. "SheilaIwanttodrink," I blurted before I'd even said "hello," or my name.

"Who this?" she asked, laughing. "Which white girl calling me 'bout wanting a drank?" *Drank* was how she said it, and the delicious silliness of it made me laugh.

"It's Allison. The Jewish one."

"Ooh, Allison, with that pretty little baby, callin' me 'bout wanting to drink. You're not even a drinker, right?"

"No," I said. "Pills. But you can't buy them on the corner."

"Not in your neighborhood, I guess," she said, and cackled. "So what you want," she said, suddenly serious, "that glass of wine or your baby? Because you know it is never just one glass of wine. Not for us. And you know where it ends, right?"

"I know," I said. I was gripping the phone tight, tight, tight. Tears were coursing down my cheeks. They'd told us that in rehab, and in group: we had given up the right to drink or take drugs like normal people. No Champagne toasts at weddings, no Vicodin after we had our teeth pulled. And what did we get in return for that sacrifice? Our lives back. Not just returned, but improved. Bernice closed every session with the Promises: "If we are painstaking about this phase of our development, we will be amazed before we are halfway through. We are going to know a new freedom and a new happiness. We will not regret the past nor wish to shut the door on it. We will comprehend the word 'serenity' and we will know peace. No matter how far down the scale we have gone, we will see how our experience can benefit others. That feeling of uselessness and self-pity will disappear. We will lose interest in selfish things and gain interest in our fellows. Self-seeking will slip away. Our whole attitude and outlook upon life will change. Fear of people and of economic insecurity will leave us. We will intuitively know how to handle situations which used to baffle us. We will suddenly realize that God is doing for us what we could not do for ourselves."

To me, it sounded like bullshit . . . maybe because I was still clinging, hard, to the notion that my life had been pretty much okay, or that I'd pulled out of my tailspin before things had gotten really bad. I didn't want better; I just wanted what I'd had before it all got so crazy, before we moved to Haverford, back when it had been the three of us in the row house in Center City. This was a point about which Bernice and I disagreed. "Don't you quit before the miracle happens," she would tell me. "I want you to experience everything this program has to offer. There's a new life out there for you, and it's better than any life you could ever have imagined. I want you to have that new life."

"Okay," I would tell her, and she'd tell me to keep doing the next right thing, and the next right thing, and the next right thing after that, and that "God" stood for Good Orderly Direction and "Fear" stood for Face Everything and Recover. All those silly sayings, those stupid platitudes, the ones I'd scoffed and rolled my eyes at. Now I wrote them down, I memorized them, I printed them out in pretty fonts and stuck them on my computer monitor, on my bathroom mirror, on my refrigerator door, and recited them to myself while I waited in supermarket lines.

In the mornings, before I put on my exercise clothes, I rolled out of bed, onto my knees, and prayed, even though I felt stupid, like an imposter, like someone acting out the idea of prayer instead of actually doing it. *Dear God,* I would think. After months and months of hearing the phrase "God of our understanding," of listening to people refer to "my Higher Power, whom I choose to call Goddess," or "Nature," I still couldn't come up with any image of God except the old tried-and-true: an ancient dude with a long white beard and a stern look on his face. *Thank you for helping me stay sober another day. Thank you for not letting me hurt Ellie, or myself, or anyone else, while I was using.* I'd run down my list, thanking God for central air-conditioning when it was hot out and my space heater when it was cold, for a favorite sweater, a comfortable pair of boots, a peaceful few minutes with my daughter.

I thanked God for my mother, who'd moved into a posh fifty-five-and-over community near Eastwood, near my dad. She'd taken up bridge, and found new friends for golf and tennis, and she came into the city two, sometimes three days a week, to spend afternoons with Ellie and give me time to go to my appointments and my meetings. I thanked God for my dad, who still, sometimes, knew who I was when I brought Ellie to visit him every other week. "Proud of you," he would tell me, and I wasn't sure what he thought he was proud of me for. Did he know I'd been in rehab, or why? Did he remember anything about how I'd become an accidental writer? Did he know that I was married and a mom? Or, in his head, was I still eighteen, with my acceptance letter from Franklin & Marshall in my hand, telling him about my big plans for my future?

I thanked God for Janet, who drove to Center City once a week to have lunch with me. I'd regale her with funny stories from my AA and NA meetings. Janet especially liked to hear about Leonard, who'd begin his recitations by thanking God "for keeping me out of the titty bars for another day." "What happens if he goes back?" she'd asked, and I'd told her how shamefaced Leonard looked when he'd stood up and said, "Well, they got me again!" We'd split a dessert and talk about our kids, our parents, and whether sex addiction was really a thing. "I love you," she would say, her face solemn, and she'd hug me at the end of every visit. Once, she'd cried, telling me that she thought she should have noticed, should have seen that I was in trouble, should have done something. I told her it was my problem and my job to solve it. "Just be my friend," I said. "That's what I need most." I thanked God that L. McIntyre was, like Dave had insisted, just a friend. "Maybe it could have been something more," he'd told me over dinner after my third week home. "But what kind of jerk cheats on his wife while she's in rehab?"

Thank God for Dave, I thought . . . and, last, I would thank God for what was, blasphemous as it sounded, the best development of my new, sober life, a small black-and-white dog named Bingo.

We'd gotten her in September, my first month back from rehab. Ellie and I had driven from Philadelphia down to Baltimore through a gorgeous fall afternoon, the sky a brilliant blue, smelling of leaves and wood smoke and, faintly, of the coming cold. Our first stop had been Target, where we'd bought everything we would need—a leash and harness made of pink nylon, a compromise between the faux-leather and rhinestone rig Ellie had fallen in love with and the plain red I preferred. We had plastic food and water dishes, a carrying crate, a ten-pound sack of dog food, a fluffy round brown-and-pink polka-dotted dog bed, a chewy toy, a squeaky toy, and the Cesar Millan video that Janet, who'd adopted three different rescue dogs, had recommended.

"Can the puppy sleep in my room?" asked Ellie.

"Fine with me," I said. Ellie had been asking for a dog ever since she'd read *Fancy Nancy and the Posh Puppy*. Of course, she'd lobbied for a teacup poodle, but had been surprisingly amenable when I'd explained that there were many dogs who needed homes, and it would be better to adopt one of them. Together, we'd spent a half hour each night online, reading about breeds, watching videos of pups, getting a season pass on TiVo for *Too Cute*. Ellie had been keeping the tantrums to a minimum, and doing her chores—making her bed and clearing her dishes and helping me make her lunches and load the dishwasher—without complaint.

"One eleven, one thirteen . . . here we go!" The house was a yellow cape, with a front yard dotted with little piles of dog poop. As we pulled into the driveway, the front door opened, and a teenage girl came out with a small white dog with black spots on a leash. The dog had a finely molded face, a whiskered snout, and a long tail that curled at its tip. One of her ears stood up straight; the other one flopped like a book page you'd turned down to mark your place.

"BINGO!" yelled Ellie, and she was out of the car almost before it had stopped rolling. She raced across the lawn, fell to her knees a few feet away from the dog, then, as instructed, held out her hand for it to sniff. The dog, who'd seemed alarmed by Ellie's charge, sniffed her hand, then wagged its tail, sat calmly, and allowed Ellie to pet it.

"She is so CUTE!" Ellie said to the girl, who looked amused at Ellie's antics. I walked over, shook her hand, and signed the papers while Ellie crooned at the puppy. She was a young adult dog, her Internet profile had said, somewhere between three and five years old. She had shown up pregnant at a shelter. They'd found her a foster family, where she'd given birth, and all five of the puppies were quickly adopted. "Now we just need to find a place for Mom," said the website, and that, of course, had made me want to drive straight to Baltimore and bring the sad-eyed little dog home. She was, according to the website, some kind of terrier mix, a solid fifteen pounds, spayed, friendly, good with kids, and with all of her shots.

"I wish we could tell you more about her," said the teenager, who had a brown ponytail and a metallic smile. "She was a good mom when the pups were here."

"I'm sure we'll figure it out," I'd said. On the application, which had struck me as astonishingly detailed, there'd been a question about whether I had ever been arrested or in jail. Nothing about rehab or addiction, but still, I wondered if I would have answered those questions honestly . . . and, if I had, whether they would have turned me down. It was crazy: Who needed a pet more than a sick person trying to get better? Who would take better care of a dog than someone trying to demonstrate to the world that she was, indeed, worthy of its trust again?

Ellie and I walked Bingo around the block, Bingo trotting briskly, Ellie clutching the leash with two hands. "Say goodbye," Ellie instructed the dog. Bingo was docile as I scooped her up and placed her in her crate, even as Ellie begged me to let the dog ride in her lap. She didn't make a sound the entire ride home. Once we were back in Philadelphia, we walked her around the neighborhood, letting her sniff the trees and hydrants. She ignored other dogs, hiding, trembling, behind my legs when they got close enough to try to sniff her. "She is SHY," said Ellie, who didn't seem to mind, as long as Bingo let her put the little tinsel collar she'd crafted around her neck, and hold the leash while they walked.

"Do you think we should try to find a better name for her?" I asked.

Ellie considered as we approached our front door. Finally, she shook her head. "I think she is a Bingo," she decided, and I told Ellie that I thought she was right.

At home, Bingo sniffed her dish full of kibble, had a few laps of water, then wormed underneath my bed, in spite of Ellie's importuning and threats to drag her out into the open. "Let's just leave her be." Ellie had gotten into her pajamas, and we read *Squids Will Be Squids* and *A Big Guy Took My Ball* before I kissed her good night and tucked her into her bed. As tempting as it was to let Ellie sleep with me every night, I'd heard enough lectures about boundaries to know that I needed to put them in place (plus, she hadn't had an accident in months, but I didn't want to take chances with my new mattress). She was my daughter, not my friend, or my comfort, or my confidante . . . and so, as much as I would have liked the feeling of another warm body in my bed, or the sweet smile she wore when she woke up (in the handful of seconds before remembering that the world and most of the people in it displeased her), I made sure she at least began each night in her own room.

So it was just me in the bedroom when Bingo inched her way out from underneath the bed and peered up at me. Her tail drooped. Her expression seemed despondent. I wondered if she missed her pups, or if she even remembered she'd had them—I knew so little about dogs!

"What is it?" I asked, putting down *A Woman's Guide to the Twelve Steps*.

Silence.

"Do you want to go out?" I guessed.

Nothing. I took her downstairs, clipped her to her leash, walked her down the steps, and stood at the edge of the sidewalk while she did her business. Upstairs, instead of going back underneath the bed, she stood at the edge and looked at me.

"Oh, okay," I said, and patted the mattress. Before the second word was out of my mouth, Bingo had hopped nimbly onto the bed and was settling down against me, folding herself into the space behind my bent knees as I lay curled up on my side.

"You're going to sleep there?" No answer. I pulled the comforter up over both of us and closed my eyes. *Thank you, God, for Bingo. Thank you for Ellie. Thank you for such beautiful weather. Thank you for helping me not take pills today.* It wasn't much of a prayer, but it was the best I could do.

Each year since we'd moved to Haverford, I'd hosted a Chanukah Happening (on the invitations, I'd spell it Chappening). Dozens of kids, parents, colleagues, and relatives and friends would fill our house, some bearing gifts for Ellie, or boxes of chocolates, or, more likely, bottles of wine. I would serve roast chickens, a giant green salad, and a table full of desserts the guests had brought. In the living room, kids would spin dreidels, and guests would be participating in the latke cook-off in the kitchen. We'd have straight potato pancakes, sweet-potato latkes, latkes with zucchini and shreds of carrots, latkes made with flour or potato starch or, once, tapioca. Barry would contribute *sufganiyot*, the sweet filled doughnuts that were also traditional Chanukah fare, and, for weeks, the kitchen would smell like a deep fryer and my hair and skin would feel lightly coated with grease.

There would be beer and wine at those parties . . . and, as the crowd got bigger and the preparations more elaborate, I'd taken more and more pills to get myself through it, to deal with the tension of whether Dave was helping me or even talking to me, pills to cope with my mom, who would show up with an eight-pound brisket and demand the use of an oven.

This year, my Chanukah Happening was limited to four people: me and Ellie, Dave and my mom. And Bingo, of course, who sat on the floor, eyes bright, tail wagging, watching the proceedings avidly, hoping that someone would drop something. Dave, I noticed, would discreetly slip her scraps, which meant that Bingo followed him around like a balloon that had been tethered to his ankle.

"Good girl," he'd say, sneaking Bingo a bit of chicken skin, then tipping his chair back and sighing. I had radically reduced the guest list, but I'd kept the menu the same: roast chicken stuffed with herbs and lemon and garlic, a salad dressed with pomegranate-seed vinaigrette, potato latkes, and a store-bought dessert—cream puffs from Whole Foods and chocolate sauce that Ellie and I had made together.

"She has a JAUNTY WALK," said Ellie, imitating Bingo's brisk stride down the street. "And at night she sleeps CURLED IN A CRULLER in Mommy's bed."

"I bet Mom likes that," he said. His eyes didn't meet mine. *I would like you better,* I thought at him.

"Hey, El, let's show Daddy how we clear the table."

"Daddy knows that I can do that." She pouted, but she got up and carefully, using two hands, carried every plate and platter from the table to the sink.

We played Sorry! after dinner—oh, irony! I tried to breathe through my discomfort, the restlessness, tried to sit with my feelings, like Bernice advised, and ignore the questions running laps in my brain. *Will he stay? Or at least come and kiss me? Does he love me a little? Is there anything left at all?*

Dave stayed as I coaxed Ellie into, then out of, her tub, combing and braiding her hair, getting her into her pajamas and reading her *This Is Not My Hat.* After I closed her bedroom door, Bingo bounded down the hallway to assume her position, curled on top of my pillow. Her tail thumped against the comforter as she watched us with her bright brown eyes.

"B-I-N-G-O," Dave sang. We were in the narrow hallway,

practically touching. "You seem well." He reached out, took a strand of my hair between his fingers, and tucked it, tenderly, behind my ear. Then his body was right up against mine, his chest warm and firm, shoulders solid in my hands. "I know they said no changes for the first year, but we've both done this a bunch of times already . . ."

I laughed, walking backward, as he maneuvered me onto the bed . . . and, later, I cried when, with my head on his chest and our bare legs entwined, he got choked up as he said, "Allison, there was never anybody else. It was always only you."

"I promise . . ." I started to say. I wanted to promise him that I'd never hurt him again, never go off the rails, never give him cause to worry again . . . but those were promises I couldn't make. One minute, one hour, one day at a time. "I never stopped loving you," I said . . . and that was the absolute truth.

We didn't move back in together. Part of me wanted it desperately, and part of me worried that we were disrupting Ellie's stable environment—some mornings Dave was in bed with me, some mornings he was at his own place, and some nights Ellie stayed there with him—but she seemed to be thriving, to be growing out of the awful yelling and stubbornness.

As for Dave and me, I often thought that we were, as coaches and sportswriters liked to say, in a rebuilding year. Not married, exactly, but not un-married. It was almost as though we were courting each other again, slowly revealing ourselves to each other. My mom or our sitter, Katrina, would come for the night, and we'd go to a concert, or out to dinner, or we'd take Bingo to the dog park where, on warm spring nights, they showed old movies, projecting the picture against a bedsheet strung between two pine trees.

"Ellie's getting big," Dave said on one of those nights. I'd been looking at the picnics other people had packed: fried chicken and biscuits and canned peaches; egg-salad sandwiches on thick-sliced whole-wheat bread; chunks of pineapple and strawberries in a fruit salad . . . and wine. Beer. Sweating thermoses of cocktails, lemon drops and Pimm's cups.

"She is," I had agreed. Every day she looked a little taller, her hair longer, or she'd bust out some new bit of vocabulary or surprisingly apt observation about the world. Sometimes at night she'd cry that her legs hurt. *Growing pains,* Dr. McCarthy had told us.

Sometimes I felt like I was having them, too. It made me think of something else I'd heard in a meeting, about how Alcoholics Anonymous can help people with their feelings. "And it's true," the speaker had said. He had a jovial grin underneath his walrus mustache. "I feel anger better, I feel sadness better, I feel disappointment better . . ."

Life on life's terms. It was an absolute bitch. There was no more tuning out or glossing over, no more using opiates as spackle to fill in the cracks and broken bits. It was all there, raw and unlovely: the little sighs and groans Dave made, seemingly without hearing them, when he ate his cereal or made the bed; the way Ellie had to be reminded, sometimes more than twice, to flush the toilet after she used it; the glistening ovals of mucus that lined the city sidewalk. Some nights, I missed my father and regretted my mother's half-assed, mostly absent-minded parenting, and there was no pill to help with it. Some nights I couldn't sleep . . . so I would lie in my bed, alone or with Dave, and stare up into the darkness and try not to beat myself up. *We will not regret the past, nor wish to shut the door on it,* The Big Book said . . . so I would try to be grateful that I'd stopped when I had instead of berating myself for letting things get as bad as they'd gotten. I had learned what I'd needed to learn, and I knew now that I was, however flawed and imperfect, however broken, undeniably a grown-up.

Then, one day, my cell phone rang, and I heard a familiar voice on the other end.

"It's a blast from your past!" said the voice, before dissolving into sniffles.

"Aubrey!" I hadn't heard from her since she'd left Meadowcrest. Mary and I e-mailed, and Shannon and I met for coffee once a month. Lena and Marissa had both disappeared, whether back into addiction or into new lives in recovery, I couldn't guess. I worried about them sometimes, but Aubrey was the one I worried about most. I'd text or call her every so often, but I had never heard back. A dozen times I'd started to type her name into Google, and a dozen times I'd made myself stop. *If she wants me to know how she's doing, she'll get in touch. Otherwise it's snooping*, I decided. Now, here she was, her voice quivering, and me clutching the phone, realizing only in that moment that I'd half believed she was dead.

"How are you?"

"I'm . . ." She gave her familiar little laugh. "I'm not so good, actually."

By now, I knew what questions to ask. Better still, I knew how to just be quiet and listen. "What's going on?"

"I've been using for . . . oh, God, months now. I was doing good at first. Then Justin started coming around his mom's house, where I was staying with Cody . . ."

I turned away so that Ellie, engrossed in an episode of *Sam & Cat*, wouldn't see my face. Justin. The fucking no-good boyfriend.

"And, you know, he made it sound like it was going to be

all different this time. Like we'd keep it under control. And I thought I could, you know, because I'd been clean for a while." She started to cry. I got the rest of the story in disjointed bursts— she'd gotten kicked out of her boyfriend's parents' house, then her mother had taken Cody and refused to let Aubrey see him until she got clean. She described couch-surfing, spending two weeks in a shelter, and then, finally, asked the question I knew was coming: "Can I crash with you for a little while?" Her voice was tiny, barely a whisper. "I could help out . . . babysit . . . I'm good with kids . . . I wouldn't ask, except I don't have anywhere else to go."

Oh, Aubrey, I thought. Aubrey, who was still more or less a kid herself. *Boundaries,* I told myself, even though I wanted nothing more than to tell her to come, to tell her that the trundle bed had fresh sheets, that Ellie would be delighted to meet her, that I would help her get well. Except I couldn't. I knew my own limits, knew how close I was to my own relapse. "I can't do that," I said. "But I can take you to a meeting. I can hook you up with Bernice. I can help you find a place to stay."

"You sound good," she said. Was she high? I couldn't tell. "I'm glad. I knew you'd do good when you got out of there."

"Aubrey, listen to me. There's a five-thirty meeting today at Fourth and Pine. That's my home group. They're really nice. They'd love to meet you. You come there, and I will meet you, and I'm going to call Bernice, and we'll find you a place."

"Ooo-kay." Definitely slurry.

"Five-thirty. Fourth and Pine." I made her say it back to me twice. Then I hung up the phone, and texted her the address, just to be sure, and started pacing, watching the door, waiting for my mother to show up for her regular Tuesday visit. Normally she was there at five at the latest, and I'd have time to grab a coffee if

I wanted one before the meeting began, but that night, of course, she was running late.

"Mommy, stop WALKING," said Ellie . . . and then, in an unprecedented move, she actually turned the TV off without being asked or prompted, and looked at me. "What are you so WORRYING about?"

"I'm not worrying," I said automatically.

"Then why are you WALKING and WALKING?" She looked at me carefully, eyes narrowed, hair gathered in a pony-tail that hung halfway down her back, pants displaying a good inch of her ankles. I'd need to go shopping again.

"I guess maybe I am a little worried." I sat down by the window, and Bingo sprang into my lap, wriggling around until her belly was exposed for a scratch. When Ronnie finally strolled into view I grabbed my bag and half trotted past Ellie.

"There's someone—a girl I knew from rehab . . ." I looked at the clock on the cable box. "I'll explain when I'm back, but I've got to go . . ."

I hurried around the corner, my keys in my hand, my purse over my shoulder, a dollar in my pocket for when they passed the basket around, my phone tucked into my bra, set on vibrate, so I'd feel it if Aubrey texted back. It was a gorgeous late afternoon, the clear, sunny sky and brilliant leaves all promising new be-ginnings, fresh starts. A young woman carrying a paper parasol walked with her Boston terrier on a red leash. An older couple on bicycles passed me. I watched them riding away and thought about all the normal people in the world, just going around, doing their business, living their lives, buying food and cooking meals, watching TV shows and movies, fighting and falling in love, without even the thought of a drink or a drug to make the good times even beter and the bad times less awful.

Don't be like me, my mother had told me, when I'd gotten out. *Don't waste your life hiding.* But still, even with so many of the rewards of sobriety making themselves known, it was hard not to crave oblivion and numbness, a pill that could keep my feelings safely at bay. Sometimes, I wondered how I'd gotten started with the drugs . . . and sometimes I wondered why everyone in the world wasn't taking them, and how I'd found the strength, somehow, to resist, even just for that day.

There was a coffee shop around the corner from where the AA meetings were held. I stuck my head in, looking for Aubrey, recognizing people at a few of the tables: the fiftyish man in a plaid shirt and glasses who'd talked about dealing with both addiction and mental illness; the woman with a buzz cut and black army boots who'd described passing out in the SEPTA station and lying on the concrete, watching rats running up and down the tracks until the cops bundled her into a cruiser; the man who dressed like a cowboy and kept his long gray hair in a ponytail tied with a rawhide loop and talked endlessly about his girlfriend who'd redecorated while he'd been in rehab, and the contractor who had unscrewed the chandelier from his dining room and stolen it, and how he was going to get that chandelier back. Sometimes I went to meetings willingly, knowing that they helped, and some nights the only thing keeping me from staying home on the couch was the promise of a chandelier update or the latest installment in the long-running saga of Leonard vs. the Titty Bars.

"What can I get for you?" asked the barista, a man who couldn't have been older than twenty-five, with thick black eyebrows and an easy smile.

I ordered an iced mocha and checked my phone again. When they called my name, I wrapped a brown paper napkin around the plastic cup. It was five-twenty. I walked around the corner to the church. In the basement with scuffed white walls and hardwood floors, fifty chairs were set up, with a group of people settling into the front rows. Once, early on, I'd made the mistake of trying to sit in the back, and the others from Bernice's group had almost collapsed laughing. *Denial Aisle! Relapse Row!* they'd shouted, as Sheila had ushered me front and center.

No Aubrey yet, but I could see Johnette and Martin, and both Brians from my group. Gregory was there, fussing with the crease of his jeans, and Alice sat next to him, with a tote bag full of knitting in her lap. "We saved you a seat," said Sheila, and tapped the empty metal chair that stood in the center of the front row. I held my cup, feeling the cool of it against my palm, and I took my place among them.

ACKNOWLEDGMENTS

I am grateful to have the support of the hands-down absolute best agent and editor in the business. Joanna Pulcini and Greer Hendricks have held my hand, helped me up, offered praise and constructive criticism, and have always been willing to listen and to read yet another draft. I'm the luckiest writer in the world to have these two women as colleagues and friends.

Judith Curr, publisher of Atria Books, and Carolyn Reidy, CEO and president of Simon & Schuster, are powerhouses and role models, and I'm lucky to work with them, as well as the team at Atria: Lisa Sciambra, Ben Lee, Lisa Keim, Hillary Tisman, Elisa Shokoff, LeeAnna Woodcock, and Kitt Reckord.

Anna Dorfman and Jeanne Lee keep my books looking good. Copyeditor extraordinaire Nancy Inglis saves me from myself at least once per page and forgives me all my sins, which include regularly confusing "like" and "as" and still not knowing when you spell out numbers versus when you just type the digits.

At Simon & Schuster UK, I'm grateful for the support of Suzanne Baboneau, Ian Chapman, and Jo Dickinson.

Nobody in the PR world does it better than Marcy Engelman, and I am so glad to have her in my corner, along with Emily Gambir and Bernice Marzan. Jessica Bartolo and her team at Greater Talent Network make my speaking engagements delightful.

Special thanks to Greer's assistant, Sarah Cantin, and Joanna's assistant Josephine Hill for their patience, enthusiasm, and attention to detail.

Thanks and love to the home team—my fantastic assistant Meghan Burnett, whose unflappable calm and unfailing good humor make my work life a joy. Terri Gottlieb cares for my girls, runs the kitchen, tends to the garden, and lets me head off to work with confidence that my daughters will be happy and my house will be standing when I return. Adam Bonin's love and support goes above and beyond—he is a wonderful father and a great friend. Susan Abrams is the best BFF anyone could ever hope for. Lucy and Phoebe—you are my heart's delight, and every day I am proud to be your mother.

Bill—you are my happy ending.

Finally, to everyone who visits my Facebook page, comes to one of my readings, indulges my tweets about *The Bachelor*, and waits patiently for my next book, my deepest thanks. None of this would be possible without you.

All Fall Down

JENNIFER WEINER

A Readers Club Guide

Topics and Questions for Discussion

1. Why does Allison initially turn to painkillers as a way to solve her problems, or at least to make her feel better for a few hours? How do her answers to the magazine quiz she takes at Ellie's doctor's office make her feel, and how does she justify taking a pill in the car just moments after she completes the quiz? How would Allison's story have been different if she had sought help immediately after taking the quiz?

2. From her work and her marriage to her role as primary caretaker for her daughter and parents, how do the pressures on Allison contribute to her addiction? Do you think that the pressures that Allison faces justify her addiction, or does she use the challenges in her life as an excuse to take more pills? How are the pressures facing Allison unique to her role as a mother and a wife, and what is the author saying about the pressures on women in society in general?

3. After Dave's book deal falls through and Allison's blogging becomes their primary source of income, how does their relationship change? Why do you think the author chose to have Allison write for a website specifically geared toward women and women's issues?

4. As Allison sinks deeper into her addiction, her relationships with her parents, husband, daughter, friends, and boss change as everyone adapts to an Allison who is less reliable, stable, and emotionally present. How do Allison's addiction and her subsequent efforts at recovery impact the people around her for better and for worse? How does Allison handle the changes she observes in the people she loves? What surprises her about her family's and friends' reactions and responses to her addiction, and what surprised you as a reader?

5. How does Allison's definition of self change when she and Dave move to the suburbs, and why? How do Allison's hopes for life in the suburbs compare to the reality of her new situation, and what does she give up to fit into the new life that Dave chose for them? Does living in the suburbs contribute to Allison's addiction, or do you think she would have faced the same issues had she stayed in the city?

6. How does Allison's ability to anonymously order pills through Penny Lane facilitate her addiction? Do you think her addiction would have reached such an extreme place if she didn't have the knowledge and resources to order pills over the Internet? What does Allison's reliance on ordering drugs online say about technology and the future of addiction?

7. When he finally confronts Allison about her addiction, Dave is extremely angry that she has put their daughter's life in jeopardy. Could Dave have interfered with his wife's addiction sooner? If you think Dave suspected that Allison was abusing drugs, why did he choose to wait so long to act? Do you think that Dave feels any responsibility for Allison's addiction?

8. At Meadowcrest, Allison meets a range of women who are addicts, including a heroin-addicted teenage mother and a devout Christian alcoholic grandmother. Did the depiction of Allison's friends at the rehab center change your perception of what an addict looks like? Which of the characters introduced at Meadowcrest did you sympathize or identify with most, and why?

9. From lying to Mrs. Dale about how impaired she was behind the wheel to her reluctance to share her full story with the women at Meadowcrest, Allison continually fabricates stories that hide the depth of her addiction. Why do you think Allison seems to be addicted to lying, and why is it so impossible for her to face the truth about her addiction? When do you think she finally realizes that she will never fully recover unless she is honest about her addiction with herself and others?

10. Compared to the women who wind up at Meadowcrest after committing felonies or losing custody of their children, Allison feels her story is "boring, bare-bones, drama-free," but Mary points out that Allison just has a "high bottom" as opposed to a "rock bottom." Discuss the concept of high bottom versus rock bottom. How does Allison's view of her addiction and her high bottom make her feel different from the other women in rehab whose situations appear more dire?

11. Despite the intense subject matter of the book, the author manages to infuse humor into Allison's journey, such as when she coaxes details about *The Bachelor* from Wanda the aide, or when she hatches her plan to escape by staging a musical about addiction and life in rehab. As a reader, how did you feel when you read these humorous scenes? Were you surprised that the author was able to bring some light to such a dark situation?

12. Even in the depths of her addiction, Allison strives to be a better mother than her own mother was to her, even sneaking out of Meadowcrest to attend Ellie's sixth birthday party. What does Allison do differently from her own mother, and in what ways are they

the same? Were you surprised when Allison's mother revealed her secret toward the end of the book? How, if at all, would Allison's life have changed if she had known the truth about her mother sooner?

13. Aubrey's phone call at the end of the book reminds Allison how quickly addiction can consume a person. Why is it so important to Allison that she refuse Aubrey's request to come stay with her? What do you think the future holds for both of them? In a year, where do you think Allison will be in terms of her relationships with her family and her work? In five years?

Enhance Your Book Club

1. Select an addiction memoir to read in tandem with *All Fall Down*, and compare the experiences of the writer with those of Allison. You may want to select a memoir written by a woman, but you don't have to. Discuss how the writer's struggles with addiction and recovery differ from Allison's, and how their stories are similar. A few books to consider include *Drinking: A Love Story* by Caroline Knapp, *Lit* by Mary Karr, and *Tweak* by Nic Sheff.

2. Read Rebecca Mead's *New Yorker* profile of Jennifer Weiner, "Written Off: Jennifer Weiner's Quest for Literary Respect" (January 13, 2014), http://www.newyorker.com/reporting/2014/01/13/140113fa_fact_mead. Discuss how the issues raised by Weiner about men, women, and writing come to light in the novel through Dave's work at the *Examiner* and Allison's work at Ladiesroom.com.

3. If you can, spend a day or an afternoon volunteering at a drug or alcohol treatment facility in your area.

4. Visit Jennifer Weiner's website at www.jenniferweiner.com to learn more about her and her books, and follow her on Twitter @jenniferweiner. Fans of *The Bachelor* and *The Bachelorette*: Be sure to tune in to her live tweets of the show on Monday nights and join the conversation!